THE **TIN**
DRUM

Also by GÜNTER GRASS

GÜNTER GRASS

THE TIN DRUM

A new translation from the
German by Breon Mitchell

HARPERVIA

An Imprint of HarperCollins *Publishers*

Boston New York

For Anna Grass

First Mariner Books edition 2010

Copyright © 1959 by Hermann Luchterhand Verlag GmbH
Copyright © 1993 by Steidl Verlag, Göttingen
Translation copyright © 2009 by Breon Mitchell

www.harpercollins.com

Library of Congress Cataloging-in-Publication Data
Grass, Günter, date.
[Blechtrommel. English]
The tin drum / Günter Grass ; a new translation by Breon Mitchell.
p. cm.
Translation of: Die Blechtrommel.
ISBN 978-0-15-101416-3
1. Germany — History — 1945–1955 — Fiction. I. Mitchell, Breon. II. Title.
PT2613.R338B5513 2009
833'.914 — dc22   2009013272

ISBN 978-0-547-33910-8 (pbk.)

Book design by Linda Lockowitz

Printed in the United States of America

23 24 25 26 27 LBC 18 17 16 15 14

Contents

BOOK THREE

Introduction

IN THE SUMMER OF 1959, I completed my first novel, *The Tin Drum*, in Paris. I had just corrected proofs and created an image for the dust jacket when a letter arrived from the legendary publisher Kurt Wolff in New York. Wolff, who had left Germany in the thirties, asked me to meet him at a hotel in Zurich. He strode up to me in the hotel lobby, a tall gentleman, with his wife and colleague Helen Wolff beside him.

"I'm thinking of publishing your book in America," he said. "Do you think the American reader will understand it?" "I don't think so," I replied. "The setting is provincial, not even Danzig itself, but a suburb. The novel is filled with German dialect. And it concentrates solely on the provinces—" "Say no more," he broke in. "All great literature is rooted in the provincial. I'll bring it out in America."

The American *Tin Drum* appeared in 1962 with Pantheon Books of New York, a firm founded by Wolff.

Later on, I was often urged to give some account of the origins of my first novel, but I didn't feel ready to sift through the circumstances and influences with a prying eye. I was almost frightened I might discover my own tricks.

Up to then I had written poetry and plays, as well as libretti for the ballet (my first wife Anna was a dancer). In 1956 Anna and I left Berlin and moved to Paris with the vague idea of writing a novel circulating in my mind. I took pleasure in art, enjoyed the varieties of form, and felt the urge to create an alternate reality on paper—in short, I had all the tools needed to undertake any artistic project, regardless of its nature. If things had gone solely according to my own desires and instinct for play, I would have tested myself against purely aesthetic norms and found my role in the scurrilous. But I couldn't. There were obstacles. The gestation of German history had brought forth piles of rubble and dead bodies, a mass of material that, once I began to clear it away, only increased from book to book.

With the first sentence, "Granted: I'm an inmate in a mental institution . . . ," the barriers fell, language surged forward, memory, imagination, the pleasure of invention, and an obsession with detail all flowed freely, chapter after chapter arose, history offered local examples, I took on a rapidly proliferating family, and contended with Oskar Matzerath and those around him over the simultaneity of events and the absurd constraints of chronology, over Oskar's right to speak in the first or third person, over his true transgressions and his feigned guilt.

The Tin Drum struck a distinctly new tone in postwar German literature, one that was greeted with enthusiasm by many critics and with annoyance by others. The poet and essayist Hans Magnus Enzensberger offered this review in 1959:

> *The Tin Drum* knows no taboos. . . . Again and again the narrative enters the forbidden sphere where disgust and sexuality, death and blasphemy meet.
>
> What differentiates Grass in this respect both from any form of pornography, and from the so-called "stark realism" of the American school, what legitimizes these blunt forays, indeed elevates them to acts of artistic brilliance, is the total objectivity with which he presents them. Unlike Henry Miller, Grass does not seek out taboos; he simply doesn't notice them. It would be unfair to accuse him of deliberate provocation. He neither avoids scandal nor invites it; but that is precisely what will give rise to scandal: Grass doesn't have a guilty conscience, he takes what we find shocking for granted.

This passage shows the wide variety of responses my work evoked in the late fifties. As a result, from the very start of my career as a novelist, I was considered controversial.

The "shocking" parts of *The Tin Drum* may have led translators and publishers in other countries to omit or shorten passages they believed their own readers might find disgusting or blasphemous. And some no doubt thought that by pruning this very long novel, written by a bra-zen young author who was still unknown, they could only improve it. I thought highly of the late Ralph Manheim, and his translations of several of my works into English were marvelous, but both literary historians and translators indicated repeatedly that his translation of *The Tin Drum* needed revision. I heard the same thing about the early translations of *The Tin Drum* into other languages.

Thus, in the early summer of 2005, ten translators, including Breon Mitchell, joined me in Gdańsk with one set goal in mind: to create new versions of my first novel in their own languages. To prepare myself for their questions, I reread *The Tin Drum* for the first time since I'd written it, hesitantly at first, then with some pleasure, surprised at what the young author of fifty years ago had managed to put down on paper.

For eight days the translators from various lands questioned the author; for eight days the author talked with them, responded to their queries. During breaks I would take them to this or that spot mentioned in the rapidly shifting narrative of the novel.

How much more relaxed the reader's attitude toward *The Tin Drum* is today, even in Catholic countries like Poland, was evident one Sunday when the author and his translators visited the Church of the Sacred Heart in the Danzig suburb of Langfuhr, where I was born and raised. In my autobiographical memoir *Peeling the Onion*, I recounted the story:

> And there, in this neo-Gothic scene of a youthful crime, a young priest with a cryptic smile, a man who bore not the faintest resemblance to Father Wiehnke, asked me to sign a Polish copy of the book in question, and the author, to the astonishment of his translators and editor, did not hesitate to place his name below the title. For it was not I who broke off the Christ Child's little watering can that day at the Altar of Our Lady. It was someone with a different will. Someone who had never renounced evil. Someone who did not wish to grow . . .

Lübeck, January 2009

The Wide Skirt

GRANTED: I'M AN INMATE in a mental institution; my keeper watches me, scarcely lets me out of sight, for there's a peephole in the door, and my keeper's eye is the shade of brown that can't see through blue-eyed types like me.

So my keeper can't possibly be my enemy. I've grown fond of this man peeping through the door, and the moment he enters my room I tell him incidents from my life so he can get to know me in spite of the peephole between us. The good fellow seems to appreciate my stories, for the moment I've finished some tall tale he expresses his gratitude by showing me one of his latest knotworks. Whether he's an artist remains to be seen. But an exhibition of his works would be well received by the press, and would entice a few buyers too. He gathers ordinary pieces of string from his patients' rooms after visiting hours, disentangles them, knots them into multilayered, cartilaginous specters, dips them in plaster, lets them harden, and impales them on knitting needles mounted on little wooden pedestals.

He often plays with the notion of coloring his creations. I advise him not to, point toward my white metal bed and ask him to imagine this most perfect of all beds painted in multiple hues. Horrified, he claps his keeper's hands to his head, struggles to arrange his somewhat inflexible features into an expression of manifold shock, and drops his polychrome plans.

My white-enameled metal hospital bed thus sets a standard. To me it is more; my bed is a goal I've finally reached, it is my consolation, and could easily become my faith if the administration would allow me to make a few changes: I'd like to have the bed rails raised even higher to keep anyone from coming too close.

Once a week Visitors Day disrupts the silence I've woven between my white metal bars. It signals the arrival of those who wish to save me, who find pleasure in loving me, who seek to value, respect, and know themselves through me. How blind, nervous, and ill-mannered they are. Scratching away at my white bed rails with their nail scissors, scribbling obscene, elongated stick figures on the enamel with ballpoint pens and blue pencils. My lawyer, having blasted the room with his hello, routinely claps his nylon hat over the left-hand bedpost at the foot of my bed. This act of violence robs me of my inner balance and good cheer for as long as his visit lasts — and lawyers always have plenty to say.

Once my visitors have placed their gifts on the little white oilcloth-covered table that stands beneath a watercolor of anemones, once they've laid out some future plan to save me, or one already under way, once they've managed to convince me, by their tireless attempts to rescue me, of the high quality of their brotherly love, they find renewed joy in their own existence and depart. Then my keeper arrives to air out the room and gather up the string from the gift wrappings. Often after airing he finds time, sitting by my bed and disentangling the string, to spread a silence so prolonged that in the end I call the silence Bruno, and Bruno silence.

Bruno Münsterberg — I'm talking about my keeper now, I'm done playing with words — bought five hundred sheets of writing paper on my behalf. Should this supply prove insufficient, Bruno, who is unmarried, childless, and hails from the Sauerland, will revisit the little stationery shop, which also sells toys, and provide me with whatever additional unlined space I need for my recollections, which I hope will be accurate. I could never have requested this favor of my visitors, my lawyer, or Klepp, say. The solicitous love prescribed for me would surely have prevented my friends from anything so dangerous as bringing me blank paper and allowing my incessantly syllable-excreting mind free use of it.

When I said to Bruno, "Oh, Bruno, would you buy me a ream of virgin paper?" he looked up at the ceiling, sent his finger pointing in that same direction to underline the comparison, and replied, "You mean white paper, Herr Oskar."

I stuck with the word virgin and told Bruno to ask for it that way at the shop. When he returned later that afternoon with the package, he seemed a Bruno lost in thought. He stared long and hard a few times at the ceiling, that source of all his bright ideas, and then announced, "That word you recommended was right. I asked for virgin paper and the salesgirl blushed bright red before she gave me what I wanted."

Fearing a long conversation about salesgirls in stationery shops, I regretted having emphasized the paper's innocence by calling it virgin, and said nothing, waited till Bruno had left the room. Only then did I open the package with the five hundred sheets of paper.

I lifted the resilient stack for a moment and tested its weight. Then I counted off ten sheets and stored the rest in my bedside table. I found the fountain pen by my photo album in the drawer: it's full, it won't fail for lack of ink; how shall I begin?

You can start a story in the middle, then strike out boldly backward and forward to create confusion. You can be modern, delete all reference to time and distance, and then proclaim or let someone else proclaim that at the eleventh hour you've finally solved the space-time problem. Or you can start by declaring that novels can no longer be written, and then, behind your own back as it were, produce a mighty blockbuster that establishes you as the last of the great novelists. I've also been told it makes a good impression to begin modestly by asserting that novels no longer have heroes because individuals have ceased to exist, that individualism is a thing of the past, that all human beings are lonely, all equally lonely, with no claim to individual loneliness, that they all form some nameless mass devoid of heroes. All that may be true. But as far as I and my keeper Bruno are concerned, I beg to state that we are both heroes, quite different heroes, he behind his peephole, I in front of it; and that when he opens the door, the two of us, for all our friendship and loneliness, are still far from being some nameless mass devoid of heroes.

I'll begin long before me, for no one should describe his life who lacks the patience to commemorate at least half of his grandparents' existence before detailing his own. To all of you forced to live confusing lives beyond the confines of my mental institution, to all you friends and weekly visitors who have no inkling of my store of paper, I introduce Oskar's maternal grandmother.

My grandmother Anna Bronski sat in her skirts late one October afternoon at the edge of a potato field. You could have seen how expertly my grandmother raked the limp potato tops into tidy piles that morning, ate a hunk of bread at noon smeared with dripping and sweetened with syrup, dug through the field one last time, and sat at last in her skirts between two nearly full baskets. Before the upturned and inwardly tilted soles of her boots, flaring up asthmatically from time to time and sending a flat layer of troubled smoke across the slightly tilted crust of the soil, smoldered a potato-top fire. The year was eighteen ninety-nine, she sat in the heart of Kashubia, near Bissau, nearer still to the brickworks, this side of Ramkau she sat, beyond Viereck, facing the road to Brentau, between Dirschau and Karthaus, with her back toward the black forest of Goldkrug she sat, shoving potatoes under the hot ashes with the charred tip of a hazel stick.

If I've singled out my grandmother's skirt for special mention, making it clear, I hope, that she was sitting in her skirts — even calling the chapter "The Wide Skirt" — it's because I know how much I owe to that article of clothing. My grandmother didn't wear just one skirt, she wore four, one atop the other. Nor did she wear one top skirt and three underskirts; she wore four so-called top skirts, each skirt wore another, but she wore all four, according to a system of daily rotation. The skirt on top the day before descended one layer on the next, her second skirt became the third. The skirt that yesterday was third now nestled right against her skin. Yesterday's inmost skirt now clearly showed its pattern, which was none at all: my grandmother Anna Bronski's skirts all preferred the same standard potato color. It must have suited her.

Aside from their color my grandmother's skirts were distinguished by a lavish expanse of material. They formed broad arcs, billowed when the wind rose, fell slack when it had had enough, rattled as it passed, and all four flew out ahead of her when the wind was in her stern. When she sat down, my grandmother gathered her skirts about her.

In addition to the four skirts that permanently billowed, drooped, draped, or stood stiff and empty by her bed, my grandmother possessed a fifth. This skirt differed in no way from the four other potato-colored ones. And this fifth skirt was not always the same fifth skirt. Like its brothers — for skirts are masculine by nature — it too was subject to rotation, was one of the four skirts she wore, and like them, when its time had come each fifth Friday, it descended into the washtub, hung Saturday on the clothesline at the kitchen window, and lay when dry on the ironing board.

When, after one of these housecleaning-baking-washing-and-ironing Saturdays, having milked and fed the cow, my grandmother climbed into the tub, tendered something to the suds, let the tub water sink once more, then sat in her grandly flowered towel on the edge of the bed, there were four skirts and the freshly washed one lying spread out before her on the floor. She propped up the lower lid of her right eye with her right forefinger, consulted no one, not even her brother Vinzent, and thus reached a speedy conclusion. Barefoot she stood and pushed aside with her toe the skirt whose potato sheen had lost the most luster. The clean one then took its place.

The following Sunday, to the greater glory of Jesus, about whom she had firm ideas, she would consecrate the new order of skirts by attending church in Ramkau. Where did my grandmother wear the freshly laundered skirt? Not only a clean woman but also somewhat vain, she wore the best one on top, and if the weather was good, in bright sunshine.

Now it was a Monday afternoon and my grandmother was sitting by the potato fire. Her Sunday skirt had moved one closer to her Monday, while the one skin-warmed on Sunday flowed atop her hips that Monday Monday dull. She whistled, with no particular tune in mind, and scraped the first baked potato from the ashes with her hazel stick. She shoved the spud far enough from the smoldering mound of tops for the breeze to caress and cool it. A sharpened stick then speared the split, charred, and crusty tuber and held it to her mouth, which no longer whistled but instead, through cracked and wind-dried lips, blew ashes and earth from the skin.

As she blew, my grandmother closed her eyes. When she thought she had blown long enough, she opened her eyes, one after the other, bit down with her peep-through but otherwise perfect front teeth, quickly released them, held the still too hot potato half, mealy and steaming, in her open mouth, and inhaling smoke and October air, stared with rounded eyes over her flaring nostrils across the field to the nearby horizon with its grid of telegraph poles and the top third of the brickworks chimney.

Something was moving between the telegraph poles. My grandmother closed her mouth, sucked in her lips, narrowed her eyes, and munched on the potato. Something was moving between the telegraph poles. Something was leaping. Three men were leaping between the poles, three made for the chimney, then round in front, when one of them doubled back, took a new running start, seemed short and stout, made it over the chimney, over the brickworks, the other two, more tall and thin, made it over the brickworks too, if only just, between the poles again, but short and stout doubled back, and short and stout was in a greater hurry than tall and thin, the other leapers, who had to head back toward the chimney because the other man was already tumbling over it, while the two, still hot on his heels, made a running start and were suddenly gone, had lost heart it seemed, and the short one too fell in midleap from the chimney and disappeared below the horizon.

And there they stayed, it was intermission, or they were changing costumes, or coating bricks and getting paid for it.

When my grandmother tried to take advantage of the intermission to spear a second potato, she missed it. For the one who seemed short and stout now climbed, in the same costume, over the horizon as if it were a picket fence, as if he'd left the two leapers who were chasing him behind the fence, among the bricks, or on the pike to Brentau, yet was still in a great hurry, trying to outrace the telegraph poles, taking long, slow leaps across the field, mud leaping from his soles as he leapt from the mud, but no matter how far he leapt, he merely crept, he crawled across the muddy earth. At times he seemed stuck to the ground, then hung suspended in air so long that short and stout he still had time to wipe his brow in midleap before planting his leg again in the freshly plowed field that furrowed toward the sunken lane by her five-acre field of potatoes.

And he made it to the sunken lane, had barely vanished short and stout into the sunken lane, when tall and thin the other two, who may have toured the brickworks meanwhile, climbed likewise over the horizon and stomped their way tall and thin but by no means slim across the field, so that my grandmother failed once more to spear her potato; because that's a sight you don't see every day, three grown men, albeit grown in quite different ways, hopping among telegraph poles, practically breaking off the brickworks chimney, then, at intervals, first short and stout, then thin and tall, but all three struggling hard, ever more mud clinging to their freshly polished boots, leaping through the field that Vinzent had plowed just two days before, and disappearing into the sunken lane.

Now all three were gone, and my grandmother dared spear a nearly cold potato. Hastily she blew earth and ashes from the skin, put the whole thing in her mouth at once, thinking, if she was thinking, that they must be from the brickworks, and was still chewing with a circular motion when one of them leapt out of the sunken lane, glanced about wildly over his black mustache, took two final leaps to the fire, stood on this, that, and the other side of the fire all at once, fled here, was scared there, didn't know where to head, couldn't go back, since tall and thin were coming up the sunken lane behind him, clapped his hands, slapped his knees, his eyes popping from his head, sweat leaping from his brow. And panting, mustache trembling, he ventured nearer, crept right up to the soles of her boots; crept right up to my grandmother, looked at my grandmother like some short, stout animal, at which she heaved a great sigh, stopped chewing her potato, tilted apart the soles of her boots, abandoned all thought of brickworks, bricks, brick makers and brick coaters, and instead lifted her skirt, no, lifted all four of them, all up at once, so that this man who was not from the brickworks could crawl short but stout beneath them, and then he was gone with his mustache, gone with his animal look, came neither from Ramkau nor Viereck, was under her skirts with his fear, his knee-slapping ended, not stout or short, yet still taking up space, panting and trembling and hands on knees now forgotten: all was as still as on the first day of Creation or the last, a slight breeze gossiped in the potato fire, the telegraph poles counted themselves in silence, the brickworks chimney stood firm, and she, my grandmother, she smoothed her top skirt over the second skirt, smooth and proper, scarcely felt him under the fourth skirt, had not yet caught on with her third to something new and amazing against her skin. And because it was amazing, though on top all was calm, and both second and third had yet to catch on, she scraped two or three potatoes from the ashes, took four raw ones from the basket by her right elbow, shoved the raw spuds into the hot ashes one by one, covered them with more ashes, and poked about until the thick smoke billowed up once more — what else could she have done?

My grandmother's skirts had barely settled down, the thick flow of smoke from the potato fire, which had lost its way during all the desperate knee-slapping, place-changing, and poking about, had barely returned to creep yellow windward across the field to the southwest, when the tall and thin pair chasing the short but stout fellow now living under her skirts spurted forth from the lane and turned out to be tall and thin and wearing the official uniform of the rural constabulary.

They almost shot past my grandmother. Didn't one of them even leap over the fire? But suddenly they had heels, and brains in their heels, dug them in, turned, stomped back, stood booted and uniformed in the thick smoke, withdrew coughing in their uniforms, pulling smoke along, and were still coughing as they addressed my grandmother, wanting to know if she'd seen Koljaiczek, she must have seen him, she was sitting by the lane and he, Koljaiczek, had escaped along the lane.

My grandmother hadn't seen any Koljaiczek, because she didn't know any Koljaiczek. Was he from the brickworks, she asked, because the only ones she knew were from the brickworks. But this Koljaiczek the uniforms described had nothing to do with bricks, he was more on the short and stout side. My grandmother thought back, recalled having seen someone like that run past, and pointed, with reference to where he was heading, with a steaming potato spitted on a sharpened stick in the direction of Bissau, which, to judge by the potato, must lie between the sixth and seventh telegraph poles, counting to the right from the chimney of the brickworks. But my grandmother had no idea if the man running was Koljaiczek, blamed her lack of knowledge on the fire at the soles of her boots; it gave her enough to do, it was burning poorly, she didn't have time to worry about people running past or standing in the smoke, in general she didn't worry about people she didn't know, the only ones she knew were from Bissau, Ramkau, Viereck, and the brickworks — and that was plenty for her.

Having said this, my grandmother heaved a gentle sigh, but loud enough that the uniforms asked why she was sighing. She nodded toward the fire to indicate that she was sighing because the little fire was burning poorly, and because of all the people standing right in the smoke, then she bit off half the potato with her widely spaced front teeth, lost herself entirely in chewing, and rolled her eyeballs up and to the left.

The men in the uniform of the rural constabulary could draw no encouragement from the distant gaze of my grandmother, nor were they sure if they should head off beyond the telegraph poles toward Bissau, so in the meantime they poked around with their bayonets in the nearby piles of potato tops not yet burning. Moved by a sudden inspiration, they simultaneously overturned both nearly full potato baskets at my grandmother's elbows, and couldn't understand why only potatoes rolled out of the woven baskets at their boots, and not Koljaiczek. Suspiciously they crept around the potato pile, as if Koljaiczek might somehow have had time to pile into it, gave it several well-aimed jabs, and were sorry when no one screamed. Their suspicions were aroused by every bush, however scraggly, every mouse hole, a colony of molehills, and time and again by my grandmother, who sat there as if rooted, emitting sighs, rolling her eyes behind her lids so that the whites showed, reciting the Kashubian names of all the saints — all of which expressed and emphasized the sorrows of a poorly burning little fire and two overturned potato baskets.

The uniforms stayed a good half-hour. They stood at varying distances from the fire, took bearings on the brickworks chimney, intending to occupy Bissau as well, postponed the attack, and held their reddish blue hands over the fire till my grandmother, without ever interrupting her sighs, gave each of them a split potato on a stick. But in the midst of their chewing, the uniforms remembered their uniforms, leapt a stone's throw into the field along the broom at the edge of the lane, and startled a hare that did not, however, turn out to be Koljaiczek. Back at the fire they recovered their mealy, hotly aromatic spuds, and pacified as well as somewhat war-weary, decided to gather up the raw spuds and return them to the baskets they had overturned earlier in the line of duty.

Only when evening began to squeeze a fine, slanting rain and an inky twilight from the October sky did they attack, briefly and listlessly, a distant, darkening boulder, but once that was taken care of they decided to call it a day. A bit more foot-stamping and hands held out in blessing over the rain-spattered little fire, its thick smoke spreading, more coughing in the green smoke, eyes tearing up in the yellow smoke, then a coughing, teary-eyed stomping toward Bissau. If Koljaiczek wasn't here, then Koljaiczek must be in Bissau. The rural constabulary never sees more than two possibilities.

11

The smoke from the slowly dying fire enveloped my grandmother like a fifth skirt, so roomy that she too, in her four skirts, with her sighs and names of saints, like Koljaiczek, found herself beneath a skirt. Only when nothing remained of the uniforms but wavering dots slowly drowning in dusk between the telegraph poles did my grandmother rise as laboriously as if she had struck root and was now interrupting that incipient growth, pulling forth tendrils and earth.

Suddenly finding himself lying short and stout in the rain without a hood, Koljaiczek grew cold. Quickly he buttoned the trousers that fear and an overwhelming need for refuge had bidden him open under her skirts. He fiddled quickly with the buttons, fearing an all too rapid cooling of his rod, for the weather carried the threat of autumnal chills.

It was my grandmother who found four more hot potatoes under the ashes. She gave three to Koljaiczek, kept one for herself, then asked before taking a bite if he came from the brickworks, though she must have known that Koljaiczek had nothing to do with the bricks. And paying no heed to his answer, she loaded the lighter basket onto him, bent beneath the heavier one herself, kept one hand free for the garden rake and hoe, and with basket, potatoes, rake, and hoe, billowed away in her four skirts toward Bissau-Abbau.

Bissau-Abbau was not Bissau proper. It lay more in the direction of Ramkau. Leaving the brickworks to their left, they headed for the black forest, where Goldkrug lay, and beyond it Brentau. But in a hollow before the forest lay Bissau-Abbau. And following my grandmother toward it short and stout came Joseph Koljaiczek, who could no longer free himself from her skirts.

Under the Raft

IT'S NOT SO EASY, lying here in the scrubbed metal bed of a mental institution, within range of a glazed peephole armed with Bruno's eye, to retrace the swaths of smoke rising from Kashubian potato fires and the fine diagonal strokes of an October rain. If I didn't have my drum, which, when handled properly and patiently, recalls all the little details I need to get the essentials down on paper, and if I didn't have the institute's permission to let my drum speak three or four hours each day, I would be a poor fellow with no known grandparents.

At any rate my drum says: On that October afternoon in eighteen ninety-nine, while Ohm Krüger was brushing his bushy anti-British eyebrows in South Africa, nearer home, between Dirschau and Karthaus, by the Bissau brickworks, beneath four skirts of a single color, beneath smoke, shock, sighs, and saints' names sorrowfully invoked, beneath the slanting rain, beneath the smoke-filled eyes and hapless questioning of two rural constables, short but stout Joseph Koljaiczek begot my mother Agnes.

Anna Bronski, my grandmother, changed her name under cover of that very night's darkness, transformed herself, with the help of a priest who was generous with the sacraments, into Anna Koljaiczek, and followed Joseph, if not into Egypt, at least to the provincial capital on the Mottlau, where Joseph found work as a raftsman and temporary respite from the rural police.

Just to heighten the suspense somewhat, I won't name that city at the mouth of the Mottlau just yet, though as my mother's birthplace it would certainly deserve mention at this point. At the end of July nineteen hundred — they were deciding to double the construction plans for the imperial navy—Mama first saw the light of day, under the sign of Leo. Self-confidence and imagination, generosity and vanity. The first house, also known as *domus vitae,* in the sign of the ascendant: the easily influenced Pisces. The constellation of the sun in opposition to Neptune, seventh house or *domus matrimonii uxoris,* would bring confusion. Venus in opposition to Saturn, called the sour planet, known to induce ailments of the spleen and liver, dominant in Capricorn and celebrating its destruction in Leo, to which Neptune offers eels and receives the mole in return, which loves belladonna, onions, and beets, which coughs lava and sours wine; he lived with Venus in the eighth house, the house of death, which spoke of accidents, while conception in the potato field gave promise of a most hazardous happiness under the protection of Mercury in the house of relatives.

Here I must insert my mama's protest, for she always denied having been conceived in the potato field. Her father—this much she admitted—had tried it there, but his situation and Anna Bronski's position were not sufficiently well chosen to provide Koljaiczek with the preconditions for conception.

"It must have happened that night, while we were on the run, or in Uncle Vinzent's box cart, or later on the island of Troyl, when we found a room and safe haven with the raftsmen."

With such words did my mama date the founding of her existence, and my grandmother, who surely must have known, would nod patiently and announce to the world, "That's right, child, maybe it was in the cart or on Troyl, but not in the field, because it was windy and raining like the dickens."

Vinzent was my grandmother's brother. Spurred on by the death of his young wife, he made a pilgrimage to Częstochowa, where the Matka Boska Częstochowska charged him to recognize her as the future Queen of Poland. From then on he spent all his time rummaging through strange books, where he found the Virgin Mother's claim to the Polish throne confirmed in every line, and let his sister handle the farmhouse and his few acres. Jan, his four-year-old son, a frail child always on the verge of tears, tended the geese, collected brightly colored cards and, steered by fate from an early age, stamps.

Into that farmhouse dedicated to the divine Queen of Poland my grandmother brought her potato baskets and Koljaiczek, whereupon

Vinzent, seeing what had happened, ran to Ramkau and drummed up a priest to come armed with the sacraments and join Anna and Joseph in marriage. No sooner had His Reverence, groggy with sleep, yawned his drawn-out blessing and, supplied with a good side of bacon, turned his consecrated back than Vinzent hitched the horse to the cart, bundled the newlyweds into the back, bedded them down on straw and empty sacks, set a shivering and weakly weeping Jan beside him on the box, and gave his horse to understand that he was to head hard and straight into the night: the honeymooners were in a hurry.

The night was dark, but almost spent, when the wagon reached the timber port of the provincial capital. Fellow raftsmen, friends of Koljaiczek, took in the fugitive couple. Vinzent turned and headed his horse toward Bissau again: a cow, the goat, a sow with her piglets, eight geese, and the farmyard dog were waiting to be fed and his son Jan to be put to bed, for he was running a slight fever.

Joseph Koljaiczek remained in hiding for three weeks, trained his hair to take a new part, shaved off his mustache, provided himself with unblemished papers, and found work as a raftsman named Joseph Wranka. But why did Koljaiczek find it necessary to appear before timber merchants and sawmills with Wranka's papers in his pocket, a man who, unbeknownst to the local authorities, had been shoved off a raft in a scuffle above Modlin and then drowned in the Bug River? Because, having given up rafting for a time, Koljaiczek worked in a sawmill near Schwetz and got into a row with the mill boss over a fence Koljaiczek had painted a provocative red and white. No fence sitter himself when it came to politics, the mill boss ripped two slats from the fence, one white and one red, and smashed them to Polish kindling across Koljaiczek's Kashubian back, grounds enough for the battered man, on the following no doubt starry night, to set the newly constructed, whitewashed sawmill ablaze in red, to the greater glory of an indeed partitioned but therefore even more firmly united Poland.

So Koljaiczek was an arsonist, and this several times over, for in the days that followed, sawmills and woodlots all over West Prussia provided tinder for the flare-up of bicolored nationalist feelings. As always when the future of Poland was at stake, the Virgin Mary appeared in the crowd at these conflagrations, and there were eyewitnesses — a few might still be alive today — who claimed to have seen the Mother of God, adorned with the crown of Poland, atop the collapsing roofs of several sawmills. The crowd that always gathers at such great conflagrations is said to have burst out in the Hymn to Bogurodzica, Mother of God — Koljaiczek's fires, we have every reason to believe, were affairs of great solemnity: solemn oaths were sworn.

While Koljaiczek was pursued as an arsonist, the raftsman Joseph Wranka — with an unblemished past and no parents, a harmless, even slow-witted fellow no one was looking for and hardly anyone even knew — had divided his chewing tobacco into daily rations till the Bug swallowed him up, leaving behind his jacket with three days' worth of chewing tobacco and his papers. Since Wranka, having drowned, could no longer show up, and no embarrassing questions were raised about him, Koljaiczek, who was about the same size and had the same round head as the drowned man, crept first into his jacket, then into his skin, complete with official papers and free of any prior conviction, gave up his pipe, took to chewing tobacco, even adopted Wranka's most characteristic trait, his speech impediment, and in the years that followed played the part of an honest and thrifty raftsman with a slight stutter who conveyed entire forests down the Niemen, the Bobr, the Bug, and the Vistula. To which must be added that he even rose to Private First Class in the Crown Prince's Leib-Hussars under Mackensen, for Wranka had not yet done his service, while Koljaiczek, who was four years older than the drowned man, had left a checkered record behind in the artillery at Thorn.

Even as they steal, murder, and set fires, the most dangerous of thieves, murderers, and arsonists are on the lookout for a more respectable trade. By effort or luck, some get that chance: Koljaiczek in the guise of Wranka made a good husband, and was so thoroughly cured of the fiery vice that the mere sight of a match made him tremble. A box of matches lying openly and smugly on the kitchen table was never safe from him, even though he might well have invented them. He cast temptation out the window. My grandmother had a hard time getting a hot lunch on the table by noon. The family often sat in darkness for lack of a match to light the oil lamp.

Yet Wranka was no tyrant. On Sunday he took his Anna Wranka to church in the lower city and allowed her, his legally wedded wife, to wear four skirts one atop the other, as she had in the potato field. In winter, when the rivers were frozen over and times were lean for the raftsmen, he sat like a good fellow on Troyl, where only raftsmen, stevedores, and dockers lived, and watched over his daughter Agnes, who seemed to take after her father, for when she wasn't crawling under the bed, she was hiding in the wardrobe, and when there were visitors she sat under the table with her rag dolls.

Thus little Agnes tried to keep hidden, seeking in her hiding place the same security, though not the same pleasure, that Joseph found under Anna's skirts. Koljaiczek the arsonist had been burned badly enough to understand his daughter's need for shelter. So when it became necessary to build a rabbit hutch on the balcony-like porch of their one-and-a-half-room flat, he added a small addition just her size. In such housing my mother sat as a child, played with dolls, and kept growing. It's said that later, when she was already at school, she threw her dolls away and, playing with glass beads and colored feathers, revealed her first taste for fragile beauty.

Since I'm burning to announce the beginning of my own existence, perhaps I may be permitted to leave the Wrankas' family raft drifting peacefully along without further comment till nineteen-thirteen, when the *Columbus* was launched at Schichau's; that's when the police, who never forget, picked up the trail of the false Wranka.

It all began in August of nineteen-thirteen, when, as he did toward the end of each summer, Koljaiczek helped man the great raft that floated down from Kiev by way of the Pripet, through the canal, along the Bug as far as Modlin, and from there on down to the Vistula. Twelve raftsmen in all, they steamed upriver on the tugboat *Radaune,* operated by the sawmill, from Westlich Neufähr along the Dead Vistula as far as Einlage, then up the Vistula past Käsemark, Letzkau, Czattkau, Dirschau, and Pieckel, and tied up that evening at Thorn. There the new sawmill manager came on board, sent to oversee the purchase of timber in Kiev. When the *Radaune* cast off at four that morning he was said to be on board. Koljaiczek saw him for the first time at breakfast in the galley. They sat opposite each other, chewing, and slurping barley coffee. Koljaiczek recognized him at once. The stout, prematurely bald man had vodka brought for the empty coffee cups. Still chewing, and while the vodka was being poured at the end of the table, he introduced himself: "Just so you know, I'm the new boss, Dückerhoff, and I run a tight ship."

At his bidding the raftsmen reeled off their names in turn as they sat, then drained their cups with bobbing Adam's apples. Koljaiczek gulped his down first, then said "Wranka" and looked Dückerhoff straight in the eye. The latter nodded just as he'd done before, repeated the name Wranka just as he had repeated those of the other men. Yet it seemed to Koljaiczek that Dückerhoff had spoken the name of the drowned raftsman with special emphasis, not pointedly but with a thoughtful air.

The *Radaune* pounded along against the muddy tide that knew but one direction, deftly avoiding sandbanks with the aid of constantly changing pilots. To right and left, beyond the dikes, the same flat landscape with occasional hills, already harvested. Hedges, sunken lanes, a hollow basin with broom, a level plain between the scattered farms, just made for cavalry attacks, for a division of uhlans to wheel in from the left onto the sand table, for hedge-vaulting hussars, for the dreams of young cavalry officers, for battles long past and battles yet to come, for an oil painting: tartars leaning forward, dragoons rearing up, Brethren of the Sword falling, grandmasters staining their noble robes, not a button missing from their cuirasses, save for one, struck down by the Duke of Mazowsze, and horses, no circus has horses so white, nervous, covered with tassels, sinews rendered with precision, nostrils flaring, crimson, snorting small clouds impaled by lowered lances decked with pennants, and parting the heavens, the sunset's red glow, the sabers, and there, in the background — for every painting has a background — clinging tightly to the horizon, with smoke rising peacefully, a small village between the hind legs of the black stallion, crouching cottages, moss-covered, thatched, and inside the cottages, held in readiness, the pretty tanks, dreaming of days to come when they too would be allowed to enter the picture, to come out onto the plain beyond the Vistula's dikes, like slender colts among the heavy cavalry.

At Włocławek, Dückerhoff tapped Koljaiczek on the jacket: "Say, Wranka, didn't you work at the mill in Schwetz a few years back? The one that burned down afterward?" Koljaiczek shook his head slowly, as if he had difficulty turning it, and his eyes were so sad and tired that Dückerhoff, exposed to that look, kept any further questions to himself.

When Koljaiczek, as all raftsmen used to do, leaned over the railing at Modlin and spat three times into the Bug as the *Radaune* entered the Vistula, Dückerhoff was standing beside him with a cigar and asked for a light. That little word, like the word match, got under Koljaiczek's skin. "You don't have to blush when I ask for a light, man. You're not some little girl, are you?"

Modlin was far behind them before Koljaiczek's blush faded, which was not a blush of shame but the lingering glow of sawmills he'd set on fire.

From Modlin to Kiev—up the Bug, through the canal linking the Bug and the Pripet, till the *Radaune,* following the Pripet, made its way to the Dnieper—nothing passed between Koljaiczek-Wranka and Dückerhoff that could be recorded as an exchange. It's of course possible that things happened on the tug, among the raftsmen, between the raftsmen and the stokers, between the stokers, the helmsman, and the captain, between the captain and the constantly changing pilots, as one assumes, perhaps rightly, they always do among men. I could imagine disputes between the Kashubian raftsmen and the helmsman, who came from Stettin, perhaps even the beginnings of a mutiny: a meeting in the galley, lots drawn, passwords given out, frog stickers sharpened.

But enough of that. There were no political disputes, no knife fights between Germans and Poles, nor a true mutiny born of social injustice to add local color. The *Radaune* chugged along eating her coal like a good girl, got hung up on a sandbank once—just beyond Ploch, I think it was—but freed herself under her own power. A brief but bitter exchange between Captain Barbusch from Neufahrwasser and the Ukrainian pilot, that was about it—and the log had little more to add.

But had I wanted or needed to keep a log of Koljaiczek's thoughts, or perhaps even a journal of Dückerhoff's inner life as a master miller, there would have been plenty of incidents and adventures to describe: suspicions aroused, suspicions confirmed, distrust, and distrust quickly quelled. They were both afraid. Dückerhoff more than Koljaiczek: for now they were in Russia. Dückerhoff could have gone overboard, as poor Wranka once had, or—by now we are in Kiev—in lumberyards so vast and confusing that a man can lose his guardian angel in the wooden labyrinth and wind up under a pile of suddenly shifting logs that can no longer be held back—or instead be saved. Saved by Koljaiczek, first to fish the mill master from the Pripet or the Bug, or, in that Kiev lumberyard bereft of guardian angels, yank Dückerhoff back in the nick of time from an avalanche of logs. How touching it would be if I could now report that a half-drowned or nearly crushed Dückerhoff, still breathing heavily, the lingering trace of death in his eyes, whispered in the ear of the ostensible Wranka, "Thanks, Koljaiczek, thanks, old man!" and then, after the obligatory pause, "We're quits now — the slate's clean."

And with gruff bonhomie, smiling awkwardly into each other's manly eyes, blinking back what might have been a tear, they exchange a shy but callused handshake.

We know this scene from magnificently filmed movies, when directors decide to turn two finely portrayed rival brothers into steadfast comrades, who now make their way together through thick and thin to face a thousand adventures.

Koljaiczek, however, found neither the opportunity to drown Dückerhoff nor to snatch him from the claws of death-dealing logs. Ever attentive and alert to his firm's advantage, Dückerhoff bought lumber in Kiev, oversaw the assembly of the nine rafts, distributed, as was customary, a large sum of Russian pocket money for the trip downriver, then boarded the train that took him by way of Modlin, Deutsch-Eylau, Marienburg, and Dirschau back to his firm, whose sawmill lay in the timber port between the shipyards of Klawitter and Schichau.

Before I bring the raftsmen, after weeks of grueling toil, from Kiev back down the rivers, through the canal, and finally into the Vistula, I ask myself if Dückerhoff had positively identified Wranka as the arsonist Koljaiczek. I would say that as long as the mill master was sitting on a steamer with the harmless, good-natured, somewhat slow-witted but generally well-liked Wranka, he hoped his traveling companion was not the hot-blooded criminal Koljaiczek. He only relinquished this hope once he had settled back into the cushions of his train compartment. And by the time the train reached its destination and rolled into Central Station at Danzig — there, now I've named it — Dückerhoff had reached the Dückerhoff Resolutions, had his luggage loaded onto a carriage, sent it rolling homeward, strode briskly, relieved of that luggage, to the nearby police station on Wiebenwall, sprang up the steps to the main entrance, and, after a brief and focused search, found the office, which functioned well enough to wring from Dückerhoff a brief report of the basic facts. Not that the mill master issued a formal complaint. He simply requested that they look into the Koljaiczek-Wranka case, which the police promised to do.

Over the following weeks, as the logs slowly glided downstream with their reed huts and raftsmen, paperwork flowed through various offices. There was the military record of Joseph Koljaiczek, a private in the such-and-such West Prussian Field Artillery Regiment. Twice the unruly private had served the standard three days in the guardhouse for shouting anarchist slogans, half in Polish, half in German, at the top of his lungs while in a state of intoxication. Those were stains not to be found on the papers of Private First Class Wranka, who had served in the Second Leib-Hussar Regiment in Langfuhr. Wranka had performed admirably, making a favorable impression on the Crown Prince during maneuvers as a battalion dispatch runner, and receiving from the Prince, who always carried a few thalers in his pocket, one Crown Prince thaler as a reward. The thaler in question was not, however, mentioned in the military record of Private First Class Wranka, but was instead reported by my loudly complaining grandmother Anna as she was being interrogated along with her brother Vinzent.

Not with that thaler alone did she dispute the term arsonist. She produced a series of documents showing that Joseph Wranka had joined the Volunteer Fire Brigade in Danzig-Niederstadt as early as ought-four as a firefighter, in the winter months, when all the raftsmen were off work, and battled blazes large and small. There was also a certificate declaring that during the great conflagration at the main rail factory on Troyl in ought-nine, Fireman Wranka not only put out the fire but also rescued two apprentice mechanics. Similar testimony was offered by Captain Hecht of the Fire Brigade, who was called as a witness. He stated for the record: "How can someone be an arsonist when he puts out fires? I can still see him now, standing there on the ladder while the church in Heubude was ablaze! A phoenix rising from ashes and flame, extinguishing not only the fire but the conflagration of this world and the thirst of our Lord Jesus Christ! Verily I say unto you: He who dares accuse this man in fireman's helmet, who always has the right of way, beloved by all insurers, bearer always of ash in his pocket, be it residue or symbol of his calling, he who dares call this splendid phoenix a firebug, deserves to have a millstone tied about his neck and . . ."

You will have noticed that Captain Hecht of the Volunteer Fire Brigade was a preacher, amply endowed with the power of the Word. Each and every Sunday he stood at the pulpit of the Church of St. Barbara in Langgarten and never missed a chance, as long as Koljaiczek-Wranka was under investigation, to hammer home to his congregation in similar terms parables of the heavenly firefighter and the infernal arsonist.

Since, however, the agents of the crime squad didn't attend church at St. Barbara's, and because the word phoenix would have sounded more like *lèse majesté* to them than a justification of Wranka's actions, the overall effect of Wranka's volunteer firefighting was simply to incriminate him further.

Evidence was gathered from various sawmills, reports sent in from hometowns: Wranka first saw the light of day in Tuchel; Koljaiczek was a native of Thorn. Minor discrepancies in the statements of older raftsmen and distant relatives. The pitcher kept going to the well; what else could it do but crack? When the interrogations had reached this point, the large raft had just entered German territory, and from Thorn on was discreetly monitored and kept under surveillance wherever it docked.

It was only below Dirschau that my grandfather first noticed those shadowing him. He'd been expecting them. A temporary spell of lethargy verging on melancholy may well have kept him from making a break for it, at Letzkau, say, or Käsemark, where, given the familiar territory and the help of a few well-disposed raftaks, as the Polish raftsmen were called, it might still have been possible. Beyond Einlage, as the rafts slowly thumped and bumped their way into the Dead Vistula, an obviously overmanned fishing boat, making a conspicuous effort to be inconspicuous, ran alongside the rafts. Just beyond Plehnendorf, the two motor launches of the harbor police shot forth from a bank of reeds and, tearing back and forth several times, slashed open the increasingly brackish water of the Dead Vistula that heralded the harbor. Beyond the bridge to Heubude the cordon of blue uniforms began. Timber fields facing the Klawitter yards, the smaller shipyards, the timber port spreading outward toward the Mottlau, the landing stages of various sawmills, their own company's dock with their families waiting for them, and blue uniforms everywhere, except across the way at Schichau, where flags were flying, where something else was going on, where something was likely being launched, where a big crowd was stir-

ring up the gulls, where some sort of celebration was under way — a celebration for my grandfather?

Only when my grandfather saw the timber port filled with blue uniforms, when the motor launches began crisscrossing more and more
ominously, sending waves washing across the rafts, only when he
grasped the full extent of the costly effort devoted to him, only then did
Koljaiczek's old arsonist heart awaken, and he spewed forth the gentle
Wranka, sloughed off Wranka the volunteer fireman, loudly and fluently renounced Wranka the stutterer, and fled, fled over the rafts, fled
over broad, shifting surfaces, barefoot over unfinished parquet, from
long log to long log toward Schichau's, where flags in the wind gaily
waved, on over the logs, where something lay in the slips, you can walk
on water after all, where they were making fancy speeches, where no
one was shouting Wranka, let alone Koljaiczek, where instead it was:
I christen you HMS *Columbus*, America, forty thousand tons, thirty
thousand horsepower, His Majesty's Ship, First-Class Smoking Salon,
Second-Class Larboard Dining Room, marble gymnasium, library,
America, His Majesty's Ship, stabilizers, promenade deck, *Heil dir im
Siegerkranz*, flag of the home port flying, Prince Heinrich at the Helm,
and my grandfather Koljaiczek barefoot, barely grazing the logs now,
heading toward the brass band, a land that has such princes, from raft
to raft, the people cheer him on, *Heil dir im Siegerkranz*, and all the
shipyard sirens and the sirens of all the ships lying in the harbor, the
tugboats and the pleasure boats, *Columbus*, America, liberty, and two
launches frantic with joy running along beside him, from raft to raft,
His Majesty's Rafts, cut off his path, play spoilsport, force him to stop
when things had been going so well, and all alone on a raft he stands
and can see America, then the launches are alongside and he has to
fling himself off — and they saw my grandfather swimming, swimming
toward a raft that was gliding into the Mottlau. And had to dive down
because of the launches and stay down because of the launches, and the
raft passed over him and seemed without end, gave birth to raft after
raft: raft of thy raft, for all eternity, raft.

The launches killed their motors. Relentless eyes searched the surface of the water. But Koljaiczek was gone for good, had escaped the
band music, the sirens, the bells of the ships and His Majesty's Ship,
Prince Heinrich's christening speech and His Majesty's frantic gulls, es-

caped *Heil dir im Siegerkranz* and His Majesty's Soap used to launch His Majesty's Ship, escaped America and the *Columbus,* escaped the police and their search beneath the endless expanse of logs.

My grandfather's body was never found. Though I firmly believe that he met his death beneath the raft, I feel compelled, in order to maintain my credibility, to recount all the versions in which he was miraculously saved.

It is said that he found a chink between the logs under the raft, just big enough to keep his respiratory organs above water. This chink supposedly narrowed toward the top in such a way that it remained invisible to the police, who continued searching the rafts and even the reed huts on the rafts far into the night. Then, under cover of darkness — so the story goes — he floated till he arrived, exhausted to be sure, but with a little luck, on the far shore of the Mottlau and the grounds of the Schichau shipyards, took cover in the scrap yard there, and later, probably with the help of Greek sailors, boarded one of those greasy tankers said to have offered asylum to many a fugitive.

Others maintained that Koljaiczek, a strong swimmer with even stronger lungs, not only swam under the raft but continued across the whole remaining breadth of the Mottlau under water and arrived with luck at the festival area of the Schichau shipyard, mingled among the workers without being noticed, then joined the enthusiastic crowd in singing *Heil dir im Siegerkranz,* listened with appreciative applause as Prince Heinrich christened His Majesty's Ship *Columbus,* and after the launch, his clothes now half-dry, drifted away with the crowd, to advance the very next day — here the first and second versions of the rescue converge — to the rank of stowaway on one of those famous infamous Greek tankers.

For the sake of completeness I should mention a third preposterous tale, according to which my grandfather floated out to sea like driftwood, where he was promptly fished out by fishermen from Bohnsack and handed over to a Swedish deep-sea fishing boat beyond the three-mile limit. There, on the Swede, the tale allows him to slowly and miraculously recover his strength, reach Malmö — and so on and so forth.

All that is nonsense and fishermen's tales. Nor do I give a fig for the reports of all those equally unreliable eyewitnesses in various ports who claim to have seen my grandfather shortly after the First World War in Buffalo, USA. Called himself Joe Colchic, they say. In the timber trade with Canada. Stockholder in match factories. Founder of fire insurance companies. Filthy rich and lonely my grandfather was, they say, sitting at a huge desk in a skyscraper, rings with glowing stones on every finger, drilling his bodyguards, who wore firemen's uniforms, could sing in Polish, and were known as the Phoenix Guard.

Moth and Light Bulb

A MAN LEFT EVERYTHING behind, crossed the great water, came to America, and grew rich. I think I'll leave it at that with my grandfather, whether he calls himself Goljaczek (Polish), Koljaiczek (Kashubian), or Joe Colchic (American).

It's not that easy, using a simple tin drum of the sort you can buy in any toy shop or department store, to search through rafts floating downriver almost to the horizon. I have, however, managed to drum my way through the timber port, through all the driftwood lurching in its inlets, tangled in the reeds, and, with less effort, through the building slips of the Schichau and Klawitter shipyards, through all the boatyards, some doing repairs only, the scrap yard at the railroad-car factory, the rancid coconut heap by the margarine factory, all the hiding places I know of on the Speicherinsel. He's dead, doesn't answer, shows no interest in imperial ship launchings, in the decline of a ship that begins with its launching and often lasts decades, in this case a ship named the *Columbus*, known as the pride of the fleet, which obviously set off for America and was later sunk, or scuttled, was perhaps raised and refitted, renamed, or scrapped. Perhaps the *Columbus*, like my grandfather, merely dived under and is still knocking about today with her forty thousand tons, smoking salon, marble gymnasium, swimming pool, and massage booths, at a depth of, say, six thousand meters, in the Philippine Trench or Emden Deep; you'll find the whole story in Weyer or in the naval calendars—I think the first or second *Columbus* was scuttled because the captain couldn't bear to go on living after some sort of disgrace connected with the war.

I read part of my raft story aloud to Bruno, and then, asking him to be objective, posed my question.

"A beautiful death!" Bruno exclaimed, and immediately began transforming my drowned grandfather into one of his knotworks. I should rest content with his response, he says, and not head for the USA with some harebrained idea of cadging an inheritance.

My friends Klepp and Vittlar came to see me. Klepp brought me a jazz record with two pieces by King Oliver, while Vittlar, with a mincing little gesture, held out a chocolate heart dangling from a pink ribbon. They clowned around, parodied scenes from my trial, and to please them, as always on Visitors Day, I put on a cheerful face and managed to laugh at even their worst jokes. In passing, as it were, and before Klepp could begin his inevitable lecture on the relationship of jazz to Marxism, I told the story of a man who, in nineteen-thirteen, shortly before all hell broke loose, wound up under a seemingly endless raft and never came up again; they never even found his body.

In reply to my question — I asked it casually, in a decidedly bored manner — Klepp twisted his head grumpily on his fat neck, buttoned and unbuttoned himself, made swimming motions, and acted as if he were under the raft. Finally he shook off my question and blamed the early hour of the afternoon for his failure to respond.

Vittlar sat stiffly, crossed his legs, taking care not to disturb the crease in his trousers, displaying that bizarre pinstriped arrogance shared perhaps only by angels in heaven: "I'm on the raft. It's pleasant on the raft. Mosquitoes are biting me, that's annoying — I'm under the raft. It's pleasant under the raft. The mosquitoes aren't biting me, that's pleasant. I think I could live under the raft if I didn't plan to live on the raft and let the mosquitoes bite me."

Vittlar paused in his practiced manner, regarded me closely, raised his already lofty eyebrows as he always did when he wished to look like an owl, and spoke with strong theatrical emphasis: "I take it the drowned man in question, the man under the raft, was your great-uncle, perhaps even your grandfather. He went to his death because, as your great-uncle, and even more so as your grandfather, he felt he owed it to you, since nothing would have been more burdensome to you than a living grandfather. You not only murdered your great-uncle, you murdered your grandfather. But since, like any true grandfather, he wished to punish you a little, he didn't give you the satisfaction of a grandchild who points proudly at a swollen, waterlogged corpse, and declaims: Behold my dead grandfather. He was a hero. He jumped in the river while they were chasing him. Your grandfather cheated the world and his grandchild of his corpse so that posterity and his grandchild would be worrying their heads about him for years to come."

Then, springing from one sort of pathos to another, a cunning Vittlar leaned slightly forward, as if placating me: "America! Be happy, Oskar! You have a goal, a task. You'll be acquitted, they'll release you here. And whither, if not to America, where you can find everything, even your long-lost grandfather."

However mocking and endlessly offensive Vittlar's answer may have been, it offered more certainty than my friend Klepp's grumbled refusal to choose between life and death, or the response of my keeper Bruno, who found my grandfather's death beautiful only because shortly thereafter the HMS *Columbus* slid down the slips and made waves. And so I praise Vittlar's America, conserver of grandfathers, a chosen goal, an ideal I can set for myself when, fed up with Europe, I choose to lay aside my drum and my pen: "Keep on writing, Oskar, do it for your filthy-rich but weary grandfather Koljaiczek, plying the timber trade in Buffalo, USA, playing with matches in his skyscraper!"

When Klepp and Vittlar had finally taken their leave, Bruno drove the disturbing smell of my friends from the room with a vigorous airing. Then I returned to my drum, but no longer drummed up death-concealing timber rafts; instead I beat out that quick erratic rhythm all men obeyed from August nineteen-fourteen on. Thus it is inevitable that my text too, as it brings us to the hour of my birth, will sketch but briefly the path taken by the group of mourners my grandfather left behind in Europe.

When Koljaiczek disappeared beneath the raft, my grandmother, her daughter Agnes, Vinzent Bronski, and his seventeen-year-old son Jan were standing frightened among the family members of the raftsmen on the sawmill's landing dock. Slightly to one side stood Gregor Koljaiczek, Joseph's older brother, who had been summoned to the city for questioning. This Gregor was wise enough to keep offering the police the following standard answer: "Hardly knew my brother. All I'm really sure of is that he was called Joseph, and the last time I saw him he was ten, maybe twelve years old. He shined my shoes and went out for beer, if Mother or I wanted some."

Even though it turned out my great-grandmother did in fact drink beer, Gregor Koljaiczek's answer was of no help to the police. But the elder Koljaiczek's existence was a great help to my grandmother Anna. Gregor, who had lived for some years in Stettin, then Berlin, and finally Schneidemühl, settled down in Danzig, got a job at the Bastion Kaninchen powder mill, and, after a year had passed, when all complications such as her marriage to the counterfeit Wranka had been cleared up and filed away, married my grandmother, who planned to stick with Koljaiczeks and wouldn't have married Gregor, or at least not so quickly, if he hadn't been a Koljaiczek.

Gregor's job at the powder mill kept him out of the colorful uniforms that soon turned uniformly gray. The three of them lived in the same one-and-a-half-room flat that had sheltered the arsonist for years. It turned out, however, that not all Koljaiczeks were necessarily alike, for after barely a year of marriage my grandmother found herself forced to rent the basement shop that was standing empty at the time in the apartment house on Troyl to try to make some extra cash by selling odds and ends ranging from pins to cabbages, since Gregor, though he made good money at the gunpowder mill, failed to provide even the bare necessities at home, but drank everything away instead. While Gregor, taking after my great-grandmother no doubt, was a real drinker, my grandfather Joseph was a man who merely enjoyed a schnapps now and then. It wasn't sorrow that drove Gregor to drink. And even when he seemed cheerful, which was seldom enough, since he tended toward melancholy, he didn't drink because he was in high spirits. He drank because he was a thorough man who liked to get to the bottom of things, including his liquor. As long as he lived, no one ever saw Gregor Koljaiczek leave a half-full shot glass of Machandel gin standing.

My mama, a plump fifteen-year-old girl back then, made herself useful, helped in the shop, pasted in food stamps, delivered groceries on Saturday, and wrote clumsy but imaginative reminders meant to bring in cash from customers who bought on credit. Too bad I don't have one of those letters. How nice it would be at this point to quote a few half-childish, half-maidenly cries of distress from the epistles of this half orphan, for whom Gregor Koljaiczek offered less than full value as a stepfather. On the contrary, my grandmother and her daughter were hard-pressed to shield their cashbox, which consisted of one tin plate clapped on top of another, filled mostly with copper and very little silver, from the melancholy gaze of the eternally thirsty powder miller Koljaiczek. Only when Gregor Koljaiczek died of the flu in nineteen-seventeen did the profit margin of the odds-and-ends shop increase slightly, but not by much; for what was there to sell in seventeen?

The smaller room in the one-and-a-half-room flat, which had been standing empty since the powder miller's death because my mama was afraid of ghosts and refused to move into it, was now taken over by Jan Bronski, my mother's cousin, around twenty years old at the time, who, having left Bissau and his father Vinzent behind, graduated with good marks from high school in Karthaus, served his apprenticeship at the post office in the small district capital, and was now entering the second stage of his career at the central post office in Danzig I. In addition to his suitcase, Jan brought an extensive stamp collection to his aunt's flat. He'd been collecting since he was a little boy; his relationship to the post office was thus not merely professional but also personal and deeply engaged. The slender young man, who stooped slightly when he walked, offered a pretty, perhaps overly sweet oval face with eyes blue enough that my mama, who was then seventeen, fell in love with him. Jan had been called up three times but had been rejected on each occasion owing to his poor physical condition, which, given that in those days anyone who could stand even halfway straight got sent to Verdun to assume the eternal horizontal on France's soil, tells you all you need to know about Jan Bronski's constitution.

Their flirtation should actually have started as they pored over stamp albums together, examining the perforations of particularly valuable items tête-à-tête. But it began, or first erupted, when Jan was called up for the fourth time. Since she had to go into town anyway, my mama accompanied him to district headquarters, waited outside next to a sentry box manned by a reservist, and felt, as Jan did, that this time he would surely be heading to France to cure his ailing chest in the iron- and lead-rich air of that land. My mama may well have been counting the reservist's buttons with varying results. It wouldn't surprise me if the buttons of all uniforms were arranged so that the last button always stood for

Verdun, or Hartmannsweilerkopf, where men got buttoned down, or some little river called the Somme or the Marne.

When, after barely an hour, the little fellow who'd been called up for the fourth time slipped through the portal of district headquarters, stumbled down the stairs, and, falling on the neck of my mama Agnes, whispered the then popular saying, "No neck and a skinny rear, rejected for another year," my mother hugged Jan Bronski for the first time, and I doubt she ever hugged him more happily.

The details of that young wartime love are not known to me. Jan sold part of his stamp collection to meet the needs of my mama, who had a lively sense for pretty, dressy, and expensive things, and is said to have kept a diary back then, which unfortunately has been lost. My grandmother seems to have tolerated the bond between the two youngsters — one can assume that it went beyond the familial — for Jan Bronski lived in the cramped flat on Troyl until shortly after the war. He didn't move out until the existence of a certain Herr Matzerath proved undeniable and undenied. My mother must have met this gentleman in the summer of nineteen-eighteen, when she was serving as an auxiliary nurse in the Silberhammer Military Hospital at Oliva. Alfred Matzerath, a native Rhinelander, lay there with a clean shot through his upper thigh and, with his merry Rhenish ways, was soon the favorite of all the nurses — Sister Agnes not excepted. Half healed, he hobbled along the corridor on the arm of this or that nurse and helped Sister Agnes in the kitchen, both because her round face looked so pretty in her little nurse's cap and because, as a passionate cook, he could convert his emotions into soups.

When his wound had healed, Alfred Matzerath stayed on in Danzig and found work straightaway as a local salesman for his Rhenish firm, one of the larger enterprises in the paper-manufacturing industry. The war had worn itself out. Peace treaties that would give cause for further wars were being crudely crafted: the region around the mouth of the Vistula — from roughly Vogelsang on the Nehrung along the Nogat to Pieckel, from there down the Vistula to Czattkau, taking a right angle leftward to Schönfließ, then tracing a hump around Saskoschin Forest to Lake Ottomin, leaving Mattern, Ramkau, and my grandmother's Bissau behind, and returning to the Baltic Sea at Klein-Katz — was now proclaimed a Free State and placed under the control of the League of

Nations. In the city itself, Poland received a free port, the Westerplatte with its munitions depot, control of the railroad, and its own post office on Heveliusplatz.

While the Free State postage stamps spread a splendid display of Hanseatic cogs and red and gold coats of arms on letters, the Poles stamped them with macabre scenes in violet illustrating the histories of Casimir and Báthory.

Jan Bronski moved to the Polish Post Office. His transfer seemed spontaneous, as did opting for Poland. There were many who felt his choice of Polish citizenship was a reaction to something my mama did. In nineteen-twenty, the year Marszałek Piłsudski defeated the Red Army at Warsaw — a Miracle on the Vistula attributed by people like Vinzent Bronski to the Virgin Mary, and by military experts to either General Sikorski or General Weygand — in that eminently Polish year, my mama became engaged to Herr Matzerath, a citizen of the German Reich. I tend to think my grandmother Anna approved of the engagement as little as Jan did. Turning over the basement shop on Troyl, which had begun to prosper in the meantime, to her daughter, she withdrew with her brother Vinzent to Bissau, that is, to Polish territory, took over the farm with its turnip and potato fields, as she had in the pre-Koljaiczek-ian era, left her increasingly grace-ridden brother to his association and conversations with the Virgin Queen of Poland, and was content to squat in her four skirts behind autumnal potato-top fires and squint out blinking toward a horizon where telegraph poles still formed a grid.

Not till Jan Bronski found and married his Hedwig, a Kashubian girl from the city, but one who still owned some farmland in Ramkau, did relations between Jan and my mama improve. At a dance in the Café Woyke, where they ran into each other by accident, she is said to have introduced Jan to Matzerath. The two gentlemen, so different by nature yet so similar in their feelings for Mama, took a fancy to each other, though Matzerath bluntly declared in his Rhenish way that Jan's transfer to the Polish Post Office was a harebrained idea. Jan danced with Mama, Matzerath with the big-boned, lanky Hedwig, whose inscrutable bovine gaze always made those around her think she was pregnant. They continued to dance with, around, and into each other all evening, always thinking as they danced of the next dance to come, a step ahead in the two-step, swept away by the English waltz, till they found their self-confidence at last in the Charleston, and settled into a sensual flow bordering on the religious during the slow-moving foxtrot.

When Alfred Matzerath married my mama in nineteen twenty-three, a year when you could paper your bedroom with zeroes for the price of a box of matches, Jan was one witness and a grocer named Mühlen the other. I can't tell you much about Mühlen. He rates a mention only because, just as the Rentenmark was being introduced, he sold Mama and Matzerath a struggling grocery store in the suburb of Langfuhr that had been nearly ruined by selling on credit. Within a relatively short time, Mama, who had acquired skills for dealing with every sort of deadbeat in the basement shop on Troyl and was blessed with cleverness, a ready wit, and a natural head for business, had lifted the fortunes of the failing business so substantially that Matzerath was forced to give up his job as a salesman in the paper industry, which was glutted in any case, in order to help out in the shop.

The two complemented each other perfectly. Mama's skills with customers were matched by the Rhinelander's rapport with agents and his deals on the wholesale market. Moreover, Matzerath's love for the cook's apron, for kitchen work including cleaning up, was a great relief to Mama, who stuck to quick meals.

The flat, which adjoined the store, was cramped and poorly laid out, but compared with living conditions on Troyl, which I've only heard stories about, it was sufficiently middle-class that Mama, at least during the early years of her marriage, must have felt comfortable on Labesweg.

In addition to a long, slightly crooked hall, stacked for the most part with boxes of Persil, there was a spacious kitchen, though it too was half-filled with goods such as canned food, sacks of flour, and packets of oatmeal. The central feature of the ground-floor flat was a living room that looked out through two windows onto the street and a front garden area adorned in summer with Baltic seashells. The wallpaper held a good deal of wine red, while the couch verged on purple. Standing black-legged on a blue carpet, a dining room leaf table with rounded corners, four black leather chairs, and a little round smoking table that was constantly shifted about. Black and gold, an upright clock, flanked by the windows. Black, pressed against the purple couch, the piano, first rented, then slowly paid for over time, with revolving stool atop a pale yellow longhair pelt. Opposite it the buffet. The black buffet with its sliding, cut-glass doors, bordered by black egg-and-dart bars, with heavy black fruit carved on the lower doors enclosing the china and linen, with black claw feet, black carved headboard — and between the crystal bowl with artificial fruit and the green loving cup won in a lottery, a gap, which thanks to my mama's business acumen was later filled by a light brown radio.

The bedroom was done in yellow and looked out on the inner courtyard of the four-story building. You'll have to take my word for it that the canopy above the broad matrimonial fortress was light blue, cast light blue light on a framed and glazed repentant Mary Magdalene above the bed, lying flesh-colored in a grotto, sighing toward the top right edge of the picture and wringing so many fingers at her breast that you had to re-count them constantly, thinking there must be more than ten. Across from the marriage bed a white-enameled wardrobe with mirror doors, to the left a little dressing table, to the right a marble-topped chest of drawers, and hanging from the ceiling, not shaded with fabric as in the living room, but on two brass arms beneath pale pink porcelain globes that left the bulbs visible, the bedroom lamp spreading its light.

Today I drummed away a long morning putting questions to my drum, wanting to know if the light bulbs in our bedroom were forty or sixty watts. It's not the first time I've asked my drum and myself this burning question. It often takes hours to find my way back to those bulbs. For must not the thousands of lights I've brought to life or put to sleep by switching them on or off when entering or leaving count-less flats first be forgotten if I'm to make my way, by the plainest and simplest of drumming, through a forest of standard bulbs back to those lights in our bedroom on Labesweg?

Mama's confinement took place at home. When the contractions started she was still standing in the shop filling blue pound and half-pound bags with sugar. It was too late to take her to the women's clinic; an elderly midwife, who took up her bag only occasionally now, had to be summoned from nearby Hertastraße. In the bedroom she helped Mama and me break free from each other.

I first saw the light of this world in the form of two sixty-watt bulbs. As a result, the biblical text "Let there be light and there was light" still strikes me today as the perfect slogan for Osram light bulbs. With the exception of the obligatory perineal tear, my birth went smoothly. Effortlessly I freed myself from the head-first position favored by mothers, embryos, and midwives alike.

Let me say at once: I was one of those clairaudient infants whose mental development is complete at birth and thereafter simply confirmed. As impervious to influence as I had been as an embryo, listening only to myself, gazing at my own reflection in the amniotic fluid, so closely and critically did I now eavesdrop upon my parents' first spontaneous remarks beneath the light bulbs. My ear was wide awake. Although it could be described as small, bent, gummed up, and of course dainty, it nonetheless caught and preserved each of those watchwords that, offered as my first impressions, were henceforth so important to me. Still more: what my ear took in, my tiniest of brains immediately evaluated, and I decided, after devoting sufficient thought to all I had heard, to do certain things and most certainly not to do others.

"It's a boy," this Herr Matzerath said, who presumed he was my father. "He'll take over the business someday. At last we know why we've been working our fingers to the bone."

Mama was thinking less about the business and more about equipping her son: "Well, I knew it would be a boy, even if I sometimes said it would be a little lass."

Thus prematurely acquainted with feminine logic, I heard the following: "When little Oskar is three years old, we'll give him a tin drum."

Weighing maternal and paternal promises against each other carefully and at some length, Oskar observed and listened to a moth that had flown into the room. Medium-sized and hairy, it wooed the two sixty-watt light bulbs, casting shadows out of all proportion to its wingspan, enveloping, filling, enlarging the room and its contents with flickering motion. What stayed with me, however, was less this light-and-shadow play than the sound produced by the moth and the light bulb: the moth chattered away as though in haste to unburden itself of its knowledge, as though it had no time for further cozy chats with fonts of light, as though this dialogue of moth and bulb were now its last confession, and once the absolution dispensed by light bulbs was granted, there'd be no further chance for sin or ecstasy.

Today Oskar says simply: The moth drummed. I've heard rabbits, foxes, and dormice drum. Frogs can drum up a storm. They say woodpeckers drum worms from their casings. And men beat on timpani, cymbals, kettles, and drums. We have eardrums and brake drums, we drum up excuses, drum into our heads, drum out of the corps. Drummer boys do that, to the beat of a drum. Composers pen concerti for strings and percussion. I might mention Tattoos, both minor and major, and Oskar's attempts up to now: all that is nothing compared with the orgy of drumming staged by that moth with two simple sixty-watt bulbs on the day of my birth. Perhaps there are Negroes in darkest Africa, and those in America who have not yet forgotten Africa, who with their innate sense of rhythm might manage, in imitation of my moth, or of African moths — which as everyone knows are larger and more splendid than those of Eastern Europe — to drum in a similar fashion: with discipline, yet freed of all restraint; I hold to my East European standards, cling to that medium-sized, powdery-brown moth of the hour of my birth, declare him Oskar's master.

It was in the first days of September. The sun was in the sign of Virgo. A late-summer storm pushed its way through the night from afar, shifting chests and cupboards about. Mercury made me critical, Uranus ingenious, Venus made me believe in modest happiness, Mars in my ambition. Libra was rising in the house of the ascendant, which made me sensitive and prone to exaggeration. Neptune entered the tenth house, the house of midlife, and anchored me between miracle and deception. It was Saturn, in the third house in opposition to Jupiter, that cast doubt on my origins. But who sent the moth, and allowed him and a late-summer thunderstorm, banging and blustering like a high school principal, to stimulate my longing for the tin drum my mother had promised me, and to steadily increase over time both my aptitude and my desire for it?

Outwardly screaming and impersonating a reddish blue baby, I reached a decision: I would reject my father's suggestion and everything else to do with the grocery store point-blank, but when the proper time came, that is, on the occasion of my third birthday, I would give favorable consideration to my mother's wish.

In addition to all this speculation about my future, I realized the following: Mama and this father Matzerath had no ear at all for my protests and decisions, and would neither understand nor in the end respect them. Lonely and misunderstood, Oskar lay beneath the light bulbs, concluded that things would go on that way for sixty or seventy years until a final short circuit cut off all fonts of light, and so lost his enthusiasm before this life beneath light bulbs even began; and only the prospect of a tin drum back then kept me from expressing more forcefully my desire to return to my embryonic head-first position.

Besides, the midwife had already cut my umbilical cord; there was nothing more to be done.

The Photo Album

I AM GUARDING A TREASURE. Through all the bad years of nothing but days to get through, I guarded it, hid it away, pulled it out again; during the trip in the boxcar I clutched it to my breast, a thing of value, and when I slept, Oskar slept on his treasure, his photo album.

What would I do without this open family grave that shows all things so clearly? It has a hundred and twenty pages. On each page, four or six or sometimes only two photos are carefully arranged, mounted in patterns that are sometimes symmetrical, sometimes less so, but always based on right angles. It's bound in leather, and the older it gets, the more leathery it smells. There were times when it was exposed to the wind and weather. The photos loosened, and I was obliged by their helpless state to seek some quiet opportunity when paste could restore those nearly lost images to their ancestral spot.

What else in this world, what novel has the epic scope of a photo album? May the good Lord in Heaven, that diligent amateur who photographs us from on high each Sunday and pastes us in his album, terribly foreshortened and more or less properly exposed, guide me safely through this my album, prevent me from any stops of unseemly length along the way, no matter how pleasurable, and refrain from nourishing Oskar's love of the labyrinthine; for I'm eager to follow up these photos with the originals.

A few incidental remarks: all sorts of uniforms here, dresses and hairstyles change, Mama gets fatter, Jan grows slacker, here are some people I don't even know, wonder who took that shot, things are starting to go downhill, and now the turn-of-the-century art photo degenerates into today's commercial photo. Take, for example, this monument to my grandfather Koljaiczek and this passport photo of my friend Klepp. Simply place Grandfather's sepia portrait side by side with that glossy passport photo of Klepp, just crying out for a rubber stamp, and it's easy to see where advances in photography have brought us. And all the paraphernalia these instant photos require. But I have more to answer for than Klepp, since, as the owner of the album, it was up to me to maintain standards. If hell's in store for us someday, one of its most refined forms of torture will be to lock a person naked in a room filled with framed photos of his era. Quick, a little pathos: O man amid candid cameras, snapshots, passport photos! O man in the glare of flashbulbs, O man standing erect beside the Leaning Tower of Pisa, O photomat man, whose right ear must be exposed to be passport-worthy. And—hold the pathos: perhaps even this hell will be bearable, because the worst pictures are never taken, but only dreamed of, or if taken, never developed.

Klepp and I had pictures both taken and developed during our early days on Jülicher Straße, having made friends while eating spaghetti. I was busy with travel plans back then. That is, I was feeling so depressed that I wanted to take a trip, and planned to apply for a passport. But since I lacked the cash to finance a proper trip, one that included Rome, Naples, or at least Paris, I was just as glad I couldn't afford it, for nothing's more depressing than traveling in a state of depression. We both had enough money for the movies, however, so Klepp and I visited cinema halls where, in keeping with Klepp's tastes, Wild West films were playing or, matching my needs, films in which Maria Schell wept as the nurse, with Borsche as head surgeon having just finished a most difficult operation, playing Beethoven sonatas by the open balcony door, the very image of responsibility. We found it a great affliction that the programs lasted only two hours. We would have liked to see some of them a second time. Often we got up at the end of a film and went to the box office to buy another ticket for the same show. But the moment we left the hall and saw the longer or shorter lines at the box-office window we lost courage. We were too ashamed to face the total strangers who stared at us with such insolence, let alone the cashier, and did not dare extend the line.

After nearly every film we saw those days, we would go to the photography shop near Graf-Adolf-Platz to have our passport photos taken.

They knew us well there and smiled to themselves as we entered, but still asked us most politely to take a seat, for we were customers and respected as such. As soon as the booth was free, a young woman, of whom I recall nothing except that she was nice, pushed us one after the other into the booth, deftly positioned and adjusted first me, then Klepp, and told us to stare at a certain spot until a flash of light synchronized with a bell announced that we were now on the plate six times in succession.

Barely photographed and still slightly stiff around the corners of our mouths, we were pressed into comfortable wicker chairs by the young woman, who asked us nicely, just being nice and also nicely dressed, to be patient for five minutes. We were happy to wait. After all, now we had something to look forward to: we were eager to see how our passport photos had turned out. After just seven minutes the nondescript but still nice young woman handed us two little paper envelopes and we paid.

The triumph in Klepp's slightly protuberant eyes. As soon as we had the envelopes, we also had an excuse to enter the nearest beer hall, for no one likes to look at his passport pictures on the open, dusty street, standing amid all the bustle, blocking the flow of traffic. Just as we were loyal to the photography shop, we always went to the same tavern on Friedrichstraße. Ordering beer, blood sausage with onions, and black bread, we spread out the slightly damp pictures before our order came, using the entire top of the round wooden table, and immersed ourselves, as our beer and blood sausage promptly arrived, in our own strained features.

We always had other pictures with us too, taken after previous visits to the movies. So there was a basis for comparison: and where there's a basis for comparison, you're allowed a second, third, and fourth glass of beer to liven things up a bit or, as they say in the Rhineland, create a little ambiance.

That's not to say that someone who's depressed can render his own depression less tangible by means of a passport photo, for true depression is intangible by its very nature; at least mine, and Klepp's as well, had no tangible basis, and demonstrated in its almost cheery intangibility a staying power that nothing seemed capable of dispersing. If there was any chance of confronting our depression then, it could only be through those photos; for in these series of snapshots, not always sharply focused to be sure, we found ourselves passive and neutralized, which was what mattered. We could treat ourselves however we wished; drink beer as we did so, torture our blood sausages, create a little ambiance, and play. We bent and folded those little pictures, cut them up with the scissors we always carried for just this purpose. We pieced old and new likenesses together, gave ourselves one eye or three, ears for noses, let our right ears speak or stay silent, browbeat our chins. Nor did we keep our montages separate; Klepp borrowed details from me, I took traits from him: we were creating new, and we hoped happier, creatures. Now and then we gave a photo away.

We — I'm speaking only of Klepp and me, leaving aside all those artificially assembled figures — got into the habit of giving the waiter, whom we called Rudi, a photo on each visit, and that beer hall saw us at least once a week. Rudi, the sort of fellow worthy of twelve children and guardianship of eight more, was familiar with our compulsion, and though he already had dozens of pictures of us in profile and even more *en face*, he always assumed a sympathetic expression and said thank you when, after lengthy consultation and a stringent selection process, we handed him the photo.

Oskar never gave a photo to the waitress at the counter or to the foxy young redhead with the cigarette tray, for women shouldn't be given photos — they always mistreat them. Klepp, however, who, for all his portliness, could never stop showing off for the ladies, was communicative to the point of folly, and was ready to bare his chest and heart to any of them, must have given a photo to the cigarette girl one day without my knowledge, for he got engaged to the saucy green slip of a thing, and even married her, because he wanted his photo back.

I've got ahead of myself and devoted too many words to the final pages of my album. Those stupid snapshots aren't worth it, except to make clear by way of comparison how grand and unrivaled — yes, even artistic — the portrait of my grandfather Koljaiczek on the first page of the album appears to me to this day.

Short and stout he stands beside a small, elaborately carved table. Unfortunately he had himself photographed as Wranka the volunteer fireman, not as the arsonist. So he's missing his mustache. But the tautly stretched fireman's uniform with its medal for bravery and the fireman's helmet transforming the table into an altar almost compensate for the arsonist's whiskers. How gravely he gazes out, how deeply aware of all that turn-of-the-century suffering. That look, proud though tragic, seems to have been both beloved and common during the Second Reich, for Gregor Koljaiczek, the drunken gunpowder maker, who appears relatively sober in his pictures, sports it too. More mystic in tone, having been taken in Częstochowa, is the image captured of Vinzent Bronski, who holds a votive candle. A youthful portrait of the slender Jan Bronski bears witness to a consciously melancholy manliness, captured by means of early photography.

The women of that period were seldom as successful at finding a look that matched their demeanor. Even my grandmother Anna, who, God knows, was a real person, sits primly behind a silly, pasted-on smile in pictures taken prior to the outbreak of the First World War, offering no hint of the breadth of her four cascading skirts and the refuge they offered.

Even during the war years women were still smiling at the photographer as he danced about under his black cloth, snapsnapping away. I have another photo, double postcard size on stiff cardboard, showing twenty-three nurses in the Silberhammer Military Hospital, Mama among them as an auxiliary nurse, timid, clustering around the staff doctor, who offers a point of support. The hospital ladies seem slightly more relaxed in a posed shot at a costume ball in which convalescent warriors also appear. Mama ventures a wink, pursing her lips for a kiss that in spite of her angel wings and tinseled hair seems to say: Even angels have a sex. Matzerath, kneeling before her, has chosen a costume he would all too happily wear in daily life: he appears as a cook in a starched chef's hat, brandishing a spoon. In uniform, on the other hand, decked out with the Iron Cross Second Class, he too, like the Koljaiczeks and Bronskis, gazes out with a knowingly tragic look, and is superior to all the women in the photos.

After the war people wore a different look. The men appear slightly demobilized, and now it's the women who know how to pose for photos, who have reason to gaze out gravely, who, even when smiling, make no effort to conceal an undertone of the sorrows they've suffered. It was quite becoming, that melancholy air of women in the twenties. Did they not manage, sitting, standing, and half reclining, with the crescents of their little black spit curls pasted to their temples, to fashion a harmonious blend of Madonna and harlot?

The picture of my twenty-three-year-old mama — it must have been taken shortly before she became pregnant — shows a young woman who bows her round, smoothly shaped head slightly forward on her firm, fleshy neck, yet looks directly at the viewer, belying the merely physical with the aforementioned melancholy smile and a pair of eyes that, more gray than blue, seem accustomed to regarding the souls of her fellow beings, as well as her own, as solid objects — a coffee cup, say, or a cigarette holder. Of course the simple word soulful would not suffice here, were I to place it as an adjective before my mama's gaze.

No more interesting, but easier to assess and therefore more revealing, are the group photos of that period. It's amazing how much more beautiful and bridal the wedding dresses were when they were signing the Treaty of Rapallo. Matzerath still wears a stiff collar in his wedding picture. He looks handsome, elegant, almost intellectual. His right foot is thrust forward, looking like some movie actor of his day, Harry Liedtke, say. Dresses were short back then. The bridal dress of my mama the bride, a white skirt with a thousand pleats that barely reaches past her knees, shows off her shapely legs and dainty dancer's feet in white strap shoes. The entire wedding party crowds into other prints. Amid the urbanely dressed guests striking various attitudes, my grandmother Anna and her blessed brother Vinzent are always conspicuous for their stern provinciality and guileless insecurity. Jan Bronski, who like my mama comes from the same potato field as his aunt Anna and his heavenly-Virgin-addicted father, manages to hide his rural Kashubian origins behind the festive elegance of a Polish postal clerk. No matter how small and endangered he stands among the robust occupiers of space, his unusual eyes and the almost feminine regularity of his features become the focal point of every photo, even when he's standing off to one side.

For some time now I've been looking at a group photo taken not long after the marriage. The matte brown rectangle compels me to reach for my drum, to try to conjure with drumsticks on lacquered tin the tristar constellation visible on the print.

The photograph must have been taken at the corner of Magdeburgerstraße and Heeresanger near the Polish student hostel, in the Bronskis' apartment, for a balcony typical only of those pasted onto the fronts of flats in the Polish quarter serves as a background, sunlit and half-overgrown with pole beans. Mama is seated, Matzerath and Jan Bronski are standing. But how she sits, and how they stand! For a time I was silly enough to try to plot the constellation formed by this triumvirate — for Mama gave the full value of a man — with a school compass Bruno had to buy for me, and a ruler and triangle. The angle of inclination of the neck, a triangle of unequal sides, led to divergent parallels, to forced congruencies, to circles of the compass that closed significantly outside the triangle, that is, in the greenery of the pole beans, and produced a central point, because I was seeking a point, believed in the point, was addicted to the point, longed for a reference point, a departure point, perhaps even a viewpoint.

Nothing resulted from this dilettantish series of measurements but tiny yet annoying holes that I dug into the most important areas of this precious photograph with the point of my compass. What was so special about this print? What made me seek, and, if you will, actually find, mathematical and, ridiculous as it seems, even cosmic references in this rectangle? Three people: a seated woman, two standing men. Her dark hair marcelled, Matzerath's curly blond, Jan's chestnut brown, combed back close to his head. All three are smiling: Matzerath more than Jan Bronski, both showing their upper teeth, the smile of the two together five times broader than Mama's, of which you see only a hint at the corners of her mouth, and nothing at all in her eyes. Matzerath rests his left hand on Mama's right shoulder; Jan is content to place his right hand lightly on the back of the chair. She, with her knees to the right, facing forward from the waist up, holding a notebook in her lap that I long took for one of Bronski's stamp albums, later for a fashion magazine, and finally for a cigarette-card collection of famous film stars. Mama's hands seem poised to turn the pages the moment the plate is exposed and the picture taken. All three appear happy, commending one another for their mutual immunity to surprises of the sort that arise only if one partner in the Triple Alliance resorts to secret drawers or keeps things concealed from the start. Since they form a set, the only reason they need the fourth person, namely Jan's wife, Hedwig Bronski *née* Lemke, who may have already been pregnant at the time with the future Stephan, is to point the camera at the three of them and the happiness the three display, so that, at least photographically, their tripartite happiness can be captured and held fast.

I've detached other rectangles from the album and placed them beside this one. Scenes in which Mama can be observed with Matzerath, or Mama with Jan Bronski. In none of these pictures is the inevitability, the sole possible outcome, as clear as in the balcony scene. Jan and Mama in one: it smells of tragedy, of gold at the end of the rainbow, and the reckless abandon that leads to surfeit, to a surfeit of reckless abandon. Matzerath next to Mama: a trickle of weekend conjugality, the Wiener schnitzels sizzling, a bit of grumbling before dinner, some yawning after the meal, a few jokes before bedtime, or complaints about the tax situation to give some intellectual substance to the marriage. Nevertheless I prefer this photographic tedium to an indecent snapshot of later years that shows Mama on Jan Bronski's lap, against the backdrop of Oliva Forest near Freudenthal. Even though the lewdness — Jan has allowed his hand to disappear under Mama's dress — records only the mad, blind passion of the unhappy pair, adulterous from the first day of Matzerath's marriage, for whom, I presume, Matzerath serves here as benumbed photographer. None of the tranquility, none of the gentle, knowing gestures of the balcony picture are visible, which were no doubt only possible when both men were standing behind or beside Mama, or lying at her feet, as on the beach at the Heubude baths; see photo.

There's yet another rectangle that shows the three most important figures of my early years forming a triangle. Although less concentrated than the balcony picture, it still radiates the same tense peace that can no doubt only be concluded among, and possibly signed by, three people. Complain all you want about the much-loved love triangle in the theater; what are two persons alone on stage to do but talk themselves to death or secretly long for a third to appear? In my little picture the three of them are together. They are playing skat. That is, they are holding their cards like well-arranged fans, but instead of checking their trumps to gauge the strength of their hands, they are looking at the camera. Jan's hand lies flat, except for his raised index finger, beside a pile of change, Matzerath is digging his nails into the tablecloth, Mama indulges in a little joke, which strikes me as rather good: she has drawn a card and shows it to the camera lens but not to her fellow card players. How easy it is, with a single gesture, by simply showing the queen of hearts in skat, to conjure up an unobtrusive symbol, for who would not swear by the Queen of Hearts!

The game of skat—which, as you probably know, can only be played by three people—was not just the most suitable game for Mama and her two men; it was their refuge, the harbor to which they always returned when life tried to lead them astray into such silly games as Sixty-six or Morris, where they were merely paired with one or the other.

That's enough for now about these three, who brought me into the world although they lacked for nothing. Before I come to myself, a word about Mama's friend Gretchen Scheffler and her master-baker husband, Alexander Scheffler. He baldheaded, she laughing with equine teeth, a good half of which were gold. He stubby-legged, never reaching the carpet when he sat on chairs, she in clothes she knitted herself in patterns that could never be busy enough. Later on, photos of both Schefflers in deck chairs or by lifeboats on the Strength through Joy ship *Wilhelm Gustloff*, or on the promenade deck of the *Tannenberg* of the East Prussian Line. Year after year they took trips and brought souvenirs from Pillau, Norway, the Azores, or Italy safely back to their house on Kleinhammerweg, where he baked rolls and she embroidered pillowcases with tiny loops called mouse teeth. When Alexander Scheffler wasn't talking, he was forever licking his upper lip with the tip of his tongue, a habit Matzerath's friend Greff, the greengrocer who lived across the way from us, found obscene and disgusting.

Though Greff was married, he was more scoutmaster than husband. A photo shows him stout, dry-skinned, and healthy, in a uniform with shorts, his scoutmaster cords, and his scout hat. Beside him, similarly outfitted, stands a boy of perhaps thirteen with overly large eyes, whom Greff, his left hand around the boy's shoulder, pulls toward him with obvious affection. I didn't know the boy, but I later met Greff through his wife Lina and came to understand him.

I'm losing myself in snapshots of Strength through Joy tourists and testaments to tender Boy Scout eroticism. Let's flip forward a few pages and come to me, my very first photographic image.

I was a handsome child. The picture was taken on Whitsuntide, nineteen twenty-five. I was eight months old, two months younger than Stephan Bronski, who appears on the very next page in the same format, radiating an indescribable ordinariness. The postcard has a scalloped edge, its verso lined for the address, no doubt printed in bulk for use by the family. The photographic portion of the extended rectangle is in the shape of an overly symmetrical egg. Nude and symbolizing the egg's yolk, I lie on my tummy on a white fur pelt that some arctic polar bear must have donated to an East European professional specializing in children's photographs. As with many photos of that period, they have chosen for my first image the warm, unmistakable sepia tone that I would term human, as opposed to the inhuman glossy black-and-white photos of our day. Dull, blurred foliage, no doubt painted, provides the dark background, relieved by a few flecks of light. While my smooth, healthy body rests tranquilly angled on the fur pelt, basking in the polar bear's native habitat, I hold my rounded baby's head strained upward, and regard with shiny eyes the various spectators of my nakedness.

A baby picture like any other, you might say. Please observe the hands: you must admit that my earliest likeness differs distinctly from the usual crop of droll little creatures in countless photo albums. You see me with clenched fists. No little sausage fingers playing absent-mindedly with tufts of polar-bear rug in response to some still obscure haptic urge. The little clutched hands hover gravely gathered at my temples, ready to strike, to sound the beat. What beat? The drum beat.

I still don't have what was promised me at birth beneath light bulbs for my third birthday; but it would be a simple matter for anyone skilled in photomontage to add a suitably reduced image of a toy drum without having to retouch the position of my body in the slightest. Only the silly stuffed animal I'm ignoring would have to be removed. It's an alien element in this otherwise harmonious composition, which strikes the theme of the astute, clearsighted age when the first milk teeth are about to come through.

Later I was no longer placed on polar-bear rugs. At eighteen months I must have been pushed along in a high-wheeled baby buggy past a fence whose pointed laths and crossbars are so clearly outlined by a layer of snow that I can only assume the picture was taken in January of nineteen twenty-six. The crude construction of the fence, its wood smelling of tar, connects it for me, on further observation, with the suburb of Hochstrieß, whose extensive barracks once sheltered Mackensen's Hussars and in my time the Free State Police. Since I can't recall anyone who lived in that suburb, however, the picture must have been taken on the occasion of a single visit my parents paid to people they never saw again, or saw only rarely.

Mama and Matzerath, flanking the baby buggy, are not wearing winter coats, in spite of the cold. On the contrary, Mama is dressed in a long-sleeved Russian blouse whose embroidered decorations suggest another wintry scene: in deepest Russia a picture is being taken of the Tsar's family, Rasputin holds the camera, I am the Tsarevich, and behind the fence crouch Mensheviks and Bolsheviks, rigging homemade bombs, plotting the destruction of my aristo-autocratic family. Matzerath's correct, Middle European, petit-bourgeois exterior, bearing, as we shall see, the seeds of the future, interrupts the telling point of the photo's moral tale. They were in the quiet suburb of Hochstrieß, had emerged for a moment, without donning their winter coats, from their hosts' flat so the master of the house could take their picture on either side of little Oskar, who obliged them with a droll expression, and were soon deliciously warming themselves with coffee, cake, and whipped cream.

There are another good dozen snapshots of Oskar lying, sitting, crawling, walking, aged one, two, two and a half. Some pictures are better than others, but taken as a whole they are a mere preliminary to the full-length portrait they had taken of me on my third birthday.

There, I have it now, my drum. There it hangs, brand-new, zigzagged white and red, on my tummy. There I am, self-assured, my face solemn and resolute, my drumsticks crossed upon the tin. There I am in my striped sweater. There I stand in gleaming patent-leather shoes. There my hair stands, like a brush ready for action atop my head, there, mirrored in each blue eye, a will to power that needs no followers. There I am back then, in a stance I found no reason to abandon. There and then I decided, there I declared, there I decreed, that I would never be a politician and most certainly not a grocer, that I would make a point instead of remaining as I was — and so I did, remained that size, kept that attire, for years to come.

Little people and big people, Little Dipper and Big Dipper, little and big ABCs, Little Hans and Karl the Great, David and Goliath, Hop-o'-My-Thumb and the Giant; I remained the three-year-old, the gnome, Tom Thumb, stayed the half-pint that's never topped up, all to bypass distinctions like big and little catechisms, to flee the clutches of a man who, while shaving at the mirror, called himself my father, to avoid, as a so-called grownup of five foot eight, being bound to a business, a grocery store that Matzerath hoped would become the grown-up world for Oskar at twenty-one. So as not to have to rattle a cash register, I stuck to my drum and didn't grow a finger's breadth from my third birthday on, remained the three-year-old, who, three times as smart, was towered over by grownups, yet stood head and shoulders above them all, who felt no need to measure his shadow against theirs, who was inwardly and outwardly fully mature while others driveled on about development well into their dotage, who merely confirmed for himself what others learned with difficulty and often painfully, who felt no need to increase his shoe and trouser size from year to year just to prove he was growing.

And yet — and here Oskar too must admit to development — something was growing, and not always to my own advantage, ultimately taking on messianic proportions; but what grownup in my day had eyes and ears for Oskar, the eternally three-year-old drummer?

Glass, Glass, Little Glass

HAVING JUST DESCRIBED a full-length photo of Oskar with drum and drumsticks, and having announced at the same time the fully matured decisions Oskar reached during that photographic session in the presence of those gathered round the birthday cake with its three candles, I must now, since the album beside me maintains a closed silence on the subject, relate other events that, though they don't explain why I remained a three-year-old, also took place, and which I initiated.

It was clear to me from the very beginning: grownups won't understand you, they will call you retarded if they can't see you grow, they'll drag you and their money to scores of doctors in search of an explanation, if not a cure, for your disorder. So to keep consultations to an endurable minimum, I had to provide a plausible explanation for my failure to grow before the doctor offered his.

A sunny day in September, my third birthday. Delicate, late summer glass-blowing, even Gretchen Scheffler's laughter was subdued. Mama at the piano intoning airs from *The Gypsy Baron,* Jan behind her at the stool, touching her shoulder, pretending to study the score. Matzerath getting supper ready in the kitchen. Grandmother Anna with Hedwig Bronski and Alexander Scheffler gathering around the greengrocer Greff, who was always full of stories, Boy Scout stories in which loyalty and courage played important roles; a grandfather clock as well, which did not miss a single quarter-hour of that gossamer September day; and since, like the clock, they were all so busy, and since a line ran from the Gypsy Baron's Hungarian countryside through Greff's Boy Scouts wandering in the Vosges, past Matzerath's kitchen, where Kashubian mushrooms with scrambled eggs and pork belly sputtered in fright in the pan, and down the hallway to the shop, I, casually sorting things out on my drum, followed that flight line and soon stood behind the counter in the shop – piano, mushrooms, and the Vosges far distant now – and saw that the trapdoor to the cellar stood open; Matzerath, who had brought up a can of mixed fruit for dessert, must have forgotten to close it.

It took me a minute or two to understand what the trapdoor to our cellar demanded of me. Not suicide, by God! That would have been far too simple. But the alternative was difficult, painful, demanded sacrifice; and even then, as always when a sacrifice is demanded of me, my brow broke out in a sweat. Above all, no harm must come to my drum; I would have to carry it safely down the sixteen well-worn steps and place it among the sacks of flour to explain its undamaged state. Then back up to the eighth step, no, down one, actually the fifth would do just as well. But from there safety and credible injury could not be combined. Back up then, too high this time, to the tenth, and finally, from the ninth step, I flung myself down, carrying a shelf laden with bottles of raspberry syrup along with me, and landed head-first on the cement floor of our cellar.

Even before the curtain descended on my consciousness, I registered the success of the experiment: the raspberry bottles I had intentionally pulled down made enough clatter to attract Matzerath from the kitchen, Mama from the piano, and the rest of the birthday party from the Vosges, luring them into the shop, to the open trapdoor, and down the stairs.

Before they arrived, I basked in the fragrance of flowing raspberry syrup, noted that my head was bleeding, and pondered – by now they were already on the stairs – whether it was Oskar's blood or the raspberries that smelled so sweet and soporific, but was greatly relieved that everything had gone so well and that thanks to my foresight my drum had sustained no damage.

I think it was Greff who carried me up. Only in the living room did Oskar emerge from that cloud consisting no doubt half of raspberry syrup and half of his own young blood. The doctor had not yet arrived; Matzerath was trying to calm Mama, who was screaming and flailing away at his face, and not just with her palm, but with the back of her hand as well, calling him a murderer.

So with a single fall, by no means harmless, but self-administered in a carefully measured dose, I managed to provide the cause grownups needed for my failure to grow — repeatedly confirmed by the doctors — and, as an added bonus, to unintentionally transform a decent and harmless Matzerath into a guilty Matzerath. He had left the trapdoor open, Mama heaped all the blame on him, and for years to come he carried the burden of that guilt, which Mama brought up only rarely but drove home without mercy when she did.

The fall earned me four weeks in the hospital, followed, except for Wednesday visits to Dr. Hollatz later on, by relative peace from the medical profession; on my first day as a drummer I had managed to give the world a sign; my case was clarified before the grownups could grasp the true nature of the condition I had initiated. From then on, the story was this: On his third birthday our little Oskar fell down the cellar stairs, he was still in one piece, but he just wouldn't grow any more.

And I began to drum. Our building had four floors. I drummed up and down the stairs, from the ground floor to the attic rooms. From Labesweg to Max-Halbe-Platz, on to Neuschottland, Anton-Möller-Weg, Marienstraße, Kleinhammerpark, the Aktien Brewery, Aktien Pond, Fröbel Meadow, the Pestalozzi School, Neuer Markt, and back again to Labesweg. My drum could take it, but grownups had a harder time, they tried to shut my drum up, to obstruct it, to trip my drumsticks — but Nature came to my aid.

The ability to drum up the necessary distance between grownups and myself on a toy drum developed soon after my fall down the cellar stairs, almost simultaneously with the emergence of a voice that allowed me to sing, scream, or sing-scream at such a high pitch and with such sustained vibrato that no one dared take away the drum that pained their ears; for when my drum was taken from me I screamed, and when I screamed something quite valuable would burst into pieces: I was able to singshatter glass; my scream slew flower vases; my song caused windows to crumple to their knees and let drafts rule; my voice sliced open display cases like a chaste and therefore merciless diamond, and, without losing its innocence, assaulted the harmonious, nobly bred liqueur glasses within, bestowed by loving hands and covered with a light film of dust.

It wasn't long before my ability was well-known up and down our street, from Brösener Weg to the housing development near the airfield, indeed throughout the entire suburb. If the neighborhood children saw me, whose games like "Pickled herring, one, two, three" or "Better start running, the Black Cook's coming!" or "I see something you don't see" held no interest for me, an entire unwashed chorus would bawl out:

Glass, glass, little glass,
Sugar and no beer,
Mother Holle runs upstairs
And sheds a tiny tear.

Just a silly, meaningless nursery rhyme. The little song hardly bothered me as I tramped through their midst behind my drum, through Little Glass and Mother Holle, while taking up the simple rhythm, not without its charm, and drumming Glass, Glass, Little Glass, drawing the children after me, though I was no Pied Piper.

Even today, when Bruno is polishing the windows in my room, for instance, I still make room on my drum for the rhythm of this nursery rhyme.

More irritating than the mocking songs of the neighborhood children, and more annoying to my parents, was the costly fact that every windowpane broken in our area by willful, ill-bred rowdies was blamed on me, or more specifically on my voice. At first Mama paid up conscientiously for kitchen windows shattered mostly by slingshots, until she too finally understood the way my voice worked, and with cool gray businesslike eyes demanded proof when damages were claimed. People in the neighborhood were indeed doing me an injustice. Nothing could have been more mistaken at the time than to assume that I was possessed by a childish urge for destruction, that I hated glass and glassware for some inexplicable reason, like children who sometimes demonstrate their strange, random dislikes by running angrily amok. Only someone at play willfully destroys. I never played, I worked on my drum, and as far as my voice was concerned, it was used, at least initially, only in self-defense. It was solely my desire to keep working on my drum that led me to use my vocal cords so single-mindedly. If with the same tones and techniques I could have cut up the boring, intricately embroidered tablecloths that sprang from Gretchen Scheffler's fantasia of patterns, or stripped the piano's gloomy varnish, I would gladly have left all glassware intact and soundly ringing. But tablecloths and varnish remained impervious to my voice. I could neither obliterate the wallpaper's pattern by incessant screaming, nor by rubbing together two long drawn-out tones with stone-age patience, allowing them to swell and ebb, produce sufficient heat to generate the spark I would have needed to set the tinder-dry curtains of our living room windows, seasoned with tobacco smoke, ablaze in decorative flames. I never sang the leg off a chair Matzerath or Alexander Scheffler was sitting in. I would gladly have defended myself in more harmless and less miraculous ways, but nothing harmless would serve; glass alone heeded me, and had to pay the price.

I made my first successful presentation of this sort shortly after my third birthday. I'd had my drum a good four weeks, and during that time, diligent as I was, had worn it out. True, the top and bottom were still joined by the cylinder of red and white flames, but the hole in the top that called the tune could no longer be ignored; and since I spurned the bottom, the hole grew bigger and bigger, frayed, and left sharp, jagged edges; tiny scraps of pounded tin splintered off and fell inside the drum, rattling about angrily at every stroke, while specks of white lacquer that could no longer endure life on my martyred drum glittered all over the living room rug and on the reddish brown planks of the bedroom floor.

It was feared I would cut myself on the treacherously sharp edges of the tin. Matzerath in particular, who had become exceedingly cautious since my fall down the cellar stairs, urged me to be careful while playing the drum. Since my arteries were always in extremely violent motion near the jagged edge of the crater, I must admit that Matzerath's fears, though exaggerated, were not entirely unfounded. A new drum would have removed all danger, of course, but that was far from their minds; instead they planned to take away the one I had, the good old drum that had fallen with me, gone to the hospital and been released with me, gone up stairs and down with me, paced cobblestones and sidewalks with me through "Pickled herring, one, two, three," past "I see something you don't see," past "Better start running, the Black Cook's coming," they planned to take that drum away from me and not replace it. A stupid piece of chocolate was offered as bait. Mama held it out, pursing her lips. It was Matzerath who reached for my crippled drum with a show of severity. I clung to the wreck. He pulled. My strength, which was barely adequate for drumming, began to fail. One red flame after another slid slowly away, the rim of the frame was about to slip from my grasp, when, for the first time, Oskar, who till that day had been deemed a quiet, almost too well-behaved child, produced his first destructively effective scream: the polished round crystal that protected the honey-yellow face of the grandfather clock from dust and dying flies shattered and fell, still splintering, to the reddish brown floorboards — for the carpet didn't quite reach to the base of the clock. The interior of the precious clock, however, was undamaged: the pendulum continued serenely — if you can say this of a pendulum — on its way, and the same for the hands. Not even the chimes, which reacted sensitively, almost hysterically, to the slightest jolt, to beer wagons rolling by on the street, gave any sign of having been impressed by my scream; only the glass gave a start, but one that startled it to bits.

"The clock is broken!" cried Matzerath, and released the drum. With a brief glance I satisfied myself that my scream had done no real damage to the clock, that only the crystal was gone. But for Matzerath, and for Mama and Uncle Jan Bronski, who was paying his usual Sunday afternoon call, more than the glass covering the clock's face seemed to have fallen to pieces. They blanched, exchanged shifting, helpless glances, reached out for the tiled stove, seized hold of piano and buffet, were afraid to stir from the spot, and Jan Bronski's dry lips moved, as he cast his eyes upward in supplication, in what I still believe today was my uncle's attempt to utter a prayer for aid and mercy, something like O Lamb of God, who taketh away the sins of the world — *miserere nobis.* And this text three times and then one Lord I am not worthy that Thou shouldst enter under my roof, say but the word . . .

Of course the Lord said not a word. After all, the clock wasn't broken, just the glass. But grownups have a strange and childish relationship to their clocks, childish in the sense in which I was never a child. Yet the clock may well be the grownups' greatest achievement. Be that as it may: to the extent that grownups can be creative, and with diligence, ambition, and a little luck actually are, they become creatures of their own epoch-making inventions the moment they create them.

But the clock remains nothing without the grownup. He winds it, sets it forward or back, takes it to the clockmaker to be checked, cleaned, and if necessary repaired. Like the cry of the cuckoo that fades too soon, like overturned saltcellars, spiders in the morning, black cats from the left, the uncle's portrait that falls from the wall when the hook pulls from the plaster, just as with mirrors, grownups see more behind and in clocks than clocks can possibly signify.

Mama, who in spite of a few whimsical fancies was the most level-headed, even if she could be flighty at times, and always interpreted any apparent sign in her favor, found words to save the situation.

"Broken glass brings good luck!" she cried, snapping her fingers, brought out dustpan and brush, and swept up the shards of good luck.

If I take my mama's words at face value, I brought my parents, my relatives, acquaintances, and even strangers plenty of good luck, for every time someone tried to take my drum, windowpanes, glasses of beer, empty beer bottles, perfume bottles redolent of spring, crystal bowls heaped with artificial fruit, in short, all glassware blown in glassworks by the glass blowers' art and sold on the market, from plain glass to art glass, were screamshattered, singshattered, shardshattered.

To limit the damage, for I've always loved fine glassware, I restricted myself, when they tried to take my drum away at night, even though it belonged in bed with me, to punishing one or more light bulbs from the fourfold effort of our living room lamp. Thus on my fourth birthday, in early September nineteen twenty-eight, I plunged the entire assembled birthday company — my parents, the Bronskis, Grandmother Koljaiczek, the Schefflers, and the Greffs, who had given me everything under the sun: tin soldiers, a sailing ship, a fire engine, but no tin drum — plunged the whole lot of them, who wanted me to waste my time playing with tin soldiers, with all this fire-engine nonsense, who begrudged me my battered but trusty drum, who planned to take it away and palm off on me instead a silly little ship with the top sails set all wrong, all those with eyes only to overlook me and my wishes — I plunged them all, with an expanding circular scream that slew all four light bulbs of our hanging lamp, into primeval darkness.

Well, you know how grownups are: after their first cries of shock and almost fervent demands for the return of light, they accustomed themselves to the dark, and by the time my grandmother Koljaiczek, who was the only person other than little Stephan Bronski with nothing to gain from the darkness, had fetched tallow candles from the shop, with Stephan sniveling at her skirts, and returned with lighted candles to brighten the room, the remnants of the totally inebriated birthday party were found strangely paired.

As might be expected, Mama was perched with disheveled blouse on Jan Bronski's lap. The sight of the short-legged baker Alexander Scheffler almost disappearing into the Greffian realm was unsavory. Matzerath licked at Gretchen Scheffler's gold and equine teeth. Only Hedwig Bronski sat alone, her bovine eyes pious in the candlelight, holding her hands in her lap, near but not too near the greengrocer Greff, who hadn't been drinking, but still sang, sang sweetly, wistfully, with drawn-out melancholy, sang urging Hedwig Bronski to join in his song. They sang a scout duet in which, according to the lyrics, a certain Rübezahl haunts the mountains of Bohemia.

Me they had forgotten. Under the table sat Oskar with the remnant of his drum, coaxing scraps of rhythm from the tin, and the spare but steady sound of drumbeats may well have proved pleasant to those who, swapped and in ecstasy, sat or lay about the room. For the drumming varnished over the kissing and sucking sounds produced by all the feverish and labored demonstrations of their diligence.

I was still under the table when my grandmother arrived like a candle-bearing angel of wrath, inspected Sodom by candlelight, spotted Gomorrah, kicked up a row that shook the candles, called the whole lot of them pigs, and put an end to idylls like Rübezahl's strolls through the mountains of Bohemia by sticking the candles on saucers, pulling a deck of skat cards from the buffet, throwing them on the table, and announcing to the still whimpering Stephan that the second half of the birthday party was about to begin. Soon thereafter Matzerath screwed new light bulbs into the old sockets of our hanging lamp, chairs were scooted up, beer bottles were popped open, and a tenth-of-a-penny game of skat got under way above me. Mama suggested a quarter-penny game at the outset, but that was more than Uncle Jan dared risk, and if the pot hadn't been considerably enlarged now and then by someone going set or making a grand with four, they would have stuck to pinching tenths of a penny.

I felt fine under the table, in the leeward shadow of the dangling tablecloth. Gently drumming, I countered the fists thumping cards above me, gave myself over to the course of the game, and declared skat in just short of an hour: Jan Bronski lost. He had good cards, but still lost. No wonder, since he paid so little attention. Had other things on his mind than diamonds without two. Had slipped the low black shoe off his left foot right at the start of the game, while still talking to his aunt, playing down the previous little orgy, and stretching his gray-stockinged left foot right past my head toward my mama, who was sitting opposite him, sought and found her knee. At the first touch Mama scooted closer to the table so that Jan, who in response to Matzerath's bid passed at thirty-three, lifting the hem of her skirt, could, first with his toe and then with his entire filled sock, which was of course fresh that day and practically clean, wander about between her thighs. You've got to admire my mama, who despite this woolen molestation under the table still managed, on the taut tablecloth above, to win the most daring games, including clubs without four, sure-handedly and accompanied by the most amusing banter, while Jan, increasingly bold below, lost several hands above that even Oskar could have taken to the bank with somnambulistic certainty.

Later on, sleepy little Stephan crept under the table too, soon fell asleep, and couldn't understand before falling asleep what his father's trouser leg was doing under my mama's dress.

Clear to partly cloudy. Occasional light showers in the afternoon. Jan Bronski came back the very next day, picked up the birthday gift he'd given me, the sailing ship, exchanged that pitiful plaything for a tin drum at Sigismund Markus in the Arsenal Arcade, returned to our flat, slightly rain-spattered, late that afternoon with the old familiar drum with its red and white pattern of flames, held it out to me, and grasped at the same time my trusty tin wreck, on which only traces of red and white lacquer remained. And while Jan clutched the worn drum and I the new one, all eyes — Jan's, Mama's, and Matzerath's — remained fixed on Oskar; I almost had to laugh — did they think I was bound to the past, that I nourished principles in my breast?

Without letting out the scream they all expected, without sounding the glass-slaying song, I relinquished the scrap-metal drum and turned at once with both hands to my new instrument. After two hours of intense drumming I hit my stride.

But not all the grownups around me proved as perceptive as Jan Bronski. Shortly after my fifth birthday, in nineteen twenty-nine — there was a good deal of talk about a stock-market crash in New York, and I wondered if my grandfather Koljaiczek, with his lumber business in far-off Buffalo, had suffered any losses — Mama, worried by my lack of growth, which was now clearly evident, took me by the hand and began our Wednesday visits to Dr. Hollatz on Brunshöferweg. I put up with these thoroughly annoying and endlessly protracted examinations because even at that age the pleasing white uniform worn by Sister Inge, who assisted at the side of Dr. Hollatz, attracted me, reminded me of the photo of Mama's days as a nurse during the war, and enabled me, by concentrating intently on the constantly changing folds of her nurse's uniform, to ignore the bellowing flood of words, by turns strongly authoritative and unpleasantly avuncular, gushing from the doctor.

His spectacles reflecting the office furnishings — there was a good deal of chrome, nickel, and polished enamel; and also shelves and glass cabinets in which stood neatly labeled jars containing snakes, newts, and toads, as well as pig, ape, and human embryos — capturing these fetuses in alcohol with his spectacles, after each examination, Hollatz would shake his head gravely as he leafed through the record of my illness, have Mama tell him yet again about my fall down the cellar stairs, and calm her as she heaped endless reproaches on Matzerath, who had left the trapdoor open, declaring him guilty now and for all time.

When, on one such Wednesday visit months later, no doubt to prove to himself, and possibly to Sister Inge as well, the success of his treatment thus far, he tried to take away my drum, I destroyed the larger part of his snake and toad collection, as well as every conceivable embryo.

Except for full glasses of beer still covered with coasters, and Mama's perfume bottle, it was the first time Oskar had tested himself on a number of full and carefully sealed glass containers. My success was unique and overwhelming, a surprise to all concerned, even to Mama, who was well aware of my relationship to glass. With my very first carefully clipped note I sliced the cabinet in which Hollatz kept his loathsome curiosities wide open, and sent a nearly square pane of glass toppling from the display side of the cabinet to the linoleum floor, where, retaining its square shape, it smashed into a thousand pieces; then, giving my scream a sharper profile and an almost profligate intensity, visited that rich note upon one jar after another.

The glass jars shattered. The greenish, partly coagulated alcohol sprayed, flowed forth, carrying its preserved, pale, somewhat gravely staring contents across the red linoleum floor of the office and filling the room with a stench so tangible, if I can use that word, that Mama got sick and Sister Inge had to open the window onto Brunshöferweg. Dr. Hollatz managed to turn the loss of his collection to his advantage. A few weeks after my assault he published an article in a professional journal called *The World of Medicine* which described the glass-slaying vocal phenomenon Oskar M. The thesis Dr. Hollatz spent over twenty pages expounding is said to have caused quite a stir in medical circles both in Germany and abroad, finding voices pro and con among qualified experts. Mama, to whom several copies of the journal were sent, was so proud of the article it gave me pause, and she could not stop reading bits of it aloud to the Greffs, the Schefflers, her Jan, and after every meal to her husband Matzerath. Even customers in the shop had to put up with passages from the essay and duly admired Mama, who mispronounced the technical terms with an imaginative flair. As for me, the fact that my given name had appeared in a journal for the first time meant next to nothing. My already finely tuned skepticism allowed me to recognize Dr. Hollatz's little essay for what it was when examined more closely: the long-winded, not unskillfully formulated irrelevancies of a doctor angling for a professorship.

Today, in the mental institution, when his voice can't even budge a toothbrush glass, when doctors of Hollatz's type are constantly coming in and out, administering so-called Rorschach tests, association tests, tests of all kinds, trying to find some high-sounding name to justify his forced confinement, today, Oskar likes to think back on the archaic early days of his voice. In that first period he sangshattered items composed of quartz sand only when necessary, but then quite thoroughly, whereas later on, during the heyday and decadence of his art, he plied his talents under no external pressure at all. Succumbing to the mannerism of a late period, a devotee of *l'art pour l'art,* out of pure playfulness, Oskar sang glass back to its original structure, and grew older as he did so.

The Schedule

KLEPP KILLS TIME by the hour drafting hourly schedules. The fact that he wolfs down blood sausage and warmed-up lentils while drafting them confirms my thesis, simply stated: Dreamers are gluttons. The fact that Klepp works fairly hard filling in the columns supports my other thesis: Only true lazybones invent laborsaving devices.

This year again Klepp spent over two weeks planning each hour of his day. When he came to see me yesterday, he behaved mysteriously for a while, then fished the piece of paper folded nine times from his breast pocket and handed it to me beaming, even smugly: he had invented yet another laborsaving device.

I skimmed the slip of paper, found little new there: breakfast at ten, meditation till lunch, a nap after lunch for an hour, then coffee – back to bed if possible, an hour of flute sitting in bed, up out of bed and an hour of bagpipes marching round the room, half an hour of bagpipes in the courtyard, every other day two hours for beer and blood sausage or two hours of movies, but in either case, before beer or movies, discreet propaganda for the illegal German Communist Party – half an hour – don't overdo it! Evenings were filled three times a week playing dance music at the Unicorn, on Saturday afternoon beer and Party propaganda were postponed till evening, afternoon being reserved for a bath including massage on Grünstraße; followed by forty-five minutes of hygiene in U9 with a girl, then coffee and cake with this same girl and her girlfriend at Schwab's, a shave just before closing time, if necessary a haircut, a quick photo at the photomat, then beer, blood sausage, Party propaganda, and relaxation.

I praised Klepp's neatly traced schedule, requested a copy, and asked what he did in his spare time. "Sleep, or think about the Communist Party," Klepp replied after the briefest reflection.

Had I told him how Oskar was introduced to his first schedule?

It began innocently enough with Auntie Kauer's kindergarten. Hedwig Bronski picked me up every morning, took me, along with her Stephan, to Auntie Kauer on Posadowskiweg, where we were forced to play ad nauseam with six to ten kids, a few of whom were always sick. Fortunately my drum counted as a toy, no building blocks were forced upon me, and a rocking horse was only shoved under me when an equestrian drummer with paper helmet was required. Auntie Kauer's black silk dress, buttoned a thousandfold, offered the score for my drum. I can safely say I dressed and undressed that skinny woman, all wrinkles, several times a day, buttoning and unbuttoning her with my drum, without ever thinking about her body.

Our afternoon walks along avenues lined with chestnut trees to Jäschkentaler Forest, up the Erbsberg, past the Gutenberg Memorial, were so pleasantly boring, so silly and carefree, that even today I still wish I could go on those picture-book walks, holding Auntie Kauer's papery hand.

Whether we were eight or twelve kids, we had to harness up. This harness consisted of a pale blue knitted cord that served as a shaft. Attached in six places to the right and left of this shaft were woolen bridles for a total of twelve kids. Bells dangled at six-inch intervals. Auntie Kauer held the reins, and we trotted klingalingalinging along in front of her, prattling, I sluggishly drumming, through autumnal suburban lanes. Now and then Auntie Kauer would strike up a song: "Jesus, for thee we live, Jesus, for thee we die," or "Star of the Sea, I greet thee," stirring the hearts of passersby as we offered up "O Mary, help me," and "Swe-ee-eet Mother of God" to the clear October air. As soon as we reached the main street the traffic had to be stopped. Trams, autos, and horse-drawn carriages came to a standstill as we sang "Star of the Sea" all the way across the avenue. Each time Auntie Kauer would thank the policeman who led us across with a papery crinkling of her hand.

"The Lord Jesus will reward you," she promised, and rustled her silken dress.

I was actually sorry that spring when, with his sixth birthday behind him, Oskar had to leave the buttonable and unbuttonable Fräulein Kauer, because of Stephan and along with him. As always when politics come into play, there had been violence. We were on the Erbsberg, Auntie Kauer was removing our woolen harnesses, the new growth glistened, and the twigs were beginning to molt. Auntie Kauer was sitting on a moss-covered stone marker on the path that pointed in different directions for one- to two-hour hikes. Like a maiden with no idea what spring does to her, she was tra-la-la-ing with jerking motions of her head normally observed only in guinea hens, and knitting us a new harness, devilishly red it was to be, but unfortunately I would never don it: for just then there were cries from the bushes, Fräulein Kauer fluttered up, and, pulling red yarn along after her, strutted with her knitting toward the bushes and the cries. I followed her and the yarn, and was soon to see more red: Stephan's nose was bleeding profusely, and a boy named Lothar, with curly locks and blue veins standing out on his temples, was squatting on the chest of the skinny tearful little fellow, and seemed determined to batter Stephan's nose in.

"Polack," he hissed between blows. "Polack!" When, five minutes later, Auntie Kauer had us back in our light blue harnesses — I alone ran free, winding up the red yarn — she said a prayer for us that was normally only spoken between Offering and Transubstantiation: "Bowed with shame, full of pain and remorse . . ."

Then down the Erbsberg and a stop at the Gutenberg Memorial. Pointing a long finger at Stephan, who was whimpering and pressing a handkerchief to his nose, she explained gently, "He can't help it if he's a little Pole." On Auntie Kauer's advice, Stephan had to withdraw from her kindergarten. Oskar, though he was no Pole and didn't think very highly of Stephan, declared his solidarity with him. Then Easter came and they decided to give the school a try. Behind his broad horn-rimmed glasses, Dr. Hollatz felt it could do no harm, and repeated his opinion out loud: "It can't do little Oskar any harm."

Jan Bronski, who intended for his part to send his Stephan to the Polish public school after Easter, couldn't be talked out of it, repeating over and over again to my mama and Matzerath that he was a Polish civil servant. The Polish state offered him an honest wage for an honest day's work at the Polish Post Office. After all, he was a Pole, and Hedwig would be too, as soon as her application was approved. Moreover, a bright child of above-average gifts like Stephan could learn German at home, and as for little Oskar — he always sighed a little when he said Oskar — Oskar was six years old just like Stephan, it's true he wasn't talking yet, and was severely retarded in general for his age, and as far as his growth was concerned, but they should try it anyway, education was compulsory, after all — always assuming the school board had no objection.

The school board expressed misgivings and demanded a doctor's certificate. Hollatz declared that I was a healthy boy, albeit the size of a three-year-old, whose mental development, though I didn't talk very well yet, was in no way inferior to that of a five- or six-year-old. He also mentioned my thyroid gland.

Through the series of examinations, through all the tests I knew so well, I remained calm, indifferent or even positive, as long as no one tried to take away my drum. The destruction of Hollatz's collection of snakes, toads, and embryos was still present in the minds of all who examined and tested me, inspiring respect and fear.

It was only at home, indeed on my first school day, that I found myself forced to demonstrate the effect of the diamond in my voice, since Matzerath, against all better judgment, demanded I set out for the Pestalozzi School opposite Fröbel Meadow without my drum, nor was I to take it into the school.

When he finally laid hands on what didn't belong to him, something he didn't know how to treat, something he lacked a feel for, I screamed an empty vase to pieces, one said to be authentic. When the authentic vase was lying in authentic pieces on the carpet, Matzerath, who was quite attached to the vase, raised his hand to strike me. But at this point Mama sprang up, and Jan, who had dropped by briefly with Stephan and his paper school cone, stepped between us.

"Alfred, please," he said in his calm and unctuous way, and Matzerath, struck by the look in Jan's blue and Mama's gray eyes, lowered his hand and stuck it in his trouser pocket.

The Pestalozzi School, decorated in the modern style with sgraffiti and frescoes, was a new, brick-red, three-story, flat-roofed elongated box that had been built by the Senate of our suburb rich in children at the vociferous insistence of the Social Democrats, who were still quite active back then. Except for its smell and the art nouveau youths playing sports in the sgraffiti and frescoes, I thought the box was not bad.

Unnaturally tiny trees that were actually turning green stood in gravel outside the gate, protected by iron bars reminiscent of crosiers. Mothers pressed forward from all directions, holding brightly colored paper cones and pulling screaming or well-behaved youths after them. Oskar had never seen so many mothers heading in the same direction. It was as if they were on a pilgrimage to a market where they planned to put their first- and second-born children up for sale.

Even in the entrance hall that school smell, described often enough, and more intimate than any known perfume in the world. On the flagstones of the hall stood four or five randomly placed granite basins out of whose depths water bubbled up simultaneously. With children, including some of my own age, crowding about them, they reminded me of my uncle Vinzent's sow in Bissau, who sometimes flung herself on her side and endured the similarly brutal and thirsty assault of her piglets.

The boys bent over the steadily collapsing towers of water in the basins, let their hair fall forward, and allowed the streams of water to poke about in their open mouths. I don't know if they were playing or drinking. Sometimes two boys would straighten up almost simultaneously with inflated cheeks and spray each other loudly in the face with mouth-warmed water, mixed, you may be sure, with saliva and breadcrumbs. For my own part, upon entering the hall I had thoughtlessly cast a glance into the adjoining open gymnasium on the left, and, having spotted the leather pommel horse, the climbing poles and climbing rope, the terrifying horizontal bar, crying out as always for a giant swing, felt a very real thirst I couldn't suppress, and would gladly have taken a drink of water like all the other boys. But I found it impossible to ask Mama, who was holding me by the hand, to lift Oskar, the toddler, over such a basin. Even if I stood on my drum, the fountain would remain out of reach. When, however, with a little jump I took a quick look over the edge of one of these basins and saw the greasy breadcrumbs nearly blocking the drain, and the nasty swill left standing in the bowl, the thirst I had stored up in my mind, and in my body as well, left me, as I wandered aimlessly past equipment in the desert wastes of the gymnasium.

Mama led me up monumental steps hewn for giants, through echoing corridors, into a room with a small plaque above the door bearing the inscription I-A. The room was full of boys my own age. The mothers of the boys pressed against the wall opposite the front windows and towering above me, held in their arms the large, brightly colored paper cones covered at the top with tissue paper which were traditional on the first day of school. Mama too was carrying a paper cone.

As I entered holding her hand, the rabble laughed, as did the rabble's mothers. A pudgy little boy who wanted to pound on my drum had to be kicked a few times in the shins to avoid singshattering glass, upon which the little brat fell over and hit his nicely combed head on a school bench, for which I received a cuff on the back of the head from Mama. The brat screamed. Of course I didn't, for I only screamed if someone tried to take my drum. Mama, who found this scene in front of other mothers embarrassing, shoved me into the first desk of a row by the windows. Of course the desk was too high. But farther back, where the rabble was ever cruder and more freckled, the desks were even higher.

I made do alone and sat quietly, having no reason to worry. Mama, who still seemed embarrassed, ducked in among the other mothers. She was probably ashamed to face her peers, owing to my so-called backward state. They acted as if they had some reason to be proud of their own little louts, who had grown far too quickly for my taste.

I couldn't look out the window at Fröbel Meadow, since the height of the windowsill was no better suited to me than the height of the school bench. But I would have liked to look over at Fröbel Meadow, where I knew that Boy Scouts were pitching tents under Greff's leadership, playing at lansquenets, and, as befitted Boy Scouts, doing good deeds. Not that I would have participated in this inflated glorification of camp life. Only the figure of Greff in short trousers interested me. His love of slim, if somewhat pale, wide-eyed boys was so great that he had clothed it in the uniform of the founder of the Boy Scouts, Baden-Powell.

Denied a worthwhile view by the insidious architecture, I simply stared at the sky and found pleasure in that. One new cloud after another emigrated from northwest to southeast, as if that direction had something special to offer. I wedged my drum, though it had not spent one drumbeat thinking about emigration, between my knees and the desk drawer. The backrest protected the back of Oskar's head. Behind me my so-called schoolmates cackled, roared, laughed, wept, and raged. They threw paper pellets at me, but I didn't turn around, finding the resolute clouds more aesthetically pleasing than the sight of a horde of grimacing, overexcited oafs.

When a woman entered and announced that she was Fräulein Spollenhauer, things settled down in class I-A. I didn't need to settle down, since I'd been waiting for what was to come in a calm, almost self-absorbed state. To tell the honest truth: Oskar wasn't even waiting for what was to come, he had no need for entertainment, and thus was not waiting, but simply holding his drum and sitting at his desk, content with the clouds behind or more properly beyond the paschally polished panes of the school windows.

Fräulein Spollenhauer wore an angularly tailored suit that gave her a dry, mannish look. This impression was reinforced by a stiff, tight collar that looked washable to me, which furrowed her neck and closed about her Adam's apple. She had scarcely entered the classroom in her flat walking shoes when, in an attempt to make herself immediately popular, she asked, "Now, dear children, how about singing a little song?"

She received a roar in answer that she must have taken for a positive response, for she set out in a prim, high-pitched voice on the spring song "In the Merry Month of May," though we were in mid-April. She had barely signaled May when all hell broke loose. Without waiting for a sign to start, without knowing the lyrics, without the slightest feeling for the simple rhythm of this ditty, the pack behind me began to loosen the plaster from the walls with their yowling.

In spite of her yellowish skin, her bobbed hair, and the man's tie peeping from beneath her collar, I felt sorry for Spollenhauer. Tearing myself free from the clouds, which apparently didn't have school that day, I rose to my feet, pulled the drumsticks from beneath my suspenders with a single motion, and drummed out the beat of the song loudly and emphatically. But the pack behind me had no ear or understanding for my efforts. Only Fräulein Spollenhauer gave me a nod of encouragement, smiled at the troop of mothers clinging to the wall, and sent a special wink toward Mama, which I took as a sign to continue drumming, simply at first, then with increased complexity, displaying all the tricks of my trade. The pack behind me had long since ceased their barbaric vocal medley. I had already begun to imagine that my drum was teaching my fellow pupils, educating them, turning them into my pupils, when Spollenhauer stopped before my desk, observed my hands and drumsticks closely, and even tried to tap along with my beat, not entirely without skill, smiling to herself, lost in thought, portraying for one brief moment a somewhat sympathetic older woman who, forgetting her teaching profession, escapes the existential caricature it prescribes and turns human, that is, childlike, curious, complex, immoral.

However, when Fräulein Spollenhauer could not follow my beat quickly and correctly, she sank back again into her old rectilinear, obtuse, and poorly paid role, pulled herself together, as teachers must from time to time, and said, "You must be little Oskar. We've heard so much about you. How nicely you drum. Isn't that so, children? Isn't Oskar a good drummer?"

The children roared, the mothers drew closer together, Spollenhauer had herself under control again. "But now," she piped in falsetto, "let's put the drum safely away in the classroom locker, it's tired and wants to sleep. Afterward, when school's out, you can have your drum back."

While she was still reeling off this hypocritical speech, she showed me her close-clipped teacher's fingernails and initiated a tenfold close-clipped assault on my drum, which, God knows, was neither tired nor wished to sleep. At first I held on tight, wrapped the arms of my sweater around the red and white flames of the cylinder, and stared at her; then, since she maintained the ancient stereotypical schoolteacher's gaze without flinching, I looked right through her, finding sufficient narrative material inside Fräulein Spollenhauer for three chapters of depravity, then tore myself loose from her inner life, since my drum was at stake, and as my gaze passed through her shoulder blades, registered the presence on her well-preserved skin of a mole the size of a gulden piece with long hairs sprouting from it.

Whether she sensed I'd seen through her, or because of my voice, with which, by way of warning, I had inflicted a small scratch, causing no real damage, on the right lens of her glasses, she abandoned the use of naked power that had chalked her knuckles white, no doubt unable to stand the glass scraping that gave her goose bumps, released my drum with a shiver and said, "You're a bad little Oskar," threw a reproachful glance at my mother, who didn't know where to look, left me my wide-awake drum, turned on her heel, marched on flat heels to her desk, rummaged through her briefcase, pulled out another pair of glasses, probably for reading, briskly removed from her nose the spectacles my voice had scraped as fingernails scrape a windowpane, acting as if I had desecrated them, placed the second pair on her nose, lifting her little finger as she did, drew herself up so stiffly you could hear her bones rattle, and announced, as she reached once more into her briefcase, "I'll now read you the schedule."

She fished out a stack of sheets from her pigskin case, took one for herself, passed the rest on to the mothers, Mama among them, and revealed at last to the six-year-olds, who were growing restless, what the schedule had to offer: "Monday: religion, writing, arithmetic, play; Tuesday: arithmetic, penmanship, singing, nature study; Wednesday: arithmetic, writing, drawing, drawing; Thursday: geography, arithmetic, writing, religion; Friday: arithmetic, writing, play, penmanship; Saturday: arithmetic, singing, play, play."

All this Fräulein Spollenhauer proclaimed as an irrevocable fate, reading out this product of a teachers' conference in strict tones that gave full weight to every letter, then, recalling her days at teacher-training college, turned gentle and progressive, burst out joyfully in pedagogical high spirits: "Now, my dear children, let's all repeat it together. All right — Monday?"

The horde roared, "Monday."

She continued: "Religion?" The baptized heathens roared out the word Religion. I spared my voice, but drummed the religious syllables on tin by way of substitute.

Behind me, spurred on by Spollenhauer, they screamed, "Wri — ting!" Twice my drum responded. "A-rith — me-tic!" Four beats this time.

The screaming continued behind me, Spollenhauer leading the litany in front of me, while I beat out the syllables soberly on my drum, putting a good face on a foolish game, till Spollenhauer — I don't know at what inner urge — sprang up, clearly annoyed — but it wasn't the louts behind me who were making her cross, no, I was the one turning her cheeks a hectic red, Oskar's poor drum was the stumbling block that made her draw the drummer keeping the beat into prayer.

"Now listen to me, Oskar: Thursday: geography?" Ignoring the word

Thursday, I struck the drum four times for geography, four times for arithmetic, twice for writing, and a triune trinity as the only true and saving drumbeats for religion.

But Spollenhauer had no ear for such distinctions. To her all drumming was equally repugnant. Ten times she bared again at me the shortest-hacked of fingernails and tried ten times to grab my drum.

Before she had so much as touched it, I unleashed my glass-slaying scream, deleting the upper panes from the three oversize windows of the classroom. The middle panes fell victim to my second scream. A mild spring breeze flowed freely into the classroom. Obliterating the lower panes with a third scream was basically superfluous, purely a matter of high spirits, for Spollenhauer had pulled in her claws when the upper and middle panes failed. Instead of assaulting those last panes in an aesthetically questionable burst of pure wantonness, God knows Oskar would have been smarter to keep his eye on the reeling Spollenhauer.

The devil knows where she conjured up that cane. At any rate it was suddenly there, vibrating in the classroom air now mingled with spring breezes, and through this airy mixture she made it whistle, rendered it flexible, hungry, thirsty, crazed for bursting skin, for *Sssst*, for all those curtains canes can imitate, bent on satisfying both herself and the cane. And she banged it down so hard on my desk that the ink in my inkwell took a violet leap. And when I wouldn't hold my hand out to be hit, she struck my drum. She struck my tin. She, that Spollenhauerite, struck my tin drum. What was she hitting it for? If she wanted to hit something, fine, but why did it have to be my drum? Weren't there enough crude louts behind me? Did it have to be my drum? Did she, who knew nothing of drumming, have to attack my drum? What was that glint in her eye? What animal longed to strike? Escaped from what zoo, seeking what prey, lusting for what? Something seized Oskar, welled up in him, rose from unknown depths through the soles of his shoes, through the soles of his feet, forced its way upward, took command of his vocal cords, and made him release a scream of passion sufficient to deglaze an entire Gothic cathedral with all its glorious windows capturing and refracting light.

In other words, I fashioned a double scream that literally pulverized both lenses of Spollenhauer's glasses. With slightly bleeding eyebrows, peering now through empty frames, she groped her way backward, then finally started to blubber in a manner far too ugly and hysterical for a schoolteacher, while the pack behind me fell into a terrified silence, some disappearing under their desks, some sitting fast with chattering teeth. Others scooted from desk to desk toward their mothers. The mothers, however, having assessed the damage and sought out the guilty party, were about to fall upon my mama, and would no doubt have done so, had I not grabbed my drum and shoved myself away from my bench.

Passing the half-blind Spollenhauer, I made my way to my mama, who was being menaced by the Furies, took her by the hand, and pulled her from the drafty room of class I-A. Echoing corridors. Stone stairs for giant children. Breadcrumbs in bubbling granite basins. In the open gymnasium boys trembled beneath the horizontal bar. Mama was still clutching her sheet of paper. Outside the portals of the Pestalozzi School I took it from her and converted the schedule into a meaningless paper ball.

But Oskar did allow the photographer, who was waiting between the columns at the entrance for the first graders with their paper cones and mothers, to take a picture of him with his own school cone, which, in spite of all the confusion, he had not lost. The sun came out, classrooms buzzed above us. The photographer posed Oskar before a blackboard on which was written: *My First Day at School.*

Rasputin and the ABCs

RELATING THE STORY of Oskar's first encounter with a schedule to my friend Klepp and my keeper Bruno, who listened with only half an ear, I said just now that the blackboard the photographer used as a traditional background for his postcard-sized pictures of six-year-old boys with knapsacks and school cones bore the following inscription: *My First Day at School.*

Of course this little phrase could only be read by the mothers, who were standing behind the photographer and acting more excited than the boys. It was at least a year before the boys in front of the blackboard could decipher the inscription, either next Easter when the new class entered or in their own earlier photos, and realize that those pretty pictures had been taken on the occasion of their first day at school.

Sütterlin script crawled across the blackboard with spiky malevolence, its curves falsely padded, chalking the inscription that marked the beginning of a new stage in life. And in fact the Sütterlin script is well suited for items of marked importance, for succinctly striking statements, for slogans of the day. And there are certain documents that, though I admit I've never seen them, I nonetheless envision in Sütterlin script. I have in mind immunization certificates, sports records, and handwritten death sentences. Even back then, when I could see through the Sütterlin script but couldn't read it, the double loop of the Sütterlin *M* with which the inscription began, malicious and smelling of hemp, reminded me of the scaffold. Nevertheless I would have preferred to read it letter for letter and not just divine its sense darkly. Let no one suppose that I spent my encounter with Fräulein Spollenhauer high-handedly singshattering glass and playing my drum in rebellious protest because I had already mastered my ABCs. Oh no, I knew only too well that simply seeing through Sütterlin script was not enough, that I lacked the most elementary schoolboy knowledge. Unfortunately the methods by which Fräulein Spollenhauer wished to educate him did not appeal to Oskar.

So I had by no means decided, having left the Pestalozzi School, that my first day at school would be my last. No more pencils, no more books, no more teacher's dirty looks. Nothing of the sort. At the very moment that the photographer was recording my image for posterity, I thought to myself: You're standing here in front of a blackboard beneath a no doubt meaningful, possibly ominous, inscription. It's true you're able to judge the inscription by the script and sense its associations, such as solitary confinement, protective custody, supervisory custody, and one-rope-fits-all, but you can't decipher the inscription. Meanwhile, in spite of your ignorance, which cries out to the partly cloudy heavens, you intend never to enter this schedule-school again. So just where, oh Oskar, do you plan to learn your big and little ABCs?

Though the little ABCs would no doubt have been enough for me, I had deduced the existence of both big and little ABCs from, among other things, the manifest existence of big people who couldn't be wished away and called themselves grownups. They never tired of offering a justification for big and little ABCs, pointing out that there were also big and little books, big and little leagues, and even state visits coded as big or little railroad stations, based on the number of arriving dignitaries and decorated diplomats for whom the red carpet had to be rolled out.

Neither Matzerath nor Mama worried about my education over the next few months. That one attempt to enroll me, so stressful and embarrassing for Mama, had been enough for them. Like Uncle Jan Bronski, they now sighed when they gazed down at me, and dredged up old stories like the one about my third birthday: "The trapdoor was open! You left it open, didn't you? You were in the kitchen, and the cellar before that, right? You brought up a can of mixed fruit for dessert, right? You left the trapdoor to the cellar open, didn't you?"

Every reproach Mama heaped on Matzerath was true, as we well know, and yet the whole was false. But he accepted all the blame and sometimes even wept, softhearted as he was. Then Mama and Jan Bronski would have to comfort him, and spoke of me, Oskar, as a cross they had to bear, a fate they could not flee, a trial they faced but knew not why.

No help was to be expected from these cross bearers, struck down by fate and plagued by trials. Aunt Hedwig Bronski, who frequently took me to Steffenspark to play in the sandbox with her two-year-old Marga, was likewise ruled out as my teacher: she was good-natured enough but dumb as the sky was blue. I was also forced to abandon the thought of Dr. Hollatz's Sister Inge, who was neither sky-blue nor good-natured, for she was no mere office girl but an extremely bright and irreplaceable assistant, and so had no time for me.

I conquered the hundred-plus steps of our four-story building several times a day, trying to drum up advice on every floor, smelled what nineteen lodgers were having for lunch, but knocked at no door, since I couldn't see old Heilandt, or the clockmaker Laubschad, and certainly not fat Frau Kater, or, much as I liked her, Mother Truczinski, as my future schoolteacher.

Under the eaves lived a musician and trumpeter named Meyn. Herr Meyn kept four cats and was permanently drunk. He played dance music at Zingler's Heights, and on Christmas Eve he and five fellow drunks would stamp through the snowy streets battling the harsh frost with carols. I met him one day in the attic: he lay on his back in black trousers and his white Sunday shirt, rolling an empty bottle of Machandel gin with his bare feet and playing the trumpet beautifully. Without lowering his trumpet, just shifting his eyes slightly to where I was standing behind him, he stole a glance at me and accepted me as his percussionist. He valued my instrument as highly as he did his own. Our duet drove his four cats out onto the roof and set the roof tiles gently vibrating.

When we finished our music and lowered our instruments, I pulled an old issue of the *Neueste Nachrichten* newspaper from under my sweater, smoothed out the pages, crouched beside Meyn the trumpeter, held out my reading matter, and asked him to teach me the big and little ABCs.

But Herr Meyer had fallen straight from his trumpet into a deep sleep. For him there were only three containers that counted: his bottle of Machandel gin, his trumpet, and sleep. It's true that for some time after that — to be precise, till he entered the SA cavalry and gave up gin —

we played unrehearsed duets in the attic for the stove, roof tiles, pigeons, and cats, but he was just never any use as a teacher.

I tried Greff the greengrocer. Without my drum, for Greff didn't like hearing it, I paid several visits to his basement shop across the way. The preconditions for a thorough course of study seemed present: scattered all about the two-room apartment, in the shop itself, behind and on the counter, even in the relatively dry potato cellar, lay books, adventure stories, song books, *Der Cherubinische Wandersmann,* the works of Walter Flex, Wiechert's *Simple Life, Daphnis and Chloe,* artists' monographs, stacks of sports magazines, and picture books filled with half-naked boys, most of whom, for some inexplicable reason, were leaping at a ball in sand dunes on the beach, displaying their oiled and gleaming muscles.

Greff was having all kinds of trouble with the shop at the time. Inspectors from the Bureau of Weights and Standards were less than pleased when they tested his weights and scales. The word fraud surfaced. Greff had to pay a fine and buy new weights. Beset by cares, only his books, youth meetings, and weekend hikes with the Boy Scouts could cheer him up.

He was filling out price tags and barely noticed me when I entered the shop; seizing the opportunity offered by this price-tagging operation, I grabbed three or four white paper tags and a red pencil, and using the finished tags as models, made a great show of imitating his Sütterlin script.

Oskar was no doubt too little for him, not wide-eyed and pale enough. So I laid the red pencil aside, chose a tome full of naked youths I thought would leap out at Greff, and held photos of bending or stretching boys I assumed meant something to him at an angle so Greff could see them.

Since as long as there were no customers in the shop demanding red beets the greengrocer kept penciling away with exaggerated precision on his price tags, I was forced to either clap the book covers loudly or flip noisily through the pages to make him emerge from his price tags and pay attention to me, the illiterate boy.

Simply put, Greff didn't understand me. When Scouts were in the shop — and there were always two or three of his lieutenants around in the afternoon—he didn't notice Oskar at all. If Greff was alone, however, nervous, strict, and annoyed by disturbances, he was quite capable of springing up and issuing orders: "Put that book down, Oskar. There's nothing in it for you. You're too dumb and too little for that. You're going to ruin it. Cost me more than six gulden. If you want to play there's plenty of potatoes and cabbages!"

He took the trashy old book away from me, leafed through it with no change of expression, and left me standing among Savoy cabbages, red cabbages, white cabbages, among sugar beets and spuds, alone and growing lonely; for Oskar didn't have his drum.

True, there was still Frau Greff, and after being brushed off by the greengrocer I would usually make my way to the couple's bedroom. Back then, Frau Lina Greff would lie in bed for weeks at a time, playing the invalid, smelling of a decaying nightgown, taking just about anything in hand except a book that might have taught me something.

In the days that followed, nursing a slight envy, Oskar eyed the school knapsacks of boys his own age, from the sides of which sponges and little rags for wiping the slates fluttered self-importantly. Nevertheless he can't recall ever having thoughts like: You brought this on yourself, Oskar. You should have put on your school game face. You shouldn't have ruined things permanently with Spollenhauer. Those urchins are getting ahead of you. They have their big or little ABCs down pat, while you still haven't learned how to hold the *Neueste Nachrichten* properly.

A slight envy, I've just said, it was no more. It took only a sniff to get a noseful of school once and for all. Have you ever gotten a whiff of those poorly rinsed, half-eaten sponges and little rags for yellow-framed flaking slates, which, in knapsacks of the cheapest leather, retain the sweat of all that penmanship, the vapor of big and little multiplication tables, the sweat of squeaking, halting, slipping, spit-moistened slate pencils? Now and then, when pupils on their way home from school laid their knapsacks down somewhere near me to play soccer or dodgeball, I would bend down to those little cloudlike sponges drying in the sun and imagine that if Satan existed, such would be the sour stench of his armpits.

So the school of slates was hardly to my taste. But Oskar can scarcely maintain that Gretchen Scheffler, who took his education in hand soon thereafter, was precisely the answer.

Everything about the furnishings of the Schefflers' flat over the bakery on Kleinhammerweg offended me. Those ornamental coverlets, those cushions embroidered with coats of arms, the Käthe Kruse dolls lurking in the corners of the sofa, those stuffed animals underfoot everywhere, all that china crying out for a bull, the souvenirs wherever you looked, all the pieces she'd started, knitted, crocheted, embroidered, woven, plaited, tatted, and trimmed in tiny mouse teeth. I could think of only one explanation for this sweetly dainty, charmingly cozy, stiflingly tiny household, overheated in winter and poisoned with flowers in summer: Gretchen Scheffler was childless, longed for little ones to ensnare in her knitting — ah, was Herr Scheffler to blame, or was she? — hungered so for a baby, would so happily have crocheted, beaded, trimmed, and covered a little one with cross-stitch kisses.

This is where I came in to learn my big and little ABCs. I made sure no piece of china or souvenir was damaged. I left my glass-shattering voice at home, so to speak, and closed one eye when Gretchen felt we'd had enough drumming for now and, baring her equine gold teeth in a smile, pulled the drum from my knees and laid it among the teddy bears.

I made friends with two of the Käthe Kruse dolls, clutched the little brats to my bosom, and strummed the lashes of their permanently startled eyes as though in love with them, so that this false and therefore even more genuine-seeming friendship with dolls might knit and ensnare Gretchen's knit-one-purl-two heart.

My plan wasn't bad. By the second visit Gretchen opened her heart, that is, she unraveled it as one unravels a stocking, showed me the whole long, threadbare thread, with little knots in places, opened all her cupboards, chests, and little boxes, spread out before me all her beaded rubbish, heaps of baby jackets, baby bibs, baby pants, enough to clothe quintuplets, held them up to me, put them on me, and took them off again.

Then she showed me Scheffler's marksmanship badges from the veterans' club, followed by photographs, sometimes the same as ours, till finally, as she turned back to the baby clothes, looking for rompers of some sort, books at last appeared: Oskar had counted fully on finding books beneath the baby clothes, had heard her talking about books with Mama, had known how eagerly the two, engaged and then married at almost exactly the same young age, had shared and borrowed books from the lending library near the Film-Palast, so that, pumped full of reading material, they could impart a more worldly scope and glamour to their grocery-store and bakery marriages.

Gretchen had little enough to offer me. Since she now devoted all her time to knitting, she no longer read, and like Mama, who never got around to reading anymore because of Jan Bronski, she no doubt gave the handsome volumes of the book club to which they both belonged for some time to people who still read because they did not knit and had no Jan Bronski.

Even bad books are books, and therefore holy. What I found was a jumble of odds and ends that no doubt came in large part from the book box of her brother Theo, who had met a seaman's death on Dogger Bank. Seven or eight volumes of Köhler's *Naval Calendar,* full of ships that sank long ago, *The Service Ranks of the Imperial Navy, Paul Benke: Naval Hero* — these could hardly have been the fare for which Gretchen's heart longed. Erich Keyser's *History of the City of Danzig,* and *A Struggle for Rome,* evidently undertaken by a man named Felix Dahn with the help of Totila and Teja, Belisarius and Narses, had no doubt likewise lost their luster and firmness of spine at the hands of her seafaring brother. To Gretchen's bookcase I attributed a book that balanced debit and credit and something about elective affinities by Goethe, as well as a thick, copiously illustrated volume entitled *Rasputin and Women.*

After hesitating for some time — the choice was so limited I didn't want to decide too quickly — I stopped, not knowing why, simply responding to that familiar inner voice, I stopped first at Rasputin and then at Goethe.

This double stop was to determine and influence my life, or at least the life I tried to live apart from my drum. To this very day — as Oskar, ever zealous to learn, gradually lures the library of the mental institution into his room — I turn up my nose at Schiller and his consorts and oscillate instead between Rasputin and Goethe, between the faith healer and the know-it-all, between the dark and gloomy figure who cast a spell on women and the luminous poet-prince who so happily allowed women to cast a spell on him. If for a time I felt closer to Rasputin and feared Goethe's intolerance, it was because I had a faint suspicion that if you, Oskar, had been drumming in Goethe's day, he would have thought you merely unnatural, condemned you as the very incarnation of the unnatural, while feeding his own nature — which you have always admired and strived for, even when it gave itself such unnatural airs — feeding his natural temperament, on sugary sweet confections, then beaten you, poor wretch, to death, if not with his fist or his *Faust,* then with a thick volume of his *Theory of Colors.*

But back to Rasputin. With Gretchen Scheffler's help he taught me my big and little ABCs, showed me how to be properly attentive to women, and consoled me when Goethe hurt my feelings.

It was no easy task to learn to read while playing the simpleton. That turned out to be harder than pretending to wet the bed for years as a child. With bed-wetting all I had to do was demonstrate each morning a failing I could easily have dispensed with. But playing the simpleton meant hiding my rapid progress under a bushel, waging a constant struggle with a nascent intellectual pride. If grownups wished to regard me as a bed wetter, I could accept it with an inner shrug, but that I had to present myself to them year in and year out as an ignoramus hurt both Oskar's feelings and those of his teacher.

The moment I rescued the books from the baby clothes, Gretchen gave a cry of joy; she recognized her vocation as a teacher then and there. I managed to lure this childless woman from the wool in which she had become entangled and made her almost happy. Actually she would have preferred to see me choose *Credit and Debit* for a reader; but I insisted on Rasputin, demanded Rasputin when she produced a proper little ABC primer for our second lesson, and finally resolved to speak up when she kept turning to idyllic stories of farm life in the mountains and fairy tales like *Dwarf Longnose* and *Tom Thumb.* "Rapupin!" I would cry, or "Rashushin!" Now and then I acted completely silly; Oskar could be heard babbling "Rashu, Rashu!" so Gretchen would know what he liked, yet remain in the dark about his awakening genius for pecking at letters.

I learned quickly and steadily without thinking much about it. Within a year I felt at home in Petersburg, in the private chambers of the autocratic ruler of all Russians, in the nursery of the sickly Tsarevich, among conspirators and popes, and not least as an eyewitness to Rasputin's orgies. There was a tone to all this that appealed to me, and it all revolved around a central figure. You could see it too in the contemporary engravings scattered throughout the book, showing a bearded Rasputin with eyes of coal among women in black stockings and little else. Rasputin's death preyed on my mind: he had been poisoned with poisoned cake and poisoned wine, and then, when he wanted more cake, they shot him with pistols, and when the lead in his chest made him feel like dancing, they tied him up and dropped him through an ice hole in the Neva. All that was done by male officers. The ladies of metropolitan Petersburg would never have given their little father Rasputin poisoned cake, though they would have given him anything else he asked for. Women believed in him, while officers had to remove him from their path before they could again believe in themselves.

Is it any wonder I wasn't the only one who took pleasure in the life and death of the athletic faith healer? Gretchen groped her way back to the reading of her early years of marriage, let herself go occasionally while reading aloud, trembled when the word orgy appeared, breathed the magical word orgy with a little gasp, was ready and willing for an orgy when she said orgy, yet had no real idea what an orgy was.

Things took a turn for the worse when Mama came along to the flat over the bakery on Kleinhammerweg and sat in on my lessons. This sometimes degenerated into an orgy, ceased to be a lesson for little Oskar and became an end in itself, turned into a duet of giggles every two or three sentences, left their lips dry and cracked, scooted the two married women closer together under Rasputin's spell, made them shift restlessly on the sofa cushions and feel like pressing their thighs tight; what began as silliness ended in sighs, and after a dozen pages of Rasputin something happened on that bright afternoon they had perhaps neither desired nor expected, but gladly accepted, something to which Rasputin would not have objected, indeed would have gladly bestowed free for all eternity.

Finally, when both women had said ohGodohGodohGod and pushed at their tousled hair in embarrassment, Mama asked with concern, "You're sure little Oskar doesn't understand any of this?" "How could he," Gretchen said soothingly. "I try so hard, but he just can't learn a thing, and he'll probably never learn to read."

To bear witness to my unshakable ignorance, she added, "Just think, Agnes, he tears pages out of our Rasputin, wads them up, and they're gone. Sometimes I feel like giving up. But when I see how happy he is with the book, I let him tear it up and ruin it. I've already asked Alex to get us a new one for Christmas."

And so I succeeded — as you will have noticed — little by little, over the course of three or four years — Gretchen Scheffler taught me that long and longer — to remove over half the pages in the Rasputin book, wadding them up carefully, while feigning wanton disregard, so that afterward, in my drummer's nook at home, I could pull the pages from under my sweater, smooth them out, and pile them up for secret reading sessions undisturbed by women. I used the same tactics with Goethe, which I demanded from Gretchen every fourth session, calling out "Döte." I didn't wish to rely solely on Rasputin, for all too soon it became clear to me that for every Rasputin in this world there is a Goethe, that Rasputin draws Goethe in his wake, or Goethe draws Rasputin, if necessary even creates the other, so he can subsequently condemn him.

When Oskar sat in the attic with his unbound book, or crouched behind bicycle frames in old Herr Heilandt's shed, shuffling loose leaves of *Elective Affinities* with a bundle of Rasputin like a deck of cards, he read the new book with growing astonishment, and at the same time with a smile, saw Ottilie strolling demurely on Rasputin's arm through gardens in central Germany, and Goethe, seated in a sleigh with a dissolute, patrician Olga, sliding from orgy to orgy through a wintry St. Petersburg.

But let us get back to my schoolroom on Kleinhammerweg. Though I seemed to be making no progress at all, Gretchen took the most maidenly pleasure in me. Beneath the invisible but still hairy hand of the Russian faith healer raised in blessing, she blossomed mightily in my presence and even swept her potted lime tree and cactuses along with her. If only Herr Scheffler had occasionally withdrawn his fingers from the flour back then and swapped the bakery rolls for another little roll. Gretchen would gladly have been kneaded, rolled, brushed, and baked by him. Who knows what might have come out of the oven? No doubt a child eventually. Gretchen would have enjoyed such baking.

There she sat, however, after the most impassioned readings of Rasputin, with fiery eyes and slightly disheveled hair, shifted her gold and equine teeth but had nothing to bite, said ohGodohGod, and thought of the primal sourdough. Since Mama, who had her Jan, after all, could not help Gretchen, the minutes following this portion of my lesson might have ended unhappily if Gretchen had not had such a joyful heart.

She would jump up and go to the kitchen, return with the coffee grinder, clutch it like a lover, sing "Dark Eyes" or "Red Sarafan" with a melancholy passion as she coarse-ground the coffee, with Mama joining in, then take her dark eyes to the kitchen, put on the water, run down to the bakery while the water heated over the gas flame, select freshly baked and day-old pastries, often over Scheffler's objections, set the little table with fancy flowered cups, a little pot of cream, a little sugar bowl and dessert forks, then strew pansies among them, pour the coffee, switch to airs from *The Tsarevich*, offer love tarts and honey almond cakes, "A Soldier Stands on the Volga Shore," Frankfurt coffee ring sprinkled with sliced almonds, "Are There Many Angels Where You Are," and meringue kisses with whipped cream, so sweet, so sweet; and as they chewed, having achieved the necessary distance, the conversation would come back to Rasputin, and now, following that brief pastry-sated interlude, they could honestly deplore the abysmal corruption of the Tsarist era.

I ate far too many pastries in those years. As can be seen in the photos, Oskar grew no taller, just got fatter and lost his figure. After those sugary sweet lessons on Kleinhammerweg I didn't know what else to do but hide behind the shop counter on Labesweg and, as soon as Matzerath was out of sight, tie a piece of dry bread on a string, dunk it in the small Norwegian barrel filled with pickled herring, and not pull it out till it was saturated to overflowing with brine. You can't imagine how effective an emetic this snack was after having overstuffed myself with pastries. To lose weight, Oskar would often throw up a gulden's worth of cakes from Scheffler's bakery into our toilet, and that was a lot of money back then.

I had to pay for Gretchen's lessons with a different coin. Since she loved to sew and knit things for children, she turned me into a doll she could dress and undress. I was obliged to try on and put up with all sorts of little smocks, bonnets, pants, and coats with and without hoods in a wide variety of styles, colors, and materials.

I don't know if it was Mama or Gretchen who transformed me, on the occasion of my eighth birthday, into a little Tsarevich who fully deserved to be shot. The Rasputin cult of the two women was then at its height. A photo taken that day shows me standing beside a birthday cake fenced in by eight non-drip candles, wearing an embroidered

Russian smock, under a Cossack cap perched at a jaunty angle, behind crossed cartridge belts, in wide white trousers and low boots.

Luckily my drum was allowed in the picture. A further piece of luck was that Gretchen Scheffler, possibly at my urging, had cut, sewn, and tailored a suit for me sufficiently Biedermeier and electively affinitive that it still conjures the spirit of Goethe in my album, bearing witness to the two souls in my breast, and enables me, with just one drum, to be in St. Petersburg and Weimar at the same time, descending to the realm of the Mothers and celebrating orgies with ladies.

Long-Distance Song Effects from the Stockturm

FRÄULEIN DR. HORNSTETTER, who drops by my room almost daily long enough to smoke one cigarette, who's supposed to be treating me but leaves the room less nervous each time I've treated her, who's so shy that the only close relationship she has is to her cigarette, steadfastly maintains that I was too isolated as a child, that I didn't play enough with other children.

Now, as far as other children are concerned, she may not be entirely wrong. Gretchen Scheffler's pedagogical venture occupied so much of my time, and I was torn so often between Goethe and Rasputin, that with the best will in the world I found no time for ring-around-the-rosy and counting games. But every time I shunned books, as scholars sometimes do, cursed them as verbal graveyards, and tried to make contact with the common folk, I ran up against the kids in our building and felt fortunate, after a few brushes with those little cannibals, to return to my reading in one piece.

Oskar could either leave his parents' flat through the shop, in which case he would be standing on Labesweg, or he could close the door to the flat behind him and stand in the stairwell, from which he could reach the street to the left, or climb four flights of stairs to the attic where Meyn played his trumpet, or, lastly, go out into the courtyard. The street was cobblestone. On the packed sand of the courtyard rabbits multiplied and carpets were beaten. The attic offered, aside from occasional duets with the drunken Herr Meyn, a view, a vista, and that lovely but deceptive feeling of freedom all tower climbers seek, which makes dreamers of all who dwell in garrets.

While the courtyard was fraught with perils for Oskar, the attic offered him security, till Axel Mischke and his gang drove him from there as well. The courtyard ran the full length of the building but measured only seven paces in depth, and was separated from three other courtyards by a tarred wooden fence sprouting barbed wire from its top. The attic offered a good overview of this labyrinth: the buildings on Labesweg, the two cross streets Hertastraße and Luisenstraße, and Marienstraße in the far distance formed an extensive quadrangle of courtyards that included a cough-drop factory and several small repair shops. Trees and bushes emerged here and there from the courtyards and advertised the season. Otherwise the courtyards indeed differed in size, but as far as rabbits and carpet beatings were concerned they all came from the same litter. While there were rabbits throughout the year, carpets were, according to house rules, beaten only on Tuesdays and Fridays. On such days the size of the courtyard complex was confirmed. Looking down from the attic, Oskar could see and hear it: over one hundred carpets, runners, and bedside rugs were rubbed with sauerkraut, brushed, beaten, and finally forced to show their patterns. One hundred women carried carpet corpses from the houses, lifting their naked round arms as they did so, their hair and hairdos protected by short knotted kerchiefs, threw the carpets over the racks, grabbed the plaited carpet beaters, and blasted the narrow courtyards with a barrage of dry blows.

Oskar hated this single-minded hymn to cleanliness. He battled the din with his drum, yet had to admit, even in the attic, which provided a certain distance, that he was powerless against the housewives. A hundred carpet-beating women could storm the heavens, could blunt the wingtips of young swallows, could bring down with a few blows the little temple Oskar had drummed up in the April air.

On days when no carpets were being beaten, the children of our building did gymnastics on the wooden carpet racks. I was rarely in the courtyard. Only old Herr Heilandt's shed offered me a degree of security, for the old man didn't allow anyone but me in his junk room and gave the children scarcely a peek at the disintegrating sewing machines, the incomplete bicycles, the vises and pulley blocks, the crooked nails pounded straight and kept in cigar boxes. That was his major occupation: when he wasn't pulling nails from crate boards, he was at the anvil straightening nails he had pulled out the previous day. Aside from the fact that he never gave up on a nail, he was the man who helped on moving day, who slaughtered rabbits for holidays, and who spat tobacco juice all over the courtyard, stairs, and attic.

One day when the children, as children do, were making soup next to his shed, Nuchi Eyke asked old man Heilandt to spit in the soup three times. The old man did so, bringing it up from his depths, then disappeared into his shanty and started pounding nails again, while Axel Mischke added a further ingredient, some pulverized brick. Oskar regarded this culinary experiment with curiosity but stood off to one side. Axel Mischke and Harry Schlager had erected a sort of tent out of blankets and rags so no grownups could peek into the soup. As the brick gruel came to a boil, little Hans Kollin emptied his pockets and contributed two live frogs he'd caught at Aktien Pond to the soup. Susi Kater, the only girl in the tent, puckered her mouth in disappointment and bitterness as the frogs sank silently into the soup, unheralded and unsung, without the slightest attempt at a last jump. Nuchi Eyke was the first to unbutton his trousers and, undeterred by Susi's presence, pee into the hotpot. Axel, Harry, and little Hans Kollin followed suit. When Little Cheese tried to show the ten-year-olds what he could do, nothing came forth. Now all eyes turned to Susi, and Axel Mischke handed her a Persil-blue enamel cook pot with a battered rim. Oskar was ready to leave by now. But he waited till Susi, who apparently had no panties on, squatted down, wrapped her arms around her knees, shoved the pot under her, gazed blankly into space, then wrinkled her nose as the pot announced with a metallic tinkle that she too had a little something to spare for the soup.

I ran away at the time. I shouldn't have run, I should have walked calmly. But because I ran, everyone who'd been fishing around in the pot with their eyes till then looked up at me. I heard Susi Kater's voice behind me saying, "He's going to rat on us, look at him run!"; her voice was still stabbing at me as I stumbled up four flights of stairs and finally caught my breath in the attic.

I was seven and a half. Susi may have been nine. Little Cheese was barely eight. Axel, Nuchi, little Hans, and Harry were ten or eleven. Then there was Maria Truczinski. She was a little older than me but never played in the courtyard, instead she played with dolls in Mother Truczinski's kitchen, or with her grown-up sister Guste, who helped out at the Protestant kindergarten.

Small wonder that to this day I can't stand to hear the sound of women urinating in chamber pots. Just when Oskar had soothed his ears by stirring his drum, felt safely removed in the attic from the soup that bubbled below, the whole contingent arrived, barefoot or in laced shoes, everyone who'd done their bit for the soup, and Nuchi had the soup with him. They surrounded Oskar, with Little Cheese bringing up the rear. They poked each other, whispering "Do it!" till Axel grabbed Oskar from behind, pinned his arms, and Susi, laughing, baring her moist, even teeth, her tongue between them, said why not? She took the spoon from Nuchi, wiped the tin to silver on her thigh, dipped the little spoon in the steaming pot, stirred around in it slowly, enjoying its mushy resistance to the full like any good housewife, blew on the spoon to cool it, and finally fed it to Oskar: she fed it to me, I've never eaten anything like it again, that taste will stay with me forever.

Not until the mob, so overly concerned with my physical well-being, had left because Nuchi had vomited into the pot, did I too crawl into a corner of the drying loft where only a few bedsheets were hanging at the time, and disgorge several spoonfuls of reddish brew, but could discover no vestiges of frog in what I threw up. I climbed up on a box under an open dormer window, gazed out at distant courtyards, grinding brick residue between my teeth, felt the urge to act, checked the distant windows of the houses on Marienstraße, glass gleaming, screamed, sang long-distance toward them, with no visible result, yet was so convinced long-distance song would work that henceforth my courtyard and all other courtyards grew too small for me, and hungering for distant climes, distant places, distant views, I seized each opportunity, alone or holding Mama's hand, that led me far from Labesweg, far from our neighborhood, and delivered me from the persecution of all those soup chefs in our small courtyard.

Every Thursday Mama went shopping in the city. She usually took me along. She always took me along when we needed to buy a new drum from Sigismund Markus in the Arsenal Arcade at Kohlenmarkt. In that period, from roughly the age of seven to ten, I wrecked a drum in two weeks flat. From ten to fourteen I would pound through the tin in less than a week. Later on I could reduce a drum to scrap metal in a single day, or, if I was in a more harmonious mood, drum firmly yet sensitively for three or four months at a time with no visible damage to my drum, apart from a few cracks in the lacquer.

But we're speaking now of the time I would leave our courtyard with its carpet racks, old man Heilandt pounding nails, the kids making new soups, and go with my mama once every two weeks to the shop of Sigismund Markus, where I was permitted to select a new instrument from his stock of tin drums. Sometimes Mama would take me along even though my drum was in a relatively sound condition, and I enjoyed those afternoons in the colorful Altstadt, which always had a museum-like quality, with bells ringing from this or that church tower.

For the most part these visits passed with pleasing regularity. A few purchases at Leiser, Sternfeld, or Machwitz, then the visit to Markus, who made a habit of addressing Mama with a carefully selected assortment of the most flattering compliments. There was no doubt that he was courting her, but so far as I know he never gave in to any greater overture than silently kissing Mama's warmly grasped hand and declaring it worth its weight in gold — except for the time he fell to his knees, which I'll tell about later.

Mama, who had inherited her full, firm, stately figure from Grandmother Koljaiczek, as well as a charming vanity coupled with good nature, submitted to the attentions of Sigismund Markus all the more willingly because of the dirt-cheap assortment of sewing silk and ladies' stockings, purchased in bulk but nonetheless flawless, that he practically gave to her. To say nothing of the tin drum he passed over the counter to me every two weeks at a ridiculously low price.

On every visit, at precisely four-thirty in the afternoon, Mama would ask Sigismund if she could leave me, Oskar, at the shop in his care, since she had important and pressing errands to attend to. Smiling oddly, Markus would bow and promise in flowery phrases to protect me like the apple of his eye while she took care of her important errands. A very gentle, by no means offensive mockery, which gave his sentences a peculiar intonation, made Mama blush on occasion and suspect that Markus knew what was what.

But I too knew the sort of errands Mama called important, to which she attended all too eagerly. For a time I was allowed to accompany her to a cheap boarding house on Tischlergasse, where she disappeared into a stairwell, returning three-quarters of an hour later, while I was left to wait with the landlady, who was usually slurping a bottle of Mampe, with a soft drink before me, silently served, always awful, till Mama came back, apparently unchanged, greeted the landlady, who didn't glance up from her half and half, and took me by the hand, forgetting that the temperature of her hand would give her away. Hot hand in hand we then visited the Café Weitzke on Wollwebergasse. Mama would order a strong Mocha coffee for herself, a lemon ice cream for Oskar, and wait till, right on time and as if by chance, Jan Bronski happened by, joined us at the table, and had his own Mocha placed on the cool, calming marble top.

They spoke quite openly in front of me, and their conversation confirmed what I'd known for some time: Mama and Uncle Jan met almost every Thursday to do it with each other for three-quarters of an hour in a room Jan rented at the boarding house on Tischlergasse. It was probably Jan who objected to these visits of mine to Tischlergasse and the Café Weitzke. He was quite prudish at times, more so than Mama, who saw no problem with my witnessing the conclusion to their hour of love, of whose legitimacy, it appears, she always remained convinced.

So at Jan's request I spent almost every Thursday afternoon from four-thirty till nearly six at Sigismund Markus's, where I could inspect and use his assortment of tin drums, even play several at once—where else could Oskar have done that?—while gazing into the hangdog face of Markus. Though I had no idea where his thoughts came from, I had a pretty good idea where they were headed: they hung around Tischlergasse, scratched at the numbered doors of rooms, or crouched like poor Lazarus beneath a marble table at the Café Weitzke, waiting for what? For crumbs?

Mama and Jan Bronski left no crumbs. They ate it all themselves. They had that ravenous hunger that's never satisfied, that swallows its own tail. They were so busy they would have sensed the thoughts of Markus beneath the table as merely the insistent caress of a draft.

On one of those afternoons—it must have been in September, for Mama left Markus's shop in a rust-brown autumn suit—when I saw that Markus was deeply immersed, completely buried, and no doubt thoroughly lost in thought behind the counter, something impelled me to carry my newly acquired drum into the Arsenal Arcade, a darkly cool tunnel lined on both sides by the windows of the choicest establishments, such as jewelry shops, delicatessens, and bookstores. But the displayed wares, no doubt reasonably priced but clearly beyond my means, could not hold me; instead that same force impelled me out of the tunnel and into the Kohlenmarkt. At its very center I stood in the dusty light before the arsenal, its basalt-gray façade studded with cannonballs of all sizes from all sorts of former sieges, iron bumps intended to remind each passerby of the city's history. The cannonballs failed to move me, for I knew they had not lodged there on their own, but that a mason who lived in the city, employed and paid by the Building Surveyor's Office in conjunction with the Office of Historical Preservation, embedded munitions from past centuries in the façades of various churches and town halls, including the front and rear walls of the arsenal.

I was headed for the Stadt-Theater, whose columned portal could be seen on the right, separated from the arsenal only by a narrow, dark lane. But since, as I expected, I found the Stadt-Theater closed at that hour — the box office for the evening performance wouldn't open till seven — I drummed off indecisively to the left, already weighing a retreat, till Oskar stood between the Stockturm and Langgasser Gate. I didn't dare pass through the gate down Langgasse and left onto Große Wollwebergasse, for Mama and Jan would be sitting there, and if they weren't yet there they might be just finishing up on Tischlergasse, or perhaps already on their way to their refreshing Mochas on the little marble table.

I don't know how I managed to cross the avenue on Kohlenmarkt, with the streetcars jangling in and out through the gate, screeching round the curve toward Kohlenmarkt, Holzmarkt, and Central Station. Perhaps some grownup — it may even have been a policeman — took me by the hand and guided me safely through the perils of the traffic.

I stood before the buttressed brick of the Stockturm, which rose steeply toward the sky, and only by chance, stirred by encroaching boredom, lodged my drumsticks between the brickwork and the ironclad frame of the tower door. From the moment I directed my gaze upward along the brick it proved hard to follow the line of the façade, for pigeons were busy taking off from niches and windows in the tower, coming to rest for brief pigeon-measured moments on waterspouts and in alcoves, then plunging down the wall, dragging my gaze along.

This pigeon business irritated me. My gaze deserved better, I withdrew it and, to dispel my irritation, used both my drumsticks in earnest as a lever: the door yielded, and before he had even pushed it fully open, Oskar was inside the tower, climbing the spiral staircase, leading with his right leg, pulling the left one after, reached the first barred dungeons, spiraled still higher, leaving behind the torture chambers with their carefully polished and instructively labeled instruments, cast a glance through a narrow barred window as he continued to climb — now leading with his left leg, pulling his right after — estimated how high he was, noted the thickness of the masonry, startled pigeons into flight, met the same pigeons one turn of the stairs higher, led with his right leg again, pulling his left after, and as Oskar, continuing to switch legs, finally reached the top, he would gladly have kept on climbing, though both his right and left legs felt heavy. But the stairs had tired too soon. He grasped the absurdity and futility of building towers.

I don't know how high the Stockturm was — and still is, for it survived the war. Nor do I have any desire to ask my keeper Bruno for a reference work on East German brick Gothic. I guess it must have been a good hundred fifty feet to the very top of the tower.

As the spiral staircase tired too soon, I had to stop at a gallery that circled the tower's dome. I sat down, thrust my legs between the little columns of the balustrade, leaned forward, and peering past a column I had wrapped my right arm around, gazed down at the Kohlenmarkt, while with my left I made sure of my drum, which had shared the entire journey.

I have no intention of boring you with a bird's-eye view of Danzig, with that panorama of bell towers, still suffused, they say, with the breath of the Middle Ages, portrayed in a thousand good engravings. Nor will I go on about the pigeons, even if it's true ten times over that pigeons, which some people call doves, are good literary material. Pigeons and doves do next to nothing for me, though gulls are somewhat more interesting. The phrase dove of peace is simply a paradox. I would sooner entrust a peace message to a hawk or even a vulture than to a dove, the most belligerent tenant under the sun. To make a long story short: there were pigeons on the Stockturm. But there are pigeons on any self-respecting tower that wants to keep up appearances with the help of its conservators.

My gaze had turned toward something totally different: the Stadt-Theater, which I'd found closed upon leaving the Arsenal Arcade. The box with its dome bore a fiendishly close resemblance to a senselessly enlarged, neoclassical coffee grinder, though it lacked the handle on the rounded top of its dome which, in that temple devoted to culture and the muses filled to the brim each evening, would have allowed it to grind to grisly scrap a five-act play with its entire assemblage of tragedians, stage sets, prompters, props, and curtains. This building, from whose column-flanked lobby windows a sagging afternoon sun, steadily applying more red, refused to depart, annoyed me.

At that hour, some one hundred fifty feet above the Kohlenmarkt, above streetcars and clerks heading home from work, high above Markus's sweet-smelling junk shop, above the cool marble tables at the Café Weitzke, above two cups of Mocha, towering above Mama and Jan Bronski, above our building, our courtyard, all other courtyards, above bent and straightened nails, leaving the neighborhood children and their brick soup far below, I, who up till then had screamed only when forced by circumstances, now screamed without cause or compulsion. Until I climbed the Stockturm, I'd only sent my piercing tones into glass, the interior of a light bulb, or a bottle of flat beer when someone tried to take away my drum; now on the tower I screamed down, though my drum was not threatened in any way.

No one was trying to take Oskar's drum away, and yet he screamed. No pigeon had sullied his drum with his droppings, to be repaid with a scream. There was verdigris on copper plates nearby but no glass, yet Oskar screamed. The pigeons had blank reddish eyes, but no glass eye eyed him, yet he screamed. What was he screaming at, what distant horizon lured him? Was it a focused attempt to demonstrate what he'd tried at random in the attic above the courtyard after enjoying his brick soup? What glass did Oskar have in mind? With what glass — and it had to be glass — did Oskar plan to experiment?

It was the Stadt-Theater, the dramatic coffee grinder, whose setting-sun windowpanes attracted my newfangled tones, first tested in our attic and bordering now, I might say, on mannerism. After a few minutes of screams of various calibers, which however produced no results, an almost soundless tone took effect, and Oskar could report with joy and telltale pride that two midlevel panes in the left window of the lobby had been forced to surrender the evening sun and now registered as two black quadrangles in need of immediate reglazing.

This success required further confirmation. Like a modern painter who, having at last found the style he's been seeking for years, bestows upon a stunned world a whole series of equally wonderful, equally bold, equally worthy, similarly formatted finger exercises in the same mode, I proceeded to put on a show.

Within a mere quarter-hour I managed to deglaze all the windows in the lobby and a portion of the doors. What appeared from above to be an excited crowd gathered in front of the theater. There are always curious bystanders. I was not particularly impressed by my admirers. Of course they forced Oskar to work with even greater rigor, even greater formal skill. I was just setting out on an even bolder experiment to lay bare the inner essence of all things, namely to project a special scream through the open lobby, through a keyhole in a lobby door, into the still darkened interior of the theater and strike the pride of all season-ticket holders, the theater's chandelier, with all its polished, reflecting, refracting, faceted claptrappery, when I spotted a rust-brown suit in the crowd outside the theater. Mama had found her way back from the Café Weitzke, had enjoyed her Mocha, had left Jan Bronski.

Admittedly, Oskar still sent a scream toward the fancy chandelier. It appeared to have had no effect, however, for the following day the newspapers reported only the mysteriously shattered panes in the lobby windows and doors. For weeks afterward semi-scientific and even scientific investigations appeared in the feature sections of the daily press, spreading one column after another of the most fantastic nonsense. The *Neueste Nachrichten* referred to cosmic rays. Staff members at the local observatory, highly qualified academics, spoke of sunspots.

I made my way down the spiral stairs of the Stockturm as quickly as my little legs would carry me and arrived somewhat breathlessly among the crowd in front of the theater portal. Mama's rust-brown autumn suit no longer stood out, she must have been inside Markus's shop, perhaps reporting the damage my voice had caused. And Markus, who accepted my so-called retarded condition, as well as my diamond voice, as the most natural thing in the world, would be wagging the tip of his tongue, so Oskar thought, and rubbing his yellow-white hands.

From the door of the shop I saw something that made me forget all my long-distance singshattering triumphs. Sigismund Markus knelt before my mama, and all the stuffed toys, bears, monkeys, dogs, even dolls with click-open eyes, fire engines, rocking horses, all the puppets hanging round guarding his shop, seemed about to kneel down with him. He, however, held Mama's two hands covered by his own, their backs showing lightly downed brownish spots, and he was crying.

Mama looked equally solemn and concerned by the situation. "Please, Markus," she said, "please, not here in the shop."

But Markus couldn't stop, and his words had an unforgettable cadence, pleading and overwrought at the same time: "Drop this Bronski business, with him and the Polish Post Office, it's bad I tell you. Don't bet on the Poles, if you got to bet on someone, bet on the Germans, they're going to be on top, sooner or later; they're partway there already, on their way up, and you're still betting on Bronski, Frau Agnes. Bet on Matzerath if you want, him you've got already. Or bet on Markus if you'd like, please, come with Markus, newly baptized and all. Let's go to London, Frau Agnes, I got people there and funds if you come, but if you won't come with Markus, if you despise him, then you despise him. But he's begging you, from his heart he's begging, please don't bet on this meshuge Bronski who sticks with the Polish Post Office when it's clear the Poles are finished once the Germans come."

Just as Mama, confused by so many possibilities and impossibilities, was about to burst into tears, Markus saw me in the shop door and, releasing one of Mama's hands, gestured toward me with five eloquent fingers: "Please, we'll take him with us to London. Like a prince he'll live, a prince!"

Now Mama looked at me too, and started to smile. Perhaps she was thinking of the paneless lobby windows of the Stadt-Theater, or felt good about the prospect of metropolitan London. But to my surprise she shook her head and said lightly, as if declining an offer to dance, "Thank you, Markus, but I can't, I really can't — on account of Bronski."

Taking my uncle's name as a cue, Markus rose at once, jackknifed a bow, and replied, "Forgive Markus, please, that's what he thought, that it wouldn't work on account of him."

As we left the shop in the Arsenal Arcade, Markus locked it from the outside, though it wasn't yet closing time, and walked with us to the stop for the Number Five line. Passersby and a few policemen were still standing outside the Stadt-Theater. I wasn't afraid, however, and scarcely recalled my triumphs over glass. Markus bent down to me, whispering more to himself than to us, "The things he can do, that Oskar. Beats his drum and raises a ruckus at the theater."

He calmed Mama's growing anxiety over the broken glass with soothing gestures, and as the tram arrived and we stepped into the second car, he implored her again softly, fearing he might be overheard, "Well, stick with Matzerath then, please, him you have, and don't bet on no more Poles."

When Oskar, lying or sitting on his metal bed today, drumming in either case, revisits the Arsenal Arcade, the words scribbled on the walls of the Stockturm's dungeons, the Stockturm itself with its oiled instruments of torture, the three lobby windows of the Stadt-Theater behind its columns, then returns to Arsenal Arcade and Sigismund Markus's shop to trace the details of that September day, he must, at the same time, seek the land of the Poles. How does he seek it? He seeks it with his drumsticks. Does he seek the land of the Poles with his soul as well? He seeks it with every organ of his being, but the soul is not an organ.

And I seek the land of the Poles that is lost, that is not yet lost. Some say nearly lost, already lost, lost once more. Here in Germany they seek Poland with credits, with Leicas, with compasses, with radar, with divining rods and delegations, with humanism, with leaders of the opposition and clubs of exiles mothballing regional costumes. While they search for the land of the Poles with the soul in this land—some with Chopin, some with revenge in their hearts—while they dismiss plans one through four for partitioning the land of the Poles and sit down to work on a fifth, while they fly with Air France to Warsaw and place a wreath in remorse where the ghetto once stood, while they seek the land of the Poles with rockets someday, I search on my drum for the land of the Poles and drum: lost, not yet lost, lost once more, lost to whom, lost too soon, lost by now, Poland's lost, all is lost, Poland is not yet lost.

The Grandstand

IN SINGSHATTERING the lobby windows of our Stadt-Theater, I sought and found my first contact with the dramatic arts. Though she was deeply engaged with the toy merchant Markus, Mama must have noticed my direct tie to the theater that afternoon, for when the Christmas holidays came, she bought four theater tickets, for herself, for Stephan and Marga Bronski, and for Oskar, and took the three of us to the Christmas play on the last Sunday of Advent. We sat in the front row of the second balcony on the side. The fancy chandelier hanging over the orchestra section was doing its best. So I was glad I hadn't shattered it from atop the Stockturm with my song.

Even back then there were far too many children. More children than mothers sat in the balcony, while the ratio of mother to child in the orchestra, where the more prosperous and procreatively cautious sat, was fairly well balanced. Why can't children sit still? Marga Bronski, who was sitting between me and the relatively well-behaved Stephan, slipped off the folding seat, tried to climb back up, soon found it more fun to do gymnastics on the balcony rail, got caught in the folding mechanism of her seat, and began to scream, but no more loudly or lengthily than the screamers around us, because Mama stuffed her silly little mouth with candy. Sucking away and prematurely exhausted by all the struggles with her seat, Stephan's little sister fell asleep soon after the performance began and had to be awakened at the end of each act to clap her hands, which she did with great enthusiasm.

The play was *Tom Thumb*, a fairy tale that gripped me from the first scene and appealed to me for obvious reasons. It was done very cleverly, you never saw Tom Thumb, just heard his voice and saw the grownups chasing after the play's invisible but very active eponymous hero. There he was, ensconced in the horse's ear, there he was, being sold at a high price to two rascals by his father, there he was, strolling about on the brim of one rascal's hat, speaking down from above; later he creeps into a mouse hole, then into a snail's shell, joins a band of thieves, sleeps in the hay, winds up with the hay in a cow's stomach. But the cow is slaughtered because it speaks with Tom Thumb's voice. The cow's stomach is thrown on a dunghill with the little fellow trapped inside and gobbled up by a wolf. Tom Thumb, however, lures the wolf to the storeroom of his father's house with a few clever remarks, then raises a din just as the wolf gets going. It ended like the fairy tale: the father kills the big bad wolf, the mother cuts open the glutton's stomach with a pair of scissors, and out pops Tom Thumb, or at least you hear his voice cry, "Oh, Father, I was in a mouse hole, and a cow's stomach, and a wolf's belly; now I'm going to stay home with you."

The end moved me, and as I blinked up at Mama, I noticed she was hiding her nose in her handkerchief; like me, she had completely identified with the action on the stage. Mama was easily moved, and in the weeks that followed, especially during what remained of the Christmas holidays, she repeatedly hugged me and kissed me, calling Oskar, laughingly, wistfully, Tom Thumb. Or: my little Tom Thumb. Or: my poor, poor Tom Thumb.

It wasn't till the summer of thirty-three that I had another chance to attend the theater. Owing to a misunderstanding on my part, the affair went badly, but it had a lasting influence on me. Even now it sounds and surges within me, for it took place at the Zoppot Opera-in-the-Woods, where summer after summer, under the night sky, the music of Wagner poured forth to Nature.

Mama was the only one who cared at all for opera. Even operettas were too much for Matzerath. Jan followed Mama's lead, gushed over arias, yet despite his musical appearance he was tone-deaf to fine music. He made up for this by knowing the Formella brothers, former schoolmates at the middle school in Karthaus, who lived in Zoppot and were in charge of lighting the pier and fountain outside the spa and casino, as well as running the lights for festival performances at the Opera-in-the-Woods.

The way to Zoppot led through Oliva. A morning in Castle Park.

Goldfish, swans. Mama and Jan Bronski in the famous Whispering Grotto. Then more goldfish and swans, working hand in glove with a photographer. Matzerath let me ride on his shoulders while the picture was taken. I propped my drum on top of his head, which elicited general laughter, both then and later, when the photo had been pasted in the album. Farewell to goldfish, swans, and the Whispering Grotto. It wasn't Sunday just in Castle Park, it was Sunday everywhere: outside the iron gate, in the streetcar to Glettkau, and at the Glettkau spa, where we had lunch while the Baltic, as if it had nothing else to do, kept on inviting us to bathe. As the beach promenade took us toward Zoppot, Sunday came out to meet us, and Matzerath had to pay admission for the lot of us.

We bathed on South Beach because it was supposedly less crowded than North Beach. The men changed on the men's side, Mama took me into a booth on the women's side; I was expected to go on the family beach naked, while she, already lushly overflowing her banks, poured her flesh into a straw-yellow bathing suit. To avoid exposing myself to all eyes on the family beach all too plainly, I held my drum before my private parts, then lay on my stomach in the sand, rejecting the inviting Baltic waters, hiding my shame in the sand instead, playing the ostrich. Matzerath and Jan Bronski looked so ridiculous and almost pitiful with their incipient paunches that I was glad when, late that afternoon, we returned to the bathing cabins, applied cream to our sunburns, and, Nivea-soothed, slipped back into our Sunday clothes.

Coffee and cake at The Starfish. Mama wanted a third helping of the five-story cake. Matzerath was against it, Jan in favor and against, Mama ordered, gave Matzerath a bite, fed Jan, satisfied both her men, then crammed the sugary sweet wedge spoonful by little spoonful into her mouth.

O holy buttercream, O clear to partly cloudy Sunday afternoon, dusted with powdered sugar! Polish nobles sat behind blue sunglasses and intense lemonades they didn't touch. The ladies played with violet fingernails and sent the insect-powder fragrance of the fur capes they'd rented for the season wafting toward us on the sea breeze. Matzerath thought they were silly. Mama would have loved to rent a fur cape like that, if only for a single afternoon. Jan claimed that the boredom of the Polish nobility had reached such heights that in spite of rising debts they no longer spoke French, but out of pure snobbishness, only the most ordinary Polish.

We couldn't just go on sitting in The Starfish staring at the blue sunglasses and violet fingernails of the Polish nobility. My mama full of cake needed some exercise. The spa park welcomed us, I had to ride on a donkey and pose for yet another photo. Goldfish, swans—the things Nature thinks of—then more goldfish and swans, enjoying the fresh water.

Between trimmed yews, which, however, did not whisper as people always claim, we met the Formella brothers, the same Formellas who served as lighting technicians for the Casino, and for the Opera-in-the-Woods. First the younger Formella had to deliver himself of all the jokes he'd heard on the job as a lighting technician. The elder Formella brother knew these jokes by heart and still managed to laugh infectiously at all the right places out of brotherly love, showing one gold tooth more than his younger brother, who only had three. We headed toward Springer's for a little Machandel. Mama said she preferred Kurfürsten. Then, still pulling jokes from his stockpile, the free-spending younger Formella invited us to dinner at The Parrot. There we met Tuschel, and this Tuschel owned half of Zoppot, a share of the Opera-in-the-Woods, and five movie theaters. He was also the Formella brothers' boss, and was pleased, as we were pleased, to meet us, to meet him. Tuschel never tired of twisting a ring on his finger, which could not, however, have been a magic ring or wishing ring, for nothing at all happened except that Tuschel in turn started telling jokes, and in fact the same jokes we'd just heard from Formella, though more long-windedly because he had fewer gold teeth. Nevertheless the whole table laughed, because Tuschel was telling them. I alone remained solemn and tried to kill his punch lines by maintaining a straight face. Ah, how the salvos of laughter, even if false, spread coziness, like the bull's-eye panes on the glass partition of our little corner booth. Tuschel was visibly grateful, kept telling jokes, ordered Goldwasser liqueur, and suddenly, drifting happily in laughter and Goldwasser, twisted his ring a different way, and something actually happened. Tuschel invited us all to the Opera-in-the-Woods, since he owned a small share of the company; unfortunately he himself couldn't, a previous engagement etc., but he hoped we could still make use of his seats, the box was padded, the little fellow could sleep if he was tired;

and he jotted down a few words in Tuschel's hand with a silver mechanical pencil on Tuschel's calling card that he said would open all doors — and so it did.

What happened can be told in a few words: a mild summer evening, the Opera-in-the-Woods sold out and full of foreigners. The mosquitoes had arrived early. But not until the last mosquito, trying as always to be fashionably late, had announced its arrival with a bloodthirsty buzz, did it well and truly start. It was a performance of *The Flying Dutchman*. A ship, looking bent more on poaching than on high-seas piracy, emerged from the woods that gave the opera company its name. Sailors sang to the trees. I fell asleep on Tuschel's padded cushions, and when I awoke, the sailors were still singing or had started up again, Helmsman keep watch . . . but Oskar went back to sleep again, glad to see, as he was drifting off, that his mama was thoroughly taken with the Dutchman, floating on the waves, and breathing deeply in true Wagnerian spirit. She hadn't noticed that Matzerath and her Jan were sawing logs of various sizes, their hands shielding their faces, nor that Wagner kept slipping through my fingers too, till Oskar finally awoke for good because a woman was standing all alone in the middle of the woods screaming. She had yellow hair, and was screaming because one of the lighting technicians, probably the younger Formella, was blinding her with a spotlight, harassing her. "No!" she cried out, "Woe is me!" and "Who hath made me suffer so?" But the Formella tormenting her didn't switch off his spotlight, and the screams of the solitary woman, whom Mama later referred to as the soloist, modulated into a whimper that now and then rose as silvery foam to wilt the leaves on the trees of Zoppot Woods before their time but could not find and destroy Formella's spotlight. Her voice, though gifted, failed her. Oskar was forced to intervene, seek out the ill-bred source of light, and with one long-distance scream, undercutting the soft urgency of the mosquitoes, kill the spotlight.

The resulting short circuit, blackout, flying sparks, and forest fire, which provoked a panic, though they finally got it under control, were consequences I hadn't counted on, for I lost more among the crowd than just Mama and her two rudely awakened men; my drum also vanished in the confusion.

This third encounter of mine with the theater gave Mama, who began, after that evening at the Opera-in-the-Woods, to domesticate Wagher in simplified arrangements on our piano, the idea of introducing me to the world of the circus in the spring of thirty-four.

Oskar has no intention of going on here about silvery ladies on the trapeze, tigers from Busch's circus, or trained seals. No one fell from the top of the circus tent. Nothing was bitten off any animal tamer. And the seals did what they'd been trained to do: they juggled balls and were tossed live herring by way of reward. I am indebted to the circus for providing entertaining children's matinees and my highly significant encounter with Bebra the musical clown, who played "Jimmy the Tiger" on bottles and directed a troupe of midgets.

We met in the menagerie. Mama and her two men were allowing themselves to be insulted at the monkey cage. Hedwig Bronski, who for once was part of the group, was showing her children the ponies. After a lion had yawned at me, I was foolish enough to get involved with an owl. I tried to stare the bird down, but it stared me down instead; and Oskar slunk away stunned, with burning ears, wounded to the core, and slipped off among the blue and white wagons, because, except for a few tethered dwarf goats, there were no animals there.

He walked past me in suspenders and slippers, carrying a pail of water. Glances crossed but fleetingly. Yet we knew each other at once. He set the pail down, tilted his great head to one side, came up to me, and I guessed that he was about four inches taller than me.

"Look at this!" came an envious growl. "These days three-year-olds don't want to grow anymore." Since I said nothing, he came at me again: "Bebra's my name, direct descendant of Prince Eugen, whose father was Louis the Fourteenth and not any old Savoyard, as they claim." I still said nothing, so he took a new run at it: "I stopped growing on my tenth birthday. A little late, but even so!"

Since he spoke so openly, I too introduced myself, but without concocting some family tree, just said I was Oskar. "Tell me, my dear Oskar, you could be fourteen now, even fifteen or sixteen. It's not possible; nine and a half, you say?"

Now I was supposed to guess his age, and made it deliberately low.

"You flatter me, my young friend. Thirty-five, that was once upon a time. In August I celebrate my fifty-third, I could be your grandfather!"

Oskar said a few nice things to him about his acrobatic clown act, praised his musical talents, and, seized by a touch of ambition, performed a little trick for him. Three light bulbs illuminating the circus grounds were taken in by it, and Herr Bebra called out bravo, bravissimo, and wanted to hire Oskar on the spot.

I still occasionally regret that I declined. I talked myself out of it, saying, "You know, Herr Bebra, I prefer to be part of the audience, to allow my little art to bloom in secret, far from all applause, but I would be the last person to fail to applaud your performances." Herr Bebra raised his crumpled forefinger and admonished me: "My dear Oskar, take it from an experienced colleague. The likes of us should never be part of the audience. We have to be on the stage, in the arena. We have to perform and direct the action, otherwise our kind will be manipulated by those who do. And they'll all too happily pull a fast one on us."

His eyes turning ancient, and almost crawling into my ear, he whispered, "They're coming! They will take over the festival grounds. They will stage torchlight parades. They will build grandstands, they will fill grandstands, they will preach our destruction from grandstands. Watch closely, my young friend, what happens on those grandstands. Always try to be sitting on the grandstands, and never standing in front of them."

Then, since my name was being called, Herr Bebra reached for his pail. "They're looking for you, my young friend. We'll see each other again. We're too little to lose each other. Bebra always says: Little people like us can squeeze into even the most crowded grandstands. And if not on the grandstand, then under the grandstand, but never in front. So says Bebra, direct descendant of Prince Eugen."

Mama, who stepped from behind a circus wagon calling for Oskar, was just in time to see Bebra kiss me on the forehead, then pick up his pail of water, and rowing with his shoulders, steer his way toward another wagon.

"Just imagine," Mama later reported indignantly to Matzerath and the Bronskis, "he was with the midgets. A dwarf kissed him on the forehead. I hope that doesn't mean anything."

Bebra's kiss on my forehead was to mean a great deal indeed to me. The political events of the following years proved him right: the era of torchlight parades and grandstand assemblies began.

Just as I followed Herr Bebra's advice, Mama took to heart one of the warnings Sigismund Markus gave her in the Arsenal Arcade and continued to repeat every Thursday. Even though she didn't go to London with Markus—I would have had no particular objection to such a move—she stayed with Matzerath, seeing Jan Bronski only discreetly and occasionally, that is, on Tischlergasse at Jan's expense, and during family skat games, which became more and more expensive for Jan, since he always lost. Meanwhile, following Markus's advice, Mama let her stakes lie, though without doubling them, and placed her bet on Matzerath, who recognized the forces of law and order relatively early on and joined the Party in thirty-four, yet even so never advanced beyond cell leader. On the occasion of this promotion, which, like any unusual event, called for a family game of skat, Matzerath introduced a new note of severity, as well as concern, to the warnings he was constantly giving Jan Bronski about his service as an official in the Polish Post Office.

Otherwise things didn't change much. The grim portrait of Beethoven hanging over the piano, a gift from Greff, was removed from its nail, and an equally grim portrait of Hitler was hung on the same nail. Matzerath, who had no interest in serious music, wanted to banish the nearly deaf composer completely. But Mama, who loved the slow movements of Beethoven sonatas, had learned to play two or three of them at a slower tempo than indicated, and occasionally let them flow slowly forth on the piano, insisted that Beethoven be placed, if not over the sofa, at least over the sideboard. This resulted in the grimmest of confrontations: Hitler and the genius hung opposite each other, stared at each other, saw through each other, yet found no joy in what they saw.

Little by little Matzerath pieced together his uniform. If I remember correctly, he began with the Party cap, which he enjoyed wearing, even in sunny weather, with the storm strap chafing his chin. For a time he donned a white shirt and black tie with this cap, or a windbreaker with an armband. When he bought his first brown shirt, he wanted to buy the shit-brown riding breeches and high boots a week later. Mama objected, and it was several weeks before Matzerath was finally in his full getup.

There were several occasions each week when he could wear this uniform, but Matzerath contented himself with joining the Sunday rallies on the Maiwiese by the Sporthalle. These, however, he never missed, appearing doggedly in even the worst weather, refusing to carry an umbrella when in uniform, and repeating time and again what was soon to become a stock phrase. "Duty is duty," Matzerath would say, "and schnapps is schnapps"; then, having prepared the noon roast in advance, he would say goodbye to Mama on Sunday mornings, and leave me in an embarrassing position, for Jan Bronski, who was well aware of the new political situation on Sundays, called on my abandoned mama in his straightforward civilian way while Matzerath was standing among the rank and file.

What could I do but keep out of the way? I had no intention of disturbing the two of them on the sofa, or watching them. So the moment my uniformed father was out of sight, and prior to the arrival of the civilian I already thought of as my presumptive father, I drummed my way out of the house and headed for the Maiwiese.

You may well ask why of all places it had to be the Maiwiese. Believe me, there was nothing going on at the waterfront on Sundays, I had no intention of hiking through the woods, and the interior of the Church of the Sacred Heart as yet meant nothing to me. True, there were Herr Greff's Boy Scouts, but at the risk of being called a fellow traveler I have to admit I preferred the commotion on the Maiwiese to that repressed eroticism.

Either Greiser or Löbsack, who was District Head of Indoctrination, was speaking. I never took much notice of Greiser. He was too moderate and was later replaced by a bolder man, a Bavarian named Forster, who became Gauleiter. But Löbsack was the sort of man to replace a Forster. Yes, if Löbsack had not had a hump, it would have been hard for the Bavarian from Fürth to find his footing on the cobblestones of our port city. Correctly assessing Löbsack's value, and seeing in his hump a sign of high intelligence, the Party had made him District Head of Indoctrination. The man knew his business. While Forster kept screaming "Home to the Reich" in his ugly Bavarian accent, Löbsack went into more detail, spoke every Low German dialect in Danzig, told jokes about Bollermann and Wullsutzki, knew how to talk to the dockers at Schichau, the common folk in Ohra, the citizens of Emaus, Schidlitz, Bürgerwiesen, and Praust. When it came to dealing with beer-earnest Communists and the feeble catcalls of a few Socialists, it was a joy to listen to the little man, whose hump was greatly enhanced by his brown uniform.

Löbsack had wit, derived all his wit from his hump, made no bones about his hump; the crowd always likes that. He was more likely to lose his hump, Löbsack claimed, than the Communists were to come to power. You could see he wasn't about to lose his hump, there was no shaking that hump, his hump was right, and with it the Party—from which we may deduce that a hump provides the ideal basis for an idea.

When Greiser, Löbsack, or, later on, Forster spoke, they spoke from the grandstand. This was the grandstand that little Herr Bebra had extolled. So for a long time I thought that Löbsack, the grandstand orator, humped and highly gifted as he appeared on the grandstand, was Bebra's brown-clad envoy in disguise, advocating Bebra's cause, and in essence mine as well, from the grandstand.

What is a grandstand? No matter for whom and by whom a grandstand is erected, it must always be symmetrical. So the grandstand on the Maiwiese by the Sporthalle was also strictly symmetrical. From top to bottom: Six swastika banners side by side. Then flags, pennants, and standards. Then a row of black SS with storm straps under their chins. Then two rows of SA, holding their hands on their belt buckles through all the singing and speechifying. Then several rows of seated Party members in uniform, behind the speaker's podium more Party members, maternal-faced leaders from the Women's Association, representatives from the Senate in civilian dress, guests from the Reich, and the Chief of Police or his representative.

The base of the grandstand was rejuvenated by the Hitler Youth, or more precisely by the regional brass band of the Hitler Young Volk and the regional drum and bugle corps of the Hitler Youth. At some rallies mixed choruses, always symmetrically arranged to left and right, were allowed to recite slogans or sing the praises of the ever popular East Wind, which, according to the text, was better suited than any other wind to unfurl flags and banners.

Bebra, who kissed me on the forehead, had added, "Oskar, never stand in front of a grandstand. The likes of us belong on the grandstand!"

Most of the time I managed to find a place among the leaders of the Women's Association. Unfortunately these women wouldn't stop caressing me for propaganda purposes during the rally. I wasn't allowed to join the kettledrums, trumpets, and snare drums at the base of the grandstand, for the lansquenet corps had rejected my tin drum. Nor did my approach to District Indoctrination Head Löbsack go well. The man was a big disappointment. Neither was he Bebra's envoy, as I had hoped, nor had he, in spite of his promising hump, the faintest understanding of my true stature.

When I approached him at the podium one grandstand Sunday, gave him the Party salute, stared at him blankly at first, then whispered to him with a wink, "Bebra is our Führer!" no light went on in Löbsack, but instead he stroked me just as the Nazi women did, then had Oskar escorted off the grandstand—after all, he had a speech to give—between two leaders of the League of German Girls, who quizzed him about "Mommy and Poppy" throughout the rally.

So it will come as no surprise that by the summer of thirty-four, though not influenced by the Röhm putsch, I was becoming disillusioned with the Party. The longer I scrutinized the grandstand from the front, the more suspicious I became of that symmetry which had been but insufficiently relieved by Löbsack's hump. You can well imagine that my criticism was aimed at the drummers and brass players in particular; and on a muggy rally Sunday in August of thirty-five I had it out with the brass band and drum and bugle corps at the base of the grandstand.

Matzerath was out of the apartment by nine. I'd helped him polish his brown leather puttees so he could leave the house on time. Even at that early hour it was unbearably hot, and dark stains were spreading under the arms of his Party shirt before he even got outside. At nine-thirty on the dot Jan Bronski turned up in an airy, light-colored summer suit with perforated, delicate-gray oxfords, wearing a straw hat. Jan played with me for a while, but even as he played he couldn't keep his eyes off Mama, who had washed her hair the night before. I soon realized that my presence was hindering their conversation, making them feel awkward, and limiting Jan's movements. Those lightweight summer trousers were clearly becoming a little too tight for him, so I toddled off, following in Matzerath's footsteps, though I didn't see him as my model. Carefully avoiding streets filled with uniformed men surging toward the Maiwiese, I approached the parade grounds for the first time by way of the tennis courts next to the Sporthalle. Thanks to this detour I had a rear view of the grandstand.

Have you ever seen a grandstand from behind? All men and women —this is merely a suggestion—should familiarize themselves with the rear view of a grandstand before they are gathered in front of one. Anyone who has examined a grandstand from behind, and examined it closely, will be marked from that hour, and thus immunized against any and all forms of magic practiced on grandstands. The same can be said for the rear view of church altars; but that's another story.

But Oskar, who has always inclined to thoroughness, was not satisfied with a simple view of the bare scaffolding in all its tangible ugliness, and recalling the words of his mentor Bebra, he approached the grandstand, meant to be seen only from the front, from its crude backside, squeezed himself and his drum, which he never left behind, through the struts, struck his head on an overhead beam, scratched his knee on a nail protruding nastily from a wooden plank, heard the boots of the Party comrades scraping above him, then the little shoes of the Women's Association, and finally reached the most sweltering and hence most representative spot for the month of August: facing the inner side of the base of the grandstand he found sufficient space and shelter behind a sheet of plywood to enjoy to the fullest and in peace the acoustic pleasures of a political rally, without being diverted by flags or visually offended by uniforms.

I crouched beneath the speaker's podium. To my right and left and above me, the younger drummers of the Young Volk and the older ones of the Hitler Youth stood spread-legged and squinting against the blinding sunlight. And then the crowd. I could smell it through the cracks of the grandstand planks. They stood and rubbed elbows in their Sunday best, they arrived on foot or by tram, they came in part from early Mass, still not fully satisfied, they came with fiancée on arm for the show, they wanted to be present when history was made, even if it took all morning.

No, said Oskar to himself, they shall not have come in vain. And placing his eye to a knothole in the planks, he noted a commotion along Hindenburgallee. They were coming! Commands rang out above him, the leader of the drum and bugle corps waggled his baton, they puffed on their trumpets, adjusted the mouthpieces to their lips, and they were off, blowing through their brightly-Sidol-polished instruments in their worst lansquenet style, hurting Oskar's ears. "Poor SA Man Brand," said he to himself, "poor Hitler Youth Quex, you've died in vain!"

As if to confirm his obituary for the martyrs of the movement, a massive thumping on taut calfskin drumheads now mingled with the trumpetry. The lane that led through the crowd to the grandstand gave a hint of uniforms approaching in the far distance, and Oskar burst out, "Now my people, now my Volk, hearken unto me!"

My drum was already in place. With divine suppleness I let the sticks play in my hands and with delicate wrists I laid a joyful waltz rhythm of consummate artistry upon my drum, sending it forth with increasing insistence, conjuring up Vienna and the Danube, until the first and second lansquenet drums above me found pleasure in my waltz, and the shallow drums of the older boys took up my prelude with greater or lesser skill. Among them were indeed a few diehards who had no ear, who kept boom-boom and boom-boom-booming away, while I was intent on the three-four time so beloved of the Volk. Oskar was almost ready to despair when the trumpet section finally saw the light, and the fifes blew Danube, oh Danube so blue. Only the directors of the brass band and the drum and bugle corps refused to bow to the king of the waltzes and kept shouting their annoying commands, but I had deposed them, the music was now mine. And the Volk thanked me for it. Laughter broke out in front of the grandstand, a few people were already singing along, oh Danube, and all across the grounds, so blue, clear to Hindenburgallee, so blue, to Steffenspark, so blue, my rhythm skipped along, amplified by the open microphone above me. And as I looked through my knothole, drumming away diligently all the while, I saw that the Volk were enjoying my waltz, they were hopping about happily, it was in their legs: nine couples were already dancing, and were soon joined by another, paired by the king of the waltzes. Only Löbsack, who, along with various district leaders and regimental commanders, with Forster, Greiser, and Rauschning and a long brown column of staff, was fuming in the midst of the crowd now blocking his way to the grandstand, seemed surprisingly immune to the rhythm of the waltz. He was accustomed to being channeled to the grandstand with linear marching music. These easygoing tones were undermining his faith in the Volk. I saw his sorrows through the knothole. A draft was coming through the hole. I may have risked an inflammation of the eye, but I still felt sorry for him and switched over to a Charleston, "Jimmy the Tiger," broke into the rhythm Bebra the clown had drummed on empty bottles of seltzer water at the circus; but the boys in front of the grandstand didn't get the Charleston. They belonged to a different generation. Of course they knew nothing about the Charleston and "Jimmy the Tiger." What they pounded out — O my good friend Bebra — wasn't "Jimmy the Tiger," they banged out any old thing at all, let Sodom and Gomorrah flourish on their trumpets. Skip, march, or dance, it's all one to us, the fifes must have thought. The angry trumpet leader chewed out every Tom, Heinz, and Harry in turn. Nevertheless the boys of the brass and the drum and bugle corps drummed, blew, and trumpeted like the devil, so that Jimmy was in seventh heaven in that hottest tigery August, till those thousands and thousands of simple Volk jostling about in front of the grandstand understood at last: Jimmy the Tiger is asking the Volk to Charleston!

And those who were not yet dancing on the Maiwiese grabbed the last available ladies before it was too late. But Löbsack had to dance with his hump, because anything wearing a skirt nearby was already occupied, and the ladies from the Women's Association who might have come to his aid were shifting about, far, far away from the lonely Löbsack, on the hard wooden rows of the grandstand. Nevertheless — as his hump advised him — he still danced, tried to put a good face on this awful Jimmy music, and save what could still be saved.

But there was nothing left to save. The Volk danced off across the Maiwiese, leaving it thoroughly trampled but green and deserted. The Volk disappeared with Jimmy the Tiger into the spacious grounds of nearby Steffenspark. There the jungle Jimmy promised was offered, tigers prowled on velvet paws, a substitute forest primeval for the Volk who had just been thronging the Maiwiese. Law and order had gone to the dogs. But whoever loved culture could still hear, on the broad, well-kept promenades of Hindenburgallee, first planted in the eighteenth century, cut down in eighteen ought-seven while under siege by Napoleon's troops and planted again in Napoleon's honor in eighteen-ten, in other words on historic ground, all those still dancing on Hindenburgallee could still hear my music, for the microphone above me had not been turned off, and I could be heard as far as Oliva Gate, nor did I let up till I and the fine young boys at the base of the grandstand had managed, with the help of Jimmy's unchained tiger, to clear the Maiwiese of everything but the daisies.

Even when I gave my drum a well-earned rest, the drummer boys kept right on. It was some time before my musical influence wore off.

A word or two about the aftermath: Oskar couldn't come out from under the grandstand immediately, since SA and SS officers were banging away at planks with their boots for over an hour, snagging tears in brown and black cloth, apparently looking for something within the framework—a Socialist, perhaps, or a team of Communist saboteurs. Without enumerating all Oskar's dodges and feints we can simply state: they didn't find Oskar, because they were no match for him.

Things finally grew quiet in the wooden labyrinth, which was about the size of the whale in which Jonah sat in oily lethargy. But Oskar was no prophet, he was feeling hungry. There was no Lord to say, "Arise, go unto Nineveh, that great city, and preach unto it." Nor did the Lord have to grow a gourd for me that a worm would then destroy at the Lord's command. I didn't bewail that biblical gourd, nor Nineveh, even one called Danzig. I had affairs of my own to attend to, tucked my non-biblical drum under my sweater, and without hitting my head or scratching myself on a nail, emerged from the bowels of a grandstand that, meant for meetings and rallies of all sorts, had the proportions of a prophet-swallowing whale merely by chance.

Who paid any attention to the little three-year-old boy, whistling as he trudged along the edge of the Maiwiese in the direction of the Sporthalle? Beyond the tennis courts my boys from the grandstand were marching with lansquenet drums, with shallow drums, fifes, and trumpets. Punitive exercises I noted, and was only moderately sorry for those at the beck and call of their leader's fife. Off to the side from his assembled staff, Löbsack was pacing up and down with his lonely hump. Turning on his heel at each end of his course, he had succeeded in completely eradicating the grass and the daisies.

When Oskar reached home, lunch was already on the table: meatloaf with boiled potatoes, red cabbage, and chocolate pudding with vanilla sauce for dessert. Matzerath didn't say a word. Mama's thoughts were elsewhere. But that afternoon there was a family fight over jealousy and the Polish Post Office. Toward evening a refreshing thunderstorm that included a cloudburst and a lovely drum solo of hail gave a lengthy performance. Oskar's exhausted drum could rest and listen.

Shop Windows

FOR A LONG TIME, till November of thirty-eight to be exact, crouching under grandstands with my drum, with greater or lesser success I broke up rallies, reduced speakers to stutters, and turned marches and hymns into waltzes and foxtrots.

Today, as a private patient in a mental institution, when all that's past history, still being eagerly forged but from cold iron, I've achieved a proper distance from my drumming under grandstands. It would never occur to me to see myself as a member of the Resistance on the basis of six or seven disrupted rallies, three or four assemblies and parade marches drummed off stride. The term is quite fashionable these days. You hear of the spirit of Resistance, of Resistance circles. There's even talk of internal resistance, what's now called Inner Emigration. To say nothing of those honorable men so well versed in the scriptures who were fined by a growling air-raid warden for having failed to black out their bedroom windows and now call themselves Resistance fighters, men of the Resistance.

Let's take another look under Oskar's grandstands. Didn't Oskar show others a thing or two with his drum? Did he not, as his teacher Bebra advised, take control of events and cause the Volk standing in front of the grandstand to break out in dance? Did he not make hash of the plans of Löbsack, District Head of Indoctrination, a man of ready wit and a smooth customer if there ever was one? Did he not, on a hotpot Sunday in August of thirty-five, and on a few later occasions, break up rallies in brown with flourishes on a tin drum that, though red and white, was not Polish?

You have to admit I did all that. But does that make me, lying here in a mental institution, a Resistance fighter? My answer must be no, and so I ask that you, who aren't inmates in a mental institution, regard me too as merely a somewhat eccentric fellow who, for private and also aesthetic reasons of his own, taking the warnings of his teacher Bebra to heart, turned down the color and cut of the uniforms, the beat and blast of the standard grandstand music, and drummed up a few protests on a simple child's toy.

In those days you could get the better of people on and in front of a grandstand with a paltry tin drum, and I grant that I developed my stage trick, as I had my long-distance, glass-slaying song, to the point of perfection. I didn't just drum down rallies in brown. Oskar sat under the grandstands of Reds and Blacks, of Boy Scouts and the spinach shirts of the PX, of Jehovah's Witnesses and the Kyffhäuser Bund, of vegetarians and the Polish Youth Fresh Air Movement. Whatever they had to sing, to blow, to pray, to proclaim: my drum knew better.

Thus my task was destruction. And what I failed to bring low with my drum I slew with my voice. In addition to my forays in broad daylight against grandstand symmetry, I initiated nighttime actions: in the winter of thirty-six/thirty-seven I played the seducer. My first lessons in seducing my fellow men came from my grandmother Koljaiczek, who opened a stand at the weekly market that harsh winter in Langfuhr, where she squatted behind a market table in her four skirts and offered goods for the holidays, crying plaintively, "Get your fresh eggs, butter gold and creamy, geese, not too fat, not too thin!" Tuesday was market day. She came from Viereck on the narrow-gauge railway, removed the felt slippers she wore for the train ride when she drew near Langfuhr, stepped into her shapeless galoshes, linked her arms under both baskets, and looked for a stand on Bahnhofstraße with a sign that said: *Anna Koljaiczek, Bissau.* How cheap eggs were back then. A mandel, which was a baker's dozen plus two, cost a mere gulden, and Kashubian butter was cheaper than margarine. My grandmother squatted between two fishmongers who called out, "Fresh flounder!" and "Pomuchel cod here!" The frost turned the butter to stone, kept the eggs fresh, honed fish scales to extra-thin razorblades, and provided a one-eyed man named Schwerdtfeger with a job and cash heating bricks over an open wood-charcoal fire, which he then wrapped in newspaper and rented out to the market women.

My grandmother had Schwerdtfeger shove a hot brick under her four skirts every hour on the dot. Schwerdtfeger did this with an iron slide. He pushed a steaming packet under her scarcely raised skirts, dumped it, lifted the other one, then Schwerdtfeger's iron slide would reappear from beneath my grandmother's skirts with a nearly cold brick.

How I envied those bricks wrapped in newspaper, storing and bestowing their heat. To this day I wish I could lie like a toasty warm brick constantly being exchanged for myself under my grandmother's skirts. And just what, you may ask, is Oskar looking for under his grandmother's skirts? Does he wish to imitate his grandfather Koljaiczek and take liberties with the old woman? Does he seek oblivion, a home, the ultimate Nirvana?

Oskar replies: I was looking for Africa under her skirts, Naples perhaps, which everyone knows you must see before dying. Where all rivers converged, where all waters divided, where special winds blew, yet calm could descend, where the rains pounded down and yet you were dry, where ships made fast or weighed anchor at last, where the good Lord, who always liked warmth, sat by Oskar, where the devil dusted his spyglass, where angels played blindman's buff; it was always summer under my grandmother's skirts, as the Christmas tree glowed, as I hunted for Easter eggs or marked every All Saints' Day. Nowhere could I live more at peace with the calendar than under my grandmother's skirts.

But she would never let me stay there at the weekly market, and only rarely otherwise. I squatted beside her on the small crate, the warmth of her arm around me in place of her skirts, watched as the bricks came and went, and learned from my grandmother the trick of tempting people. She would throw Vinzent Bronski's old coin purse, with a cord attached, onto the hard-packed snow of the sidewalk, which was so darkened and dirtied by the sand spreaders that only my grandmother and I could see the string.

Housewives came and went, not buying anything, even though her wares were so cheap, wanting produce for free or with a little something thrown in; then a lady would bend down for Vinzent's castoff purse, and just as her fingers touched the leather, my grandmother would reel in the line along with the slightly embarrassed customer, draw the well-dressed fish to the crate on which she sat, and say good-naturedly,

"Well, ma'am, how about a little butter, gold and creamy, or a mandel of eggs for a gulden?"

That's how Anna Koljaiczek sold her produce. Meanwhile I grasped the magic of temptation, but not the temptation that lured fourteen-year-old boys into the basement with Susi Kater to play doctor. That didn't tempt me, I stayed well away from that, once the brats in our building, using me as their patient, with Axel Mischke and Nuchi Eyke as serum donors and Susi Kater as the doctor, forced me to swallow doses that were not as grainy as the brick soup but left an aftertaste of rotten fish. The temptation I offered was almost ethereal, and I kept a proper distance from those I tempted.

Long after darkness had fallen, one or two hours after the shop had closed, I slipped away from Mama and Matzerath. Into the winter night I went, and took up my position. On silent, nearly deserted streets, from the recesses of doorways sheltered from the wind, I observed the shop windows across the way: delicatessens, haberdasheries, all those shops with their shoes, clocks, and jewelry on display, all those easily portable, desirable items. Not every display was illuminated. I even preferred shops that kept their displays in semidarkness, at some distance from streetlamps, for light attracts all people, even the most ordinary, while only the chosen will linger in semidarkness.

I wasn't interested in those who merely glanced in brightly lit shop windows as they passed, more concerned with price tags than with merchandise, or those who used the windowpane's reflection to make sure their hats were on straight. The customers I lay in wait for in the crisp, dry, windless cold, behind flurries of large snowflakes, amid silent, thick snowfall, or beneath a frosty waxing moon, were those customers who stopped before shop windows as if in answer to a call, scanned the shelves briefly, and quickly brought their gaze to rest on a single item.

My pursuit was that of the hunter. It required patience, sang-froid, a clear view, and a steady eye. Only when all these preconditions obtained did it fall to my voice, spilling no blood and causing no pain, to bag my prey, to lure it on — but toward what?

Toward theft: for with my most silent of screams I cut a circular section from the shop window at the lowest level of the display opposite the desired object, and with a last lift of my voice pushed the glass disk into the interior of the display case, so that a quickly muffled tinkle, which was not however the tinkle of breaking glass, was heard — not by me, for Oskar stood too far away; but that young woman with a rabbit-fur collar on her brown winter coat, surely reversed at least once by now, she heard the glass disk and gave a start that made her rabbit fur quiver, started off through the snow, but paused, perhaps because it was snowing, and when it's snowing, if it's snowing hard enough, all things are permitted. Yet she looked around, suspicious of the snowflakes, looked around as if there might be something else beyond the snowflakes, kept looking around as her right hand glided out of a muff covered in that same rabbit fur. And looked around no more, but reached through the circular opening, first pushing aside the glass disk that had fallen on top of what she wanted, pulled first the right and then the left black pump through the hole, without scratching the heels, without cutting her hand on the sharp edges. Left and right the shoes disappeared in her coat pockets. For a moment that lasted five snowflakes long, Oskar saw a pretty but empty profile, had time to think, that's a mannequin from Sternfeld's department store, walking about by some miracle, then she dissolved into the falling snow, only to reappear beneath the next streetlamp, then, beyond its circle of light, be it as young newlywed or emancipated mannequin, she vanished.

Having completed my work — and waiting, lurking without the comfort of my drum, then singing toward icy glass and thawing it out was hard work — there remained nothing to do but, like the thief, with no spoils it's true, but with a similarly inflamed and deeply chilled heart, to head home.

I did not always manage, as I did in the mannequin case described above, to employ the art of seduction with such clear success. One of my ambitions was to transform a pair of lovers into a pair of thieves. Either both were unwilling, or he grabbed and she pulled his hand back; or she was bold enough, and he fell to his knees and begged till she complied and henceforth despised him. And once I seduced what seemed to be a very young pair of lovers in the falling snow outside a perfume shop. He was playing the hero and stole a bottle of cologne. She wailed and claimed she was giving up perfume. He wanted her fragrant, however, and had his way as far as the next streetlamp. But there, demonstratively and blatantly, as if the young thing wanted to annoy me, she kissed him, standing on tiptoe, till he retraced his steps and returned the cologne to the shop window.

I had similar experiences on occasion with elderly gentlemen, from whom I expected more than their brisk pace through the winter night promised. They stood before a cigar-shop display with rapt attention, their thoughts in Havana, in Brazil, or on the Bissago Islands, but when my voice produced its custom-made incision and the disk fell at last onto a box of Black Wisdom, a pocketknife snapped closed in these gentlemen. They turned around, rowed their way across the street with their canes, and hurried past me and my doorway without spotting me, while their disturbed old faces, which looked as if the devil had given them a good shaking, brought a smile to Oskar's lips — a smile that bore a trace of concern, for the gentlemen, mostly cigar smokers advanced in years, had broken out in a cold sweat, and thus ran the risk, particularly with a change in the weather, of catching cold.

Insurance companies had to pay substantial claims that winter to many of the shops in our suburb, most of which were insured against theft. Though I never allowed things to progress to the point of grand larceny, and intentionally kept the excised panes of glass small enough that only one or two items could be removed from a display at a time, the number of what were termed burglaries still increased so greatly that the criminal-investigation units never had a quiet moment, yet were still criticized by the press for doing a poor job. From November of thirty-six till March of thirty-seven, when Colonel Koc formed a National Front government in Warsaw, a total of sixty-four attempted and twenty-eight successful burglaries of the same type were reported. Of course the police were able to recover part of the loot from elderly women, counter jockeys, maids, and retired schoolteachers, none of whom were truly enthusiastic thieves, or else the amateur window-weasel would decide, after losing a night's sleep over the object of his desire, to go to the police the next day and say, "Oh, I'm so sorry. It'll never happen again. A hole just appeared in the window, and when I'd nearly recovered from the shock and the broken window was three streets behind me, I found an expensive pair of men's leather gloves, probably cost a fortune, illegally lodged in the left pocket of my overcoat."

Since the police don't believe in miracles, everyone they caught, and all those who turned themselves in, served from four weeks to two months in jail.

I myself was put under house arrest from time to time, for of course Mama suspected, though she did not admit it to herself, or — wisely enough — to the police, that my glass-shattering voice was involved in this crime spree.

Matzerath, playing the law-abiding citizen, conducted an interrogation at which I offered no statement of any kind, but hid instead with ever increasing skill behind my drum and the permanently stunted stature of a three-year-old. At the end of such interrogations Mama would always cry, "It's all that midget's fault, kissing Oskar on the head and all. I knew right away it meant something, Oskar never used to be that way."

I admit Herr Bebra exerted a gentle but persistent influence on me. Even the house arrests couldn't keep me from escaping for an hour or so, with a little luck and of course without leave, to sing one of those notorious round holes in the window of a haberdashery shop and turn the promising young man enjoying the display into the proud owner of a genuine burgundy silk tie.

If you were to ask, was it Evil that bid Oskar to increase the already strong temptation of a brightly polished shop window by adding a hand-sized opening, I would have to reply, it was. It was Evil by the very fact that I stood in dark doorways. For as we all know, a doorway is Evil's favorite spot. On the other hand, without wishing to downplay the evil nature of the temptations I offered, I feel compelled, now that I have lost all opportunity or inclination for such acts, to say to myself and my keeper Bruno: Oskar, not only did you fulfill the small and medium-sized dreams of those who strolled silently through wintry nights in love with some special object, you helped them, as they stood before those shop windows, to know themselves. Many a respectable, elegant lady, many an upstanding uncle, many an elderly spinster still youthful and vigorous in her religious beliefs, would never have recognized the thief that dwells within had your voice not led them to steal, nor would they have undergone such a change as citizens, who till then had regarded every maladroit petty pickpocket as a dangerous scoundrel deserving eternal damnation.

After I'd lain in wait for him evenings on end, watching as three times he refused to steal before finally reaching out to become a thief the police never found, Dr. Erwin Scholtis, district attorney and a dreaded prosecutor for the Higher Regional Court, is said to have become a mild, indulgent jurist whose sentences were almost humane, and all because he sacrificed to me, the little demigod of thieves, and stole a genuine badger-hair shaving brush.

In January of thirty-seven I stood shivering for some time across the way from a jewelry shop, which, despite its quiet location on a suburban avenue bordered at regular intervals by maples, was well-known by name and reputation. The shop window with its watches and jewels attracted all sorts of game that I would have snared without a second thought as they faced displays of silk stockings, velour hats, or bottles of liqueur.

That's what jewelry does to you: you become selective, take your time, adapt yourself to the endless chain of necklaces, measure time not in minutes but in a string of pearl years, proceed on the assumption that pearls outlast the neck, that the wrist, not the wristband, will wither, that rings will be found in tombs where fingers have long since failed them; in short, I would find one window shopper too pretentious, another too small-minded, to care to bedeck them with jewels.

The shop window of Bansemer Jewelers was not overcrowded. A few choice watches, Swiss-quality articles, an assortment of wedding rings on pale blue velvet, and in the center of a display of perhaps six, or better seven, of the choicest items: a triply coiled snake, fashioned in varicolored gold, its finely chased head adorned and enriched with a topaz, two diamonds, and two sapphire eyes. As a rule I don't like black velvet, but it was a perfect setting for the Bansemer Jewelers' snake, as was the gray velvet that spread a tingling calm beneath the enchantingly simple articles of silverwork with their harmonious forms. A ring set with a stone so lovely you could see it would wear out the hands of equally lovely women, becoming lovelier and lovelier, till it achieved that degree of immortality reserved, it seems, for jewelry alone. There were chain-necklaces not to be donned with impunity, chains that would wear out the wearer, and finally, on a pale yellow velvet cushion in the simplified form of the base of a neck, a collier necklace of infinite delicacy. Finely articulated, a playful border, a mesh repeatedly pierced. What spider had secreted that golden web into which six small rubies and one large stone had wandered? And where was she sitting, that spider, and waiting for what? Surely not for more rubies, but for someone whose gaze would be riveted by the rubies that glowed in the web like sculpted blood — in other words: to whom, for my own purposes or those of that gold-spinning spider, should I give this necklace?

On the eighteenth of January, nineteen thirty-seven, on crunchy, hard-trodden snow, in a night that smelled of more snow to come, smelled of all the snow a person who wished to leave it all up to the snow could possibly want, I saw Jan Bronski cross higher up the street on the right from where I was posted, pass the jewelry store without glancing up, then hesitate, or better yet pull up, as if in response to a challenge; he turned, or was turned — and there Jan stood, before the shop window, among the hushed maples laden in white.

The stylish, always slightly plaintive Jan Bronski, submissive at work, ambitious in love, imprudent and obsessed by beauty in equal measure, who lived from the flesh of my mama, who, as I still believe and doubt to this day, begot me in Matzerath's name, stood in his elegant winter coat, worthy of a Warsaw tailor, and became a statue of himself, or so it seemed to me, so petrified, so symbolically did he stand before the windowpane, his gaze, like that of Parsifal standing in the snow staring at the blood in the snow, fastened upon the rubies of the golden necklace.

I could have called him back, drummed him back. I had my drum with me, after all. I could feel it under my coat. All I had to do was loosen one button and it would have swung out into the frosty night on its own. One hand in my pocket would handle the sticks. Hubertus the huntsman didn't shoot that special stag he had within range. Saul became Paul. Attila turned round when Pope Leo raised his finger with the ring. But I fired my shot, was neither changed nor turned back, stayed Oskar the huntsman intent on the goal, loosed no button, no drum to the frost, crossed no cudgels on a wintry-white drum, nor turned that January night into one for drummers, but screamed instead in silence, screamed as a star might scream, or a fish deep down, screamed at the very texture of frost, so new snow could fall at last, then screamed into glass, into glass that was thick, into glass that was dear, into glass that was cheap, into glass that was clear, into glass that divided, into glass between worlds, into virginal, mystical shop-window glass that stood between Jan and that necklace of rubies, screamed a hole I knew was the size of Jan's glove, dropped the glass like a trapdoor, like the portals of heaven and the gates of hell: and Jan didn't flinch, let his fine leather hand emerge from his pocket and enter heaven; then the glove left hell behind, stole a necklace from heaven or hell whose rubies looked good on all angels flying or fallen — and he let that handful of rubies and gold slide back in his pocket, and still he stood by the gaping window, in spite of the danger, though no rubies bled now to force his gaze or that of Parsifal in one unchanging direction.

Oh, Father, Son, and Holy Spirit! Something had better move the Holy Spirit, or it will be the end of Jan the Father. Oskar, the Son, quickly unbuttoned his coat, yanked out his drumsticks, and cried on his drum, Father, Father! till Jan turned round, slowly, much too slowly, crossed the street, and found me, Oskar, in the doorway.

How good that at the very moment Jan looked at me, his face still expressionless but soon to thaw, it started to snow. He held out a hand, but not the glove that had touched the rubies, to me, and led me, silent but not dejected, home, where Mama was worrying about me, and Matzerath, with his usual feigned severity but no serious intent, was threatening to call the police. Jan offered no explanation, didn't stay long or join the game of skat Matzerath invited him to while placing beer on the table. As he was leaving he patted Oskar, who didn't know whether he was asking for his silence or his friendship.

Soon thereafter Jan Bronski gave my mama the necklace. Surely aware of its origin, she only wore it a few hours at a time when Matzerath was away, either just for herself or for Jan Bronski, and possibly for me.

Shortly after the war I traded it on the black market in Düsseldorf for twelve cartons of Lucky Strikes and a leather briefcase.

No Miracle

Today, in the bed of my mental institution, I often miss the power I had back then to penetrate the wintry night, thaw frost flowers, lay open shop windows, and guide the hand of thieves.

How I would like, for example, to deglaze the glazed peephole in the upper third of my door so Bruno, my keeper, could observe me more directly.

How my voice's impotence pained me the year before I was sent to the institution. If, on some street at night, I released a scream longing for success and yet achieved none, I, who abhor all violence, was quite capable of picking up a stone from some wretched suburban lane in Düsseldorf and taking aim at a kitchen window. I would have been so glad to put on a show, especially for Vittlar, the window dresser. If after midnight, his upper body screened by a curtain, I recognized his green and red wool socks in the window of some men's store on Königsallee or at a perfume shop near the old Concert Hall, I would gladly have sung-shattered glass for him, since he is in fact my disciple, or might be, for I still don't know if I should call him Judas or John.

Vittlar is of noble birth, and his given name is Gottfried. After my futile and embarrassing attempt at song had failed, I drummed lightly on the undamaged shop window to get the window dresser's attention, and when he came out onto the street for a quarter of an hour to chat with me, making light of his own decorative abilities, I simply called him Gottfried, because my voice had not produced the miracle that would have entitled me to call him John or Judas.

The song at the jewelry shop that transformed Jan Bronski into a thief and my mama into the owner of a ruby necklace put a temporary end to singing at shop windows with desirable displays. Mama turned pious. What made her pious? Her affair with Jan Bronski, the stolen necklace, the sweet strain of an adulterous woman's life, produced both piety and a lust for sacraments. The routine of sin establishes itself so easily: on Thursdays they met in the city, left little Oskar with Markus, engaged in a strenuous and generally satisfactory workout on Tischlergasse, refreshed themselves afterward in the Café Weitzke with Mocha and pastries, she picked up the boy at the Jew's place, accepted a few of his compliments along with a package of sewing silk he practically gave her for free, caught the Number Five streetcar, enjoyed the ride past Oliva Gate along Hindenburgallee, smiling, her thoughts far away, scarcely noticed the Maiwiese by the Sporthalle where Matzerath spent his Sunday mornings, tolerated the curve around the Sporthalle — how ugly that box could be when one had just experienced something beautiful — a further curve to the left and there behind the dust-covered trees was the Conradinum with its red-capped schoolboys — how nice little Oskar would have looked in a red cap like that with its golden C; twelve and a half he would be, sitting in the third form, ready for Latin, behaving like a true little Conradinian: hardworking, slightly cheeky, and arrogant.

Beyond the railway underpass, heading toward Reichskolonie and the Helene Lange School, Frau Agnes Matzerath's thoughts of the Conradinum and her son Oskar's missed opportunities faded away. Another curve leftward past the Church of Christ with its onion dome to alight at Max-Halbe-Platz in front of Kaisers-Kaffee, where she glanced briefly in the competition's shop windows, then toiled along Labesweg as if passing through the stations of the cross: the incipient disgust, the abnormal child holding her hand, her guilty conscience, the desire for more of the same; satiated yet still wanting more, with a mixture of loathing and good-natured affection for Matzerath, Mama toiled down Labesweg with me, with my new drum, with her package of practically free sewing silk, to the shop, to rolled oats, to kerosene and casks of herring, to currants, raisins, almonds, and gingerbread spices, to Dr. Oetker's Baking Powder, to Persil Tried and True, to Urbin's the One, to Maggi and Knorr, to Kathreiner and Kaffee Hag, to Vitello and Palmin, to Kühne's Vinegar and four-fruit jam, to those two fly strips abuzz at different pitches that dangled honey-sweet above our counter and had to be changed every other day in summer, while Mama, with a similarly oversweet soul that attracted sins buzzing high and low throughout the year, summer and winter alike, entered the Church of the Sacred Heart each Saturday and confessed to the Right Reverend Father Wiehnke.

Just as Mama took me along to the city on Thursdays to share in her guilt, so to speak, she took me on Saturdays through the portals onto the cool Catholic flagstones, having first stuffed my drum under my sweater or my little overcoat, for I couldn't do without my drum, and without my drum at my stomach I would never have crossed myself in Catholic fashion, touching my forehead, chest and shoulders, or knelt down as though to put on my shoes, or behaved and sat still on the polished church wood as the holy water slowly dried on the bridge of my nose.

I still remembered the Church of the Sacred Heart from my baptism: my heathen name caused problems, but the family insisted on Oskar, as Jan, my godfather, made clear at the church door. Then Father Wiehnke blew in my face three times to drive Satan out, the sign of the cross was made, a hand was laid upon me, salt was sprinkled and a few further measures taken against Satan. Inside the church a second stop at the actual baptismal chapel. I kept quiet as the Apostles' Creed and Our Father were tendered to me. After which Father Wiehnke found it advisable to pronounce another Satan Depart, and imagined he was awakening my senses as he touched Oskar's nose and ears, though I had known what was what right from the start. Then he wanted to hear it once more, loud and clear, asking, "Dost thou renounce Satan? And all his works? And all his pomp?"

Before I could shake my head—for I had no intention of rejecting anything—Jan answered in my stead, saying three times, "I do renounce."

Without my having said anything to spoil my relations with Satan, Father Wiehnke anointed me on the breast and between my shoulder blades. Another Apostles' Creed before the baptismal font, then finally water three times, anointing of the scalp with chrism, a white garment to stain, the candle for days of darkness, the dismissal—Matzerath paid—and as Jan carried me outside the doors of the Church of the Sacred Heart to where the taxi stood waiting in clear to partly cloudy weather, I asked Satan within me, "Did you make it through?"

Satan hopped up and down and whispered, "Did you see those church windows, Oskar? All glass, all glass!"

The Church of the Sacred Heart was built during the early years of the German empire, and its style could thus be identified as Neo-Gothic. Since it had been faced with rapidly darkening brick, and the copper dome of the tower had quickly taken on the traditional verdigris, the distinctions between early Gothic brick churches and Neo-Gothic ones were evident and disturbing only to experts. Confession was heard identically in churches old and new. Hundreds of other Right Reverend Fathers sat in the confessional on Saturday after the offices and shops had closed exactly as the Right Reverend Father Wiehnke did, holding a hairy priestly ear against the polished black grille while the congregation attempted to slip their strings of sins with bead after bead of sinfully tawdry jewels through the lattice and into his priestly ear.

While Mama, following the model Mirror of Confession, was communicating her omissions and commissions, her conduct in thought, word, and deed, to the highest authorities of the only true Church by way of Father Wiehnke's auditory canal, I, who had nothing to confess, slid down from the church wood too smoothly polished for my liking and took my stand upon the flagstones.

I admit that the flagstones in Catholic churches, the odor of a Catholic church, Catholicism as a whole, still inexplicably fascinates me, like a red-haired girl, even though I'd like to re-dye that red hair and even though Catholicism moves me to blasphemies that repeatedly betray my futile, yet still irrevocable, baptism as a Catholic. Even during the most mundane of activities, like brushing my teeth, even during bowel movements, I catch myself running through commentaries on the Mass such as: In the Holy Mass Christ's blood sacrifice is renewed, his blood is shed again for the remission of your sins, this is the chalice of his blood, the wine is transformed whenever Christ's blood is shed, the true blood of Christ is present, through the vision of his most sacred blood, the soul is sprinkled with the blood of Christ, the precious blood, washed in the blood, in the consecration the blood flows, the bloodstained flesh, the voice of Christ's blood rings through all the heavens, the blood of Christ diffuses fragrance before the face of God.

You must admit I have retained a certain Catholic tone. In earlier days I couldn't wait for a streetcar without thinking of the Virgin Mary. I called her blessed, full of grace, virgin of virgins, mother of divine grace,

Thou blessed among women, Thou who art worthy of all veneration, Thou who hast borne the . . . , mother most amiable, mother inviolate, virgin most renowned, let me savor the sweetness of the name of Jesus as Thou savoredst it in thy heart, for it is just and meet, right and for our salvation, Queen of Heaven, thrice-blessed. . . .

From time to time, and particularly when Mama and I went to the Church of the Sacred Heart on Saturday, that little word "blessed" so sweetened and poisoned me that I thanked Satan inside me for having survived the baptism and for providing me with an antidote that permitted me to stride across the flagstones of the Church of the Sacred Heart as a blasphemer, but still unbowed.

Jesus, after whose heart the church was named, was present not only in the sacraments, but also appeared in several small, bright paintings of the stations of the cross, and three times in painted sculpture in various poses.

One was in painted plaster. Longhaired he stood in sandals and a Prussian-blue garment on a golden pedestal. Opening his robe at his chest, he displayed, in the center of his thorax, completely contrary to nature, a tomato-red, glorified, and stylized bleeding heart so the church could name itself for this organ.

During my very first inspection of this openhearted Jesus I couldn't help but notice how embarrassingly perfect the resemblance was between the Savior and my godfather, uncle, and presumptive father Jan Bronski. Those blue, naively self-confident fanatic's eyes. That blossoming bud of a mouth, constantly ready to cry. That manly suffering, traced by the line of the eyebrows. Full, ruddy cheeks, longing to be chastised. They both had that slap-me face women are drawn to caress, along with effeminately weary hands, well manicured and adverse to labor, displaying their stigmata like the finest works of a court jeweler. I was tormented by those Bronski eyes painted in Jesus' face, regarding me with fatherly misunderstanding. After all, I had that same blue look, one that could inspire but not convince.

Oskar turned from the Sacred Heart in the right nave and hastened past the first station of the cross, where Jesus takes up the cross, to the seventh station, where he falls for the second time beneath its weight, to the high altar, above which hung the second sculpted Jesus. This one, however, whether from fatigue or in an attempt to concentrate more deeply, kept his eyes closed. What muscles the man had! This man with his decathlete body instantly made me forget the Sacred Hearted Bronski, drew me to the high altar, each time Mama confessed to Father Wiehnke, to gaze devoutly at the gymnast. I prayed, believe me. Sweet model gymnast, I called him, athlete of athletes, champion in cross-hanging from one-inch publican's nails. And never a twitch out of him. The perpetual flame twitched, but he maintained perfect discipline and received the highest possible score for the event. The stopwatches ticked away. They timed him. Back in the sacristy somewhat grimy acolyte fingers were already polishing the gold medal that was his due. But Jesus didn't compete in this sport for the honors he gained. Faith came to me. I knelt down, as best my knee would allow, beat out the sign of the cross on my drum, and tried to connect words like blessed or afflicted with Jesse Owens and Rudolf Harbig, with last year's Olympics in Berlin — which wasn't always successful, since I had to admit that Jesus had not played fair with the two thieves. So I disqualified him and turned my head to the left, where, arousing new hope, I saw the third sculpture of the heavenly gymnast in the Church of the Sacred Heart.

"Let me not pray till I've seen you thrice," I stammered, then set my soles once more on the flagstones, used the chessboard pattern to reach the left nave, and sensed at every step: He's watching you walk away, the saints are watching you, Peter, who was nailed to a cross head-down, Andrew, who was nailed to a slanting cross — thus St. Andrew's cross. And there's the Greek cross, the Latin or Passion cross. Crosslet crosses, Teutonic crosses, Calvary crosses appearing in textiles, pictures, and books. I saw Greek crosses, anchor crosses, budded crosses crossing each other in relief. The fleurie cross handsome, the Maltese cross prized, the hooked cross, or swastika, forbidden, de Gaulle's cross the cross of Lorraine, St. Anthony's cross for crossing the T in battles at sea. The ankh on a chain, the thief's cross too plain, the Pope's cross too papal, that Russian cross known as Lazarus too. Then there's the Red Cross. The Blue Cross that crosses itself blue in the face. Yellow cross poisons me, crossfire kills me, crusades cross to convert me, cross spiders bite me, I cross you at crosswalks, we crisscross, we cross-talk, and crosswords cry solve me. Weighed down with more crosses than I could bear, I turned and left him behind, turned my back on that gymnast nailed to the cross, who, it crossed my mind, might be cross enough to kick me in the back, for I was approaching the Virgin Mary, who held the child Jesus on her left thigh.

Oskar stood before the left side-altar of the left nave. Mary wore the expression his mama must have had as a seventeen-year-old shop girl back on Troyl when she had too little money for the movies and made up for it by gazing longingly at film posters of Asta Nielsen.

She was paying no attention to Jesus but was gazing instead at the other boy by her right knee, whom, to avoid any possible misunderstanding, I'll identify at once as John the Baptist. Both boys were my size. If pressed, I would have said Jesus was an inch taller, though according to the texts he was younger than the boy Baptist. The sculptor had amused himself by portraying the three-year-old Savior naked and pink. Because he later spent time in the wilderness, John was wearing a chocolate-colored shaggy pelt that hid half his chest, his tummy, and his little watering can.

Oskar would have done better to linger by the high altar or beside the confessional rather than near those two quite precocious boys whose grave mien bore such a shocking resemblance to his own. Naturally they had blue eyes and his chestnut hair. The only thing the sculpting barber had failed to do was give the two of them Oskar's crew cut and trim off those silly corkscrew curls.

I don't want to dwell too long on the boy Baptist, who was pointing with his left forefinger at the boy Jesus as if he were about to count off, "Eeny, meeny, miny, moe . . ." Without entering into counting games, I name Jesus at once and realize: we're identical twins! He could have been my twin brother. He had my stature, and my little watering can, still used only for watering back then. He stared into the world with my Bronski eyes cobalt blue, and assumed—and this I resented most—my own special pose.

My double raised both his arms, closed his hands into fists you wouldn't hesitate to thrust something into—my drumsticks, for example—and had the sculptor done so, and plastered my red and white drum on his pink little thighs as well, it would have been I, the most perfect of Oskars, sitting up there on the Virgin's knee, drumming up a congregation. There are things in this world which — no matter how sacred — just can't be left as they are.

Three steps pulled a carpet up to the Virgin robed in silvery green, to the chocolate-colored shaggy pelt of John, to the boy Jesus the color of boiled ham. Before them stood a small altar to the Virgin Mary with anemic candles and flowers in all price ranges. The green Virgin, the brown John, and the pink Jesus had halos the size of dinner plates stuck to the back of their heads. Gold leaf enriched the plates.

Had there not been steps in front of the altar I would never have climbed them. Steps, door latches, and shop windows enticed Oskar back then, nor does he remain indifferent to them even today, when his hospital bed should be all that he needs. He let himself be enticed from one step to the next, though always remaining on the same carpet. The group surrounding the little altar to the Virgin Mary was quite near to Oskar, allowing his knuckle a disdainful yet respectful percussion of all three. He scraped paint off the plaster with his fingernails. The drapery of the Virgin made its way by diverse paths down to her toes on the cloud bank. The Virgin's barely intimated shinbone gave the impression that the sculptor had first applied the flesh, then submerged it in drapery. As Oskar carefully examined the boy Jesus' little watering can, which should have been circumcised but wasn't, stroking and cautiously squeezing it, as if trying to make it move, he felt something at once pleasant and confusing in his own little watering can, at which point he left Jesus' alone in hopes that his would leave him alone.

Circumcised or not, I let things rest there, pulled the drum from under my sweater, removed it from my neck, and hung it, without damaging his halo, around Jesus. That was somewhat difficult for me given my size. I had to climb up on the sculpture so that, from the cloud bank that served as a pedestal, I could provide Jesus with an instrument.

Oskar didn't do this in January of thirty-seven, on his first visit to church after being baptized, but during Holy Week that same year. All that winter his mama had been hard-pressed to stay on top of her affair with Jan Bronski in the confessional. So Oskar found ample time on Saturdays to work out his plan, reject it, justify it, plan it anew, examine it from every angle, and then at last, casting aside all prior plans, simply, directly, and aided by the prayers at the foot of the altar on Passion Monday, carry it out.

Since Mama needed to confess before the high point of the Easter doings, she took me with her on the evening of Passion Monday, leading me by the hand along Labesweg, past Neuer Markt corner, down Elsenstraße, Marienstraße, past Wohlgemut's butcher shop, turning left at Kleinhammerpark, through the railway underpass, which was oozing nasty yellow stuff as always, to and into the Church of the Sacred Heart across from the railway embankment.

It was late when we arrived. Only two old women and an embarrassed young man still waited outside the confessional. While Mama was searching her conscience — she was leafing through the Mirror of Confession, licking her thumb as if going through a business ledger or concocting a tax return — I slipped down from the oak pew and, without passing beneath the eyes of the Sacred Heart or the gymnast on the cross, sought out the left side-altar.

Though it had to be done quickly, I did not omit the Introitus. Three steps: *Introibo ad altare Dei.* To God, who giveth joy to my youth. The drum removed from my neck, drawing out the Kyrie, up to the cloud bank, no lingering now by the watering can, no, just before Gloria, the drum around Jesus' neck, watch out for the halo, down from the cloud bank, remission, pardon, forgiveness, but first the sticks in those hands just made for them, one, two, three steps, I lift my eyes unto the hills, a little more carpet, the flagstones at last and a prayer stool for Oskar, who knelt down on the cushion and folded his drummer-boy hands at his face — *Gloria in excelsis Deo* — looked up past his folded hands toward Jesus and his drum and awaited the miracle: will he drum now, or can't he drum, or isn't he allowed to drum, either he drums or he's no real Jesus; if he doesn't drum now, Oskar's more Jesus than Jesus is.

If you want a miracle, you have to be patient. So I waited, patiently at first, perhaps not patiently enough, for the longer I kept repeating the text "All eyes attend thee, O Lord," replacing eyes with ears to match the situation, the more disappointed Oskar found himself on his prayer stool. He gave the Lord every chance, closed his eyes so the Lord might decide, since no one was looking, to make a start, even if somewhat awkwardly, but at last, after the third Credo, after Father, maker, visible and invisible, and the only begotten Son, of the Father, very of very, begotten, not made, being of one with the, by whom, for us and for our, came down, was incarnate, was made, was also, for, under, was buried, rose again, according to, ascended into, sitteth on the, shall come, to judge, and the dead, no end, I believe in, with the, together, spake by, believe in one holy catholic and . . .

No, all that remained for me of Catholicism was its smell. One could no longer speak of faith. Nor did I care about the smell, I was looking for something else: I wanted to hear my drum, wanted Jesus to oblige me with a little something, a small, quiet miracle. It wouldn't have to be anything resounding, with Vicar Rasczeia rushing in, Father Wiehnke laboriously lugging his flabby flesh to the miracle, with protocols to the Bishop's seat in Oliva and bishopric reports headed for Rome. No, I wasn't in the least ambitious, Oskar had no desire to be canonized. He just wanted a small private miracle, something he could see and hear, something to clarify once and for all if Oskar should drum for or against, something to proclaim which of the two blue-eyed, identical twins would henceforth have the right to call himself Jesus.

I sat and waited. Meanwhile I began to worry: Mama should be in the confessional by now and might have already finished the sixth commandment. The old man who is always tottering through churches tottered past the high altar and finally reached the left side-altar, greeted the Virgin and the boys, may have seen the drum but failed to register it. He shuffled on, growing older.

Time passed, I say, but Jesus did not beat the drum. I heard voices from the choir. I hope no one starts playing the organ, I thought anxiously. They'll start up rehearsing for Easter and create a clamor that drowns out the first paper-thin drumroll of the boy Jesus.

They didn't play the organ. Jesus didn't drum. There was no miracle, and I rose from the cushion, my knees cracking, and led myself by the nose, bored and morose, across the carpet, pulled myself up step by step, skipping all known prayers at the foot of the altar, mounted the plaster clouds, knocking over flowers in the mid-price range, and was about to remove my drum from that dumb naked child.

I admit it openly and always will: it was a mistake to try to teach him. Why did I have to take the sticks from him, leaving him the drum, then drum something for him, drumming softly at first, but then like an impatient teacher, show this false Jesus how to drum, then thrust the sticks back into his hands so he could show what he'd learned from Oskar?

Before I could take the sticks and drum away from this most stubborn of pupils, with no thought for his halo, Father Wiehnke was behind me—my drumming had tested the height and breadth of the church—Vicar Rasczeia was behind me, Mama behind me, the old man behind me, and the Vicar grabbed me, and the Right Reverend smacked me and Mama wept at me, and the Right Reverend whispered to me, and the Vicar fell to his knees and leapt up and snatched the sticks from Jesus, knelt again and jumped up for the drum, took the drum from him, snapped the halo, bumped his watering can, chipped off a bit of cloud, and fell back onto the steps, one knee, the other knee, refused me the drum, made me even angrier, made me kick the Right Reverend and put Mama to shame, and she was indeed ashamed when I kicked and bit and scratched and tore myself free from the Right Reverend, Vicar, old man, and Mama, stood at the high altar, felt Satan hopping up and down in me, and heard him as I had at my baptism: "Oskar," Satan whispered, "look around, windows everywhere, all glass, all glass."

And past the gymnast on the cross, who didn't twitch, who kept his silence, I sang at the three high windows of the apse depicting the twelve apostles in red, yellow, and green on blue. But it was not at Mark or Matthew that I aimed. I aimed at the dove standing on its head above them celebrating Pentecost, aimed at the Holy Spirit, began to vibrate, pitted my diamond against the bird and—was it my fault? Was it the gymnast, who, by not twitching, intervened? Was this the miracle, and no one knew it? They saw me trembling, soundlessly pouring forth toward the apse what everyone but Mama took for prayers, though it was broken glass I sought; but Oskar failed, his time had not yet come. I fell to the flagstones and wept bitterly, because Jesus had failed, because Oskar had failed, because the Right Reverend and Rasczeia misunderstood me and even babbled of my repenting. But Mama did not fail. She understood my tears, though she was surely glad there'd been no broken glass.

Then Mama took me in her arms, recovered the drum and sticks from the Vicar, promised the Right Reverend to pay for the damage, and received belated absolution from him, since I had interrupted her confession; Oskar received his share of the blessing too, but it meant nothing to me.

As Mama carried me from the Church of the Sacred Heart, I ticked off on my fingers: Today is Monday, tomorrow Tuesday, then Wednesday, Holy Thursday, Good Friday, then it's all over for that character who can't even drum, who won't even treat me to a little broken glass, who looks like me yet is false, who must descend to the grave while I keep on drumming and drumming but will never again ask for a miracle.

Good Friday Fare

AMBIVALENT: THAT MIGHT be the word for my feelings between Passion Monday and Good Friday. On the one hand, I was annoyed by that plaster boy Jesus who refused to drum; on the other, the drum was now reserved for me alone. If, on one side, my voice failed vis-à-vis the church windows, on the other, the intact and colorful glass allowed Oskar to retain that remnant of Catholic faith which was later to inspire him to any number of desperate blasphemies.

Yet a further ambivalence: if I succeeded, on one hand, in singshattering a mansard window to test my powers on the way home from the Church of the Sacred Heart, on the other the feat my voice performed vis-à-vis the profane made me keenly aware from then on of my defeats in the sacred sector. Ambivalent, I say. This cleavage remained, could not be healed, and remains open to this day, since I am at home in neither the sacred nor the profane, and in consequence am housed on the fringes, in a mental institution.

Mama paid for the damage to the left side-altar. Business was good that Easter, even though, at the insistence of Matzerath, who was Protestant, the shop had to be closed on Good Friday. Mama, who generally had her way in most matters, gave in on Good Fridays and closed the shop, demanding in return the right on Catholic grounds to close the shop for Corpus Christi, to replace the boxes of Persil and display packages of Kaffee-Hag in the window with a small, colorful picture of Mary, illuminated with electric lights, and to take part in the procession in Oliva.

There was a cardboard sign that read on one side: *Closed for Good Friday.* The other side of the card stated: *Closed for Corpus Christi.* On the Good Friday that followed that drumless and voiceless Passion Monday, Matzerath hung the card with *Closed for Good Friday* in the shop window, and shortly after breakfast we mounted the tram for Brösen. To stay with our word: Labesweg behaved ambivalently. The Protestants went to church, the Catholics washed their windows and beat anything that even vaguely resembled a carpet so vigorously and resoundingly in their backyards that it sounded as if biblical workers were nailing multiple saviors to multiple crosses in the courtyards of every building in the neighborhood.

We, however, left the Passion-filled pounding of carpets behind and seated ourselves in our customary arrangement—Mama, Matzerath, Jan Bronski, and Oskar—in the Number Nine streetcar, rode down Brösener Weg past the airfield, past the old and new drill grounds, then waited on a siding by Saspe Cemetery for the car coming from Neufahrwasser-Brösen to pass. Mama used the stop as an occasion for lightly uttered yet gloomy observations. The small abandoned graveyard with its stunted shore pines and tilted, moss-covered tombstones from the previous century struck her as lovely, romantic, and charming.

"I wouldn't mind lying there if they still used it," Mama said warmly. But Matzerath felt the soil was too sandy, complained about the rampant shore thistles and barren oats. Jan Bronski pointed out that the noise from the airfield and the shunting of streetcars near the cemetery might disturb the tranquility of the otherwise idyllic spot.

The approaching streetcar shunted around us, the conductor rang the bell twice, and leaving Saspe and its cemetery behind, we headed for Brösen, a beach resort that at this time of year, toward the end of March, looked strange and desolate. The refreshment stands boarded up, the spa hotel shut tight, the pier bereft of flags, two hundred fifty empty booths lined up at the bathhouse. On the weather board traces of last year's chalk—air: twenty degrees centigrade; water: seventeen; wind: northeast; forecast: clear to partly cloudy.

At first we all decided to walk to Glettkau, then, without discussing it, we turned in the opposite direction, toward the jetty. Broad and lazy, the Baltic lapped at the beach. As far as the harbor mouth, from the white lighthouse to the jetty with the sea marker, not a soul to be seen. Rain had fallen that morning, imprinting upon the sand a regular pattern we took pleasure in destroying, leaving our barefoot prints behind. Matzerath sent smoothly polished disks of brick the size of gulden pieces skipping across the greenish water, trying to outdo the others. Jan Bronski, less skilled, searched for amber between throws, found a few chips and a piece the size of a cherry pit which he gave to Mama, who was walking along barefoot like me, constantly glancing over her shoulder, seemingly in love with her footprints. The sun shone cautiously. It was cool, windless, clear; you could see the strip on the horizon that was Hela Peninsula, two or three fading plumes of smoke, and the superstructure of a cargo steamer climbing over the horizon with a leaping motion.

One after the other, at varying intervals, we reached the first granite blocks at the base of the jetty. Mama and I put our shoes and socks back on. She helped me tie them while Matzerath and Jan were already hopping along the rugged crest of the jetty from stone to stone toward the open sea. Damp beards of seaweed grew in disorderly fashion from the seams of the foundation. Oskar felt like combing them. But Mama took me by the hand and we followed the men, who were behaving like schoolboys up ahead. My drum banged against my knee at every step; even here I wouldn't let them take it from me. Mama wore a light blue spring coat with raspberry-colored lapels. The granite blocks were giving her high-heeled shoes trouble. As on all Sundays and holidays, I was in my sailor's jacket with its gold anchor buttons. An old ribbon from Gretchen Scheffler's souvenir collection bearing the legend *SMS Seydlitz* encircled my sailor's cap and would have fluttered had it been windy enough. Matzerath unbuttoned his brown greatcoat. Jan, stylish as always, in his ulster with its shimmering velvet collar.

We leapt along until we reached the sea marker at the end of the jetty. An elderly man with a docker's cap and padded jacket was sitting at the foot of the sea marker. Beside him lay a potato sack with something twitching and wriggling inside. The man, who probably lived in Brösen or Neufahrwasser, was holding the end of a clothesline. The line, matted with seaweed, disappeared into the brackish waters of the Mottlau, which, still muddy here at its mouth, slapped against the stones of the jetty without any help from the open sea.

We wondered why the man in the docker's cap was fishing with an ordinary clothesline and apparently without a float. Mama asked him in a good-natured but teasing way, calling him Uncle. Uncle grinned, showed us the stubs of his tobacco-stained teeth, and with no further explanation, spat a long, lumpy stream of juice that tumbled in the air and landed in the slop between the tar-and-oil-covered granite humps below. The spittle rocked back and forth until a seagull arrived and, nimbly avoiding the stones, snatched it up in flight, drawing other screeching gulls in its wake.

Just as we were about to leave, since it was cold on the jetty and the sun was no help, the man in the docker's cap began hauling the line in hand over hand. Mama still wanted to leave. Matzerath, however, wouldn't budge. Even Jan, who always granted Mama's slightest wish, offered no support this time. Oskar didn't care either way. But since we stayed, I watched. As the docker, pulling steadily hand over hand, gathered the line between his legs, stripping away the seaweed at each pull, I noted that the cargo steamer, which a mere half-hour ago had barely cleared the horizon with its superstructure, had now changed course and, lying low in the water, was heading for the harbor. Lying that low, she must be a Swede carrying ore, Oskar guessed.

I turned away from the Swede as the docker rose with some effort. "Well now, let's just take a little look and see what we got." This he said to Matzerath, who had no idea what he was talking about but still concurred. Steadily repeating "let's just take" and "a little look," the docker kept hauling on the line, but with more effort now, then climbed down the stones alongside the line and thrust—Mama didn't turn away in time—thrust his whole arm into the blubbering bay between the granite stones, felt around, got hold of something, grabbed tight, pulled, and crying out to us to stand back, swung something upward, something heavy and dripping, a spraying, living clump, into our midst: a horse's head, a fresh head, a real one, the head of a black horse with a black mane, which only yesterday or the day before may still have been whinnying, for the head was not yet rotten, did not stink, smelled at most of the Mottlau, like everything else on the jetty.

The man with the docker's cap, which was now pushed far back on his head, was standing over the horseflesh, from which small light green eels were furiously wriggling. The man had a hard time catching them, for eels move quickly and surely over smooth stone, especially when it's damp. Seagulls and the screech of seagulls were instantly above us. They pecked away, three or four of them easily handling a small to medium-sized eel, nor could they be driven off, for the jetty was their domain. Nevertheless the docker, thrusting his arm forcefully among the gulls and grabbing hold, managed to stuff perhaps two dozen smaller eels into his sack, which Matzerath, helpful as ever, held out for him. He was too busy to see Mama's face turn the color of cheese, as she laid first her hand and then her head on Jan's shoulder and velvet collar.

But when the small and middle-sized eels were in the sack, and the docker, whose cap had fallen from his head as he went about his business, started squeezing thicker, darker eels from the cadaver, Mama had to sit down; Jan tried to turn her head aside, but she wouldn't allow it, staring steadily with large cow's eyes directly into the very middle of the docker's work as he wormed out the eels.

"Take a little look!" he grunted now and then. "Let's just see!" He wrenched open the horse's mouth with the help of his rubber boot and forced a stick between the jaws, so that the great yellow horse teeth seemed to be laughing. And when the docker — you could see now that his head was bald and egg-shaped — reached into the horse's gullet with both hands and pulled out two at once, at least as thick as his arm and just as long, my mama's jaw dropped: she spewed her whole breakfast, clumps of egg white with yolk trailing threads among lumps of bread in a gush of coffee and milk, onto the stones of the jetty, and kept retching till nothing more would come, since she hadn't had much breakfast, for she was overweight and trying to slim down, had tried all sorts of diets, but could seldom stick to them — she snacked in secret — and the only thing she held to strictly were her Tuesday exercises with the Women's Association, though Jan and even Matzerath laughed at her when they saw her carrying her gym bag to join those comical heifers and swing Indian clubs in her shiny blue outfit, and still she lost no weight.

Mama spewed half a pound at most onto the stones, and no matter how hard she retched, she could lose no more. Nothing came but green phlegm — and the gulls. They came as soon as she started vomiting, circled lower, descending sleek and smooth, fought over my mama's breakfast with no fear of getting fat, could not be driven off — and certainly not by Jan Bronski, who was afraid of gulls and shielded his pretty blue eyes with his hands.

Nor did they listen to Oskar, who weighed in against the gulls with his drum and battled their whiteness with a whirl of his sticks on white lacquer. But that didn't help, at most turned the gulls even whiter. Matzerath, however, was not worried in the least about Mama. He laughed and mimicked the docker, showed how strong his nerves were, and when the docker was practically done and with a final flourish pulled a huge eel out through the horse's ear, causing the white gruel of the horse's brain to dribble out with it, Matzerath's face too turned the color of cheese, but he still couldn't stop showing off, bought two medium-sized and two large eels from the docker for practically nothing, then tried to talk him down even further.

I had to admire Jan Bronski. He looked as if he wanted to cry, but even so helped Mama to her feet, put one arm around her, held the other out before her, and led her away, which looked comical, Mama tottering in her high heels from one stone to the next toward the beach, one leg or the other giving way at every step, and still she never broke an ankle.

Oskar remained with Matzerath and the docker, because the latter, having replaced his cap, was explaining to us why his potato sack was half-full of coarse salt. There was salt in the sack so the eels would wriggle themselves to death in the salt, so the salt would draw the slime from their skin and innards. Eels can't stop wriggling once they're put in salt, they keep squirming till they die and leave their slime in the salt. That's what you do if you want to smoke your eels afterward. Of course it's outlawed by the police and the Society for the Prevention of Cruelty to Animals, but that doesn't stop the eels from squirming. How else are you supposed to get the slime off them, and out of them? Afterward the dead eels are wiped clean with dry peat and hung in a smoking barrel over beech wood.

Matzerath felt it was just to leave the eels wriggling in salt. After all, they crawled into the horse's head, he said. And into human corpses too, said the docker. They say the eels were mighty fat after the Battle of Skagerrak. And just a few days ago a doctor here at the mental hospital told me about a married woman who tried to satisfy herself with a live eel. But the eel bit firmly into her; she had to be committed, and they say she could never have children after that.

The docker closed the sack with the eels in salt and threw it over his shoulder as it continued to thrash about. He hung the coiled clothesline around his neck and trudged off, just as the cargo steamer was entering the harbor, heading toward Neufahrwasser. The steamer was about eighteen hundred tons and wasn't a Swede but a Finn, carrying not ore but lumber. The docker with the sack must have known a few men on the Finn, for he waved over at the rusty tub and yelled something. Those on the Finn waved and yelled something in reply. But why Matzerath waved and roared out something silly like "Ship ahoy!" was a mystery to me. As a native Rhinelander he didn't know the first thing about ships, nor did he know a single Finn. But he made it a habit to wave when anyone else did, and to yell, laugh, or clap whenever anyone else yelled, laughed, or clapped. That's why he joined the Party relatively early on, when it was still totally unnecessary, offered no advantages, and simply tied up his Sunday mornings.

Oskar followed slowly behind Matzerath, the man from Neufahrwasser, and the overloaded Finn. Now and then I looked back, for the docker had left the horse head at the base of the sea marker. There was nothing to be seen of the head now, however, for it was powdered over with gulls. A white, weightless hole in the bottle-green sea. A freshly laundered cloud that might rise at any moment, clean and pure, into the air, screeching loudly, hiding a horse's head that did not whinny but screamed.

When I'd had enough, I ran away from the gulls and Matzerath, striking my drum with my fist as I leapt along, passed the docker, who was now smoking a stubby pipe, and caught up with Jan Bronski and Mama at the head of the jetty. Jan was holding Mama just as he had been, but one hand had disappeared beneath her lapel. That Mama also had one hand in Jan's trouser pocket was something Matzerath could not see, for he was far behind us, wrapping the four eels the docker had stunned with a stone in a piece of newspaper he'd found among the rocks on the jetty.

When Matzerath caught up with us, he waved the bundle of eels about and bragged, "One-fifty he wanted. But I gave him a gulden and *basta!*"

Mama's face was looking better now, both hands were together again, and she declared, "Just don't think I'm going to eat any of that eel. I'm never eating another fish, least of all eel."

Matzerath laughed. "Don't make such a fuss, girl. You've always known what eels do and you still ate them, fresh ones too. We'll see once your humble servant has cooked them just right with all the trimmings and a little salad."

Jan Bronski, who had removed his hand in time from Mama's coat, said nothing. I drummed away steadily till we reached Brösen so they wouldn't start up about the eels again. At the tram stop, and inside the second car, I continued to prevent the three grownups from talking. The eels remained relatively still. No stop at Saspe, because the other tram had already arrived. Just beyond the airfield, in spite of my drumming, Matzerath started going on about how enormously hungry he was. Mama didn't react and stared past everyone till Jan offered her one of his Regattas. As he gave her a light and she adjusted the gold tip to her lips, she smiled at Matzerath, for she knew he didn't like to see her smoke in public.

At Max-Halbe-Platz we got off, and despite everything Mama took Matzerath's arm and not, as I had expected, Jan's. Jan walked beside me, holding my hand as he finished Mama's cigarette.

On Labesweg the Catholic housewives were still beating their carpets. While Matzerath was unlocking the door to the flat, I saw Frau Kater, who lived on the fifth floor next to the trumpeter Meyn, on the stairs. She was holding a rolled-up brownish carpet on her right shoulder with her powerful reddish blue arms. Her blond hair, matted and salty with sweat, blazed from both armpits. The carpet hung down both in front and behind. She could easily have been carrying a drunken man, but her husband was no longer living. As she lugged her fat self past me in a shiny black taffeta dress her effluvium struck me: ammonia, pickles, carbide — she must have been having her monthlies.

Shortly thereafter the rhythmic blows of carpet beating rose from the courtyard and drove me through the flat, pursued me till I escaped at last by crouching in the wardrobe of our bedroom, where the dangling winter coats muffled the worst of the pre-paschal noise.

But it wasn't just the carpet-beating Frau Kater who sent me scurrying to the wardrobe. Mama, Jan, and Matzerath had not yet removed their coats when they started arguing about the Good Friday meal. And it wasn't restricted to eels, I had to be trotted out again, with my famous fall down the cellar steps: "It's your fault, it was your fault too, I'm making eel soup, don't be such a sissy, cook what you want but not eel, there's plenty of canned goods in the cellar, bring up some mushrooms but shut the trapdoor so something like that doesn't happen again, forget that old song and dance, we're having eels and that's it, with milk, mustard, parsley, and boiled potatoes and a bay leaf on top and a clove, no, no, come on, Alfred, if she doesn't want any, now don't you stick your nose in, I didn't buy those eels for nothing, they'll be nicely cleaned and washed, no, no, we'll just see once they're on the table, we'll see who eats and who doesn't."

Matzerath slammed the living room door behind him and disappeared into the kitchen, where we could hear him banging away. He killed the eels with a crosscut slice below the head while Mama, who had an overly lively imagination, had to sit down on the sofa, where she was quickly joined by Jan Bronski, and a moment later the two were holding hands and whispering in Kashubian.

When the three grownups had assumed their respective positions in the flat, I was not yet sitting in the wardrobe but still in the living room. There was a child's chair by the tile stove. There I sat swinging my legs, with Jan staring at me, and I could tell I was in the way, though they couldn't really do much, since Matzerath was right behind the living room wall, threatening them silently but unmistakably with half-dead eels that he swung like a whip. So they exchanged hands, squeezed and tugged on twenty fingers, cracked their knuckles, and drove me to distraction with their noise. Wasn't Frau Kater's carpet pounding in the courtyard enough? Didn't it penetrate every wall, drawing ever closer though it grew no louder?

Oskar slid down from his little chair, crouched for a moment beside the tile stove, so that his departure would not be too obvious, and then, totally immersed in his drum, scooted across the threshold into the bedroom.

To avoid making any noise, I left the bedroom door half-open, and noted with satisfaction that no one called me back. I was still trying to decide if Oskar should crawl under the bed or climb into the wardrobe. I chose the wardrobe because my nice navy blue sailor's uniform might have got dirty under the bed. I could just reach the wardrobe key, turned it once, pulled the mirrored doors apart, and used my drumsticks to push aside the hangers with coats and winter clothes lined up on the pole. To reach the heavy woolens and move them I had to stand on my drum. The gap left in the center of the wardrobe was not large, but it was big enough to accommodate an incoming and crouching Oskar. I even managed with some effort to pull the mirrored doors inward and, using the overlapping slat, to jam them with the help of a shawl I found on the cupboard floor in such a way that a finger-wide gap allowed me to see out if necessary and even let in some air. I placed my drum on my knee but didn't strike it, not even lightly, allowed myself instead to be enveloped and penetrated by the vapors of winter coats.

How good that the wardrobe existed with its heavy woolens that barely breathed, allowing me to gather nearly all my thoughts, to bundle them together and present them to an ideal figure who was rich enough to receive this gift with measured and scarcely noticeable joy.

As always, when I concentrated and made proper use of my powers, I transported myself to the office of Dr. Hollatz on Brunshöferweg and enjoyed the one part of my weekly Wednesday visits I cared about. Thus my thoughts centered less on the doctor with his increasingly detailed examinations and more on his assistant, Sister Inge. She was allowed to undress and dress me, she alone was permitted to measure me, weigh me, test me; in short, all the experiments Dr. Hollatz conducted upon me were carried out by Sister Inge, correctly but somewhat sullenly, and reported, not without a touch of mockery, as total failures, which Hollatz termed partial successes. I seldom looked Sister Inge in the eye. My gaze and my sometimes racing drummer's heart found repose on the clean, starched white of her nurse's uniform, on the weightless edifice she wore as a cap, on a smooth pin decorated with a red cross. How pleasant it was to follow the constantly renewing folds of her uniform. Did she have a body beneath that fabric? Her aging face and her well-cared-for yet rawboned hands indicated that Sister Inge was indeed a woman. Of course the sort of smells that would have revealed a physical state similar to my mama's when Jan, or even Matzerath, unveiled her before my eyes, those Sister Inge did not breed. She smelled of soap and soporific medications. How often I was overcome by sleep as she auscultated my small and supposedly ailing body: a shallow sleep, born from the folds of white fabric, a carbolic-cloaked sleep, a dreamless sleep; unless in the distance her pin expanded into who knew what: a sea of banners, an alpine glow, a splash of poppy field, ready to revolt, who knew against whom: against red Indians, cherries, nosebleeds, against cockscombs, red blood cells, coalescing to a red that filled my vision and gave background to a passion that I found, both then and now, quite understandable, but could not name, because the small word red says nothing, and nosebleeds do nothing, and banners fade, and if in spite of all I still say red, red won't have me, turns its coat: back to black, the Cook is coming, scares me yellow, makes me blue, blue won't do, blue's untrue, turns me green, green grows the grass above my grave, green turns me white: calls me black, black scares me yellow, yellow makes me blue, blue won't turn green, green blooms me red, red was Sister Inge's pin, the red cross she wore, to be precise, upon the washable collar of her nurse's uniform; but things seldom stopped with this most monochromatic of all images, nor did they in the wardrobe.

A highly colorful din, pushing its way in from the living room, pounded at my wardrobe doors, awakening me just as I was falling into a doze devoted to Sister Inge. Sober and thick-tongued I sat holding my drum on my knees among winter coats of all styles, smelled Matzerath's Party uniform, felt his military belt, leather shoulder straps with hooks, beside me, but found no remnant of the folds of the nurse's white uniform: wool dangled, worsted hung, cord creased flannel, and above me four years' fashion in hats, at my feet large shoes, little shoes, polished puttees, heels with and without taps, a strip of light falling in from outside that outlined everything; Oskar was sorry he'd left a gap between the mirrored doors.

What could those people in the living room have to offer me? Perhaps Matzerath had caught the two of them on the sofa, though that was highly unlikely, for Jan always maintained a certain degree of caution, and not just when he was playing skat. Probably — and this proved to be the case — Matzerath had placed the slaughtered, cleaned, washed, cooked, spiced, and sampled eels in the large terrine and set it on the living room table as a ready-to-serve eel soup with boiled potatoes, and then, because no one would join him, had dared to start singing the praises of his dish, listing all its ingredients and reciting the recipe like a prayer. Mama shouted. She shouted in Kashubian. Which Matzerath could neither stand nor understand, yet still he had to listen, and no doubt got the drift of it; she had to be talking about eels, and as always when Mama started shouting, it was about my fall down the cellar steps. Matzerath replied in kind. They knew their parts well. Jan raised objections. Without him there would have been no show. Finally Act Two:

The piano lid banged open, without a score, by heart, feet on both pedals, up, down, and sideways resounded the Huntsmen's Chorus from the *Freischütz:* What thing on earth resembles . . . And right in the midst of the Halali the piano lid bangs, feet off the pedals, the piano stool tips over, and Mama's on her way, already in the bedroom, takes a last glance at herself in the mirror of the wardrobe door, and throws herself, I saw it through the gap, across the marriage bed beneath the blue canopy, weeping and wringing her hands with as many fingers as the penitent, gold-framed Mary Magdalene in the color print at the head of the matrimonial fortress.

For a long time I heard nothing but Mama's whimpering, the soft creaking of the bed, and faint murmurs from the living room. Jan was calming Matzerath down. Matzerath asked Jan to calm Mama down. The murmuring thinned out, Jan entered the bedroom. Act Three: He stood by the bed, observing Mama and the repentant Mary Magdalene in turn, sat gingerly on the edge of the bed, stroked Mama, who was lying on her stomach, on the back and buttocks, spoke to her soothingly in Kashubian, and finally — since words no longer helped — slid his hand under her dress, until she ceased whimpering and Jan could remove his gaze from the many-fingered Magdalene. You should have seen how Jan stood up when his work was finished, dabbed at his fingers with his handkerchief, then spoke aloud to Mama, no longer in Kashubian, emphasizing every word so that Matzerath could hear him from the living room or kitchen: "Come on now, Agnes, let's just forget the whole thing. Alfred took the eels and dumped them in the toilet long ago. Let's have a good game of skat, quarter-penny for all I care, and when we've all forgotten this and made up, Alfred will fix us mushrooms with scrambled eggs and fried potatoes."

Mama said nothing, rolled from the bed, smoothed out the yellow quilt, shook her hair into place before the wardrobe's mirrored doors, and followed Jan from the bedroom. I took my eye from the observation slit, and the next thing I heard was the shuffling of cards. Subdued, cautious laughter, Matzerath cut, Jan dealt, and they started to bid. I think Jan must have outbid Matzerath. He passed at twenty-three. Whereupon Mama bid Jan up to thirty-six, then he too had to back down, and Mama played a grand, which she just barely lost. Jan won the following diamond simple hands down, while Mama just managed to bring home the third round, a heart hand without two.

Certain that this family game of skat, interrupted briefly for scrambled eggs, mushrooms, and fried potatoes, would stretch well into the night, I barely listened to the following rounds but instead tried to find my way back to Sister Inge and her white, soporific uniform. But my stay in Dr. Hollatz's office was to remain a gloomy experience. Not only did green, blue, yellow, and black constantly interrupt the redness of the Red Cross pin, the events of that morning pressed in as well: whenever the door to the consultation room and to Sister Inge opened, what was offered was not the pure and delicate sight of the nurse's uniform, but instead the docker on the harbor jetty at Neufahrwasser with the sea marker pulling eels from a dripping, wriggling horse's head, and what posed as white, what I tried to connect with Sister Inge, were seagull wings, which, for a moment, covered the carcass and the eels inside it deceptively, till the wound opened once more, yet did not bleed red blood, but black was the horse, bottle-green the sea, some rust appeared, brought by the Finn that loaded lumber, and the gulls — let's have no more talk of doves — clouded the victim and dipped in their wingtips and threw the eel to my own Sister Inge, who caught it, celebrated it, and turned into a gull, took its form, not that of a dove, yet still Holy Spirit, and in the form that's called a gull, sank down as cloud on flesh and celebrated Pentecost.

Abandoning the effort, I abandoned the wardrobe as well, pushed open the mirrored doors angrily, climbed forth from the cupboard, found myself unchanged in front of the mirrors but relieved that Frau Kater was no longer beating her carpets. Good Friday had ended for Oskar, but only when Easter was over would his Passion begin.

Tapering toward the Foot

AND FOR MAMA TOO it was only after that Good Friday with the eel-wriggling horse head, after Easter Sunday with Grandmother and Uncle Vinzent in rural Bissau along with the Bronskis, that an ordeal set in which even the smiling May weather could not assuage.

It's not true that Matzerath made Mama start eating fish again. Just two weeks after Easter, entirely on her own and driven by some mysterious urge, she started devouring fish in such quantities and with so little thought for her figure that Matzerath said, "Stop eating all that fish — you act like someone's making you!"

She started out with sardines in oil for breakfast, then, two hours later, if there were no customers in the store, she would raid a plywood box of Bohnsack sprats, demand fried flounder or cod in mustard sauce for lunch, and be reaching for the can opener again by afternoon: jellied eel, rollmops, pickled herring — and if Matzerath refused to fry or boil fish for supper she didn't say a word, raised no complaint, just rose quietly from the table and returned from the shop with a chunk of smoked eel, at which we would all lose our appetite, for she would scrape every smidgen of fat from both sides of the eel's skin with a knife, and in general ate nothing but fish with a knife from then on. She had to vomit several times a day. Matzerath was worried sick: "Are you pregnant, or what?"

"Rubbish," Mama would say, if she said anything, and one Sunday, when boiled eel with parsley and new potatoes swimming in May butter arrived at the dinner table, Grandmother Koljaiczek banged her hand between the plates and cried out, "Agnes, what's going on? Why are you eating fish when it don't agree with you, are you off your rocker?" and

Mama just shook her head, shoved the potatoes aside, pulled the eel through the May butter, and chewed away steadily as if she had a job to do. Jan Bronski said nothing. Once when I surprised the two of them on the sofa, holding hands as usual with their clothes in the normal disarray, I was struck by Jan's tear-stained eyes and Mama's general apathy, which, however, was quickly transformed into its opposite. She jumped up, clutched me, lifted me and squeezed me, revealing a void that nothing, not even those vast quantities of fried, boiled, pickled, and smoked fish, could ever fill.

A few days later I saw her in the kitchen as she not only gobbled up those damned sardines as usual but poured the leftover oil from several old tins she'd saved into a small saucepan, heated the mess up over the gas flame, and drank it down, while, standing at the kitchen door, I almost dropped my drum.

That same evening Mama had to be taken to the city hospital. Matzerath cried and carried on before the ambulance arrived: "Why don't you want the child? Who cares whose it is? Or is it still that damn horse's head? If only we'd never gone there. Forget all that, Agnes. I didn't do it on purpose."

The ambulance arrived, Mama was carried out. Children and grownups gathered on the sidewalk; the ambulance drove off with her, and soon it was apparent that Mama had forgotten neither the jetty nor the horse's head, that she carried the memory of that horse — whether it was named Fritz or Hans — with her. Her organs recalled that Good Friday outing with painful clarity and, for fear of repeating it, allowed my mother, who was at one with her organs, to die.

Dr. Hollatz spoke of jaundice and fish poisoning. At the hospital they discovered that Mama was three months pregnant and gave her a private room, and for four days she showed those of us allowed to visit her a face devastated by pain and nausea, a nausea through which she sometimes smiled at me.

Even though she tried to please her visitors, just as I take pains to seem happy when my friends arrive on Visitors Day, she still couldn't prevent the occasional bouts of retching that repeatedly racked her slowly succumbing body, though it could come up with nothing more by the fourth day of that difficult death than the last gasp we all must expel to gain our death certificate.

We all sighed with relief when nothing remained in my mama to set off the retching that so disfigured her beauty. The moment she had been washed and lay there in her shroud, she showed once more her familiar, round, naïve yet clever face. The head nurse closed Mama's eyes, since Matzerath and Jan were blinded by their tears.

I could not weep, because the others, the men and Grandmother, Hedwig Bronski, and fourteen-year-old Stephan, were all weeping. Besides, my mama's death had come as no great surprise to me. To Oskar, who accompanied her on Thursdays into the Altstadt and to the Church of the Sacred Heart on Saturdays, it seemed as if she'd been seeking a chance for years to dissolve her triangular relationship in such a way that Matzerath, whom she may have hated, would bear the guilt for her death, while Jan Bronski, her Jan, could keep working at the Polish Post Office thinking: She died for me, she didn't want to stand in my way, she sacrificed herself.

Though both Mama and Jan were coldly calculating when it came to finding a safe love nest, they showed an equal talent for romance: one might see them as Romeo and Juliet, or those two royal children kept apart because the water was too deep. While Mama, who had taken the last sacraments just in time, lay cold and unmoved by the priest's prayers, I found time and leisure to observe the hospital nurses, who were mostly Protestant. They folded their hands differently from Catholics, more self-confidently I might say, recited the Lord's Prayer with words that varied from the original Catholic text, and didn't cross themselves the same way Grandmother Koljaiczek, the Bronskis, and I did. My father Matzerath — I call him that now and then, even if his role remains presumptive — he, the Protestant, differed from other Protestants in prayer by not holding his hands anchored at his chest, but instead switched his fingers from one religion to the other by clenching them at the level of his private parts, and was obviously ashamed to be seen praying. My grandmother, kneeling beside her brother Vinzent at the deathbed, prayed loudly and effusively in Kashubian, while Vinzent merely moved his lips, presumably in Polish, though his widened eyes brimmed with spirituality. I would have liked to play my drum. After all, I had my poor mama to thank for all those red and white drums. As a counterweight to Matzerath's desires, she had laid the maternal promise of a tin drum in my cradle, and now and then, particularly when she was slimmer and didn't have to exercise, Mama's beauty had served as a score for my drumming. Finally, no longer able to contain myself, I shaped the ideal vision of her gray-eyed beauty on my drum at Mama's deathbed, and was amazed that it was Matzerath who took my side and softened the immediate protest of the head nurse, whispering, "Let him be, Sister, they were so close."

Mama could be very cheerful. Mama could be very timid. Mama forgot things quickly. Mama nonetheless had a good memory. Mama threw me out with the bathwater yet sat in the tub with me. Mama was sometimes lost, but I always found her. When I sangshattered glass, Mama sold lots of putty. She sometimes put her foot in it when she could have put her foot down elsewhere. Even when Mama buttoned up, she stayed an open book to me. Mama feared drafts but generated storms. She lived on what she charged but hated paying taxes. I was the flip side of her top card. When Mama played a heart hand, she always won. When Mama died, the red flames on my drum turned pale; but the white lacquer grew whiter, so dazzling that, blinded, even Oskar had to shut his eyes.

My poor mama was not buried at Saspe Cemetery, as she had sometimes wished, but in the small, peaceful cemetery in Brentau. Her stepfather, the gunpowder miller Gregor Koljaiczek, who died of influenza in nineteen-seventeen, lay there too. There was a large crowd of mourners, as might be expected at the funeral of a popular grocer; the faces of her steady customers appeared, of course, but also salesmen from various wholesale houses and even a few competitors, like the grocer Weinreich and Frau Probst from the store over on Hertastraße. The chapel of Brentau Cemetery couldn't hold the crowd. It smelled of flowers and black clothing in mothballs. In the open coffin my poor mama's face was yellow and worn. During the interminable ceremony I couldn't shake the feeling: Her head is going to bob up, she'll have to vomit again, something inside her still wants out — not just the three-month-old fetus who, like me, doesn't know which father to thank, who wants to come out and ask for a drum as Oskar did, and not just the fetus, there's still fish in there, not sardines, and I don't mean flounder, I mean a small chunk of eel, a few greenish white tendrils of eel meat, eel from the naval battle at Skagerrak, eel from the harbor jetty at Neufahrwasser, Good Friday eel, eel that sprang from the head of the horse, perhaps even eel from Joseph Koljaiczek her father, who slipped under a raft and fell prey to the eels, eel of thine eel, for eel thou art, and to eel returnest . . .

But she did not retch. She kept it down, took it with her, was going to bury the eel beneath the earth, so there might at last be peace.

When the men lifted the coffin lid and started to cover my poor mama's nauseated yet resolute face, Anna Koljaiczek held the men back and, trampling the flowers beside the coffin, threw herself across her daughter and wept, tearing at the expensive white shroud and wailing in Kashubian.

There were many who later said she cursed my presumptive father Matzerath and called him her daughter's murderer. There was also talk of my fall down the cellar steps. She took the tale over from Mama and never allowed Matzerath to forget his supposed guilt for my supposed accident. Again and again she accused him, even though Matzerath, in spite of his politics, showed an almost grudging reverence for her, and kept her stocked throughout the war years with sugar and synthetic honey, with coffee and kerosene.

The greengrocer Greff and Jan Bronski, who was weeping in a high-pitched feminine register, led my grandmother away from the coffin. The men could now fasten the lid and assume at last the faces pallbearers always assume when they take up their positions beneath the coffin. At the semirural cemetery at Brentau, with its two fields on either side of the avenue lined with elms, with its little chapel that looked like a pasteboard set for a Nativity play, with its draw-well, with its quick and lively bird world, on the neatly raked cemetery lane, right behind Matzerath at the head of the procession, I took pleasure for the first time in the coffin's shape. Since then I've often had occasion to let my gaze glide over the black or dark brown wood employed for ultimate ends. My poor mama's coffin was black. It tapered in a wonderfully harmonious way toward the foot. Is there any other shape in the world so admirably suited to the human form?

If only beds narrowed like that toward the foot. If only all our familiar and occasional couches tapered so clearly toward the foot. For we can strut about all we like; in the end, the broad expanse of the head, shoulders, and torso always tapers down to the narrow base of our feet.

Matzerath walked directly behind the coffin. He carried his top hat in his hand and did his best, in spite of his sorrow, to hold himself erect during the slow march. Whenever I looked at his neck I felt sorry for him: the bulge at the back of his head and those two rigid tendons that climbed from collar to hairline.

Why was it Mother Truczinski who took my hand and not Gretchen Scheffler or Hedwig Bronski? She lived on the second floor of our building, apparently had no first name; everyone called her Mother Truczinski.

Ahead of the coffin, Father Wiehnke with acolytes and incense. My gaze slipped from Matzerath's neck to the crisscrossed furrows of the pallbearers' necks. Oskar had to fight a wild desire: to climb up on the coffin. To sit right on top and drum. To drum with his sticks on the lid of that coffin and not on his drum. To ride on the top as they carried it swaying. While the Right Reverend followed in prayer from behind, Oskar would lead by drumming in front. As the coffin was placed over pit, planks, and ropes, he would keep calmly poised on the wood. Midst sermon, incense, holy water, and bells he'd drum out the Latin on top of the wood and stay as they lowered both him and the box by the ropes. Would descend to the grave with Mama and fetus. Would stay down below while those left behind cast handfuls of earth, and not come back up, but sit on the tapered foot drumming, even under the earth if he could, just keep right on drumming, till the sticks in his hands, the wood of his sticks, till his Mama for him, till he for her, till each for the other, had rotted away, given their flesh to the earth and its tenants; and Oskar would gladly have played something more with his little knuckles for the tender cartilage of the fetus, had that only been possible and permitted.

No one sat on the coffin. It swayed bare beneath the elms and weeping willows of Brentau Cemetery. Among the graves, the sexton's speckled hens, pecking for worms, reaping though they had not sown. Then through the birches. I behind Matzerath, holding Mother Truczinski's hand, Grandmother right behind me — Greff and Jan escorting her — Vinzent Bronski on Hedwig's arm, little Marga and Stephan hand in hand ahead of the Schefflers. Laubschad the clockmaker, old Herr Heilandt, Meyn the trumpeter, but without his instrument and relatively sober.

Not till it was all over and people began offering their condolences did I notice Sigismund Markus. Dressed in black and embarrassed, he joined those who wanted to shake hands with Matzerath, me, my grandmother, and the Bronskis, and murmur something. At first I didn't understand what Alexander Scheffler wanted of Markus. They hardly knew each other, perhaps they'd never even met. Finally Meyn the musician joined in and said something to the toy merchant. They stood behind a waist-high hedge of the sort of greenery that leaves a stain and tastes bitter when you rub it between your fingers. Frau Kater with her daughter Susi, who had grown somewhat too quickly and was grinning behind her handkerchief, were expressing their condolences to Matzerath and didn't miss the chance to pat me on the head. The altercation behind the hedge grew louder but remained indistinct. The trumpeter Meyn poked Markus on his black suit with his index finger, pushed him backward, then took Sigismund's left arm while Scheffler linked arms on the right. Both were careful to see that Markus, who was stepping backward, didn't stumble over the borders of the graves, pushed him onto the main path, and showed Sigismund the way to the cemetery gate. He appeared to thank them for the information, walked away toward the exit, putting on his top hat as he did so, and did not look back, as Meyn and the baker watched him.

Neither Matzerath nor Mother Truczinski noticed that I had evaded them and the condolences. Acting like a little boy who has to go, Oskar sneaked off past the gravedigger and his helper, then ran, with no regard for the ivy, and reached both the elms and Sigismund Markus at the exit.

"Little Oskar!" Markus said in surprise. "Why are they treating Markus like this? What's he done to deserve it?"

I didn't know what Markus had done, took him by his hand, clammy with sweat, led him through the wrought-iron cemetery gate, which stood open, and the two of us, the keeper of my drums and I, the drummer, possibly his drummer, ran into Crazy Leo, who shared our belief in paradise.

Markus knew Leo, for Leo was well-known around town. I had heard of Crazy Leo, knew that one sunny day, while he was still at the seminary, the world, the sacraments, the confessions, heaven and hell, life and death, had driven him so mad that from then on Leo's worldview, though mad, was radiant with perfection.

Crazy Leo's occupation was to turn up after every funeral — and no one took leave without his knowledge — wearing white gloves and a shiny black suit several sizes too big for him, to await the mourners. Markus and I both understood that he was standing there at the wrought-iron gate of Brentau Cemetery in a professional capacity, his glove oozing sympathy, his watery eyes crazed, his drooling mouth drooling toward the mourners.

Mid-May: A bright, sunny day. Hedges and trees filled with birds. Cackling hens, symbolizing immortality by and through their eggs. Humming in the air. A fresh coat of green without dust. Crazy Leo carried his faded silk hat in his gloved left hand, approached lightly, like a dancer, for he was truly touched by grace, with five mildewed glove fingers thrust forth toward Markus and me, then stood before us, leaning to one side as if in a wind, though not the slightest breeze stirred, tilted his head and babbled, dribbling threads, as Markus, hesitantly at first and then firmly, placed his bare hand in the clutching glove: "What a beautiful day. Now she's where everything's cheap. Did you see the Lord? *Habemus ad Dominum.* He passed by in a hurry. Amen."

We said amen, and Markus assured Leo the day was beautiful, even said he'd seen the Lord.

Behind us we heard the approaching hum of the mourners from the cemetery. Markus let his hand fall from Leo's glove, still found time for a tip, gave me a Markus look, and scurried off to the taxi waiting for him outside the Brentau post office.

I was still watching the cloud of dust that cloaked a disappearing Markus when Mother Truczinski took me by the hand again. They arrived in larger and smaller groups. Crazy Leo offered his condolences to all, called their attention to the beautiful day, asked them if they had seen the Lord, and received, as usual, larger or smaller tips, or none at all. Matzerath and Jan Bronski paid the pallbearers, the gravedigger, the sexton, and Father Wiehnke, who with an embarrassed sigh allowed Crazy Leo to kiss his hand, and with kissed hand sent gestures of blessing after the slowly dispersing crowd of mourners.

Meanwhile we — my grandmother, her brother Vinzent, the Bronskis with their children, Greff without his wife, and Gretchen Scheffler — seated ourselves in two one-horse box carts. We were taken past Goldkrug through the forest and across the nearby Polish border to Bissau-Abbau for the funeral banquet.

Vinzent Bronski's farmyard lay in a hollow. Poplars stood before it to ward off lightning. They took the barn door off its hinges, laid it across wooden trestles, and spread tablecloths over it. More people came from the surrounding area. The meal lasted a long time. We banqueted in the entrance to the barn. Gretchen Scheffler held me on her lap. The food was greasy, then sweet, then greasy again, potato schnapps, beer, a goose and a piglet, cake and sausage side by side, pumpkin in vinegar and sugar, red fruit jelly with sour cream, toward evening a breeze through the open barn, mice rustled, as did the Bronski children, who in league with the neighborhood brats took over the farmyard.

With the oil lamps the skat cards appeared on the table. The potato schnapps stayed. There was also eggnog, homemade. That cheered things up. And Greff, who didn't drink, sang songs. The Kashubes sang too, and Matzerath dealt first. Jan was second and the foreman from the brickworks third. Only then did I truly realize poor Mama was gone. They played well into the night, but none of the men could win a heart hand. When Jan Bronski inexplicably lost a heart hand without four, I heard him say to Matzerath in a low voice, "Agnes would have won that for sure."

With that I slipped from Gretchen Scheffler's lap and found my grandmother and her brother Vinzent outside. They were sitting on a wagon shaft. Vinzent was muttering to the stars in Polish. My grandmother could cry no more but let me under her skirts.

Who will take me under her skirts today? Who will switch off the daylight and lamplight for me? Who will give me the smell of that yellow, slightly rancid melted butter that my grandmother stockpiled, sheltered, and seasoned as fare for me under her skirts and gave me once upon a time, a fare I liked, and came to long for.

I fell asleep beneath her four skirts, close to my poor mama's beginnings, and found a peace almost as still, if not as breathless, as she found in that box which tapered toward the foot.

Herbert Truczinski's Back

NOTHING CAN TAKE a mother's place, they say. Soon after Mama's burial I began to miss my poor mama. The Thursday visits to Sigismund Markus stopped, I was no longer taken to Sister Inge's white uniform, and Saturdays in particular brought home my mama's death with painful clarity: Mama no longer went to confession.

So I was cut off from the Altstadt, the office of Dr. Hollatz, the Church of the Sacred Heart. I'd lost all interest in rallies. And how was I supposed to lure passersby to shop windows when even the tempter's trade now seemed bland and insipid to Oskar? There was no more Mama to take me to the Stadt-Theater for the Christmas play, or to the Krone or Busch circus. Conscientiously if somewhat morosely, I pursued my studies on my own, tediously tracing the rectilinear streets of the suburb toward Kleinhammerweg to visit Gretchen Scheffler, who told me of Strength through Joy trips to the Land of the Midnight Sun, while I kept on comparing Goethe with Rasputin, never coming to the end of such comparisons, escaping that constant cycle of radiance and darkness most often through historical studies. *A Struggle for Rome*, Keyser's *History of the City of Danzig*, and Köhler's *Naval Calendar*, my old standard works, gave me a worldwide half knowledge. To this very day I can give you precise details on the armor, firepower, launching, manufacture, and crew strength of every ship that participated, sank, or was damaged in the Battle of Skagerrak.

I was almost fourteen, loved solitude, and often went on walks. My drum came along, but I plied its tin sparingly, for Mama's departure called into question the timely delivery of drums both then and in the future.

Was it in the fall of thirty-seven or the spring of thirty-eight? At any rate I was tripping along Hindenburgallee toward the city, had just about reached the Café Vierjahreszeiten, leaves were falling, or buds were bursting, at any rate Nature was up to something, when I ran into my friend Master Bebra, who was a direct descendant of Prince Eugen and consequently of Louis the Fourteenth.

We hadn't seen one another in three years, and yet we recognized each other at twenty paces. He was not alone; on his arm hung a dainty southern beauty almost an inch shorter than Bebra, three finger-breadths taller than me, whom he presented in the course of the introductions as Roswitha Raguna, Italy's most famous somnambulist.

Bebra invited me for a cup of Mocha at the Café Vierjahreszeiten. We sat in the Aquarium Room, and the coffee-drinking biddies hissed, "Look at the midgets, Lisbeth, did you see? Do you think they're at Krone's circus? We ought to try and go."

Bebra smiled at me and showed a thousand barely visible tiny wrinkles.

The waiter who brought our Mocha was very tall. As Frau Roswitha ordered a small tart she gazed up at the towering man in tails.

Bebra looked me over: "He doesn't seem to be doing so well, our glass slayer. What's wrong, my friend? Is the glass unwilling, or is the voice a little too weak?"

Young and impetuous as I was, Oskar wanted to give a little sample of his still vibrant art then and there. I looked about me and focused on the large glass surface of the aquarium with its ornamental fish and aquatic plants, but Bebra spoke up before I could break out in song: "Hold on, my friend! We believe you. Let's not destroy anything, please, no floods, no dying fish."

Shamefaced, I apologized, particularly to Signora Roswitha, who had pulled out a miniature fan and was agitatedly stirring up a breeze.

"My mama died," I tried to explain. "She shouldn't have done that. I'm very upset with her. People always say that a mother sees all, feels all, forgives all. Mother's Day clichés. She saw me as a midget. She would have done away with me if she could. But she couldn't do away with me, since children, even midgets, are recorded and you can't just get rid of them. Then too, I was *her* midget, if she'd done away with me she would have done away with herself, and that would have stopped her. It's either me or the midget, she said to herself, then ended it all, ate nothing but fish, not even fresh fish, took leave of her lovers, and now that she's lying in Brentau they all say, all the lovers, all the customers at the store: The midget drummed her to her grave. She didn't want to go on living because of little Oskar, he killed her!"

I was exaggerating wildly, perhaps in hopes of impressing Signora Roswitha. After all, most people blamed Matzerath, and especially Jan Bronski, for Mama's death. Bebra saw right through me.

"You're exaggerating, my good friend. You're upset with your dead mama out of pure jealousy. You feel slighted because it wasn't you but those tiresome lovers who sent her to her grave. You're wicked and vain, as befits a genius."

Then, after a sigh and a sidelong glance at Signora Roswitha: "It's not easy to persevere in life when you're our size. To remain human without growing visibly, what a task, what a calling!"

Roswitha Raguna, the Neapolitan somnambulist with the smooth yet wrinkled skin, whose age I put at eighteen springtides and in the next breath admired as an old woman of eighty or perhaps ninety years, Signora Roswitha stroked Herr Bebra's elegant tailored suit, cut in the English style, then projected her cherry-black Mediterranean eyes at me, while her dark voice filled with the promise of fruit moved me, yet chilled me too: "*Carissimo,* Oskarnello! How I understand that pain! *Andiamo,* come with us: Milano, Parigi, Toledo, Guatemala!"

My head began to reel. I seized Raguna's ancient, childlike hand. The Mediterranean beat against my coast, olive trees whispered in my ear: "Roswitha will be your mama, Roswitha will understand. She, the great somnambulist, who sees through everyone, knows everyone, except herself, *mammamia,* except herself. *Dio!*"

Oddly enough, Raguna had barely begun to see through me and illuminate me with her somnambulistic gaze when she jerked her hand back in fright. Had my hungry fourteen-year-old heart terrified her? Had she grasped that Roswitha was still Roswitha to me, be she girl or old woman? She whispered in Neapolitan, trembled, crossed herself so often it seemed the terrors she read in me were endless, then disappeared without a word behind her fan.

Confused, I sought an explanation, asked to have a word with Bebra. But even Bebra, in spite of his direct descent from Prince Eugen, had lost his composure, stammered, till I finally understood: "Your genius, my young friend, the divine but certainly devilish nature of your genius, has confused my good Roswitha somewhat, and I too must confess that a certain wild abandon that erupts in you is foreign to me, though not entirely incomprehensible. But" — Bebra gathered himself — "regardless of the nature of your character, come with us, perform in Bebra's Miracle Show. With a little self-discipline and moderation you should be able to find an audience, even in the present political circumstances."

I understood at once. Bebra, who'd advised me always to be on the grandstands, not standing in front of them, had taken his place among the rank and file, even if he continued to perform in the circus. So he wasn't at all disappointed when I declined his offer with polite regret. And the Signora released an audible sigh of relief behind her fan and showed me her Mediterranean eyes once more.

We chatted for another hour or so, I asked the waiter to bring me an empty glass, sang a heart-shaped opening into it, sang a curving inscription with flourishes beneath, *From Oskar to Roswitha,* gave her the glass, which pleased her, Bebra paid, and added a large tip before we left.

They both accompanied me to the Sporthalle. I pointed with my drumstick toward the naked grandstand at the other end of the Maiwiese and — now I remember, it was in the spring of thirty-eight — told Master Bebra about my career as a drummer under grandstands.

Bebra gave an embarrassed smile, Raguna's face was stern. And while the Signora stood a few paces off to the side, Bebra whispered in my ear as he took his leave: "I've failed, my friend, how could I be your teacher now? Oh, the dirty politics."

Then he kissed me on the forehead, as he had years ago when I met him among the circus wagons, Lady Roswitha held out a hand like porcelain, and I bent politely, almost too smoothly for a fourteen-year-old, over the fingers of the somnambulist.

"We'll meet again, my son!" Herr Bebra winked. "Regardless of the times, people like us don't lose each other."

"Forgive your fathers!" the Signora admonished me. "Accustom yourself to your own existence, so that your heart may be at peace and Satan discomforted!"

I felt as if the Signora had baptized me a second time, but once again in vain. Satan, depart — but Satan did not depart. I looked after them sadly and with an empty heart, waved as they entered a taxi and disappeared within, for the Ford was built for grownups and looked empty, as if cruising for customers, as it roared away with my friends.

I tried to get Matzerath to take me to the Krone circus, but Matzerath could not be moved, he was devoting himself entirely to mourning my poor mama, whom he had never possessed entirely. But who had possessed Mama entirely? Not even Jan Bronski, if anyone me, Oskar, for Oskar suffered most from her absence, which upset his daily life, even called it into question. Mama had cheated me. I could expect nothing from my fathers. Master Bebra had found his own master in Goebbels, Minister of Propaganda. Gretchen Scheffler was spending all her time in Winter Aid work. Let no one go hungry, let no one be cold, that was the watchword. I turned to my drum and perfected my loneliness on its once white tin, now drummed thin. In the evenings Matzerath and I sat across from each other. He leafed through his cookbooks, I lamented on my instrument. Sometimes Matzerath wept and hid his head in the cookbooks. Jan Bronski's visits to the house were more and more infrequent. In light of the political situation, both men agreed caution was called for, you never knew which way the rabbit might jump or the wind might blow. Skat games with various third partners grew increasingly infrequent, and when they did take place it was late at night, in our living room, under the hanging lamp; all mention of politics was avoided. My grandmother Anna no longer seemed to find her way from Bissau to our place on Labesweg. She held a grudge against Matzerath, perhaps against me too; after all, I'd heard her say, "My Agnes died because she couldn't stand the drumming no more."

Even if I did cause my poor mama's death, I clung all the more tightly to my despised drum, for it didn't die as a mother does, you could buy a new one, have it repaired by old man Heilandt or Laubschad the clockmaker, it understood me, always gave the right answer, it stuck with me, and I stuck with it.

If the apartment grew too cramped for me back then, the streets too short or too long for my fourteen years, if by day there was no chance to play tempter at shop windows, and the temptation not strong enough when evening came to stand as a plausible tempter in darkened doorways, I would stomp up the four flights of stairs, beating out the time, counting one hundred sixteen steps, pause on each landing, and breathe in the smells that seeped through the five apartment doors on every floor, since the smells, like me, found the two-room flats too cramped.

At first I had occasional luck with Meyn, the trumpeter. Drunk, lying among the bedsheets hung out to dry in the attic, he could still blow his trumpet with amazing musical feeling and bring joy to my drum. In May of thirty-eight he gave up Machandel and told everyone, "I'm starting a new life!" He joined the Mounted SA to play in the band. In boots and leather-seated breeches, cold sober, I saw him taking the steps five at a time from then on. He kept his four cats, one of them named Bismarck, because, as you might expect, the Machandel gained the upper hand now and then and brought out his musical side.

I seldom knocked at the door of Laubschad the clockmaker, a silent man among a hundred noisy clocks. I couldn't stand the excessive wear and tear of time more than once a month.

Old man Heilandt still had his shed in the courtyard of the apartment house. He still hammered crooked nails straight. And there were rabbits, and rabbits from those rabbits, as in the old days. But the brats in the courtyard had changed. Now they wore uniforms and black ties, and were no longer brewing brick-dust soup. What grew there, towering above me, I scarcely knew by name. It was a new generation, while my generation had finished school and were now apprentices: Nuchi Eyke was at a barber's, Axel Mischke wanted to be a welder at Schichau, Susi Kater was training as a salesgirl in Sternfeld's department store and had a steady boyfriend. How things can change in three or four years. The old carpet rack was still there and the house rules still read, *Tuesdays and Fridays — carpet beating,* but the blows resounded only occasionally on those two weekdays, and with a hint of embarrassment: since Hitler had come to power there were more and more households with vacuum cleaners; the carpet racks grew lonely and served only the sparrows.

All that was left to me were the stairwell and the attic. Beneath the roof tiles I studied my trusty reading material, in the stairwell I knocked at the first door on the left on the second floor whenever I felt the need for human company. Mother Truczinski always answered. Ever since taking my hand at Brentau Cemetery and leading me to my poor mama's grave, she opened up whenever Oskar signaled on the door with his drumsticks.

"Don't drum so loud, little Oskar. Herbert's still sleeping, he had a rough night again and they had to bring him back in the car." Then she pulled me into the flat, poured me some barley coffee and milk, and added a stick of brown rock candy on a string to dip in it and lick. I drank, sucked away on the candy, and gave my drum a rest.

Mother Truczinski had a small round head, covered so transparently with thin ash-gray hair that her pink scalp showed through. The sparse strands all strove toward the farthest point at the back of her head where they formed a bun, which in spite of its modest size—it was smaller than a billiard ball—could be seen from all sides, no matter which direction she turned. Knitting needles held the bun together. Each morning Mother Truczinski rubbed her round cheeks with red paper from chicory packages till they seemed pasted on her face when she laughed. She glanced about like a mouse. Her four children were named Herbert, Guste, Fritz, and Maria.

Maria was my age, had just finished grade school, and lived as an apprentice housekeeper with a family of civil servants in Schidlitz. Fritz, who worked in the railroad-car factory, was seldom seen. He had two or three young women he danced with at The Racetrack in Ohra, who took turns making his bed. He kept rabbits, Vienna Blues, in the apartment-house courtyard, but Mother Truczinski had to feed them, since Fritz had his hands full with his girlfriends. Guste, a calm young woman around thirty, was a waitress at the Eden Hotel by the railroad station. Still unmarried, she lived on the top floor of the Eden, along with the rest of the staff of that first-class hotel. Herbert, the oldest and the only one living with his mother—if one leaves aside an occasional overnight visit from Fritz the mechanic—worked as a waiter in the waterfront suburb of Neufahrwasser. He's the one I want to tell you about. After the death of my poor mama, for a brief but happy period Herbert Truczinski was the goal toward which I strove: to this day I call him my friend.

Herbert worked as a waiter for Starbusch. That was the name of the host and owner of the Swedish Bar. It lay opposite the Protestant Seaman's Church, and the customers—as can be easily guessed from its name—were mostly Scandinavians. But a few Russians came too, Poles from the Free Port, dockers from Holm, and sailors from German warships that had dropped in for a visit. Being a waiter in this truly European bar was not without its dangers. Only the experience he'd gained at The Racetrack in Ohra—Herbert had worked as a waiter in the third-class dance bar before going to Fahrwasser — enabled him to rise commandingly above the bubbling confusion of tongues he encountered in the Swedish Bar with his suburban Plattdeutsch, interspersed with scraps of English and Polish. Even so, once or twice a month an ambulance would bring him home, against his will but free of charge.

Then Herbert would have to lie face down, breathing heavily, for he weighed well over two hundred pounds, and burden his bed for a few days. Mother Truczinski kept up a steady stream of complaints on such occasions while caring for him untiringly, removing a knitting needle from her bun each time she changed his bandages and tapping it on the glass of a picture opposite his bed, the retouched photograph of a solemnly staring man with a mustache who closely resembled some of the mustaches inhabiting the opening pages of my photo album.

The gentleman indicated by Mother Truczinski's knitting needle was not, however, a member of my family, it was the father of Herbert, Guste, Fritz, and Maria.

"You'll end up just like your father," she needled into the ear of the heavily breathing, groaning Herbert. Yet she never said clearly how and where the man in the black lacquered frame had met, or perhaps sought, his end.

"Who was it this time?" the gray-haired mouse asked above her folded arms.

"Swedes and Norskis, same as always." Herbert shifted his weight, and the bed creaked loudly.

"Same as always, same as always. Don't act like they're the only ones. Last time it was some lads from that there training ship, what's its name, come on, yes, from the *Schlageter,* just like I said, and you talk about Swedes and Norskis!"

Herbert's ear — I couldn't see his face — turned red all the way past its rim: "Damn Heinis, always shooting their mouths off and throwing their weight around!"

"Let them, those guys. What do you care? When they're on leave in town they always look decent enough. You told them your ideas about Lenin, didn't you, or started spouting off about the Spanish Civil War?"

Herbert made no further response, and Mother Truczinski shuffled back to the kitchen and her barley coffee.

The moment Herbert's back was healed, I was allowed to look at it.

He would sit on a kitchen chair, let his suspenders fall across his blue-clad thighs, and slowly, as if grave thoughts were giving him pause, strip off his woolen shirt.

His back was round, mobile. Muscles wandered tirelessly. A rosy landscape strewn with freckles. Below the shoulder blades fox-red hair grew rankly on either side of a spine embedded in fat. Downward it curled till it disappeared into the long underwear Herbert wore even in summer. Upward, covering his back from the top of his underwear to the muscles of his neck, interrupting the growth of hair, obliterating the freckles, puckering the skin into folds, ranging in color from blue-black to greenish white, itching at each change in the weather, ran thick, puffy scars. These scars I was allowed to touch.

What have I, lying here in bed, looking out the window, observing the outbuildings of the mental institution and the Oberrath Forest beyond for months on end without ever really seeing them, what to this very day have I been allowed to touch that was as hard, as sensitive, and as disconcerting as the scars on Herbert Truczinski's back? To wit: the parts of a few young girls and women, my own member, the plaster watering can of the boy Jesus, and that ring finger the dog brought me from the rye field barely two years ago, which a year ago I was still allowed to keep, in a glass jar to be sure where it couldn't be touched, yet so clear and complete that even now I can feel each joint of the finger and count them off by just taking my drumsticks in hand. Whenever I wished to recall the scars on Herbert Truczinski's back, I sat down and drummed with that canning jar and finger before me, drumming up memories. Whenever I traced a woman's body, which happened rarely enough, and Oskar was not sufficiently convinced by the scarlike parts of the woman, I would conjure up Herbert Truczinski's scars. But I could just as easily say: the first touch of those welts on the broad back of my friend already promised knowledge and even temporary possession of those transient indurations characteristic of women ready for love. The signs on Herbert's back likewise promised me at that early date the ring finger, and before Herbert's scars made their promises, it was the drumsticks that, from my third birthday on, promised me scars, reproductive organs, and finally the ring finger. Yet I must reach even further back: even as a fetus, before Oskar was even called Oskar, the game with my umbilical cord promised me in succession drumsticks, Herbert's scars, the occasionally erupting craters of younger and older women, finally the ring finger, and time and again, from the watering can of the boy Jesus on, my own sex, which I resolutely carry with me as a moody monument to my impotence and limited possibilities.

Today I return to my drumsticks. In any case it is only by way of the detour my drum provides that I recall scars, soft parts, and my own only occasionally functioning equipment. I will have to turn thirty to celebrate my third birthday a second time. I'm sure you've guessed by now: Oskar's goal is a return to the umbilical cord; that's the sole purpose of all this effort, why I've lingered over Herbert Truczinski's scars.

Before I go on to describe and interpret my friend's scars in greater detail, one preliminary remark: except for a bite wound on his left shin that a prostitute from Ohra left behind, there were no scars on the front of his powerful body, though it offered a target so large as to be nearly indefensible. They could only attack him from behind. They could only get at him from behind, his back alone was marked by Finnish and Polish knives, by the frog stickers of dockers from Speicherinsel, by the sailor's knives of cadets from the training ship.

When Herbert had finished his lunch—three times a week they had potato pancakes, which no one could bake so thin, so greaseless yet crispy, as Mother Truczinski—when Herbert shoved his plate aside, I handed him the *Neueste Nachrichten*. He dropped his suspenders, peeled off his shirt, and let me question his back while he read. Mother Truczinski usually sat with us at the table during these question sessions, unraveling old wool socks, offering remarks of approval or disapproval, and not omitting an occasional reference to the—one presumes—horrible death of her husband, who, photographed and retouched, hung behind glass on the wall across from Herbert's bed.

The questioning began when I would tap on a scar with my finger. At times I tapped with one of my drumsticks.

"Press on it again, boy. I don't know which one it is. It seems to be asleep today." Then I would press again, a little harder.

"Oh, that one. That was a Ukrainian. He got into a scrap with a guy from Gdingen. At first they were sitting at the same table like brothers. Then the guy from Gdingen calls the other one a Russki. The Ukrainian wasn't going to take that lying down, no way was he a Russki, anything but. He'd floated logs down the Vistula and a few rivers before that, and now he had a wad of money in his boot, with half a bootful already laid out buying rounds from Starbusch, when the guy from Gdingen says Russki, and I have to jump right in and push them apart, gently, the way I always do. So Herbert has his hands full, when the Ukrainian up and calls me a Water Polack, and the Polack, who spends his day hauling up muck on a dredger, adds something that sounds like Nazi. Well, Oskar, you know Herbert Truczinski: the one from the dredger, a pasty-faced guy, looks like a stoker, is soon lying in a heap by the cloakroom. And I'm just about to explain to the Ukrainian the difference between a Water Polack and a fine Danzig lad when he sticks me from behind—and that's the scar."

Whenever Herbert said "and that's the scar," he would turn a page of the newspaper to emphasize his words and take a gulp of his barley coffee before I was allowed to press the next scar, once or sometimes twice.

"Oh, that one! It don't amount to much. Two years or so ago it was, a whole fleet of torpedo boats from Pillau tied up here, swaggered about playing sailor boy in blue and the Danzig girls went crazy. How a skinny rag like that ever got into the navy is a mystery to me. And he was from Dresden, Oskar, can you believe it, from Dresden! You got no idea how odd that sounds, a sailor from Dresden."

Herbert's thoughts now lingered about in the beautiful city of Dresden on the Elbe, and to lure them back to their home in Neufahrwasser, I tapped again on that scar he thought didn't amount to much.

"Yeh, like I was saying. A signalman on the torpedo boat he was. Talked high and mighty, starts ribbing a quiet Scotsman with a tub in dry dock. Starts in with Chamberlain, umbrellas, and the like. I advise him gently, the way I always do, to stow that sort of talk, since the Scot can't cop a word anyway and was just drawing pictures on the tabletop with schnapps. And when I say, Drop it, boy, this ain't your home, this here's the League of Nations, the torpedo fritz calls me 'German booty,' in Saxon you understand—and I whack him a time or two, which quiets him down. A half-hour later, when I'm bending down to fish out a gulden that'd rolled under the table and can't see nothing, since it's dark under there, the Saxon hauls out his pik-pik and piks me quick!"

Herbert turned the page of the *Neueste Nachrichten* and laughed, then added, "And that's the scar," pushed the newspaper over to a grumbling Mother Truczinski, and prepared to rise. Quickly, before Herbert could head for the toilet — I could tell from his face where he was headed — while he was still pressing his hands on the edge of the table to rise, I tapped on a blackish violet stitched scar as broad as a skat card is tall.

"Herbert's got to go to the can, son. I'll tell you when I'm back." But I tapped again, stamped my feet, played the three-year-old; that always helped.

"All right, then. Just to keep you quiet. But I'm making it short." Herbert sat down again. "It was Christmas nineteen-thirty. Nothing going on at the harbor. Dockers hanging out on street corners seeing how far they could spit. After midnight mass — we'd just finished mixing the punch — the Swedes and the Finns come pouring out of the Seaman's Church across the way, all neatly combed and polished in their blues. I've already got a feeling they're up to no good, stand there in the doorway watching those real pious faces, thinking why are they fiddling around with their anchor buttons? And all of a sudden they're at it: long are the knives and short is the night. Well, Finns and Swedes have always had a thing about each other. But why Herbert Truczinski gets mixed up with them, the devil only knows. When something's up, the monkey bites him and Herbert's got to join in. I was out the door with Starbusch calling after me, 'Watch yourself, Herbert.' But Herbert's on a mission to save the pastor, a small young fella, fresh from the seminary at Malmö, who'd never spent a Christmas with Finns and Swedes in one church before, he's going to take him under his wing, get him home safe and sound, so I've barely got ahold of the churchman's sleeve when there's a nice clean blade in my back and I think 'Happy New Year,' though it's only Christmas Eve. When I come to, I'm lying on the bar at our place, with my beautiful blood filling the beer glasses free of charge, and Starbusch comes with his Red Cross kit and wants to give me so-called first aid."

"What'd you want to stick your nose in for?" Mother Truczinski said angrily, and pulled a knitting needle from her bun. "You don't never go to church. Never ever!"

Herbert waved her off, headed for the can, his suspenders dangling, his shirt trailing along behind him. He went angrily, added angrily, "And that's the scar!" and undertook the journey as if to distance himself once and for all from the church and all its knife fights, as if the can were the one place to sit where one is, becomes, or remains a freethinker.

A few weeks later I found Herbert wordless and in no mood for a question session. He appeared grief-stricken but didn't have the customary bandage on his back. Instead I found him lying quite normally on his back on the living room sofa. He wasn't lying in bed like a wounded man and yet he seemed severely wounded. I heard Herbert groan, cry out to God, Marx, and Engels, and curse them. Now and then he shook his fist in the air, then let it fall to his chest, joined in with the other fist, and hammered himself like a Catholic crying *mea culpa, mea maxima culpa.*

Herbert had killed a Latvian sea captain. The court had acquitted him — he'd acted, as so often in his profession, in self-defense. But the Latvian remained a dead Latvian in spite of the acquittal and weighed on the waiter like a ton of bricks, even though the captain was supposedly frail and delicate, with a bad stomach to boot.

Herbert stopped going to work. He'd quit his job. Starbusch, the owner, visited several times, sat by the sofa near Herbert or at the kitchen table with Mother Truczinski, pulled a bottle of Stobbes Machandel Double Null from his briefcase for Herbert, and a half-pound of unroasted real coffee from the Free Port for Mother Truczinski. He tried either to talk Herbert into coming back, or to talk Mother Truczinski into talking Herbert into coming back. But Herbert was now hardened, or softened — whichever way you see it — he no longer wished to be a waiter, and certainly not in Neufahrwasser, across from the Seaman's Church. He no longer wished to be a waiter at all; for waiters always get stabbed, and one fine day someone who's stabbed will strike a little Latvian captain dead, just because he's trying to make him keep his distance, because he's not about to let a Latvian knife add its Latvian scar to all the Finnish, Swedish, Polish, Free Port, and German scars that crisscross the plowed back of a Herbert Truczinski.

"I'd sooner go to work for customs than go back to waiting in Fahrwasser," said Herbert. But he didn't go to work for customs.

Niobe

IN NINETEEN THIRTY-EIGHT the customs duties were raised and the borders between Poland and the Free State temporarily closed. My grandmother could no longer take the narrow-gauge railway to the weekly market in Langfuhr and had to close down her stand. She was left sitting on her eggs, so to speak, but in no mood to brood. In the harbor the herring stank to high heaven, the goods piled up, and statesmen met and reached an agreement; it was only my friend Herbert who lay on the sofa, jobless and at odds with himself, brooding like a man with plenty to brood about.

Meanwhile the customs service offered bread and wages. It offered a green uniform and a green border worth guarding. Herbert didn't want to work for customs, had no wish to wait tables, he just wanted to lie on the sofa and brood.

But a man must work. Mother Truczinski wasn't the only one who thought so. Though she'd declined Starbusch's request to talk her son Herbert into going back to Fahrwasser as a waiter, she was all in favor of getting Herbert off the sofa. He too soon grew tired of the two-room flat, his brooding became purely pro forma, and he started reading through the Help Wanted ads in the *Neueste Nachrichten* and, reluctantly, the Nazi *Vorposten,* in search of some temporary dock job.

I wanted to help him. Other than a proper occupation in the harbor suburb, should a man like Herbert really have to go looking for makeshift ways to earn money? Part-time dock work, odd jobs, burying rotten herring? I couldn't imagine Herbert on the Mottlau bridges spitting at gulls, falling prey to chewing tobacco. It occurred to me that I could enter into a partnership with Herbert: two hours of concentrated work once a week, or even once a month, and we would have it made. Oskar, with his still diamond-hard voice, his wits sharpened by long experience in the field, would slice open shop windows with valuable displays and play lookout, while Herbert would, as they say, be light-fingered. We would need no blowtorches, skeleton keys, or tool kits. Nor any brass knuckles or shooting irons. Green Minna, as we called the Black Maria, and us — two worlds, and never the twain should meet. And Mercury, the god of thieves and trade, would bless us, since, born in the sign of Virgo, I possessed his seal, which I stamped now and then on solid objects.

It would be pointless to pass over this episode. I'll record it briefly, then, though I'm not making a confession: Herbert and I committed two relatively minor break-ins at delicatessens while he was unemployed, and one juicy burglary at a furrier's which netted us three blue foxes, a sealskin, a Persian lamb muff, and one pretty, but not terribly valuable, pony coat that my poor mama would surely have enjoyed wearing.

What caused us to give up our life of crime was not so much the misplaced yet oppressive sense of guilt we occasionally felt as it was the growing difficulty we had fencing the goods. To unload goods profitably, Herbert had to take them to Neufahrwasser, since that was where the only reliable middlemen hung out. But since the place was a constant reminder of the skinny Latvian sea captain with the bad stomach, he tried to move the goods anywhere else he could, on Schichaugasse, in Hakelwerk, in Bürgerwiesen, anywhere but Fahrwasser, where the furs would have sold like buttered hotcakes. Fencing our loot was thus such a long-drawn-out affair that the delicatessen items finally wound up in Mother Truczinski's kitchen, and Herbert even gave her the Persian lamb muff, or at least tried to.

When Mother Truczinski saw the muff, the fun was over. She'd accepted the food quietly enough, perhaps justifying it as sanctioned theft based on necessity. But the muff was a luxury and luxury meant irresponsibility and irresponsibility meant prison. Such was Mother Truczinski's simple, straightforward line of thought, she made mouse eyes, jerked a knitting needle from her bun, said with the knitting needle, "You're going to end up just like your father!" and shoved the *Neueste*

Nachrichten at Herbert, or the *Vorposten*, which was the same as saying: Now look for some honest work, and not any old odd job, or I'm done cooking for you.

Herbert lay for another week on his brooding sofa, was insufferable and unavailable for questioning about his scars or an assault on promising shop windows. I was very understanding with my friend, let him drain his sorrow to the dregs, hung around Laubschad the clockmaker and his time-devouring timepieces, tried Meyn the musician again, but he no longer touched schnapps, chased nothing but Mounted SA band tunes with his trumpet, gave off a well-groomed and energetic air, while his four cats, relics of a drunken but highly musical era, were so poorly fed that they were slowly going to the dogs. On the other hand I would often find Matzerath, who drank only socially while Mama was alive, sitting glassy-eyed behind a shot glass at some late hour. He would be leafing through the photo album, trying, as I do now, to bring Mama to life in the small, more or less properly exposed rectangles, cried himself elegiac around midnight, then spoke to Hitler or Beethoven, who still faced each other gloomily, addressing them with the familiar *du*, and seemed to be answered by the genius, though he was deaf, while the tee-totaling Führer said not a word, since Matzerath, a small-time drunken cell leader, was unworthy of Providence.

One Tuesday — my drum allows me to recall this precisely — things came to a head: Herbert spruced himself up, that is, he let Mother Truczinski brush his flared blue trousers with cold coffee, squeezed into his low shoes, stuffed himself into the jacket with anchor buttons, sprayed the white silk scarf he had from the Free Port with eau de cologne that had likewise mushroomed from the duty-free dung heap of the Free Port, and soon stood stiff and square beneath his blue peaked cap.

"I'm going to look round a bit for a job," said Herbert, tilting his Prince Heinrich Memorial Cap rakishly to the left, and Mother Truczinski let her newspaper sink.

The next day Herbert had a job and a uniform. Decked out in dark gray and not customs green, he was a guard at the Maritime Museum.

Like everything worth preserving in this city, itself so deserving of preservation, the treasures of the Maritime Museum filled an old patrician mansion that had its own historic air, having retained its imposing stone porch, a playfully yet richly ornamented façade, and an interior carved in dark oak and spiral-staircased. Here was displayed the carefully catalogued history of our seaport city, whose fame had always been based on growing and remaining filthy rich in the midst of several powerful but largely impoverished neighbors. Ah, those privileges purchased from Teutonic knights and Polish kings and invested in detail by charter! Those color engravings of the endless sieges of the fortress at the mouth of the Vistula! There stands the unhappy Stanisłaus Leszczyński, holed up within the city walls, fleeing his rival the Saxon anti-king. One can see in the painting just how frightened he is. The primate Potocki and the French ambassador de Monti are equally frightened, for the Russians under General Lascy are besieging the city. Everything is clearly labeled, even the names of the French ships sailing under the fleur-de-lis banner are legible. An arrow indicates: On this ship King Stanisłaus Leszczyński had to flee to Lorraine when the city was forced to surrender to the third Augustus. The majority of the items on display, however, were trophies from war victories, for lost wars seldom if ever provide a museum with trophies.

The pride of the collection was the figurehead from a large Florentine galleon, which, though its home port was Bruges, belonged to the Florentine merchants Portinari and Tani. The Danzig pirates and city captains Paul Beneke and Martin Bardewiek had managed to capture the galleon in April of fourteen seventy-three while tacking off the coast of Zeeland near the port city of Sluys. Soon after its capture, most of the crew, as well as the officers and captain, were put to the sword. The ship and its cargo were brought to Danzig. A folding triptych of the Last Judgment by the artist Memling and a golden baptismal font — both commissioned by the Florentine Tani for a church in Florence — were displayed in the Church of the Virgin Mary; the Last Judgment, so far as I know, brings pleasure to this day to the Catholic eye of Poland. What became of the figurehead after the war remains unclear. In my day it was kept in the Maritime Museum.

A voluptuous wooden woman, green and naked, her arms raised and languidly crossed, all fingers on view, gazed ahead with sunken amber eyes across breasts striving toward their goal. This woman, this figurehead, brought disaster. The merchant Portinari had commissioned it, modeled on a Flemish maiden he was close to, from a sculptor who'd made a name for himself carving figureheads. The carved green figure was barely mounted beneath the bowsprit of the galleon when the maiden, as was customary back then, was tried for witchcraft. Before she went up in flames, having been asked a few painful questions with regard to her patron, she accused the merchant from Florence as well as the sculptor who had measured her so carefully. It's said Portinari hanged himself, because he feared the fire. As for the sculptor, they chopped off both his gifted hands to prevent him from turning any more witches into figureheads. While the trials were still under way in Bruges and causing a stir, since Portinari was a rich man, the galleon with its figurehead fell into the piratical hands of Paul Beneke. Signore Tani, the second merchant, fell beneath a pirate's grappling iron, Paul Beneke was next: a few years later he fell out of favor with the patricians of his native city and was drowned in the courtyard of the Stockturm. Ships to whose bows the figurehead was affixed after Beneke's death burst into flames while still in the harbor shortly after she was in place, and spread fire to other ships; everything burned, except of course for the figurehead itself, it was fireproof and with its shapely curves always found new admirers among the ship owners. No sooner had this woman taken her accustomed place, however, than once peaceful crews broke out in mutiny behind her back and decimated each other. The failed expedition of the Danzig fleet against Denmark in the year fifteen twenty-two under the leadership of the highly talented Eberhard Ferber led to Ferber's downfall and bloody insurrection in the city. History speaks of religious conflicts — in twenty-three a Protestant pastor named Hegge led a mob in an iconoclastic assault on the city's seven parish churches — but we prefer to place the blame for this long-standing disaster on the figurehead: she graced the bow of Ferber's ship.

When, fifty years later, Stefan Báthory besieged the city in vain, Kaspar Jeschke, abbot of the cloister at Oliva, delivered penitential sermons in which he blamed the figurehead, the sinful woman. The king of the Poles, who had received her as a gift from the city, took her along to his field camp, and was badly advised by her. The extent to which the wooden lady influenced the Swedish campaign against the city and impelled the long incarceration of Dr. Ägidius Srach, who had conspired with the Swedes and had demanded that the green maiden, who'd meanwhile found her way back to the city, be burned, is unknown. A somewhat murky report maintains that a poet by the name of Opitz fled Silesia and sought refuge for a few years in the city, but died an early death because he hunted down the insidious carving in a storeroom and tried to sing verses to her.

Only toward the end of the eighteenth century, at the time of the various partitions of Poland, did the Prussians, who were forced to take the city by storm, issue a royal Prussian decree against the "wooden figure Niobe." For the first time she was mentioned by name in an official document, and evacuated to, or, more precisely, incarcerated in, that same Stockturm in the courtyard of which Paul Beneke was drowned and from the gallery of which I successfully tested my first long-distance song, so that, confronted by the most refined products of human imagination, instruments of torture, she would hold her peace for the whole of the nineteenth century.

When in nineteen thirty-two I climbed the Stockturm and ravaged the lobby windows of the Stadt-Theater with my voice, Niobe — popularly known as "the green maiden" — had, thank God, long since been removed from the tower's torture chamber. Otherwise who knows whether my assault on that neoclassical edifice would have succeeded.

It must have been some uninformed museum director from out of town who fetched Niobe from the torture chamber where she'd been held in check and installed her in the newly furnished Maritime Museum, shortly after the founding of the Free State. Soon thereafter the overzealous man died from a case of blood poisoning he'd brought on himself while putting up a sign saying that the lady displayed above it was a figurehead answering to the name of Niobe. His successor, a cautious man well acquainted with the city's history, wanted to move Niobe out again. His idea was to present the dangerous wooden maiden to the city of Lübeck, and it was only because the citizens of Lübeck refused the gift that, except for its brick churches, the little city on the Trave made it through the wartime air raids relatively unscathed.

So Niobe, or "the green maiden," remained in the Maritime Museum, and over a period of barely fourteen years of museum history caused the death of two directors — not the cautious one, he'd managed to get himself transferred — the expiration of an elderly priest at her feet, the violent end of a student from the engineering school and two seniors from St. Peter's Gymnasium who had just passed their final exams, and the demise of four reliable museum guards, most of them married.

They were all found, including the engineering student, with transfigured countenances and chests impaled by sharp instruments of the sort kept only in the Maritime Museum: sailor's knives, grapnel, harpoons, finely chiseled spear-tips from the Gold Coast, sailmakers' needles; and only the last of the gymnasium students had been forced to resort first to his pocketknife and then to his school compass, since shortly before his death all sharp objects in the museum had either been chained up or placed behind glass.

Although the detectives from the homicide squad described each death as a tragic case of suicide, a rumor ran through the city and the newspapers too: "The green maiden's doing it with her own hands." Niobe was seriously suspected of having dispatched men and boys to the other world. The discussions went back and forth, columns were set aside in newspapers for the free expression of opinions on the Niobe case; people termed them sinister events. The city administration spoke of outmoded superstition: they had no intention of taking any precipitate action till they had proof that something supernatural had really and truly occurred.

And so the green wooden figure remained the showpiece of the Maritime Museum, since the Regional Museum in Oliva, the City Museum on Fleischergasse, and the administration of the Artushof all refused to take in the man-crazy creature.

There was a shortage of museum guards. And they weren't the only ones who wanted nothing to do with the wooden virgin. Museum visitors also avoided the room with the amber-eyed woman. For a long time silence reigned behind the Renaissance windows that lent the necessary lateral light to the fully rounded sculpture. Dust piled up. The cleaning ladies no longer came to clean. The photographers who had once been so obtrusive, one of whom had died shortly after taking a photo of the figurehead — a natural death, but one that still raised eyebrows, given the connection — no longer furnished the press of the Free City, Poland, Germany, and even France with flash photos of the homicidal statue, but instead destroyed whatever portraits of Niobe they had in their archives and henceforth photographed only the arrival and departure of various presidents, heads of state, and exiled kings, living in the sign of whatever stood in the program of the day: poultry shows, National Party congresses, auto races, and spring floods.

And so things remained, till Herbert Truczinski, who no longer wanted to be a waiter and least of all to work for customs, donned the mouse-gray uniform of a museum guard and took his place on the leather chair by the door of the room popularly known as "the green maiden's parlor."

On his very first day at work, I followed Herbert to the tram stop on Max-Halbe-Platz. I was worried about him.

"Go home, little Oskar. I can't take you along." But I stood so steadfastly before my big friend with my drum and drumsticks that Herbert said, "Well, come along then as far as Hohes Tor. And then be a good boy and go home." At Hohes Tor I refused to get on the Number Five; Herbert took me along to Heilige-Geist-Gasse, tried to get rid of me again on the museum steps, sighed, and bought me a child's ticket at the desk. I was fourteen and should have paid full price, but that was no business of theirs.

We had a pleasant, quiet day. No visitors, no supervisors. Now and then I would drum for a half-hour or so, now and then Herbert slept for about an hour. Niobe gazed ahead with amber eyes and strove double-breasted toward some goal that was not our goal. We paid scant attention to her. "Not my type anyway." Herbert gestured dismissively. "Take a look at those rolls of fat and that double chin."

Herbert tilted his head and let his mind roam: "And those hips, like a barn door. Herbert's more for dainty little doll-like creatures."

I listened as Herbert described his type of woman at length and in detail, and watched his powerful shovel-hands knead and mold the contours of a graceful feminine figure that long remained, in fact remains to this day, even when camouflaged beneath a nurse's uniform, my ideal of womanhood.

By the third day of our museum sojourn we ventured forth from the chair by the door. Under the pretext of tidying the room, which really did look bad, we made our way, wiping things off, sweeping cobwebs and daddy longlegs from the oak paneling, turning the room in the literal sense into a true "green maiden's parlor," toward the light-flooded, shadow-casting, green wooden body. I can't say that Niobe left us entirely cold. She bore her ample but by no means shapeless beauty before her all too clearly. We didn't just enjoy this sight with the eyes of someone who wished to possess her. We cultivated instead the objective vision of connoisseurs making a detailed appraisal. Herbert and I, two cool-headed, soberly intoxicated aesthetes, took the measure of female proportions, our thumbs moving up and down, finding in the classic eight head-lengths a measure to which Niobe, with the exception of her too short thighs, conformed, while all that was broad about her, her pelvis, shoulders, and chest, demanded a standard more Dutch than Greek.

Herbert let his thumb fall: "She'd be too busy in bed for me. Herbert's had plenty of wrestling matches in Ohra and Fahrwasser. I don't need no woman for that." Herbert's fingers had been burned. "If she was just a handful, a delicate little thing you had to be careful with because of her size, Herbert wouldn't mind at all."

Of course if it came right down to it, we wouldn't have had anything against Niobe or her wrestler's body either. Herbert was well aware that the passivity or activity he sought from naked or half-clad women wasn't offered just by the slim and graceful or withheld by the shapely and voluptuous; there are gentle girls who can't lie still, and women who can take on five men at a time and, like some sleepy inland waterway, scarcely betray a current. We were intentionally oversimplifying, reducing everything to a pair of common denominators, deliberately insulting Niobe in a manner that became increasingly inexcusable. Herbert lifted me up in his arms so I could beat on the woman's breasts with my drumsticks till absurd little puffs of sawdust rose from her treated and thus untenanted but numerous wormholes. As I drummed, we stared into those amber stones that simulated eyes. Nothing twitched, twinkled, teared, or overflowed. Nothing narrowed to menacing eye slits discharging hatred. Both polished drops, more yellow than reddish, reflected, in convex distortion, the entire contents of the exhibition room and a portion of the sunlit windows. Amber is deceptive, we all know that. And we know about the treacherous ways of this resin product elevated to the rank of jewelry. Nevertheless, continuing in our obtuse masculine fashion to divide all things womanly into active and passive, we interpreted Niobe's apparent indifference in our own favor. We felt safe. Chuckling sardonically, Herbert pounded a nail into her kneecap: my knee smarted at every blow, but she never lifted an eyebrow. We engaged in all sorts of horseplay right under the eyes of the green, swelling wood: Herbert threw on the coat of an English admiral, armed himself with a spyglass, donned the admiral's matching hat. With a little red waistcoat and an allonge wig I turned myself into an admiral's page. We played Trafalgar, bombarded Copenhagen, scattered Napoleon's fleet at Abukir, rounded this and that cape, assumed historical poses, then contemporary ones, all this before a figurehead with the proportions of a Dutch witch, who, we felt, either approved of everything we did or paid no attention at all.

Today I know that all things are watching, that nothing goes unseen, that even wallpaper has a better memory than human beings. It's not God in his heaven who sees everything. A kitchen chair, a clothes hanger, a half-filled ashtray, or the wooden replica of a woman named Niobe can serve perfectly well as an unforgetting witness to our every deed.

For fourteen days or more we performed our duties at the Maritime Museum. Herbert gave me a drum as a present and brought home his weekly wages to Mother Truczinski for a second time with an added hazard bonus. One Tuesday, for the museum was closed on Mondays, the cashier refused to issue me a child's ticket, nor would he let me enter. Herbert wanted to know why. The cashier, grouchy but well-intentioned, told us that an official request had been submitted, and children were no longer let in. The boy's father had objected, he didn't mind if I stayed below at the cashier's desk, since as a businessman and widower he didn't have time to take care of me himself, but I was no longer allowed in the gallery, in the green maiden's parlor, because I was irresponsible.

Herbert was ready to give in, but I poked and prodded him, and he told the cashier that while all that was true, I was still his good-luck charm, his guardian angel, spoke of childish innocence that would protect him; in short, Herbert practically made friends with the cashier and managed to get me into the Marine Museum for what the cashier said was one last time.

And so, holding my big friend's hand, I mounted once more the ornate, always freshly oiled spiral staircase to the second floor, where Niobe lived. It was a peaceful morning and an even more peaceful afternoon. Herbert sat with half-closed eyes on the leather chair with the yellow studs. I crouched at his feet. My drum stayed voiceless. We blinked up at the cogs, the frigates, the corvettes, at the five-masters, the galleons and sloops, the coastal sailing vessels and clippers dangling from the coffered oak ceiling, awaiting a favorable wind. We mustered the model fleet, watched with them for a fresh breeze, dreaded the doldrums of the parlor, and all just to avoid gazing at Niobe in fear. What we would have given for the sound of a woodworm at work, for proof that the interior of the green wood was slowly but surely being penetrated and hollowed out, that Niobe was perishable. But no worm ticked. The conservator had wormproofed the wooden body and rendered it immortal. So we were left with the model fleet and the foolish hope for a fair wind, playing an eccentric game with our fear of Niobe, whom we shunned, strenuously ignored, and might well have forgotten had not the afternoon sun suddenly scored a direct hit on her left amber eye and set it ablaze.

And yet that inflammation should scarcely have surprised us. We knew those sunny afternoons on the second floor of the Maritime Museum, knew what hour had struck or would strike when the light fell from the cornice and boarded the cogs. The churches of Rechtstadt, Altstadt, Pfefferstadt did their bit too, striking the passing hours of dust-whirling sunlight and adding the sounds of historical bells to our collection of historical objects. Small wonder then if the sun itself seemed part of history, ripe for exhibition, suspiciously in league with Niobe's amber eyes.

On that afternoon, however, when we had neither the desire nor the courage for games or provocative nonsense, the blazing eye of the otherwise dull woodcarving struck us with redoubled force. Dejectedly we waited through the final half-hour that faced us. At five sharp the museum closed.

The next day Herbert took up his post alone. I accompanied him to the museum but didn't feel like waiting by the cashier, and instead found a place opposite the old patrician mansion. I sat with my drum on a granite ball, from the back of which a tail grew that grownups used as a banister. It goes without saying that the other side of the stairs was guarded by a similar ball with the same cast-iron tail. I drummed only occasionally, but then terribly loudly, protesting against the mostly female passersby, who seemed to enjoy pausing beside me, asking my name, and patting my beautiful, short but slightly curly hair with their sweaty hands. The morning passed. At the end of Heilige-Geist-Gasse the brick hen of St. Mary's, red-black and green-steepled, brooded beneath its fat, overgrown tower. Pigeons pushed one another repeatedly from gaps in the tower walls, settled nearby, talked all sorts of nonsense, and hadn't the faintest idea how long she would be brooding, what she was hatching, or whether, after all these centuries, brooding had not become an end in itself.

At noon Herbert came out onto the street. From his lunch box, which Mother Truczinski had stuffed so full that it could not be closed, he fished out a sandwich with dripping and finger-thick blood sausage and handed it to me. When he saw I didn't want it, he nodded mechanically to encourage me. In the end I ate it, and Herbert, who ate nothing, smoked a cigarette. Before the museum swallowed him up again, he disappeared into a pub on Brotbänkengasse for two or three Machandels. I watched his Adam's apple as he tipped the glasses. I didn't like the way he was tossing them down. Long after he'd mounted the museum's spiral staircase again and I was sitting once more on my granite ball, Oskar could still see the Adam's apple of his friend Herbert jerking.

The afternoon crept across the pale, polychromatic façade of the museum. It swung from curlicue to curlicue, rode nymphs and horns of plenty, devoured plump angels plucking flowers, ripened ripely painted grapes beyond their prime, burst into the midst of a country fête, played blindman's buff, swung in a swing of roses, ennobled burghers bargaining in baggy breeches, caught a stag the dogs were after, and reached at last that second-story window through which the sun, briefly yet forever, illuminated an amber eye.

Slowly I slid from my granite ball. My drum banged hard against the hammered stone. Lacquer from the white casing of the drum and a few flakes of lacquered flame sprang off and lay white and red on the stone steps of the porch.

I may have recited something, rattled off a prayer, run through a list: shortly thereafter the ambulance pulled up in front of the museum. Passersby flanked the entrance. Oskar managed to slip into the building with the emergency team. I made my way up the stairs more quickly than they did, though they must have known the museum's layout from earlier accidents.

I had to laugh when I saw Herbert. He was hanging from the front of Niobe, he had tried to mount the wooden statue. His head covered hers. His arms clung to her raised, crossed arms. He had no shirt on. It was later found neatly folded on the leather chair by the door. His back displayed all its scars. I read that script, counted the letters. Not one was missing. But not even the start of some new mark could be seen.

The emergency team who came rushing into the room not far behind me had a hard time dislodging Herbert from Niobe. In a frenzy of lust he had torn a short, double-edged ship's ax from its security chain, pounded one blade into Niobe's wood, then drove the other into his own flesh as he assaulted the woman. In spite of the perfect bond above, he had been unable, below, where his trousers gaped open, where he still thrust forth, stiff and at a loss, to find ground for his anchor.

As they spread a blanket bearing the words *Municipal Emergency Service* over Herbert, Oskar found his way back, as always when he'd lost something, to his drum. He was still beating on it with his fists as members of the museum staff led him out of the green maiden's parlor, down the stairs, and finally home in a police car.

Even now, in the institution, as he recalls this attempt at love between wood and flesh, he must work with his fists to wander once more through the labyrinth of scars on Herbert Truczinski's back, puffy, multicolored, hard and sensitive, foretelling all, anticipating all, surpassing all in hardness and sensitivity. Like a blind man he reads the script of that back.

Only now, when they have taken Herbert down from his loveless carving, does Bruno, my keeper, arrive with his desperate pear-shaped head. Gently he removes my fists from the drum, hangs the drum over the left bedpost at the foot of my metal bed, and smooths the blanket over me.

"Herr Matzerath," he admonishes me, "if you keep drumming so loudly, others are bound to hear that someone's drumming too loudly. Won't you stop for a while, or drum more quietly?"

Yes, Bruno, I will try to make the next chapter I dictate to my drum a quieter one, though its theme cries out for a roaring, ravenous orchestra.

Faith Hope Love

ONCE UPON A TIME there was a musician named Meyn, and he played the trumpet too beautifully for words. He lived on the fourth floor of an apartment house, just under the roof, kept four cats, one of them named Bismarck, and drank from morning till night from a bottle of Machandel gin. This he did till disaster struck and sobered him up.

Even today, Oskar doesn't truly believe in omens. Nevertheless, there were plenty of omens of a disaster that was donning larger and larger boots, taking longer and longer strides in those larger and larger boots, and had every intention of spreading. Then my friend Herbert Truczinski died from a chest wound inflicted by a wooden woman. The woman didn't die. She was put under seal and stored in the cellar of a museum, supposedly for restoration. But disaster can't be sealed in a cellar. It drains through the pipes with the sewage, it seeps into gas lines, invades every household, and no one who sets his kettle of soup on bluish flames suspects in the least that disaster is bringing his grub to a boil.

When Herbert was buried at Langfuhr Cemetery, I saw Crazy Leo again, whose acquaintance I'd made at Brentau Cemetery. To all of us — Mother Truczinski, Guste, Fritz, and Maria Truczinski, the stout Frau Kater, old Heilandt, who slaughtered Fritz's rabbits for Mother Truczinski on holidays, my presumptive father Matzerath, who, generous as he could be at times, was paying half the burial costs, and Jan Bronski, who scarcely knew Herbert and had only come to see Matzerath, and possibly me, on neutral burial ground — to all of us Crazy Leo, drooling and trembling, extended his white, mildewed glove, offering confused condolences in which joy and pain seemed indistinguishable.

As Crazy Leo's glove fluttered toward Meyn the musician, who had arrived half in civilian dress, half in SA uniform, there was a further sign of impending disaster.

Startled, the pale cloth of Leo's glove darted up and flew off across the tombs, pulling Leo with it. You could hear him screaming; but those weren't words of sympathy left hanging as scraps in the cemetery shrubbery.

No one moved away from Meyn the musician. Yet, recognized and singled out by Crazy Leo, he stood alone among the mourners, fiddling in embarrassment with his trumpet, which he'd brought along on purpose, and upon which he had just played too beautifully for words over Herbert's grave. Beautifully because Meyn had done something he hadn't done for a long time; moved by Herbert's death, who was about his own age, he had gone back to drinking Machandel, while that same death had silenced me and my drum.

Once upon a time there was a musician named Meyn, and he played the trumpet too beautifully for words. He lived on the fourth floor of our building, just under the roof, kept four cats, one of them named Bismarck, and drank from morning till night from a bottle of Machandel, until, toward the end of thirty-six or early in thirty-seven I believe, he joined the Mounted SA, and as a trumpeter in the band made far fewer mistakes, but no longer played too beautifully for words, because, having slipped on those leather-seated riding breeches, he gave up the Machandel bottle, and from then on his playing was merely loud and sober.

When the SA man Meyn lost his old friend Herbert Truczinski, who back in the twenties had been a fellow dues-paying member of a Communist youth group, and later joined the Red Falcons with him, when that friend was to be laid in the ground, Meyn reached for his trumpet and his Machandel bottle. For he wished to play too beautifully for words and not soberly, having kept his ear for music even while riding on a brown horse, and therefore took one last swig at the cemetery, then kept his civilian coat on over his uniform while he played his trumpet, though he'd planned to blow across the graveyard soil in brown, even if he couldn't wear his cap.

Once upon a time there was an SA man, who kept his coat on over his Mounted SA uniform while he played the trumpet with Machandel brilliance and too beautifully for words at the grave of an old friend. When Crazy Leo, a type found at all graveyards, extended his sympathy to each of the mourners, each mourner heard him in turn. Only the SA man could not grasp his white glove, for Leo saw what he was and with a loud cry of fear withdrew both sympathy and glove. The SA man headed home with no sympathy and a cold trumpet, where, in his flat just under the roof of our building, he found his four cats.

Once upon a time there was an SA man named Meyn. As a relic of the days when he drank Machandel all day and played the trumpet too beautifully for words, Meyn still kept four cats in his flat, one of them named Bismarck. When SA Man Meyn returned one day from the funeral of his old friend Herbert Truczinski, sad and sober again because someone had withheld his sympathy, he found himself alone with his four cats in the flat. The cats rubbed against his riding boots and Meyn gave them a newspaper full of herring heads, which got them away from his boots. The flat smelled more strongly than usual that day of cats, all of them toms, one of them named Bismarck, who padded about black on white paws. But Meyn had no Machandel in his flat. So the smell of cats, or tomcats, grew stronger and stronger. He might have bought some in our store if his flat hadn't been on the fourth floor right under the roof. But he dreaded the stairs and he dreaded his neighbors, having sworn before them on numerous occasions that not another drop of Machandel would ever cross his musician's lips, that he was starting a new life of total sobriety, that from now on he would lead an orderly existence far removed from the drunken excesses of a wasted and unstable youth.

Once upon a time there was a man named Meyn. One day when he found himself alone in his flat under the roof with his four tomcats, one of them named Bismarck, the tomcat smell was particularly annoying, because something unpleasant had happened to him that morning, and because there was no Machandel in the flat. Since his displeasure and thirst increased and the tomcat smell intensified, Meyn, a musician by trade and a member of the Mounted SA band, reached for the poker beside the cold slow-combustion stove and flailed away at the tomcats till it was safe to assume that all four, including the tomcat named Bismarck, were dead and done for, even if the smell of tomcats in the flat had lost none of its intensity.

Once upon a time there was a clockmaker named Laubschad, and he lived on the first floor of our building in a two-room flat with windows overlooking the courtyard. Laubschad the clockmaker was unmarried, a member of the National Socialist Welfare Organization and the SPCA. Laubschad had a good heart and helped all tired humans, sick animals, and broken clocks back on their feet. As the clockmaker sat musing at the window one afternoon, thinking back on a neighbor's funeral he'd attended that morning, he saw Meyn the musician, who lived on the fourth floor of the same building, lowering a half-full potato sack that seemed to be wet on the bottom and dripping, into one of the two garbage cans. But since the garbage can was three-fourths full, the musician had a hard time getting the lid back on.

Once upon a time there were four tomcats, one of them named Bismarck. These tomcats belonged to a musician named Meyn. Since the tomcats hadn't been fixed they had a strong and pungent smell, and one day, when for personal reasons he found the smell particularly annoying, the musician slew the four cats with a poker, put the cadavers in a potato sack, carried the sack down the four flights of stairs, and quickly deposited the bundle in a courtyard garbage can by the carpet rack, because the sack was leaky and already dripping by the time he reached the second floor. But since the can was fairly full, the musician had to compress the garbage along with the sack in order to put on the lid. No sooner had he exited onto the street from the building — for he had no desire to go back to a catless flat that still smelled of cats — than the compressed garbage began to expand, lifting the sack and with it the lid.

Once upon a time there was a musician who slew his four cats, stuffed them in a garbage can, left the building, and went to visit friends.

Once upon a time there was a clockmaker who sat lost in thought at his window and observed how Meyn the musician stuffed a half-full sack in the garbage can, then left the courtyard, and how, a few moments after Meyn's departure, the lid of the garbage can began to rise and kept on rising.

Once upon a time there were four cats who, because they smelled more strongly than usual on a particular day, were killed, stuffed in a sack, and buried in a garbage can. But the cats, one of them named Bismarck, weren't dead yet, being tough, like most cats. They shifted about in the sack, set the garbage-can lid in motion, and confronted

Laubschad the clockmaker, who still sat pensively at his window, with a question: Guess what's in the sack that Meyn the musician stuffed in the garbage can?

Once upon a time there was a clockmaker who couldn't look on quietly while something was stirring in the garbage can. So he left his flat on the first floor of the building, went into the courtyard, removed the lid from the garbage can, opened the sack, and took the four battered but still living cats to his flat to care for them. But they died the following night under the clockmaker's hands, which left him no recourse but to lodge a complaint with the SPCA, of which he was a member, and inform local Party headquarters of a case of cruelty to animals which might damage the Party's reputation.

Once upon a time there was an SA man who killed four cats, was betrayed by them, since they weren't quite dead, and was informed against by a clockmaker. This resulted in judicial proceedings, and the SA man had to pay a fine. The case was discussed in the SA as well, and the SA man was expelled from the SA for dishonorable conduct. Even the conspicuous bravery he demonstrated during the night of the ninth to the tenth of November thirty-eight, which later came to be known as Kristallnacht, when he joined others in torching the Langfuhr Synagogue on Michaelisweg, and his active participation the following morning in emptying several shops that had been carefully marked in advance, all his zeal could not prevent his expulsion from the Mounted SA. He was reduced in rank for inhuman cruelty to animals and struck from the membership list. A year passed before he gained admittance to the Home Guard, which was later incorporated into the Waffen-SS.

Once upon a time there was a grocer who closed his shop one November day because something was going on in the city, took his son Oskar by the hand and traveled with the Number Five tram to Langgasser Gate, because the synagogue there was on fire, as were those in Zoppot and Langfuhr. The synagogue was burned almost to the ground, and the firemen were making sure the fire didn't spread to the surrounding buildings. Outside the ruins, civilians and men in uniforms were piling up books, sacral objects, and strange pieces of cloth. The mound was set ablaze, and the grocer took the opportunity to warm his hands and his passions at the public fire. His son Oskar, however, seeing his father so involved and inflamed, slipped away unnoticed and hurried off toward the Arsenal Arcade, because he was worried about his drums of white and red lacquered tin.

Once upon a time there was a toy merchant named Sigismund Markus, and he sold, among other things, white and red lacquered tin drums. Oskar, mentioned above, was the major customer for these tin drums, for he was a drummer by trade, and could neither live without a drum nor wished to. He hurried away from the burning synagogue to the Arsenal Arcade, for there dwelt the keeper of his drums; but he found him in a state that made it impossible for him ever to sell tin drums again in this world.

The same ordnance specialists I, Oskar, thought I'd run away from had visited Markus before I got there, had dipped a brush in paint and written the words Jewish Swine across his shop window in Sütterlin script, then, perhaps displeased with their own handwriting, had kicked in the window with the heels of their boots, so that the slur they had cast on Markus could now only be guessed at. Disdaining the door, they had made their way into the shop through the window and were now playing in their own deliberate way with the toys.

I found them at play, as I too stepped into the shop through the window. A few had pulled down their trousers, had deposited brown sausages, in which half-digested peas could still be discerned, on sailing ships, fiddling monkeys, and my drums. They all looked like Meyn the musician, were wearing Meyn's SA uniform, but Meyn wasn't there, just as those who were there weren't somewhere else. One of them had drawn his dagger. He was slicing dolls open and seemed disappointed each time nothing but sawdust flowed forth from plump bodies and limbs.

I was worried about my drums. They didn't like my drums. My own drum couldn't stand up to their rage, had to keep quiet and bend at the knee. But Markus had escaped their rage. When they wished to speak with him in his office, they didn't bother to knock at the door but broke it down instead, although it wasn't locked.

Behind his desk sat the toy merchant. He was wearing sleeve protectors as usual over his dark gray everyday jacket. Dandruff on his shoulders revealed a scalp problem. A man with Punch and Judy dolls on his fingers poked him woodenly with Punch's grandmother, but Markus was no longer in, could no longer be harmed. Before him on the desktop stood a water glass that thirst must have urged him to empty at the very moment the splintering cry of a window in his shop turned his throat dry.

Once upon a time there was a tin-drummer named Oskar. When they took away his toy merchant and destroyed the merchant's shop, he sensed that bad times were ahead for midget tin-drummers like him. So as he left the shop he pulled one undamaged drum and two slightly damaged ones from the debris, and left the Arsenal Arcade for the Kohlenmarkt with the drums round his neck to look for his father, who might be looking for him. It was a late November morning. Outside the Stadt-Theater, near the tram stop, stood pious women and shivering, ugly girls handing out religious tracts, collecting money in tin cans, and displaying between two poles a banner with an inscription from First Corinthians, chapter thirteen. "Faith — Hope — Love" — Oskar read those three little words and played with them like a juggler with bottles: faith healer, hope chest, lovebird, Old Faithful, Hope Diamond, Lovers' Leap, with love as always, hope to see you again, faithfully yours. An entire gullible nation believed faithfully in Santa Claus. But Santa Claus was really the Gasman. In faith I believe it smelled of walnuts and almonds. But it smelled of gas. Soon it will be what's called first Advent. And the first and second through fourth Advent will be turned on like a gas cock, so that it smells believably of walnuts and almonds, so that all those nutcrackers can take comfort in belief:

He's coming! He's coming! And who came? The Christ Child, the Savior? Or was it the heavenly Gasman with the gas meter under his arm, ticking away? And he said: I am the Savior of this world, without me you can't cook. And he was open to reason, he offered special rates, turned on the freshly polished gas cocks and let the Holy Spirit pour forth, so that the dove could be cooked. And gave out walnuts and almonds in the shell, which were promptly cracked, and they too poured forth Spirit and gas, so that the gullible were easily gulled, saw all the gasmen in the increasingly thick and bluish air outside the department stores as Santa Clauses and Christ Children in all sizes and prices. And so they believed in the only true and saving Gas Company, which symbolized fate with its rising and falling gas meters, and staged an Advent season at standard prices, one many in fact believed would bring them the Christmas they expected, but only those for whom the store of walnuts and almonds was insufficient survived the holidays—though all had believed there was plenty for everyone.

But once belief in Santa Claus turned out to be faith in the Gasman, they tried love, abandoning the order of things in Corinthians: I love you, they said, oh, I love you. Do you love yourself too? Do you love me, tell me, do you really love me? I love myself too. And out of sheer love they called each other little radish, loved little radishes, bit into each other, one little radish biting off the other's little radish in love. And told one another stories of wonderful heavenly love among little radishes, and earthly love too, and whispered just before biting down, fresh, hungry, and sharp: Tell me, little radish, do you love me? I love myself too.

But after they had bitten off each other's little radishes out of love, and faith in the Gasman was proclaimed the state religion, after faith and pre-anticipated love, there remained only the third white elephant from the Epistle to the Corinthians: hope. And while they still had little radishes, walnuts, and almonds to nibble on, they hoped that it would soon end, so they could start anew or continue, after the final fanfare or even during the final fanfare, that the end would soon come. And still didn't know what it was that would end. Just hoped it would soon end, end tomorrow, but, they hoped, not today; for what would they do, how begin anew, if it ended so suddenly? And when the end came, they quickly turned it to a hopeful beginning; for in our country an end is always a beginning and there is always hope in any end, even the most definitive of ends. And so it is written: As long as man hopes, again and again he will begin anew with endings full of hope.

As for me, I just don't know. I don't know, for example, who hides behind Santa Claus beards today, don't know what Ruprecht his helper has in his sack, don't know how to wring the necks of gas cocks, nor how to choke them off, for Advent is flowing forth again, or flows forth still, and I don't know if it's some trial run, don't know for whom, don't know if I believe in all good faith that they are polishing those gas cocks, one hopes with love, so they will crow, on what morn or eve I do not know, nor if it matters what hour of day; for Love knows no hour, and Hope knows no end, and Faith knows no boundaries, but knowing and not knowing are bound by time and boundaries, and generally end before their time with beards, and sacks on back, and almonds that crack, so I say again: I just don't know, don't know, for example, what's in those sausage casings, whose guts they need to fill, don't know, though the price of fillings, coarse or fine, is clearly marked, what all's included in the price, don't know which dictionaries they filch the names of fillings from, don't know what fills those dictionaries, fills those casings, don't know what flesh, don't know what tongue: a word has a meaning, a butcher is silent, I cut slices off, you open books up, I read what I like, you don't know what you like: slices of sausage and quotes from those casings and books — and we'll never know who had to fall silent, to say not a word, so guts could be filled and books could be heard, stuffed tight, jam-packed, thickly written, and still I don't know, and yet I sense it darkly: the same butchers fill both dictionaries and guts with language and sausage, and there is no Paul, the man was called Saul, and Saul he remained and wrote as Saul to the people of Corinth in praise of those amazingly low-priced sausages he called Faith, Hope, and Love, so easy to digest, which, in the ever changing form of Saul, he palms off on mankind to this very day.

As for me, they took away my toy merchant, tried to banish all toys from the world along with him.

Once upon a time there was a musician named Meyn, and he played the trumpet too beautifully for words.

Once upon a time there was a toy merchant named Markus, and he sold white and red lacquered tin drums.

Once upon a time there was a musician named Meyn, and he had four cats, one of them named Bismarck.

Once upon a time there was a tin-drummer named Oskar, and he depended on the toy merchant.

Once upon a time there was a musician named Meyn, and he slew his four cats with a poker.

Once upon a time there was a clockmaker named Laubschad, and he belonged to the SPCA.

Once upon a time there was a tin-drummer named Oskar, and they took away his toy merchant.

Once upon a time there was a toy merchant named Markus, and he took along all the toys when he left this world.

Once upon a time there was a musician named Meyn, and if he's not dead, he's still alive today, playing his trumpet again, too beautifully for words.

Scrap Metal

VISITORS DAY: Maria brought me a new drum. She passed the drum over the bed rails and was about to hand me the receipt as well, but I waved it off and pressed the button at the head of my bed till Bruno, my keeper, arrived and did what he always does when Maria brings me a new tin drum wrapped in blue paper. He undid the string on the package, let the wrapping paper fall open, lifted out the drum with almost ceremonial solemnity, and carefully folded the paper. Only then did Bruno stride — and when I say stride, I mean stride — to the washbasin with the new drum, run hot water, and without scraping the white and red lacquer, carefully loosen the price tag from the frame.

When, after a brief and not overly tiring visit, Maria prepared to depart, she took along the old drum I'd battered to death during my description of Truczinski's back, the galleon's wooden figurehead, and my somewhat overly personal interpretation of the First Letter to the Corinthians, to store it in our cellar with all the other worn-out instruments that had served both my professional and private needs.

Before Maria left, she said, "The cellar's getting mighty crowded. Just where am I supposed to put the winter potatoes?"

Smiling, I ignored this complaint from the housewife in Maria and asked her to duly record the retired drum by numbering it in black ink and entering the data and concise details concerning its career, which I'd indicated on a slip of paper, in the log that's been hanging on the inside of the cellar door for some years now and which knows all about my drums from nineteen forty-nine on.

Maria nodded in resignation and kissed me goodbye. She still finds my sense of order incomprehensible and somewhat weird. Oskar can well understand Maria's reservations; indeed, he hardly knows himself why this odd pedantry has led him to collect worn-out tin drums. He doesn't want to lay eyes again on that pile of scrap metal in the potato cellar of the Bilk apartment for as long as he lives. He knows from experience that children scorn their fathers' collections, and that one day, when his son Kurt inherits all those unfortunate drums, he won't give a rap for or on them.

What drives me then, every three weeks, to issue instructions to Maria which, if regularly followed, will one day fill our cellar and leave no room for winter potatoes?

Not until several dozen drums had already been stored in the cellar did the idée fixe seize me that some museum might eventually find my disabled drums of interest, an idea that flares up less and less frequently these days. So that can't have been the source of my passion for collecting. Rather — and the more I think about it, the more likely this seems — the source of this passion for collecting has a simple psychological explanation: that there might be a shortage of tin drums someday, that they might become rare, be banned, fall prey to total destruction. That someday Oskar might find himself forced to have a few of the less damaged ones repaired by a tinsmith, so that with the aid of those patched-up veterans I might survive a drumless and terrible era.

The doctors at the mental institution say much the same thing about the source of my obsession, though they use different terms. Fräulein Dr. Hornstetter even wanted to know the exact date of the birth of my complex. I could tell her with some precision: it was the tenth of November in thirty-eight, for that was the day on which I lost Sigismund Markus, the custodian of my storehouse of drums. Even though it had been difficult to procure new drums in a timely fashion following my poor mama's death, which of necessity brought the Thursday visits to the Arsenal Arcade to an end, while Matzerath was slipshod at best about my drums and Jan Bronski came by our place less and less often, my situation became all the more hopeless when the toy merchant's shop was destroyed and the sight of Markus sitting at his bare desk made perfectly clear: Markus won't be giving you drums anymore, Markus no longer deals in toys, Markus has broken off all business relations with the firm that used to manufacture and deliver beautifully lacquered red and white tin drums to you.

Nevertheless I refused to believe back then that the toy merchant's end meant the end of my early, relatively cheerful era of drumming, and instead grabbed from the rubble that was now Markus's shop one unscathed drum and two whose rims were merely dented, carried this booty back home, and felt I'd made provisions for the future.

I treated these pieces with care, drummed only occasionally, as a last resort, denied myself entire drummer-boy afternoons and, quite reluctantly, the drummer-boy breakfasts that made my whole day bearable. Oskar practiced asceticism, lost weight, was taken to Dr. Hollatz and his increasingly bony assistant Sister Inge. They gave me sweet, sour, bitter, and tasteless medicine and declared my glands at fault, which in Dr. Hollatz's opinion were damaging my health by alternating between underactivity and overactivity.

To escape Dr. Hollatz, Oskar moderated his asceticism, started gaining weight again, and by the summer of thirty-nine was his former three-year-old self, having won back his chubby cheeks at the cost of the complete destruction of the last of Markus's drums. The tin gaped, flapped, shed white and red lacquer, rusted, and hung discordantly at my tummy.

There was no point in appealing to Matzerath for help, though he was helpful by nature, and even kindly. Since my poor mama's death the man thought of nothing but Party business, passed his time at Party meetings, or, toward midnight, after a good deal of alcohol, engaged in loud but intimate conversations with the black-framed portraits of Hitler and Beethoven in our living room, letting the Genius of Destiny and the Führer of Providence speak their minds, and in a sober state saw collecting for Winter Aid as his providential destiny.

I don't like to recall those collection Sundays. On one such day I made a futile attempt to obtain a new drum. Matzerath, who had collected money that morning outside the art cinema on Hauptstraße, and outside Sternfeld's department store, came home at noon and warmed up some Königsberg meatballs for himself and me. After the meal, which I still recall was a tasty one — even as a widower, Matzerath loved to cook and did so splendidly — the weary collector lay down upon the sofa to take a little nap. No sooner did his breathing suggest sleep than I grabbed the half-full collection box from the piano, disappeared under the shop counter with the thing, which was shaped like a tin can, and violated that most preposterous of all tin cans. Not that I wanted to enrich myself with those pennies. My absurd idea was to try the thing out as a drum. No matter how I struck it and plied the sticks, it always gave the same answer: Give a little something to Winter Aid. Let no one be hungry, let no one be cold. Give a little something to Winter Aid!

After half an hour I gave up, fished five pennies from the shop till, gave them to the relief fund, and returned the collection box thus enriched to the piano so Matzerath could find it and kill the rest of his Sunday rattling it for the cold and hungry.

This misguided attempt cured me forever. Never again did I make a serious effort to use a tin can, an overturned bucket, or a washtub bottom as a drum. And if I did, I try to forget those inglorious episodes, and have conceded them little or no space in these pages. A tin can is no tin drum, a bucket is a bucket, and a washtub is for washing yourself or your socks. Just as there's no substitute today, there was none back then; a tin drum with red and white flames speaks for itself and needs no spokesman.

Oskar was alone, betrayed and sold out. How could he preserve his three-year-old face over time when he lacked the most basic necessity, his drum? All the deceptions I'd attempted over the years — my occasional bed-wetting, the babbling of childish prayers each evening, my fear of Santa Claus, whose real name was Greff, the tireless repetition of typically droll three-year-old questions: why do cars have wheels? — all the rubbish grownups expected of me, I now had to handle without my drum, and so, nearly ready to give up, I sought in my despair the man who was not my father but who had most likely begotten me: Oskar waited near the Polish settlement on Ringstraße for Jan Bronski.

In spite of their beautiful shared memories, the relationship, verging at times on friendship, between Matzerath and my uncle, who had been promoted to post office clerk in the meantime, loosened and dissolved after my poor mama's death, not suddenly or all at once, but gradually and with finality as political conditions became increasingly critical. With the disintegration of my mama's slender soul and voluptuous body, the friendship of the two men, who had been mirrored in that soul and nourished by that flesh, also disintegrated, and lacking the nourishment and the convex mirror, the two were reduced to the companionship of their politically opposed groups, who had nothing in common but the brand of tobacco they smoked. However, the Polish Post Office and shirtsleeve Party meetings could not replace a beautiful woman who had been tenderhearted even in adultery. With appropriate caution — Matzerath had to consider his customers and the Party, Jan the postal administration — my two presumptive fathers met several times between the death of my poor mama and the end of Sigismund Markus.

Two or three times a month, around midnight, Jan's knuckles could be heard on the panes of our living room window. Matzerath would draw back the curtain and open the window a crack, leaving both men thoroughly embarrassed, till one or the other would break the ice and suggest a late-night game of skat. They would fetch Greff from his greengrocery, and if he declined because of Jan's presence, since as a former scoutmaster — he'd disbanded his troop in the meantime — he had to be careful, and was a poor player who didn't like skat all that much anyway, then it was mostly Alexander Scheffler, the baker, who sat in as third man. It's true the master baker didn't like sitting at the same table with my uncle Jan either, but a certain attachment to my poor mama, transferred like an heirloom to Matzerath, as well as Scheffler's maxim that retailers had to stick together, caused the short-legged baker to hurry over from Kleinhammerweg whenever Matzerath called, take his place at our living room table, shuffle the cards with his pale fingers dusted with worm-eaten flour, and deal them out like buns to the hungry multitude.

Since these forbidden games usually started after midnight and had to break off by three in the morning so Scheffler could get back to his bakery, it was only on rare occasions that I managed to slip from my little bed in my nightshirt, avoiding any sound, and reach the shaded corner under the table unseen and drumless.

As you will already have noted, I always indulged in the easiest of all observations under tables: I made comparisons. How things had changed since my poor mama died. No more Jan Bronski, cautious above, yet losing hand after hand, bold below, seeking conquests between my mama's thighs with his shoeless sock. There was no erotic play under the skat table in those years, and certainly no love. Six trouser legs displaying a variety of fishbone patterns covered six more or less hairy men's legs — naked or in long underwear according to preference, making a sixfold effort to avoid even the most casual contact—which extended and diversified above into torsos, heads, and arms deeply engaged in a game that should have been forbidden on political grounds, but which in every case, whether the game was won or lost, provided both justification and triumph: Poland has lost a grand hand; the Free City of Danzig has just won a sure-fire diamond single for the Greater German Reich.

The day could be foreseen on which these war games would come to an end—as all games must one day end—and on an expanded scale, in response to some so-called national emergency, turn into hard facts.

Early in the summer of thirty-nine it became clear that in the course of his weekly Party meetings Matzerath had found less compromising skat partners than Polish postal clerks and former scoutmasters. Jan Bronski was forced to recall what camp he was in, and stuck with the post office staff, the lame janitor Kobyella for instance, who, since his service in Marszałek Piłsudski's legendary legion, stood an inch or two short on one leg. In spite of his limp, Kobyella was an excellent janitor and thus also a skilled craftsman, who, I hoped, might eventually be kind enough to fix my ailing drum. So it was that every afternoon about six, even in the most oppressive August heat, simply because I could only reach Kobyella through him, I would stand near the Polish settlement waiting for Jan, who normally quit right on time and headed home. He didn't arrive. Without actually asking myself, what is your presumptive father doing after closing time?, I waited, as I often did, till seven or seven-thirty. But he didn't arrive. I could have gone to Aunt Hedwig. Jan might be ill, running a fever, or nursing a broken leg in a plaster cast. Oskar stayed where he was and made do with staring now and then at the window and curtains of the postal clerk's flat. A strange shyness kept Oskar from visiting his aunt, whose warm, motherly, bovine eyes saddened him. Nor did he particularly like the children the Bronski marriage had produced, who were his presumptive half brother and half sister. They treated him like a doll. They wanted to play with him, use him as a toy. Why did fifteen-year-old Stephan, who was almost the same age as Oskar, think he had the right to act like a father, always lecturing and talking down to him? And ten-year-old Marga with her pigtails and a face in which the moon was always rising fat and full: did she think Oskar was a spineless doll she could dress, comb, brush, pat into place, and instruct for hours on end? Of course they both saw me as an abnormal, pitiful midget and themselves as healthy, highly promising children who were indeed the darlings of my grandmother Koljaiczek, who, given the way I acted, found it hard to see in me a darling. I had no real interest in fairy tales and picture books. What I wanted from my grandmother, what I picture even today in broad and pleasurable brushstrokes, was quite clear-cut and thus rarely achieved: the moment Oskar saw her he wished, in eager emulation of his grandfather Koljaiczek, to dive beneath her and, if possible, never draw another breath outside her sheltered lee.

The tricks I tried to get under my grandmother's skirts! I can't say she disliked having Oskar sitting there. But she hesitated, refused me for the most part, might well have offered refuge to anyone halfway resembling Koljaiczek, but I, who had neither the build nor the ready matchstick of the arsonist, had to invent Trojan horses to enter the fortress.

Oskar sees himself as a real three-year-old playing with a rubber ball, notices that Oskar has accidentally allowed the ball to roll under her skirts, then follows the spherical pretext before his grandmother can see through the ruse and give the ball back. When grownups were around, my grandmother wouldn't tolerate me under her skirts for long. The grownups made fun of her, reminding her with a few often risqué phrases of her bridal day in the autumnal potato fields, till my grandmother, who was not naturally pale in any case, would blush loud and long, which didn't look bad on a sixty-year-old with nearly white hair.

But when my grandmother Anna was alone—which happened rarely, and I saw her less and less often after my poor mama's death, and scarcely at all once she was obliged to give up her booth at the weekly market in Langfuhr—she put up with having me under her potato-colored skirts more readily, more willingly, and for longer periods of time. I didn't even need my silly trick with that even sillier rubber ball to gain admittance. Scooting across the floorboards with my drum, doubling up one leg and pushing off with the other against the furniture, I shoved myself toward the grandmotherly mountain, and having reached its foot, lifted the fourfold garment with my drumsticks, moved quickly underneath, let the curtain fall fourfold, rested quietly for a moment, and, breathing in with all my pores, surrendered myself totally to the pungent smell of rancid butter, which, unaffected by the seasons, always reigned beneath those four skirts. Only then did Oskar begin to drum. He knew what his grandmother liked to hear, and so I drummed the sounds of October rain, similar to what she must have heard beside the potato-top fire as Koljaiczek ducked in beneath her with the smell of a hotly pursued arsonist. I let a fine, slanting rain fall on the drum till sighs and saints' names sounded above me, and now it's up to you to recognize those sighs and saints' names, last heard in ninety-nine, as my grandmother sat in the rain and Koljaiczek in the dry.

As I waited for Jan Bronski across from the Polish settlement in August of thirty-nine, I often thought of my grandmother. She might have been visiting Aunt Hedwig. Tempting as the thought of sitting beneath her skirts and breathing in the smell of rancid butter was, I still didn't climb the two flights of stairs or ring at the door with the nameplate: *Jan Bronski*. After all, what did Oskar have to offer his grandmother? His drum was battered, his drum had nothing to say, his drum had forgotten what rain sounds like as it falls fine and slanting on a potato field in October. And since his grandmother could only be swayed by a background of autumnal rainfall he stayed outside on Ringstraße, gazing at the streetcars as they approached and receded, jangling their way up and down Heeresanger, all serving the Number Five line.

Was I still waiting for Jan? Hadn't I already given up, wasn't I still standing at my station simply because I could think of no acceptable way to give up? A long wait can be educational. But it can also tempt one to imagine an encounter in such detail that it destroys any chance for a real surprise. Jan surprised me nonetheless. Motivated by the desire to spot him first while he was still unprepared, so I could drum at him on the remnant of my drum, I stood tensely at my station with my sticks at the ready. Without going into long explanations, I planned to make my hopeless situation clear by a loud hue and cry from my drum: five more streetcars, I told myself, three more, this last one, imagined my worst fears in vivid detail, that the Bronskis had been transferred to Modlin or Warsaw at Jan's request, saw him as head postal clerk in Bromberg or Thorn, waited, breaking all my previous oaths, for one last streetcar, and was already turning for home when Oskar was grabbed from behind, a grownup covered his eyes.

I felt soft, pleasingly dry male hands, smelling of expensive soap; I felt Jan Bronski.

As he released me, turned me toward him with a loud laugh, it was too late to demonstrate my desperation on my drum. So I stowed both drumsticks behind the linen suspenders of my knee-length trousers, which, since no one was looking after me at the time, were dirty and frayed at the pockets. My hands now free, I lifted high the drum hanging from a wretched string, high in accusation, high above eye level, high the way his highness Wiehnke lifts high the host at Mass, and could have added, This is My flesh and blood, but said not a word, just lifted high the flayed metal, sought no fundamental transubstantiation or miracle, asked nothing more than that my drum be repaired.

Jan immediately broke off his improper laughter, in which I'd detected nervousness. He saw my drum, which he could hardly miss, looked away from the crumpled tin, sought my blank eyes, still seemingly those of a true three-year-old, saw nothing in them at first but the same empty blue iris twice over, with highlights, reflections, all those things they claim make eyes expressive, then, having realized that my look was in no way different from that of any shiny puddle in the street, gathered all his goodwill, all his tangible memories, and forced himself to rediscover in my eyes those of my mama, admittedly gray but of a similar cast, which, after all, had reflected back everything from goodwill to passion for him over several years. But he may also have been bewildered by some semblance of himself, which still doesn't mean that Jan was my father, or, more precisely, my begetter. For his eyes, Mama's, and my own were all distinguished by the same naively shrewd, radiantly imprudent beauty found in almost all the Bronski faces, including Stephan's, to a lesser degree Marga Bronski's, but above all in those of my grandmother and her brother Vinzent. But for all my black lashes and blue eyes there was no denying a shot of Koljaiczek arsonist blood in me — just think of my glass-slaying song — while it would have been difficult to ascribe any Rhenish Matzerath traits to me at all.

The moment I lifted high the drum and let my eyes take effect, Jan himself, who gladly avoided such questions, would, if asked directly, have had to confess: his mother Agnes is looking at me. Or perhaps I'm looking at myself. His mother and I had far too much in common. Then again my uncle Koljaiczek might be looking at me, who's in America or at the bottom of the sea. Matzerath's the only one who's not looking at me, and that's just as well.

Jan took the drum from me, turned it about, tapped it. He, an impractical fellow who couldn't even sharpen a pencil properly, assumed the air of a man who knew something about repairing tin drums, obviously reached some decision, which he seldom did, took me by the hand — which surprised me, for I wasn't in all that big a hurry — crossed the Ringstraße with me, reached the streetcar island at Heeresanger still holding my hand, and as the Number Five tram arrived, pulled me with him into the trailer car where smoking was permitted.

As Oskar suspected, we were heading into the city, to Heveliusplatz, to the Polish Post Office and the janitor Kobyella, who had the tools and the skill Oskar's drum had been craving for weeks.

This tram ride might have turned into a peaceful pleasure jaunt had not the Number Five lead car and trailer jangled its way toward the city, filled from Max-Halbe-Platz on with tired yet noisy bathers from the seaside resort at Brösen, on the eve of the first of September nineteen thirty-nine. What a late-summer evening would have awaited us, drinking a soft drink through a straw in the Café Weitzke after delivering the drum, had not the battleships *Schlesien* and *Schleswig-Holstein* dropped anchor in the harbor mouth opposite Westerplatte and presented their steel hulls, revolving dual turrets, and casemate guns to the red brick wall with the ammunition depot lying beyond. How lovely it would have been to ring at the porter's lodge of the Polish Post Office and entrust an innocent toy drum to the janitor Kobyella for repair, had not the interior of the post office been fitted out for months with armored plates and transformed into a fortress garrison manned by previously innocent postal staff, officials, and mailmen, trained on weekends at Gdingen and Oxhöft.

We were approaching Oliva Gate. Jan Bronski was sweating, staring into the dusty foliage of the trees on Hindenburgallee and smoking more of his gold-tipped cigarettes than his natural thriftiness allowed. Oskar had never seen his presumptive father sweat so, except for the two or three times he had watched him on the sofa with his mama.

But my poor mama was long since dead. So why was Jan Bronski sweating? After noticing that almost every time we came to a tram stop he thought of getting off and then, recalling my presence just as he was about to descend, sat back down only because of me and my drum, I realized he was sweating over the Polish Post Office, which as a civil servant he was required to defend. He'd already fled it once, but then he found me and my scrap-metal drum on the corner of Ringstraße and Heeresanger, decided to return to his civil duty, and dragged me along, though I was neither a civil servant nor fit to defend a post office, and now he sat sweating and smoking. Why didn't he get off again? I certainly would not have stopped him. He was still in the prime of life, not yet forty-five. Blue were his eyes, brown his hair, well manicured his trembling hands, and had he not perspired so pitifully it would have been eau de cologne and not cold sweat that Oskar smelled as he sat beside his presumptive father.

At Holzmarkt we got off and walked down Altstädtischer Graben. A windless late-summer evening. As always toward eight o'clock, the bells of the Altstadt bronzed the sky. Chimes sent pigeons up in clouds: "Be true and upright to the grave." It was beautiful and made you want to cry. But all about was laughter. Women with sunburned children, terrycloth bathrobes, brightly colored beach balls and toy sailboats, descended from trams bearing freshly bathed multitudes from the seaside resorts of Glettkau and Heubude. Drowsy girls licked raspberry ice cream with lithe tongues. A fifteen-year-old dropped her cone, bent to retrieve it, then hesitated, abandoned the melting delicacy to the pavement and the soles of future passersby; soon she would be one of the grownups and no longer lick ice cream in the street.

We turned left into Schneidemühlengasse. Heveliusplatz, to which the little lane led, was blocked off by the SS Home Guard standing about in groups: youngsters, also older family men with armbands and police carbines. It would have been easy to make a detour around the blockade and reach the post office by way of Rähm. Jan Bronski went straight up to the Home Guard. His intention was clear: he wanted to be stopped before the eyes of his superiors, who were surely keeping watch on Heveliusplatz from the post office, and sent back, so that, a thwarted hero cutting a reasonably honorable figure, he could return home on the same Number Five tram that had brought him here.

The Home Guard let us through, probably never dreaming that this well-dressed gentleman with a three-year-old boy by the hand meant to enter the post office. They politely advised us to be careful and didn't yell stop till we'd passed through the iron gate and stood outside the main entrance. Jan turned around uncertainly. Then the heavy door opened slightly and we were pulled in: we stood in the pleasantly cool half-light of the main hall of the Polish Post Office.

Jan Bronski received a less than cordial greeting from his colleagues. They mistrusted him, had probably already given up on him, and stated openly their clear suspicion that he, Postal Clerk Bronski, meant to run away. Jan had a hard time fending off their accusations. They didn't even listen to him, just shoved him into a line of men who had taken on the task of passing sandbags from the cellar to the bank of windows in the main hall. These sandbags and similar nonsense were being stacked in front of the windows, while heavy pieces of furniture such as filing cabinets were being shoved near the main door so the entrance could be quickly barricaded across its entire width if necessary.

Someone asked who I was, but had no time to wait for Jan's answer. The men were nervous, calling out loudly, then whispering more cautiously than necessary. My drum and its predicament seemed forgotten. Kobyella the janitor, on whom I had pinned my hopes, who was supposed to restore the pile of scrap metal at my tummy to respectability, was nowhere in sight, and was probably working away on the first or second floor of the post office at the same feverish pitch as the mailmen and window clerks in the main hall, piling up overstuffed sandbags that were supposedly bulletproof. Jan Bronski was embarrassed by Oskar's presence. So I slipped away the moment a man the others called Dr. Michon started giving Jan instructions. After a brief search, and carefully dodging this Herr Michon, who was wearing a Polish steel helmet and was obviously the postmaster, I found the stairs to the first floor and there, almost at the end of the hallway, a medium-sized, windowless room where no one was carrying crates of ammunition or piling up sandbags.

Laundry baskets on wheels, filled with brightly stamped letters, stood crowded together on the wood floor. The room was low, the wallpaper ocher. There was a faint smell of rubber. A light bulb burned unprotected. Oskar was too tired to look for the switch. In the far distance the bells of St. Mary's, St. Catherine's, St. John's, St. Bridget's, St. Barbara's, Trinity, and Corpus Christi rang out their reminders: It's nine o'clock, Oskar, you must go to bed. And so I lay down in one of the mail baskets, bedded my drum, which was as exhausted as I was, by my side, and fell asleep.

The Polish Post Office

I SLEPT IN a laundry basket full of letters headed for Łódz, Lublin, Lwów, Torun, Krakow, and Częstochowa, coming from Lodz, Lublin, Lemberg, Thorn, Krakau, and Tschenstochau. But I dreamed neither of the Matka Boska Częstochowska nor of the Black Madonna, nibbled in dreams neither on Marszałek Piłsudski's heart preserved in Cracow nor on the gingerbread that has made the city of Thorn so famous. I didn't even dream of my still unrepaired drum. Lying dreamless on letters in a laundry basket on wheels, Oskar heard none of the whispers, murmurs, and small talk, none of those indiscretions they say can be heard when letters lie in a heap. To me those letters breathed not a word, I was expecting no mail, no one could see in me a recipient or even a sender. Imperiously I slept with retracted antennae on a mountain of mail that, brimming with news, might well have stood for the world.

So of course I wasn't awakened by the letter that a certain Pan Lech Milewczyk from Warsaw wrote to his niece in Danzig-Schidlitz, a letter alarming enough to awaken a millennial tortoise; I was awakened either by machine-gun fire close at hand or by the distant salvos from the twin turrets of the battleships in the Free Port.

It's so easily written: machine guns, twin turrets. Might it not have been a cloudburst, a hailstorm, the deployment of a late-summer thunderstorm like the one that accompanied my birth? I was too sleepy, such speculations were beyond me, and so, the sounds still fresh in my ear, like all sleepyheads I simply and aptly called a spade a spade: Now they are shooting!

Scarcely having climbed from the laundry basket, unsteady on his sandals, Oskar turned his attention to the well-being of his delicate drum. With both hands he dug into the basket that had sheltered his slumbers, scooped out a hole in the loosely piled yet interlocked letters, but was not brutal—he neither tore nor bent nor defaced them; no, I cautiously separated the jumbled mail, treated each letter, even the postcards, stamped *Poczta Polska* in violet for the most part, with care, made sure no envelope came open; for even in the face of inescapable, world-shaking events, the privacy of the post must always be maintained.

As the machine-gun fire increased, so the crater in that laundry basket full of letters deepened. Finally I let well enough alone, bedded my terminally ill drum down in the freshly dug site, and covered it not in three but in ten or twenty layers of overlapping envelopes, fitting them with care, as masons do bricks when they wish to build a solid wall.

No sooner had I completed these precautionary measures, with which I hoped to shield my drum from shrapnel and bullets, than the first antitank shell exploded against the post office façade facing Heveliusplatz, at about the level of the main hall.

The Polish Post Office, a massive brick building, could easily absorb a number of such hits with no fear that the Home Guard would make short work of things and quickly open a breach wide enough for the frontal assault they had practiced so often.

I left my safe, windowless mailroom, enclosed by three offices and the first-floor corridor, to go looking for Jan Bronski. While I was keeping an eye out for my presumptive father Jan, I was of course seeking, perhaps even more eagerly, the disabled janitor Kobyella. After all, I had given up my supper the evening before, taken the tram into the city to Heveliusplatz, and entered the post office, to which I was otherwise totally indifferent, solely in order to get my drum repaired. If I did not find the janitor in time, that is, before the all-out attack that was sure to come, a painstaking reinforcement of my rickety drum would be out of the question.

So Oskar looked for Jan with Kobyella in mind. He traversed the long, tiled corridor repeatedly, his arms folded across his chest, a solitary marcher. He could indeed differentiate the scattered rifle shots coming from the post office from the wasted barrage of the Home Guard, but the thrifty postal sharpshooters must have exchanged their rubber stamps for alternate means of leaving their mark, and stayed in their offices. In the corridor no squad of men stood by or lay in readiness to launch a possible counterattack. Oskar patrolled the hall alone, unarmed and drumless, exposed to the history-making introitus of Aurora at a far too early hour, adorned in lead instead of gold.

Nor did I find a single soul in the offices on the courtyard side. Very careless, I thought. The building should have been secured on the Schneidemühlengasse side as well. The police headquarters located there, separated from the post office courtyard and the parcel ramp by a bare wooden fence, offered a picture-perfect opportunity for an attack. I went through the offices, the registered parcel room, the money-order room, the payroll department, the telegraph office: there they lay. Behind armored plates and sandbags, behind overturned office furniture they lay, firing hesitantly, almost sparingly.

In most of the rooms a few windowpanes had already been introduced to the Home Guard's machine guns. I undertook a quick survey of the damage, making comparisons with the windows that had collapsed under the impact of my diamond voice in calm, deep-breathing times of peace. Well now, if I were asked to do my bit in defense of the Polish Post Office, if, say, that little wiry Dr. Michon were to approach me in his military rather than his postal capacity, to enlist me in the defense and service of Poland, my voice would not be found wanting: for Poland and Poland's economy, which grows wild but always bears fruit, I would gladly have smashed the panes of all the buildings across the way on Heveliusplatz, the glazing of all the buildings on Rähm, the glassy row along Schneidemühlengasse, including the police station, and, with greater long-distance effect than ever, the brightly polished windowpanes of Altstädtischer Graben and Rittergasse, reducing them all within minutes to black, drafty holes. That would have spread confusion among the Home Guard and the onlooking burghers. It would have replaced several high-caliber machine guns, it would have instilled a belief in miracle weapons right from the start of the war, but it would not have saved the Polish Post Office.

Oskar was not sent into action. This Dr. Michon with a Polish steel helmet on his postmaster's head did not enlist me, but instead, as I rushed down the stairs to the main hall and got tangled in his legs, gave me a painful box on the ear, then, cursing loudly in Polish, returned to his defensive duties. I could only submit to this blow. The men, and Dr.

Michon too, who bore the burden of responsibility, were agitated and frightened; they had to be forgiven.

The clock in the main hall told me it was twenty past four. At twenty-one past four I inferred that the initial hostilities had not damaged its works. It was running, and I didn't know whether to interpret this indifference on the part of Time as a good or bad omen.

In any case I stayed in the main hall for the time being, looked for Jan and Kobyella, kept out of Dr. Michon's way, found neither my uncle nor the janitor, noted the damaged glass in the hall, the cracks and ugly gaps in the plaster by the main entrance, and was privileged to witness the first two wounded men being carried in. One of them, an older gentleman with gray hair still neatly parted, spoke in a steady, agitated stream while they bandaged his upper right arm, which had been grazed by a bullet. No sooner had this slight wound been swathed in white than he was ready to jump up, grab his rifle, and throw himself once more behind the apparently not so bulletproof sandbags. Fortunately a slight dizziness brought on by substantial blood loss forced him back to the floor and prescribed the rest without which an elderly gentleman who's just been wounded is unlikely to recover his strength. Moreover, the energetic little fifty-year-old wearing a steel helmet, but from whose civilian breast pocket the triangle of a silk handkerchief peeked forth, this gentleman with the noble gestures of a knight in government service, this same Dr. Michon who had interrogated Jan Bronski so sternly the evening before, ordered the older wounded gentleman in the name of Poland to keep still and rest.

The second wounded man lay breathing heavily on a straw mattress and showed no further interest in sandbags. At regular intervals he screamed loudly and without shame, for he'd been shot in the gut.

Oskar was just about to inspect the row of men behind the sandbags again in hopes of finding those he sought, when two shells struck home almost simultaneously above and beside the main entrance, rattling the hall. The cabinets that had been shoved against the door burst open and released bundles of bound files that, having lost all decent control, fluttered loosely to the floor and touched and covered slips of paper whose acquaintance they had no right to make under any proper bookkeeping system. Needless to say, the rest of the window glass shattered, and larger and smaller patches of plaster fell from the walls and the ceiling. Yet another wounded man was lugged through clouds of chalk and plaster into the center of the room, but then, at the command of Dr. Michon's steel helmet, hauled up the stairs to the first floor.

Oskar followed the men bearing the postal clerk, who groaned at every step; no one called him back, asked where he was going, or felt it necessary, as Michon had a short time before, to box his ear with a rough manly hand. Of course he was careful not to run between the grownup post-office-defender legs.

When I reached the first floor behind the men trudging up the stairs, my suspicions were confirmed: they were taking the wounded man to the windowless and therefore safe mailroom I'd reserved for myself. And since there were no mattresses, they decided that the mail baskets, though rather too short, would provide soft padding for the wounded. I was already regretting having lodged my drum in one of those rolling laundry baskets full of undeliverable mail. Wouldn't the blood of these roughly opened and perforated mailmen and postal clerks seep through ten or twenty layers of paper and color my drum a hue it knew only as lacquer? What did my drum have in common with the blood of Poland! Let them dye their files and blotting paper with that sap! Let them dump the blue from their inkwells and refill them with red! Let them color half of every handkerchief and starched white shirt a good Polish red! After all, Poland was at stake, not my drum. If they insisted that Poland, if lost, be lost in red and white, must my drum, rendered suspect by its fresh coat, be lost as well?

Slowly the thought took root in me: this isn't about Poland, it's about my warped drum. Jan had lured me to the post office to give the clerks, for whom Poland was an insufficient rallying cry, a rousing battle standard. At night, while I slept in the rolling mail basket yet neither rolled nor dreamed, the clerks standing guard had whispered it like a password: A dying toy drum has sought refuge with us. We are Poles, we must protect it, especially since England and France are bound by treaty to defend us.

While useless and abstract speculations of this sort hampered my discretionary actions outside the half-open door to the mailroom, machine-gun fire could be heard for the first time in the courtyard. As I had predicted, the Home Guard was launching its initial attack from Police Headquarters on Schneidemühlengasse. Soon thereafter we were all knocked off our feet: the Home Guard had managed to blow in the door to the parcels area at the head of the loading ramp. A moment later they were in the parcel room, then in the parcel-post reception area, and the door to the corridor leading to the main hall stood open.

The men who had carried the wounded man upstairs and bedded him down in the mail basket that sheltered my drum rushed out; others followed. From the noise I gathered that they were fighting in the corridor on the ground floor, then in the parcel-post reception area. The Home Guard was forced to withdraw.

Hesitantly at first, then with more confidence, Oskar entered the dead-letter room. The wounded man's face was grayish yellow; he was baring his teeth and working his eyeballs behind his closed lids. He spat thread-trailing blood. But since his head was hanging over the edge of the mail basket, there was little danger that he would soil the letters. Oskar had to stand on tiptoe to reach inside the basket. The man's bottom bore down heavily on the exact spot where his drum was buried. Finally Oskar managed, gingerly at first, taking care not to hurt the wounded man or the letters, then pulling harder, in the end yanking and tearing them to pieces, to drag several dozen envelopes from under the groaning man.

Today let me say that I had just felt the rim of my drum when men came storming up the stairs and down the corridor. They were coming back, had driven the Home Guard from the parcel room, were at least momentarily the victors; I heard them laughing.

Hidden behind one of the mail baskets, I waited near the door till they were at the wounded man's side. At first shouting and gesticulating, then cursing softly, they bandaged him.

Two antitank shells struck home, level with the main hall — another two, then silence. The salvos of the battleships in the Free Port, across from the Westerplatte, rolled in the distance, grumbling on good-naturedly at a steady pace — you got used to it.

Unnoticed by the men with the wounded clerk, I slipped out of the dead-letter room, left my drum in the lurch, and resumed my search for Jan, my presumptive father and uncle, and for Kobyella the janitor.

On the second floor was the official residence of Postmaster General Naczelnik, who seemed to have sent his family off to Bromberg or Warsaw just in time. After searching through a few storerooms on the court-yard side, I found Jan and Kobyella in the nursery of Naczelnik's flat.

A bright, pleasant room with cheery wallpaper, which had unfortu-nately been wounded here and there by stray bullets. In more peaceful times one could have stood at the double windows enjoying the view onto Heveliusplatz. A rocking horse, as yet unwounded, a variety of balls, a medieval castle full of toppled tin soldiers, on foot and on horse-back, an open cardboard box full of railroad tracks and miniature box-cars, several dolls looking more or less the worse for wear, dollhouses in which disorder reigned—in short, a plethora of toys revealed that Post-master General Naczelnik must have been the father of two thoroughly spoiled children, a boy and a girl. How fortunate that the brats had been evacuated to Warsaw, that I was spared an encounter with a pair of sib-lings of the sort I already knew from the Bronskis. A gentle schaden-freude ran through me as I imagined how painful it must have been for the postmaster general's little rascal to bid farewell to his childhood par-adise full of tin soldiers. Perhaps he stuck a few uhlans in his pocket to reinforce the Polish cavalry later on at the battle for Modlin Fortress.

Oskar is talking too much about tin soldiers and still can't squeeze his way past a confession: on the top shelf of a rack for toys, picture books, and parlor games stood a row of toy musical instruments. A honey-yellow trumpet stood soundlessly beside a glockenspiel that was participating in the hostilities, that is, it chimed every time a shell struck. On the outer right a brightly painted accordion dangled crook-edly. The parents had even been crazy enough to give their offspring a real little violin with four real strings. Next to the violin, displaying its white, undamaged circle, held in place by a few building blocks so it wouldn't roll off, stood—you won't believe it—a red and white lac-quered tin drum.

I didn't even try to pull the drum down from the rack on my own. Oskar was well aware of his limited reach, and in cases where his gnome-like stature resulted in helplessness, took the liberty of soliciting favors from grownups.

Jan Bronski and Kobyella lay behind sandbags that blocked the lower third of the tall windows. Jan had taken the left window. Kobyella was on the right. I realized immediately that the janitor would have no time to retrieve and repair my drum, which lay beneath the wounded man who was spitting blood, and was undoubtedly being crushed flat, for Kobyella was fully occupied: he was firing his rifle at regular intervals through a gap in the sandbag wall across Heveliusplatz toward the corner of Schneidemühlengasse, where an antitank gun had taken up position just short of Radaune Bridge.

Jan lay cowering, hiding his head and trembling. I recognized him only by his elegant dark gray suit, now dusted with chalk and sand. The lace of his right shoe, gray as well, had come undone. I bent down and tied it in a bow for him. As I pulled the knot tight, Jan twitched, raised his far too blue eyes above his left sleeve and turned an incredibly blue and watery gaze upon me. Though not wounded, as Oskar ascertained with a quick inspection, he was weeping silently. Jan Bronski was frightened. I ignored his blubbering, pointed toward the tin drum of Naczelnik's evacuated son, and with crystal-clear gestures asked Jan to make his way, as carefully as possible, taking advantage of the dead corner of the nursery, to the rack and hand the drum down to me. My uncle didn't understand. My presumptive father didn't see what I was driving at. My poor mama's lover was so busy with his fear, so filled with it, that my pleading gestures had no effect but to increase that fear. Oskar wanted to scream at him but was worried he might be discovered by Kobyella, who seemed to be listening only to his rifle.

So I lay down with Jan behind the sandbags, pressed myself against him, trying to transfer some portion of my customary sang-froid to my unhappy uncle and presumptive father. Soon he seemed somewhat calmer.

My steady breathing helped to restore a degree of regularity to his pulse. When I then drew Jan's attention once again to Naczelnik junior's tin drum, all too soon of course, by trying to turn his head, slowly and gently but still insistently, in the direction of the wooden rack loaded with toys, Jan still didn't understand. Fear invaded him from head to toe, surged back from toe to head, encountered such strong resistance below, perhaps because of the inner soles, that it tried to vent itself, but was flung back, fleeing past stomach, spleen, and liver, occupying his poor head so that his blue eyes bulged and the whites disclosed intricate little veins that Oskar had never before had the opportunity to observe in the eyes of his presumptive father.

It cost me time and effort to drive my uncle's eyeballs back in place, to make his heart behave itself. All my diligence in the service of aesthetics was in vain, however, when the Home Guard employed their midrange field howitzers for the first time, and firing directly at the iron fence in front of the post office, sighting through a scope, laid it flat with admirable precision, revealing a high level of training, blasting away at the knees of one brick pillar after another until they were forced to kneel once and for all, dragging the iron fence with them. My poor uncle Jan felt the collapse of each of the fifteen to twenty pillars with heart and soul, and was so passionately stricken one would have thought those weren't just pedestals being reduced to dust, but that along with those pedestals, standing upon them, imaginary statues of gods were being cast down, gods my uncle knew intimately and without whom he could not live.

This alone can explain why each time a howitzer hit, Jan responded with a shrill scream that, had it only been shaped and aimed more consciously, would, like my glass-slaying scream, have had the glass-cutting virtue of a diamond. Jan screamed fervently but to no purpose, merely causing Kobyella to throw his bony, disabled janitor's body over toward us, lift his lean, lashless bird's head, and scan our mutual-aid society with watery gray pupils. He shook Jan. Jan whimpered. He unbuttoned his shirt, checked Jan's body hastily for wounds — I almost had to laugh — then, having failed to find the slightest scratch, turned him on his back, seized Jan's chin, jerked it around so hard that it cracked, forced Jan's blue Bronski eyes to endure the watery gray flare of Kobyella's predatory gaze, cursed him in Polish, spraying saliva in his face as he did so, then finally tossed him the rifle that Jan had so far left untouched at his own loophole; the safety hadn't even been released. The rifle butt struck Jan's left kneecap dully. The brief pain, the first physical pain he'd felt after so much mental torment, seemed to do him good, for he seized the rifle, took fright as he felt the cold gunmetal in his fingers and soon thereafter in his blood, but then, urged on by a cursing, coaxing Kobyella, crawled to his post.

For all the tender lushness of his imagination, my presumptive father had such a detailed and realistic concept of war that he found it difficult, even impossible, to be brave. Without surveying the field of fire or selecting a worthwhile target through his loophole, holding his rifle at an angle and at arm's length, he fired away blindly across the rooftops of the buildings on Heveliusplatz, quickly emptied his magazine, then crawled back empty-handed to hide behind the sandbags. The sheepish look Jan gave the janitor from his hiding place, imploring his forgiveness, seemed that of a sulky and embarrassed schoolboy admitting he hadn't done his homework. Kobyella worked his lower jaw several times, laughed loudly and seemingly uncontrollably, then broke off with frightening abruptness, kicked Jan Bronski, a postal clerk who was after all his superior, three or four times in the shins, drew back his bulky laced shoe to deliver a blow to Jan's ribs, but then, as machine-gun fire ticked off the remaining upper panes of the nursery one by one and roughed up the ceiling, lowered his orthopedic shoe, threw himself behind his rifle, and as if trying to make up for the time he'd wasted on Jan, started firing grouchily and hastily, shot after shot — all of which added to the ammunition consumed during the Second World War.

Hadn't the janitor noticed me? He, who was otherwise so severe and unapproachable, who demanded the sort of respectful distance only disabled war veterans can, allowed me to remain in this drafty den, where the air was so rich in iron. Did Kobyella say to himself: It's a nursery after all, so why shouldn't Oskar stay here and play during lulls in the battle?

I don't know how long we lay that way: I between Jan and the left wall of the room, both of us behind the sandbags, Kobyella behind his rifle, shooting for two. Around ten o'clock the firing died down. Things got so quiet I could hear flies buzzing, caught voices and commands coming from Heveliusplatz, and now and again lent an ear to the dull drone of the battleships at work in the harbor. A clear to partly cloudy September day, the sun coating everything in antique gold, paper-thin, sensitive, yet still hard of hearing. My fifteenth birthday was coming up in a few days. And as I did every year in September, I wanted a tin drum, nothing less than a tin drum; renouncing all the treasures of this world, my mind was set only and forever on a tin drum, lacquered red and white.

Jan didn't stir. Kobyella wheezed so evenly that Oskar assumed he was asleep, taking advantage of the short break in the action for a little nap, for don't all men, even heroes, need a refreshing little nap now and then? I alone was wide awake and focused on that drum with all the stubbornness of youth. It was hardly as if Naczelnik junior's tin drum had come to mind again just now, amid the growing stillness and dying buzz of a fly wearied by summer. Throughout the fighting, with the roar of battle about him, Oskar had never let it out of his sight. Now, however, an opportunity presented itself which my every thought urged me not to waste.

Oskar got up slowly and, avoiding the shattered glass, moved quietly but single-mindedly toward the wooden rack with the toys, mentally constructing a pedestal of boxes on a nursery chair, tall and stable enough to make him the owner of a brand-new tin drum, when Kobyella's voice and then the janitor's horny hand caught up with me. I pointed to the drum in despair. Kobyella pulled me back. I stretched both arms out toward the drum. The disabled man was already weakening, was about to stretch forth his hand and grant me happiness, when machine-gun fire entered the nursery and antitank shells exploded at the main entrance; Kobyella flung me into the corner with Jan Bronski, flung himself behind his gun, and loaded for a second time while my eyes remained fixed on the tin drum.

There lay Oskar, and Jan Bronski, my sweet blue-eyed uncle, didn't even lift his nose when the bird-head with the clubfoot and the watery eyes with no lashes brushed me aside just short of my goal and shoved me into the corner behind the sandbags. But Oskar didn't cry. Rage bred within me. Fat, bluish white, eyeless maggots multiplied, searching for a worthwhile corpse: What did Poland mean to me? Or the Poles, for that matter? They had their own cavalry. Let them mount up. They kissed the ladies' hands and always realized too late that those weren't the languid fingers of a lady but the unrouged muzzle of a field howitzer. By then she'd already vented her feelings, that virgin from the house of Krupp. She smacked her lips in a poor yet convincing imitation of the sounds of battle heard in weekly newsreels, peppered the main entrance of the post office with inedible exploding bonbons, tried to open a breach, opened a breach through the ruptured main hall and nibbled away at the staircase so no one could go up or down anymore. And her retinue behind the machine guns and in the elegant armored scout cars painted with pretty names like "Ostmark" and "Sudetenland" just couldn't get enough, rolled back and forth outside the post office, clattering, armored, scouting: two studious and cultured young ladies who wished to visit the castle, but the castle was still closed. Then the spoiled young beauties grew impatient, couldn't wait to get in, began casting lead-gray, penetrating glances, all of the same caliber, toward every chamber of the castle they could see into, making things hot, cold, and uncomfortable for the castle stewards.

One of the armored scout cars — I think it was the "Ostmark" — was just rolling toward the post office again from Rittergasse, when my uncle Jan, who'd been totally lifeless for some time, shoved his right leg up to the loophole and lifted it in hopes that the scout car might spot it and take a shot at it, or that some stray bullet would take pity on him and graze his calf or heel, providing the wound that lets a soldier retreat with an exaggerated limp.

This leg posture must have been hard for Jan Bronski to hold for very long. He was forced to abandon it from time to time. Not until he rolled onto his back did he find sufficient strength, propping his leg up with both hands at the knee, to offer calf and heel more steadily, and with more hope of success, to aimed or errant bullets.

No matter how deeply I sympathized with Jan, both then and today, I could well understand Kobyella's rage when he saw his superior, Postal Clerk Jan Bronski, in such a miserable and desperate posture. With one leap the janitor was on his feet, with the second beside us, over us, had grabbed hold, seized Jan's jacket and with the jacket Jan, raised the bundle up, smashed it down, grabbed it again, banged it down, hauled off with his left, held back with his right, hauled off with his right, then dropped his left, caught hold of his right with his left in flight, made one great fist of left and right, drew back for the one great blow that would lay my uncle Jan Bronski low, lay Oskar's presumptive father low — when something whirred, as angel wings may whir to honor God, something sang, as radios sing through the ether, but did not strike Jan Bronski, struck Kobyella instead, a shell had delivered a colossal joke and bricks now laughed themselves to chips, shards to dust, plaster to flour, wood found its ax, the whole droll nursery hopped on one leg, Käthe Kruse dolls split their sides, the rocking horse bolted and longed for a rider to throw, faulty structures arose from Märklin block boxes, Polish uhlans occupied all four corners of the room — and finally the toy rack toppled: the glockenspiel rang Easter in, the accordion cried out, the trumpet may have blown something or other, all sounded their keynotes at once, like an orchestra tuning up; screaming, splitting, neighing, ringing, smashing, bursting, gnashing, screeching, chirping on high yet unearthing our deepest foundations below. But finding myself, as befits a three-year-old, in the guardian-angel corner of the nursery right under the window when the shell struck, the drum, the drum made of tin fell to me — no holes at all and scarcely a crack, Oskar's new tin drum.

When I looked up from my newly won prize, which had rolled to my feet in the blink of an eye, I saw I'd have to help Jan Bronski. He was having trouble shifting the janitor's heavy body off him. At first I thought Jan had been hit too, for he was whimpering very realistically. When we finally managed to roll Kobyella, whose moans were equally realistic, to one side, Jan's bodily injuries proved negligible — splintered glass had scratched his right cheek and the back of one hand. A quick comparison allowed me to note that my presumptive father's blood was paler than the janitor's, whose trousers were stained at the thighs with a dark sap.

It was of course no longer clear who had ripped and twisted Jan's elegant gray jacket. Was it Kobyella or the shell? It hung in tatters from his shoulders, the lining had been loosened, the buttons freed, the seams split, and the pockets turned inside out.

I hope you'll excuse my poor Jan Bronski for scraping together everything that had been shaken from his pockets by that rough storm before dragging Kobyella out of the nursery with my help. He recovered his comb, the photos of his loved ones, including a half-length portrait of my poor mama; his coin purse hadn't even come open. The only difficulty he had, and one that was not without its dangers, since the protective sandbags had been partly swept away, was gathering up the skat cards scattered all over the room; he wanted all thirty-two of them, and was desperately unhappy when he couldn't find the thirty-second; when Oskar found it, found it between two devastated dollhouses, and handed it to him, he smiled, even though it was the lowly seven of spades.

After we'd dragged Kobyella from the nursery and finally got him into the corridor, the janitor found the strength to utter a few words that Jan Bronski managed to make out. "Is everything still there?" he asked with concern. Jan reached into the man's trousers, between his old man's legs, found a handful, and nodded to Kobyella.

We were all happy: Kobyella had kept his pride, Jan Bronski had found all thirty-two skat cards, including the seven of spades, and Oskar had a new drum that banged against his knee at every step while Jan and a man Jan called Viktor carried the janitor, weakened by loss of blood, down one floor and into the dead-letter room.

House of Cards

VIKTOR WELUHN HELPED us move the janitor, who, though steadily losing blood, grew heavier and heavier. Viktor, who was very nearsighted, still had his glasses at the time and didn't stumble on the stone steps. Strange as it sounds for someone as nearsighted as Viktor, he delivered money for the post office. Today, whenever Viktor's name comes up, I call him poor Viktor. Just as my mama became my poor mama after a family outing to the harbor jetty, Viktor, who delivered money orders, became poor Viktor when he lost his glasses—though other factors came into play as well.

"Have you ever run into poor Viktor again?" I always ask my friend Vittlar on Visitors Day. But since that streetcar ride from Flingern to Gerresheim—I'll speak of that later on—Viktor Weluhn has been lost to us. We can only hope that the bloodhounds who are after him are having an equally difficult time, that he's found his glasses or at least a suitable substitute and is now delivering money orders as before, if not for the Polish Post Office, then for the Federal Republic, nearsighted but bespectacled, blessing people with colored banknotes and hard coins.

"Isn't it awful?" panted Jan, who had grabbed Kobyella on his left.

"And what if the English and the French don't come?" said Viktor with concern, bearing the janitorial load on the right.

"They'll come all right. I heard Rydz-Śmigły just yesterday on the radio saying we have their pledge: if it kicks off, the whole of France will rise as one man." Jan had difficulty maintaining his conviction to the end of the sentence, for though the sight of his own blood on the back of his scratched hand did not in itself call the Polish-French treaty into question, it did raise the possibility that he might bleed to death before the whole of France rose up as one man and, true to their pledge, over-ran the Siegfried Line.

"I'm sure they're on their way right now. And the English fleet must be plowing through the Baltic this very minute!" Viktor Weluhn, who loved strong, ringing phrases, paused on the stairs with the wounded body of the janitor draped over his right shoulder, threw one hand in the air on the left as if he were on stage, and let all five fingers speak: "Come, you proud and mighty Britons!"

While the two men slowly bore Kobyella toward the emergency aid station, earnestly deliberating Polish-French-English relations, Oskar mentally leafed through Gretchen Scheffler's books for relevant passages. Keyser's *History of the City of Danzig*: "During the Franco-German War of eighteen-seventy, on the afternoon of the twenty-first of August, four French warships entered Danzig harbor, crossed the roads, and trained their guns on the harbor and the city; the following night, however, the propeller-driven corvette *Nymphe* under Lieutenant-Commander Weickmann forced the formation, which had anchored in the small inner bay at Putzig, to withdraw."

Shortly before we arrived at the dead-letter room on the first floor, I reached a troubling conclusion, which was later to be confirmed: while the Polish Post Office and the whole plain of Poland was under assault, the English home fleet lay more or less comfortably sheltered in some firth in northern Scotland; the grand army of France was still dawdling over lunch, confident that a few scouting patrols in the general vicinity of the Maginot Line had fulfilled the Franco-Polish mutual-defense treaty.

Outside the mailroom-cum-emergency-aid station we were intercepted by Dr. Michon, still wearing his steel helmet, the silk handkerchief peeking from his breast pocket, and a delegate from Warsaw, a man by the name of Konrad. Jan Bronski's fear was immediately activated across a broad spectrum, simulating the most serious of wounds. While Viktor Weluhn, who was not wounded, and equipped with his glasses should make a good marksman, was sent down to the main hall, we were given permission to enter the windowless room, dimly lit by tallow candles since the Municipal Power Plant of Danzig was no longer prepared to provide current to the Polish Post Office.

Dr. Michon, who had his doubts about Jan's wounds but no high opinion of Jan's military prowess in defense of the post office either, ordered his postal clerk to watch over the wounded men in a sort of quasimedical capacity, and — he patted me briefly, and with what I sensed was a touch of despair — urged him to keep an eye on me too, lest the child wander into the action.

The field howitzer scored a hit on the main hall below. We were tossed about like dice. Michon the steel helmet, Konrad the Warsaw delegate, and Weluhn the money-order man raced to their battle stations. Jan and I found ourselves with seven or eight wounded men inside the sealed-off room where the sounds of combat were muffled. The candles hardly flickered when the howitzer got down to business outside. It was quiet in spite of the moaning around us, or perhaps because of it. With awkward haste Jan wrapped strips of torn sheets around Kobyella's thighs, then started to tend to himself; but my uncle's cheek and the back of his hand had stopped bleeding. The cuts maintained a crusty silence, but they must have been painful enough to feed Jan's fear, which found no outlet in the stuffy, low-ceilinged room. Nervously he searched through his pockets and found the full deck. Then, till the final collapse of our defenses, we played skat.

Thirty-two cards were shuffled, cut, dealt, and played. Since all the mail baskets were already occupied by casualties, we propped Kobyella against a basket, and then, when he kept sliding down, bound him to it with another wounded man's suspenders, sat him up at attention, and forbade him to drop his cards, for we needed Kobyella. How could we have done without a third for skat? Those men in the mail baskets could hardly tell black from red and had lost all interest in games. In fact Kobyella didn't feel much like skat either. All he wanted was to lie down. Just leave it to chance, let things slide, that's what he wanted. To witness the final demolition work with his janitorial hands idle for once, as he closed his lashless lids. But we weren't about to put up with such fatalism, we bound him fast, forced him to play third, while Oskar played second — and no one was surprised at all that the toddler could play skat.

When I lent my voice to grownup speech for the first time and said "Eighteen!" Jan did, it's true, emerge from behind his cards and give me a brief and incredibly blue look, then nodded, to which I responded, "Twenty?" Jan didn't miss a beat: "Keep going." "Two!" I said, "And three?

Twenty-four?" Jan gave up: "Pass." And Kobyella? He'd nearly collapsed in spite of the suspenders. But we hoisted him back up and waited for the noise of a shell that had struck somewhere far from our card room to die away so Jan could hiss into the sudden stillness, "Twenty-four, Kobyella! Didn't you hear the boy's bid?"

I don't know from where or what depths the janitor surfaced. It looked as if he was raising his eyelids with a winch. At last his watery gaze strayed over the ten cards that Jan had discreetly pressed into his hand, taking care not to peek at them.

"Pass," said Kobyella. That is, we read it from his lips, which were too dry for speech.

I played a club single. Jan, who was playing contra, had to shout at the janitor and give him a sharp, good-natured poke in the ribs during the early tricks to get him to pull himself together and follow suit; first I drew all the trumps from the two of them, sacrificed my king of clubs, which Jan took with the jack of spades, but since I was void in diamonds I trumped Jan's ace of diamonds, regained the lead, and captured his ten with the jack of hearts — Kobyella discarded the nine of diamonds and there I sat with a run of hearts that was good: one-hand-two-contra-three-schneider-four-times-clubs-is-forty-eight-makes-twelve-pfennigs. It wasn't till the next hand — I risked a more than risky grand without two — when Kobyella, who had both jacks but stopped bidding at thirty-three, took my jack of diamonds with the jack of clubs, that the game began to liven up. The janitor, emboldened, it seemed, by having taken a trick, came back with the ace of diamonds, I had to follow suit, Jan snapped down the ten, Kobyella raked in the cards, pulled out his king, I should have trumped but didn't, discarded the eight of clubs instead, Jan threw on whatever points he could, even led a ten of spades, I trumped in, and damned if Kobyella didn't top it with his jack of spades, which I'd forgotten or thought Jan had, but it was Kobyella who over-trumped me and guffawed, came back with a spade, of course, I had to discard something, Jan threw on what points he could, and they finally led a heart to me, but it was far too late: I'd counted fifty-two in all the back and forth: without-two-one-hand-three-times-grand-minus-sixty-one-hundred-twenty-makes-thirty-pfennigs. Jan loaned me two gulden in change and I paid up, but in spite of having won the hand, Kobyella collapsed a second time, didn't take his money, and even the first antitank shell to strike the staircase, which landed just then, didn't mean a thing to the janitor, though it was his staircase, which he'd never tired of cleaning and polishing over the years.

Fear overcame Jan again, however, as the door to our mailroom rattled and the flames of the tallow candles had no idea what was happening to them or which way to head. Even when relative calm returned to the staircase and the next antitank shell exploded some distance away, against the façade, Jan Bronski shuffled as if he'd gone crazy and misdealt twice, but I let it pass. As long as they were firing outside, Jan was unreceptive to any comment, he was overwrought, failed to follow suit, even forgot to discard the skat, and constantly kept one of his small, well-formed, sensuously fleshy ears trained outside while we waited impatiently for him to play. Though Jan's attention to the game was rapidly losing focus, Kobyella, when he wasn't about to collapse and needed a poke in the ribs, was always in it. His play wasn't nearly as bad as the state he was in. He never collapsed till he'd won a hand or spoiled a grand for Jan or me. Winning or losing no longer mattered to him. He was playing for the game itself. And while we counted and re-counted the score, Kobyella the janitor hung there at an angle in his borrowed suspenders, giving no sign of life but the terrifying spasms of his Adam's apple.

This three-man skat game was putting a strain on Oskar too. Not that the sounds and concussions connected with the siege and defense of the Polish Post Office placed too great a burden on my nerves. It was this first sudden abandonment of all disguise, which I resolved was only temporary. Up till then I'd been my true unvarnished self only with Master Bebra and his somnambulistic Lady Roswitha, but now I laid myself bare to my uncle and presumptive father, as well as a disabled janitor — men who would never come into question as later witnesses — as the fifteen-year-old adolescent indicated on my birth certificate, playing skat somewhat recklessly but not without skill. This strain, which was not too much for my will but far too much for my gnomelike proportions, produced the severest of headaches and bodily pains after barely an hour of skat.

Oskar felt like giving up, and could easily have slipped away at some point, between two blasts that rattled the building in quick succession, say, had not a previously unknown feeling of responsibility told him to hold on and counter his presumptive father's fear by the only effective means available: a game of skat.

And so we played, and would not let Kobyella die. He just couldn't get around to it. I made sure the cards kept circulating. And when the tallow candles fell beneath the onslaught of an explosion in the stairwell and gave up their little flames, it was I who had the presence of mind to do the obvious thing and reach into Jan's pocket for his matches, pulling Jan's gold-tipped cigarettes out with them, I who restored light to the world, lit a calming Regatta for Jan, and set one little flame after another alight in the darkness before Kobyella could take advantage of that darkness to make his getaway.

Oskar stuck two candles on his new drum, placed the cigarettes close at hand, disdained tobacco himself, but kept passing them to Jan, hung one in Kobyella's crooked mouth, and things went better, the game got livelier, the tobacco comforted, calmed, but could not stop Jan Bronski from losing game after game. He sweated and, as always when deeply involved, tickled his upper lip with the tip of his tongue. He got so fired up that in his excitement he called me Alfred or Matzerath, thought Kobyella was my poor mama playing. And when someone out in the hall yelled, "They got Konrad!" he looked at me reproachfully and said, "Please, Alfred, turn that radio off. I can hardly hear myself think."

Jan really got annoyed when the door to the dead-letter room was torn open and Konrad, who was at the end of his rope, was dragged in.

"Shut the door, there's a draft!" he protested. There really was a draft. The candles flickered wildly and didn't calm down till the men, who had stuffed Konrad into a corner, closed the door behind them. The three of us appeared strangely romantic. The candles lit us from below, gave us the look of all-powerful magicians. And when Kobyella bid his heart without two, calling out, no, gurgling out twenty-seven, thirty, his eyes rolling out of sight, and something lodged in his right shoulder started pushing its way out, twitched, seemed crazily alive, quieted down at last, then tipped Kobyella forward, set the basket he was tied to rolling, the basket filled with letters and the suspenderless dead man, Jan brought Kobyella and the laundry basket to a standstill with one powerful blow, whereupon Kobyella, hindered once more from departing, finally piped up with "heart hand," Jan hissed "contra," and Kobyella forced out his "double contra," Oskar understood then and there that the defense of the Polish Post Office had succeeded, that those attacking had lost the war from the very start, even if they managed in the course of that war to occupy Alaska and Tibet, the Easter Islands and Jerusalem.

The only sad thing was that Jan, having declared schneider schwarz, was unable to play out his wonderful bulletproof grand hand with four.

He began with his club run, called me Agnes now, thought Kobyella was his rival Matzerath, played the jack of diamonds as innocent as could be — I preferred being Agnes for him to Matzerath, by the way — then the jack of hearts — under no circumstances did I wish to be confused with Matzerath — Jan waited impatiently for Matzerath, who in reality was an incapacitated janitor named Kobyella, to make his discard; that took some time, but then Jan slapped the ace of hearts down on the floor and simply couldn't understand, couldn't believe, could never understand, was always just a blue-eyed boy who smelled of cologne, never understood much of anything, couldn't understand why Kobyella suddenly dropped all his cards, tilted the laundry basket with the letters and the dead man at an angle, till first the dead man, then a layer of letters, and finally the entire carefully woven basket tipped over, delivering a flood of mail as if it were meant for us, as if the thing for us to do now was to shove our playing cards aside and start reading these epistles or collecting stamps. But Jan didn't want to read, didn't want to collect, had spent too much time collecting as a boy, he wanted to play, to play out his grand hand, wanted to win, did Jan, to triumph. And he lifted Kobyella up, set the basket back on its wheels, but left the dead man lying there, didn't shovel the letters back in, didn't put enough weight in the basket, and seemed surprised even so when Kobyella, hanging from the now unstable basket, showed no staying power, leaned farther and farther forward, till Jan yelled at him, "Alfred, please don't be a spoilsport. Just this one last hand and we'll go home."

Oskar rose wearily, overcame the increasing pain in his limbs and his head, laid his little, tough drummer-boy hands on Jan Bronski's shoulders, and forced himself to speak, softly but insistently: "Leave him alone, Papa. He's dead and can't go on. If you want we can play Sixty-six."

Jan, whom I'd just addressed as my father, released the janitor's bodily remains, stared at me with those blue eyes, the blue overflowing, and wept: Nonononono. . . . I stroked him, but he kept saying no.

I kissed him with meaning, but he couldn't get his mind off the grand hand he hadn't finished.

"I would have won it, Agnes. I'm sure I could have brought it home." Thus he lamented to me in my poor mama's stead, and I — his son — threw myself into the role, agreed with him, swore he would have won, that he'd already basically won, he just had to believe in it firmly and listen to his Agnes. But Jan believed neither me nor my mama, wept loudly at first in high lament, then fell into a soft, unmodulated babbling, scratched skat cards from beneath cold Mount Kobyella, mined between his legs, the letter landslide yielded a few, Jan didn't rest till he'd gathered up all thirty-two. Then he cleaned off the sticky sap that had seeped onto them from Kobyella's trousers, working hard on each card, shuffled, and started to deal again, when his finely shaped forehead, which was by no means low but somewhat too smooth and impenetrable, finally admitted the thought that there was no third skat man left in this world.

A deep silence fell over the dead-letter room. Outside as well, an extended minute of silence was devoted to the last skat player and third man. It seemed to Oskar that someone had quietly opened the door. And looking over his shoulder, expecting some sort of supernatural apparition, he saw Viktor Weluhn's strangely blind and empty face. "I've lost my glasses, Jan. Are you still here? We've got to run for it. The French aren't coming, or they'll be too late. Come with me, Jan. Show me the way, I've lost my glasses."

Perhaps poor Viktor thought he was in the wrong room. For when he received neither answer nor glasses nor Jan's flight-ready arm, he withdrew his unspectacled face and shut the door, and I listened for a few more steps as Viktor, feeling his way forward through the fog, set out in flight.

Who knows what comical incident transpired in Jan's small head to make him break into laughter, softly at first, still amid tears, then loudly and joyfully, to let his tongue play, pink, poised for tender caresses, to throw the deck of skat cards high and catch them, and finally, since a windless Sunday-like calm fell over the room holding the silent men and letters, he began, with careful, well-balanced movements and bated breath, to construct an extremely delicate house of cards: the seven of spades and the queen of clubs provided the base. Both were topped by the king of diamonds. Then he built a second base beside the first from the nine of hearts and the ace of spades, topped by the eight of clubs. Then he connected both bases with tens and jacks set upright, with queens and aces laid crosswise, so that all parts supported the whole. Then he decided to place a third story upon the second, and did so with spellbinding hands my mother must have known from similar rituals. And when the queen of hearts leaned against the king with the heart of red, the edifice did not collapse; no, airily it stood, sensitive, breathing softly in that room full of breathless dead and living beings with bated breath, and permitted us to fold our hands, allowed even a skeptical Oskar, who saw through a house of cards and what held it up as well as anyone, to forget the acrid smoke and stink that crept sinuously and sparingly through the cracks of the mailroom door, making it seem that the little chamber with the house of cards stood door to door with Hell.

They'd brought in flamethrowers and, shying away from a frontal assault, had decided to smoke out the remaining defenders. This had moved Dr. Michon to take off his steel helmet, seize a bedsheet, and when that didn't seem enough, pull out his silk handkerchief, wave them both, and offer the surrender of the Polish Post Office.

And out they came, some thirty scorched, half-blind men with arms raised and hands crossed behind their necks, from the left side entrance to the post office, then stood by the courtyard wall, waiting for the slowly advancing Home Guard. It was said later that during the brief interval before the attack force arrived, while the defenders were still standing in the courtyard, three or four escaped by way of the post office garage, passing through the adjoining police garage into houses on Rähm that had been evacuated and were hence unoccupied. There they'd found clothes, complete with Party badges, had washed, tidied themselves up, and slipped away one by one; and one of them, it's said, visited an optician's shop on Altstädtischer Graben and got fitted with a pair of glasses, having lost his own during the battle at the post office. Newly bespectacled, Viktor Weluhn, for it was he, even had a beer, and then another, for the flamethrowers had made him thirsty, and then, with his new glasses, which indeed lightened the fog he gazed into, but by no means lifted it as his old glasses had done, set out on a flight that continues to this day, so persistent have been his pursuers.

But the others—and as I say, there were around thirty who decided not to run—were already standing by the wall opposite the side entrance when Jan leaned the queen of hearts against the king of hearts and withdrew his hands in happiness.

What more can I say? They found us. They yanked the door open, screamed "Rausss!," stirred up the air, created a breeze, brought down the house of cards. They didn't have the nerve for that kind of architecture. They swore by concrete. They built for eternity. They paid no attention to Postal Clerk Bronski's indignant, offended face. And as they dragged him out, they didn't notice that Jan had reached in among the cards and taken something with him, or that I, Oskar, wiped the candle stubs from my newly won drum and took the drum along, disdaining the candle stubs since far too many flashlights were trained upon us; they didn't see that their miserable lamps blinded us, so that we could barely find the door. They screamed behind torchlamps and raised carbines, "Rausss!" They kept screaming "Rausss!" when Jan and I had already reached the hall. Their "Rausss!" was meant for Kobyella and Konrad from Warsaw, for Bobek and little Wischnewski, who, when he lived, sat at the telegram window. Their refusal to obey frightened the men. I laughed so loud when they kept shouting "Rausss!" that the Home Guard finally realized they were making themselves ridiculous, stopped shouting, said "Ach, so," and took us to join the thirty men in the courtyard with raised arms and hands crossed behind their necks, who were thirsty and were being filmed for the weekly newsreels.

We'd just been led out the side entrance when the newsreel crew swung the camera they'd mounted on a car toward us and shot that short film which was later shown in all the movie houses.

I was separated from the cluster standing by the wall. Recalling his gnomelike stature, knowing that no one would hold a three-year-old responsible for anything, beset once more by pains in my limbs and head, Oskar fell to the ground with his drum, thrashing about in a seizure he half felt and half faked, but throughout which he clung to his drum. And as they picked him up and stuck him in an official SS Home Guard car, Oskar could see, as the car carried him off to the municipal hospital, Jan, poor Jan, smiling foolishly and happily to himself, holding a few skat cards in his upraised hands and waving one in his left — I think it was the queen of hearts — toward Oskar, his departing son.

He Lies in Saspe

I'VE JUST READ through my last paragraph again. Even if I'm not satisfied, Oskar's pen has every right to be, for in its succinct summary it has managed, as succinctly summarizing treatises often do, to embellish now and then, if not to lie.

But I'd like to stick to the truth, stab Oskar's pen in the back, and report, first of all, that Jan's last hand, which alas he was unable to play out to the end and win, was not a grand but a diamond without two; second, that before leaving the mailroom, Oskar picked up not only his new tin instrument but also his old broken one, which had fallen from the laundry basket that held the dead man without suspenders and the letters. To which must be added: no sooner had Jan and I left the mailroom, as ordered by the Home Guard with their "Rausss!" and their flashlights and carbines, than Oskar, seeking protection, inserted himself between two avuncular and seemingly good-natured members of the Home Guard, put on a show of pathetic weeping, and pointed at Jan, his father, with accusatory gestures, transforming the poor man into a villain who had dragged an innocent child to the Polish Post Office in typically barbaric Polish fashion to use as a human shield.

Oskar hoped this Judas performance would produce certain benefits vis-à-vis his intact drum and his damaged one, and he was right: the Home Guard kicked Jan in the small of the back, struck him with their rifle butts, but left me both drums, and one of the men, a somewhat older member of the Home Guard with the careworn creases of a paterfamilias alongside his nose and mouth, patted my cheek, while another towheaded fellow with eyes that were always laughing and therefore narrowed to slits and permanently invisible, lifted me up in his arms, which embarrassed Oskar greatly.

Today, since I'm occasionally ashamed of my disgraceful behavior, I like to tell myself that Jan didn't notice, that he was preoccupied with his cards and remained so to the end, that nothing, neither the funniest nor the most fiendish notion of the Home Guard, could lure him from those skat cards. Jan had already entered the eternal realm of card houses, dwelt happily in one of those houses that trust in good fortune, whereas the Home Guard and I — for Oskar counted himself among the Home Guard — stood amid brick walls, on tiled corridor floors, under roofs with stucco cornices, with walls and partitions so tightly interlocked that one could only expect the worst on that day when, in response to some set of circumstances or other, all this patchwork we call architecture would come unglued.

Of course this belated insight hardly excuses me, especially since the mere sight of scaffolding turns my thoughts toward demolition, and a belief in card houses as the only dwellings worthy of humankind was not at all foreign to me. To which must be added the incriminating family factor. I was firmly convinced that afternoon that Jan Bronski was not only my uncle but also my actual and not merely presumptive father. Which put him ahead of Matzerath for good: for Matzerath was either my father or nothing at all.

The first of September nineteen thirty-nine — and I assume that you too, on that less than blissful afternoon, recognized the blissful Jan Bronski who played with cards as my father — that day marks the assumption of my second great burden of guilt.

I can never silence that inner voice, be it ever so plaintive: It was my drum, no, it was I myself, Oskar the drummer, who sent first my poor mama, then Jan Bronski, my uncle and father, to the grave.

Yet on days when a rude feeling of guilt simply refuses to leave the room and presses me back into the cushions of my hospital bed, I tend, like everyone else, to make allowances for my ignorance, an ignorance that was just then coming into fashion and, like a jaunty hat, still looks oh so good on many a person today.

Oskar, sly and ignorant, an innocent victim of Polish atrocities, was transported to the municipal hospital running a fever and suffering from inflammation of the nerves. Matzerath was notified. He'd reported me missing the previous evening, though it was still unclear whether I was his to miss.

The thirty men with upraised arms and hands crossed behind their necks, plus Jan, having been filmed for the newsreels, were taken first to Victoria School, which had been evacuated, then received at Schießstange Prison, and finally, in early October, by the porous sand behind the wall of the rundown abandoned cemetery at Saspe.

How does Oskar know this? I heard it from Crazy Leo. For of course there was no official announcement as to the sort of sand the thirty-one men had been shot on, or against what wall, or in what sand the thirty-one had been buried.

Hedwig Bronski first received an eviction notice for the flat on Ringstraße, which was taken over by the family of a high-ranking officer in the Luftwaffe. While Stephan was helping her pack and prepare for the move to Ramkau—where she owned a few acres of farmland and forest, along with the tenant's cottage—the widow received notification of something that her eyes, reflecting but not grasping the pain of this world, deciphered only slowly, with the help of her son Stephan, something that rendered her a widow in black and white.

It read as follows:

Department of Justice
Staff Headquarters
Eberhardt Subsection 41/39
Zoppot, 6 Oct. 1939

Frau Hedwig Bronski,
You are hereby informed that Bronski, Jan, has been found guilty of irregular military activity by military tribunal, sentenced to death, and executed.

Zelewski
(Inspector of Courts-Martial)

As you see, not a word about Saspe. Out of solicitude for the family members, wishing to spare them the expense of caring for such a large and flower-devouring mass grave, the authorities took full responsibility for its maintenance and any future relocation by leveling out Saspe's sandy soil and gathering up all the empty shells but one—for one is always left behind — since empty shells lying about spoil the looks of any decent cemetery, even an abandoned one.

But the empty shell that's always left behind, the one that counts, was found by Crazy Leo, from whom no burial, be it ever so secret, could remain hidden. He, who knew me from my poor mama's funeral and that of my scar-crossed friend Herbert Truczinski, and who surely knew where they had buried Sigismund Markus — though I never asked him that — was elated and nearly overwhelmed by joy that late November — I'd been released from the hospital — when he passed the telltale shell to me.

But before I take you and the already slightly oxidized housing that may have harbored the very kernel of lead meant for Jan to Saspe Cemetery, following Crazy Leo, I must ask you to compare the metal bed in the children's ward of Danzig Municipal Hospital with the one in this mental institution. Both enameled in white yet different. The bed in the children's ward was shorter with respect to length, but higher if we measure the rails with a ruler. Though I prefer the shorter but higher cage of nineteen thirty-nine, I've found the modest peace I now seek in my compromise grownup's bed, and leave it to the institution's administration to accept or deny the request I submitted some months ago for higher bed rails, likewise metal and enameled.

Though I'm nearly defenseless now against my visitors, in the children's ward a towering fence separated me on Visitors Day from Visitor Matzerath, Visiting Couples Greff and Scheffler, and toward the end of my hospital stay my bars divided that mountain in four rotating skirts named after my grandmother Anna Koljaiczek into worried, heavily breathing sections. She came, sighed, lifted those large hands with so many wrinkles, disclosing her pink cracked palms, then let both hands and palms fall despondently to her thighs with a slap whose sound I can still hear today, though I can only begin to approximate it on my drum.

On her very first visit she brought along her brother Vinzent Bronski, who clutched the bed rails and spoke, or sang, or spoke as he sang, softly but insistently and without pause, about the Virgin Mary, Queen of Poland. Oskar was glad to have one of the nurses nearby. For my visitors accused me. Turned their unclouded Bronski eyes upon me, expected me, struggling as I was to recover from the nervous fever I'd acquired during the skat game in the Polish Post Office, to provide a commentary, condolences, an exculpatory report on Jan's final hours of life, filled with fear and cards. They wanted to hear a confession that would exonerate Jan—as if I could exonerate him, as if my testimony would carry any weight.

What would my affidavit to the Eberhardt Subsection have said: I, Oskar Matzerath, hereby declare that on the eve of the first of September I lay in wait for Jan Bronski, who was returning home, and on the pretext of a drum in need of repair, lured him into the Polish Post Office, which he'd just left because he did not wish to defend it.

Oskar didn't submit this testimony, did not exonerate his presumptive father, but on the contrary fell into such powerful convulsions the moment he started to bear witness that at the request of the head nurse his visiting hours were curtailed and further visits from his grandmother Anna and his presumptive grandfather Vinzent were forbidden.

As the two old folk—they'd walked all the way from Bissau, and had brought apples for me—left the children's ward, helplessly, moving with exaggerated caution, as country folk do, my guilt, my most grievous guilt, grew in direct proportion to the increasing distance from my grandmother's four swaying skirts and her brother's black Sunday suit, smelling of cow dung.

So many things happened at once. While Matzerath, the Greffs, and the Schefflers crowded round my bed with fruit and cake, while Grandmother and Vinzent arrived on foot from Bissau by way of Goldkrug and Brentau because the railway line from Karthaus to Langfuhr had not yet been cleared, while nurses, white and anesthetic, babbled hospital gossip and stood in for angels in the children's ward, Poland was not yet lost, then nearly lost, then finally, after those famous eighteen days, Poland was lost, though it soon turned out that Poland was not yet lost, just as today, in spite of Silesian and East Prussian Societies, Poland is not yet lost.

O insane cavalry!—picking blueberries on horseback. With wimpled lances, red and white. Squadrons of melancholy and tradition. Picturebook charges. Over the fields of Łódz and Kuno. Modlin, freeing the fortress. Galloping so brilliantly. Always awaiting the setting sun. Only then does the cavalry attack, when both foreground and background are splendid, for battle is so picturesque, and Death the artist's model, one leg engaged and one leg free, then plunging, nibbling blueberries, rose-hips tumble and burst, release the itch that spurs the cavalry to charge. Uhlans, itching again, wheel their horses about where shocks of straw are standing — this too a striking image — and gather round a man called Don Quixote in Spain, but this one's name is Pan Kichot, a pureblood Pole of sad and noble mien, who's taught his uhlans how to kiss a lady's hand on horseback, so now they always kiss the hand of Death as if he were a lady, but gather first with sunset at their backs — for atmosphere and mood are their reserves — the German tanks before them, stallions from the stud farms of Krupp von Bohlen and Halbach, nobler steeds there never were. But that half-Spanish, half-Polish knight so in love with death — brilliant Pan Kichot, too brilliant — lowers his red-white wimpled lance, bids you all to kiss the lady's hand, cries out so that the evening glows, red-white storks clatter on the rooftops, cherries spit out their pits, and he cries to the cavalry, "Ye noble Poles on horseback, those are not tanks of steel, they are windmills or sheep. I bid you all to kiss the lady's hand!"

And so the squadrons charged the steel-gray flanks, and gave a further tinge of red to evening's glow upon the land. I hope you'll forgive Oskar for adding this final couplet and for the poetic nature of the battle scene. I might have done better to indicate the number of men lost by the Polish cavalry, and commemorate the so-called Polish Campaign with dry but impressive statistics. But if asked, I could introduce an asterisk here, add a footnote, and let the poem stand.

Up to about the twentieth of September I could hear the salvos of the artillery batteries firing from the heights of the Jäschkental and Oliva forests while lying in my hospital bed. Then the final pocket of resistance on Hela Peninsula surrendered. The Free Hanseatic City of Danzig celebrated the Anschluß of its Gothic brick to the Greater German Reich and gazed jubilantly into the blue eyes of the Führer — which had one trait in common with Jan Bronski's blue eyes: success with women — the eyes of German Chancellor Adolf Hitler, who stood tirelessly in his black Mercedes delivering one rectangular salute after another, almost without pause.

Oskar was released from the municipal hospital in mid-October. I found it hard to say goodbye to the nurses. And when one of them — I think her name was Sister Berni, or perhaps Erni — as Sister Erni or

Berni handed me my two drums, the beat-up one that occasioned my guilt and the undamaged one I had captured during the defense of the Polish Post Office, I realized that there was something else in this world I cared for besides tin drums: nurses.

Equipped with instruments and with new knowledge, I left the municipal hospital holding Matzerath's hand, returned to Labesweg, a permanent three-year-old still slightly wobbly on my sandals, and gave myself up to everyday life, to everyday boredom, and to the special boredom of Sundays in those early war years.

One Tuesday toward the end of November — I was out on the streets again for the first time after weeks of convalescence — Oskar was drumming along morosely to himself, hardly noticing the cold, wet weather, when, at the corner of Max-Halbe-Platz and Brösener Weg, he ran into the former seminarian Crazy Leo.

We stood for some time exchanging embarrassed smiles, and it was not until Leo reached into his pockets, pulled out his kid gloves, and slowly stretched the whitish yellow, skinlike casings over his fingers and palms that I realized whom I had met and what this meeting would yield — and Oskar was afraid.

We spent a little more time looking in the shop windows at Kaisers-Kaffee, watched a few Number Five and Nine trams cross Max-Halbe-Platz, followed the uniform row of buildings along Brösener Weg, circled an advertising pillar several times, studied an announcement about when and how to exchange Danzig guldens for German marks, scratched at a Persil poster and found something red beneath the blue and white, left it at that, and were just heading back toward the square when Crazy Leo pushed Oskar into the entranceway of a building with both gloved hands, reached back with his left gloved fingers, lifted his coattails, poked around in his trouser pocket, sifted the contents, found something, tested his find with his fingers still in the pocket, then, satisfied with what he'd found, removed his closed hand from his pocket, let his coattail fall, slowly extended his gloved fist, extended it farther, forced Oskar back against the wall, his long arm long — the wall solid — and just as I was starting to think that his arm would pull right out of its socket, break free, push against my chest, pass through it, exit between my shoulder blades, and penetrate the wall of the musty stairwell — that Oskar would never find out what Leo had in his hand, would learn at best the text of the house rules on Brösener Weg, which were not substantially different from those on Labesweg—he opened his five sheathed fingers.

Stopping just short of my sailor's jacket, already pressing on an anchor button, Leo opened the glove so quickly I heard his joints crack: on the fusty, shiny cloth protecting the palm of his hand lay an empty shell.

When Leo closed his fist again, I was ready to follow him. That little piece of metal spoke directly to me. Side by side, we walked down Brösener Weg, Oskar on Leo's left, no longer stopping at shop windows or advertising pillars, crossed Magdeburger Straße, turned left behind the two tall, boxy buildings at the end of Brösener Weg, topped at night by warning lights for planes that were taking off and landing, tramped along the periphery of the fenced-in airfield for a time, then finally switched over to the drier asphalt street and followed the rails of the Number Nine tram toward Brösen.

We didn't say a word, but Leo still held the empty shell in his glove. When I hesitated and started to turn back because of the cold and the rain, he opened his fist, made the little piece of metal hop up and down in his palm, lured me on a hundred paces, then another hundred smaller paces, and when, just before we reached the Saspe grounds, I made a serious decision to retreat, he even resorted to music. He turned on his heel, held the shell with its open end upward, pressed the hole like the mouthpiece of a flute against his protruding lower lip, and sent a raspy tone, now shrill, now muffled as though by fog, into the ever more intensely falling rain. Oskar was freezing: it wasn't just the music on the empty shell that made him shiver, the lousy weather, arriving as if on cue to fit the mood, played its part too, so that I didn't even try to hide my miserable state.

What lured me to Brösen? Well, yes, Leo the Pied Piper, piping on his empty shell. But other things piped to me too. Beyond November's laundry-room fog, from the roadstead and Neufahrwasser, the sirens of the steamships and the hungry howl of a torpedo boat running in or out reached us over Schottland, Schellmühl, and Reichskolonie, so that with foghorns, sirens, and a whistling shell, it was child's play for Leo to draw a freezing Oskar after him.

Not far from where the wire fence curved off toward Pelonken, separating the airfield from the new drill ground with its encircling trenches, Crazy Leo paused, his head cocked to one side, slobbering over the empty shell, and observed for a time my shivering, trembling body. He sucked at the shell, held it with his lower lip, and following a sudden inspiration, flailed his arms about, pulled off his long-tailed frock coat and threw the heavy cloth, smelling of damp earth, over my head and shoulders.

We set off again. I don't know if Oskar was any less cold. Now and then Leo would leap forward five paces, pause, and strike a figure in his rumpled yet shockingly white shirt that might have sprung mysteriously from some medieval dungeon—the Stockturm, say—with the harshly bright shirt that style demands of the insane. Whenever Leo turned to see Oskar tottering along in his frock coat, he would burst out laughing and flap his wings like a croaking raven. Indeed I must have looked like some strange bird, if not a raven, then a crow, since my coattails dragged behind me like a train, mopping up the asphalt street, leaving behind a broad, majestic track that made Oskar proud each time he glanced back over his shoulder, and foreshadowed, perhaps even symbolized, a tragic fate that slept within him and was gradually to awaken.

Even before leaving Max-Halbe-Platz, I suspected that Leo had no intention of taking me to Brösen or Neufahrwasser. From the very start the only possible goal of this march was Saspe Cemetery and the training trenches, near which a modern rifle range had been set up for the police.

From the end of September through the end of April, the trams to the seaside resorts ran only every thirty-five minutes. As we were leaving the suburb of Langfuhr, a single-car tram approached. A few moments later the tram that had been waiting for it on the siding at Magdeburger Straße overtook us. We had almost reached Saspe Cemetery, where a second siding had been installed, when another tram jangled past, then the moist, yellow headlight of a tram we'd seen waiting ahead in the mist came toward us.

The flat, morose face of the tram driver was still sharp in Oskar's mind as Crazy Leo led him off the asphalt street through loose sand hinting at the sand dunes on the beach. A wall that enclosed the cemetery formed a square. A small gate on the south side, ornately rusted and only pretending to be locked, permitted us to enter. Unfortunately Leo left me no time to inspect more closely the slanted gravestones, heading for a fall or already flat on their faces, carved mostly from black Swedish granite or diorite, rough-hewn on their backs and sides, their fronts polished smooth. Five or six stunted beach pines, which had taken various detours as they grew, filled in as decorative trees for the cemetery. When Mama was alive and gazing out from the streetcar she always preferred this little rundown spot to any other final resting place. Now she lay in Brentau. The soil was richer there; elms and maples grew.

Before I could find my footing in all that romantic decay, Leo led me out of the cemetery through a small, gateless portal in the northern wall. Just beyond the wall we found ourselves on sandy level ground. Broom, pines, and rosehip shrubs drifted off toward the coast with striking clarity through a misty brew. Looking back at the cemetery, I saw at once that a portion of the northern wall had been freshly whitewashed.

Leo busied himself before the seemingly new wall, its harsh brightness matching his rumpled shirt. He strained to take long strides, seemed to be counting them, counted aloud in what Oskar believes to this day was Latin. And chanted a text too, one he might have learned in the seminary. Approximately thirty feet from the wall Leo marked a point, then placed a wooden stick near the whitewashed section, which I imagine had also been repaired, all this with his left hand, for in his right he held the empty shell, and finally, after interminable searching and measuring, he removed the wooden stick and replaced it with that hollow metallic cylinder, somewhat narrowed at the tip, which had housed a lead kernel till someone tightened his index finger, sought the pressure point, and smoothly, without jerking, issued the lead's eviction notice and ordered its death-dealing relocation.

We stood and stood. Crazy Leo drooled threads of spittle. Wringing his gloves, he chanted a few more Latin phrases, then fell silent, as there was no one present who knew the responses. Then Leo turned round, peered over the wall toward Brösener Landstraße with peevish impatience, and kept turning his head that way every time the trams, empty for the most part, pulled onto the siding and jangled past each other, then distanced themselves again. Leo was probably waiting for mourners. But no one arrived on foot or by tram to whom he could offer his glove in sympathy.

Some planes roared overhead, coming in for a landing. We didn't look up, submitted to the noise of the engines, had no desire to satisfy ourselves that three Ju 52s with blinking lights on their wingtips were coming in to land.

Shortly after the engines left us — the stillness was as painful as the wall we faced was white — Crazy Leo reached into his shirt, pulled something out, stepped up beside me, tore his crow's coat from Oskar's shoulders, leapt off toward the broom, rosehips, and beach pines, heading for the coast, and in bounding away, with a calculating gesture suggesting it was meant to be found, let something drop.

Only when Leo had disappeared for good — he roamed about in the foreground like a ghost till milky tendrils of fog clinging to the ground swallowed him up — only when I found myself totally alone in the rain, did I pick up the small rectangle of cardboard stuck in the sand: it was a skat card — the seven of spades.

A few days after this meeting at Saspe Cemetery, Oskar met his grandmother Anna Koljaiczek at the weekly market in Langfuhr. Now that there was no longer any border or customs at Bissau, she could take her eggs, butter, even green kale and winter apples to market. People were busy buying all they could, for food would soon be rationed and they had to lay in stores. The very moment Oskar saw his grandmother squatting behind her wares, he felt the skat card against his bare skin, beneath his coat, sweater, and undershirt. At first, having hopped on the tram free of charge at the conductor's urging, I'd meant to tear up the seven of spades on the way back from Saspe to Max-Halbe-Platz.

Oskar didn't tear up the card. He gave it to his grandmother. She was startled behind her green kale when she saw him. She may have thought that Oskar's presence could bode no good. Nevertheless, she waved the three-year-old, who was half hiding behind some baskets of fish, over to her. Oskar took his time, looked over a live cod nearly a yard long lying on damp seaweed, then watched some pocket crabs from Lake Ottominer still hard at work practicing their crabwalk in a basket; then Oskar tried this method of locomotion himself, approaching his grandmother's stand with the back of his sailor's jacket, and didn't show her his golden anchor buttons till he bumped against one of the wooden trestles under her display and set the apples rolling.

Schwerdtfeger came with his hot bricks wrapped in newspaper, shoved them under my grandmother's skirts, drew out the cold bricks with a slide as he always did, made a mark on the slate tablet dangling from him, moved on to the next stand, and my grandmother handed me a shiny apple.

What could Oskar give her when she gave him an apple? He handed her the skat card and then the empty shell, for he hadn't wished to leave it lying in Saspe either. Anna Koljaiczek stared uncomprehendingly at those two quite disparate objects for some time. Then Oskar's mouth approached her gristly old woman's ear beneath her scarf, and casting all caution to the wind, I whispered, thinking of Jan's small but fleshy pink ear with the long, nicely shaped lobes: "He lies in Saspe," Oskar whispered, and dashed off, upsetting a shoulder basket of green kale.

Maria

WHILE HISTORY, BLARING special communiqués at the top of its lungs, drove, swam, and flew like a well-oiled machine through Europe's streets, waterways, and skies, conquering them all, my own affairs, which were limited to wearing out lacquered tin drums, slowed, sputtered, and finally came to a halt. While others were flinging high-priced metal lavishly about, I was running out of tin again. It's true Oskar had managed to rescue a new, nearly unscathed instrument from the Polish Post Office and thus provide some justification for the latter's defense, but given the fact that it took me a mere eight weeks to transform a drum into scrap metal when I was at my best, how much could Herr Naczelnik junior's tin drum mean to me?

Soon after my release from the city hospital, lamenting the loss of my nurses, I released a mighty drumroll and started to drum mightily. That rainy afternoon in Saspe Cemetery had not stilled my handiwork; on the contrary, Oskar redoubled his efforts and devoted all his energy to the task of destroying the last witness of his shameful conduct with the Home Guard, his drum.

But it held firm, responded, struck back accusingly each time I struck it. Strangely enough, in the midst of all these slugfests, which were intended solely to eradicate a certain limited segment of my past, I kept thinking of Viktor Weluhn, the postal money-order clerk, though he was surely too nearsighted to bear witness against me. But had he not escaped in spite of being nearsighted? Could it be that nearsighted people see more than we do, that Weluhn, whom I usually call poor Viktor, scanned my gestures like those of a black and white silhouette, recognized my Judas act, and carried Oskar's secret shame with him on his flight into the wider world?

It wasn't till mid-December that the accusations of the lacquered, red-flamed conscience round my neck began to lose their persuasive power: the lacquer showed hairline cracks and started to peel. The tin began to yield, grow thin, and split before turning transparent. As always when something is suffering and struggling toward its end, the eyewitness wishes to shorten its sufferings, to end things more rapidly. Oskar speeded up during the final weeks of Advent, worked so hard the neighbors and Matzerath held their heads in their hands, was determined to settle his accounts by Christmas Eve; for on Christmas Eve I hoped to receive a new, guiltless drum.

I made it. On the eve of the twenty-fourth of December I rid my body and my soul of a crumpled, flapping, rusty something, reminiscent of a wrecked car, and with that I hoped the defense of the Polish Post Office had also been crushed once and for all.

Never has any human being — if you are prepared to accept me as one — experienced a more disappointing Christmas than Oskar, who found beneath the Christmas tree a whole range of presents set out for him save one — a tin drum.

There was a set of building blocks I never even opened. A rocking swan, meant as a very special present, was supposed to turn me into Lohengrin. Just to annoy me, no doubt, they had the nerve to place three or four picture books on the gift table. The only items that appeared useful were a pair of gloves, some laced boots, and a red sweater Gretchen Scheffler had knitted. Dismayed, Oskar let his gaze glide from the building blocks to the swan, stared at the picture-book teddy bears meant to be cute, holding all sorts of musical instruments in their paws. One of these adorable, mendacious beasts even held a drum, looked as if he knew how to drum, as if he were about to launch into a drum solo, as if he were drumming away; and I had a swan but no drum, probably more than a thousand building blocks but not a single drum, had mittens for all those bitter-cold winter nights but nothing round, smooth, ice-cold, lacquered, and tinny in my mittened fists to carry into the winter night so the frost could finally hear something truly white.

Oskar thought to himself: Matzerath has hidden the drum. Or Gretchen Scheffler, who's come with her baker husband to polish off our

Christmas goose, is sitting on it. They want to share my pleasure in the swan, the building blocks, and the picture books before they pull out the real treasure. I gave in, leafed like a fool through the picture books, mounted the swan, and rocked back and forth in utter disgust for at least half an hour. Then in spite of the overheated apartment I let them try the sweater on me, slipped into the boots with Gretchen Scheffler's help — meanwhile the Greffs had arrived too, since the goose would serve six — and after wolfing down the goose, stuffed with dried fruit, masterfully prepared by Matzerath, during dessert — plums and pears — desperately clutching a picture book Greff had added to my other four, after soup, goose, red cabbage, boiled potatoes, plums and pears, breathed on by a hot tile stove, we all sang — and Oskar sang too — a Christmas carol and another verse, Rejoice, and Ochristmastreeochristmastreehow-lovelyarethy-ringbellsgotingalingaling-everyyearatchristmas and felt it was about time — they were already ringing the bells outside — I wanted my drum — the drunken brass band that Meyn the musician had once belonged to blew so loud the icicles at the window ledges . . . but I wanted, and they weren't giving, weren't bringing out, Oskar "Yes!" the others "No!" — and then I screamed, I hadn't screamed in a long time, I filed my voice to a sharp, glass-cutting instrument once more, after its long rest, and didn't slay vases, or beer glasses, or light bulbs, sliced open no showcase window, blinded no spectacles — instead my vocal resentment was directed at all those resplendent glass balls, bells, silvery shining bubbles, and treetop baubles spreading good cheer on the Ochristmastree: ringadinging and tingalingalinging, the Christmas tree ornaments were shattered to dust. Quite superfluously, several dustpans' worth of pine needles detached themselves at the same time. But the candles went on burning, silent and holy, and Oskar still didn't get his drum.

Matzerath simply lacked judgment. I don't know if he was trying to raise me properly or if he just didn't think of providing me with an ample supply of drums in a timely fashion. Things were headed for disaster, and it was only because it was impossible to hide the mounting disorder in our grocery shop at the very moment of my impending disaster that help arrived — as one always thinks it will when times are hard — and saved both me and the shop.

Since Oskar possessed neither the necessary height nor the inclination to stand behind the store counter selling Ryvita, margarine, and synthetic honey, Matzerath, whom I'll resume calling my father for the sake of simplicity, hired Maria Truczinski, my poor friend Herbert's youngest sister, to work in the store.

Maria wasn't just named for a saint, she was one. Not only did she manage, within a few weeks, to restore the good reputation of our shop, she also showed, along with her friendly but firm approach to business, to which Matzerath gladly submitted, some true understanding for my situation.

Even before taking her place behind the counter, Maria had offered me an old washbasin on several occasions as a substitute for the scrapheap I held at my tummy as I stamped accusingly up and down the hundred-plus steps of the stairwell. But Oskar would accept no substitute. He steadfastly refused to drum on an overturned washbasin. No sooner had Maria gained a firm foothold in the business, however, than she managed, in spite of Matzerath, to accommodate my wishes. Of course Oskar could not be persuaded to enter a toy store at her side. The interiors of those brightly colored, overstocked shops would surely have evoked painful comparisons with Sigismund Markus's devastated shop. Maria, gentle and compliant, let me wait outside, or went shopping on her own, brought me a new drum every four or five weeks as needed, and during the final years of the war, when even tin drums were rare and rationed, offered the shopkeepers sugar or an ounce of real coffee and received my drum under the table, as so-called UT goods. All this she did without sighing, shaking her head, or glancing heavenward, but with the same serious, attentive, and matter-of-fact air she assumed when she dressed me in freshly laundered, properly mended trousers, socks, and smocks. Though relations between Maria and me have remained in constant flux over the intervening years, and are unsettled to this day, the way in which she hands me my drum remains unchanged, though the price of tin drums has risen substantially since nineteen-forty.

Today, Maria subscribes to a fashion magazine. She looks more elegant from one Visitors Day to the next. And back then?

Was Maria beautiful? She had a round, freshly washed face, gazed out coolly but not coldly from slightly protruding gray eyes with short but thick lashes beneath strong, dark eyebrows that merged above the bridge of her nose. Clearly defined cheekbones — with skin that grew taut, turned bluish, and chapped painfully in cold weather — lent a calming regularity to her features, barely interrupted by a diminutive nose that was by no means unattractive or comical in any way, but rather, in spite of its delicacy, nicely shaped. Her forehead was small and round, and even early on marked by thoughtful vertical creases above the brows that merged over her nose. Rounded too was the slightly curly brown hair at her temples, which still has the sheen of wet tree trunks today, drawn back tightly, like Mother Truczinski's, to span a small, round skull that barely revealed its back. When Maria donned her long white smock and took her place behind our shop counter, she still wore braids behind her flushed, robustly healthy ears, whose earlobes unfortunately were not free but attached, growing straight into the flesh of her lower jaws, without any ugly creases to be sure, but still degenerate enough to draw conclusions about Maria's character. Later, Matzerath talked the young girl into a permanent wave and her ears remained hidden. These days Maria lets her attached earlobes show beneath a short, stylish hairdo, but hides this blemish by means of large and slightly tasteless clip-ons.

Just as Maria's small, easily encompassed head displayed full cheeks, high cheekbones, and generously large eyes on both sides of its almost inconspicuous, inset nose, so her body, which was more small than medium, was provided with somewhat overly broad shoulders, full breasts swelling right from her armpits, and an opulent bottom to match her pelvis, which was supported in turn by legs that were strong but too slender, leaving a visible gap beneath her pubic hair.

Perhaps Maria was a bit knock-kneed back then. And her permanently reddened hands always struck me, compared to her fully grown, fully developed body, as somewhat childlike, with fingers a bit like sausages. To this day she can't deny that she has little paws. Her feet, on the other hand, which trudged about in bulky walking shoes back then and somewhat later in my poor mama's little shoes, which were stylish but old-fashioned and didn't really fit her, gradually lost their childish redness and drollness in spite of being forced into those hand-me-downs, and eventually fit modern models from West Germany and even Italy.

Maria didn't talk much but liked to sing while she washed dishes and while she filled blue pound and half-pound sacks with sugar. After the shop closed, while Matzerath busied himself with his accounts, on

Sundays too, and whenever she could take a half-hour break, she would pick up the harmonica her brother Fritz had given her when he was drafted and sent to Groß-Boschpol.

Maria could play pretty much anything on the harmonica. Scout songs she'd learned evenings at the League of German Girls, tunes from operettas, and hits she'd heard on the radio or learned from her brother Fritz, who came back to Danzig for several days on official business at Easter in nineteen-forty. Oskar recalls that Maria could play "Raindrops" with flutter tongue, and coax "The Wind Told Me a Tale" from her harmonica without imitating Zarah Leander. Maria never pulled her Hohner out during business hours. Even when there were no customers she refrained from playing and wrote out price tags and inventory lists in round, childlike letters.

Though you couldn't help seeing that she was in charge of the shop and had won back a number of the customers who'd switched to the competition after my poor mama's death, she maintained a respect for Matzerath that bordered on servility, which he didn't find in the least embarrassing, since he always thought highly of himself.

"After all, I'm the one who hired the girl and taught her the business," his argument ran, whenever the greengrocer Greff and Gretchen Scheffler started teasing him. So simple were the thought processes of this man, who grew refined, sensitive, and therefore interesting only while engaged in his favorite pastime, namely cooking. Oskar had to hand it to him: his Kassler ribs with sauerkraut, his pork kidneys in mustard sauce, his fried Wiener schnitzel, and above all his carp with cream and horseradish, were sights to behold, not to mention smell and taste. There wasn't much he could teach Maria in the shop, because the girl brought an inborn talent for small business with her, and Matzerath, who was almost totally lacking in the fine art of countertop commerce, was fit only for dealing with wholesalers, but he did teach Maria how to boil, roast, and stew, for in spite of spending two years as a maid to a family of civil servants in Schidlitz, she couldn't even boil water when she came to us.

Soon Matzerath had things the way they were in my poor mama's lifetime: he reigned in the kitchen, outdid himself from Sunday roast to Sunday roast, spent hours contentedly washing dishes, while on the side, so to speak, he handled purchases, orders, and payments with wholesale firms and the Rations Office—increasingly difficult during those war years—conducted correspondence with the tax bureau with a certain shrewdness, decorated the shop window every other week, not half badly, showing imagination and good taste, fulfilled his Party nonsense conscientiously, all of which, while Maria stood firm as a rock at the counter, kept him very busy.

You may well be thinking: What's the point of all these preparatory remarks, this detailed concern with a young girl's cheekbones, eyebrows, earlobes, hands, and feet? I totally agree; I don't like describing a person this way any more than you do. Oskar is firmly convinced he's done nothing thus far but distort Maria's image, if not permanently falsify it. So one final sentence that I hope will clarify everything: Maria was, leaving aside all those anonymous nurses, Oskar's first love.

I realized my state while listening to myself drum one day, which I rarely did, and noticed something new: insistently yet gently, Oskar was communicating his passion to the drum. Maria responded to my drumming. Though I didn't much like it when she picked up her harmonica, furrowed her brow in an ugly way, and felt she had to accompany me. But often, when she was darning socks or filling sacks with sugar, she would lower her hands, gaze past the drumsticks at me, gravely and attentively, her face completely calm, and before resuming her darning, with a soft, sleepy motion, run her hand over my short, stubbly hair.

Oskar, who couldn't bear even the slightest contact otherwise, no matter how affectionately intended, accepted Maria's hand, and became so addicted to that caress that he often played for hours, deliberately beating out the seductive rhythm on his drum that led to the caress, till Maria's hand at last obeyed and brought him pleasure.

After a time Maria began putting me to bed each night. She undressed me, washed me, helped me into my pajamas, advised me to empty my bladder again before going to sleep, said an Our Father with me, though she was Protestant, three Hail Marys, and now and then a Jesusiliveforyoujesusidieforyou, and finally tucked me in with a friendly, sleepy-making face.

As pleasant as I found those final minutes before the lights went off—I gradually replaced the Our Father and Jesusiliveforyou with the tenderly allusive Staroftheseaigreetthee and Maryilovethee—the nightly preparations before going to bed embarrassed me and nearly undermined my self-control, reducing me, despite my normal mastery over my features, to the traitorous blush of teenage flappers and lovesick young men. Oskar admits: each time Maria undressed me, placed me in the zinc tub and leached and scrubbed the dust of a day's drumming from my skin with a washcloth, brush, and soap, each time I realized that I, a nearly sixteen-year-old boy, was standing stark naked before a nearly seventeen-year-old girl, I blushed deeply and continued to glow for some time.

But Maria didn't seem to notice the change in the color of my skin. Did she think her brush and washcloth had heated me up so? Did she tell herself it must be hygiene stoking Oskar's fire? Or was Maria modest and tactful enough that she saw through my daily evening glow and simply ignored it?

I'm still a slave to this sudden flush that's impossible to hide and often lasts five minutes or so. Like my grandfather Koljaiczek the arsonist, who turned fire-engine rooster red at the mere mention of the word match, the blood courses through my veins the moment anyone, even a total stranger, tells of small children being plied with washcloth and brush each evening in a bathtub. Oskar stands there like a red Indian; the world smiles, calls me strange, even perverse: for what can it mean to the world if little children are soaped up, scrubbed off, and visited by a little washcloth in the most private of places.

But Maria, who was a child of nature, did the most daring things in my presence without embarrassment. Every time she mopped the living room and bedroom floors she would reach halfway up her thighs and pull off the stockings Matzerath had given her, because she wanted to spare them. One Saturday after closing — Matzerath was busy at local Party headquarters — Maria removed her skirt and blouse, stood beside me in the living room in her worn but clean slip, and started removing spots from her skirt and artificial silk blouse with gasoline.

What could it have been that gave Maria, once she had taken off her outer garments, and as soon as the smell of gasoline had evaporated, the pleasant, naively bewitching smell of vanilla? Did she rub herself with the root? Was there some cheap perfume that tended in that olfactory direction? Or was this fragrance as specific to her as the fumes of ammonia Frau Kater exuded, or the smell of slightly rancid butter beneath my grandmother Koljaiczek's skirts? Oskar, who always liked to get to the bottom of things, investigated the vanilla: Maria didn't rub it on herself. Maria just smelled that way. Yes, I'm convinced to this day that she wasn't even aware of the scent that clung to her, for if on a Sunday, after roast veal with mashed potatoes and cauliflower in brown butter, a vanilla pudding trembled on the table because I was kicking the table leg with my boot, Maria, who went into ecstasies over a red berry dessert, ate but little of it and with evident distaste, while to this very day Oskar is in love with this simplest and perhaps most banal of all puddings.

In July of nineteen-forty, shortly after special communiqués had announced the rapid success of the campaign in France, bathing season opened on the Baltic. While Maria's brother Fritz, now an airman second class, was mailing his first picture postcards from Paris, Matzerath and Maria decided Oskar ought to go to the beach, the sea air would do him good. Maria was to take me to the Brösen beach at midday—the shop closed from one to three—and if she stayed on till four, Matzerath said, that wouldn't be a problem, he enjoyed taking a turn behind the counter now and then and showing himself to the customers.

A blue bathing suit with an anchor sewn on it was purchased for Oskar. Maria already had a green one trimmed in red that her sister Guste had given her for confirmation. Into a beach bag from Mama's day were stuffed a white terrycloth bathrobe of the same vintage and, quite superfluously, a little pail and shovel and various sandcake molds. Maria carried the bag. My drum I carried myself.

Oskar was apprehensive about the tram ride past the cemetery at Saspe. Was it not to be feared that the sight of that so silent yet eloquent spot would spoil his enthusiasm for the beach, which wasn't all that great anyway? What will the spirit of Jan Bronski do, Oskar asked himself, when the agent of his undoing, lightly clad for summer, jangles past his grave on a tram?

The Number Nine rolled to a stop. The conductor called out Saspe. I stared fixedly past Maria toward Brösen, where the oncoming tram grew slowly larger as it crept toward us. Don't let your eyes wander. What was there to see anyway? Twisted beach pines, ornate rusted iron, a jumble of loose gravestones whose inscriptions only beach thistles and wild oats could read. Better to look out the open window and upward: there they were, droning overhead, the fat Ju 52s, as only tri-engine planes or very fat flies could drone in a cloudless July sky.

We set off, jingling and jangling, and the other tram blocked our view. Just past the trailing car my head turned of its own accord: I caught the whole rundown cemetery, including a portion of the north wall with a noticeably white patch that lay in shadow, but was still extremely embarrassing . . .

And then we were past it, we approached Brösen, and I looked at Maria again. She filled out a light, flowery summer dress. About her softly glowing neck, on her well-padded collarbone, lay a necklace of antique red wooden cherries, all the same size and looking ready to burst. Was it my imagination, or did I actually smell it? Oskar leaned forward slightly — Maria was taking her vanilla scent along with her to the Baltic — took a deep breath of the fragrance, and instantly vanquished the moldering Jan Bronski. The defense of the Polish Post Office had receded into history before the flesh had even fallen from the defenders' bones. Oskar, the survivor, had totally different smells in his nostrils from those of his once so elegant and now crumbling presumptive father.

In Brösen Maria bought a pound of cherries, took me by the hand — she knew that Oskar allowed her alone to do this — and led us through the stand of beach pines to the bathhouse. In spite of my nearly sixteen years — the bath attendant had no eye for that — I was allowed into the women's side. Water: eighteen degrees centigrade; air: twenty-six; wind: east — continued fair, stood on the black slate next to a poster for the Lifesavers' Association showing various techniques for artificial respiration accompanied by clumsy, old-fashioned drawings. All of the drowned were wearing striped bathing suits, the lifesavers wore mustaches, straw hats floated on treacherously dangerous waters.

The barefoot bath attendant led the way. She wore a cord around her body like a penitent, and from the cord hung a mighty key that unlocked all the cabins. Boardwalks. The railings of the walks. A rough coconut-fiber runner outside all the cabins. We were given cabin 53. The wood of the cabin was warm, dry, of a natural bluish white color I'd call blind. Beside the cabin window, a mirror that no longer took itself seriously.

Oskar had to undress first. I did this with my face to the wall, accepting help only reluctantly. Then Maria turned me around with her practical firm grip, held out my new bathing suit, and forced me ruthlessly into the tight-fitting wool. No sooner had she buttoned my shoulder straps than she lifted me up onto the wooden bench against the back wall of the cabin, put the drum and drumsticks down on my lap, and began to undress with rapid, energetic movements.

At first I drummed a little and counted the knotholes in the floorboards. Then I stopped drumming and counting. I still don't know why Maria was whistling to herself with comically pursed lips as she stepped from her shoes, two high notes, two low notes as she stripped off her socks, whistled like a beer-truck driver, removed her flowered dress, whistled as she hung her slip over the dress, let her bra fall, still straining to whistle but without finding a tune as she pulled her underpants, which were actually gym shorts, down to her knees, let them fall to her ankles, stepped from her rolled-up shorts, and kicked them off into a corner with her left foot.

Maria frightened Oskar with her hairy triangle. Of course he knew from his poor mama that women weren't bald down there, but to him Maria wasn't a woman in the sense in which his mama had shown herself to be a woman with Matzerath or Jan Bronski.

And I recognized her at once. Rage, shame, indignation, disappointment, and a half-comic, half-painful incipient stiffening of the little watering can under my bathing suit made me forget both drum and drumsticks in favor of a newly grown stick.

Oskar jumped up and flung himself at Maria. She caught him with her hair. His face was now overgrown. It grew between his lips. Maria laughed and tried to push him away. But I was drawing more and more of her in, tracking down that vanilla scent. Maria was still laughing. She even let me reach her vanilla, it seemed to amuse her, for she didn't stop laughing. Only when my legs slipped and I hurt her — for I didn't let go of her hair, or it wouldn't let go of me — only when the vanilla brought tears to my eyes, only when I tasted mushrooms or something else sharp and pungent, but no longer vanilla, only when this earthy smell that Maria concealed behind the vanilla nailed the moldering Jan Bronski to my brow and infected me for all time with the taste of the transient nature of all things — only then did I let go of her.

Oskar slid down onto the blind-colored boards of the bathhouse cabin and was still crying as Maria, who was laughing again, lifted him up into her arms, caressed him, and pressed him to her necklace of wooden cherries, the only thing she was still wearing.

Shaking her head, she picked her hairs from my lips and said in surprise, "You are such a little rascal! Head for it but don't know what it is, and then you cry."

Fizz Powder

Do you know what that is? It came in little flat packets and you could buy it all year round. In our shop my mama sold a vomit-green packet of woodruff-flavored fizz powder. A packet that borrowed its color from half-ripened oranges styled itself fizz powder with orange flavor. You could get raspberry too, and another one that hissed, bubbled, and acted excited when you added clear tap water, and if you drank it before it settled down, it tasted very faintly and remotely of lemon, was lemon-colored in the glass, but even more so: an artificial yellow masquerading as poison.

What else was shown on the little packet besides its flavor? All-Natural Product, it said—Patented—Keep Dry—and below a dotted line: Tear Here.

Where else could you buy fizz powder? It wasn't sold just in my mama's shop, every grocery store in town—except for Kaisers-Kaffee and the Konsum cooperatives—stocked the little powder. A packet cost three pfennigs there and at any refreshment stand.

Maria and I got our fizz powder free. But when we couldn't wait till we got home, we would wind up paying three pfennigs at some grocery store or refreshment stand, or even six, since we could never get enough of it and sometimes asked for two packets.

Who started with the fizz powder? That old lovers' quarrel. I say Maria started it. Maria never claimed Oskar did. She left the question open, found such interrogations painful, and if pressed might well have said, "The fizz powder started it."

Of course everyone will say Maria was right. Oskar alone could not accept the verdict. I could never admit to myself that a little three-pfennig packet of fizz powder had managed to seduce Oskar. I was sixteen years old and set great store by declaring myself to blame, or possibly Maria, but certainly not fizz powder you had to keep dry.

It began a few days after my birthday. According to the calendar, the bathing season was drawing to a close. The weather, however, would hear nothing of September. After a rainy August, summer was showing its mettle; its belated accomplishments could be read on the board nailed up beside the Lifesavers' Association poster in the bathing attendant's cabin — air: twenty-nine degrees centigrade; water: twenty; wind: southeast; mostly fair.

While Fritz Truczinski was writing postcards as an airman second class in the Luftwaffe from Paris, Copenhagen, Oslo, and Brussels — the fellow was always traveling on official business — Maria and I managed to acquire a bit of a tan. In July we had our regular little spot by the sun shield in the family area. Since Maria was never safe there from the awkward horseplay of senior boys from the Conradinum in their red gym shorts and the boring, long-winded declarations of love of a student from the Petri School, we abandoned the family area in mid-August and found a quieter spot near the water in the women's area, where fat ladies, short of breath and wheezing like the short-lived waves of the Baltic, ventured into the water up to the varicose veins at the back of their knees, where little urchins, naked and badly behaved, struggled against fate: that is, saw how high they could pile sand towers before they collapsed.

The women's area: when women are by themselves and think they're unobserved, a young man of the kind that Oskar knew how to keep hidden back then should keep his eyes closed rather than become an unwilling witness to unabashed womanhood.

We lay in the sand. Maria in her green bathing suit trimmed in red, I having adjusted to my blue. The sand slept, the sea slept, the shells were crushed and not listening. Amber, which allegedly keeps you awake, was off somewhere else, the wind, from the southeast as the weatherboard said, fell slowly asleep, the broad expanse of sky, which had surely overexerted itself, could not stop yawning; Maria and I were somewhat tired ourselves, we'd already been in the water, had eaten after, not before, going in. Now our still-moist cherry pits lay on the beach beside last year's dried-white, weightless ones.

At the sight of so much transience, Oskar let the sand with its year-old, thousand-year-old, and still-oh-so-young cherry pits trickle onto his drum as if through an hourglass, and tried to enter into the role of Death playing with bones. Beneath Maria's warm, sleepy flesh I pictured parts of her surely wide-awake skeleton, relished the gap between ulna and radius, played counting games up and down her spine, poked through both holes in her hipbones, and amused myself with the base of her sternum.

Despite all the fun I was having as Death with a beach-sand hourglass, Maria stirred. She reached blindly into the beach bag, relying solely on touch, and looked for something while I poured the rest of the sand with the last of the cherry pits onto the drum, which was already half-covered. When Maria didn't find what she was looking for, probably her harmonica, she turned the bag inside out; a moment later something lay on the beach towel, but it wasn't her harmonica — it was a packet of woodruff fizz powder.

Maria acted surprised. And perhaps she really was. I was certainly surprised and kept asking myself, still ask myself today: How did fizz powder, this cheap stuff bought only by children of temporary dockworkers and the unemployed, because they had no money for regular soft drinks, how did this slow-selling article get into our beach bag?

While Oskar was still mulling this over, Maria grew thirsty. Even I, interrupting my thoughts, had to admit against my will to an urgent thirst. We had no cup, and drinking water was at least thirty-five strides away if Maria went for it, and nearly fifty if I did. Borrowing a cup from the bathhouse attendant and turning on the faucet by the cabin meant making your way between mounds of flesh gleaming with Nivea oil lying on their backs or bellies, and enduring the burning sand.

We both dreaded the trip, so we left the packet lying there on the beach towel. Finally I picked it up before Maria showed any signs of doing so. But Oskar put it back on the towel so Maria could take it. But Maria didn't take it. So I took it and gave it to Maria. Maria gave it back to Oskar. I thanked her and made a present of it to her. But she wasn't accepting any presents from Oskar. I had to put it back on the towel. It lay there a long time without stirring.

Oskar wishes to make clear that it was Maria who, after an awkward pause, picked up the packet. Not only that: she tore off a strip of paper right on the dotted line where it said *Tear Here*. Then she held the open packet out to me. This time I was the one who declined with thanks. Maria managed to feel hurt. She replaced the open packet firmly and resolutely on the towel. What was I to do except pick it up myself before any sand got into it, and offer it to Maria.

Oskar wishes to make clear that it was Maria who made one finger disappear into the opening of the packet, who coaxed it out again and held it up vertically for inspection: something bluish white appeared on the tip of her finger, fizz powder. Of course I took it. Though it made my nose prickle, my face managed to mirror pleasure at the taste. It was Maria who cupped her hand. And Oskar couldn't avoid sprinkling a little fizz powder into that pink bowl. She didn't know what to do with the little heap. The mound in her palm was too new to her, too amazing. Then I leaned forward, gathered all my saliva, added it to the fizz powder, did it again, and didn't lean back till I had no more spittle left.

In Maria's hand a hissing and foaming set in. The woodruff erupted like a volcano. The greenish rage of who knew what native tribe was boiling over. Something was going on that Maria had neither seen nor probably ever felt before; her hand twitched, trembled, tried to fly away, for woodruff nipped at her, woodruff penetrated her skin, woodruff excited her, gave her a feeling, a feeling, a feeling . . .

The green grew greener, but Maria grew red, brought her hand to her mouth, licked her palm with her long tongue, again and again, and so frantically it seemed to Oskar that her tongue, instead of stilling the woodruff feeling that stirred her so, was intensifying it to the limit, perhaps even past the limit, normally set for any feeling.

Then the feeling ebbed. Maria giggled, looked around to make sure there were no witnesses to the woodruff, and seeing only listless Nivea-brown sea cows in bathing suits, she sank to the beach towel; her blush of shame gradually faded against its ever so white surface.

The seaside air that noonday hour might even have lulled Oskar to sleep had not Maria straightened up a brief half-hour later and dared to reach again for the fizz powder packet, which was still half-full. I don't know if she struggled with herself before pouring the rest of the powder into that hollow hand which was no longer a stranger to the effects of woodruff. For about as long as it takes a man to polish his glasses, she held the packet in her right hand, and opposite it, its motionless counterpart, the little pink bowl of her left hand. Not that she directed her gaze at the packet or her hollow hand, or let it wander back and forth between half-full and empty; Maria stared straight between the two, darkly and sternly. But it was soon evident how much weaker that stern look was than the half-full packet. The packet approached the hollow hand, the hand drew near the packet, her gaze lost its sternness sprinkled with melancholy, took on an aroused curiosity, and then was simply aroused. With painstakingly feigned indifference, Maria heaped the rest of the woodruff fizz powder in the well-padded palm of her hand, which was dry in spite of the heat, dropped the packet and her indifference, propped up her full hand with the one now free, let her gray eyes linger for a time on the powder, then looked at me, gazed at me grayly, her gray eyes demanding something of me, she wanted my spit, why didn't she use her own, Oskar had hardly any left, she surely had much more, spittle doesn't renew itself that quickly, she should use her own please, it was just as good, if not better, and anyway she surely had more than I did, I couldn't come up with more that fast, and she was bigger than Oskar.

Maria wanted my spit. From the very beginning it was clear that only my spit would do. She kept her demanding gaze trained on me, and I blamed this cruel intransigence on those earlobes, attached, not hanging free. So Oskar swallowed, thought of things that normally made his mouth water, and yet — perhaps it was the sea air, perhaps the salt air, perhaps the salty sea air — my saliva glands failed me, I had to rise, driven by Maria's look, and set out on my way. It was a matter of taking over fifty strides across the hot sand, looking neither left nor right, climbing the even hotter steps to the bathhouse attendant's cabin, turning on the water faucet, angling my head under its open spout, taking a drink, swilling it around, and swallowing, so that Oskar could replenish his spittle.

When I had conquered the stretch between the bathing attendant's cabin and our white towel, as endless and ringed with ghastly sights as that path was, I found Maria lying on her stomach. She had nestled her head in her crossed arms. Her braids lay languid on her round back.

I poked her, for now Oskar had spittle. Maria didn't stir. I poked her again. Not interested. Cautiously I opened her left hand. She didn't resist: the hand was empty, as though it had never seen woodruff. I straightened the fingers of her right hand: pink was her palm, its lines moist, hot, and empty.

Had Maria used her own spittle after all? Couldn't she wait? Or had she blown the fizz powder away, stifled that feeling before she felt it, rubbed her hand on the beach towel until Maria's familiar little paw resurfaced, with its slightly superstitious Mound of the Moon, its fat Mercury, and its tightly padded Belt of Venus?

We went home right after that, and Oskar will never know if Maria foamed the fizz powder a second time that same day or if it was a few days later that a mixture of fizz powder and my spittle first became, through repetition, a vice we both fell prey to.

It happened by chance, or perhaps chance responding to our wishes, that on the very evening of the beach visit just described — we were eating blueberry soup followed by potato pancakes — Matzerath informed Maria and me, ever so circumspectly, that he had joined a little skat club at his local Party gathering, and that he would be meeting with his new skat brothers, all cell leaders, two evenings a week at Springer's restaurant, and that Selke, the new local group leader, would sit in now and then, which in itself meant he had to go and, unfortunately, leave us by ourselves. Probably the best thing to do would be to billet Oskar at Mother Truczinski's on skat evenings.

Mother Truczinski agreed, since this solution pleased her far more than the one Matzerath had suggested the day before without Maria's knowledge, which was that rather than my staying overnight at Mother Truczinski's, Maria would spend the night with us twice a week and sleep on our sofa.

Up till then Maria had been sleeping in the broad bed where my friend Herbert had formerly lodged his scarred back. That heavy piece of furniture stood in a small back room. Mother Truczinski's bed was in the living room. Guste Truczinski, who still worked as a waitress at the Hotel Eden's snack bar and also lived there, came home occasionally on her days off but seldom spent the night, and when she did she slept on the sofa. But if Fritz Truczinski came home from the front bearing gifts from distant lands, whether on leave or on duty, he slept in Herbert's bed, while Maria slept in Mother Truczinski's bed and the old woman camped on the sofa.

This order of things was disrupted by my demands. At first I was to bed down on the sofa. I rejected this notion briefly but firmly. Then Mother Truczinski offered to relinquish her old woman's bed and put up with the sofa. Here Maria raised an objection, couldn't bear to see her old mother's nightly rest disturbed by such discomfort, and without wasting words, declared herself prepared to share Herbert's former waiter's bed with me: "Little Oskar and me can fit into one bed. He's just a half-pint anyways."

So, starting the following week, Maria carried my bedclothes twice weekly from our ground-floor flat up two stories and prepared the night's lodging for me and my drum on the left side of her bed. On Matzerath's first skat night nothing at all happened. Herbert's bed seemed huge to me. I lay down first, Maria came in later. She had washed in the kitchen and entered the bedroom in a ridiculously long and old-fashioned starched nightgown. Oskar had expected her to be naked and hairy, and was disappointed at first, but happy even so, since the gown from great-granny's drawer was reminiscent of the white folds of nurse uniforms, and built pleasant bridges to them.

Standing before the chest of drawers, Maria undid her braids, whistling all the while. Whenever Maria dressed or undressed, did or undid her braids, she whistled. Even when she was combing her hair she never tired of squeezing those two notes through her pursed lips, though she never found a tune.

As soon as Maria put down the comb, the whistling stopped. She turned, shook her hair out, and arranged things on her chest of drawers with a few deft movements, which put her in high spirits: she threw a kiss to her mustached father, photographed and retouched in a black ebony frame, then leapt into bed with exaggerated energy, bounced up and down a few times, grabbed the eiderdown on her last bounce, and disappeared up to her chin under the mound, didn't touch me at all as I lay under my own quilt, reached out from under the eiderdown with a round arm from which the sleeve of her gown slid back, felt over her head for the cord to click off the light, found it, clicked it, and only when it was dark, said to me much too loudly, "Good night!"

Maria was soon breathing evenly. I don't think she was pretending, she probably did fall asleep quickly, for the hours of good solid work she put in each day led of necessity to similarly good solid hours of sleep.

For some time Oskar was beset by absorbing images that kept him awake. In spite of the thick darkness that reigned between the walls and the blackout paper over the window, blond nurses bent over Herbert's scarred back, Crazy Leo's white rumpled shirt turned quite naturally into a seagull that flew away, then smashed in flight against a cemetery wall, which instantly took on a freshly whitewashed look, and so on, and so on. Not until the steadily intensifying, sleepy-making smell of vanilla made the pre-slumber film first flicker, then break, did Oskar's breathing fall into the calm rhythm that Maria's had long since achieved.

Three days later Maria presented an equally demure image of maidenly modesty going to bed. She arrived in her nightgown, whistled as she undid her braids, kept whistling as she combed out her hair, put the comb away, stopped whistling, arranged things on top of the chest of drawers, threw a kiss, made her exaggerated leap into bed, bounced, reached for the eiderdown, and caught sight—I was contemplating her back—caught sight of a little packet—I was admiring her long, lovely hair—discovered something green on the eiderdown—I closed my eyes, waiting for her to grow used to the sight of the fizz powder—then the springs cried out beneath a Maria flopping back down, there was a click, and when I opened my eyes at the click, Oskar confirmed what he already knew: Maria had turned out the light, her breath in the dark was uneven, she had not grown used to the sight of the fizz powder; but the question remained whether the darkness she'd summoned might not have granted the fizz powder an even more intense existence, brought woodruff to full bloom, and ordained a mixture of bubbling carbonate for the night.

I almost think the darkness was on Oskar's side. For after a few minutes—if one can speak of minutes in a pitch-black room—I could make out movements at the head of the bed; Maria was fishing for the cord, the cord bit, and an instant later I was again admiring the long, lovely hair cascading down Maria's sitting nightgown. How steady and yellow shone the light bulb behind its pleated lampshade! The eiderdown still rose plump, turned up, and untouched at the foot of the bed. The little packet atop the mound hadn't dared budge in the darkness. Maria's granny nightshirt rustled, a sleeve of the gown lifted along with its plump little hand, and Oskar gathered spit in his mouth.

Over the following weeks the two of us emptied over a dozen little packets of fizz powder, mostly woodruff flavored, and then when the woodruff ran out, lemon and raspberry, always following the same routine, using my spittle to make it bubble and provoking a feeling that Maria grew to appreciate more and more. I became skilled in gathering saliva, used tricks to make my mouth water quickly and copiously, and was soon able, with the contents of a single packet of fizz powder, to bestow the sensation Maria longed for three times in rapid succession.

Maria was pleased with Oskar, hugged him sometimes, even kissed him two or three times after a fizz-powder pleasuring, somewhere on his face; then Oskar would hear her giggle briefly in the darkness and quickly fall asleep.

I was finding it increasingly difficult to fall asleep. I was a sixteen-year-old with a lively imagination and a sleep-depriving urge to endow my love for Maria with even more amazing possibilities than those slumbering in the fizz powder, which, awakened by my spittle, invariably aroused the same sensation.

Oskar's meditations were not confined to the period after the light clicked off. During the day I brooded behind my drum, leafed through my well-thumbed Rasputin excerpts, recalled earlier educational orgies between Gretchen Scheffler and my poor mama, consulted Goethe, whose *Elective Affinities* I had excerpted as I had Rasputin, took on the faith healer's animal drive, tempered it with the noble poet's world-embracing feel for nature, gave Maria first the traits of the Tsarina, then the Grand Duchess Anastasia, chose ladies from Rasputin's retinue of eccentric nobles, but soon, repelled by so much animal passion, saw Maria take on the celestial transparency of an Ottilie, or as Charlotte, masking a disciplined, fully mastered passion. Oskar saw himself by turns as Rasputin, then as his murderer, often as the Captain, more rarely as Charlotte's vacillating husband, and once — I have to admit — as a genius with the well-known features of Goethe, hovering over a sleeping Maria.

Strangely enough, I received more inspiration from literature than from actual, naked life. Jan Bronski, for example, whom I'd seen tilling the flesh of my poor mama often enough, taught me next to nothing. Though I knew that this tangle consisting by turns of Mama and Jan or Matzerath and Mama — sighing, straining, then moaning in exhaustion, falling apart, trailing sticky threads — meant love, Oskar still couldn't believe that love was love, and moved by love sought other loves, yet always returned to that same tangle-love, hated that love till he'd practiced that love himself and was forced to defend it in his own eyes as the only true and possible love.

Maria took the fizz powder lying down. Since her legs generally started twitching and fidgeting the moment the powder started to fizz, her nightgown often rode high up her thighs after the first sensation. By the second fizzing the gown had usually managed to climb over her belly and roll up under her breasts. Spontaneously, without having had a chance to consult Goethe or Rasputin beforehand, after weeks of filling her left hand, I shook the rest of the raspberry fizz-powder packet into her hollow bellybutton and let my spittle flow onto it before she could protest, and as the crater started to seethe, Maria lost track of any arguments she might have used in protest, for the seething, bubbling bellybutton had obvious advantages over her hollow hand. It was still the same fizz powder, my spittle was still my spittle, and the feeling had not changed, it was simply more intense, much more intense. The sensation reached such a pitch that Maria could barely stand it. She bent over and tried to switch off the fizzing raspberry in her little bellybutton pot with her tongue, just as she used to slay the woodruff in her hollow hand when it had done its duty, but her tongue wasn't long enough; her bellybutton was farther away than Africa or Tierra del Fuego. But Maria's bellybutton was right beside me, and I sank my tongue into it, went looking for raspberries and found more and more, grew so lost in picking them that I wandered toward regions where no wardens checked licenses to pick berries, felt duty-bound to pluck each and every raspberry, had eyes, mind, heart, ears, and nose only for raspberries, was so intent on raspberries that Oskar merely noted in passing: Maria is pleased by your berry-picking zeal. That's why she's clicked off the light. That's why she's fallen asleep so trustingly and lets you keep on looking; for Maria was rich in raspberries.

And when I found no more, I found, as if by chance, mushrooms in other places. And since they grew more deeply hidden under moss, my tongue failed, and I grew an eleventh finger, since my ten fingers failed too. And so Oskar acquired a third drumstick — he was old enough for it. And I drummed not on tin but on moss. And I no longer knew: am I drumming? Is it Maria? Is that my moss or her moss? Do the moss and eleventh finger belong to someone else, and only the mushrooms to me?

Did the gentleman down there have a mind and a will of his own? Who was doing the begetting: Oskar, he, or I?

And Maria, asleep above and awake below, guileless vanilla and pungent mushrooms under moss, who longed for fizz powder but not for the little gentleman who raised his own head, who declared independence, who did what he felt like doing, whom I didn't want either, who proposed things I never suggested, who rose up when I lay down, whose dreams were not my dreams, who could neither read nor write yet signed for me, who goes his own way to this very day, who left me the first time I noticed him, a foe I must repeatedly join forces with, who betrays me and leaves me in the lurch, whom I'd gladly betray in turn, who makes me ashamed, who's fed up with me, whom I wash, who befouls me, who sees nothing and sniffs out everything, who's such a stranger I hardly know him, whose memory is not Oskar's memory: for when Maria enters my room today and Bruno slips discreetly into the hall, he no longer recognizes her, neither can nor will, lolls about phlegmatically, while Oskar's surging heart makes me stammer out, "Listen to me, Maria, just tender suggestions: I could buy a compass and trace a circle about us, could use that compass to measure the angle of inclination of your neck as you read, sew, or, as now, turn the dial on my portable radio. Leave the radio alone, just tender suggestions: I could inoculate my eyes and shed tears again. Oskar will put his heart through the next butcher's meat grinder if you'll do the same with your soul. We could buy a stuffed animal to have some quiet between us. If I decided on worms and you on patience, we could go fishing and be happier. Or the fizz powder back then, do you remember? You call me Woodruff, I bubble up, you want more, I give you the rest — Maria, fizz powder, just tender suggestions.

"Why do you keep turning those knobs, keep listening to that radio, as if you have a mad passion for special communiqués?"

Special Communiqués

IT'S HARD TO EXPERIMENT on my drum's white disk. I should have known that. My tin always wants the same wood. It wants to be asked striking questions and give striking answers, or be plied with easy, conversational rolls that leave both question and answer open. My drum is neither a frying pan that startles raw meat with artificial heat nor a dance floor for couples who aren't sure if they belong together. So even in his loneliest hours Oskar has never sprinkled fizz powder on his drum, added his spit, and put on a show he's not seen for years, one I sorely miss. It's true that Oskar could not entirely forgo an experiment with said powder, but he proceeded more directly and left his drum out of it; and in doing so I exposed myself, for without my drum I'm always defenseless and exposed.

It was hard to get hold of fizz powder at first. I sent Bruno to every grocery store in Grafenberg, had him take the tram to Gerresheim. I asked him to try in the city too, but even at refreshment stands like the ones in tram terminals Bruno couldn't find any fizz powder. The younger salesgirls had never heard of it, older shopkeepers recalled it long-windedly, rubbed their foreheads pensively — as Bruno reported — and said, "Man, what's that you want? Fizz powder? Long time back that was, when you could get it. Back in Wilhelm's day, and early on under Adolf, in shops. Those were the days! But how about a soda or a cola?"

My keeper drank several bottles of soda and cola at my expense but couldn't find what I wanted, yet Oskar received help in the end. Bruno proved relentless: yesterday he brought me a little white packet without a label; the lab technician at the mental institution, a certain Fräulein Klein, was very understanding and agreed to open her containers, drawers, and reference books to take a few grams of this and a few grams of that, and finally, after several trials, produced a fizz powder that, Bruno reported, fizzed, prickled, turned green, and tasted very discreetly of woodruff.

And today was Visitors Day. Maria came. But Klepp arrived first. We spent almost three-quarters of an hour laughing about something forgettable. I spared Klepp and his Leninist leanings, didn't bring up current events, didn't mention the special communiqué I'd heard on my little portable radio — Maria gave it to me a few weeks ago — reporting Stalin's death. But Klepp seemed to know all about it, for awkwardly sewn on the sleeve of his brown-checked overcoat was a black band. Then Klepp arose and Vittlar came in. The two friends were apparently quarreling again, for Vittlar greeted Klepp with a laugh and made devil's horns with his fingers: "Stalin's death caught me by surprise while shaving this morning!" he taunted and helped Klepp on with his coat. With unctuous piety shining on his broad face Klepp lifted the black band on his sleeve. "That's why I'm in mourning," he sighed, and imitating Armstrong's trumpet, he intoned the funereal opening bars of the New Orleans Function — trrrah trahdada traah dada dadada — then slipped out the door.

Vittlar stayed, however, refused to sit down, danced about instead in front of the mirror, and we smiled at each other knowingly for about a quarter of an hour without mentioning Stalin.

I don't know if I wanted to confide in Vittlar or if I meant to drive him away. I motioned him over to my bed, motioned his ear closer, and whispered into his large-lobed spoon, "Fizz powder! Do you know what that is, Gottfried?"

A horrified leap carried Vittlar back from my crib; he assumed his accustomed air of theatrical pathos, thrust his index finger toward me, and hissed, "Wilt thou seduce me, Satan, with fizz powder? Dost thou not yet know I am an angel?"

And like an angel Vittlar winged away, but not before checking himself once more in the mirror over the washbasin. The young people outside this mental institution are quite odd and affected.

And then Maria arrived. She's had a new spring suit tailor-made and is wearing an elegant mouse-gray hat with a refined touch of straw-yellow trim, a creation she does not remove even inside the room. She gave me a cursory greeting, proffered her cheek, and turned on the portable radio, which she had, in fact, given to me but seemed to reserve for her own use, for that vile plastic box always replaces a part of our conversation on visiting days. "Did you hear the communiqué this morning? That's really something. Or did you miss it?" "Yes, Maria," I replied patiently. "They weren't hiding Stalin's death from me, but please, turn off the radio."

Maria obeyed without a word and sat down, still wearing her hat, and we talked as usual about little Kurt.

"Just think, Oskar, the little rascal don't want to wear long socks no more, and it's March and getting colder, they said so on the radio." I tuned out the weather report but sided with little Kurt about the long socks. "The boy's twelve years old, Maria, he's ashamed to wear wool socks around his school chums."

"Well, it's his health I'm worried about, and he's wearing those socks till Easter."

This appointed date was stated so firmly that I gingerly offered a compromise: "Then you should buy him ski pants, because those long wool socks are really ugly. Just think back when you were his age. In the courtyard on Labesweg? What did they do to Little Cheese, who had to wear long socks till Easter? Nuchi Eyke, who fell on Crete, Axel Mischke, who got his in Holland right near the end, and Harry Schlager — what did they do to Little Cheese? They smeared those long wool socks of his with so much tar they stuck to him and he had to go to the hospital."

"That was Susi Kater's fault, she's to blame and not the socks!" Maria burst out angrily. Even though Susi Kater had joined the women's telegraph corps at the very start of the war and supposedly got married in Bavaria later on, Maria bore the sort of grudge against Susi, who was a few years her senior, that only women seem able to sustain from childhood to grannyhood. Nevertheless my reference to Little Cheese's tar-smeared wool socks had some effect. Maria promised to buy little Kurt ski pants. Our conversation could take another turn. There was praise to report for our Kurt. Principal Könnemann had offered a few words of recognition at the last parents' meeting. "Just imagine! He's second in his class. And he helps me in the shop, I can't tell you all he does."

I nodded approvingly, listened as she described her newest purchases for the delicatessen. I encouraged Maria to open a branch in Oberkassel. Times are favorable, I said, and the economic outlook is good — I'd picked that up from the radio, by the way — and then I decided it was time to ring for Bruno. He came in and handed me the little white packet containing the fizz powder.

Oskar had thought out his plan. Without explanation of any kind I asked Maria for her left hand. First she gave me her right, then corrected herself, offered the back of her left hand, shaking her head and laughing, probably expecting me to kiss it. She showed no surprise till I turned her palm toward me and poured powder from the little packet into a little pile between the Mound of the Moon and the Mound of Venus. She allowed this, however, and was startled only when Oskar bent over her hand and let his spittle flow freely over the fizz-powder mound.

"Stop that foolishness, Oskar!" she said indignantly, jumped up, stepped back, and stared in dismay at the bubbling, frothy green foam. Maria blushed from her forehead down. I was just starting to hope when she reached the washbasin with three quick strides, turned on the tap, and let water, disgusting water, first cold, then warm, flow over our fizz powder, then washed her hands with my soap.

"You're really impossible sometimes, Oskar! What will Herr Münsterberg think of us?" Pleading for him to be lenient with me, she looked at Bruno, who had taken a stand at the foot of the bed during my attempt. To spare Maria any further embarrassment, I sent my keeper from the room, and as soon as he'd closed the door behind him, called Maria back to the bed: "Don't you remember? Please, surely you remember. Fizz powder. Three pfennigs a packet. Just think back: woodruff, raspberry, how beautifully it foamed and fizzed, and that feeling, Maria, that feeling!"

Maria didn't remember. She was silly enough to be afraid, trembled a little, hid her left hand, tried desperately to change the topic, told me again about little Kurt's success in school, about Stalin's death, about the new icebox at Matzerath's delicatessen, about plans for the new branch in Oberkassel. But I remained true to the woodruff: fizz powder, I said, she stood up, fizz powder, I begged, she said a quick goodbye, plucked at her hat, unsure if she should leave, twisted the radio's dial, the radio blared, I shouted above it: "Fizz powder, Maria, surely you remember!"

Then she stood in the doorway, wept, shook her head, left me alone with the blaring, whistling radio, closed the door so quietly she might have been leaving a dying man.

So Maria no longer remembers fizz powder. But for me, as long as I can breathe and drum, that fizz powder will never stop foaming; for it was my spittle in the late summer of nineteen-forty that brought woodruff and raspberry to life, awakened the feelings that sent my flesh out questing, that made me a gatherer of chanterelles, morels, and other mushrooms as yet unknown to me but no doubt equally edible, that made a father of me, yes, a father, so young a father, from spittle to father, awakening feelings, a father, gathering and begetting; for by early November there was no room for doubt, Maria was pregnant, Maria was in her second month, and I, Oskar, was the father.

I believe it to this very day, for the business with Matzerath occurred much later; it was two weeks, no, ten days after I had impregnated a sleeping Maria in her richly scarred brother Herbert's bed, in that darkened room, between walls and blackout paper, and in full view of the postcards from her younger brother, the airman second class, that I found a Maria no longer sleeping but instead busily gasping for air on our sofa; she lay beneath Matzerath and Matzerath lay on top of her.

Oskar, who'd been meditating in the attic, stepped from the hallway into the living room with his drum. The two of them didn't notice me. Had their heads toward the tile stove. Hadn't even undressed properly. Matzerath's shorts were hanging about his knees. His trousers in a pile on the carpet. Maria's dress and slip had rolled up over her bra to her armpits. Her panties were dangling from her right foot, which, along with her leg, hung twisted at an ugly angle from the sofa. Her left leg lay hooked over the backrest, as if it weren't involved. Between her legs Matzerath. With his right hand he turned her head aside, the other widened her opening to guide him on his way. Through Matzerath's spread fingers Maria stared sideways at the carpet and seemed to follow its pattern under the table. He'd bitten down on a velvet-covered cushion and only let up on the velvet when they talked. For sometimes they talked, without interrupting their labors. Only when the clock struck three-quarters did they both hesitate for as long as it took the chimes to do their duty, and he said, working away as he had before the chimes began, "It's a quarter of." And then he wanted to know from her if it was good that way, how he was doing it. She said yes several times and asked him to be careful. He promised her he would. She told him again, urged him to watch it this time. Then he asked if she was nearly there. And she said: I'm nearly there. Then she must have had a cramp in the foot hanging from the sofa, for she thrust it into the air, with her panties still clinging to it. Then he bit into the velvet cushion again and she cried out go away, and he tried to but could not, because before he was away Oskar was on top of them both, because I'd plunked my drum down on the small of his back and my drumsticks on the tin, because I could no longer stand to hear go away, because my drum drowned out her words, because I could not let him leave as Jan Bronski always left Mama; for Mama too had always cried to Jan to go away, had cried to Matzerath, go away. Then they would fall apart and let the snot splat down somewhere, onto a towel they'd brought, or if they couldn't reach that, onto the sofa or even on the carpet. But I couldn't bear to see that. After all, I hadn't gone away. And I was the first one not to, so I'm the father and not Matzerath, who believed to the very end he was my father. And yet Jan Bronski was. And that's something I inherited from Jan, that I was there before Matzerath and didn't go away, that I stayed in, let go inside; and what came out was my son, not his. He didn't have a son. He was no real father. Even if he married my poor mama ten times over and married Maria too, because she was pregnant. And that's what people in our building and on our street will surely think. Of course they thought: Matzerath's knocked up Maria and now he's marrying her, with her only seventeen and a half and him forty-five. But she's a hard worker for her age, and as for little Oskar, he should be happy to have her for a stepmother, Maria's more than a stepmother to the poor child, she's like a real mother, though Oskar's not quite right in the head and should really be in an institution, like Silberhammer or the one in Tapiau.

On Gretchen Scheffler's advice, Matzerath decided to marry my beloved. So if I call my presumptive father my father, it follows that my father married my future wife, called my son Kurt his son Kurt, expected me to acknowledge his grandson as my half brother, to accept my beloved vanilla-scented Maria as my stepmother, and to tolerate her presence in his bed, which stank of fish roe. When, however, I realized: this fellow Matzerath is not even your presumptive father, he's a complete stranger, deserving neither sympathy nor antipathy, a good cook, who while cooking well has cared for you after a fashion up till now in your father's place, because your poor mama left you in this man's care, who has now snatched from you, of all people, the best of all women, making you witness a wedding and five months later a baptism as a guest at two family celebrations you yourself should have been hosting, for you should have been the one taking Maria to the registry office, you should have chosen the godparents—when, therefore, I regarded the major roles in this tragedy and was forced to note that the performance suffered from a total miscasting of the lead role, I despaired of the theater: for Oskar, the true character actor, had been assigned the role of an extra, one that could easily have been dispensed with altogether.

Before I give my son the name Kurt, a name he never should have had—for I would have named the boy after his real great-grandfather Vinzent Bronski—before I resign myself to Kurt, Oskar will not conceal how, during Maria's pregnancy, he defended himself against the coming birth.

On the evening of the day on which I surprised the two of them on the sofa, the day I was drumming on Matzerath's sweat-covered back, and prevented the precautions Maria had urged, I made a desperate attempt to win back my beloved.

By the time Matzerath managed to shake me off it was already too late. So he hit me. Maria took Oskar under her wing and reproached Matzerath for not being careful enough. Matzerath defended himself like an old man. It was Maria's fault, he said, trying to talk his way out of it, she should have been satisfied with doing it once, but she could never get enough. Then Maria started crying and said things didn't go that quick for her, just in and out and done, he'd have to find someone else for that, yes, she knew she wasn't very experienced, but her sister Guste at the Eden knew what was what, and told her things don't go that quick, Maria should watch out, some men just wanted to shoot their snot, and Matzerath was probably one of them, but she wasn't putting up with it anymore, she had to have her bell rung too, like that last time. But that meant he had to be careful, he owed her that, he should show her a little consideration. Then she cried and kept on sitting there on the sofa. And Matzerath shouted in his shorts that he was fed up with her bawling; then he felt bad he'd lost his temper and renewed his assault on

Maria, that is, he reached under her dress, where she was still bare, and tried to stroke her, which made Maria furious.

Oskar had never seen her like that. Red spots appeared on her face, and her gray eyes grew darker and darker. She called Matzerath a limp-dick, whereupon he picked up his trousers, pulled them on, and buttoned them up. He could buzz off, Maria yelled at him, go back to his group leaders, they were a bunch of quick-squirts too. Matzerath grabbed his jacket, then the door handle, and assured her he would be making some changes, he was fed up with women; if she was so hot, she should get her hooks in some foreign worker, the Frenchy who brought the beer, he could surely do it better. To him, Matzerath, love was something more than just swinishness, he was going to play some skat now, at least there he knew what to expect.

And then I was alone with Maria in the living room. She had stopped crying and was thoughtfully pulling on her panties, whistling only sparingly. She spent a long time smoothing out her dress, which had suffered on the sofa. Then she turned on the radio, tried to listen as the water levels on the Vistula and the Nogat were reported, and then, after the gauge reading for the lower Mottlau had been announced, as a waltz was first promised and could then be heard, she suddenly and unexpectedly pulled off her panties again, went into the kitchen, plunked down a kettle, turned on the tap; I heard the gas puff and gathered that Maria had decided on a sitz bath.

To dispel this rather embarrassing image, Oskar concentrated on the strains of the waltz. If I recall correctly, I even drummed a few bars of Strauß and enjoyed it. Then the radio station interrupted the waltz for a special communiqué. Oskar bet on news from the Atlantic and was not mistaken. Several U-boats had managed to sink seven or eight ships of so-and-so-many thousand tons to the west of Ireland. Other subs had managed to send a nearly equal number of registered tons to the bottom of the Atlantic. One submarine in particular had distinguished itself, under the command of Lieutenant-Captain Schepke, or perhaps Lieutenant-Captain Kretschmer — anyway, one or the other, or some third famous lieutenant-captain — had sunk the most tonnage, and into the bargain, or over and above it, a British destroyer of the XY class.

While I played variations on "Sailing against England," which followed the special communiqué, and almost turned it into a waltz on my drum, Maria came into the living room with a Turkish towel over her arm. In an undertone she asked Oskar, "Do you hear that, little Oskar, another special communiqué! If they keep on like that . . ."

Without revealing to Oskar what would happen if they managed to keep on like that, she sat down in the chair on which Matzerath usually hung his jacket. Maria twisted the wet towel into a sausage and whistled along with "Sailing against England," rather loudly and even correctly. She repeated the final chorus a second time when those on the radio had already stopped, then switched off the box on the sideboard the moment strains of the immortal waltz set in again. She left the sausaged towel on the table, sat down, and placed her little paws on her thighs.

Then things grew very quiet in our living room, only the grandfather clock spoke more and more loudly, and Maria seemed to be wondering if it might not be best to turn the radio back on. But she made another decision. She pressed her head against the sausaged towel on the tabletop, let her arms dangle past her knees toward the carpet, and wept silently and steadily.

Oskar wondered if Maria was ashamed because I'd caught her in such an embarrassing position. I decided to cheer her up, slipped out of the living room and found in the dark shop, next to packages of pudding and sheets of gelatin, a little packet that in the twilight of the corridor turned out to be a packet of woodruff-flavored fizz powder. Oskar was pleased by his find, for at the time I thought Maria preferred woodruff to any other flavor.

As I entered the living room, Maria's right cheek still rested on the towel twisted into a sausage. And her arms still dangled helplessly between her thighs. Oskar approached from the left and was disappointed to find her eyes closed and tearless. I waited patiently till she lifted her lids with their slightly sticky lashes, then held the little packet out to her, but she didn't notice the woodruff, seemed to stare right through the little packet and Oskar too.

She's probably been blinded by her tears, I thought, excusing her, and decided, after a brief internal deliberation, on a more direct approach. Under the table climbed Oskar, crouched at Maria's pigeon-toed feet, took her left hand, which was almost touching the carpet with its fingertips, turned it till I could see the palm, tore open the packet with my teeth, poured half the contents of the paper package into the bowl thus listlessly relinquished to me, added my spittle, and had just enough time to see it start to fizz before Maria gave me a painful kick in the chest that hurled Oskar to the carpet directly under the living room table.

In spite of the pain I was back on my feet in an instant and out from under the table. Maria was standing too. We stood across from each other breathing hard. Maria grabbed the Turkish towel, wiped her left hand clean, slung the towel at my feet, and called me a dirty pig, a nasty dwarf, a crazy midget that should be thrown in the nuthouse. Then she grabbed me, slapped the back of my head, reviled my poor mama for having brought a brat like me into the world, and just as I was about to aim a scream at all the glass in the living room and in the whole world, she stuffed my mouth with that Turkish towel, which was tougher than tough beef when you clamped down on it.

Not until Oskar managed to turn red and blue did she release me. Now I could easily have screamshattered all the glasses and window-panes, including the crystal covering the dial of the grandfather clock again. But I didn't scream; instead I allowed a hate to possess me that's so deep-seated I still feel it today every time Maria walks in the room, feel it like that towel between my teeth.

Capricious as Maria could be, she let up on me, laughed good-naturedly, turned the radio on with a flick of the dial, came toward me, whistling along with the waltz, to stroke my hair the way I always liked and make up.

Oskar let her get right up close and then struck her an uppercut with both fists right where she'd admitted Matzerath. And when she caught my fists before I could hit her a second time, I bit down hard on that same accursed spot and fell to the sofa with her, still biting Maria hard, heard the radio break for another special communiqué, but Oskar had no wish to hear it; and so he can't tell you who sank what and how many, for a violent fit of tears loosened my jaws and I lay motionless on Maria, who was crying in pain, while Oskar was crying with hate, and with a love that turned to leaden helplessness and yet could never die.

Carrying My Helplessness to Frau Greff

I DIDN'T LIKE Greff. Greff didn't like me. Later on, when Greff built the drum machine for me, I still didn't like him. Even today, when Oskar barely has the strength for such sustained antipathies, I don't much care for Greff, even if he no longer exists.

Greff was a greengrocer. But don't fool yourself. He didn't believe in potatoes or Savoy cabbages, but still he knew a great deal about growing vegetables and liked to think of himself as a gardener, a friend of Nature, a vegetarian. But precisely because Greff didn't eat meat, he was no true greengrocer. He found it impossible to talk about vegetables as mere vegetables. "Consider, please, this extraordinary potato," I would often hear him tell his customers, "this swelling, bursting fruity pulp, constantly creating new forms, yet so chaste. I love a potato, for it speaks to me." Of course no true greengrocer would ever embarrass his customers with talk like that. Even in the best potato years, my grandmother Anna Koljaiczek, who grew old amid potato fields, never uttered more than some brief remark such as "Them spuds are a bit bigger than last year." Yet Anna Koljaiczek and her brother Vinzent Bronski were far more dependent on the potato harvest than the greengrocer Greff, who could always make up for a bad potato year with a good one in plums.

Everything about Greff was overdone. Did he have to wear a green apron in the shop? What presumption to smile at his customers, point sagely at his spinach-green bib, and call it "God's green garden-apron." Nor could he give up scouting. True, he'd been forced to disband his troop in thirty-eight — the little rogues were fitted out in brown shirts and dashing black winter uniforms instead — but his former scouts came by regularly, in civilian clothes or their new uniforms, to see their former scoutmaster, and as he plucked a guitar against the garden-apron God had loaned him, sang morning songs, evening songs, hiking songs, soldier's songs, harvest songs, church songs, and folk songs native and foreign. Since Greff had joined the National Socialist Motor Corps just in time and, from forty-one on, called himself both a greengrocer and an air-raid warden, and since he could count on the support of two of his former scouts who had risen in the Hitler Youth, one to squad leader and the other to platoon leader, the evenings of song in Greff's potato cellar could be considered more or less approved by the Hitler Youth District Bureau. Greff had also been asked by Löbsack, the District Director of Training, to set up song evenings for training sessions at the school in Jenkau. Early in nineteen-forty, Greff and a schoolteacher were commissioned to compile a young people's songbook entitled *Sing Along!* for the district of Danzig–West Prussia. The book turned out well. The greengrocer received a letter from Berlin, signed by the Reich Youth Leader, and was invited to attend a gathering of song leaders in Berlin.

Greff was a practical man. Not only did he know all the verses of all the songs, he could also pitch a tent, kindle and extinguish campfires without setting the woods ablaze, and find his way easily with a compass; he was on a first-name basis with every star in the sky, rattled off jokes and told tall tales, knew all the legends of the land of the Vistula, gave home lectures on "Danzig and the Hanseatic League," and could list all the Grand Masters of the Teutonic Knights along with their dates; nor did he stop at that: he could also tell you all sorts of things about the Germanic mission in the territories of the Order, and only on rare occasions did he weave an obvious Boy Scout maxim into his lectures.

Greff loved young people. He loved boys more than girls. In fact he didn't love girls at all, he only loved boys. Often he loved boys more than he could express in song. It may well be that his wife, Frau Greff, a slovenly woman with a bra that was always greasy and holes in her underwear, forced him to seek a purer measure of love among those wiry, squeaky-clean boys. But one might also lay bare another root of the tree on whose branches Frau Greff's dirty underwear bloomed throughout the year. I think Frau Greff turned slovenly because the greengrocer and air-raid warden had no appreciation for her carefree and somewhat dimwitted voluptuousness.

Greff loved the taut, the muscular, the hardened. When he said Nature, he meant asceticism. When he said asceticism, he meant a particular type of physical culture. Greff knew his body well. He cared for it meticulously, exposed it to heat and, in particularly inventive ways, to cold. While Oskar sangshattered glass at both near and long distances, thawing frost-flowers from windows now and then, melting icicles and sending them tinkling down, the greengrocer was a man who attacked ice directly with hand tools.

Greff chopped holes in the ice. In December, January, February he chopped holes in the ice with an ax. Early in the morning, while it was still dark, he would bring his bicycle up from the cellar, wrap the ice ax in an onion sack, ride through Saspe to Brösen, follow the snow-covered beach promenade from there toward Glettkau, dismount between Brösen and Glettkau, and, as the sky gradually brightened, push his bicycle with the ax in the onion sack across the icy beach and then several hundred feet out onto the frozen Baltic. Coastal fog held sway over the entire scene. No one could have seen from the beach how Greff laid down his bicycle, unwrapped the ax from the onion sack, stood for a while in devout silence, listening to the foghorns of the icebound freighters on the roads, then dropped his jacket, did a few exercises, and finally began to chop away, strongly and steadily, hacking a round hole in the Baltic Sea.

Greff needed a good three-quarters of an hour for his hole. Don't ask me how I know. Oskar knew just about everything back then. So I knew how long Greff took for his hole in the ice too. He was sweating, and his sweat sprang salty from his high-domed forehead into the snow. He chopped efficiently, drove the traced circle all the way round to its beginning, then, gloveless, lifted the round plug of ice, which was about ten inches thick, out of the broad expanse of ice, which presumably stretched clear to Hela, or even Sweden. Water stood in the hole, ancient and gray, studded with ice grits. It steamed a little but was no hot spring. The hole attracted fish. That is, they say holes in the ice attract fish. Greff could have caught lampreys or a twenty-pound cod. But he wasn't fishing, instead he was taking off his clothes, stripping naked; for whenever Greff took off his clothes, he stripped naked.

Oskar has no wish to send wintry shivers up and down your spine. Let me be brief: During the winter months the greengrocer Greff bathed twice weekly in the Baltic. On Wednesdays he bathed alone at the crack of dawn. He left around six, was there around six-thirty, hacked out the hole by seven-fifteen, flung off his clothes with quick, exaggerated movements, rubbed himself down with snow, jumped in the hole, began to shout, and at times could be heard singing: "Wild geese are flying through the night" or "Oh, how we love the storm . . . ," he sang, bathed, shouted for two or at most three minutes, then with a single leap he stood terrifyingly distinct on the surface of the ice: a mass of steaming, crab-red flesh racing around the hole, still shouting, still glowing, then back in his clothes at last and onto the bike. Shortly before eight Greff was at Labesweg again and opened his shop right on time.

Greff took a second ice bath on Sundays, in the company of several boys. Oskar makes no claim to have ever seen this, nor did he. But word got around. Meyn the musician told stories about the greengrocer, trumpeted them through the whole neighborhood, and one of those trumpet-tales ran like this: Each Sunday during the roughest winter months, Greff would bathe in the company of several boys. But even Meyn didn't claim that the greengrocer forced the boys to jump into the ice hole naked, as he did. He was satisfied if they frolicked around on the ice, sinewy and tough, half-naked or nearly naked youths, and rubbed each other down with snow. Indeed, the boys in the snow gave Greff so much pleasure that before or after bathing he often frolicked with them, helped rub down one or two, and let the whole horde rub him down; and Meyn the musician claims that in spite of the coastal fog, he saw from the Glettkau beach promenade an appallingly naked, singing, shouting Greff pull two of his naked pupils to him, lift them up, and naked bearing the naked, tear off across the thick Baltic ice like a shouting, runaway troika.

As you might imagine, Greff was no fisherman's son, though there were lots of fishermen in Brösen and Neufahrwasser named Greff. Greff the greengrocer hailed from Tiegenhof, but Lina Greff, née Bartsch, met her husband in Praust. He was helping an enterprising young vicar there run the Catholic journeymen's club, and Lina was drawn to the parish house each Saturday by same vicar. A photo she must have given me, for it's still pasted today in my photo album, shows the twenty-year-old Lina as strong, plump, merry, good-natured, flighty, dumb. Her father ran a good-sized fruit and vegetable farm in Sankt Albrecht. She was twenty-two and, as she always swore later, totally inexperienced when she followed the vicar's advice and married Greff, then opened the vegetable shop in Langfuhr with her father's money. Since they got a large part of their produce—almost all their fruit, for example—at low cost from their father's farm, the business practically ran itself, and Greff could do little damage.

In fact if it hadn't been for the greengrocer's childish tendency to tinker with things, the shop could easily have turned into a gold mine, for it was favorably located in a suburb swarming with children and far removed from competitors. But when an inspector from the Bureau of Weights and Standards appeared for the third or fourth time to examine the scales, then confiscated the weights, locked the scales, and imposed assorted fines on Greff, a number of regular customers turned elsewhere, bought at the weekly market, and passed the word: the produce at Greff's is always high quality, and the prices aren't bad, but something fishy is going on; the people from Weights and Standards were there again.

Yet I'm sure Greff wasn't trying to cheat anyone. What happened was that the large potato scales were weighing to Greff's disadvantage after the greengrocer had made a few adjustments. So shortly before the war he built a set of chimes into the scales that would play a little tune depending on the weight of the potatoes. With twenty pounds of potatoes the customer was regaled, as a sort of bonus, with "On the sunny shores of the Saale," fifty pounds of potatoes got you "Always true and honest be," a hundred pounds of winter potatoes lured from the chimes the naively bewitching tones of the little song "Ännchen von Tharau."

Though I could see how the Bureau of Weights and Standards might not like such musical pleasantries, Oskar himself was in tune with the greengrocer's flights of fancy. Lina Greff too indulged her husband's eccentricities, for the Greffs' marriage was founded precisely on the mutual indulgence of such eccentricities. In this sense the Greffs' marriage was a good one. The greengrocer didn't beat his wife, never cheated on her with other women, was neither a drunkard nor a glutton; instead he was a cheerful, respectably dressed man who was well liked for his affability and helpful nature, not only by young boys but also by those of his customers who bought his music along with his potatoes.

So Greff too watched calmly and indulgently from year to year as his Lina turned into an increasingly foul-smelling slattern. I saw him smile when people who meant well called her that. Blowing on his hands, which were well kept in spite of the potatoes, and rubbing them together, I sometimes heard him say to Matzerath, who disapproved of Greff's wife, "Of course you're perfectly right, Alfred. She is a bit slovenly, our good Lina. But don't you and I have our faults too?" If Matzerath didn't let up, Greff would end such discussions in a firm yet friendly manner: "You may be right on the whole, but still she has a good heart. I know my Lina."

And he may indeed have known her. But she hardly knew him at all. Like the neighbors and customers, she never saw anything more in Greff's relations with the young boys and striplings who visited him so often than their youthful enthusiasm for a nonprofessional yet ardent friend and mentor of the young.

As for me, Greff neither roused my enthusiasm nor served as my mentor. Nor was Oskar his type. Had I chosen to grow, I might have grown into his type, for my son Kurt, who's now around thirteen, embodies in all his bony lankiness exactly what Greff liked, even though he takes after Maria on the whole, bearing little resemblance to me and none whatever to Matzerath.

Greff and Fritz Truczinski, who was home on leave, served as witnesses at the wedding of Maria Truczinski and Alfred Matzerath. Since Maria, like her bridegroom, was Protestant, they simply went to the registry. This was in mid-December. Matzerath said his I do in Party uniform. Maria was in her third month.

The stouter my beloved grew, the more Oskar's hate mounted. I had nothing against her pregnancy. But the fact that the fruit of my loins would one day bear the name of Matzerath destroyed any pleasure in my future son and heir. So when Maria was in her fifth month, much too late of course, I made my first attempt at an abortion. It was around Carnival time. Maria wanted to attach a few paper streamers and two clown masks with bulbous noses to the brass rod over the counter hung with sausages and bacon. The ladder, which normally leaned firmly against the shelves, was placed precariously against the counter. Maria far above, with her hands among the streamers, Oskar far below, at the foot of the ladder. Using my drumsticks as a lever, and helping with my shoulder and the firmest resolve, I lifted the steps up and to the side: Maria gave a soft and terrified cry from among the streamers and masks, the ladder swayed, Oskar sprang aside, and Maria, brightly colored streamers, sausage, and masks all came tumbling down.

It looked worse than it was. She had only sprained an ankle, had to lie in bed and take it easy, but had suffered no other injury, grew bulkier still, and didn't even tell Matzerath who had helped her sprain her ankle.

It wasn't till May, about three weeks before she was due, after I made a second try at abortion, that she spoke to her husband Matzerath, without revealing the full extent of the truth. At table, and in my presence, she said, "Little Oskar's so rough lately when he plays, and hits me in the belly sometimes. Maybe he should stay with Mama till the baby comes, she's got lots of room."

Matzerath heard it and believed it. In reality a fit of murderous rage had led to a very different sort of encounter with Maria.

She was lying on the sofa during the noon break. Having washed the lunch dishes, Matzerath was in the shop arranging the window display. All was silent in the living room. A fly perhaps, the clock as usual, the radio turned low, reporting the exploits of paratroopers on Crete. I pricked up my ears only when they put on the great boxer Max Schmeling. From what I could gather, he had sprained his world-champion ankle when he parachuted onto Crete's rocky soil, and had to lie down and take it easy now — like Maria, who had to take to bed after her fall from the ladder. Schmeling spoke calmly, modestly; then less prominent paratroopers came on and Oskar stopped listening: silence, a fly perhaps, the clock as usual, very low the radio.

I sat by the window on my little bench and watched Maria's belly on the sofa. She was breathing heavily and had closed her eyes. From time to time I plied my drum morosely. She didn't stir, but still forced me to breathe in the same room with her belly. Of course there was still the clock, the fly between pane and curtain, and the radio with the rocky island of Crete in the background. All of that faded for me in a split second, I could see nothing but her belly, knew neither in what room that belly swelled nor to whom it belonged, scarcely knew who'd made that belly so big, knew only one desire: That belly has to go, it's a mistake, it's blocking your view, you've got to stand up and do something. So I stood up. You've got to see what can be done. So I went over to the belly and took something with me as I went. You need to let a little air out there, that's a bad case of flatulence. Then I raised what I'd brought with me and sought a spot between Maria's little paws as they breathed along on her belly. You've got to decide once and for all, Oskar, otherwise Maria is going to open her eyes. I could already sense I was being watched, but kept my eyes on Maria's slightly trembling left hand, noticed that she'd drawn back her right hand, that her right hand was planning something, and was not particularly astonished when Maria twisted the scissors from Oskar's grip with her right hand. I may have remained standing there for a few seconds with raised but empty hand, heard the clock, the fly, the announcer's voice on the radio concluding the report from Crete, then I turned and, before the next program could begin — light music from two to three — left our living room, which in view of that space-filling belly was now too crowded for me.

Two days later Maria bought me a new drum and took me up to Mother Truczinski's second-floor flat, smelling of ersatz coffee and fried potatoes. At first I slept on the sofa, since Oskar declined to sleep in Herbert's former bed, which I feared might still bear traces of Maria's vanilla scent. A week later old man Heilandt lugged my wooden cot up the stairs. I let them set it beside the bed that had remained still and silent beneath me, Maria, and our shared fizz powder.

Oskar grew calmer, or more apathetic, at Mother Truczinski's. After all, I no longer saw that belly, for Maria shied away from climbing stairs. I avoided our ground-floor flat, the shop, the street, even the courtyard of our building, where, as food shortages became increasingly serious, rabbits were again being raised.

For the most part Oskar sat with the postcards Airman Second Class Fritz Truczinski sent or brought with him from Paris. They gave me various ideas about Paris, and when Mother Truczinski handed me a postcard of the Eiffel Tower, I began to drum up Paris, entering into the bold ironwork of that construction, began to drum a musette without ever having heard one.

On the twelfth of June, fourteen days early, according to my calculations, in the sign of Gemini, and not as I had expected in the sign of Cancer, my son Kurt was born. The father in a Jupiter year, the son in a Venus year. The father ruled by Mercury in Virgo, which made him skeptical and ingenious; the son likewise ruled by Mercury, but in the sign of Gemini, endowed with a cold, ambitious intelligence. What in my own case was tempered by Venus with Libra in the house of the ascendant, was aggravated in my son by Aries in the same house; I would come to feel his Mars.

Mother Truczinski delivered the news like an excited mouse: "Just think, little Oskar, the stork's brought you a little brother. And just when I was thinking, man, just so it's not a lass, with all sorts of trouble later." I scarcely interrupted my drumming on the Eiffel Tower and a newly arrived view of the Arc de Triomphe. Even now that she was Grandma Truczinski, Mother Truczinski didn't seem to expect me to congratulate her. Though it wasn't Sunday, she decided to put on a little rouge, reached for the good old chicory paper, rubbed it on her cheeks to color them, left her rooms freshly rouged, and went down to the ground floor to help Matzerath, the presumptive father.

As I've said, it was June. A deceptive month. Victories on every front — if you want to call victories in the Balkans victories — but even greater victories lay ahead in the east. A massive army was advancing there. The railroads were kept busy. Even Fritz Truczinski, who had been having such a good time in Paris, had to set out on a journey eastward that would not soon end and could not possibly be mistaken for leave. But Oskar sat quietly before the shiny postcards, lingering in a mild, early-summer Paris, casually drumming "Trois jeunes tambours," with no connection to the German occupation army, and thus with nothing to fear from the partisans who might think of throwing him off the bridges of the Seine. No, clad as a civilian I climbed the Eiffel Tower with my drum, enjoyed the vista from the top as expected, felt so good and, in spite of the tempting height, so free from bittersweet thoughts of suicide, that it was only on descending, when I stood three foot one at the base of the Eiffel Tower, that I remembered the birth of my son.

Voilà, a son! I thought to myself. When he's three years old, he'll get a tin drum. We'll see who the father is — this Herr Matzerath or me, Oskar Bronski.

In the heat of August — I believe the successful conclusion of another encircling action had just been announced, at Smolensk this time — my son Kurt was baptized. But how did my grandmother Anna Koljaiczek and her brother Vinzent Bronski come to be invited? If I accept once more the version where Jan Bronski is my father, and the calm and increasingly eccentric Vinzent my grandfather on my father's side, there were ample grounds for the invitation. After all, my grandparents were the great-grandparents of my son Kurt.

Of course this line of reasoning never occurred to Matzerath, who issued the invitation. Even in moments of greatest self-doubt — after losing his shirt in a game of skat, for example — he always regarded himself as a begetter, father, and provider twice over. Oskar saw his grandparents again owing to other factors. The two old people had been Germanized. They were no longer Poles, and only their dreams remained Kashubian. Ethnic Germans they called them, Ethnic Group Three. In addition, Hedwig Bronski, Jan's widow, had married a Baltic German who ran the Local Farm Association in Ramkau. Petitions had already been submitted which, once granted, would allow Marga and Stephan Bronski to take on the name of their stepfather Ehlers. Seventeen-year-old Stephan had volunteered, he was at the Infantry Training Camp at Groß-Boschpol, and chances were good he'd get to visit various European theaters of war, while Oskar, who would soon be of military age himself, would have to wait behind his drum until the army, navy, or perhaps even the air force could think of a way to use a three-year-old tin-drummer boy.

Local Farm Leader Ehlers took the initiative. Two weeks before the baptism he pulled up at Labesweg in a carriage and pair with Hedwig on the box beside him. He was bowlegged, had a bad stomach, and didn't come close to measuring up to Jan Bronski. He sat a full head shorter beside the cow-eyed Hedwig at the living room table. Even Matzerath was surprised at his appearance. No one could think of anything to say. They discussed the weather, agreed that all sorts of things were happening in the east, that they were making good progress, much better than they had in nineteen-fifteen, as Matzerath, who'd been there in nineteen-fifteen, recalled. They were all at pains to avoid any mention of Jan Bronski till I drew a line through their silent calculations by giving a droll, childish pout and crying out loudly several times for Oskar's uncle Jan. Matzerath gave a start, and made a few amiable remarks followed by some thoughtful words about his former friend and rival. Ehlers quickly chimed in at some length, though he'd never laid eyes on his predecessor. Hedwig even produced a few authentic tears that rolled slowly down her cheeks and offered the concluding observation on Jan: "A good man he was. And wouldn't hurt a fly. Who'd think he'd end like that, he was always such a scaredy-cat, scared of the least little thing."

Moved by these words, Matzerath asked Maria, who was standing behind him, to fetch a few bottles of beer, and asked Ehlers if he played skat. Ehlers was sorry to say he didn't, but Matzerath was magnanimous enough to forgive the Local Farm Leader this minor shortcoming. He even clapped him on the shoulder and assured him, with beer already in their glasses, that it didn't matter if he couldn't play skat, they could still be friends.

So Hedwig Bronski found her way back to our flat as Hedwig Ehlers, and, along with her Local Farm Leader, brought her former father-in-law Vinzent Bronski and his sister Anna to my son Kurt's baptism. Matzerath seemed to be in the know, gave the old folks a loud, friendly welcome on the street, beneath the neighbors' windows, and said in the living room, when my grandmother reached under her four skirts and pulled out the baptismal gift, a fine fat goose, "You didn't have to do that, dearie. I'm just glad you came, even if you didn't bring a thing." But that didn't sit right with my grandmother, who wanted some appreciation for her goose. She slapped her flat palm on the fat bird in protest: "Don't be like that, Alfie. This is no Kashubian goose, it's ethnic German, and tastes just like before the war."

That solved all the ethnic problems, and there were no further difficulties till the baptism, when Oskar refused to set foot in the Protestant church. Even when they fetched my drum from the taxi, used it as bait, and kept assuring me that drums could be carried openly in Protestant churches, I remained the blackest of Catholics and would sooner have poured a brief, summary confession into Father Wiehnke's pastoral ear than listen to a Protestant baptismal sermon. Matzerath gave in. He probably dreaded my voice and attendant claims for damages. So while the baptism took place in the church I stayed in the taxi and examined the back of the driver's head, scrutinized Oskar's face in the rearview mirror, and recalled my own baptism all those years ago and Father Wiehnke's repeated attempts to drive Satan from the infant Oskar.

After the baptism we ate. Two tables were shoved together and we started with mock turtle soup. Spoons and bowl rims. The country folk slurped. Greff crooked his little finger. Gretchen Scheffler bit into the soup. Guste smiled broadly over her spoon. Ehlers talked with the spoon in his mouth. With a shaky hand Vinzent searched with his spoon. Only the old women, Grandmother Anna and Mother Truczinski, were devoting themselves wholly to their spoons, while Oskar, dropping the spoon so to speak, slipped off while they were still spooning, and sought his son's cradle in the bedroom, for he wanted to think about his son, while the others shriveled up behind their spoons with blank minds, spooned out, in spite of all the soup they were spooning in.

Light blue tulle heavens over the little basket on wheels. Since the basket's rim was too high, all I could spot at first was something reddish blue and pinched. I placed my drum under me and watched my son twitching nervously in his sleep. O paternal pride, always seeking grandiose phrases. Since I could think of nothing in the infant's presence but the brief sentence, When he's three years old he'll get a drum — since my son offered no information about the inner world of his thoughts, since I could only hope that, like me, he might belong to the race of clairaudient infants, I again promised him a tin drum on his third birthday, repeated it several times, descended from my own drum, and tried my luck once more with the grownups in the living room.

They were just finishing off the mock turtle soup. Maria brought out the sweet green canned peas in butter. Matzerath, who was responsible for the pork roast, served it himself from the platter: he removed his jacket, cut slice after slice in his shirtsleeves, and looked with such unabashed tenderness at the tender juicy meat that I had to avert my eyes.

The greengrocer Greff was served separately. He was given canned asparagus, hardboiled eggs, and radishes with cream, since vegetarians don't eat meat. Like everyone else, however, he took a dollop of homemade mashed potatoes, but didn't pour sauce from the roast over them, using instead the browned butter an attentive Maria brought him from the kitchen in a sizzling pan. While the others drank beer, Greff had a glass of fruit juice. They talked about the encirclement of Kiev, counted up the number of prisoners on their fingers. Ehlers, the Baltic native, was particularly deft at this; he shot up a finger for each hundred thousand, and then when his spread hands had reached a million, he continued to count by lopping the top off one finger after another. When they'd exhausted the subject of Russian prisoners of war, who grew increasingly worthless and uninteresting as their numbers increased, Scheffler told us about the U-boats in Gotenhafen, and Matzerath whispered in my grandmother Anna's ear that two submarines a week were being launched at Schichau. Upon which the greengrocer Greff explained to the guests why submarines had to be launched sideways rather than stern first. He tried to give them a vivid picture of the whole procedure, using gestures that a few of the guests, who were fascinated by U-boats, imitated attentively and awkwardly. Vinzent Bronski knocked over his beer glass with his left hand trying to duplicate a diving U-boat. My grandmother scolded him. But Maria calmed her down, said it didn't matter, the tablecloth was going into the wash tomorrow anyway; you had to expect a few stains at a baptismal dinner. And there came Mother Truczinski with a rag to sop up the puddle of beer, and in her left hand she held the big crystal bowl full of chocolate pudding with cracked almonds.

Oh, if that chocolate pudding had only had some other sauce, or none at all! But it had to be vanilla. Vanilla sauce: flowing thick and yellow. A totally banal vanilla sauce, commonplace, yet unparalleled. There may be nothing in this world as joyous as vanilla sauce, nor anything as sad. The vanilla gently released its fragrance, enveloping me more and more in Maria, prime source of all vanilla, so that I could no longer bear to look at her, sitting there by Matzerath, holding his hand in hers.

Oskar scooted down off his little chair, clinging tightly to Frau Greff's skirts as he did so, remained lying at her feet as she spooned away, and partook for the first time of Lina Greff's own particular effluvium, which instantly shouted down, swallowed up, killed off all vanilla.

As sourly as it struck me, I persevered on this new aromatic course till all my memories connected with vanilla seemed numbed. Slowly, silently, and steadily, I was overcome by a liberating nausea. While the mock turtle soup, chunks of roast pork, nearly intact canned green peas, and a few small spoonfuls of chocolate pudding with vanilla sauce escaped me, I realized my helplessness, floundered in my helplessness, spread Oskar's helplessness out at the feet of Lina Greff—and decided from then on to carry my helplessness daily to Frau Greff.

Seventy-five Kilos

VYAZMA AND BRYANSK; then the era of mud set in. In mid-October of forty-one Oskar too began wallowing robustly in mud. I hope you will indulge me if I draw a parallel between the mud-logged victories of Army Group Center and my victories in the trackless and equally muddy terrain of Frau Lina Greff. Just as tanks and trucks bogged down outside Moscow, so I too bogged down; of course the wheels did not stop spinning there, throwing up mud, nor did I slacken my efforts — I managed literally to whip up a little froth in the Greffian mud — but no territory of any note was gained outside Moscow, or in the bedroom of the Greffian flat.

I'm not yet ready to abandon this comparison: just as future strategists would draw lessons from those bogged-down muddy campaigns, I drew my own conclusions from my battle with that Greffian phenomenon of nature. One should not underestimate these campaigns on the home front during the last world war. Oskar was seventeen back then, yet in spite of his youth he developed into a man on the treacherously convoluted training grounds of Lina Greff. Abandoning the military comparisons, let me now measure Oskar's progress in artistic terms: if Maria taught me the minor modes in her naively bewitching vanilla fog, familiarizing me with lyrical forms like fizz powder and mushroom gathering, I found in the stringent, sour, and multilayered Greffian effluvium that expansive epic breath which today allows me to combine victories on the front and victories in bed in a single sentence. Music! From Maria's childlike and sentimental yet ever so sweet harmonica straight to the conductor's stand; for Lina Greff offered me an orchestra of a depth and range found only in Bayreuth or Salzburg. There I learned to blow, strum, puff, pluck, and bow, whether it involved continuo or counterpoint, twelve-tone or atonal, the entry to the scherzo or the tempo of the andante, my emotional tone was at once rigorously precise and softly flowing; Oskar drew all there was from Frau Greff and, though satisfied, remained dissatisfied, like any true artist.

It was only twenty short steps from our grocery store to the Greffs' vegetable shop. Their shop was conveniently located just across and down the street, and was far easier to reach than the flat of Alexander Scheffler, the master baker, on Kleinhammerweg. It may have been due to this more favorable location that I made more progress in female anatomy than in the study of my masters Goethe and Rasputin. Perhaps this gaping disparity in knowledge, which persists to this very day, may be explained and even excused by the difference between my two female teachers. While Lina Greff had no interest in educating me but simply placed her riches straightforwardly and passively at my disposal, to be viewed and experimented with as I wished, Gretchen Scheffler took her role as a teacher all too seriously. She wanted to see progress, wanted me to read aloud, wanted to see my drummer-boy fingers engaged in penmanship, wanted me to make friends with fair Grammatika and even profit from that friendship herself. When Oskar nonetheless refused to show any visible signs of progress, Gretchen Scheffler lost patience, and soon after my poor mama's death, following what had after all been seven years of instruction, returned to her embroidery and, since her baker's marriage remained childless, merely favored me now and then, particularly on major holidays, with sweaters, socks, and mittens she had knitted herself. There was no more talk of Goethe and Rasputin, and it was only thanks to the excerpts from the works of both masters which I continued to stash away here and there, mostly in the drying attic of our building, that this side of Oskar's studies didn't bog down entirely; I educated myself and formed my own judgments.

The ailing Lina Greff was confined to her bed, however, and could neither avoid nor abandon me, for her illness was indeed a lingering one, but not serious enough that Death could snatch my teacher Lina from me before her time. But since nothing on this star lasts forever, it was Oskar who abandoned the bedridden woman the moment he considered his studies complete.

You will say: What a narrow world this young man was reduced to for his education! Forced to piece together his armor for a later manly life from a grocery store, a bakery, and a vegetable shop. Though I must admit that Oskar received his first, all so important impressions in extremely stuffy petit-bourgeois surroundings, he also had a third teacher. To this man fell the task of opening up the world to Oskar, of making him what he is today, a person upon whom, for want of any better designation, I bestow the inadequate title cosmopolitan.

I'm referring, as the most attentive among you will have noted, to my teacher and master Bebra, direct descendant of Prince Eugen, scion of the house of Louis the Fourteenth, the dwarf and musical clown Bebra. When I say Bebra, I include of course the lady at his side, the great somnambulist Roswitha Raguna, the timeless beauty to whom my thoughts were often drawn during those dark years after Matzerath took my Maria from me. How old, I wondered, can she be, the Signora? Is she a blooming girl of twenty, or even nineteen? Or is she that delicately graceful ninety-nine-year-old lady, who, a hundred years from now, will still indestructibly embody the small-scale format of eternal youth?

If I recall correctly, I ran into these two kindred souls again shortly after the death of my poor mama. We drank Mochas together in the Café Vierjahreszeiten, then parted ways. There were slight, but not insignificant, political differences; Bebra had close connections with the Reich's Ministry of Propaganda, frequented, as I clearly gathered from hints he dropped, the privy chambers of Herr Goebbels and Herr Goering, and went to the greatest lengths to explain and justify this political derailment. He spoke of the influential role of court jesters in the Middle Ages, showed me reproductions of pictures by Spanish masters depicting some Philip or Carlos with his royal retinue, and in the midst of those rigidly formal groups a few jesters could be seen in ruffles, peaked caps, and baggy pantaloons who were about Bebra's size, and Oskar's as well. Precisely because I liked these pictures — for today I am an ardent admirer of the brilliant painter Diego Velázquez — I refused to let Bebra off that easily. So he gave up trying to compare the role of dwarfs in the court of Philip the Fourth of Spain to his own position in the entourage of the Rhenish upstart Joseph Goebbels. He spoke of difficult times, of the weak, who must temporarily give way, of resistance that blooms in secret, in short, the phrase "inner emigration" was uttered, and that was the parting of the ways for Bebra and Oskar.

Not that I bore the master any ill will. In the years that followed I scanned every poster pillar, looking for Bebra's name among the placards for circuses and variety shows, and found it listed twice, along with Signora Raguna, but did nothing that might have led to a meeting with my friends.

I left it up to chance, but chance failed me, for had Bebra and I crossed paths in the fall of forty-one, instead of the following year, Oskar would never have become a pupil of Lina Greff, but instead a disciple of Master Bebra. As it was, however, I would cross Labesweg every day, often at an early morning hour, enter the vegetable shop, spend a half-hour or so for appearance's sake with the grocer, who was developing more and more into an oddball amateur mechanic, watch as he built his whimsical, jingling, wailing, screeching machines, and poke him when a customer entered, for at the time Greff hardly noticed the world around him. What had happened? Why was this gardener and friend of the young, who had once been so open and convivial, now silent; what caused this loneliness and isolation, what was turning him into a crank, and a rather poorly groomed older man?

The young no longer came to see him. The new generation didn't know him. The war had scattered his Boy Scout entourage to all fronts. Field-post letters arrived, then only field-postcards, and one day news reached Greff indirectly that his favorite, Horst Donath, first a scout, then a squad leader in the Hitler Youth, had fallen as a lieutenant on the Donets.

Greff began to age that same day; he neglected his appearance and threw himself totally into his tinkering, till there were more jingling machines and wailing contrivances visible in his vegetable shop than potatoes and cabbages. Of course the general food shortage played a role too; deliveries to the shop were few and far between, and Greff was not, like Matzerath, able to fall back on a good customer's connections with the wholesale market.

The shop had a dismal air, and one could only be grateful for the decorative way in which Greff's absurd noisemakers, even if they did seem ludicrous, filled up the space. The creations that sprang from Greff's increasingly confused tinkerer's mind appealed to me. When I examine my keeper Bruno's string knotworks today, I'm reminded of Greff's display. And just as Bruno enjoys my smiling yet serious interest in his artistic flights of fancy, Greff was happy, in his distracted way, whenever he noticed that one or another of his music machines gave me pleasure. He who for years had paid no attention to me was now visibly disappointed when, after a brief half-hour, I left the store he had transformed into a workshop and visited his wife, Lina Greff.

What shall I tell you about my visits to the bedridden Lina, which usually lasted two to two and a half hours? When Oskar entered, she beckoned from the bed: "Oh, it's you, little Oskar. Come on closer and get under the feathers if you want, it's cold in here and Greff's so stingy with the heat." So I slipped in under the featherbed with her, left my drum and both the drumsticks I'd just been using by the bed, and allowed only a third drumstick, worn and somewhat frayed, to come along with me and pay a visit to Lina.

Not that I undressed before getting in bed with her. In wool, velvet, and leather shoes I climbed in, and long afterward, in spite of the heat generated by my strenuous efforts, I emerged from the matted feathers in the same nearly undisturbed clothes.

After I'd gone several times to the greengrocer straight from the Linabed while still steeped in his wife's effluvia, a ritual was adopted that I all too gladly observed. As I lingered in bed going through my final exercises with his wife, the greengrocer would come into the bedroom with a basin of warm water, set it down on a little stool, place a hand towel and soap beside it, and leave the room without a word, not having burdened the bed with a single glance.

Generally Oskar tore himself free quickly from the warm nest, went over to the washbasin, and subjected himself and the former drumstick that had functioned so well in bed to a thorough cleansing; I could readily understand that Greff found his wife's smell unbearable, even if it assailed him secondhand.

But freshly washed, I was welcomed by the amateur inventor. He demonstrated all his machines and their noises to me, and I wonder to this day why, despite this late intimacy, no real friendship ever developed between Oskar and Greff, why Greff remained a stranger to me, arousing my interest but never my sympathy.

In September of forty-two—I'd just put my eighteenth birthday behind me, unheralded and unsung, while on the radio the Sixth Army took Stalingrad — Greff built the drum machine. He suspended two evenly balanced pans filled with potatoes in a wooden frame, then removed one potato from the left pan: the scales tipped and released a lever that freed a drumming mechanism installed on top of the frame: it rolled, banged, rattled, scraped, pans clashed together, a gong rang, and the whole thing came to a final, clattering, tragically discordant finale.

The machine pleased me. I had Greff demonstrate it for me time and again. For Oskar believed that the tinkering greengrocer had invented and built it especially for him. Soon my error became all too clear. Greff may have received an inspiration or two from me, but the machine was meant for him, and its finale was his finale.

It was an early, fresh October morning, as only the north wind delivers free of charge to your doorstep. I'd left Mother Truczinski's flat in good time, stepped onto the street just as Matzerath was raising the roller-shutter in front of the shop door. I stood next to him as the green painted slats rattled upward, was engulfed by a cloud of grocery-store odors that had been pent up overnight inside the shop, and then received Matzerath's morning kiss. I crossed Labesweg before Maria had put in an appearance, casting a long shadow westward across the cobbled pavement, for to the right, in the east, over Max-Halbe-Platz, the sun was rising under its own power, using the same trick that Baron Münchhausen must have used as he pulled himself out of the swamp by his own pigtail.

Anyone who knew the greengrocer Greff as well as I did would have been equally surprised to see his display window and shop door still shuttered and shut at that hour. It's true that the past few years had rendered Greff increasingly peculiar. Still, up to now, he had always managed to open the store on time. Perhaps he's sick, Oskar thought, and quickly rejected the notion. For how could Greff, who as recently as last winter, though perhaps not as regularly as in past years, was still chopping holes in the Baltic Sea to bathe in, how could this man of Nature, despite a few signs of age, fall ill from one day to the next? The privilege of staying in bed was already being fully exercised by Greff's wife; I knew, moreover, that Greff scorned soft beds, that he preferred sleeping on field cots and hard plank beds. The illness didn't exist that could confine the greengrocer to his bed.

I took up a position outside the closed vegetable store, looked back at our shop, saw that Matzerath had gone back inside, and only then rapped out a few cautious beats on my drum, banking on Frau Greff's sensitive ear. Just a few sounds and the second window to the right of the shop door opened. La Greff in her nightgown, her hair up in rollers, clutching a pillow to her breast, appeared above the window box with its winter flowers. "Come on in, little Oskar. What are you waiting for, it's cold out there!"

By way of explanation I tapped one of my drumsticks against the metal slats shielding the display window.

"Albrecht!" she cried, "Where are you, Albrecht? What's going on?" Still calling out for her husband, she withdrew from the window. Doors slammed, I heard her rattling around in the shop, and shortly thereafter she started screaming. She was screaming in the cellar, but I couldn't see what she was screaming about, because the hatch they dumped potatoes through on delivery days, which were increasingly rare during the war years, was also closed tight. When I pressed my eye against the tarred boards of the hatch I saw that the electric light was burning in the cellar. And I could make out the top part of the cellar steps with something white lying on them, probably Frau Greff's pillow.

She must have dropped the pillow on the steps, for she was no longer in the cellar but screaming again in the shop and a moment later in the bedroom. She picked up the phone, screamed and dialed, then screamed into the phone; but Oskar couldn't understand what she was saying, all he could catch was accident and the address 24 Labesweg, which she screamed several times, then hung up and soon thereafter filled the window in her nightgown, without pillow but still in her rollers, screaming, poured herself and her entire double stockpile, with which I was well acquainted, onto the window box with the winter flowers, thrust both hands into the fleshy, pale red leaves, and screamed into the air so that the street seemed to narrow, and Oskar thought, Now La Greff's going to start singshattering glass; but not a pane broke. Windows were thrown open, neighbors appeared, women called out questions, men came running, Laubschad the clockmaker, still pulling on his jacket, old man Heilandt, Herr Reißberg, the tailor Libischewski, Herr Esch, from the nearest buildings, even Probst, not the barber, the one who sold coal, came with his son. Matzerath sailed up in his white shop apron while Maria stood in the doorway of the grocery store with little Kurt in her arms.

It was easy for me to submerge myself in the swarm of excited grown-ups and evade Matzerath, who was looking for me. He and the clockmaker Laubschad were the first to spring into action. They tried to enter the flat by way of the window. But La Greff wasn't letting anyone up, let alone in. Scratching, flailing, and biting all the while, she still found time to scream, more and more loudly, and to some extent intelligibly. They should wait for the ambulance to come, she'd already called, no one else needed to, she knew what to do in cases like this. They should mind their own business. Things were bad enough already. Curiosity, that's all it was, pure curiosity, you always learned who your friends were when disaster struck. And in the midst of all her hue and cry she must have spotted me in the crowd outside her window, for she called out to me, stretched out her bare arms toward me, having meanwhile shaken them free of men, and someone — Oskar still believes it was the clockmaker Laubschad — lifted me up, tried to hand me in over Matzerath's objections, and in fact Matzerath almost caught me just short of the flower box, but Lina Greff already had me in her grasp, pressed me to her warm gown, and stopped screaming, just wept in a high whimper, gasped in a high whimper for breath.

As the screams of Frau Greff had whipped the neighbors into a frenzy of shameless gesticulation, so now her thin, high whimpering transformed the throng below those winter flowers into a silent, embarrassed, foot-scraping mob that hardly dared face her tears, and turned all its hope, all its curiosity, and all its interest toward the eagerly anticipated ambulance.

Oskar found Frau Greff's whining less than pleasant himself. I tried to scoot lower so I wouldn't be so near those sounds of lamentation. And I did manage to let go of her neck and seat myself partly on the flower box. Oskar felt all too closely observed, for Maria stood in the shop door with the boy in her arms. So I gave up this perch as well, fully aware of the embarrassing position I was in, and, thinking only of Maria — I couldn't have cared less about the neighbors — I cast off from the Greffian coast, which trembled more than I cared for and always meant bed.

Lina Greff didn't notice my flight, or else she no longer had the strength to hold back that small body which for the longest time had so diligently served her as a substitute. Perhaps Lina also sensed that Oskar was slipping away from her forever, that with her screams a sound was born which on the one hand would become a wall, a sound barrier between the bedridden woman and the drummer boy, and on the other would shatter a wall that existed between Maria and me.

I stood in the Greffian bedroom. My drum dangled uncertainly at an angle. Oskar knew the room well, could have recited the length and breadth of the sap-green wallpaper by heart. Yesterday's washbasin with its gray soapsuds still sat on the stool. Everything was in its place, and yet the furniture, nicked up, rubbed bare, worn through, and slept hollow, looked fresh to me, or at least refreshed, as if everything standing there stiffly on four legs or on four feet against the wall had needed those screams of Lina Greff, followed by her high whimper, to achieve this new and terrifyingly cold radiance.

The door to the shop stood open. Against his will, Oskar let himself be drawn into that room, redolent of dry earth and onions and divided into strips of swirling dust by the daylight coming in through cracks in the shutters. Most of Greff's noise and music machines remained in semidarkness; the light picked out a few details—a little bell, a plywood strut, the lower part of the drum machine—and showed me the evenly balanced potatoes.

The trapdoor to the cellar, which was located, just as in our shop, behind the counter, stood open. Nothing supported the plank cover, which Frau Greff must have flung open in her screaming haste, though she hadn't hooked it to the latch on the counter. Oskar could have given it a little push and tipped it over, closing off the cellar.

Motionless, I stood halfway behind those planks, breathing in their smell of dust and decay, and stared at the brightly lit square framing part of the stairs and a portion of the concrete cellar floor. Into the rectangle, from the upper right, protruded a section of a stepped platform, presumably a new acquisition of Greff's, for I'd never seen it before on my occasional visits to the cellar. But Oskar would never have peered into the cellar so long and intently at a mere platform had not two filled wool socks in black-laced shoes, oddly foreshortened, entered the upper right-hand corner of the picture. Even though I couldn't inspect the soles, I recognized them immediately as Greff's hiking shoes. That can't be Greff, I thought to myself, standing there in the cellar ready for a hike, because the shoes aren't standing there, they're dangling above the platform; unless the tips of the shoes, sharply angled downward, have managed to touch the boards, if only barely. So for a second I pictured Greff standing there on tiptoe, for this comic but strenuous exercise would be just like him, gymnast that he was, and nature lover.

To convince myself of the accuracy of my hypothesis, and to have a good laugh at the greengrocer's expense if it proved to be true, I climbed cautiously down the steep stairs, drumming, as I recall, something to create and dispel fear: "Better start running, the Black Cook's coming! Ha! Ha! Ha!"

Only when Oskar stood firmly on the concrete floor did he allow his gaze to wander indirectly over bundles of empty onion sacks and stacks of equally empty fruit crates until, gliding across timberwork he'd never seen before, it approached the spot where Greff's hiking shoes must be hanging or standing on tiptoe.

Of course I knew that Greff was hanging. The shoes were hanging, thus the coarsely knit dark green socks were hanging too. Bare male knees above the edges of the socks, hairy thighs to the edges of the knee pants; then a prickling, stabbing sensation rose slowly from my private parts, followed my buttocks along my numbing back, ascended my spinal column, settled in the back of my neck, struck me hot and cold, bounded down between my legs, shriveled my already tiny sack, leapt right over my now bent back and lodged itself once more behind my head, contracting there — to this day Oskar still gags, still feels that stab whenever anyone mentions hanging, even hanging out the laundry, in his presence; it was not just Greff's hiking shoes, wool socks, knees, and knee pants that were hanging there; the whole of Greff was hanging by the neck, and the strained expression on his face above the cord was not entirely free of theatrics.

The contracting, stabbing sensation faded surprisingly quickly. The sight of Greff returned to normal, for the posture of a hanging man looks as normal and natural as a man walking on his hands or standing on his head, or a man making a true spectacle of himself by mounting a four-legged horse for a ride.

And then there was the setting. Only now did Oskar grasp the lengths to which Greff had gone. The frame, the setting in which Greff hung, was most carefully chosen, studied almost to the point of extravagance.

The greengrocer had aimed at a form of death appropriate to him, one that was carefully balanced. He who in his lifetime had had difficulties and unpleasant exchanges by post with the Bureau of Weights and Standards, whose weights and scales had been confiscated on more than one occasion, who had been fined for weighing fruit and vegetables inaccurately, had balanced his weight to the gram with potatoes.

The dully gleaming cord, which had no doubt been soaped, was led by pulleys over two beams, which he had fashioned for his final day into a scaffold whose sole purpose was to serve as his final scaffold. Since the wood was of the highest quality, I gathered that the greengrocer had spared no expense. Given the scarcity of building materials in wartime, it must have been difficult to procure those planks and beams. Greff had obviously done some bartering, getting wood in exchange for fruit. Thus the scaffolding was not lacking in even superfluous and merely decorative braces. The three-part stepped podium — one corner of which Oskar had seen from the shop — lifted the whole edifice onto an almost sublime plane.

As with the drum machine, which may have served the home mechanic as a model, Greff and his counterweight hung within the scaffolding. In striking contrast to the four whitewashed corner posts, a small, delicate green ladder stood between him and the produce, which also dangled in the air. The potato baskets had been attached to the main cord by means of an ingenious knot of the sort boy scouts are skilled at. Since the interior of the scaffold was illuminated by four light bulbs, which, though painted white, still shone brightly, Oskar was able, without stepping onto the platform and desecrating it, to read the inscription on a little cardboard sign wired to the Boy Scout knot above the potato baskets: *seventy-five kilos (less one hundred grams).*

Greff was hanging in a scoutmaster's uniform. On the last day of his life he had returned to the uniform of his prewar years. It was too tight for him now. He had not managed to fasten the two top buttons or the belt, a jarring note in his otherwise neat appearance. Greff had crossed two fingers on his left hand according to Boy Scout custom. Before hanging himself, he had tied his scout hat to his right wrist. The neckerchief he'd been forced to forgo. Since, as with his knee pants, he hadn't managed to fasten the buttons at his collar, curly black chest hair sprang through the opening.

A few asters lay on the steps of the platform, and also, looking out of place, some stalks of parsley. He had probably run out of flowers as he was strewing them about, since he'd used most of the asters, as well as a few roses, to wreathe four small photos hanging on the four main posts of the scaffolding. On the left front post, behind glass, Sir Baden-Powell, the founder of the Boy Scouts. On the left rear, unframed, the saintly Saint George. On the right rear, without glass, the head of Michelangelo's *David*. Framed and glazed on the right front post, the photo of an expressively handsome lad of around sixteen. An early photo of his favorite, Horst Donath, who fell as a lieutenant on the Donets.

Perhaps I should also mention the four scraps of paper on the platform steps among the asters and parsley. They lay in a way that made it easy to piece them together. Oskar did so and deciphered a court summons stamped several times by the vice squad.

The rest may be summed up briefly: The insistent cry of the ambulance awakened me from my meditations on the death of a greengrocer. A moment later they stumbled down the stairs, mounted the platform, and laid hands on the dangling Greff. No sooner had they lifted the grocer, however, than the counterbalancing potato baskets came crashing down, setting in motion a now freed mechanism, similar to the drum machine, which Greff had cleverly encased in plywood above the scaffolding. While the potatoes rattled across the platform and onto the concrete floor, a banging on tin, wood, bronze, and glass sounded from above, a frenzied orchestra of drums, hammering out Albrecht Greff's grand finale.

Today Oskar faces the difficult task of reproducing on his drum an echo of that avalanche of potatoes—a windfall, by the way, for a few of the medics—and the organized din of Greff's drum machine. No doubt because my drum had a decisive influence on the shape and design of Greff's death, I sometimes manage to translate Greff's death into a well-rounded composition for percussion on Oskar's drum, and when friends or my keeper Bruno ask me what I call it, I tell them: Seventy-five Kilos.

Bebra's Theater at the Front

In MID-JUNE of forty-two, my son Kurt turned one year old. Oskar, his father, took it in stride, thought to himself: Just two short years to go. In October of forty-two the greengrocer Greff hanged himself on a gallows of such formal perfection that I, Oskar, have henceforth considered suicide one of the sublime forms of death. In January of forty-three there was a good deal of talk about the city of Stalingrad. Since Matzerath referred to this city in the same tone he'd used earlier for Pearl Harbor, Tobruk, and Dunkirk, I paid no more attention to it than any other place I knew from special communiqués; for war reports and special communiqués had become a sort of geography lesson for Oskar. How else could I have learned where rivers like the Kuban, the Mius, and the Don flowed, who could have explained the location of the Aleutian islands Attu, Kiska, and Adak better than the detailed radio reports on events in the Far East? Thus, though I learned in January of forty-three that the city of Stalingrad is situated on the Volga, I wasn't as worried about the Sixth Army as I was about Maria, who was suffering from a slight case of the flu at the time.

While Maria's flu faded, the radio continued its geography lesson: Oskar can still find the little towns of Rzev and Demyansk on any map of Soviet Russia with his eyes closed. Maria had barely recovered when my son Kurt came down with whooping cough. While I tried to remember the most difficult names of a few hotly contested oases in Tunisia, little Kurt's whooping cough and the Africa Corps both came to an end.

O the merry month of May: Maria, Matzerath, and Gretchen Scheffler were making preparations for little Kurt's second birthday. Oskar attached a greater significance to the upcoming celebration too, for after the twelfth of June in forty-three, only one short year remained. Had I been present on little Kurt's second birthday, I could have whispered in my son's ear, "Just wait, soon you too will be drumming." And it came to pass in those days that on the twelfth of June in forty-three, Oskar was no longer in Danzig-Langfuhr but in the ancient Roman village of Metz. Indeed, he had been away for so long that he had a hard time getting back to the familiar environs of his still undamaged native city by the twelfth of June in forty-four to help celebrate little Kurt's third birthday.

What business took me away? I won't beat around the bush: outside the Pestalozzi School, which had been converted into barracks for the Luftwaffe, I met my master Bebra. But Bebra alone could not have talked me into a trip. On Bebra's arm hung La Raguna, Signora Roswitha, the great somnambulist.

Oskar was coming from Kleinhammerweg. He'd paid a visit to Gretchen Scheffler, leafed through the *Struggle for Rome*, discovered that even back then, in the time of Belisarius, things were constantly in flux, with victories or defeats at various cities and river crossings being celebrated or bemoaned with a fine geographical sweep.

I crossed Fröbel Meadow, which in the course of the last few years had been turned into a construction camp for the Todt Organization, with my thoughts on Taginae — where Narses defeated Totila in the year five fifty-two — yet it wasn't the victory that caused my thoughts to linger on Narses, the great Armenian, it was the general's figure I liked: misshapen and humpbacked, Narses was small, a dwarf, a gnome, a midget was Narses. Perhaps only a child's head taller than Oskar, I reflected, and standing outside the Pestalozzi School I examined by way of comparison the rows of ribbons on a few Luftwaffe officers who had shot up too quickly, told myself that Narses surely never wore ribbons, had no need of them, when there in the main entrance to the school stood the great general himself with a lady hanging on his arm — why shouldn't Narses have a lady on his arm? And then they approached, dwarfed by Luftwaffe giants, and yet they were central figures, wrapped in the aura of history, old as the hills among these newly minted airforce heroes — what does a whole barracks full of Totilas and Tejas, of tree-tall Ostrogoths, mean in the face of a single Armenian dwarf called

Narses — and Narses drew nearer Oskar step by tiny step, waved to Oskar, and the lady on his arm waved too: Bebra and Signora Roswitha Raguna greeted me — the Luftwaffe stepped aside respectfully — I placed my lips near Bebra's ear, whispered, "Dear master, I took you for the great general Narses, whom I hold in much higher esteem than that muscle man Belisarius."

Bebra modestly waved this aside. But my comparison pleased Raguna. How prettily her lips moved as she spoke: "Come now, Bebra, is he so mistaken, our young *amico*? Does not the blood of Prince Eugen flow in your veins? *E Lodovico quattordicesimo*? Is he not your ancestor?"

Bebra took my arm and led me aside, for the airmen kept staring at us in admiration, which was becoming annoying. Finally, after a lieutenant and a moment later two airmen first class came to attention and saluted Bebra — the master was wearing a captain's stripes on his uniform, and a band on his sleeve with the inscription *Propaganda Corps* — after the beribboned airmen asked for and received autographs from Raguna, Bebra beckoned for his official car, we climbed in, and put up with the enthusiastic applause of the Luftwaffe as we pulled away.

We drove along Pestalozzistraße, Magdeburger Straße, Heeresanger. Bebra sat beside the driver. We'd barely reached Magdeburger Straße when Raguna used my drum as an opening. "Are you still faithful to your drum, my dear friend?" she whispered in those Mediterranean tones I had not heard for so long. "And how faithful have you been otherwise?" Oskar didn't reply, spared her his tiresome stories about women, but smilingly permitted the great somnambulist to caress first his drum, then his hands, which were clutching the drum rather convulsively, to caress them with an increasingly southern warmth.

As we turned onto Heeresanger and followed the rails of the Number Five line, I even responded, that is, I caressed her left hand with my left while she fondled my right with her right. Soon we'd left Max-Halbe-Platz behind. It was too late for Oskar to get out; then I saw Bebra's shrewd, light brown, age-old eyes in the rearview mirror, watching our mutual caresses. Wishing to spare my friend and master, I tried to withdraw my hands, but Raguna held them fast. Bebra smiled into the rearview mirror, then looked away and started up a conversation with the driver, while on her part Roswitha, warmly caressing and pressing my hands, opened a conversation in Mediterranean tones that flowed directly and sweetly into Oskar's ear alone, took a brief practical turn, then became even sweeter, tones in which all my misgivings and attempted escape bogged down. We were at Reichskolonie, heading toward the Women's Clinic, when Raguna confessed to Oskar that she'd never stopped thinking of him all these years, that she still had the glass from the Café Vierjahreszeiten that I'd singscribed a dedication into back then, that Bebra was a splendid friend and excellent colleague, but marriage was out of the question; Bebra has to live alone, Raguna replied when I broke in, she allowed him total freedom, and though he was quite jealous by nature, over the course of the years he had come to see that Raguna could not be tied down either, and anyway, as director of the Theater at the Front, the dear man would hardly have time to perform any possible conjugal duties, but the theater itself was first-rate, with a show that could have played at the Wintergarten or La Scala in peacetime, wouldn't I, Oskar, with all my God-given talent, like to try it for a year, I was certainly old enough, she could arrange it, but I, Oskar, probably had other obligations, no? — then so much the better, they were leaving today, they'd had their last matinee in the military district of Danzig–West Prussia, now they were heading for Lothringen, then on to France, the Eastern Front was out of the question for the time being, that was safely behind them, I, Oskar, could count myself lucky that the East was passé, they were headed for Paris now, yes of course to Paris, had I, Oskar, ever been to Paris? Well then, *amico,* if Raguna can't seduce your hard drummer's heart, let Paris do so, *andiamo!*

The car pulled to a stop with these final words of the great somnambulist. At regular intervals, green and Prussian, the trees of Hindenburgallee. We climbed out, Bebra told the driver to wait; I didn't want to go to the Café Vierjahreszeiten, my somewhat confused brain needed fresh air. So we strolled through Steffenspark: Bebra on my right, Roswitha on my left. Bebra explained the nature and purpose of the Propaganda Corps. Roswitha related little anecdotes from the daily life of the corps. Bebra chatted about war artists, war correspondents, and his Theater at the Front. Roswitha referred in Mediterranean tones to distant cities I'd heard mentioned on the radio when special communiqués were issued. Bebra said Copenhagen. Roswitha sighed Palermo. Bebra sang Belgrade. Roswitha offered a tragedienne's lament: Athens. But both raved over and over about Paris, promised Paris would make up for all the cities they'd just mentioned, and finally, in his professional capacity as director and captain of a Theater at the Front, Bebra made me what sounded like an official offer: "Join us, young man, drum, sing-shatter beer glasses and light bulbs! The German Army of Occupation in fair France, in a Paris eternally young, will thank you and hail you."

Purely for form's sake, Oskar asked for time to think it over. For a good half-hour, at some remove from Raguna, from my friend and master Bebra, I paced through the vernal green of the shrubbery, assumed a pensive and troubled air, rubbed my forehead, listened to the little birds in the forest, which I'd never done before, pretended I wanted some little robin or other to tell me what to do, and said, when a particularly loud and conspicuous chirp arose from the greenery, "Mother Nature in her wisdom and benevolence advises me to accept your offer, my dear master. You may regard me henceforth as a member of your Theater at the Front."

Then we went to the Vierjahreszeiten after all, drank an anemic Mocha, and discussed the details of my flight, which we referred to not as a flight but as a departure.

Outside the café we recapitulated all the details of the planned action. Then I took my leave of Raguna and Captain Bebra of the Propaganda Corps, who insisted on placing his official car at my disposal. While the two of them strolled up Hindenburgallee toward the city, the captain's driver, a somewhat older corporal, drove me back to Langfuhr and dropped me off at Max-Halbe-Platz, for I could hardly go all the way to Labesweg: the arrival of Oskar in an official Wehrmacht car would have excited too much inopportune attention.

I didn't have much time left. A farewell visit to Matzerath and Maria. I stood for a long time by the playpen of my son Kurt, even came up with a few fatherly thoughts as I recall, tried to pat the blond rascal, but little Kurt was having none of that, while Maria accepted my caresses, the first she'd received in years, with some surprise, and returned them graciously. I found it strangely hard to take leave of Matzerath. The man was standing in the kitchen, cooking kidneys in mustard sauce, entirely at one with his cooking spoon, even happy perhaps, so I didn't dare disturb him. It wasn't till he reached back blindly and groped for something on the kitchen table that Oskar anticipated him, picked up the little wooden board with chopped parsley, and handed it to him — and to this day I assume he stood holding that little wooden board with parsley in surprise and bewilderment long after I'd left the kitchen, for Oskar had never before picked up, held out, or handed anything to Matzerath.

I ate supper at Mother Truczinski's, let her wash me, put me to bed, waited till she was under her featherbed and snoring with a soft whistle, then slipped on my slippers, grabbed my clothes, slipped through the room where the gray mouse was whistling, snoring, and growing older, struggled a while with the key in the hall but finally managed to coax the bolt from the lock, tumbled up the stairs to the drying attic with my bundle of clothes, still shoeless and in my little nightshirt, and found in my hiding place, behind piles of roofing tiles and bundled newspapers, stored there in defiance of air-defense regulations, stumbling over the air-defense sand pile and the air-defense bucket, I found the brand-new drum I'd stashed away unbeknownst to Maria, and found Oskar's reading material too: Rasputin and Goethe in one volume. Should I take my favorite authors along?

As Oskar slipped on his clothes and shoes, slung the drum around his neck, and stowed the drumsticks behind his suspenders, he was simultaneously negotiating with his gods Apollo and Dionysus. While the god of blind intoxication advised him to take no reading matter at all with him, or if he must, just a stack of Rasputin, the overly clever and far too sensible Apollo tried to talk me out of the trip to France altogether, then, once he saw that I was set on going, insisted there be no gap in my luggage; I would have to take along that polite yawn Goethe issued centuries ago, but out of spite, and because I knew that *Elective Affinities* could never solve all my sexual problems, I took Rasputin along too, and his world of naked women in black stockings. If Apollo strove for harmony and Dionysus for intoxication and chaos, Oskar was a diminutive demigod who harmonized chaos and intoxicated reason, with one advantage, in addition to his mortality, over all the gods recognized throughout the ages: Oskar could read what he pleased, whereas the gods censored themselves.

How accustomed one grows to a building and the kitchen smells of nineteen tenants. I took my leave at every step, every floor, every door with its nameplate: O Meyn the musician, declared unfit for service and sent home, who was playing his trumpet again, drinking Machandel again and waiting for them to return again — and later they did come for him, but this time they made him leave his trumpet behind. O bulky Frau Kater, whose daughter Susi called herself a telegraph girl. O Axel Mischke, what have you traded your whip for? Herr and Frau Woiwuth, who were always eating rutabaga. Herr Heinert had a bad stomach, so he was at Schichau and not in the infantry. And next door Heinert's parents, who were still called Heimowski. O Mother Truczinski; softly slept the mouse behind the apartment door. My ear to the wood heard her whistle. Little Cheese, whose real name was Retzel, had made lieutenant, even though he'd been forced to wear long wool socks as a child. Schlager's son was dead, Eyke's son was dead, Kollin's son was dead. But the clockmaker Laubschad was still alive and brought dead clocks to life. And old man Heilandt was alive and still hammering crooked nails straight. And Frau Schwerwinski was sick, and Herr Schwerwinski was healthy, yet he died before she died. And across the way on the ground floor, who lived there? Alfred and Maria Matzerath lived there, and a little rascal almost two years old named Kurt. And who was leaving that large building, breathing heavily in the middle of the night? That was Oskar, little Kurt's father. What did he carry out to the darkened street? He carried his drum and the big book he was learning from. Why did he pause amid all the blacked-out buildings that believed in air defense before one blacked-out building that believed in air defense? Because the widow Greff lived there, who had not educated him but had taught him certain delicate skills. Why did he remove his cap before the black building? Because he was thinking of the greengrocer Greff, who had curly hair and an aquiline nose, who weighed and hanged himself both at the same time, who as a hanged man still had curly hair and an aquiline nose, but whose brown eyes, which normally lay pensive in their hollows, bulged forth overstrained. Why did Oskar put his sailor's cap with the flowing ribbon back on again and stride away capped? Because he had an appointment at the Langfuhr freight-train station. Did he arrive on time at the appointed spot? He did.

At the very last minute, that is, I reached the railway embankment near the Brunshöferweg underpass. Not that I'd stopped outside the office of Dr. Hollatz nearby. I took leave of Sister Inge in my thoughts, sent my greetings to the baker's flat on Kleinhammerweg, but did all that as

I walked past, and only the portal of the Church of the Sacred Heart made me call a halt that almost made me late. The door was locked. Nevertheless, I pictured all too vividly the naked, pink boy Jesus on the left thigh of the Virgin Mary. There she was again, my poor mama. She was kneeling in the confessional, pouring her grocery-wife sins into Father Wiehnke's ear, just as she used to pour sugar into blue pound and half-pound sacks. And Oskar was kneeling at the left side-altar, trying to teach the boy Jesus how to drum, but the rascal wouldn't drum, offered no miracle. Oskar had sworn back then and swore again outside the locked church door: I'll teach him to drum yet. Sooner or later.

Since I had a long trip ahead of me, I settled for later, turned my drummer boy's back on the church door, certain I wouldn't lose track of Jesus, scrambled up the railway embankment near the underpass, losing a little Goethe and Rasputin in the process but still managing to get the major portion of my educational assets to the top, stood on the tracks, stumbled a stone's throw farther on over ties and gravel, and almost knocked down Bebra, who was waiting in the dark.

"There's our virtuoso drummer!" cried the captain and musical clown. Then, urging mutual caution, we groped our way over tracks and crossings, lost our way among the shunted boxcars, and finally found the furlough train, in which a special compartment had been set aside for Bebra's troupe.

Oskar already had many a tram ride under his belt, and now he was going to ride on a train. When Bebra pushed me into the compartment, Raguna looked up from something she was sewing, smiled, and, smiling, kissed me on the cheek. Still smiling, but without taking her fingers from her sewing, she introduced me to the two remaining members of the troupe: the acrobats Felix and Kitty. Honey-blond, of a slightly gray complexion, Kitty was not without physical allure and was about the size of the Signora. A slight Saxon accent added to her charm. The acrobat Felix was without doubt the tallest of the group. He measured nearly four foot six. The poor man suffered from this very noticeable height. My own arrival at three foot one added fuel to his complex. The acrobat's profile also bore a certain resemblance to that of a thoroughbred racehorse, so Raguna had nicknamed him "Cavallo" or "Felix Cavallo." Like Captain Bebra, the acrobat wore a field-gray uniform, but with the insignia of a corporal. The women were also dressed in field-gray suits, tailored for travel and not particularly becoming. The sewing Raguna held in her hands proved to be field-gray cloth as well: it was to become my uniform, Felix and Bebra had purchased the outfit, and Roswitha and Kitty took turns sewing, cutting more and more cloth until the jacket, trousers, and field cap fit me. But there was no way they could have found shoes Oskar's size in any Wehrmacht clothing depot. I had to rest content with my civilian laced shoes, and do without army boots.

My papers were forged. The acrobat Felix proved particularly adept at this delicate work. As a matter of simple courtesy I could hardly protest when the great somnambulist passed me off as her brother — her older brother, mind you: Oskarnello Raguna, born on the twenty-first of October nineteen hundred twelve in Naples. I've gone by all sorts of names in my time. Oskarnello Raguna was one of them, and certainly not the least mellifluous.

And then it was all aboard, as they say, and we pulled out. We traveled by way of Stolp, Stettin, Berlin, Hanover, and Cologne to Metz. Of Berlin I saw next to nothing. We had a five-hour layover. Of course the air-raid sirens were wailing. We had to go down into the Thomaskeller. Soldiers on furlough were packed like sardines into the vaulted rooms. Greetings were shouted as an MP tried to squeeze us in. A few boys from the Eastern Front who knew Bebra and his troupe from earlier guest appearances clapped and whistled while Raguna threw them kisses. They wanted a show, and a stage of sorts was hastily set up at one end of the former beer hall. Bebra could hardly refuse, especially when an Air Force major asked him affably, and with exaggerated deference, if he couldn't oblige the men with a little something.

For the first time Oskar was to take the stage in an actual theatrical performance. Although I didn't go on entirely unprepared — Bebra had rehearsed my number with me several times on the train — I was still so struck by stage fright that Raguna took the occasion to soothe me by stroking my hands.

The boys were eager for action. Our theatrical gear had barely arrived when Felix and Kitty launched into their acrobatic routine. Both were made of rubber — they tied themselves in knots, kept twisting in, out, and around each other, adding and subtracting parts, exchanging arms and legs, and gave the gawking, thronging soldiers aching limbs and sore muscles that would last for days. While Felix and Kitty were still knotting and unknotting, Bebra embarked on his musical clown number. On bottles that ranged from full to empty, he played all the most popular wartime hits, plunked out "Erika" and "Mamatchi Give Me a Pony," made "Stars of the Homeland" twinkle and resound from the necks of the bottles, and when that failed to set the house on fire, fell back on his old standby, sending an enraged "Jimmy the Tiger" prowling through the bottles. That appealed both to the soldiers on furlough and to Oskar's fastidious ear; and when, after a few foolish magic tricks that were surefire crowd pleasers, Bebra announced Roswitha Raguna, the great somnambulist, and Oskarnello Raguna, the glass-slaying drummer, the audience was thoroughly warmed up, and Roswitha and Oskar were assured of success. I opened our act with a gentle drumroll, led up to climaxes with rolling crescendos, and called for applause after each turn with a loud, artful ta-ta-boom. Raguna would invite a soldier or two, even an officer, to come up out of the audience, ask leathery old corporals or shy but brash cadets to sit down beside her, pick one or two, look into their hearts — yes, she could do that — then give the crowd facts from the pay book of each that always turned out to be right, along with a few intimate details from their private lives. She did all this with sensitivity and tact, was witty in her revelations, then, in what the audience assumed was a sort of parting gift, handed the exposed man a full bottle of beer, asked him to hold it above his head so that everyone could see it clearly, and gave me, Oskar, the sign: a drumroll crescendo, child's play for a voice made for larger tasks, and the beer bottle exploded, leaving behind the stunned, beer-splattered face of a corporal who thought he'd seen everything, or a milky-skinned cadet still wet behind the ears — and then came the applause, loud and long, mingled with the sounds of a major air raid on the capital.

What we offered wasn't world-class, of course, but it entertained the audience, made them forget the front and their furlough, released a wave of laughter that seemed endless; for as the blockbusters rained down upon us, shaking and burying the beer cellar and everything in it, dousing both lights and emergency lights, when everything lay scattered about, laughter still rose through the dark, stifling coffin, "Bebra!" they cried, "We want Bebra!" and good old indestructible Bebra answered the call, played the clown in the dark, drew salvos of laughter from the buried mob, and when they cried for Raguna and Oskarnello he blared out, "Signora Raguna is verrry tired, my dear tin soldiers. And little Oskarnello has to take a little nap too for the grrreater glory of the Gerrrman Reich and final victory!"

Raguna, however, lay with me and was frightened. Oskar, though not frightened, lay with Raguna. Her fear and my courage brought our hands together. I explored her fear, she explored my courage. Toward the end I became slightly frightened, but she gained courage. And when I had banished her fear the first time and given her courage, my manly courage arose a second time. While my courage was eighteen glorious years old, she fell prey again, standing in I know not what year of her life, recumbent for I know not how many times, to the well-practiced fear that gave me courage. For like her face, her body, sparingly measured but complete in every way, had nothing in common with a Time that leaves its traces. Timelessly courageous and timelessly fearful, Roswitha gave herself to me. And no one will ever learn if, during a major air raid on the capital, that midget who lost her fear beneath my courage before the air-raid wardens dug us out of a collapsed Thomaskeller was nineteen or ninety-nine years old; and Oskar finds it easy to be discreet, since he himself has no idea if this first embrace that truly matched his own bodily proportions was granted by a courageous old woman or a young girl made willing by fear.

Inspecting Concrete— or Mystical Barbaric Bored

FOR THREE WEEKS we performed every night within the venerable casemates of the Roman garrison city of Metz. We put on the same show for two weeks in Nancy. Châlons-sur-Marne received us hospitably for a week. A few French phrases were already tripping off Oskar's tongue. In Rheims one could admire ruins from the First World War. The stony menagerie of the world-famous cathedral, disgusted by humanity, spat water unceasingly onto the cobblestones: that is, it rained daily in Rheims, and nightly too. In exchange, we had a sunny, mild September in Paris. I celebrated my nineteenth birthday by strolling along the *quais* with Roswitha on my arm. Though I knew the city from Airman First Class Fritz Truczinski's postcards, Paris didn't disappoint me in the least. As Roswitha and I stood arm in arm at the foot of the Eiffel Tower — I was three foot one, she was three foot three — we looked up and realized for the first time how special we were, sensing our true stature. We kissed on the street, which in Paris doesn't mean much.

Oh, the glorious associations with art and history! As I paid a visit to the Dôme des Invalides, still with Roswitha on my arm, and meditated on the great emperor, who though great was not all that tall, and therefore dear to both our hearts, I spoke Napoleon's words. Just as he had proclaimed at the tomb of the second Friedrich, who was no giant himself, "If he were still alive, we would not be standing here!" I whispered tenderly into my Roswitha's ear, "If the Corsican were still alive, we would not be standing here, would not be kissing beneath the bridges, on the *quais, sur le trottoir de Paris.*"

As part of a long program, we appeared in the Salle Pleyel and at the Théâtre Sarah Bernhardt. Oskar quickly accustomed himself to big-city stages, refined his repertoire, and adapted to the jaded tastes of the army of occupation: I no longer sangshattered ordinary German beer bottles, no, I reduced to shards with my song the most exquisite, gracefully curved, paper-thin blown vases and fruit bowls from French castles. My act was structured on a cultural-historical point of view, began with glasses from the reign of Louis XIV, then crushed Louis XV glassware to glassdust. Vehemently, with revolutionary fervor, I ravaged the goblets of poor Louis XVI and his heedless and headless Antoinette, then a little Louis Philippe, and for a finale took issue with the vitreous fantasies of French art nouveau.

If the field-gray masses in the stalls and balconies could not follow my historical presentation and applauded the shards simply as ordinary shards, there were also occasional staff officers and journalists from the Reich who admired my historical sense as well as the shards. A scholarly type in uniform offered a few flattering remarks on my artistic skills when we were introduced to him following a gala performance for garrison headquarters. Oskar was particularly grateful to the correspondent of a leading newspaper of the Reich in the city on the Seine who identified himself as an expert on France and discreetly drew my attention to a few small errors, not to say stylistic inconsistencies, in my program.

We spent the entire winter in Paris. They lodged us in first-class hotels, and I won't hide the fact that throughout the whole of that long winter, Roswitha repeatedly tested and confirmed at my side the advantages of the French bed. Was Oskar happy in Paris? Had Oskar forgotten his loved ones back home, Maria, Matzerath, Gretchen and Alexander Scheffler, had Oskar forgotten his son Kurt and his grandmother Anna Koljaiczek?

Though I had not forgotten them, I didn't miss them either. I sent no postcards home, gave no sign of life, but offered them instead a chance to live for a year without me; for I'd already decided when I left that I would return, and of course I wanted to see how they would fare in my absence. On the street, and during performances too, I sometimes searched among the soldiers for familiar faces. Perhaps, Oskar speculated, Fritz Truczinski or Axel Mischke had been transferred to Paris from the Eastern Front, and once or twice he thought he recognized Maria's dashing brother in a horde of infantrymen; but it wasn't him: field-gray can be misleading.

The only thing that made me homesick was the Eiffel Tower. Not that I climbed it and let the vista awaken in me an urge to head for home. Oskar had climbed the tower so often on postcards and in his mind that an actual physical ascent could only have resulted in a disappointed descent. At the foot of the Eiffel Tower, but without Roswitha, standing or even squatting alone beneath the boldly curved base of the iron structure, that vault, through which I could indeed see, but which still covered me, became the sheltering hood of my grandmother Anna: when I sat beneath the Eiffel Tower, I sat beneath her four skirts, the Champ de Mars was transformed into a Kashubian potato field, a Paris October rain slanted down tirelessly between Bissau and Ramkau; on such days it seemed the whole of Paris, including the metro, smelled of slightly rancid butter, and I turned silent, meditative, while Roswitha treated me with kindness, aware of my sorrow, for she was a sensitive soul.

In April of forty-four—amid reports that our lines were being successfully shortened on all fronts—we had to pack up our theatrical gear, leave Paris, and regale the Atlantic Wall with Bebra's Theater at the Front. We began the tour in Le Havre. Bebra seemed taciturn, distracted. Although he never gave a bad performance, and kept the laughers on his side as always, his age-old Narses face would turn to stone the moment the final curtain fell. At first I saw him as a jealous man, and worse yet, one ready to capitulate to the vigor of my youth. Roswitha cleared things up for me in whispers, knew nothing for sure, just rumors about officers visiting Bebra behind closed doors after his performances. It looked as if the master was emerging from his inner emigration, as if he was planning some direct action, as if the blood of his ancestor Prince Eugen was stirring within him. His plans had taken him so far from us, had led him into a realm of such broad and far-reaching import, that Oskar's narrow and purely personal relationship with his former Roswitha might at most have lured a weary smile to his wrinkled face. When—in Trouville it was, we were lodged at the spa hotel—he surprised us intertwined on the carpet of the dressing room we all shared, he waved off our attempt to pull apart and spoke into his makeup mirror: "Enjoy each other, my children, kiss while you can, for it's concrete tomorrow, then concrete grit between your lips, and an end to joy in kissing."

That was in June of forty-four. In the meantime we'd slogged all along the Atlantic Wall, from the Bay of Biscay to Holland, but remained for the most part in the hinterlands, saw little of the legendary pillboxes, and it wasn't till Trouville that we performed right on the coast. We were offered a chance to inspect the Atlantic Wall. Bebra accepted. A final performance in Trouville. We moved that night to the little village of Bavent, just short of Caen, four kilometers from the sand dunes. We were billeted with farmers. Broad meadows, hedgerows, apple trees. Calvados, the apple brandy, was distilled there. We drank some and slept well. A brisk breeze came through the window, a frog pond croaked till morning. Some frogs can really drum. I heard them in my sleep and told myself: You have to go home, Oskar, your son Kurt will soon be three, you have to give him his drum, you promised! When, thus admonished, Oskar the tormented father would awake from hour to hour, he felt beside him to make sure his Roswitha was still there, breathed in her smell: Raguna smelled faintly of cinnamon, crushed cloves, and nutmeg; she smelled like the cake spices that heralded Christmas, retained her fragrance even in summer.

In the morning an armored personnel car pulled up in front of the farmyard. We all stood shivering slightly at the gate. It was early, cool, we chatted into the breeze coming off the sea, climbed in: Bebra, Raguna, Felix and Kitty, Oskar, and a Lieutenant Herzog, who was taking us to his battery west of Cabourg.

When I say Normandy is green, I pass over in silence the brown-and-white-spotted cows engaged in their ruminant profession on both sides of the country road that ran straight as a string through the slightly misty meadows wet with dew, cattle that greeted our armored car with such indifference that the armor plates would have turned bright red with shame had they not previously received a coat of camouflage. Poplars, hedgerows, creeping underbrush, the first of the hulking, empty beach hotels, their shutters banging; we turned onto the promenade, climbed out, and followed behind the lieutenant, who showed Captain Bebra a slightly overbearing but still properly military respect, plodding through the dunes into a wind filled with sand and the sound of the surf.

It was no gentle Baltic, bottle-green and sobbing like a maiden, that awaited me. The Atlantic was testing his age-old maneuver: storming forward at high tide, retreating at low.

Then there it was, our concrete pillbox. We could admire it and pet it: it held still. "Achtung!" someone cried out inside, and flew forth at full stretch from the pillbox, which was shaped like a flattened turtle, lay between two sand dunes, was called "Dora Seven," and gazed out on high and low tides with its gun embrasures, observation slits, and small-caliber hardware. It was a man named Corporal Lankes, reporting to Lieutenant Herzog and to our Captain Bebra.

LANKES, *saluting:* Dora Seven, sir, one corporal, four men. Nothing special to report!

HERZOG: Very good! At ease, Corporal Lankes. You hear that, Captain, nothing special to report. It's been like that for years.

BEBRA: But even so, high and low tides. The performances of Nature.

HERZOG: That's just what keeps our men busy. That's why we keep building one pillbox after another. We're already sitting in each other's line of fire. Soon we'll have to blow up a few pillboxes just to clear room for new concrete.

BEBRA *knocks on the concrete; his troupe does likewise:* And you have faith in concrete, Lieutenant?

HERZOG: That's hardly the right word. We haven't much faith in anything anymore. Right, Lankes?

LANKES: Yes, sir, not anymore!

BEBRA: But they keep on mixing and pouring.

LANKES: Just between you and me: We're getting valuable experience here. I never knew how to build anything, spent some time as a student, then the war broke out. I'm hoping to use my knowledge working with cement when it's over. Everything's going to have to be rebuilt back home. Just take a look at that concrete, take a close look. *Bebra and his troupe with their noses right on it.* You see that? Seashells. We've got everything right at our doorstep. Just have to gather and mix it. Stones, seashells, sand, cement . . . What more can I say, Captain, you're an artist and an actor, you know how it is. Lankes! Tell the captain what we put in the concrete.

LANKES: Yes, sir! Tell the captain what we put in the concrete. We put puppies in. There's a puppy buried in the foundation of every pillbox.

BEBRA'S TROUPE: A puppy?

LANKES: Soon there won't be another puppy between Caen and Le Havre.

BEBRA'S TROUPE: No more puppies.

LANKES: That's how hard we've been working.

BEBRA'S TROUPE: That's how hard.

LANKES: We'll have to start using kittens soon.

BEBRA'S TROUPE: Meow!

LANKES: But cats aren't as good as puppies. So we're hoping there's some action here soon.

BEBRA'S TROUPE: The gala performance! *They applaud.*

LANKES: We've rehearsed long enough. And if we run out of puppies . . .

BEBRA'S TROUPE: Oh!

LANKES: . . . we can't build any more pillboxes. Cats are bad luck.

BEBRA'S TROUPE: Meow, meow!

LANKES: But if you'd like to know in a nutshell, sir, why we use puppies . . .

BEBRA'S TROUPE: Puppies!

LANKES: Personally I think it's all bunk . . .

BEBRA'S TROUPE: Phooey!

LANKES: But most of my comrades are country boys. And even today, when they build a house or a barn or a village church, they feel they have to wall in something living, and . . .

HERZOG: That will do, Lankes. At ease. As you've heard, Captain, we indulge in what you might call superstition here on the Atlantic Wall. Just like you people in the theater, where you don't dare whistle before an opening night, and actors spit over their shoulders before the curtain goes up . . .

BEBRA'S TROUPE: Toi, toi, toi! *They spit over each other's shoulders.*

HERZOG: But all joking aside. You have to let the men have their fun. And even the little seashell mosaics and concrete decorations they've started adding to pillbox entrances are tolerated by orders from the very top. People need to keep busy. And so I always say to our CO, who doesn't like the concrete curlicues: Better curlicues in concrete than in their brains, Major. We Germans like to tinker. What can you do.

BEBRA: Well, we're trying to do our bit too, entertaining the waiting army at the Atlantic Wall . . .

BEBRA'S TROUPE: Bebra's Theater at the Front sings for you, plays for you, rallies you to final victory!

HERZOG: You're certainly right about that, you and your troupe. But the theater alone is not enough. We're on our own for the most part, so we do what we can. Right, Lankes?

LANKES: Yes, sir! We do what we can!

HERZOG: You see. And now if you'll excuse me, sir. I have to go over to Dora Four and Dora Five. Take your time looking over the pillbox, it's worth it. Lankes will show you everything . . .

LANKES: Everything, sir! *Herzog and Bebra exchange salutes. Herzog exits right. Raguna, Oskar, Felix, and Kitty, who had been standing behind Bebra, spring forward. Oskar holds his tin drum, Raguna carries a picnic basket, Felix and Kitty climb up onto the concrete roof of the pillbox, start practicing their acrobatic exercises. Oskar and Roswitha play in the sand beside the bunker with a little pail and shovel, make it plain they're in love, call out happily, and tease Felix and Kitty.*

BEBRA, *offhandedly, after he has inspected the pillbox from all sides:* Tell me, Lankes, what do you do for a living?

LANKES: I'm a painter, sir. But that was long ago.

BEBRA: You paint houses?

LANKES: Houses too, sir, but more in the way of art.

BEBRA: Hear, hear! So you emulate the great Rembrandt, or Velázquez perhaps?

LANKES: Sort of in between the two.

BEBRA: But my God, man! Why are you mixing, pouring, and guarding concrete? You should be in the Propaganda Corps. War artists are what we need!

LANKES: Haven't got it in me, sir. My stuff's too oblique for present tastes. Got a cigarette, sir? *Bebra hands him a cigarette.*

BEBRA: Oblique? You mean modern?

LANKES: Who knows what's modern? Before these people turned up with their concrete, oblique was modern for a while.

BEBRA: It was?

LANKES: Yep.

BEBRA: Do you lay it on thick? With a spatula, maybe?

LANKES: That too. And I work with my thumb, just press it in and stick in nails and studs, and before thirty-three I stuck barbed wire on cinnabar for a while. Got good reviews. A private collector in Switzerland has them now, soap manufacturer.

BEBRA: This war, this terrible war! And now you're pouring concrete. Hiring out your genius for fortification work. Well, I must admit that Leonardo and Michelangelo did the same in their day. Designed mechanical swords and erected bulwarks when they didn't have a Madonna on commission.

LANKES: You see! There's always a niche somewhere. A true artist has to express himself. Take a look at those ornaments over the bunker entrance, sir. I did them.

BEBRA, *after thorough study:* Amazing! What richness of form, what rigorous power of expression!

LANKES: You could call the style Structural Formations.

BEBRA: And does your creation, this relief, this image, have a title?

LANKES: Like I said: Formations, or Oblique Formations, if you like. A new style. No one's ever done it before.

BEBRA: But that's just it, you're the creator, you should give the work a distinctive title ...

LANKES: Titles, what's the point of titles? If it weren't for exhibition catalogues they wouldn't exist.

BEBRA: Now don't put on airs, Lankes. Think of me as an art lover, not an officer. Cigarette? *Lankes takes it.* Well?

LANKES: Well, if you put it that way. What I thought to myself was this: When this is all over — and it will be over someday, one way or the other — these pillboxes will still be standing, because pillboxes always remain standing, even when everything else collapses. And then Time will come into play. The centuries will pass, I mean — *He tucks away the last cigarette.* Got another cigarette, sir? Much obliged! And the centuries will come and go as if they're nothing. But the pillboxes will remain, just as the pyramids have always remained. And one fine day a so-called archaeologist will arrive and say to himself, What an artistically impoverished age that was back then, between the first and the seventh world wars: dull gray concrete, a few amateurish, awkward curlicues in folk style over bunker entrances—and then he'll run across Dora Four, Dora Five, Six, Dora Seven, he'll see my structurally oblique formations, and say to himself: Let's have a look at this. Interesting. One might almost say magical; menacing, yet imbued with striking spirituality. A genius, perhaps the only genius of the twentieth century, expressed himself here clearly, and for all time. Does the work bear a title? Did the master reveal himself through a signature? And if you'll look closely, sir, and tilt your head at an oblique angle, then between these rough Oblique Formations . . .

BEBRA: My glasses. Help me, Lankes.

LANKES: All right, here's what it says: Herbert Lankes, anno nineteen hundred and forty-four. Title: MYSTICAL, BARBARIC, BORED.

BEBRA: You have given our century its name.

LANKES: You see!

BEBRA: Perhaps five hundred or a thousand years from now, when restoration work is under way, they will find a few puppy bones in the concrete.

LANKES: Which will only reinforce my title.

BEBRA, *excited:* What is our age, and what are we, dear friend, if not our works . . . but look: Felix and Kitty, my acrobats, are doing gymnastics on the pillbox.

KITTY *For some time now a piece of paper has been passing back and forth between Roswitha and Oskar, between Felix and Kitty, all of whom have been writing on it. Kitty, in a slight Saxon accent:* See, Herr Bebra, what you can do on concrete. *She walks on her hands.*

FELIX: And nobody ever did a *salto mortale* on concrete before. *He does a somersault.*

KITTY: We need a real stage like this.

FELIX: Though it's a bit windy up here.

KITTY: But it's not as hot and smelly as those stupid movie houses. *She ties herself in knots.*

FELIX: And we even wrote a poem up here.

KITTY: What do you mean, we? Oskar made it up, and Signora Roswitha.

FELIX: Well, we helped when they needed a rhyme.

KITTY: Just one more word and it's done.

FELIX: Oskar wants to know what those spikes on the beach are called.

KITTY: He has to put them in the poem.

FELIX: They're too important to leave out.

KITTY: So tell us, soldier, what are those spikes called?

FELIX: Maybe he can't, because enemy ears are listening.

KITTY: We won't tell anyone.

FELIX: Otherwise it won't scan right.

KITTY: He's worked so hard, has Oskarnello.

FELIX: And he can write so beautifully, in Sütterlin script.

KITTY: I wonder where he learned it.

FELIX: The only thing he doesn't know is what those spikes are called.

LANKES: Do I have your permission, Captain?

BEBRA: Unless it's some vital military secret.

FELIX: Oskar really wants to know.

KITTY: The poem won't work without it.

ROSWITHA: We're all so curious to know.

BEBRA: I'm making it an order.

LANKES: All right, we put them up to ward off tanks and landing craft. And we call them Rommel asparagus, because that's what they look like.

FELIX: Rommel . . .

KITTY: . . . asparagus? Does it fit, Oskarnello?

OSKAR: It fits! *He writes the words on the paper, hands the poem to Kitty on the bunker. She ties herself into a tighter knot and recites the following lines like a school poem.*

KITTY:

ON THE ATLANTIC WALL
Still staring from guns, with camouflaged teeth,
Rommel asparagus, poured concrete,
we're already off to the Land of Slippers,
with scrambled eggs and Friday's kippers,
and Sunday's roast with leaves of bay:
The bourgeois life is on its way!

Still sleeping in snarls of sharp barbed wire,
We plant our mines in latrine mire

while dreaming above of garden bowers,
of bowling teams and lovely flowers,
of pretty gargoyles, birds in May:
The bourgeois life is on its way!

Though Death has many still to take,
and many a mother's heart must break,
at least Death's always nicely dressed
in parachute silk that's properly pressed,
ruffled with feathers of peacock and jay:
The bourgeois life is on its way!

Everyone applauds, including Lankes.

LANKES: It's low tide now.

ROSWITHA: Then it's time we had breakfast! *She swings the large picnic basket, which is decorated with bows and artificial flowers.*

KITTY: Yes, let's picnic outside.

FELIX: Nature whets the appetite.

ROSWITHA: O sacred ritual of dining, which binds all nations, as long as men eat breakfast.

BEBRA: Let's have our feast on concrete. It will provide the proper foundation! *Everyone except Lankes climbs up on the bunker. Roswitha spreads out a bright, flowered tablecloth. She pulls small cushions with tufts and fringes from the bottomless basket. A parasol, pink and bright green, is opened, a tiny gramophone with speaker is set up. Little plates, little spoons, eggcups, napkins are distributed.*

FELIX: I'd like some of that pâté de foie gras.

KITTY: Is there any of that caviar we rescued from Stalingrad?

OSKAR: Don't spread the Danish butter on too thick, Roswitha.

BEBRA: That's right, son, watch out for her figure.

ROSWITHA: But I like it, and it's good for me. Oof! When I think of that cake with whipped cream the Luftwaffe served us in Copenhagen.

BEBRA: The Dutch chocolate in the thermos is still nice and hot.

KITTY: I just love these tins of American cookies.

ROSWITHA: Be sure and put this South African ginger marmalade on them.

OSKAR: Don't pile it on, Roswitha, please.

ROSWITHA: You've been taking inch-thick slices of that awful English corned beef yourself.

BEBRA: What about you, soldier? A paper-thin slice of raisin bread with yellow plum jam?

LANKES: If I wasn't on duty, sir . . .

ROSWITHA: You have to give him an official order.

KITTY: Yes, an official order.

BEBRA: All right, Corporal, I hereby order you to take some raisin bread with French plum jam, a Danish soft-boiled egg, Soviet caviar, and a small cup of genuine Dutch chocolate.

LANKES: Yes, sir! Genuine Dutch chocolate! *He joins them on top of the bunker.*

BEBRA: Don't we have another cushion for the soldier?

OSKAR: He can have mine. I'll sit on my drum.

ROSWITHA: But don't catch cold, darling. Concrete is treacherous, and you're not used to it.

KITTY: He can have my cushion too. I'm going to knot myself up a little so the bread and honey goes down better.

FELIX: But stay over the tablecloth, let's not get honey on the concrete. That would weaken our defenses. *Everyone giggles.*

BEBRA: Ah, the sea air feels so good.

ROSWITHA: Yes it does.

BEBRA: The chest expands.

ROSWITHA: Yes it does.

BEBRA: The heart sheds its skin.

ROSWITHA: The heart indeed does.

BEBRA: The soul bursts forth from its cocoon.

ROSWITHA: How beautiful the sea air makes us look.

BEBRA: Sight is freed, takes wing . . .

ROSWITHA: It flies . . .

BEBRA: Flaps away, across the sea, the endless sea . . . Say, Corporal, I see something black down there on the beach, five of them.

KITTY: I do too. With five umbrellas!

FELIX: Six.

KITTY: Five! One, two, three, four, five!

LANKES: It's the nuns from Lisieux. They were evacuated with their kindergarten and shipped over here.

KITTY: But Kitty can't spot any children. Just five umbrellas.

LANKES: They always leave the children in the village, in Bavent, and come at low tide to gather shellfish and prawns caught in the Rommel asparagus.

KITTY: Poor things.

ROSWITHA: Should we offer them corned beef and a few cookies?

OSKAR: I suggest raisin bread with plum jam, since it's Friday and nuns can't eat corned beef on Friday.

KITTY: Now they're running. Sailing along with their umbrellas.

LANKES: They always do that when they've gathered enough. They start playing. Especially Agneta, the novice, a young thing who still doesn't know which way is up — got another cigarette, sir? Many thanks. And the one bringing up the rear, the fat one who can't keep up, that's the Mother Superior, Sister Scholastika. She doesn't want them playing on the beach, it might be against the rules of the order. *Nuns with umbrellas run about in the background. Roswitha starts up the gramophone: "Sleigh Bells in St. Petersburg" rings out. The nuns dance to it and shout with joy.*

AGNETA: Yoo-hoo! Sister Scholastika!

SCHOLASTIKA: Agneta, Sister Agneta!

AGNETA: Ha, ha, Sister Scholastika!

SCHOLASTIKA: Come back, my child. Sister Agneta!

AGNETA: I can't! I'm carried away.

SCHOLASTIKA: Then pray, Sister, for a conversion!

AGNETA: A sorrowful one?

SCHOLASTIKA: A merciful one.

AGNETA: A joyful one?

SCHOLASTIKA: Pray, Sister Agneta!

AGNETA: I'm praying, I keep onnn praying. But I'm still being carried away!

SCHOLASTIKA, *her voice dying away*: Agneta, Sister Agneta!

AGNETA: Yoo-hoo! Sister Scholastika! *The nuns disappear. Now and then their umbrellas appear in the background. The phonograph record runs down. Beside the entrance to the bunker the telephone rings. Lankes springs down from the top of the pillbox, lifts the receiver; the others continue eating.*

ROSWITHA: Even here, in the midst of boundless nature, there has to be a telephone.

LANKES: Dora Seven here. Corporal Lankes.

HERZOG *enters slowly from the right with telephone receiver and cable, stops several times to speak into the phone:* Are you asleep, Lankes? There's something moving in front of Dora Seven. Plain as day.

LANKES: Those are nuns, sir.

HERZOG: What do you mean, nuns? And what if they aren't nuns?

LANKES: But that's what they are. Plain as day.

HERZOG: Ever hear of camouflage? Fifth column? The English have been at it for centuries. Come with their Bibles and then suddenly all hell breaks loose.

LANKES: They're gathering prawns, sir ...

HERZOG: Clear the beach immediately, is that understood?

LANKES: Yes, sir. But they're just gathering prawns.

HERZOG: Man your machine gun, Lankes!

LANKES: But they're just looking for prawns, at low tide, for their kindergarten ...

HERZOG: I'm giving you an order ...

LANKES: Yes, sir! *Lankes disappears into the pillbox. Herzog exits right with the telephone.*

OSKAR: Better hold your ears, Roswitha, there's going to be shooting, just like in the newsreels.

KITTY: Oh, how awful! I'll tie myself in a tighter knot.

BEBRA: I'm almost inclined to believe we'll hear something.

FELIX: We should turn on the gramophone again. That helps some. *He turns on the gramophone: The Platters sing "The Great Pretender." The machine gun rattles in time with the slow, tragically drawn-out music. Roswitha holds her ears. Felix stands on his head. In the background five nuns with umbrellas fly heavenward. The record sticks, repeats itself, then silence. Felix ends his handstand. Kitty unties herself. Roswitha hastily clears away the tablecloth with the breakfast leftovers and puts them in the picnic basket. Oskar and Bebra help her. They leave the roof of the bunker. Lankes appears in the entrance.*

LANKES: Got another cigarette, sir?

BEBRA, *his frightened troupe behind him:* Soldier, you smoke too much.

BEBRA'S TROUPE: Smoke too much.

LANKES: It's the concrete, sir.

BEBRA: And if there's no more concrete someday?

BEBRA'S TROUPE: No more concrete someday.

LANKES: It's immortal, sir. But we and our cigarettes . . .

BEBRA: I know, I know, we vanish with the smoke.

BEBRA'S TROUPE, *slowly exiting:* With the smoke!

BEBRA: But they'll still be inspecting concrete a thousand years from now.

BEBRA'S TROUPE: A thousand years from now!

BEBRA: They'll find puppy bones.

BEBRA'S TROUPE: Little puppy bones.

BEBRA: And your oblique formations in concrete.

BEBRA'S TROUPE: MYSTICAL, BARBARIC, BORED!

Lankes, alone, smoking.

Though Oskar said little or nothing during that breakfast on the pillbox, he could not resist recording this dialogue on the Atlantic Wall, for such words were indeed spoken on the eve of the invasion; and we will run into our concrete artist Corporal Lankes again on another page, when we assess the postwar period and our now blossoming bourgeois era.

On the beach promenade the armored personnel car was still waiting for us. With long strides Lieutenant Herzog joined those entrusted to his care. Breathlessly he apologized to Bebra for the minor incident. "Off limits means off limits," he said, helped the ladies into the car, gave the driver a few final instructions, and back we headed for Bavent. We were in a rush, barely had time for lunch, for we had announced a show at two that afternoon in the grand hall of the charming little Norman château that lay behind poplars at the edge of the village.

We had just half an hour to test the lighting, then Oskar raised the curtain with a drumroll. We were playing to an audience of noncoms and enlisted men. They laughed loud and often. We laid it on thick. I sangshattered a glass chamber pot containing a pair of Viennese sausages with mustard. His face boldly outlined, Bebra shed clown tears over the broken pot, dug the sausages from the shards, added more mustard, and wolfed them down, to boisterous laughter from the field-gray crowd. Kitty and Felix had been appearing for some time now in snappy lederhosen and Tyrolean hats, which lent a special touch to their gymnastic exercises. Roswitha, in a close-fitting silvery gown with long pale green gloves, and gold-embroidered sandals on her tiniest of feet, kept her bluish eyelids lowered while her somnambulistic Mediterranean tones produced their usual effect of daemonic magic. Have I already mentioned that Oskar needed no costume? I wore my good old sailor cap with the stitched inscription *SMS Seydlitz*, my navy blue shirt beneath my jacket with the little gold anchor buttons, my knee pants peeping out below, rolled knee-length socks in my thoroughly worn shoes, and my red and white lacquered tin drum, with five more just like it safely stockpiled in my theatrical gear.

That evening we repeated the performance for the officers and the telegraph girls from a communications center in Cabourg. Roswitha was a trifle nervous, though she made no mistakes, but in the midst of her routine donned a pair of blue-rimmed sunglasses, altered her tone of voice, and became more direct in her revelations, informing, for example, a somewhat pale, embarrassed, and therefore slightly snippy telegraph girl that she was having an affair with her commanding officer. This seemed to me in rather poor taste, but it drew plenty of laughs from the audience, since the officer in question was no doubt the one sitting next to the telegraph girl.

After the show the regimental staff officers, who were billeted at the château, gave a party. Bebra, Kitty, and Felix stayed on, but Raguna and Oskar quietly took their leave, went to bed, fell asleep quickly after such a busy day, and slept till five A.M., when the invasion woke us up.

What shall I tell you about the invasion? Canadians landed in our sector, near the mouth of the Orne. Bavent had to be evacuated. We'd already loaded our luggage. We were to withdraw along with the regimental staff. A steaming, motorized field kitchen had pulled up in the courtyard of the château. Roswitha asked me to bring her a cup of coffee, since she hadn't had breakfast yet. Slightly nervous, and worried that I might miss pulling out with the other trucks, I refused, and was even a trifle rude to her. Whereupon she jumped from the truck herself, ran over to the field kitchen in her high heels with the mess kit, and reached her hot morning coffee at precisely the same moment as an incoming naval shell.

O Roswitha, I know not how old you were, I only know that you were three foot three, that the Mediterranean spoke through you, that you smelled of cinnamon and nutmeg, that you could see into the hearts of men but could not look into your own, or else you would have stayed with me and not gone running after that coffee, which was all too hot.

In Lisieux, Bebra managed to get us marching orders for Berlin. When he emerged and rejoined us outside garrison headquarters, he spoke for the first time since Roswitha's passing: "We dwarfs and fools should not dance on concrete that's been poured and hardened for giants. If only we'd stayed under the grandstands, where no one suspected our presence."

In Berlin I parted from Bebra. "What will you do in all those air-raid shelters without your Roswitha?" he said with a smile as thin as a spider web, kissed me on the forehead, provided Kitty and Felix with travel papers to escort me to Central Station in Danzig, and presented me with the five remaining drums from the theatrical gear; and thus provided for, still armed with my book, I arrived on the eleventh of June in forty-four, the day before my son's third birthday, in my native city, which, still undamaged and medieval, rang forth the hours with bells of various sizes from church towers of various heights.

The Imitation of Christ

AH, YES, THE HOMECOMING! At twenty-four minutes past twenty hundred hours the furlough train pulled into Danzig Central. Felix and Kitty accompanied me as far as Max-Halbe-Platz, said goodbye, with Kitty getting teary-eyed, then, shortly before twenty-one hundred hours, proceeded to the control station in Hochstrieß while Oskar plodded down Labesweg with his luggage.

The Homecoming. There's an unfortunate tendency nowadays to regard every young man who forges a small check, joins the Foreign Legion, then returns home in a few years, slightly older and full of stories, as a modern-day Ulysses. Some absent-minded fellow climbs onto the wrong train, winds up in Oberhausen instead of Frankfurt, has some sort of encounter on the way — how could he not? — and starts bandying about names like Circe, Penelope, and Telemachus the minute he gets home.

Oskar was no Ulysses, if for no other reason than that he found things unchanged at his homecoming. His beloved Maria, to whom the role of Penelope would have fallen, was not surrounded by lecherous suitors, she still had her Matzerath, whom she had chosen over Oskar long before his departure. And I do hope the more classically minded among you don't see my poor Raguna as a man-beguiling Circe simply because she was once a professional somnambulist. Finally, as far as my son Kurt is concerned, he didn't lift a finger to help his father, and so was certainly no Telemachus, even if he did fail to recognize Oskar.

If a comparison is necessary — and I understand that homecomers must put up with comparisons — then I prefer to be viewed as the Prodigal Son, for Matzerath opened the door and welcomed me like a father, and not just a presumptive one. Yes, he showed such joy at Oskar's homecoming, shedding genuine, wordless tears, that from that day forth I no longer called myself exclusively Oskar Bronski but Oskar Matzerath as well.

Maria received me with less emotion but was by no means unfriendly. She was sitting at the table, pasting in food stamps for the Office of Economic Affairs, and had already stacked a few wrapped birthday presents for Kurt on a little side table. Practical as she was, the first thing she thought of was my physical well-being; she undressed me, bathed me as in days of old, ignoring my blushes, and sat me at the table in my pajamas, where Matzerath had meanwhile served up fried eggs and roasted potatoes. They gave me milk to drink too, and while I ate and drank, the questioning began: "Where were you, we searched everywhere, and the cops searched like mad, and we had to go to court and swear we hadn't bumped you off. Well, you're back now. But you made plenty of trouble for us, and more to come, because now we have to tell them you're back. Let's just hope they don't stick you in some home. That's what you deserve. Running away and not saying nothing!"

Maria proved to be right. There was plenty of trouble. An officer from the Ministry of Health arrived and spoke in private with Matzerath, but Matzerath cried out loudly enough so we could all hear, "It's out of the question, I promised my wife on her deathbed, I'm his father, not the health authorities!"

So I wasn't sent to a home. But from then on an official letter arrived every two weeks asking Matzerath for a simple signature; Matzerath refused to sign, but his face grew lined with care.

Oskar's getting ahead of himself, and must smooth Matzerath's face again, for the evening I arrived his face beamed; he was far less worried than Maria and asked fewer questions, just enjoyed my happy homecoming, behaved like a true father, and said, as I was taken up to a somewhat bewildered Mother Truczinski at bedtime, "Won't little Kurt be happy to have a little brother again. And just think, tomorrow is Kurt's third birthday."

On his birthday table my son Kurt found, in addition to the cake with three candles, a wine-red sweater knitted by Gretchen Scheffler to which he paid no attention. There was a nasty yellow rubber ball he sat on, then rode all about and finally punctured with a kitchen knife. Then he sucked from the rubber wound that sickeningly sweet fluid that gathers in all inflated balls. Scarcely had the ball been given its permanent dent than little Kurt began to unrig the sailboat and transform it into a shipwreck. A humming top and its whip lay untouched, but frighteningly close at hand.

Oskar, who had planned for his son's birthday far in advance, who had rushed eastward amid the ultimate fury of historical events, determined not to miss the third birthday of his son and heir, stood to one side, looked upon his son's destructive efforts, admired the boy's resolution, compared his own physical dimensions with those of his son, and was forced to admit with some concern: Little Kurt has outgrown you while you were away, the three feet you've managed to hold yourself down to for almost seventeen years, ever since your third birthday, this little boy has clearly topped by an inch; it's time to turn him into a tin-drummer and call an energetic "Halt!" to this precipitous growth.

From my theatrical gear, which I had stowed behind the roof tiles in the attic along with my large one-volume course of study, I fetched a shiny brand-new tin drum, resolved to offer my son the same opportunity—since none of the grownups would—that my poor mama, keeping her promise, had offered me on my third birthday.

Matzerath had once hoped that I would take over the grocery store, and since I'd let him down, I had good reason to believe that Matzerath now saw little Kurt as the future grocer. If I say that had to be prevented at all costs, please don't regard Oskar as an outright enemy of retail trade. I would have felt exactly the same way had either one of us been asked to take over a factory or inherit a kingdom with all its colonies. Oskar wanted no hand-me-downs, and he hoped his son would reject them too; I wanted him—and therein lay my logical error—to be a drummer eternally three years old, as if taking over a drum weren't just as revolting for a hopeful young man as taking over a grocery store.

Oskar sees that today. But back then he was consumed by one desire: to set a drumming son beside a drumming father, to drum as a duo looking up at the grownups from below, to establish a drumming dynasty capable of perpetuating itself, passing on his work from generation to generation on red and white lacquered tin.

What a life lay before us! Drumming away beside each other, but also in different rooms, side by side, but he at times on Labesweg, I on

Luisenstraße, he in the cellar, I in the attic, little Kurt in the kitchen, Oskar in the toilet, father and son, here and there, and now and then in tandem, and should the fortunate occasion have arisen, we could both have slipped under the skirts of my grandmother and his great-grandmother Anna Koljaiczek to live and drum and breathe in the smell of slightly rancid butter. Crouching by her portal, I would have said to little Kurt, "Take a look inside, my son. That's where we come from. And if you're very, very good, we may be allowed to return there for a brief hour or so and visit those who await us."

And there beneath the skirts, little Kurt would have bent low, risked a peep, and politely asked me, his father, to explain things.

"That beautiful woman," Oskar would have whispered, "sitting in the middle, playing with her beautiful hands, with an oval face so lovely it brings tears to your eyes, that's my poor mama, your dear grandmother, who died from eating eel soup or from her own overly tender heart."

"Go on, Papa, go on!" little Kurt would have clamored. "Who's the man with the mustache?"

Then, with an air of mystery, I would have lowered my voice: "That's your great-grandfather, Joseph Koljaiczek. Note his flickering arsonist's eyes, the divine Polish eccentricity and the practical Kashubian cunning crowning the bridge of his nose. Observe as well the webs between his toes. In nineteen-thirteen, as the *Columbus* was being launched from the slips, he wound up under a raft of logs, then swam and swam, all the way to America, where he became a millionaire. But sometimes he takes to the water again, swims back, and dives in here, where he first found refuge as an arsonist and contributed his part toward my mama."

"But what about that handsome man who's been hiding behind the lady who is my grandmother, but is sitting beside her now, caressing her hands? His eyes are as blue as yours, Papa!"

Then, wicked and traitorous son that I am, I would have gathered all my courage to answer my dear child: "Those are the dreamy blue eyes of the Bronskis looking at you, Kurt. It's true your own eyes are gray. You got them from your mother. Yet like Jan, who is kissing my poor mama's hand, and like his father Vinzent, you are a Bronski, a dreamer through and through, yet with a Kashubian practicality. One day we'll return there, return to the source that spreads the slightly rancid smell of butter. Rejoice!"

According to my theories at the time, it was only inside my grandmother Koljaiczek, or, as I put it in jest, in the grandmotherly butter tub, that true family life was possible. Today, when God the Father, his only begotten Son, and, most important of all, the Holy Spirit himself are such a short hop away that I could jump right over them — for in addition to all my other callings, I am reluctantly committed to the Imitation of Christ — and though nothing is farther from me now than the entrance to my grandmother, I still picture the most beautiful of family scenes in the circle of my forebears.

I envision them mostly on rainy days: My grandmother sends out invitations and we all meet inside her. Jan Bronski arrives with flowers, carnations perhaps, stuck in the bullet holes in his Polish Post Office defender's breast. Maria, who has received an invitation at my behest, approaches my mama shyly and, trying to curry favor, shows her the account books Mama set up and Maria has carried on flawlessly, at which Mama releases her Kashubian laugh, draws my beloved to her, kisses her cheek, and says with a wink, "Dear little Maria, who cares? After all, we both wed a Matzerath and nursed a Bronski!"

I must sternly forbid myself any further thoughts along these lines, any speculation for example about a son sired by Jan, carried to term by my mama inside Grandmother Koljaiczek, and finally born in the butter tub. For this would surely have drawn further consequences. Thus my half brother Stephan Bronski, who after all belonged in this circle, might have hit on the Bronskian idea of casting first an eye, and soon much more, at my Maria. My imaginative powers prefer to focus on an innocent family gathering. Renouncing a third and fourth drummer, I rest content with Oskar and little Kurt, narrate for those present something on my drum about that Eiffel Tower which replaced my grandmother in foreign climes, and am pleased if the guests, including our hostess Anna Koljaiczek, enjoy our drumming and slap one another's knees in time to the rhythm.

Enticing as it is to unfold the world and its relationships inside one's own grandmother, to be multilayered within restricted levels, Oskar must now — since, like Matzerath, he is a merely presumptive father — limit himself to recounting the events of the twelfth of June, nineteen forty-four, little Kurt's third birthday.

To repeat: the boy had received a sweater, a ball, a sailboat, and a whip and humming top, to which I was about to add a red and white lacquered tin drum. He'd barely finished unrigging the sailboat when Oskar approached, holding his tin gift hidden behind his back, with his own battered drum dangling at his tummy. We stood only a step apart: Oskar, the toddler; Kurt, the inch-taller toddler. He had a furious, pinched look on his face — still bent on destroying the sailboat — and at the very moment I drew forth the drum and held it up, he broke off the final mast of the *Pamir*, for that was the windjammer's name.

Kurt dropped the wreck, accepted the drum, held it, turned it about, and his face grew calmer, though it was still tense. Now it was time to hand him the drumsticks. Unfortunately he misunderstood my dual gesture, felt threatened, knocked the sticks from my hands with the edge of his drum, reached behind him as I bent for the sticks, and as I offered them to him a second time, struck me with his birthday gift: struck me, not the top grooved for the whip, tried to make me, his father, hum and spin like a top, whipped me, thought just you wait little brother; thus did Cain whip Abel till Abel spun, still wobbling at first, then with ever increasing speed and precision, and found his way darkly through a low, grumbling humming to a higher song, sang the song of the humming top. Higher and higher Cain enticed me with his whip, my voice chalky, a tenor pouring forth his morning prayer, I sang as silver-chased angels might sing, or the Vienna Boys' Choir, or well-drilled castrati — as Abel may have sung before he fell, as I now fell, collapsing beneath the whip of the boy child Kurt.

When he saw me lying there in misery, my hum dying away, he cracked his whip in the air several more times, as if his arm hadn't had enough. He also kept a mistrustful eye on me during his thorough examination of the drum. First the red and white lacquer was banged against the corner of a chair, then my gift fell to the floor and little Kurt sought and found the massive hull of the former sailboat. With this he beat the drum. He didn't play the drum, he beat it to pieces. His hand did not attempt the simplest rhythm. He just pounded away steadily with an expression of frantic concentration on an instrument that had never expected such a drummer, that was made to withstand playful rolls of lightweight drumsticks but not blows with a bulky wreck used as a battering ram. The drum buckled, tried to escape by breaking away from its frame, tried to turn invisible by shedding its red and white lacquer and letting its gray-blue tin beg for mercy. But the son showed no mercy to his father's birthday gift. And when his father tried to mediate again, making his way across the carpet, in spite of all his aches and pains, to where his son sat on the wooden floor, the whip intervened once more. And the weary top, knowing that mistress well, gave up spinning and humming, just as the drum gave up once and for all on finding a sensitive drummer, strong but not brutal, who would playfully ply his drumsticks.

When Maria walked in, the drum was ready for the scrapheap. She picked me up, kissed my swollen eyes and my torn ear, licked my blood and the welts on my hands.

Oh, if only Maria had not kissed the maltreated, backward, deplorably abnormal child! If only she had recognized the beaten father and in every wound the lover. What a consolation, what a true, secret husband I could have been for her during the dark months ahead.

The first blow—which had little direct impact on Maria—fell on my half brother Stephan Bronski, serving on the Arctic Front and recently promoted to lieutenant, who was still going by his stepfather's name Ehlers, and found his career as an officer suddenly placed on permanent hold. While Stephan's father Jan, shot during the defense of the Polish Post Office, bore a skat card under his shirt at the cemetery in Saspe, the lieutenant's jacket was decorated with the Iron Cross Second Class, the Infantry Badge, and the so-called Cold Storage Medal.

Toward the end of June Mother Truczinski suffered a slight stroke when the mailman delivered bad news. Airman First Class Fritz Truczinski had fallen for three things simultaneously: his Führer, his Volk, and his Fatherland. This had happened in the Center Sector, and Fritz's wallet with snapshots of pretty young women, most of them laughing, from Heidelberg, Brest, Paris, Bad Kreuznach, and Saloniki, his Iron Cross First and Second Class, a medal for some wound or other, his bronze bar for close combat, and two loose antitank patches, along with a few letters, had been sent by a certain Captain Kanauer directly from the Center Sector to Labesweg, Langfuhr.

Matzerath helped as best he could, and Mother Truczinski soon improved, though she never really recovered. She sat stuck in her chair by the window, asked me or Matzerath, who brought something up for her two or three times a day, just where this "Center Sector" was, if it was far away, and if you could get there by train on a Sunday.

Much as he would have liked to, Matzerath couldn't tell her. So, based on the geography lessons I'd learned from special communiqués and military broadcasts, it was left to me to spend long afternoons with Mother Truczinski, who sat motionless except for her wobbling head, drumming out various versions of the Center Sector's now rapidly shifting location.

Maria, on the other hand, who was deeply attached to the dashing Fritz, turned religious. At first, all through July, she tried to make do with the religion she'd been raised in, going to Pastor Hecht at the Church of Christ on Sundays, accompanied at times by Matzerath, though she preferred to go alone.

Protestant services were not enough for Maria. One weekday — was it a Thursday or a Friday? — before closing time, turning the shop over to Matzerath, she took me, the Catholic, by the hand, we headed toward Neuer Markt, then turned on Elsenstraße, again on Marienstraße, passed Wohlgemuth's butcher shop, reached Kleinhammerpark — Oskar was already thinking, we're headed for Langfuhr Station, we're going to take a little trip, to Bissau perhaps in Kashubia — when we swung to the left, waited superstitiously at the underpass for a freight train to go by, entered the underpass, which was dripping nastily, and went through, not straight ahead to the Film-Palast, but left along the railway embankment. I thought: Either she's dragging me to Dr. Hollatz's office on Brunshöferweg or she's heading for the Church of the Sacred Heart to convert.

Its portal faced the railway embankment. Between the embankment and the open door we came to a stop. A late August afternoon, the air humming. Behind us, on the ballast between the rails, Ukrainian women in white kerchiefs were hacking and shoveling. We stood and peered into the shadowy, cool-breathing belly of the church: far to the back, deftly seductive, a severely inflamed eye — the Eternal Light. Behind us on the embankment the women stopped shoveling and hacking. A horn tooted, a train was approaching, it arrived, it was there, was still there, not gone yet, then it was gone, and the horn tooted, Ukrainians shoveled. Maria wavered, perhaps unsure which foot to put forward, placed the burden of responsibility on me, by birth and baptism closer to the only true Church; for the first time in years, since those two weeks filled with fizz powder and love, Maria resigned herself to Oskar's guidance.

Then we left the embankment and its sounds, August and its August hum. Rather mournfully, gently tapping my drum with the tips of my fingers beneath my smock, as outwardly a look of indifference settled on my face, I recalled masses, pontifical offices, vesper services, and Saturday confessions at my poor mama's side, who shortly before her death was rendered pious by her all too intense involvement with Jan Bronski, and sought relief in confession Saturday after Saturday, strengthened herself each Sunday with the sacrament, and thus relieved and strengthened would meet Jan on Tischlergasse the following Thursday. Who was the priest back then? It was Father Wiehnke, and he was still pastor at the Church of the Sacred Heart, delivered sermons that were pleasantly soft and unintelligible, sang the Credo so faintly and plaintively that even I might have been overcome by something resembling faith back then if it hadn't been for that left side-altar with the Virgin, the boy Jesus, and the boy Baptist.

And yet it was that altar that impelled me to pull Maria from the sunshine into the portal, then across the flagstones into the nave.

Oskar took his time, sat quietly beside Maria on the oak pew, growing calmer, cooler. Years had passed, and yet it seemed to me that the same people still awaited Father Wiehnke's ear, leafing methodically through the Mirror of Confession. We sat somewhat off to the side, but nearer the central aisle. I wanted to leave the choice up to Maria and make it easier for her. She wasn't so near the confession box as to be confused by it, leaving her free to convert in a quiet, unofficial way; yet she could see how people behaved prior to confession and, while watching, reach her own decision about making her way into the box to the Father's ear to discuss the details of her conversion to the only true Church. I felt sorry for her, small and with still unpracticed hands, kneeling amid incense, dust, plaster, sinuous angels, refracted light, and convulsed saints, before, beneath, and amid all that sweet, sorrow-laden Catholicism, crossing herself backward the first time. Oskar tapped Maria, demonstrated how it should be done, showed the eager pupil where behind her forehead, where deep in her breast, where exactly in the joints of her shoulder Father, Son, and Holy Spirit dwell, and how the hands must be folded to finish it off with Amen. Maria did so, brought her hands to rest in Amen, and with her Amen began to pray.

At first Oskar tried to pray too, for a few of the dead, but as he supplicated the Lord on behalf of his Roswitha, trying to negotiate eternal peace for her and admission to the joys of heaven, he so lost himself in earthly details that eternal peace and heavenly joys wound up in a Paris hotel. I took refuge in the Preface, where there is nothing much to pin you down; for all eternity, I said, *sursum corda, dignum et justum* — it is just and right, left it at that, and began watching Maria from the side.

Catholic prayer was becoming to her. She was pretty as a picture in her devotions. Prayer lengthens the eyelashes, arches the brows, inflames the cheeks, renders the brow somber, the neck supple, makes the nostrils quiver. Maria's face, blossoming in sorrow, nearly seduced me into an attempted caress. But one must never disturb those in prayer, one must neither seduce nor be seduced by them, however pleasant and conducive to prayer it may be for those praying to know someone thinks they're worth watching.

So I slid from the polished church bench and quietly folded my hands on the drum that bulged beneath my smock. Oskar fled from Maria, crossed the flagstones with his drum, passed the stations of the cross in the left nave, not pausing at Saint Anthony — pray for us — having lost neither a purse nor a house key, to our left Saint Adalbert of Prague, slain by the Prussians of old, never resting, hopping from stone to stone — a chessboard spread before us — till a carpet announced the steps to the left side-altar.

I can assure you that nothing in the Neo-Gothic brick Church of the Sacred Heart, and consequently nothing in the left side-altar either, had changed. The naked-pink boy Jesus still sat on the left thigh of the Virgin, whom I will not call the Virgin Mary, lest you confuse her with my own Mary, my Maria busy converting. Still pressed against the right knee of the Virgin was the boy Baptist, scantily clad in his chocolate-colored shaggy pelt. She herself pointed at Jesus as before with her right finger while looking at John.

Yet even after years of absence, Oskar was less interested in the Virgin's maternal pride than in the build of the two boys. Jesus was about the size of my son Kurt on his third birthday, and thus almost an inch taller than Oskar. John, who according to the evidence was older than the Nazarene, was my height. Both, however, had the same precocious expression, which as a permanent three-year-old I too bore. Nothing had changed. They had stared out with that same precocity when I used to visit the Church of the Sacred Heart at my poor mama's side all those years ago.

Over and up the carpeted steps, but without the Introitus. I examined each fold of drapery, slowly traced the painted plaster of both little nudists with my drumstick, more sensitive than all my fingers combined, omitting nothing: thighs, belly, arms, counted the rolls of fat, the dimples — that was Oskar's exact build, my healthy flesh, my strong, slightly plump knees, my short but muscular drummer's arms. And he held them the same way, the rascal. He sat on the thigh of the Virgin and lifted his arms and fists as though about to drum, as though Jesus and not Oskar was the drummer, as though he was just waiting for my drum, as if this time he had every intention of pounding out something rhythmically pleasing on it for the Virgin, John, and me.

I did what I'd done years before, removed the drum from my tummy and put Jesus to the test. Cautiously, careful not to damage the painted plaster, I pushed Oskar's red and white drum onto his rosy thighs, but this time for my own satisfaction, not in the stupid expectation of some miracle but to witness sculptural impotence, for even though he sat there with upraised fists, even though he was my size and had my own sturdy build, even though he could easily provide a plaster copy of the three-year-old I had sustained with such effort and the greatest of privations — he still couldn't drum, could only pretend, thinking no doubt: if I had one I could; now you've got one, I said, and you can't, and doubled over with laughter. I stuck both sticks into his ten sausage fingers — now drum, sweetest Jesus, painted plaster drumming on tin, Oskar backs down the three steps, from carpet to flagstones, come on, drum, Jesus boy, Oskar steps farther back. Maintains his distance and laughs himself silly, for Jesus just sits there, can't drum though he wants to. Boredom starts gnawing at me as if I were a rind of bacon — and then he struck, and all at once he was drumming!

While all remained motionless: he crossed over nicely, first with his right, then his left, then with both sticks, his drumroll not half-bad, he took it seriously, loved to change tempo, was as good when the rhythm was simple as he was when he made it complex, and yet he avoided all gimmicks, just stuck to his drum, his style not even religious or that of some warmed-over trooper, but simply and purely musical, nor did he scorn popular hits, playing, among others, one that was on everyone's lips back then, "Everything Passes," and of course "Lili Marleen," then slowly, a little jerkily perhaps, he turned his curly head with the blue Bronski eyes toward me, smiled somewhat arrogantly, and delivered a potpourri of Oskar's favorites: it began with "Glass, Glass, Little Glass," skimmed through "The Schedule," the rascal played Rasputin off against Goethe just as I did, climbed the Stockturm with me, crawled under the grandstand with me, caught eels off the harbor jetty, strode at my side behind my poor mama's coffin, tapering toward the foot, and, what stunned me most, appeared again and again beneath the four skirts of my grandmother Anna Koljaiczek.

Oskar stepped nearer. Something drew him forward. He wanted to stand on the carpet, not the flagstones. One altar step passed him on to the next. So I climbed up, though I would rather have seen him climb down. "Jesus" — I scraped together the remnants of a voice — "that wasn't our bargain. Give me back my drum right now. You have your cross, that's all you need!" Though he didn't break off abruptly, he ended his playing, crossed the sticks on the drum with exaggerated care, and without a word of objection handed me what Oskar had so thoughtlessly loaned him.

I was ready to run like ten devils down the steps with no thanks and away from Catholicism when a pleasant but imperious voice touched my shoulder: "Dost thou love me, Oskar?" Without turning I responded, "Not that I know of." And he in the same voice, without raising it in the least: "Dost thou love me, Oskar?" Crossly I replied, "Sorry, no, not at all!" Then he needled me a third time: "Oskar, dost thou love me?" Now Jesus saw my face: "I hate you, little fellow, you and your bag of tricks!"

Strangely enough, my hostility lifted him to vocal triumph. He raised his forefinger like a lady schoolteacher and gave me an assignment: "Thou art Oskar, the rock, and upon this rock I will build my church. Follow thou me!"

You can imagine my indignation. Rage turned my skin to soup-chicken flesh. I broke off one of his plaster toes, but he no longer moved. "Say that again," Oskar hissed, "and I'll scratch the paint right off you!"

Not another word came, nothing came but the old man who now and forever is shuffling through churches. He bowed to the left side-altar, took no notice of me, shuffled onward, and had already reached Adalbert of Prague when I too stumbled down the steps from carpet to flagstones and, without looking back, made my way across the chess-board pattern to Maria, who just then made the Catholic cross correctly in accordance with my instructions.

I took her by the hand, led her to the holy-water font, and when she had almost reached the portal, had her cross herself once more toward the high altar from the rear of the church but did not join in, pulling her instead, just as she was about to kneel, out into the sun.

It was early evening. The women laborers from the east had disap-peared from the embankment. In their place a freight train was being shunted just outside the local station at Langfuhr. Clusters of gnats hung in the air. Bells rang down from above. The sounds of shunting cars ab-sorbed their ringing. The gnats still hung in clusters. Maria's face was tear-stained. Oskar wanted to scream. What should I do about Jesus? I felt like loading my voice. What did I have to do with his cross? But I knew that my voice was no match for his church windows. Let him keep building his temple on people named Petrus, or Petri, or East Prussian Petrikeit. "Watch out, Oskar, don't break those church windows!" Satan whispered inside me. "He'll ruin your voice if you do." And so I cast one solitary glance upward, took the measure of one of those Neo-Gothic windows, and then tore myself away, didn't sing, didn't follow Him but instead trotted along beside Maria to the underpass on Bahnhofstraße, through the dripping tunnel, up the hill to Kleinhammerpark, right onto Marienstraße, past Wohlgemuth's butcher shop, left onto Elsen-straße, across Strießbach to Neuer Markt, where they were building a water tank for air-raid defense. Labesweg seemed endless, and then, at last, we were there: Oskar left Maria, climbed over ninety steps to the attic. Bedsheets were hanging there, and behind the sheets a mound of air-defense sand, and behind sand and buckets, behind bundles of newspapers and stacks of roof tiles, my book and my store of drums from the Theater at the Front days. And, in a shoebox, a few burned-out but still bulbous light bulbs. Oskar took the first of these, sangshattered it, took the second, reduced it to glassdust, sliced off the plumper half of the third quite neatly, sangscribed the calligraphic letters *JESUS* on the fourth, then pulverized both bulb and script, and was about to repeat the exercise when he saw he was out of light bulbs. Exhausted, I sank down on the air-defense sand: Oskar still had his voice. Jesus may have had a follower. But as for me, the Dusters would be my first disciples.

The Dusters

OSKAR WAS NOT CUT OUT to follow in Christ's footsteps, if only because gathering disciples presented me with insuperable difficulties, but the call reached my ear by various circuitous routes and turned me into his follower, though I did not believe in my predecessor. Yet true to the rule, He who doubts believes, and the unbeliever believes longest, I did not manage to bury the small miracle offered to me in private inside the Church of the Sacred Heart beneath my doubts, but tried instead to persuade Jesus to repeat his performance.

Oskar returned to the brick church several times without Maria. I could always slip away from Mother Truczinski, who was after all stuck in her chair and couldn't get at me. What did Jesus have to offer me? Why did I remain half the night in the left nave of the church and let the sexton lock me in? Why did Oskar stand at the left side-altar till his ears turned brittle and his limbs grew stiff? For in spite of my crushing humility and my equally crushing blasphemies, I never got to hear my drum or the voice of Jesus again.

Miserere! Never in all my life have I heard my teeth rattle as noisily as they did in those midnight hours on the flagstones of the Church of the Sacred Heart. What jester could ever have found a better rattle than Oskar? I imitated an entire frontline sector of freewheeling machine guns, had a whole insurance office full of secretaries and typewriters lodged between my upper and lower jaws. Back and forth it resounded, drawing echoes of applause. Columns shivered, vaulted grottos got goose-flesh, then my cough hopped one-legged across the flagstone chessboard, down the way of the cross in reverse, up the central nave, hoisted itself to the choir, coughed sixtyfold — a Bach society that didn't sing but had been trained to cough instead—and just when I was hoping that Oskar's cough had crawled into the organ pipes and wouldn't be heard from again till the Sunday chorale—a cough came from the sacristy, then from the chancel, and finally died down, still coughing, behind the high altar, behind the gymnast on the cross—where it quickly coughed up its soul. It is finished, coughed my cough; but nothing was finished. The boy Jesus held my drumsticks stiffly and impudently, immune to the cold, held my drum on rosy plaster and would not drum, would not confirm me as his follower. Oskar wished he had it in writing, that command to follow Christ.

I still have a habit, a bad one, left over from those days: in spite of the strongest of constitutions, the moment I touch the flagstones of a church, or even the best known of cathedrals, I break out in a persistent cough, which, depending on the style, height, and breadth of the church in question, turns Gothic or Romanesque, Baroque as well, and permits me even after many years to allow those coughs from the cathedrals of Ulm, Münster, or Speyer to echo again on Oskar's drum. But back then, as I submitted to the sepulchral chill of Catholicism in mid-August, trips to churches in foreign climes were only possible if you were in uniform and part of planned withdrawals, noting perhaps in the little diary one always carried along: "Withdrew from Orvieto today, fantastic church, come back with Monika when the war's over and take a closer look."

I found it easy to become a churchgoer, for there was nothing to keep me at home. There was Maria. But Maria had Matzerath. There was my son Kurt. But the rascal was becoming more and more unbearable, threw sand in my eyes, and clawed me so hard his fingernails broke off in my parental flesh. In addition, my son showed me a pair of fists with knuckles so white that the mere sight of that pugnacious twin made blood gush from my nose.

Strangely enough, Matzerath defended me, somewhat awkwardly but nevertheless with feeling. Astonished, Oskar let this man, who had never meant anything to him, draw him onto his lap, hug him, gaze at him, even kiss him once, going all teary-eyed and saying more to himself than to Maria, "I just can't do it. Not to my own son. Even if he goes ten times and the doctors all say the same. They just jot those things down. Probably don't have any kids of their own."

Maria, who sat at the table pasting food stamps onto sheets of newspaper as she did every evening, looked up. "Calm down, Alfred. You're acting like I don't care. But if they say that's how it's done these days, I just don't know what to think."

Matzerath pointed at the piano, which had produced no music since my poor mama's death: "Agnes would never have done it or allowed it!"

Maria glanced over at the piano, lifted her shoulders, and let them fall again as she spoke: "Well, you can understand that, her being the mother and all, always hoping he might get better. But you can see he's not, he's just shoved here and there and don't know how to live or how to die!"

Was it the portrait of Beethoven, which still hung above the piano, gloomily staring at a gloomy Hitler, that gave Matzerath his strength? "No," he cried, "never!" and banged his fist on the table, on damp, sticky pages of stamps, had Maria pass him the letter from the institute, read it, read and read and read, then tore it up and threw the pieces among the bread stamps, lard stamps, grocery stamps, travel stamps, heavy-labor stamps, extra-heavy-labor stamps, and stamps for expectant and nursing mothers. Though Oskar, thanks to Matzerath, did not fall into the hands of those doctors, a vision arose before him — and still does today, whenever he lays eyes on Maria — of a beautiful clinic located in the finest mountain air, and within this clinic a bright, modern, cheerful operating room, where, outside its padded door, a shy but trusting Maria hands him over with a smile to first-class doctors who are smiling too, inspiring trust, while behind their white, sterile aprons they hold first-class, trust-inspiring, instantly effective syringes. So the whole world had forsaken me, and on several occasions only the shadow of my poor mama, which fell with paralyzing force on Matzerath's hand whenever he started to sign a document from the Reich's Ministry of Health, prevented me, the forsaken, from forsaking this world.

Oskar does not wish to seem ungrateful. I still had my drum. And I still had my voice, which hardly offers you anything new, since you know all about my triumphs over glass, and may even bore those of you who like a change of pace — but to me Oskar's voice above his drum was eternally fresh proof of my existence, for as long as I sangshattered glass I existed; as long as my focused breath could knock the breath out of glass, there was life still left in me.

Oskar sang a lot back then. He sang with a desperate edge. Whenever I left the Church of the Sacred Heart at some late hour I would singshatter something. I headed for home, picked some target at random, a poorly blackened window beneath a mansard roof or a streetlamp painted a proper air-defense blue. Each time I went to church I chose a different way home. Once Oskar walked along Anton-Möller-Weg to Marienstraße. Another time he trudged up Uphagenweg, circled the Conradinum, splintered the glass in the school door, and reached Max-Halbe-Platz by way of Reichskolonie. One day toward the very end of August, when I arrived late at the church and found the door locked, I decided to take an even longer detour to walk off my rage. I strode along Bahnhofstraße killing every third streetlamp, turned right behind the Film-Palast onto Adolf-Hitler-Straße, spared the windows of the infantry barracks, but cooled my little bout of rage on a nearly empty tram coming toward me from Oliva by stripping its left side of all its dreary, blackened panes.

Oskar barely noted his triumph, let the tram screech to a halt, let the passengers get out, curse, and get on again, then set out in search of a dessert for his rage, some tasty morsel in those times so poor in tasty morsels, and didn't stop in his laced-shoe tracks till he'd reached the outskirts of suburban Langfuhr and saw, between Berendt's carpentry shop and the spacious hangars of the airfield, the headquarters of the Baltic Chocolate Factory lying in the moonlight.

My rage having cooled somewhat, I did not immediately introduce myself to the factory in my customary manner. I took my time, counted the windows the moon had counted before me, reached the same result as the moon, and felt ready to begin introductions, but first I wanted to know what those youngsters were up to who had been following me since Hochstrieß, perhaps even beneath the chestnut trees on Bahnhofstraße. Six or seven of them were standing around or inside the tram shelter at the Hohenfriedberger Weg stop. Five more I could make out behind the trees on Zoppoter Chaussee.

I was about to postpone my visit to the chocolate factory, make a wide detour around them, and sneak across the railway bridge, past the airfield, and through the allotment gardens to the Aktien Brewery on Kleinhammerweg, when Oskar heard an exchange of whistled signals, some coming from the bridge. There was no longer any doubt: the troops were being deployed with me in mind.

In such situations, in the short span of time when the pursuers have been spotted but the chase has not yet begun, one runs through the remaining chances to save oneself with particular pleasure: Oskar could have yelled for his mama and papa. I could have drummed up who knows what, possibly a policeman. I could certainly have sought help from grownups, given my stature; but I rejected — principled as Oskar could be on occasion — the help of passing grownups, or the intervention of a policeman, and spurred by curiosity and self-confidence, having decided to let things take their course, did the dumbest of all possible things: I scanned the tarred fence of the chocolate-factory grounds for a hole, found none, saw the youngsters leave the shelter, the shade of the trees on Zoppoter Chaussee, Oskar moving on, along the fence, now they were coming from the bridge too, and still the board fence had no hole, they weren't moving quickly, just strolling along, one by one, Oskar could look a bit longer, they gave me just enough time to find a hole in the fence, but when I finally found one single plank missing and, feeling something snag and tear, squeezed through the gap, there were four of them standing before me in windbreakers on the other side, their paws bulging in the pockets of their ski pants.

Since I quickly realized there was no way out of my situation, I felt for the snag I'd torn in my clothes squeezing through the gap in the fence. It was on the right rear of my trousers. I measured it with two spread fingers, found it annoyingly large, put on a show of indifference, and waited to look up till all the boys from the tram shelter, the Chaussee, and the bridge had clambered over the fence, for the hole in the fence was too small for them.

This happened toward the very end of August. The moon veiled itself now and then with a cloud. I counted around twenty. The youngest was fourteen, the oldest sixteen, going on seventeen. The summer of forty-four was hot and dry. Four of the taller boys were wearing Air Force Auxiliary uniforms. Forty-four was a good year for cherries, I remember. They stood around Oskar in small groups, talking in undertones, using a jargon I didn't even try to understand. They called one another by odd names, only a few of which I caught. One, a little fifteen-year-old with slightly hazy doe eyes was called Jackrabbit, or sometimes Thumper. The one next to him was PuttPutt. The smallest, but surely not the youngest, with a protruding upper lip and a lisp, they called Pinchcoal. An Air Force auxiliary answered to Mister, and another, aptly enough, to Chickenface; there were historical names too: Lionheart, a milk-faced Bluebeard, names I knew well like Totila and Teja, two even had the impudence to call themselves Belisarius and Narses; Störtebeker, who wore a raincoat that was too long for him and a genuine velour hat with its crown dented into a duck pond, I examined more closely: in spite of being only sixteen, he was the leader of the gang.

They paid no attention to Oskar, probably trying to soften him up, and so, with weary legs, half amused, half annoyed with myself for getting involved in what was clearly some sort of adolescent romanticism, I sat down on my drum, looked up at the nearly full moon, and tried to dispatch a portion of my thoughts to the Church of the Sacred Heart.

Perhaps he'd drummed today, even said a word or two, and here I was sitting in the yard of the Baltic Chocolate Factory playing cops and robbers. Perhaps he was waiting for me, perhaps he planned, after a brief introductory drum solo, to open his mouth again, to clarify what it meant to imitate Christ, and was disappointed that I hadn't come, perhaps he was raising his eyebrows with customary arrogance. What would Jesus have thought of these brats? What was Oskar, his likeness, his follower and vicar, supposed to do with this horde? Could he have addressed the words of Jesus, "Suffer the little children to come unto me!" to a gang of teenagers who called themselves PuttPutt, Thumper, Bluebeard, Pinchcoal, and Störtebeker?

Störtebeker approached. Beside him, Pinchcoal, his right-hand man. Störtebeker: "Stand up!"

Oskar's eyes were still on the moon, his thoughts still at the left side-altar of the Church of the Sacred Heart, he did not stand, and at a sign from Störtebeker, Pinchcoal kicked the drum out from under me.

As I stood up I pulled the drum to me to protect it from further harm, and put it under my smock.

A handsome rascal, this Störtebeker, thought Oskar. Eyes a bit too deep-set and narrow, but the mouth lively and imaginative.

"Where are you from?"

The interrogation was under way, then, and since I didn't like his

greeting, I turned back to the disk of the moon, imagined the moon —
which puts up with anything you care to imagine — as a drum, and
smiled at my harmless megalomania.

"He's grinning, Störtebeker."

Pinchcoal looked me over, suggested something to his chief called
"a dusting." Others in the background, the pimply Lionheart, Mister,
Thumper, and PuttPutt, also favored a dusting.

Still with the moon, I spelled out the word dusting. A pretty little
word, but it surely did not stand for anything pleasant.

"I'll decide when it's time for a dusting!" Störtebeker said, bringing
the murmurs of his gang to an end, then turned to me again: "We've
seen you plenty of times on Bahnhofstraße. What are you doing there?
Where you coming from?"

Two questions at once. Oskar had to answer at least one of them if he
wanted to maintain control of the situation. So I turned my gaze from
the moon, looked at Störtebeker with my persuasive blue eyes, and said
quietly: "I'm coming from church."

Murmuring behind Störtebeker's raincoat. They filled in my answer.
Pinchcoal figured out that by church I meant the Church of the Sacred
Heart.

"What's your name?"

This question was bound to come up. It lay in the very nature of the
encounter. This particular formulation plays an important role in human
conversation. Answering that question provides the substance of entire
plays, both short and long, as well as whole operas — see *Lohengrin*.

I waited for the moonlight to emerge between two clouds, let it shim-
mer in the blue of my eyes and work on Störtebeker for the length of
three spoonfuls of soup, then spoke, named myself, envious of the word's
effect — for the name Oskar would only have made them laugh — "My
name is Jesus," Oskar declared; a long silence followed this confession,
till Pinchcoal cleared his throat and said, "We really have to dust him,
Chief."

Pinchcoal wasn't the only one in favor of dusting him. Störtebeker
gave his permission with a snap of his fingers and Pinchcoal grabbed
me, ground his knuckles into my upper right arm, rubbed them rapidly,
dry, hot, and painful until Störtebeker signaled stop with a second snap
of his fingers — so that was dusting.

"Now what was that name?" The chief in his velour hat acted bored, shot his right arm out like a boxer, pulling back the overly long sleeve of his raincoat, showed his wristwatch in the moonlight, and whispered past me to my left, "You've got one minute to think it over. Then I close up shop."

For another full minute Oskar could gaze at the moon with impunity, search for refuge in its craters, and question the decision he once made to follow in Christ's footsteps. Because I didn't like the sound of the phrase close up shop, and because I had no intention of allowing these brats to patronize me with their deadlines, after about thirty-five seconds Oskar declared, "I am Jesus."

What happened next was very effective, though I hadn't planned it. The moment I repeated my confession as Christ's follower, and before Störtebeker could snap his fingers or Pinchcoal could start dusting — an air-raid siren sounded.

Oskar said, "Jesus," took another breath, and the word was confirmed one after the other by the sirens at the nearby airfield, the siren at the headquarters of the infantry barracks in Hochstrieß, the siren on the roof of the Horst Wessel School just outside Langfuhr Forest, the siren on Sternfeld's department store, and far in the distance, from Hindenburgallee, the siren at the School of Engineering. It was some time before all the sirens in the suburb, like a choir of long-winded and emphatic archangels, took up the message I had delivered, set the night rising and falling, caused dreams to flicker and break, crept into the ears of the sleeping, and gave the moon, which was beyond all influence, the terrible significance of a heavenly body that could not be blacked out.

While Oskar knew that the air-raid alarm was entirely on his side, the sirens made Störtebeker nervous. A part of his gang was addressed directly and clearly by the alarm. He had to send the four Air Force auxiliaries over the fence to their batteries to man the eight-comma-eights between the tram depot and the airfield. Three of his people, Belisarius among them, were air-raid wardens at the Conradinum, and also had to leave immediately. The rest of them, around fifteen in number, he kept together, and since nothing was going on in the sky, he resumed the interrogation: "So if we understood you right, you're Jesus. Let's leave it at that. One more question: How do you do that thing with the streetlights and windowpanes? Don't try to get out of it, we know what's going on!"

But in fact they had no idea what was going on. At most they had witnessed one or another of my vocal triumphs. Oskar told himself not to be too hard on the youngsters, who today would simply be called hooligans. I tried to forgive their direct and somewhat awkward single-mindedness, to be gentle and objective. So these were the notorious Dusters the whole city had been talking about for the past few weeks, a gang of youths the police and several Hitler Youth patrols were after. Schoolboys, as it later turned out, from the Conradinum, Petri School, and Horst Wessel School. There was also a second gang of Dusters in Neufahrwasser, led by schoolboys but made up largely of apprentices from the Schichau shipyards and the railroad-car factory. The two gangs worked separately, joining forces only for nighttime forays by way of Schichaugasse to Steffenspark and Hindenburgallee, combing them for leaders heading home from evening classes of the League of German Girls at the youth hostel on Bischofsberg. Quarrels between gangs were avoided, their respective territories were clearly demarcated, and Störtebeker considered the leader of the Neufahrwasser group more as a friend than a rival. The Dusters attacked everything. They raided the offices of the Hitler Youth, grabbed medals and insignia from soldiers on furlough necking with their girls in the park, stole weapons, ammunition, and gasoline from anti-aircraft batteries, aided by their Air Force auxiliaries, and had been planning a major attack on the Office of Economic Affairs from the very start.

Oskar knew nothing about the Dusters' organization and plans back then, but feeling forsaken and dejected, a sense of security stole over him in the company of these youths. I was already secretly starting to feel I belonged with them, cast our age difference to the wind — I would soon be twenty — and thought: Why not give them a sample of your art? The young are always eager to learn. You too were fifteen or sixteen once. Give them an example, a little demonstration. They'll admire you, may even make you their leader. You can exercise your influence, sharpened by long experience; answer your calling now, gather disciples and follow in the footsteps of Christ.

Störtebeker may have sensed that my meditative silence was well founded. He gave me time, and I was thankful to him. The end of August. A moonlit night with scattered clouds. Air-raid sirens. Two or three spotlights on the coast. Probably a reconnaissance flight. Paris was being evacuated. Across from me the multiwindowed façade of the Baltic Chocolate Factory headquarters. After a long march back, Army Group Center had dug in at the Vistula. Of course Baltic no longer sold retail, but made chocolate for the Air Force. So Oskar had to get used to the idea of General Patton's soldiers strolling about beneath the Eiffel Tower in their American uniforms. That was painful for me, and Oskar lifted a drumstick. All those hours with Roswitha. And Störtebeker noticed my gesture, his eyes followed my stick toward the chocolate factory. While Japanese soldiers were being cleaned out of a small island in the Pacific in broad daylight, here the moon lay in all the factory windows at once. And Oskar said to all who had ears to hear, "Jesus will now singshatter glass."

Even before I'd finished off the first three panes, I heard the buzz of a fly high above me. While two further panes were surrendering their moonlight, I thought: That fly's dying, or it wouldn't be buzzing so loud. Then I blackened the rest of the windows on the top floor of the factory with my voice, and convinced myself that several spotlights must be suffering from anemia, before eliminating reflected lights — probably from the battery near Camp Narvik — on the two lower floors. First the coastal batteries fired; then I let the middle floor have it. A moment later the Altschottland, Pelonken, and Schellmühl batteries opened up. Three windows on the ground floor — and night fighters were taking off from the airfield, streaking low over the factory. Before I'd finished off the ground floor the anti-aircraft guns had stopped firing, leaving it to the night fighters to shoot down the four-engine long-range bomber, which was being honored by three spotlights at once over Oliva.

At first Oskar was worried that the simultaneity of his own presentation with the spectacular efforts of the anti-aircraft guns might divide the gang's attention, or even lure their gaze from the factory into the night sky.

Thus, when my work was done, I was all the more astonished to find the entire band still staring at the chocolate factory with no windowpanes. Even when applause and bravos erupted from nearby Hohenfriedberger Weg as from a theater, because the bomber had been hit and was in flames, offering a general spectacle as it crash-landed in Jäschkentaler Forest, only a few members of the gang, PuttPutt among them, tore themselves away from the deglazed factory. But neither

Störtebeker nor Pinchcoal, the ones I cared about, paid any attention to the downing.

Then the heavens were bare once more of all but the moon and the petty jewelry of the stars. The night fighters landed. Far in the distance fire engines howled. Then Störtebeker turned, showing me the usual contemptuous curve of his lip, gave the boxer's jab that freed the wristwatch from the sleeve of his oversize raincoat, removed the watch, handed it to me without a word, and, breathing heavily, tried to say something but had to wait for the all-clear sirens to die away before declaring, to the applause of his gang, "OK, Jesus. You're in if you want. We're the Dusters, if that means anything to you!"

Oskar weighed the wristwatch in his hand, then gave the rather fine piece with its luminous dial showing twenty-three minutes past midnight to little Pinchcoal. He looked up inquiringly at his chief. Störtebeker nodded his assent. And Oskar said, as he adjusted his drum snugly for the trip home, "Jesus will lead the way. Follow thou me!"

The Christmas Play

THERE WAS A GOOD deal of talk in those days about miracle weapons and final victory. We Dusters didn't talk about either, but we had the miracle weapon.

Oskar's first move when he took over leadership of the thirty to forty members of the gang was to have Störtebeker introduce me to the chief of the Neufahrwasser group, Moorskiff, a limping seventeen-year-old, the son of a high official in the Neufahrwasser Pilot Office, who because of his disability — his right leg was almost an inch shorter than his left — had not been taken in as an Air Force auxiliary or as a recruit. Even though Moorskiff displayed his limp openly and assertively, he was shy and soft-spoken. This young man, who bore a constant and somewhat crafty smile on his lips, was considered the top student in the graduating class at the Conradinum and had every expectation — so long as the Russian Army raised no objection — of passing his final exam with flying colors; Moorskiff planned to study philosophy.

Like Störtebeker, who gave me his unconditional respect, this lame boy accepted me as Jesus, leader of the Dusters. Oskar asked both gangs right at the start to show him the storeroom and the cash box, for they both kept their loot in the same cellar. This dry and spacious room was located in a quiet, elegant villa on Jäschkentaler Weg in Langfuhr. The house, covered with ivy and creeping vines and set well back from the street at the top of a gently rising lawn, was the abode of PuttPutt's parents, who were named "von Puttkamer" — though Herr von Puttkamer, who had been awarded the Knight's Cross and was of Pomeranian-Polish-Prussian stock, was off commanding a division in fair France, while Frau Elisabeth von Puttkamer, who was in poor health, had been in upper Bavaria for several months now, trying to recover. Wolfgang von Puttkamer, whom the Dusters called PuttPutt, was lord of the manor, for we never saw the old, nearly deaf maid who cared for the young master in the upper reaches of the villa, since we entered the cellar through the laundry room.

The storeroom was piled high with canned goods, tobacco, and several bolts of parachute silk. Hanging from one shelf were two dozen army watches, which PuttPutt was under orders from Störtebeker to keep running and properly synchronized. He also had to clean the two submachine guns, the assault rifle, and the pistols. I was shown a bazooka, machine-gun ammo, and twenty-five hand grenades. All this and an imposing row of gasoline cans were meant for storming the Office of Economic Affairs. Oskar's first order, which I spoke as Jesus, ran as follows: "Bury the weapons and gasoline in the garden. Hand over all the firing pins to Jesus. Our weapons are of a different kind!"

When the gang showed me a cigar box full of stolen medals and decorations I smiled and granted them permission to keep them. But I should have taken away the paratrooper knives. Later on they made use of those blades, which fit so neatly inside their handles and were just crying out to be used.

Then they brought me the cash box. Oskar had them count out the money, re-counted it himself, and recorded the cash on hand as two thousand four hundred and twenty Reichsmarks. This was at the beginning of September, in forty-four. And when, in mid-January of forty-five, Konev and Zhukov broke through on the Vistula, we were forced to surrender our cellar cash box. PuttPutt confessed, and thirty-six thousand Reichsmarks lay stacked and bundled on the bench of the Higher Regional Court.

True to my nature, Oskar stayed in the background during the action. By day, on my own usually, or at most with Störtebeker, I would seek out a suitable target for our nightly forays, then leave the planning to Störtebeker or Moorskiff, and would singshatter — now I've named our miracle weapon — with greater long-distance effect than ever before, and without leaving Mother Truczinski's flat, from my bedroom window, at some late hour, the ground-floor windows of several Party offices, the courtyard window of a printing shop that turned out food-ration cards, and once, when requested, and reluctantly, the kitchen windows of a high school principal the boys bore a grudge against.

This was in November. V1s and V2s were winging toward England, and I sang out over Langfuhr, followed the trees of the Hindenburgallee, hopped over Central Station, Altstadt, and Rechtstadt, sought out Fleischergasse and the museum, and sent my gang in to look for Niobe, the wooden galleon figurehead.

They didn't find her. In the room beside me Mother Truczinski sat stuck in her chair, her head wobbling, sharing some things she had in common with me; for while Oskar sang long-distance, she thought long-distance, searching heaven for her son Herbert, and the front lines of the Center Sector for her son Fritz. And she also searched distant Düsseldorf for her eldest daughter Guste, who'd gone off to get married in the Rhineland in forty-four, since that was where Köster the headwaiter lived, though now he was spending time in Courland; Guste had only a brief two-week furlough to have him to herself and get to know him.

Those were peaceful evenings. Oskar sat at Mother Truczinski's feet, improvised a bit on his drum, fetched a baked apple from the oven in the tile stove, disappeared into the darkened bedroom with the wrinkled fruit meant for old women and little children, lifted the blackout paper, opened the window a crack, letting a little of the frosty night into the room, and sent forth his carefully aimed long-distance song, not toward any trembling star or some point in the Milky Way, but aimed instead at Winterfeldplatz, not at the radio building, but at the boxlike structure across the way, where the office doors of the Hitler Youth district headquarters stood all in a row.

In clear weather my work took barely a minute. Meanwhile the baked apple had cooled off a little by the open window. Munching, I returned to Mother Truczinski and my drum and soon went to bed, with every assurance that while Oskar slept, the Dusters were stealing Party cash boxes, food-ration cards, and, most important of all, official rubber stamps, preprinted forms, or a membership list of the Hitler Youth Patrol, all in Jesus' name.

Indulgently I let Störtebeker and Moorskiff engage in all sorts of nonsense with falsified documents. The gang's main enemy was now the Patrol Service. They could kidnap and dust their adversaries to their hearts' content, or, for all I cared—to use Pinchcoal's phrase for the practice, which he oversaw himself—polish their balls.

Since I kept my distance from these events, which were all a mere prologue, revealing nothing of my real plans, I can't say for sure whether it was the Dusters who, in September of forty-four, tied up two high-ranking officers of the Patrol Service, one the dreaded Helmut Neitberg, and drowned them in the Mottlau above the Kuhbrücke.

But as Oskar and Jesus, double leader of the bands, I must challenge later claims that there were connections between the Dusters and the Edelweiß Pirates in Cologne on the Rhine, or that Polish partisans from Tuchlerheide influenced our actions, perhaps even directed them; all this must be banished to the realm of legend.

At the trial we were also accused of having ties with the perpetrators of the July Twentieth conspiracy, because PuttPutt's father, August von Puttkamer, had been close to Field Marshal Rommel and had committed suicide. PuttPutt, who had seen his father perhaps four or five times during the war, and then just briefly enough to note his changing insignia of rank, first heard this story about the officers, which left us totally indifferent, at the trial, and wept so wretchedly and shamelessly that Pinchcoal, who was sitting beside him, had to give him a dusting right in front of the judges.

Only once in the course of our activities did grownups try to approach us. Some shipyard workers—with Communist leanings, as I could guess at once—tried to gain influence over our Schichau apprentices and turn us into a Red underground movement. The apprentices weren't even particularly opposed to the idea. But the high school students opposed all political tendencies. Mister, the Air Force auxiliary who was the band's cynic and theoretician, formulated his position during a gang meeting: "We have nothing to do with parties, we're fighting against our parents and all grownups, regardless of what they may be for or against."

Mister may have put it a bit too strongly, but the schoolboys all agreed; and so there was a schism within the Duster gangs. The Schichau apprentices—they were good lads, I was sorry to see them go—formed a club of their own, but, over the objections of Störtebeker and Moorskiff, still called themselves Dusters. At the trial—for their shop went bust at the same time ours did—the fire on the training submarine in the shipyards was laid at their doorstep. Over one hundred captains and midshipmen met a terrible death on the submarine. Fire broke out on deck, preventing the crew sleeping below from leaving their quarters, and when the young midshipmen of barely eighteen tried to squeeze out the portholes to the safety of the harbor waters, their hips got stuck; caught from behind by the rapidly spreading flames, they screamed so loudly and for so long that motor launches were brought alongside and they had to be shot.

We didn't set that fire. Perhaps the Schichau apprentices did, or it may have been members of the Westerland Society. The Dusters were no arsonists, though I, their spiritual rector, may have tended toward arson on my grandfather Koljaiczek's side.

I remember well the mechanic who'd been transferred to Schichau from the Deutsche Werke in Kiel and visited us shortly after the gangs split up. Erich and Horst Pietzger, sons of a docker on Fuchswall, brought him to us in the cellar of the Puttkamer villa. He examined our storehouse carefully, deplored the absence of usable weapons, but still found a few grudging words of praise, and when he asked to see the gang leader and was directed, at once by Störtebeker and more hesitantly by Moorskiff, to me, he succumbed to such a gale of arrogant laughter that Oskar was within a hair of turning him over to the Dusters for a dusting.

"What kind of gnome is that?" he said to Moorskiff, jerking his thumb over his shoulder at me.

Before Moorskiff, who smiled awkwardly, could reply, Störtebeker answered with ominous calm, "That's our Jesus."

This proved too much for the mechanic, whose name was Walter, and he felt free to burst out angrily right in our own headquarters, "Say, are you political activists or a bunch of choirboys practicing for a Christmas play?"

Störtebeker opened the cellar door, gestured to Pinchcoal, let the blade of his paratrooper knife spring from the sleeve of his jacket, and said, more to the gang than to the mechanic, "We're choirboys practicing for a Christmas play."

But the mechanic suffered no harm. He was blindfolded and led from the villa. Soon we were left to ourselves, for the apprentices from the Schichau shipyards dropped out and started a gang of their own under the mechanic's leadership, and I'm sure they're the ones who set the training submarine on fire.

From my point of view, Störtebeker had answered correctly. We were politically neutral, and once the Hitler Youth patrols were intimidated enough that they rarely left their quarters, or at most checked the identity papers of flighty young girls hanging around Central Station, we shifted our field of action to the churches and, in the words of the radical left-wing mechanic, began rehearsing for Christmas plays.

Our first concern was to find replacements for the apprentices, good members all, who had been wooed away. At the end of October, Störtebeker swore in the brothers Felix and Paul Rennwand, choirboys from the Church of the Sacred Heart. Störtebeker had approached them through their sister Luzie. In spite of my protests, this young girl, who was not yet seventeen, was at the swearing-in ceremony. The Rennwand brothers had to place their left hands on my drum, which the gang, overly romantic as they could sometimes be, regarded as some sort of symbol, and repeat the Duster oath: a text so daft and filled with hocus-pocus that I can no longer remember it.

Oskar watched Luzie during the ceremony. She hunched her shoulders, held a slightly trembling sausage sandwich in her left hand, gnawed on her lower lip, held her triangular fox face rigid, burned her eyes into Störtebeker's back, and I feared for the future of the Dusters.

We started redecorating our cellar. Operating out of Mother Truczinski's flat, working with the choirboys, I directed the acquisition of our furnishings. From St. Catherine's we brought in what turned out to be an authentic sixteenth-century half-size Joseph, a few candelabra, some utensils from the Mass and a Corpus Christi banner. A nocturnal visit to Trinity Church yielded a trumpet-blowing wooden angel of no particular artistic interest and a colored tapestry to decorate our walls. A copy based on an earlier work, it showed a foppish young lady with a mythical beast known as the unicorn, who was entirely devoted to her. Though Störtebeker was right when he said that the woven smile of the lady in the tapestry had the same playful cruelty as the smile on Luzie's fox face, I still hoped my lieutenant was not as prone to devotion as that fabulous unicorn. When the tapestry was hanging on the far wall of the cellar, which had formerly been decorated with all sorts of nonsense like Black Hands and Death's Heads, and the unicorn motif at last dominated our deliberations, I asked myself: Why oh why, Oskar, when Luzie sniggers behind your back, why this second woven Luzie, who turns your lieutenants into unicorns, when living and woven she has eyes for you alone, for you alone, Oskar, are truly fabulous, the solitary beast with the decoratively spiraled horn.

How fortunate that Advent season was upon us, allowing me to block off the tapestry with life-size, crudely carved nativity figures evacuated from neighborhood churches, so the tapestry's fable no longer incited the boys. In mid-December Rundstedt began his offensive in the Ardennes, and we completed preparations for our major coup.

After attending ten o'clock Mass several Sundays in a row hand in hand with Maria, who to Matzerath's consternation was entirely immersed in Catholicism, and having ordered the entire Duster gang to attend church too, I was well enough acquainted with the layout that, on the night of the eighteenth to the nineteenth of December, with the help of the choirboys Felix and Paul Rennwand, and without Oskar's having to singshatter any glass, we were able to break into the Church of the Sacred Heart.

Snow fell but didn't stick to the ground. We stowed the three handcarts behind the sacristy. The younger Rennwand had the key to the main entrance. Oskar went in first, led the gang one by one to the holy-water font, had them kneel toward the high altar in the central nave. Then I ordered them to cover the statue of Jesus of the Sacred Heart with a Labor Service blanket, lest his blue gaze interfere with our work. Thumper and Mister carried the tools down the left nave to the left side-altar. First the stable full of nativity figures and evergreen boughs had to be evacuated to the central aisle. We already had all the shepherds, angels, sheep, asses, and cows we needed. Our cellar was filled with extras; only the leading players were still missing. Belisarius cleared the flowers off the altar table. Totila and Teja rolled up the carpet. Pinchcoal unpacked the tools. Oskar knelt behind a small prayer stool and supervised the dismantling.

First the boy Baptist in his chocolate-colored shaggy pelt was sawed off. It's a good thing we'd brought along a hacksaw. Inside the plaster, finger-thick metal rods connected the Baptist to the cloud. Pinchcoal sawed. He did it like a grammar-school boy, awkwardly. Once again the apprentices from the Schichau shipyards were sorely missed. Störtebeker took over for Pinchcoal. Things went a little better, and after half an hour's rasping we were able to shift aside the boy Baptist, wrap him in a wool blanket, and immerse ourselves in the nocturnal silence of the church.

Sawing off the boy Jesus took longer, since his whole bottom was attached to the Virgin's left thigh. Thumper, the elder Rennwand, and Lionheart spent a good forty minutes at it. But where was Moorskiff? He'd planned to come straight from Neufahrwasser with his gang and meet us at the church so our approach wouldn't attract too much attention. Störtebeker was in a bad mood and seemed nervous. He kept asking the Rennwand brothers about Moorskiff. When, as we all had expected, Luzie's name came up, Störtebeker asked no more questions, grabbed the hacksaw from Lionheart's clumsy hands, and finished off the boy Jesus in a grim and savage flurry.

While the figure was being shifted its halo broke off. Störtebeker apologized to me. With difficulty I repressed the irritability that had taken hold of me and had them gather the pieces of gilded plaster plate in two caps. Pinchcoal thought he could repair the damage with a little glue. The sawed-off Jesus was cushioned with pillows, then wrapped in two wool blankets.

Our plan was to saw off the Virgin above the pelvis and then make a second cut between the soles of her feet and the cloud. We would leave the cloud in the church and cart the two halves of the Virgin, Jesus for sure, and if possible the boy Baptist to the Puttkamer cellar. As it turned out, we had overestimated the weight of the plaster pieces. The entire group was hollow cast, the walls were no more than an inch thick, and only the iron framework posed difficulties.

The boys were exhausted, especially Pinchcoal and Lionheart. They had to be given a break, since the others, even the Rennwand brothers, couldn't saw. The gang sat scattered on the pews, shivering. Störtebeker stood crumpling his velour hat, which he'd removed upon entering the church. I didn't like the mood. Something had to be done. The gang was suffering from the effects of the sacred architecture, empty and nocturnal. Moorskiff's absence was causing some tension too. The Rennwand brothers seemed to be afraid of Störtebeker; they stood off to one side whispering till Störtebeker ordered them to quiet down.

Slowly, and with a sigh as I recall, I rose from my prayer cushion and went straight up to the Virgin, who was still in her place. Her gaze, meant for John, now rested on the altar steps filled with plaster dust. Her right forefinger, hitherto aimed at Jesus, pointed off into the void, or, rather, into the darkness of the left nave. I climbed one altar step after another, then looked back, sought Störtebeker's deep-set eyes; they were lost in thought till Pinchcoal jabbed him and awakened him to my summons. He looked at me with an uncertainty I'd never seen before, didn't understand, then finally understood, or understood in part, approached slowly, much too slowly, but took the altar steps in a single bound and lifted me onto the white, somewhat jagged surface of the Virgin's left thigh, which bore witness to a poorly wielded saw and roughly reproduced the impression of the boy Jesus' behind.

Störtebeker turned round at once, was on the flagstones in a single stride, ready to immerse himself again in his thoughts, but then turned his head, narrowed his closely set eyes to flickering pilot lights, and along with the rest of the gang in the pews, could not conceal the impact I made sitting there so matter-of-factly in Jesus' place, ready for and worthy of their worship.

He soon saw what I was after, quickly grasped my plan and even enlarged upon it. He ordered Narses and Bluebeard to aim the two flashlights they'd used during the dismantling directly at me and the Virgin, and since the torches blinded me, told them to use the red beam, waved the Rennwand brothers over, whispered with them, he wanted something they didn't want, Pinchcoal approached without being summoned by Störtebeker and bared his knuckles for a dusting; the brothers gave in and disappeared into the sacristy, shadowed by Pinchcoal and Mister. Oskar waited calmly, adjusted his drum, and was by no means surprised when Mister, who was tall, came back in priest's robes, along with the Rennwand brothers got up as red and white choirboys. Pinchcoal, wearing most of the curate's garb, had everything necessary for a Mass, spread the equipment out on the cloud, and slipped away. The older Rennwand held the censer, the younger the bells. In spite of the robes, which were much too large for him, Mister gave a fair imitation of Father Wiehnke, at first with schoolboy cynicism, but then, carried away by the text and sacred ritual, offered us all, and myself in particular, not some silly parody but a Mass that the court always referred to later as a Mass, albeit a black one.

The three boys began with the preparatory prayers at the altar steps: the gang in the pews and on the flagstones genuflected and crossed themselves, and Mister, who knew most of the words and was backed up by the trained choirboys, began to sing the Mass. With the Introitus I had already begun cautiously plying the tin with my drumsticks. The Kyrie I accompanied more forcefully. *Gloria in excelsis Deo* — I praised on my drum, summoned to prayer, substituted a long drum solo for the Epistle from the daily mass. I was particularly pleased with my performance for the Hallelujah. During the Credo I could see that the boys believed in me, drummed rather more softly during the Offertory, had Mister present bread, mix wine with water, waft incense over me and the chalice, watched to see how Mister would handle the Lavabo. *Orate, fratres,* I drummed in the red glow of the flashlights, led up to the Transubstantiation: This is My body. *Oremus,* sang Mister, reminded by holy pattern — the boys in the pews offered me two different versions of the Lord's Prayer, but Mister managed to unite Catholics and Protestants in one Communion. While they were still partaking, I drummed the Confiteor into them. The Virgin pointed her finger at Oskar, the drummer. I took up the Imitation of Christ. The Mass went smooth as silk. Mister's voice rose and fell. How beautifully he pronounced the benediction — pardon, absolution, and remission — and when he confided the final words, *ite, missa est* — Go, it is the dismissal — to the church's interior, the dismissal was a true spiritual release, and secular imprisonment could henceforth only befall a gang of Dusters strong in faith, strengthened in Oskar's and Jesus' name.

I had heard the cars during the Mass. Störtebeker turned his head too, so we were the only ones not surprised when voices sounded at the entrance, the sacristy, and from the right side door, and boot heels rang out on the flagstones.

Störtebeker wanted to lift me off the Virgin's thigh. I waved him away. He understood Oskar, nodded, forced the band to keep kneeling, to await the cops kneeling, and the boys stayed down, a few trembling fell to both knees, but all waited silently till they made their way to us down the left aisle of the central nave and from the sacristy and surrounded the left side-altar.

Several harshly glaring flashlights, not set on red. Störtebeker rose, crossed himself, stepped toward the flashlights, handed his velour hat to the still kneeling Pinchcoal, and advanced in his raincoat toward a bloated shadow with no flashlight, toward Father Wiehnke, pulled something skinny that flailed about from the shadow into the light, Luzie Rennwand, and slapped away at the girl's pinched triangular face under the beret till a blow from a policeman sent him flying into the pews.

"Man, Jeschke," I heard one of the cops cry from my perch on the Virgin, "that's the chief's son!"

Oskar, with a sense of modest satisfaction at having had the son of a police chief as an able lieutenant, let himself be taken into custody without a struggle, playing the role of a whimpering three-year-old misled by teenagers: Father Wiehnke picked me up in his arms.

The police were the only ones shouting. The boys were led away. Father Wiehnke, feeling faint and sinking onto the nearest pew, had to put me down on the flagstones. I stood by our equipment and discovered, behind the chisels and hammers, the basket full of sausage sandwiches that Thumper had prepared before we started on our mission.

I grabbed the basket and went up to Luzie, who was shivering in her thin coat, and offered her the sandwiches. She picked me up, held me in her right arm, hung the basket with the sausage sandwiches over her left, a sandwich moved rapidly from her fingers to her teeth, and I watched her burning, beaten face with its crowded features: the eyes restless behind two black slits, the skin as if hammered, a chewing triangle, doll, Black Cook, devouring sausage and skin, growing skinnier as she fed, more ravenous, more triangular, more doll-like — a look that left its mark upon me. Who will remove that triangular mark from my brow, and from my mind? How long will it chew away inside me, chewing sausage, skin, and men, and smiling as only that triangle and ladies in tapestries taming unicorns can smile?

As Störtebeker was led away between two officers and turned his blood-smeared face to Luzie and Oskar, I looked right past him, no longer recognized him, and surrounded by four or five cops, was carried along behind my former Duster gang in the arms of the sandwich-eating Luzie.

What stayed behind? Father Wiehnke stayed behind with our two flashlights, still set on red, surrounded by hastily cast-off choir robes and priest's garments. Chalice and monstrance remained on the altar steps. A sawed-off John and a sawed-off Jesus remained with the Virgin once meant to serve as a counterweight to the tapestry with lady and unicorn in our Puttkamer cellar.

Oskar, however, was carried away toward a trial that I still call the second trial of Jesus, a trial that ended with my acquittal, and hence that of Jesus.

The Ant Trail

IMAGINE, IF YOU PLEASE, a swimming pool tiled in azure blue, and in that pool, feeling suntanned and athletic, people swimming. At the edge of the pool men and women recline outside the bathing cabins. Some music from a loudspeaker perhaps, playing softly. Healthy boredom, an easygoing, casual eroticism that tautens swimsuits. The tiles are smooth, but no one slips. A few signs with rules; but these too are unnecessary, for those who swim have come for just an hour or two and break the rules elsewhere. Now and then someone dives from the three-meter board but does not merit the attention of those swimming or tempt those lying at poolside to look up from their magazines. Suddenly a breeze. No, not a breeze. A young man, slowly, resolutely climbing the ladder of the ten-meter tower, rung by rung. The magazines with commentaries from Europe and abroad droop, eyes rise with him, bodies at rest now stretch, a young woman shades her eyes, someone loses his train of thought, a word remains unspoken, a minor flirtation, barely begun, comes to a sudden end in midsentence — for now he stands on the platform, well built, virile, takes a little hop, leans against the gently curving tubular steel railing, gazes down as if bored, casts off from the rail with an elegant thrust of the hips, ventures out upon the diving board towering high above, which dips at each step, looks down, his gaze tapering to an azure, startlingly small pool below in which red, yellow, green, white, red, yellow, green, white, red, yellow bathing caps constantly rearrange themselves. His friends must be sitting there, Doris and Erika Schüler, Jutta Daniels with her boyfriend, who's not at all right for her. They wave, Jutta waves too. Careful not to lose his balance, he waves back. They call out. What do they want? Do it, they call out, dive, cries Jutta. But he wasn't planning on that at all, just wanted to see what it looked like from up there and then climb back, slowly, rung by rung. And now they're shouting to him, so that everyone can hear, shouting loudly: Jump! Go on! Jump!

You have to admit that's a hell of a situation, no matter how close the diving board is to heaven. The Dusters and I found ourselves in a similar situation, though it wasn't the season for swimming, in January of forty-five. We had ventured high above, were now jostling about on the diving board, while below us, forming a solemn horseshoe around an empty pool, sat judges, associates, witnesses, and bailiffs.

Then Störtebeker stepped out onto the springy board with no railing.

"Jump!" the judges shouted.

But Störtebeker didn't jump.

Then the slim figure of a young girl in a short Berchtesgaden jacket and a gray pleated skirt rose from the benches of the witness stand. She raised a pale but not blurred face—which I still maintain formed a triangle—like a blinking target; and Luzie Rennwand did not shout but whispered instead, "Jump, Störtebeker, jump!"

Then Störtebeker jumped, and Luzie sat back down on the wooden witness bench, pulling the sleeves of her knitted Berchtesgaden jacket over her fists.

Moorskiff limped onto the diving board. The judges urged him to jump. But Moorskiff didn't feel like it, examined his fingernails with an embarrassed smile, waited till Luzie freed her sleeves, lowered her fists from the wool, and showed him her triangle of a face, black-framed, with slits for eyes. Then he jumped, plunging toward the triangular target, yet never reached it.

Pinchcoal and PuttPutt, who had it in for each other even as they ascended, came to blows on the diving board. PuttPutt got a dusting and Pinchcoal didn't let go of him even when he jumped.

Thumper, who had long, silky lashes, closed his unfathomably sad doe eyes before he jumped.

The Air Force auxiliaries had to remove their uniforms before they jumped.

Nor could the Rennwand brothers jump from the diving board into heaven as choirboys; Luzie, their little sister, sitting in the witness stand, dressed in threadbare wartime wool and encouraging this jumping game, would never have stood for it.

Countering history, Belisarius and Narses jumped first, then Totila and Teja.

Bluebeard jumped, Lionheart jumped, the foot soldiers of the Dusters, Nosey, Bushman, Tanker, Piper, Hotsauce, Yatagan, and Cooper, jumped.

When Stuchel, a high school student so cross-eyed it was confusing to look at him, only loosely involved with the Dusters, and that almost by accident, had jumped, only Jesus remained on the diving board and, as Oskar Matzerath, was urged in chorus by the judges to jump, an invitation Jesus declined. And when a stern Luzie rose from the witness stand with her scrawny Mozart pigtail between her shoulder blades, spread her knitted sleeves, and without moving her pinched mouth, whispered, "Jump, sweet Jesus, jump!" I understood the seductive nature of the ten-meter diving board, little gray kittens tumbled about in the hollows of my knees, hedgehogs mated beneath the soles of my feet, fledgling swallows took wing in my armpits, and the whole world lay at my feet, not just Europe. There were Americans and Japanese, dancing a torch dance on the island of Luzon. There were slant-eyes and round-eyes, losing buttons on their uniforms. But at the same moment a tailor in Stockholm was sewing buttons on a pinstriped evening suit. There was Mountbatten, feeding the elephants of Burma with shells of every caliber. But at the same moment a widow in Lima was teaching her parrot to say "caramba." There were two powerful aircraft carriers, decked out like Gothic cathedrals, heading for each other in the Pacific, sending up their planes and then sinking each other. But the planes had nowhere to land, hung in the air like helpless, allegorical angels, roaring, burning up their fuel. But that didn't disturb a tram conductor in Haparanda, just home from work. He broke eggs into a pan, two for him and two for his fiancée, whose arrival he awaited with a smile, planning everything in advance. Of course as expected the armies of Konev and Zhukov were on the move again; as it rained in Ireland, they broke through on the Vistula, took Warsaw too late and Königsberg too early, and still couldn't keep a woman in Panama with five children and only one husband from burning the milk on her gas stove. And thus did the threads of current events, still hungry in front, coil about and create a story already being woven into History behind. And I saw too that activities like thumb-twiddling, brow-wrinkling, head-nodding, hand-shaking, baby-making, coin-faking, light-dousing, tooth-brushing, man-killing, and diaper-changing were being engaged in all over the world, if not always with equal skill. I was bewildered by so many purposeful actions. And so I turned my thoughts back to the trial being staged in my honor at the foot of the diving board. "Jump, sweet Jesus, jump," whispered Luzie Rennwand, the precocious witness. She sat on Satan's lap, which emphasized her virginity. He tempted her desire by handing her a sausage sandwich. She took a bite, yet retained her chastity. "Jump, sweet Jesus, jump!" she chewed, and offered me her triangle, still intact.

I didn't jump, nor will I ever jump or dive from a diving tower. That wasn't Oskar's final trial. They've attempted to persuade me to jump many times, even quite recently. At the ring-finger trial — which I prefer to call the third trial of Jesus — just as at the Dusters' trial, there were plenty of spectators at the edge of the empty, azure-tiled pool. They sat on witness benches, intending to live through and beyond my trial.

But I turned around, stifled the fledgling swallows in my armpits, squashed the hedgehogs celebrating their marriage beneath my soles, starved the gray kittens from the hollows of my knees — and stepped stiffly to the rail, scorned the exhilaration of the jump, swung onto the ladder, descended, confirming with every rung that one could not only climb diving towers, but leave them without diving.

Maria and Matzerath waited for me below. Father Wiehnke blessed me unasked. Gretchen Scheffler had brought me a little winter coat and some cake. Little Kurt had grown and refused to recognize me as his father or half brother. My grandmother Koljaiczek held her brother Vinzent by the arm. He knew the world and mumbled incoherently.

As we left the courthouse, an official in civilian clothes came up to Matzerath, handed him a document, and said, "You really should think this over, Herr Matzerath. You've got to get that child off the streets. You see how easy it is for certain elements to misuse such a poor helpless creature."

Maria wept and draped my drum around me, which Father Wiehnke had taken charge of during the trial. We walked to the tram stop at Central Station. Matzerath carried me the last part of the way. I looked back over his shoulder, searching for a triangular face in the crowd, wanted to know if she would climb to the diving board too, if she would jump after Störtebeker and Moorskiff, or if, like me, she would avail herself of the second possibility, and descend the ladder.

To this very day I have not cured myself of the habit of keeping a lookout on streets and squares for a skinny teenage girl, neither pretty nor ugly, who devours men like a shark. Even in my bed at the mental institution I'm frightened whenever Bruno announces an unknown visitor. My fear is this: Luzie Rennwand has come back as a scary Black Cook to urge you to jump one last time.

For ten days Matzerath pondered whether or not to sign the letter and send it back to the Ministry of Health. When, on the eleventh day, he sent it off signed, the city already lay under artillery siege, and it was questionable whether the post office would have a chance to send it on. The tanks leading the way for Marshal Rokossovski's army pressed forward to Elbing. The second army, under Weiß, took up positions on the heights surrounding Danzig. Life in the cellar began.

As we all know, our cellar was under the shop. It could be reached through the door in the hall across from the toilet, by descending eighteen steps, past the cellars of Heilandt and Kater, and before Schlager's. Old man Heilandt was still there. But Frau Kater, as well as Laubschad the clockmaker, the Eykes, and the Schlagers, had all departed with a few bundles. They were later said to have boarded a former Strength through Joy ship, along with Gretchen and Alexander Scheffler, and taken off in the direction of Stettin or Lübeck, or into the skies, having hit a mine; in any case, over half of the flats and cellars were empty.

Our cellar had the advantage of a second entrance, as we also know, through a trapdoor behind the counter in the shop. So no one could see what Matzerath took to the cellar or brought up from it. Nor would anyone have tolerated the provisions Matzerath managed to store there during the war. The dry, warm room was filled with such foodstuffs as dried beans, noodles, sugar, synthetic honey, wheat flour, and margarine. Boxes of Ryvita rested on boxes of Palmin. Tin cans of Leipzig Mixed Vegetables were stacked beside cans of yellow plums, baby peas, and prunes on shelves Matzerath the handyman had built himself and pegged to the walls. Midway through the war, at Greff's suggestion, he had wedged a few beams between the ceiling and the concrete floor of the cellar, so that the storeroom was as safe as a regulation air-raid shelter. Matzerath had wanted to knock these beams down again at various times, since Danzig had not suffered any serious bombardments other than nuisance raids. But when Greff the air-raid warden was no longer there to raise the issue, Maria asked Matzerath to leave the props in place. She demanded security for little Kurt and sometimes even for me.

During the first air raids at the end of January, old man Heilandt and Matzerath joined forces to carry the chair along with Mother Truczinski down to the cellar. Thereafter, either at her request or to avoid the effort, they left her by the window in her flat. After the big air raid on the inner city, Maria and Matzerath found the old lady with her jaw hanging down and squinting so oddly you'd think a small, sticky fly had flown into her eye.

So the door to the bedroom was lifted off its hinges. Old man Heilandt fetched his tools and a few crate boards from his workshop. Smoking Derby cigarettes that Matzerath had given him, he started taking measurements. Oskar helped him with his work. The others disappeared into the cellar because the artillery had started firing again from the heights.

He meant to do the job quickly and construct a simple, untapered box. But Oskar preferred the traditional form of the coffin, refused to relent, and held the boards so firmly in place beneath the saw that Heilandt finally decided to taper it toward the foot after all, giving it the shape every human corpse has the right to demand.

The coffin ended up fine. Lina Greff washed Mother Truczinski, took a freshly laundered nightgown from the wardrobe, trimmed her fingernails, arranged her bun, and gave it the support it needed with three knitting needles; in short, she made sure that in death as in life, Mother Truczinski looked like a gray mouse who liked to drink barley coffee and eat potato pancakes.

But since the mouse had stiffened in her chair during the air raid and couldn't fit in the coffin with her knees drawn up, old man Heilandt waited until Maria had left the room for a few minutes with little Kurt in her arms, then broke both legs so the coffin could be nailed shut.

Unfortunately we had no black paint but only yellow. So Mother Truczinski was carried out of her flat and down the stairs in unpainted boards, which, however, tapered toward the foot. Oskar carried his drum behind and examined the coffin lid, which read *Vitello-Margarine—Vitello-Margarine—Vitello-Margarine*—three times in succession, evenly spaced, in posthumous confirmation of Mother Truczinski's taste. During her lifetime she had preferred good old Vitello Margarine made from pure vegetable oil to the finest butter, because margarine is wholesome and nutritious, stays fresh, and lifts the spirits.

Old man Heilandt loaded the coffin onto a flatbed cart from Greff's vegetable shop and pulled it down Luisenstraße, Marienstraße, along Anton-Möller-Weg—where two houses were on fire—toward the Women's Clinic. Little Kurt stayed in our cellar with the widow Greff. Maria and Matzerath pushed, Oscar sat on the cart, would have liked to climb up on the coffin, but wasn't allowed to. The streets were clogged with refugees from East Prussia and the Delta. It was almost impossible to get through the railway underpass by the Sporthalle. Matzerath suggested digging a grave on the school grounds at the Conradinum. Maria was against it. Old man Heilandt, who was Mother Truczinski's age, waved it off. I was opposed to the school grounds too. We had to forgo the city cemetery, though, since from the Sporthalle on, Hindenburgallee was closed to all but military traffic. So we couldn't bury the mouse next to her son Herbert, but did find a place for her beyond the Maiwiese in Steffenspark, which lay across from the city cemetery.

The ground was frozen. While Matzerath and old man Heilandt took turns plying the pickax and Maria tried to dig up some ivy from around the stone benches, Oskar slipped off to be on his own and was soon among the tree trunks on Hindenburgallee. What traffic! The tanks retreating from the heights and the Delta were towing one another off. From the trees—lindens, if I remember rightly—dangled Volkssturm men and soldiers. Cardboard signs on their uniform jackets were fairly legible and indicated that the men hanging from the trees, or lindens, were traitors. I stared into the strained faces of several hanged men, made a few general comparisons, then specific ones with the hanged greengrocer Greff. I also saw clusters of youngsters strung up in uniforms too large for them, kept thinking I saw Störtebeker—though all hanged youngsters look alike—and said to myself: So now they've hanged Störtebeker—I wondered if they've strung up Luzie Rennwand?

This thought gave Oskar wings. He searched the trees left and right for a skinny dangling girl, ventured between the tanks to the other side of the avenue, but found only doughboys, elderly Volkssturmers, and youngsters who looked like Störtebeker. Disappointed, I searched along the avenue up to the half-demolished Café Vierjahreszeiten, returned only reluctantly, and when I stood once more at Mother Truczinski's grave, strewing ivy and foliage over the mound with Maria, I still retained the clear and detailed image of a dangling Luzie.

We didn't return the widow Greff's cart to the vegetable shop. Matzerath and old man Heilandt took it apart but stowed the pieces by the shop counter, and the grocer said as he stuck three packets of Derby cigarettes in the old man's pockets, "We may need the cart again. At least it's fairly safe here."

Old man Heilandt said nothing, but helped himself to several packages of noodles and two bags of sugar from the nearly empty shelves. Then he shuffled out of the shop in the same felt slippers he'd worn at the burial and all the way there and back, leaving it to Matzerath to clear his meager remaining stock from the shelves and carry it to the cellar.

Now we seldom emerged from our hole. The Russians were said to be in Zigankenberg and Pietzgendorf and on the outskirts of Schidlitz. In any case they must have occupied the heights, for they were firing straight down on the city. Rechtstadt, Altstadt, Pfefferstadt, Vorstadt, Jungstadt, Neustadt, and Niederstadt, built up over the past seven hundred years, burned to the ground in three days. But it wasn't the first time Danzig had been put to the torch. Pomerelians, Brandenburgers, Teutonic Knights, Poles, Swedes and Swedes again, French, Prussians and Russians, Saxons too, making history, had found the city worthy of burning every few decades — and now it was the Russians, Poles, Germans, and English who were baking the Gothic bricks for the hundredth time, without improving the baker's art. Häkergasse, Langgasse, Breitgasse, Große and Kleine Wollwebergasse, were burning, Tobiasgasse, Hundegasse, Altstädtischer Graben, Outer Graben, the ramparts burned, as did Lange Brücke. Crane Gate was made of wood and burned beautifully. On Tailor Lane the fire had itself measured for several flashy pairs of trousers. St. Mary's Church burned from the inside out, its lancet windows lit with a festive glow. Those bells that had not yet been evacuated from St. Catherine's, St. John's, Saints Brigitte, Barbara, Elisabeth, Peter, and Paul, from Trinity and Corpus Christi, melted in their tower frames, dripping without song or sound. In the Great Mill they were grinding red wheat. Butchers Lane smelled of burned Sunday roast. At the Stadt-Theater *Dreams of Arson,* a one-act play of ambiguous import, was given its world premiere. The town fathers in Rechtstadt decided to raise the firemen's wages retroactively after the fire. Holy Spirit Lane blazed in the name of the Holy Spirit. The Franciscan monastery blazed joyfully in the name of St. Francis, who loved fire and sang hymns to it. The Lane of Our Lady glowed for Father and Son alike. Needless to say, the Hay Market, Coal Market, and Lumber Market burned to the ground. In Bakers Lane the buns never made it out of the oven. In Milk Churn Lane the milk boiled over. Only the West Prussian Fire Insurance building, for purely symbolic reasons, refused to burn down.

Oskar never had much interest in fires. So I would have stayed in the cellar when Matzerath bounded up the steps to watch Danzig burn from the attic windows, had I not been thoughtless enough to store my few, highly flammable possessions in that same attic. It was a matter of saving the last of the drums from my Theater at the Front stockpile and my Goethe and Rasputin. I also kept a paper-thin, delicately painted fan between the pages of my book, one that my Roswitha, La Raguna, had wielded gracefully in her lifetime. Maria remained in the cellar. But little Kurt wanted to come up to the roof with Matzerath and me and watch the fire. Though my son's uncontrolled enthusiasm annoyed me, Oskar told himself the boy must get that from his great-grandfather, my grandfather Koljaiczek, the arsonist. Maria kept little Kurt below while I went up with Matzerath, gathered my things, glanced out the attic window, and was amazed to see the scintillating burst of vitality our venerable old city had managed to summon up.

When shells began landing nearby, we left the attic. Matzerath wanted to go up again later, but Maria wouldn't let him. He caved in, and wept as he gave a detailed account of the fire to the widow Greff, who had remained below. He went back to the flat again and turned on the radio, but there was no longer any signal. You couldn't even hear the crackle of the flames at the burning station, let alone a special communiqué.

Matzerath stood in the middle of the cellar, as hesitant as a child who isn't sure if he should go on believing in Santa Claus, tugged at his suspenders, expressed doubt for the first time about the final victory, and on the widow Greff's advice, removed his Party pin from his lapel, then didn't know what to do with it, since the cellar had a concrete floor, Lina Greff wouldn't take it, and Maria said he should bury it among the winter potatoes, but the potatoes didn't seem safe enough to Matzerath and he didn't dare go back upstairs, for they were bound to arrive soon, if they weren't already there, he'd seen them fighting in Brentau and Oliva from the attic, and he kept wishing he'd left the little bonbon up there in the air-defense sand, because if they found him holding it down here — then he dropped it on the concrete, was about to stamp on it, a man of action, but little Kurt and I both pounced on it, I got to it first and held tight as little Kurt started hitting the way he always did when he wanted something, but I wouldn't give my son the Party pin for fear of endangering him, because you didn't fool around with the Russians. Oskar remembered that from reading Rasputin, and I wondered, as little Kurt flailed away at me and Maria tried to separate us, whether it would be White Russians or Great Russians, Cossacks or Georgians, Kalmucks or Crimean Tartars, Ruthenians or Ukrainians, or maybe even Kirghizes, who would find the Party pin on little Kurt if Oskar relented beneath the blows of his son.

When Maria pulled us apart with the help of the widow Greff, I clutched the little bonbon victoriously in my left fist. Matzerath was glad to be rid of his badge. Maria was tending to the howling Kurt. The open pin was sticking into my palm. As usual, I just couldn't acquire a taste for the thing. But just as I was trying to pin Matzerath's bonbon on the back of his jacket — after all, what did I care about his Party — they were in the shop above us, and to judge by the screaming women, most likely in the adjoining cellars as well.

When they lifted the trapdoor, the open pin was still pricking me. What else could I do but crouch at Maria's trembling knees and watch ants as they crawled along an army trail leading diagonally from the winter potatoes across the concrete floor of the cellar to a sack of sugar. A mixed assortment of totally ordinary Russians, I judged, a half-dozen or so crowding down the cellar steps with big eyes above their tommy guns. In the midst of all the screaming, it was reassuring to see that the ants were unmoved by the arrival of the Russian Army. They were thinking only of potatoes and sugar, while those holding the tommy guns had other conquests in mind. It struck me as perfectly normal that the grownups raised their hands. I knew that from newsreels, and I'd seen a similar show of submissiveness following the defense of the Polish Post Office. But it wasn't at all clear to me why little Kurt aped the grownups. He should have taken his example from me, his father — or if not from his father, then from the ants. Since three of the boxy uniforms instantly warmed toward the widow Greff, a little life was introduced into the somewhat stiff company. Lina Greff, who was hardly expecting such a spirited throng after her long widowhood and the lean years that preceded it, let out a few screams of surprise at first, but soon reaccustomed herself to that almost forgotten position.

I had read in Rasputin that Russians love children. In our cellar I saw it firsthand. Maria, trembling needlessly, couldn't understand why the four men who weren't busy with the widow Greff allowed little Kurt to remain sitting on her lap instead of taking their own turns at it; on the contrary, they fondled little Kurt, said dadada to him, patted his cheek and Maria's too.

Someone picked me and my drum up off the concrete floor and thus prevented me from continuing my observation of the ants, comparing and gauging the march of events by their resolute diligence. My drum dangled at my belly, and the brawny fellow with large pores tapped out a few beats with his fingers, not at all badly for a grownup, to which we might have danced. Oskar would have been glad to reply in kind, would gladly have offered a few examples of his art on tin, but couldn't because Matzerath's Party pin was still sticking into his left palm.

Things grew almost calm and cozy in our cellar. La Greff lay with increasing composure beneath the three men taking turns, and when one of them had had enough, my talented drummer handed Oskar over to a sweaty, slightly slant-eyed fellow I assume was a Kalmuck. Holding me with his left hand, he buttoned his trousers with his right, and took no offense when his predecessor, my drummer, did the reverse. For Matzerath, however, nothing had changed. He was still standing in front of the shelf filled with tins of Leipzig Mixed Vegetables, his hands in the air, displaying his lined palms, which no one cared to read. The women, meanwhile, proved to be remarkably quick learners: Maria was picking up her first few words of Russian, her knees no longer trembled, she even laughed and would have played her harmonica, had it been at hand.

Oskar couldn't adjust that easily, however, and looking about for something to take the place of his ants, shifted his attention to several flat, grayish brown creatures strolling along the edge of my Kalmuck's collar. I wanted to catch one and examine it more closely, for I'd read a good deal about lice, not so much in Goethe, but relatively often in Rasputin. Since I was having a hard time catching the louse with one hand, I decided to get rid of the Party pin. And to explain my conduct, Oskar says: Since the Kalmuck already had several medals on his chest, I held out the bonbon that had been pricking me and keeping me from catching a louse to Matzerath, who was standing beside me, keeping my hand loosely closed all the while.

Now you might say I shouldn't have done that. But you might also say that Matzerath didn't have to reach out for it.

He reached out for it. I was rid of the bonbon. Matzerath grew more and more terrified as he felt the Party pin between his fingers. With my hands newly freed, I had no wish to witness what Matzerath did with it. Too distracted to pursue the louse, Oskar tried to concentrate again on the ants, but couldn't help seeing the quick movement of Matzerath's hand, and since he can no longer recall what he thought then, he says now: It would have been wiser to keep the colored button in his closed hand.

But he wanted to get rid of it, and in spite of his often-tested imagination as cook and grocery-store window dresser, could think of no other hiding place than his mouth.

How important such a trifling gesture can be! From hand to mouth, it was enough to startle the two Ivans who had been sitting quietly on either side of Maria and send them leaping up from the air-defense cot. They stood with their tommy guns thrust at Matzerath's belly and anyone could see that Matzerath was trying to swallow something.

If only he had at least closed the Party pin first with three fingers. Now he was choking on the sticky bonbon, turning red; his eyes bulged, he coughed, cried, laughed, and with all this turmoil of emotions, was no longer able to keep his hands in the air. But the Ivans would have none of that. They shouted at him to show them his palms. But Matzerath was directing his entire attention to his respiratory system. He could no longer even cough properly, breaking instead into a little dance and flinging his arms about, sweeping a few tin cans full of Leipzig Mixed

Vegetables from the shelf, all of which provoked my Kalmuck, who had been watching calmly up till then through narrowed eyes, to set me down carefully, reach behind him, bring something into horizontal position, and fire from the hip, emptying the whole magazine, firing before Matzerath could choke to death.

The strange things one does when fate steps on the stage. Without thinking or noticing, while my presumptive father swallowed the Party and died, I crushed a louse I'd just picked off the Kalmuck between my fingers. Matzerath had fallen across the ant trail. The Ivans left the cellar by way of the stairs to the shop, taking along a few packets of synthetic honey. My Kalmuck was the last to leave, but took no honey, for he was busy inserting a new magazine into his tommy gun. The widow Greff hung exposed and twisted between crates of margarine. Maria hugged little Kurt to herself as if she wanted to smother him. A phrase ran through my mind, one I had read in Goethe. The ants found the situation altered but didn't mind making a detour, forming their new army trail around a doubled-up Matzerath, for the sugar that trickled from the burst sack during the occupation of Danzig by the army of Marshal Rokossovski had lost none of its sweetness.

Should I or Shouldn't I

FIRST CAME THE RUGII, then the Goths and Gepidae, then the Kashubes, from whom Oskar descends in a direct line. Soon thereafter the Poles sent Adalbert of Prague. He came with the Cross and was slain with the Ax by either Kashubes or Borussians. This happened in a fishing village, and the name of that village was Gyddanyzc. Gyddanyzc became Danczik, Danczik became Dantzig, later spelled Danzig, and now called Danzig-Gdańsk.

Before this spelling was settled upon, however, the Kashubes had been followed to Gyddanyzc by the dukes of Pomerelia. They had names like Subislaus, Sambor, Mestwin, and Swantopolk. The village became a small town. Then the savage Borussians came and wreaked a little havoc in the city. Then the Brandenburgers came from afar and wreaked a little havoc of their own. Boleslaw of Poland had a little havoc to wreak too, and the Teutonic Knights made sure with their knightly swords that the recently repaired damage showed forth clearly again.

For centuries now, the dukes of Pomerelia, the grandmasters of the Teutonic Knights, the kings and antikings of Poland, counts of Brandenburg, and bishops of Włocławek had been replacing each other as they played their little game of destruction and reconstruction. The master builders and demolition experts were called Otto and Waldemar, Bogussa, Heinrich von Plotzke — and Dietrich von Altenberg, who built the fortress of the Teutonic Knights on the spot later named Heveliusplatz, where, in the twentieth century, the defense of the Polish Post Office took place.

The Hussites came, set a few fires here and there, and withdrew. Then the Teutonic Knights were thrown out of the city and their fortress demolished, because no one wanted a fortress in the city. The Polish took over and things didn't go too badly. The king who managed that was Kazimierz, called the Great, son of the first Władysław. Then came Louis of Hungary, and after Louis, Hedwig. She then married Jagiello of Lithuania, founder of the Jagiellon dynasty. A third Władysław followed Władysław the Second, then another Kazimierz, who wasn't all that enthusiastic about it but nevertheless spent thirteen long years squandering the good money of Danzig merchants waging war against the Teutonic Knights. Johann Albrecht, on the other hand, spent more time on the Turks. Sigismund the Elder, also called Zygmunt Stary, followed Alexander. Following the chapter on Sigismund August in history books comes the chapter on Stefan Báthory, for whom the Poles like to name their ocean liners. He laid siege to the city and bombarded it over a long period of time — as one can read in books — but could never capture it. Then the Swedes came and did the same thing. They had such a good time laying siege to the city that they did so again on several occasions. And the Gulf of Danzig proved so attractive to the Dutch, Danes, and English during this period that several foreign ship captains became sea heroes merely crossing and recrossing the Danzig roadstead.

The Peace of Oliva. How pretty and peaceful it sounds. There the great powers noticed for the first time that the land of the Poles is admirably suited for partition. Sweden, Sweden, and again Sweden — Swedish earthworks, Swedish punch, Schwedensprung. Then the Russians and the Saxons came because poor King Stanisław Leszczyński of Poland was hiding in the city. Eighteen hundred houses were destroyed because of this one king, and when poor Leszczyński fled to France because that's where his son-in-law Ludwig lived, the citizens of the city had to cough up a million.

Poland was then partitioned three times. The Prussians came uninvited and painted their own bird over the royal Polish eagle on every city gate. The schoolmaster Johannes Falk barely had time to write his Christmas carol "Oh du fröhliche . . ." before the French arrived. Napoleon's general was named Rapp, and after a long and terrible siege the Danzigers were forced to give a rap, to the tune of twenty million francs. There's no reason to doubt that the French occupation was horrific. But it only lasted seven years. Then the Russians and Prussians came and set Speicherinsel ablaze with their artillery. That put an end to the Free State that Napoleon had envisioned. The Prussians took the opportunity to repaint their bird on the city gates, and did so diligently, after first, in true Prussian fashion, establishing a garrison consisting of the 4th Regiment of Grenadiers, the 1st Artillery Brigade, the 1st Battalion of Engineers, and the 1st Regiment of Hussar Guards. The 30th Infantry Regiment, the 18th Infantry Regiment, the 3rd Regiment of Foot Guards, the 44th Infantry Regiment, and Fusilier Regiment No. 33 were only temporarily stationed in Danzig. The famous Infantry Regiment No. 128, on the other hand, didn't depart until nineteen-twenty. And for the sake of completeness it should be added that during the Prussian era the 1st Artillery Brigade was expanded to include the 1st Battalion of Fortress Artillery and the 2nd Infantry Division of East Prussian Artillery Regiment No. 1. They were joined by Pomeranian Artillery Regiment No. 2, which was later relieved by West Prussian Artillery Regiment No. 16. The 1st Regiment of Hussar Guards was followed by the 2nd Regiment of Hussar Guards. The 8th Regiment of Uhlans, on the other hand, remained within the city walls for only a short time. Outside the walls, however, West Prussian Quartermaster Battalion No. 17 was stationed in the suburb of Langfuhr. In the days of Burckhardt, Rauschning, and Greiser there were only green-clad Security Police in the Free State. Things changed in thirty-nine under Forster. The brick barracks were filled with happily laughing men in uniform, juggling all sorts of weapons. We could now go on to list all the units stationed in Danzig and environs from thirty-nine to forty-five, and those that shipped out from Danzig for the Arctic Front. But Oskar will skip that and simply say: Then, as we have seen, came Marshal Rokossovski. Seeing the undamaged city, he recalled his great international precursors and set the city ablaze with his artillery, so that those who came after him could work off their excess energy by rebuilding it.

This time, strangely enough, it wasn't Prussians, Swedes, Saxons, or Frenchmen who came after the Russians; it was the Poles who came.

With bag and baggage the Poles came, from Vilna, Białystok, and Lemberg, looking for housing. A gentleman called Fajngold came to us, single, but acting as if he were surrounded by a large family he had to take care of. Herr Fajngold took over the grocery store without further ado, showed his wife Luba, who remained invisible and unresponsive, the decimal scales, the kerosene tank, the brass rod to hang sausage on, the empty cash box, and, overjoyed, the provisions in the cellar. Maria, whom he immediately installed as salesgirl and introduced verbosely to his imaginary wife Luba, showed Herr Fajngold our Matzerath, who had been lying for three days under a piece of canvas in the cellar, since we didn't dare bury him, given all the Russians on the street trying out bicycles, sewing machines, and women.

When Herr Fajngold saw the corpse, which we had turned on its back, he clapped his hands to his head in the same expressive gesture Oskar had seen his toy merchant, Sigismund Markus, make years ago. He called his whole family, not just his wife Luba, into the cellar, and it was clear he saw them all coming, for he called each by name, Luba, Lev, Jakub, Berek, Leon, Mendel, and Zonja, explained to them all who it was lying there dead, then explained to us that everyone he'd called lay like that before they were put in the ovens at Treblinka, along with his sister-in-law and her other brother-in-law, who had five small children, and all of them lay there, except Herr Fajngold, who did not lie there because he had to spread lime.

Then he helped us carry Matzerath up to the shop, but had his family round him again, asked his wife Luba to help Maria wash the corpse. She didn't help, but that went unnoticed by Herr Fajngold, who was busy bringing up provisions from the cellar. Nor did Lina Greff, who had washed Mother Truczinski, lend us a hand this time, for she had a flat full of Russians; you could hear them singing.

Old man Heilandt, who had found work as a cobbler during the first days of the occupation, resoling Russian boots worn through during their advance on the city, didn't want to make us a coffin at first. But when Herr Fajngold drew him into a business deal, offering him Derby cigarettes from our shop in exchange for an electric motor from his shed, he laid his boots aside and picked up other tools, along with his crate boards.

At the time—until we were evicted and Herr Fajngold turned the cellar over to us—we were living in Mother Truczinski's flat, which had been stripped bare by neighbors and newly arrived Poles. Old man Heilandt took the door between the kitchen and the living room off its hinges, since the door from the living room to the bedroom had already been used for Mother Truczinski's coffin. Below in the courtyard he was smoking Derby cigarettes and assembling the box. We stayed upstairs, and I took the only chair that had been left in the room, pushed open the shattered window, and was annoyed to see the old man knocking together the box, taking no pains at all, and omitting the proper tapering.

Oskar didn't see Matzerath again, for when the coffin was lifted onto the widow Greff's flatbed cart, the Vitello Margarine slats had already been nailed down, though Matzerath not only refused to eat margarine during his lifetime but even despised its use in cooking.

Maria asked Herr Fajngold to come with us, since she was afraid of the Russian soldiers on the streets. Fajngold, who was sitting cross-legged on the shop counter spooning synthetic honey from a paper cup, had some misgivings at first, fearing his wife Luba might be suspicious, but then evidently received his wife's permission to go along, for he slid down from the counter and handed me the synthetic honey, which I passed on to little Kurt, who cleaned up every drop, while Herr Fajngold had Maria help him into a long black coat with gray rabbit fur. Before he locked up the shop and told his wife not to open the door for anyone, he placed himself under a top hat too small for him, which Matzerath had formerly worn to various funerals and weddings.

Old man Heilandt refused to pull the cart clear to the city cemetery. He still had boots to sole, he said, and had to make it quick. At Max-Halbe-Platz, with smoke still rising from its ruins, he turned left onto Brösener Weg, and I sensed he was heading for Saspe. The Russians sat outside the houses in the feeble February sun, sorting wristwatches from pocket watches, polishing silver spoons with sand, trying bras on as earmuffs, practicing bicycle tricks on an obstacle course they'd erected with oil paintings, grandfather clocks, bathtubs, radio sets, and hat stands, peddling through them in figure eights, helixes, and spirals, carefully avoiding the baby carriages, chandeliers, and the like that were being thrown out of windows, and were applauded for their skill. When we passed by, the sport paused for a few seconds. A few men wearing women's lingerie over their uniforms helped us push, then grabbed for Maria too, but Herr Fajngold, who spoke Russian and carried an official pass, managed to keep them at bay. A soldier in a lady's hat gave us a birdcage with a live budgie on its perch. Little Kurt, who was hopping along beside the cart, immediately grabbed for the brightly colored feathers, ready to pull them out. Maria, who was afraid to turn down the gift, lifted the cage out of little Kurt's reach and handed it up to me on the cart. Oskar, who wasn't about to budge for a budgie, set the cage and bird on Matzerath's oversize margarine crate. I sat clear at the back with my legs dangling and looked into Herr Fajngold's face, which, furrowed and pensive to the point of moroseness, gave the impression of a man mentally rechecking a complicated bill that just wouldn't add up.

I beat my drum a little, kept it cheery, and tried to dispel Herr Fajngold's gloomy thoughts. His brow remained furrowed, his gaze off somewhere, in distant Galicia for all I knew, but he didn't see my drum. Oskar gave up, and only the sound of Maria weeping and the rumbling of the wheels remained.

What a mild winter, I thought, as the last houses in Langfuhr fell away behind us, and took some notice of the budgie too, fluffing its feathers in response to the afternoon sun that stood over the airfield.

The airfield was under guard, the road to Brösen closed. An officer spoke with Herr Fajngold, who held his top hat between his outspread fingers during the interrogation and showed his thin, reddish blond hair, blown about by the wind. Rapping briefly on Matzerath's box as if to examine its contents, and teasing the budgie with his finger, the officer let us pass, but gave us two boys, who couldn't have been more than sixteen, with caps too small and tommy guns too large, as guards or escorts.

Old man Heilandt pulled without ever turning around. And he was even able to light a cigarette with one hand as he did so, without stopping the cart. Airplanes hung in the air. You could hear the engines so clearly because it was late February or early March. Only a few small clouds remained near the sun and gradually took on color. Bombers headed for Hela or returned from Hela Peninsula, where scattered units of the Second Army were still holding out.

The weather and the droning of the planes depressed me. There's nothing more tedious, nothing more tiring, than a cloudless March sky filled with the roar of airplanes swelling and dying. To make matters worse, the two Russian boys kept struggling in vain to march in step the whole way.

Perhaps a few boards of the hastily assembled crate had loosened during the journey, first over cobblestones and then on asphalt with potholes, and also we were heading into the wind; at any rate, it smelled of dead Matzerath, and Oskar was glad when we reached Saspe Cemetery.

We couldn't make it all the way to the wrought-iron gate because a burned-out T 34 was angled across the street just short of the cemetery, blocking it off. Other tanks advancing toward Neufahrwasser had been forced to detour around it and had left their tracks in the sand to the left of the street, flattening a portion of the cemetery wall. Herr Fajngold asked old man Heilandt to take the rear. They carried the coffin, which sagged slightly in the middle, along the tracks of the tank, hoisted it with some difficulty over the crumbling wall and, with what remained of their strength, a few steps on between the fallen and tilted gravestones. Old man Heilandt sucked greedily at his cigarette and blew the smoke toward the foot of the coffin. I carried the cage with the budgie on its perch. Maria dragged two shovels behind her. Little Kurt carried the pickax, or, rather, brandished it about, risking life and limb as he hacked away at the gray granite in the cemetery, till Maria took the pick away from him and, strong as she was, helped the two men dig.

It's a good thing the soil's sandy here and not frozen, I said to myself, and went looking for Jan Bronski's place on the other side of the north wall. It must have been here, or perhaps there. I could no longer tell for sure, for the changing seasons had softened the once telltale fresh whitewash to a crumbling gray that matched all the other walls in Saspe Cemetery.

I made my way back through the iron gate at the rear, glanced up at the stunted pines, and said to myself, trying to avoid idle thoughts: Now they're burying Matzerath too. I sought and found at least partial meaning in the fact that the two skat brothers, Bronski and Matzerath, now lay beneath the same sandy soil, even if my poor mama wasn't here to keep them company.

Funerals always make you think of other funerals.

The sandy soil didn't give in easily; no doubt it demanded more experienced gravediggers. Maria paused, leaned panting on the pickax, and started to cry again when she saw little Kurt throwing stones from some distance at the budgie in the cage. Little Kurt didn't score any hits, kept overthrowing it, while Maria wept loudly and sincerely because she'd lost Matzerath, because she'd seen something in Matzerath I don't believe was ever there, but which, in her eyes, would remain clear and worthy of love forever. Herr Fajngold offered her a few words of comfort and took the opportunity to pause briefly himself, since the work was wearing him down. Old man Heilandt seemed to be digging for gold, so steadily did he wield the shovel, tossing each shovelful behind him, expelling even his cigarette smoke in measured intervals. The two Russian boys sat on the cemetery wall a short distance away and chatted into the wind. Above, airplanes and a steadily ripening sun.

They may have dug down about a meter, while Oskar stood by idly and at a loss amid the old granite, amid the stunted pines, between the widow Matzerath and a little Kurt still throwing stones at the budgie.

Should I or shouldn't I? You're going on twenty-one, Oskar. Should you or shouldn't you? You're an orphan. It's high time you did. You've been a half orphan since your poor mama died. You should have made up your mind back then. Next they laid your presumptive father, Jan Bronski, just under the crust of the earth. That made you a presumptive full orphan, and you stood here on this sand called Saspe, holding a slightly oxidized shell in your hand. It was raining, and a Ju 52 was coming in for a landing. Wasn't "Should I or shouldn't I?" already clear, if not in the sound of the falling rain, then in the drone of the landing transport plane? You told yourself, it's the sound of the rain, it's the noise of the engines; any text could be read into that sort of monotony. You wanted it to be absolutely clear, and not just presumptive.

Should I or shouldn't I? Now they're digging a hole for Matzerath, your second presumptive father. To the best of your knowledge, you have no more presumptive fathers. So why keep juggling two empty glass-green bottles: Should I or shouldn't I? Who else is there to question? These stunted pines, themselves so questionable?

Then I found a slender cast-iron cross with crumbling ornaments and crusted letters that spelled Mathilde Kunkel — or Runkel. Then — should I or shouldn't I — in the sand between thistles and wild oats — should I — I found — or shouldn't I — three or four rusty, flaking metal wreaths the size of dinner plates, which at one time — should I — may have depicted oak leaves or laurel — perhaps I shouldn't — weighed them in my hand — perhaps I should — aimed — should I — at the top of the cross — or not — with a diameter of — should I — perhaps an inch and a half — or not — moved back about six feet — should I — and tossed — or not — missed — should I try again — the cross too far aslant — should I —

Mathilde Kunkel, or was it Runkel—should I, Kunkel, should I, Runkel—took my sixth toss, took a seventh, and six times I should not, and threw a seventh—should!—looped it over—should!—wreathed Mathilde—should!—adorned with laurel Fräulein Kunkel—asked a young Frau Runkel should I—yes! Mathilde said; she died so young, at twenty-seven, born in sixty-eight. But I was nearly twenty-one when that seventh toss succeeded, when I reduced my "Should I, shouldn't I?" to a confirmed, wreathed, targeted, triumphant "I should!"

And as Oskar headed for the gravediggers with the new "I should!" on his tongue and "I should!" in his heart, the budgie squawked; little Kurt had struck home, and yellow-blue feathers flew. I wondered what question had moved my son to barrage a budgie with pebbles till one finally hit home and gave the answer.

They had moved the crate beside the pit, which was about four feet deep. Old man Heilandt was in a hurry, but had to wait because Maria was offering up Catholic prayers, while Herr Fajngold held his top hat to his chest with his eyes somewhere off in Galicia. Little Kurt came closer now too. He'd no doubt reached a decision after his direct hit and was approaching the grave with some purpose or other in mind, just as resolutely as Oskar.

The uncertainty was killing me. After all, this was my son who had decided for or against something. Had he decided to recognize and love me at last as the only true father? Or had he decided, now that it was too late, to take up the tin drum? Or was his decision: Death to my presumptive father Oskar, who killed my presumptive father Matzerath with a Party pin simply because he was fed up with fathers. Was he too only able to express the childlike affection desirable between fathers and sons by an act of homicide?

While old man Heilandt dropped more than lowered the crate with Matzerath, the Party pin in Matzerath's windpipe, and the bullets of a Russian machine gun in Matzerath's belly, into the grave, Oskar confessed to himself that he had deliberately killed Matzerath because of the high probability that he was not only his presumptive father, but his real father as well; and because he was fed up with having to haul a father around with him all his life.

Nor was it true that the Party pin was open when I picked the bonbon up off the concrete floor. The pin was first opened within my closed hand. I passed the sticky bonbon on to Matzerath, pointed and jagged, so they would find the badge on him, so he would place the Party on his tongue, so that he would choke on it—on the Party, on me, on his son; for this had to stop!

Old man Heilandt began to shovel. Little Kurt helped him, awkwardly but eagerly. I never loved Matzerath. Sometimes I liked him. As a cook he took better care of me than as a father. He was a good cook. If I still miss Matzerath on occasion, it's his Königsberg dumplings, his pork kidneys in vinegar sauce, his carp with horseradish and cream, dishes like eel soup with dill, Kassler ribs with sauerkraut, and all his unforgettable Sunday roasts, which I can still feel on my tongue and between my teeth. They forgot to put a cook's spoon in the coffin of this man who turned feelings into soups. They forgot to put a deck of skat cards in his coffin. He cooked better than he played skat. But he still played better than Jan Bronski, and nearly as well as my poor mama. Such were his gifts, such was his tragedy. I could never forgive him for Maria, though he treated her well, never beat her and generally gave in when she picked a fight. Nor did he turn me over to the Reich Ministry of Health, and he hadn't signed the letter till they were no longer delivering the mail. When I was born beneath light bulbs he chose the shop as my career. To avoid standing behind a shop counter, Oskar spent over seventeen years behind a hundred or more drums lacquered red and white. Now Matzerath lay flat and could stand no more. Smoking Matzerath's Derby cigarettes, old man Heilandt was shoveling him in. Oskar was supposed to take over the shop. But in the meantime Herr Fajngold, with his large, invisible family, had done so. What remained fell to me: Maria, little Kurt, and the responsibility for them both.

Maria was still weeping and praying in true Catholic fashion. Herr Fajngold tarried in Galicia or solved knotty sums. Little Kurt was growing tired but kept right on shoveling. On the cemetery wall the Russian boys sat chatting. With morose regularity old man Heilandt shoveled the sand of Saspe Cemetery onto the margarine crate boards. Oskar could still make out three letters of the word *Vitello,* then took his drum from around his neck, dropped "Should I or shouldn't I?" said instead "It must be!" and threw his drum on top of the coffin, which was already sufficiently covered with sand that it made little clatter. I added the drumsticks as well. They stuck in the sand. My drum came from my Duster days. One of my Theater at the Front stockpile. Bebra gave me those drums. What would the Master have thought of my deed? Jesus had drummed on that tin, and a boxy Russian with large pores. There wasn't much life left in it now. But when a shovelful of sand struck its surface, it managed a sound. And at the second shovelful it made a slightly smaller sound. By the third shovelful it fell silent, just showing a small patch of white lacquer, till the sand covered that too with more sand, with more and more sand, sand gathered on my drum, piled higher, and grew — and I too began to grow, which was announced by a violent nosebleed.

Little Kurt was the first to notice the blood. "He's bleeding, he's bleeding!" he screamed, calling Herr Fajngold back from Galicia, pulling Maria from her prayers, even forcing the two Russian boys, who were still sitting on the wall, chatting in the direction of Brösen, to glance up startled.

Old man Heilandt dropped his shovel in the sand, took the pickax, and laid the back of my neck against the blue-black iron. The cold took effect. My nosebleed eased somewhat. Old man Heilandt went back to his shoveling, and there wasn't much sand left beside the grave when my nosebleed stopped entirely, though my growth continued, announcing itself to me by an inner grinding, popping, and cracking.

When old man Heilandt had finished the grave, he pulled a dilapidated wooden cross with no inscription from another grave and thrust it into the fresh mound somewhere halfway between Matzerath's head and my buried drum. "That's it!" the old man said, and picked up Oskar, who was unable to walk, in his arms, carrying him along and leading the others, including the Russian boys with the tommy guns, out of the cemetery, across the flattened wall, along the tank tracks to the cart on the streetcar rails where the tank was angled across the street. I looked back over my shoulder toward Saspe Cemetery. Maria was carrying the cage with the budgie, Herr Fajngold carried the tools, little Kurt carried nothing, the two Russians carried caps too small and tommy guns too large for them, and the beach pines too were bent over.

From the sand to the asphalt street. On the wrecked tank sat Crazy Leo. High overhead, planes coming from Hela, heading for Hela. Crazy

Leo was being careful not to blacken his gloves on the charred T 34. The sun and its saturated little clouds descended on Turmberg near Zoppot. Crazy Leo slid down from the tank and stood at attention.

The sight of Crazy Leo amused old man Heilandt: "Did you ever see the like? The world's falling to pieces, but you can't keep Crazy Leo down!" He clapped his free hand good-naturedly on the black frock coat and explained to Herr Fajngold, "This here's our Crazy Leo. He's here to share our sorrow and shake our hands."

And so he was. Leo fluttered his gloves, drooled out his sympathy to each person present, as was his wont, and asked, "Did you see the Lord, did you see the Lord?" No one had seen Him. Maria gave Leo the cage with the budgie; why, I don't know.

When Crazy Leo approached Oskar, whom old man Heilandt had laid on the handcart, his face dissolved, and the wind billowed his clothing. A dance seized hold of his legs. "The Lord, the Lord!" he cried, and shook the budgie in its cage. "Look at the Lord, how He is growing, look at Him grow!"

He was tossed into the air along with the cage, and he ran, flew, danced, staggered, fell, fled with the screeching bird, himself a bird, taking wing at last, fluttering across the field toward the sewage farms. And you could hear him cry through the voices of both tommy guns, "He's growing, he's growing!" and screaming still as the two Russian boys were busy reloading, "He's growing!" And even as the tommy guns fired again, as Oskar plunged down stepless stairs into a growing, all-embracing faint, I could still hear the bird, the voice, the raven — Leo proclaiming: "He's growing, he's growing, he's growing . . ."

Disinfectant

LAST NIGHT I was beset by hasty dreams. They were like friends on Visitors Day. Each dream held the door for the next and departed, having told me what dreams find worth telling: inane stories filled with repetitions, monologues you can't help listening to because they're declaimed so insistently, with the gestures of incompetent actors. When I tried to tell the stories to Bruno at breakfast, I couldn't rid myself of them because I had forgotten them all; Oskar has no talent for dreaming.

While Bruno cleared away breakfast, I asked, as if in passing, "My dear Bruno, how tall am I actually?"

Bruno placed the little dish of jam on top of my coffee cup and said in a worried voice, "But Herr Matzerath, you haven't touched your jam."

I'm all too familiar with this reproach. It's always trotted out after breakfast. Every morning Bruno brings me a dab of strawberry jam that I cover immediately by folding my newspaper into a tent over it. I can't stand the sight or taste of jam, and so I dismiss Bruno's reproach calmly and firmly: "You know how I feel about jam, Bruno—just tell me how tall I am."

Bruno has the eyes of an extinct octopod. The moment he's required to think, he trains his prehistoric gaze at the ceiling and speaks toward it for the most part, so that this morning too he said to the ceiling, "But it's strawberry jam!" Only after a long pause—for my silence kept the question of Oskar's height in play—when Bruno's gaze had found its way back from the ceiling and was clinging to the bars of my bed, did I hear that I measured one meter and twenty-one centimeters, or just under four foot tall.

"Won't you please measure me again, dear Bruno, just to be sure?"

Without batting an eyelash, Bruno pulled out a folding rule from his hip pocket, threw back my covers with almost brutal force, pulled my tangled nightclothes down over my nakedness, unfolded the stark-yellow rule, broken off at one meter seventy-eight, held it up to me, adjusted it by hand and carefully, but with his gaze in the Saurian age, and finally, as if reading out the result, let the rule come to rest on me: "Still one meter and twenty-one centimeters."

Why does he have to make so much noise folding his rule and clearing away breakfast? Doesn't he like my height?

When Bruno left the room with the breakfast tray, with the yolk-yellow folding rule next to the revolting, natural-colored strawberry jam, he glued his eye to the peephole in the door from the corridor for one last look — his gaze made me feel as old as the hills, until he finally left me alone with my four foot height.

So Oskar's that tall! Almost too tall for a dwarf, a gnome, or a midget. What was the altitude of my Roswitha, La Raguna's summit? What height did Master Bebra, descended from Prince Eugen, choose to maintain? Nowadays I could even look down on Kitty and Felix. Whereas all those I mentioned once looked down in friendly envy on Oskar, who until his twenty-first year had measured a mere ninety-four centimeters, or three foot one.

It wasn't till that stone hit me on the back of the head at Matzerath's burial in Saspe Cemetery that I began to grow.

Oskar says stone. So it seems I've decided to expand my report on events at the cemetery.

After I had discovered, by a little game, that "Should I or shouldn't I?" no longer existed for me, but only "I should, I must, I will!" — I unslung my drum, tossed it and the sticks into Matzerath's grave, decided to grow, suffered an immediate roaring in my ears, and was only then hit on the back of the head by a stone about the size of a walnut, which my son Kurt had flung with all his four-and-a-half-year-old might. Though not surprised by the blow — I'd sensed that my son had something in mind for me — I still plunged into Matzerath's grave right behind my drum. Old man Heilandt pulled me from the pit matter-of-factly with an old man's dry grip but left my drum and drumsticks below, and, once my nosebleed was evident, laid the back of my neck against the iron of the pickax. The nosebleed soon abated, as we know, but my growth progressed, albeit at such a slow pace that only Crazy Leo, fluttering and light as a bird, noticed and proclaimed it with a loud screech.

So much for this addendum, which is basically superfluous; for my growth began before the stone was thrown and I fell into Matzerath's grave. As far as Maria and Herr Fajngold were concerned, however, from its onset there was only one reason for my growth, which they termed an illness: the stone on the back of the head, my fall into the grave. Maria spanked little Kurt right there at the cemetery. I felt sorry for Kurt, for he may well have meant to help with his stone, to speed up my growth. Perhaps he wanted a real grownup father at last, or at least a substitute for Matzerath; for he has never acknowledged or honored the father in me.

In the course of my growth, which went on for nearly a year, there were plenty of male and female doctors who confirmed that the stone and my unfortunate fall were to blame, who stated and entered into my medical records: Oskar Matzerath is deformed because a stone hit him in the back of the head — and so on and so forth.

At this point let us recall my third birthday. What did the grownups say about the actual start of my story? At the age of three Oscar Matzerath fell down the cellar steps onto the concrete floor. His growth was cut short by this fall, and so on and so forth. . . .

One recognizes in these explanations mankind's reasonable desire to provide a rational basis for every miracle. Oskar has to confess that he too examines miracles from all angles before casting them aside as totally implausible fantasies.

Returning from Saspe Cemetery, we found new lodgers in Mother Truczinski's flat. A Polish family of eight populated the kitchen and both rooms. They were nice people and offered to take us in till we found something else, but Herr Fajngold, who objected to such mass overcrowding, suggested we move back into his bedroom and said he would make do temporarily with the living room. Maria opposed that in turn. She found it improper, in her newly widowed state, to share such close quarters with an unattached gentleman. Fajngold, who was unaware at the time that he no longer had a wife named Luba and a family, and constantly sensed his energetic wife looking over his shoulder, could see Maria's point. Both propriety and his wife Luba spoke against that plan, but he could still turn the cellar over to us. He even helped us rearrange the storeroom, but wouldn't let me move into the cellar with the others. Because I was ill, so miserably ill, a temporary cot was set up for me in the living room beside my poor mama's piano.

It was hard to find a doctor. Most of the doctors had left the city along with the troops, since the West Prussian Insurance Fund had already been transferred westward in January, and many doctors had trouble conceiving of people as true patients anymore. After a long search, Herr Fajngold managed to scare up a female doctor from Elbing who was amputating limbs at the Helene Lange School, where wounded soldiers from the Wehrmacht and the Red Army lay side by side. She promised to come around, and four days later she did, sat down by my sickbed, smoked three or four cigarettes in a row as she examined me, and fell asleep while still on the fourth.

Herr Fajngold was afraid to wake her. Maria poked her timidly. But the doctor didn't stir till the cigarette burned down and singed her left forefinger. She immediately stood up, stamped out the butt on the carpet, said tersely and irritably, "Sorry. Haven't slept in three weeks. Trying to get kids trucked in from East Prussia on the ferry at Käsemark. No go. Troops only. Four thousand kids. Blown to bits." Then she patted my growing kid's cheek as tersely as she'd told of the kids blown to bits, stuck a new cigarette in her mouth, rolled up her left sleeve, pulled an ampoule from her case, and said to Maria as she gave herself a pickup shot in the arm, "Can't say what's wrong with the boy. Got to get him to a clinic. But not here. Be sure you get away, and head west. His knee, wrist, and shoulder joints are swollen. His head is bound to start swelling too. Make cold compresses. I'll leave you a few pills in case he can't sleep."

I liked this terse doctor who didn't know what was wrong with me and said so. Over the coming weeks Maria and Herr Fajngold made numerous cold compresses, which helped, but couldn't keep the joints of my knees, wrists, and shoulders from continuing to swell painfully, along with my head. My expanding head scared Maria and Herr Fajngold the most. The pills they gave me ran out all too quickly. Herr Fajngold started charting the curve of my fever with a ruler and pencil, but wound up experimenting as he did so, recording my temperature in a boldly executed graph, measuring it five times daily with a thermometer he obtained on the black market in exchange for synthetic honey, a graph which then appeared on Herr Fajngold's tables as a shockingly jagged mountain chain—I thought of the Alps, the snowy peaks of the Andes—while in reality my temperature wasn't half that adventurous: in the morning it was usually thirty-eight-point-one centigrade, or one hundred point five, by the evening it would rise to thirty-nine; the highest point it reached during the period of my growth was thirty-nine point four, or one hundred two point seven. I saw and heard all sorts of things in my fever; it was like riding a carousel I wanted to get off but couldn't. I was sitting with a lot of little children in fire engines, scooped-out swans, on dogs, cats, pigs, and stags, round and round and round, wanting to get off but unable to. All the little children were crying, wanted out of the fire engines and scooped-out swans as much as I did, wanted off the cats, dogs, stags, and pigs, wanted to end the carousel ride but couldn't. The Good Lord stood beside the carousel owner and kept treating us to yet another ride. And we prayed: "Oh, Our Father who art in heaven, we know you have lots of loose change and like watching us ride the carousel, that you enjoy proving to us that the world is round and round. Please put your purse away, cry stop, halt, *fertig,* shop's closed, everybody off, *basta, stoi*—we poor little kids are dizzy, they've trucked four thousand of us to Käsemark on the Vistula, but we can't cross, because your carousel, your carousel . . ."

But the dear Lord Our Father, the carousel owner, smiled as the good book says, let another coin hop from his purse, and four thousand little children, with Oskar among them, were whirled about in fire engines and scooped-out swans, on cats, dogs, pigs, and stags, and each time my stag—I still think I was on a stag—carried me past Our Father the carousel owner, he had a different face: there was Rasputin, laughing and biting the coin for the next ride with his faith healer's teeth; there was Goethe, prince of poets, plucking coins from his finely embroidered purse, each one stamped with the profile of Our Father, then Rasputin drunk, then Herr von Goethe sober. A little craziness with Rasputin, then for reason's sake a little Goethe. The extremists with Rasputin, the forces of order with Goethe. The masses in revolt with Rasputin, calendar mottoes from Goethe . . . and finally someone bent down—not because the fever abated, but because some soothing presence always bends down in a fever—Herr Fajngold bent down and stopped the carousel. He turned off the fire engine, swan, and stag, cashed in Rasputin's coins, sent Goethe down to the Mothers, sent four thousand dizzy little children floating off from Käsemark across the Vistula into the kingdom of heaven—and lifted Oskar from his sickbed, then sat him on a cloud of Lysol; that is to say, he disinfected me.

It began because of the lice, then it became a habit. He first discovered lice on little Kurt, then on me, Maria, and himself. The lice were probably left behind by the Kalmuck who took Matzerath from Maria. The cries Herr Fajngold let out when he discovered the lice! He summoned his wife and children, suspected that the whole family was infested with vermin, traded synthetic honey and rolled oats for a wide variety of disinfectants, and began to administer a daily dose of disinfectants to himself, his whole family, little Kurt, Maria, and me, as well as my cot. He rubbed, sprayed, and powdered us. And while he sprayed, powdered, and rubbed, my fever blossomed, his words flowed, and I learned of whole boxcars filled with carbolic acid, chlorine, and Lysol, which he had sprayed, strewn, and sprinkled when he was still disinfector at Treblinka, where every afternoon at two, as Disinfector Mariusz Fajngold, he sprinkled a daily dose of Lysol over the streets of the camp, the barracks, the shower rooms, the cremation ovens, the bundled clothes, over those who were waiting, having not yet showered, over those lying still, having already showered, over all that emerged from the ovens, over all yet to enter the ovens. And he listed the names, for he knew every one: he told me of Bilauer, who on one of the hottest days in August told him to sprinkle the camp streets of Treblinka with kerosene rather than Lysol. Herr Fajngold did so. And Bilauer had the match. And old Zev Kurland from the ŻOB administered oaths to the lot of them. And the engineer Galewski broke into the arsenal. And Bilauer shot Hauptsturmführer Kutner. And Sztulbach and Warynski took care of Zisenis. And the others handled the Trawniki men. And still others cut open the fence and died. But Unterscharführer Schöpke, who always made little jokes while taking a group to the showers, stood at the camp gate firing. But it was no use, they all fell on him at once: Adek Kave, Motel Levit, and Henoch Lerer; Hersz Rotblat and Letek Zagiel were there too, and Tosias Baran with his Debora. And Lolek Begelmann cried out, "Get Fajngold too, before the planes arrive." Herr Fajngold was still waiting for his wife Luba. But even then she no longer came when he called. So they seized him left and right. On the left Jakub

Gelernter and on the right Mordechaj Szwarcbard. And running before him little Dr. Atlas, who had advised sprinkling Lysol liberally at Treblinka and later in the woods near Vilna, who maintained: Lysol is more important than life! And Herr Fajngold could confirm this, for he had sprinkled the dead with Lysol, not just one corpse, no, but the dead, why bother with numbers, the dead. And named names for so long it grew tedious, since for me, floating in Lysol, the question of the life and death of a hundred thousand names was less important than the question of whether life, and if not life, then death, had been disinfected in time and thoroughly enough with Herr Fajngold's disinfectants.

But my fever waned, and April arrived. Then my fever rose again, the carousel spun round once more, and Herr Fajngold sprinkled Lysol on the living and the dead. Then my fever waned again, and April drew to a close. By early May my neck grew shorter and my chest grew larger, pressing upward till I could rub Oskar's chin against my collarbone without lowering my head. Then more fever and Lysol. And I heard Maria whispering words that floated in Lysol: "If only he don't grow crooked. If only he don't wind up with a hump. If only he don't get water on the brain!"

Herr Fajngold consoled Maria, however, recalling stories of people he'd known who managed to make something of themselves in spite of a hump and water on the brain. He told of a certain Roman Frydrych who had emigrated to Argentina with his hump and opened a sewing-machine business that later expanded into a large concern and made a real name for itself.

The story of Frydrych the successful hunchback did little to console Maria, but it catapulted its narrator, Herr Fajngold, into such a state of enthusiasm that he decided to give our grocery store a facelift. In mid-May, shortly after the war ended, new merchandise showed up in the shop. The first sewing machines appeared, along with spare parts, while groceries remained for some time and helped ease the transition. Idyllic times. Almost no one ever paid in cash. Things were traded and re-traded, and synthetic honey, rolled oats, the remaining packets of Dr. Oetker's Baking Powder, sugar, flour, and margarine were transformed into bicycles, the bicycles and spare parts into electric motors, these into work tools, the tools into furs, and the furs, as if by magic, Herr Fajngold transformed into sewing machines. Little Kurt made himself useful at this trade-and-retrade game, brought in customers, helped make deals, adjusted to the new line much more quickly than Maria. It was almost like the old days with Matzerath. Maria stood behind the counter, served those of the old customers who were still around, and tried to decipher the wishes of the newly arrived customers with her painfully limited Polish. Little Kurt was a gifted linguist. Little Kurt was all over the place. Herr Fajngold could count on little Kurt. Though not quite five, little Kurt became an expert, picking out high-quality Singer and Pfaff sewing machines with ease from a hundred poor to mediocre models being offered on the black market on Bahnhofstraße; and Herr Fajngold valued little Kurt's knowledge. When, toward the end of May, my grandmother Anna Koljaiczek came on foot from Bissau to Langfuhr by way of Brentau to visit us, and plopped herself down on the sofa breathing heavily, Herr Fajngold praised little Kurt to the skies and extolled Maria too. When he told my grandmother the story of my illness in lengthy detail, pointing out again and again the efficacy of his disinfectants, he found words of praise for Oskar too, because I'd been so calm and well-behaved, and never once cried throughout the whole ordeal.

My grandmother wanted kerosene, because Bissau had no electricity. Fajngold told her about his experience with kerosene in the camp at Treblinka, and about his multifarious duties as camp disinfector, had Maria fill two liter bottles with kerosene, added a package of synthetic honey and a broad assortment of disinfectants, and listened, nodding absently, as my grandmother reported on all the things that had burned to the ground in Bissau and Bissau-Abbau in the course of the fighting. She also described the damage in Viereck, which was now called Firoga again. And Bissau was once more Bysewo, as before the war. As for Ehlers, who was once Party leader of the Local Farm Association in Ramkau and very able, who had married her brother's son's wife Hedwig, whose Jan had stayed at the post office, the farmhands had hanged him outside his office. And almost hanged Hedwig too, because she'd switched as a wife from a Polish hero to the Party leader of the Local Farm Association, and Stephan had been a lieutenant and Marga had been in the League of German Girls.

"Well," said my grandmother, "they couldn't hurt Stephan no more, cause he was killed up in the Arctic. They wanted to take Marga away and stick her in a camp. But Vinzent started jawing and talking like he never did before. So now Hedwig is with Marga, helping in the fields. All that talking near wore Vinzent out, and he might not last much longer. As for Granny, her heart's bad and everything else, her head too, where some oaf whacked her because he thought he ought."

Thus the lamentations of Anna Koljaiczek; stroking my growing head and holding her own, she delivered a few meditative insights: "That's Kashubes for you, little Oskar. Always getting hit on the head. But you are going where things are better now, and leaving old Granny behind. Because Kashubes don't move around a lot, they always stay put, and hold their heads still for others to whack, because we ain't really Polish and we ain't really German, and Kashubes ain't good enough for Germans or Pollacks. They want everything cut and dried."

My grandmother laughed loudly, stowed the kerosene bottles, the package of synthetic honey, and the disinfectants under her four skirts, which, in spite of the extreme violence of military, political, and world-historical events, had lost none of their potato color.

As she was about to leave, Herr Fajngold asked her to wait a moment, since he wanted to introduce his wife Luba and the rest of his family to her, and when Frau Luba failed to appear, Anna Koljaiczek said, "Well, let her be then. I'm always calling out, Agnes, that's my daughter, come help your old ma wring out the wash, and she don't come, just like your Luba. And Vinzent, that's my brother, goes out sick or not in the dark at night and wakes up the neighbors, crying out for his son Jan that was at the post office and got killed."

She was standing in the door, pulling on her scarf, when I called out from my bed, "Babka, Babka!" which means Grandma, Grandma. And she turned, lifted her skirts slightly, as if she wanted to let me in under them, take me with her, when she probably recalled the kerosene bottles, the synthetic honey, and the disinfectants already occupying that space — and left, left without me, left without Oskar.

At the beginning of June the first convoys headed west. Maria said nothing, but I could see she too was taking leave of the furniture, the shop, the flat, taking leave of the graves on both sides of Hindenburg-allee and the mound in Saspe Cemetery.

Sometimes in the evening, before she went down to the cellar with little Kurt, she would sit beside my cot at my poor mama's piano, holding the harmonica in her left hand and trying to accompany her little tune with one finger of her right hand.

The music made Herr Fajngold sad, he asked Maria to stop, yet the moment she lowered the harmonica and started to close the piano, he would ask her to play a little more.

Then he proposed to her. Oskar had seen this coming. Herr Fajngold called his wife Luba less and less often, and one summer evening full of buzzing flies, when he was certain she was gone, he proposed to Maria. He would take care of her and both children, Oskar the sick one too. He offered her the flat and a partnership in the business.

Maria was twenty-two then. Her early beauty, which had seemed pieced together almost by chance, had firmed up, perhaps even hardened. The last few months of the war and its aftermath had deprived her of the permanents Matzerath always paid for. Though she no longer wore braids, as she had in my day, her hair hung down to her shoulders, lending her the aura of a somewhat serious, perhaps even embittered young woman—and this young woman said no, rejected Herr Fajngold's proposal. Maria stood on the carpet that was once ours, holding little Kurt in her left arm, gestured with her right thumb toward the tile stove, and Herr Fajngold and Oskar heard her say, "Can't do it. Things are all washed up here. We're going to my sister Guste in the Rhineland. She married a headwaiter in the hotel business there. His name's Köster and he'll take us in for now, all three of us."

The very next day she filled out the applications. Three days later we had our papers. Herr Fajngold no longer spoke, closed the store, sat in the dark shop on the counter near the scales while Maria packed, and didn't even feel like spooning out synthetic honey. Only when Maria came to say goodbye did he slide down from his perch, fetch his bicycle with its cart, and offer to accompany us to the station.

Oskar and the baggage—each person was allowed fifty pounds—were loaded into the two-wheeled cart, which ran on rubber tires. Herr Fajngold pushed the bicycle. Maria held little Kurt's hand and looked back one last time from the corner as we turned left onto Elsenstraße. I couldn't turn toward Labesweg, since it hurt me to twist my neck. Oskar's head thus remained at rest between his shoulders. Only with my eyes, which had retained their mobility, did I take leave of Marienstraße, Strießbach, Kleinhammerpark, the underpass to Bahnhofstraße, still dripping nastily, my undamaged Church of the Sacred Heart and the Langfuhr suburban railway station, which was now called Wrzeszcz, a name that almost defied pronunciation.

We had to wait. When the train finally rolled in, it was a freight train. There were hordes of people, and far too many children. Our baggage was inspected and weighed. Soldiers threw a bale of straw into each boxcar. No music played. But at least it wasn't raining. Clear to partly cloudy it was, with a breeze from the east.

We climbed into the fourth-to-last car. Herr Fajngold stood below us on the tracks with his thin, reddish hair blowing in the wind, and when the locomotive announced its arrival with a jolt, he stepped closer, handed Maria three packages of margarine and two of synthetic honey, and as orders in Polish, cries, and weeping signaled our departure, added a package of disinfectants to our provisions—Lysol is more important than life—and we were off, leaving Herr Fajngold behind, who, as is proper and fitting when a train departs, grew smaller and smaller with his reddish hair blowing in the wind, then was merely something waving, then nothing at all.

Growth in a Boxcar

I FEEL THE PAIN to this day. It flung my head to the pillows just now. It brings out the joints of my ankles and knees, turns me into a grinder — by which I mean that Oskar must grind his teeth to keep from hearing the grinding of his bones in their sockets. I observe my ten fingers and have to admit that they're swollen. A final try on my drum shows that Oskar's fingers are not only swollen, they're not up to the job right now; they just can't hold the drumsticks.

Nor will my fountain pen submit to my guidance. I'll have to ask Bruno for cold compresses. Then, with hands, feet, and knees wrapped and cool, and a cloth on my brow, I'll give my keeper Bruno paper and pencil, for I don't like to lend out my fountain pen. Will Bruno be willing and able to listen properly? And will his retelling do justice to that trip in a boxcar which began on twelve June of forty-five? Bruno sits at the little table beneath the picture of anemones. Now he turns his head, shows me that side called the face, and stares past me right and left with the eyes of a mythical beast. He's slanted the pencil across his thin, sour lips, trying to look like a man waiting. But even assuming he's actually waiting for me to speak, for the signal to start recreating my narrative — his thoughts are circling about his own knotworks. He'll be tying string, while it remains Oskar's task to disentangle my tangled prehistory in a wealth of words. Now Bruno writes:

I, Bruno Münsterberg, from Altena in the Sauerland, unmarried and childless, am a keeper in the private wing of the local mental institution. Herr Matzerath, who has been here for over a year, is my patient. I have other patients I can't speak of here. Herr Matzerath is my most harmless patient. He never gets so upset that I have to call in other keepers.

He writes and drums a little too much. To spare his overstrained fingers, he's asked me to write for him today and not create my knotted figures. Nevertheless I've stuck some string in my pockets and while he's telling his story I'll start on the lower limbs of a figure I plan to call "Eastern Refugee," in line with Herr Matzerath's story. It won't be the first figure I've based on my patient's stories. So far I've knotted his grandmother, whom I call "Potato in Four Skirts": strung together his grandfather, the raftsman, titled rather daringly "Columbus"; his poor mama as "The Beautiful Fish Eater"; I knotted his two fathers, Matzerath and Jan Bronski, as a pair called "Two Skat-Playing Card Thumpers"; I cast the scar-studded back of his friend Herbert Truczinski in string, and titled the raised relief "Rough Road Ahead"; and knot by knot, I built such buildings as the Polish Post Office, the Stockturm, the Stadt-Theater, the Arsenal Arcade, the Maritime Museum, Greff's vegetable cellar, the Pestalozzi School, the Brösen Bathhouse, the Church of the Sacred Heart, the Café Vierjahreszeiten, the Baltic Chocolate Factory, several bunkers on the Atlantic Wall, the Eiffel Tower in Paris, Stettin Station in Berlin, Rheims Cathedral, and, last but not least, the building in which Herr Matzerath first saw the light of day; the gates and gravestones of the cemeteries at Saspe and Brentau offered their decorative ornaments to my string, I set the Vistula and the Seine flowing in wave after wave of string, sent the rolling Baltic and the cresting Atlantic dashing against coasts of string, turned Kashubian potato fields and Norman pasturelands to string, and populated the resulting landscape — which I called simply "Europe" — with groups like: Defenders of the Post Office. Grocery Store Owners. People in the Grandstands. People in Front of the Grandstands. Schoolboys with Paper Cones. Museum Guards Dying Out. Young Hooligans Preparing for Christmas. Polish Cavalry at Sunset. Ants Making History. Theater at the Front Performs for NCOs and Soldiers. Standing Men Disinfecting Men Lying Motionless at Camp Treblinka. And now I'm starting on Eastern Refugee, which will probably develop into a group of Eastern Refugees.

On the twelfth of June in forty-five, around eleven in the morning, Herr Matzerath pulled out of Danzig, which at that time was already called Gdańsk. He was accompanied by the widow Maria Matzerath, whom my patient refers to as his former mistress, and Kurt Matzerath, my patient's alleged son. He says there were another thirty-two people in the boxcar, including four Franciscan nuns in their habits, and a young woman in a scarf, whom Herr Matzerath claimed to have recognized as a certain Fräulein Luzie Rennwand. Upon further questioning on my part, however, my patient admits that the young woman's name was Regina Raeck, but continues to speak of a nameless triangular fox face he repeatedly refers to by name as Luzie; which does not stop me from entering the young woman's name here as Fräulein Regina. Regina Raeck was traveling with her parents, her grandparents, and a sick uncle who bore a bad case of stomach cancer westward along with his family, was a big talker, and announced the moment the train pulled out that he was a former Social Democrat.

As far as my patient can recall, the trip was uneventful as far as Gdynia, which had been called Gotenhafen for the past four and a half years. Two women from Oliva, several children, and an elderly gentleman from Langfuhr cried all the way past Zoppot, while the nuns withdrew into prayer.

The train had a five-hour layover in Gdynia. Two more women and their six children were ushered into the car. The Social Democrat protested because he was ill and, as a prewar Social Democrat, felt he deserved special treatment. But the Polish officer in charge of the convoy boxed him on the ear when he refused to make room, and told him in fluent German that he wasn't familiar with the term Social Democrat. He'd been forced to spend a good deal of the war in various parts of Germany, he said, and he'd never heard the words Social Democrat. The Social Democrat with stomach problems never managed to explain the aims, nature, and history of the German Social Democratic Party to the Polish officer, because the officer left the car, shoved the doors closed, and bolted them from the outside.

I've forgotten to write that everyone was sitting or lying on straw. As the train pulled out late that afternoon a few women cried, "We're going back to Danzig!" But they were mistaken. The train was only shunted onto another track, then headed west toward Stolp. It took four days to reach Stolp, I'm told, because the train was constantly being stopped in the open countryside by former partisans and bands of Polish youths. The youths opened the sliding doors of the boxcar, letting a little fresh air in and a little stale air out, along with a portion of the travelers' luggage. Whenever the youths entered Herr Matzerath's boxcar, the four nuns would stand up and hold their crosses high on their chains. The four crucifixes made a deep impression on the young men. They always crossed themselves before throwing the backpacks and suitcases of those on board onto the railway embankment.

When the Social Democrat showed the boys the paper from the Polish authorities in Danzig or Gdańsk certifying that he had been a dues-paying member of the Social Democratic Party from thirty-one to thirty-seven, the young men didn't cross themselves but instead knocked the papers from his hands and seized his two suitcases and his wife's rucksack; the fine winter coat with the large checks, on which the Social Democrat was lying, was also carried out into the cool Pomeranian air.

Nevertheless, Herr Oskar Matzerath maintains that the boys seemed well disciplined and made a favorable impression on him. He attributes this to the influence of their leader, who despite his tender age of barely sixteen springs, already showed a strong personality that reminded Herr Matzerath, to his pleasure and sorrow, of Störtebeker, the leader of the Dusters.

The young man who so resembled Störtebeker was trying to pry the rucksack from Maria Matzerath's hands and finally did so, but not before Herr Matzerath had seized the photo album, which luckily was lying on top. The gang leader was about to fly into a rage. But when my patient opened the album and showed the boy a photo of his grandmother Koljaiczek, he dropped Frau Maria's rucksack, probably thinking of his own grandmother, touched two fingers to the brim of his pointed Polish cap, turned toward the Matzerath family, said "Do widzenia!" and having grabbed some other traveler's suitcase in place of the Matzerath rucksack, left the car with his men.

Inside the rucksack, which thanks to the family photo album remained in the family's possession, were, in addition to a few items of underwear, the account books and tax returns for the grocery store, their bankbooks, and a ruby necklace that had once belonged to Herr Matzerath's mother, which my patient had hidden in a package of disinfectant; the educational tome, composed half of extracts from Rasputin and half of selections from Goethe, also traveled along on the trip westward.

My patient maintains that he kept the photo album on his knees for most of the trip, and now and then his educational tome, leafed through them both, and although he suffered extreme pain in his joints, both books are said to have afforded him many pleasant though sobering hours of reflection.

Moreover, my patient would like to state that all the jolting and shaking, the switches and intersections crossed while he lay at full length on the constantly vibrating front axle of the boxcar, furthered his growth. He no longer grew wider, he says, but now gained in height. His swollen but not inflamed joints had a chance to loosen. Even his ears, nose, and male member, I'm told, grew perceptibly, aided by the pounding of the rails. As long as the convoy's journey was unimpeded, Herr Matzerath evidently felt no pain. Only when the train came to a stop for another visit by partisans or some gang of youths did the stabbing, cramping pains return, which he countered, as noted, with the soothing effects of the photo album.

In addition to the Polish Störtebeker, several other young bandits took an interest in the family photos, as did an older partisan. The old warrior even sat down, pulled out a cigarette, and leafed thoughtfully through the album without omitting a single rectangle, starting with the picture of Grandfather Koljaiczek, and following the photo-rich rise of the family through to the snapshots showing Frau Maria Matzerath with her one-, two-, three-, and four-year-old son Kurt. My patient even saw him smile now and then at an idyllic family scene. Only a few all too evident Party insignias on the suits of the deceased Herr Matzerath and the lapels of Herr Ehlers, who was Party leader of the Local Farm Association and married the widow of Jan Bronski, the defender of the post office, met with the partisan's disapproval. With the point of a breakfast knife, my patient tells me, before the man's critical eyes and to his evident satisfaction, he scratched off the Party insignias from each photo.

This partisan — Herr Matzerath now sees fit to inform me — was an authentic partisan, as opposed to many who are inauthentic. For he maintains there is no such thing as a part-time partisan, true partisans are always and forever hoisting fallen governments back into the saddle and, with the aid of other partisans, pulling the governments they've helped up into the saddle back down again. Incorrigible partisans, constantly infiltrating one another's groups, are, according to Herr Matzerath's thesis — which I actually thought made sense — the most artistically gifted of all politicians, for they immediately reject whatever they have just created.

My own situation is somewhat similar. Are not my own knotted figures, barely hardened in plaster, often smashed with a blow of my fist? I'm thinking in particular of a work my patient commissioned a few months ago, a figure in ordinary string who was to combine Rasputin, the faith healer, and Goethe, the German prince of poets, into a single person who, moreover, would bear a striking resemblance to himself. I don't know how many kilometers of string I've already knotted to combine these two extremes into a single satisfactory knotwork. Yet like the partisan Herr Matzerath praises as a model, I remain restless and dissatisfied; what I knot with my right hand, I undo with my left, what my left hand forms, my right fist destroys.

But Herr Matzerath can't keep his story moving in a straight line either. Aside from the four nuns he sometimes calls Franciscans and sometimes Vincentians, it's that young thing with her two names and her one face he claims is triangular and foxlike which keeps throwing the story off, so that in retelling it, I should really record two or more versions of that trip from the East to the West. But that's not my job, so I'll stick with the Social Democrat, who never altered his face throughout the journey, or indeed, my patient tells me, the story he told several times before reaching Stolp, that until the year thirty-seven he'd spent his free time as a partisan of sorts, pasting up posters, risking his health, for he was one of the few Social Democrats who pasted up posters even when it rained.

He is said to have been telling this story yet again when the convoy was stopped for the umpteenth time just outside Stolp for another large gang of youths who wished to pay a visit. But since there was almost no luggage left, the boys started taking the clothes of those on board. Sensibly, they stuck to male outer garments. The Social Democrat failed to understand why, however, maintaining that a clever tailor could make several excellent suits from the flowing habits of the nuns. The Social Democrat was, as he proclaimed in the voice of a true believer, an atheist. But the young bandits, without proclaiming themselves true believers, were partial to the one true Church, and bypassed the nuns' ample wool robes for the single-breasted suit of the atheist, even though it contained a good dose of wood fiber. But he did not wish to remove his jacket, vest, and trousers, repeating instead the tale of his brief but brilliant career as a Social Democratic poster-paster, and when he wouldn't stop talking and proved reluctant to remove his suit, he was kicked in the stomach with a boot formerly belonging to the German Wehrmacht.

The Social Democrat vomited long and hard, finally coughing up blood. He had no thought for his suit and the boys lost all interest in the stained garment, although it could have been saved with a thorough dry cleaning. Turning from men's garments, they removed a light blue artificial silk blouse from Frau Maria Matzerath and a knitted Berchtesgaden jacket from the young woman whose name was not Luzie Rennwand but Regina Raeck. Then they shoved the boxcar doors closed, but not completely, and the train pulled off while the death of the Social Democrat got under way.

Two or three kilometers outside Stolp the train was shunted onto a siding and remained there throughout the night, which was clear and starry, I'm told, but cool for the month of June.

That night—Herr Matzerath reports—indecently, cursing God loudly, urging the working class to arise, toasting freedom with last words he'd probably heard at the movies, then falling prey to a fit of coughing that horrified the whole boxcar, the Social Democrat who was all too strongly attached to his single-breasted suit died.

This did not occasion any outbreak of weeping, my patient says. The boxcar fell silent and remained so. The only sound came from the chattering teeth of Frau Maria, who was freezing without her blouse, and had laid what underclothing remained over her son Kurt and Herr Oskar. Toward morning two plucky nuns took advantage of the open door to clean out the boxcar, throwing damp straw, the feces of children and grownups, and the vomit of the Social Democrat out onto the embankment.

In Stolp the train was inspected by Polish officers. At the same time, warm soup and a drink resembling barley coffee were distributed. The corpse in Herr Matzerath's car was seized for fear of contagion and carried off on a scaffold plank by medical orderlies. At the nuns' request a superior officer allowed the family to offer a brief prayer. They were also allowed to remove the dead man's shoes, socks, and suit. During the stripping of the garments—the corpse on the plank was later covered with empty cement sacks—my patient observed the stripped man's niece. Even if her name was Raeck, she still reminded him, with loathing and fascination, of Luzie Rennwand, whose image in knotted string I have entitled The Sausage Sandwich Eater. The girl in the boxcar, it's true, did not reach for a sausage sandwich and eat it skin and all in front of her pillaged uncle, but instead joined in the pillage, inheriting her uncle's vest, which she pulled on in place of her stolen knitted jacket; then she checked out her new look, which was not at all unbecoming, in a pocket mirror, and in that same mirror, my patient says — arousing a panic he still feels today — captured him and his resting place, and, mirrored and smooth, coolly observed him from eyes that were slits in a triangle.

The trip from Stolp to Stettin took two days. There were frequent involuntary stops, to be sure, and more visits, which were slowly becoming a habit, from teenagers armed with paratroopers' knives and tommy guns, but the visits grew shorter and shorter, since there was almost nothing left to take from those on board.

My patient claims that during the trip from Danzig-Gdańsk to Stettin, within a single week, he grew three and a half to four inches. His upper and lower legs stretched out, while his chest and head barely changed. On the other hand, though my patient lay on his back throughout the trip, he could not prevent the growth of a hump, rather high up and slightly displaced to the left. Herr Matzerath also admits that beyond Stettin — German railway staff had taken over the convoy in the meantime — the pain increased and could no longer be forgotten by simply leafing through the family photo album. He screamed aloud and at length on several occasions, but did not damage any train station windows with his screams — Matzerath: My voice had lost its glass-slaying power — but his screams did summon up the four nuns, who gathered about his resting place and remained in a state of constant prayer.

A good half of his fellow travelers, among them the Social Democrat's family along with Fräulein Regina, left the convoy in Schwerin. Herr Matzerath was sorry to see them go, for the sight of the girl had become so familiar and necessary to him that once she was gone, he was overcome by violent, convulsive fits accompanied by a high fever that left him shaken. According to Frau Maria Matzerath, he cried out desperately for someone named Luzie, called himself a mythical beast, a unicorn, and seemed frightened of falling, wanted to fall, from a ten-meter diving board.

In Lüneberg Herr Oskar Matzerath was taken to a hospital. There he made the acquaintance of a few nurses in his fevered state, but was soon transferred to the university clinic in Hanover. There they managed to lower his fever. Herr Matzerath saw Frau Maria and her son Kurt only rarely, and not on a daily basis until she found a job as a cleaning lady at the clinic. Since there was no place for Frau Maria and little Kurt to stay at the clinic, or even in the neighborhood, and because life in the refugee camp was becoming increasingly unbearable — Frau Maria had to travel three hours a day in overcrowded trains to reach the clinic, often standing on the running board — the doctors agreed, in spite of grave misgivings, to transfer the patient to City Hospital in Düsseldorf, especially since Frau Maria could produce a residence permit: her sister Guste, who had married a headwaiter living there during the war, had made one room of her two-and-a-half-room apartment available to Frau Matzerath, since the headwaiter wasn't taking up any space; he was currently in a Russian prison.

The flat was conveniently located. City Hospital could be easily reached without having to change lines on any of the trams leaving Bilk Railway Station in the direction of Wersten or Benrath.

Herr Matzerath remained hospitalized there from August nineteen forty-five till May of forty-six. For over an hour now he's been telling me about several nurses at once. Their names are Sister Monika, Sister Helmtrud, Sister Walburga, Sister Ilse, and Sister Gertrud. He recounts long snatches of hospital gossip from memory and seems obsessed by the minor details of the nurses' daily lives and their uniforms. Not a word about the hospital food, which if I remember correctly was terrible in those days, or the poorly heated rooms. Just nurses, nurses, and the extremely boring social life of nurses. Someone whispered something in strictest confidence, Sister Ilse mentioned it to the head nurse, the head nurse had the nerve to search the quarters of the nurses in training just after lunch hour, something had indeed been stolen, and a nurse from Dortmund — Gertrud, I think he said — was unfairly accused. Then he tells long-winded tales of young doctors who want only one thing from the nurses — cigarette stamps. An inquiry into an abortion that some lab assistant, not a nurse, supposedly gave herself, or attempted with the help of an intern, strikes him as worth retelling. It's beyond me how my patient can waste his intellect on such trivialities.

Herr Matzerath has just asked me to describe him. I'm happy to oblige, and to skip over a number of those stories which, because they deal with nurses, he paints with a broad brush and embellishes with fancy phrases.

My patient measures one meter and twenty-one centimeters, or just under four feet tall. He carries his head, which would be too large even for someone of normal stature, between his shoulders on a nearly atrophied neck; his chest and back, which can only be termed hunched, protrude noticeably. He gazes forth from brilliant, at times ecstatically widened blue eyes alive with intelligence. His dark brown hair is thick and slightly wavy. He likes to display his arms, which are powerful in comparison to the rest of his body, and his hands, which he himself describes as beautiful. Especially when Herr Oskar drums — which the administration allows him to do three to four hours daily — his fingers seem to take on a life of their own, to belong to another, more successfully formed body. Herr Matzerath has grown rich through his recordings and still earns money from them. Interesting people seek him out on Visitors Day. Even before his trial was under way, before he was sent here, I knew his name, for Herr Oskar Matzerath is a prominent artist. Personally, I believe he is innocent, so I'm not sure whether he will remain with us or be released and resume his successful career. Now he wants me to measure him, although I just did so two days ago.

Without bothering to read over what my keeper Bruno has written, I, Oskar, now take up my pen.

Bruno has just measured me with his rule. He held it up to me, then left the room proclaiming the result aloud. He even dropped the knotwork he was secretly fashioning as I was telling my story. I assume he's calling Fräulein Dr. Hornstetter.

Yet before the doctor comes and confirms Bruno's measurements, Oskar can tell you himself: Over the course of the three days in which I told my keeper the story of my growth, I gained — dare we call it a gain? — a good two centimeters in height, or almost an inch.

As of today, then, Oskar is almost four foot one. He will now relate how he fared after the war, when he was released from City Hospital in Düsseldorf as a deformed yet otherwise relatively healthy young man who could speak easily, write slowly, and read fluently, to begin — as one always assumes upon being released from a hospital — a new and now grownup life.

BOOK

THREE

Flintstones and Gravestones

FAT, SLEEPY, GOOD-NATURED: there was no need for Guste Truczinski to change when she became Guste Köster, especially since Köster had only been able to work on her during their two-week engagement, shortly before he was shipped off to the Arctic Front, and for a few nights later on, spent mostly in air-raid shelter beds, when he was home on leave and they'd married. Though there was no word on Köster's whereabouts following the army's surrender in Courland, Guste, when asked about her husband, would reply with assurance and a jerk of her thumb toward the kitchen door, "Ivan's got him locked up over there. There'll be some changes round here once he's back."

The changes in store for the Bilk apartment upon Köster's return involved Maria as well as little Kurt. Having been released from the hospital, after taking my leave of the nurses and promising to visit whenever I got the chance, I boarded the tram toward Bilk, the sisters, and my son Kurt, where I found, on the second floor of an apartment house burned out from the third floor to the roof, a black-market headquarters run by Maria and my son, six years old and counting on his fingers.

Maria, still true to Matzerath even on the black market, was dealing in synthetic honey. She poured from unlabeled pails, slapped the stuff on the kitchen scales, and put me to work — barely arrived and still getting used to the cramped conditions — making up quarter-pound cartons.

Little Kurt sat behind a Persil crate as if it were a counter, looked up, it's true, at his homecoming father, but trained his always somewhat wintry gray eyes on some item of interest that could evidently be seen directly through me. He held a sheet of paper before him on which he was arranging imaginary columns of numbers, and after a scant six weeks of schooling in overcrowded and poorly heated classrooms, had the look of a brooder and a go-getter.

Guste Köster was drinking coffee. Real coffee, Oskar noted when she pushed a cup over to me. While I dealt with the honey, she regarded my hump with curiosity and no small sympathy for her sister Maria. It was all she could do to stay seated and not stroke my hump, for all women think stroking a hump brings good luck, and good luck in Guste's case meant the return of Köster, who would change everything. She held back, stroked her coffee cup instead, but with no luck, and let out a loud sigh I was to hear daily over the coming months: "You can bet your life on it, when Köster gets home there'll be some changes round here, quick as a wink!"

Guste condemned black-market activities, but was happy enough to drink the real coffee provided by synthetic honey. When customers came she left the living room and shuffled off into the kitchen, where she banged about loudly in protest.

There were plenty of customers. The bell would start ringing at just past nine, right after breakfast: short — long — short. Late in the evening, around ten o'clock, often over the objections of little Kurt, who had to miss half the business day because of school, Guste would switch off the bell.

"Any synthetic honey?" people asked. Maria nodded gently and replied, "Quarter or half pound?" But there were some who didn't want honey. They would ask, "Any flintstones?" Upon which little Kurt, whose school alternated between mornings and afternoons, would emerge from his columns of numbers, reach for the little cloth sack under his sweater, and call out figures into the living room air with a brightly demanding little boy's voice: "Would you like three, or four? Better take five. They'll be up to twenty-four soon. They were eighteen last week, this morning I had to ask twenty, and if you'd come two hours ago, right after school, I could have said twenty-one."

Little Kurt was the only dealer in flintstones in a four-by-six street area. He had a source, one he never revealed but mentioned constantly, even before he went to bed, saying in place of a nightly prayer, "I've got a source!"

As a father, I was determined to assert my right to know my son's source. So when he announced, self-confidently and without the slightest air of mystery, "I have a source!" my question quickly followed: "Where do you get those flints? Tell me right now where you get them!"

Maria's standard response in the months I was trying to learn his source was: "Leave the boy alone, Oskar. First of all it's none of your business, second I'll do the asking if need be, and third don't be acting like you're his father. A few months ago you couldn't even say boo!"

When I wouldn't stop, and pursued little Kurt's source too stubbornly, Maria would slap her hand down on a pail of honey and get so riled up she'd attack both me and Guste, who occasionally backed me up in my search for a source: "A fine lot you are! Trying to ruin the boy's business. Biting the hand that feeds you. When I think of the dab of extra calories Oskar gets on sick relief, then wolfs down in two days, it makes me sick, but I have to laugh!"

Oskar has to admit: I was blessed with a good appetite, and it was thanks to little Kurt's source, which brought in more than the honey did, that Oskar regained his strength after the meager fare at the hospital.

So the father was reduced to shamefaced silence, and with a decent allowance provided by little Kurt's childish benevolence, absented himself from the apartment in Bilk as often as possible, so as not to confront his disgrace.

All sorts of well-placed critics of the German Economic Miracle are waxing nostalgic these days, and the less they remember what things were really like back then, the more enthusiastic they are: "Ah, those were the days, before the currency reform! There was always something happening. People's stomachs were empty, but they still lined up for theater tickets. And those spur-of-the-moment parties with potato schnapps were just marvelous, so much more fun than parties today, with all that champagne and Dujardin."

So speak the romantics of lost opportunities. I could easily sound the same lament, in fact, for in the years when little Kurt's flintstone source was still bubbling, I educated myself at almost no cost in the company of thousands determined to learn, to make up for the education they'd missed, took courses in night school, was a regular visitor at the British Center, called Die Brücke, or The Bridge, discussed collective guilt with

Catholics and Protestants, shared that guilt with all who thought: Let's get it over with now, be done with it, and later, when things get better, there'll be no need to feel guilty.

At any rate, I am indebted to night school for what education I received, which was indeed modest, though generous in its gaps. I read a great deal in those days. The readings that, prior to my growth, led me to simply divide the world evenly between Rasputin and Goethe, and the knowledge I gained from Köhler's *Naval Calendar* from ought-four to sixteen, no longer sufficed. Not that I remember what I read. I read on the toilet. I read while standing in line for hours for theater tickets, squeezed between young women with Mozart pigtails who were also reading. I read while little Kurt sold flintstones, read while I packed synthetic honey. And when the power was interrupted, I read by the light of tallow candles; thanks to little Kurt's source, we had a few.

I'm ashamed to say that what I read in those years did not stick with me but passed through me instead. A few phrases, some blurbs, remain. And the theater? Names of actors: Hoppe, Peter Esser, Flickenschildt with her special way of pronouncing *r*'s, drama students trying to improve on Flickenschildt's *r* on studio stages, Gründgens all in black as Tasso, removing the laurel wreath called for by Goethe because the greenery supposedly seared his locks, and the same Gründgens all in black as Hamlet. And Flickenschildt claiming Hamlet was fat. And Yorick's skull made an impression on me because of some very impressive things Gründgens had to say about it. *Draußen vor der Tür* played before a shaken audience in an unheated theater, and I imagined Beckmann, the Man Outside with his broken glasses, as Guste's husband, Köster, coming home to make some changes and stop up the source of my son Kurt's flintstones forever.

Today, with all that behind me, and knowing that a postwar binge is just a binge, and that the hair of the dog that barks up the wrong tree, reducing to history that which but yesterday was fresh and bloody deed or misdeed, offers no cure at all for the hangover, today I praise the lessons I received from Gretchen Scheffler amid Strength through Joy souvenirs and her own knitting: not too much Rasputin, Goethe in moderation, key phrases from Keyser's *History of the City of Danzig*, the armaments of a battleship long since sunk, the speed in knots of all the Japanese torpedo boats that took part in the Battle of Tsushima, as well as Belisarius and Narses, Totila and Teja, Felix Dahn's *Struggle for Rome*.

In the spring of forty-seven I gave up night school, the British Centre, and Pastor Niemöller, and took my leave, from the second balcony, of Gustaf Gründgens, who was still on the program as Hamlet.

Not two years had passed since I'd stood beside Matzerath's grave and resolved to grow, and already I'd lost interest in grownup life. I longed for the lost proportions of a three-year-old. I had an unshakable desire to be three foot one again, smaller than my friend Bebra, than the dearly departed Roswitha. Oskar missed his drum. He took long walks that ended near City Hospital. Since he had to see Professor Irdell once a month anyway, who referred to him as an interesting case, he paid repeated visits to the nurses he knew, and even when they had no time for him, just being around all that white cloth in a hurry, promising recovery or death, made him feel good, almost happy.

The nurses liked me, played childish but not malicious games with my hump, gave me good things to eat, and let me in on their endless, convoluted, pleasantly soporific stories about the hospital. I listened, gave advice, even served as a go-between in smaller disputes, since I enjoyed the sympathy of the head nurse. Among twenty to thirty young women camouflaged in nurse's uniforms, I was the only male, and in some strange way an object of desire.

As Bruno has already said, Oskar has beautiful, expressive hands, fine wavy hair, and — amply blue — those ever so winning Bronski eyes. Perhaps my hump and the narrow, vaulted chest that starts just under my chin accentuated the beauty of my hands, eyes, and pleasing head of hair, at any rate often enough when I was sitting in the nurses' ward they would take my hands in theirs, play with my fingers, and fondle my hair, then say to one another as they left, "When you look into his eyes, you could just forget all the rest."

So I could rise above my hump and would certainly have resolved to make a conquest or two at the hospital had I still been in command of my drum back then, and sure of my well-tested potency as a drummer. Shamefaced, uncertain, not trusting the contingent impulses of my body, I would depart the hospital after such tender foreplay, having avoided any frontal assault, and unburden myself, wandering through the garden or along the wire fence surrounding the hospital grounds, which, with its finely meshed geometric pattern, awakened in me a mood of serenity that set me whistling. I watched the trams heading for Wersten or Benrath, strolled in pleasant boredom along the walks near the bicycle paths, and smiled at Nature's efforts to play Spring and make buds burst like tiny firecrackers right on time.

Across the way, the greatest Sunday painter of them all was daily adding a little more sap green, fresh from the tube, to the trees of Wersten Cemetery. I have always been attracted to cemeteries. They are well kept, straightforward, logical, manly, full of life. You can summon up courage and reach decisions in cemeteries, life takes on clear contours — and I'm not referring to burial plots — in cemeteries, and, if you will, a meaning.

A street called Bittweg ran along the northern wall of the cemetery. Seven gravestone manufacturers competed there. Large firms like C. Schnoog or Julius Wöbel. Between them the smaller artisans, with names like R. Haydenreich, J. Bois, Kühn & Müller, and P. Korneff. A jumble of sheds and workshops, large signs, freshly painted or barely legible, on the roofs with inscriptions under the firm's name like *Gravestones — Monuments and Borders — Natural and Artificial Stone — Mortuary Art*. Above Korneff's shop I could barely make out: *P. Korneff Stonecutter and Gravestone Sculptor*.

Between the workshop and the wire fence enclosing the yard stood staggered lines of tombstones for single to four-person graves, so-called family plots, set on single or double pedestals. Just beyond the fence, patiently bearing the lozenge-patterned shadow of the wire on sunny days, were shell-limestone cushions meant for modest budgets, polished diorite slabs with unpolished palm branches, and standard thirty-two-inch children's gravestones of slightly smoky Silesian marble with running fluted borders and sunken reliefs on the top third, mostly showing broken roses. Next came a row of standard meter-high stones, taken from the Main-sandstone façades of bombed-out banks and department stores and celebrating here their resurrection, if that can be said of gravestone. In the midst of this display stood the showpiece: a monument of bluish white Tyrolean marble set on three pedestals and consisting of two side pieces and a richly carved center slab. On this central slab rose in sublime relief what is known in the trade as a corpus. This was a corpus with its head and knees to the left, with a crown of thorns and three nails, beardless, hands open, and a wound in its side bleeding in stylized fashion, five drops I think it was.

Though there were more than enough monuments on Bittweg with a corpus turned to the left — prior to the spring season there would often be ten or more of them spreading their arms — I was particularly taken with Korneff's Jesus Christ, because, well, because he bore the closest resemblance to my gymnast above the main altar in the Church of the Sacred Heart, flexing his muscles, expanding his chest. I spent hours at that fence. I let a stick purr along the finely meshed wire net, wishing for this and that, thinking all sorts of thoughts or none at all. For a long time Korneff remained in hiding. A stovepipe emerged from one of the workshop windows, flexed its elbows a few times, and finally jutted high above the flat roof. Thick yellow smoke from cheap coal barely rose, fell back on the roofing pasteboard, trickled down the windows, along the gutters, and lost itself among the unworked stones and slabs of brittle Lahn marble. Outside the sliding door of the workshop a three-wheeled truck waited under several tarps, as if camouflaged against low-flying planes. Sounds from the workshop — wood striking iron, iron chipping stone — betrayed the stonemason at work.

In May the tarps were off the three-wheeler, the sliding door stood open. Gray on gray I saw stones tilted against a bench inside the shop, the gallows of a polisher, shelves with plaster models, and, finally, Korneff. He walked with a stoop, his knees permanently bent. His head he held stiffly thrust forward. Pink adhesive tape blackened with grime crossed the back of his neck. Korneff stepped out with a rake and raked, since spring had come, between the gravestones standing on display. He did so thoroughly, leaving alternating tracks in the gravel and picking off a few of last year's leaves that still clung to the monuments. Right by the fence, while the rake was being carefully guided between shell-limestone cushions and diorite slabs, his voice surprised me: "Well, son, don't they want you at home no more?"

"I really like your gravestones," I said flatteringly.

"Don't say that aloud or you may wind up under one."

Now he made an effort to turn his neck for the first time, and his sidewise glance took me in, or rather my hump: "What've they done to you? Don't that make it hard to sleep?"

I let him have his laugh, then explained that a hump doesn't necessarily get in the way, that I was more than a match for it, that there were girls and even grown women who seemed attracted to a hump, who adapted to the special position and potentialities of a hunchbacked man, women who, to put it plainly, found a hump fun.

Korneff leaned his chin on the rake handle and pondered this: "You might be right there, I've heard tell of it."

Then he told me about his days in the Eifel, when he worked in the basalt quarries and had something going with a woman who had a wooden leg, the left one I believe, which could be unbuckled, to which he compared my hump, though there was no unbuckling what he called my "box." The stonecutter recalled the whole story from start to finish in long-winded detail. I waited patiently till he was through and the woman had buckled her leg back on, then asked if I could see his workshop.

Korneff opened the sheet-metal gate in the wire fence, pointed his rake toward the open sliding door by way of invitation, and I crunched across the gravel till the smell of sulfur, lime, and moisture engulfed me.

Heavy pear-shaped wooden mallets, flattened on top, with frayed hollows from the same constantly repeated blow, rested on roughly hewn slabs formed by four of those blows. Points for boasting mallets, points with billet heads, freshly reforged cold chisels still blue from tempering, long, springy etching chisels and bull chisels for marble, compact broad-track bush chisels on a slab of Blaubank, polishing paste drying on four-cornered wooden sawhorses, and, on wooden rollers, ready to roll out, standing on end, matte and fully polished, a travertine slab, oily, yellow, cheesy, porous, for a double plot.

"This here's a bush hammer, that's a spoon chisel, that's a groove cutter, and this"—Korneff lifted a board a hand's breadth wide and three paces long, examined its edge closely—"this here's a marking level. I uses it to whack the tyros on the head if they don't do what I say."

My question was not merely polite: "So you take on apprentices?"

Korneff launched into complaints: "I got work enough for five. But you can't get none. They're all in the black market these days, the bunglers!" Like me, the stonecutter opposed the sort of shady dealing that hindered many a promising young man from learning a useful trade. While Korneff demonstrated the polishing qualities of various coarse to fine grinding stones on a Solnhof slab, I was playing with a little idea. Pumice stones, the chocolate-brown shellac stone for prepolishing, tripoli to tripol a dull surface shiny, and still there, but gleaming more brightly now, my little idea. Korneff showed me lettering samples, told me of lettering in relief and lettering in blind, of gilding, and that using gold isn't as crazy as you might think: with one good, old-fashioned thaler you could gild an entire horse and rider, and my thoughts flew off to Kaiser Wilhelm on the Heumarkt in Danzig, eternally riding off along Sandgrube, whose statue the Polish authorities in charge of monuments might now decide to gild, but in spite of horse and rider covered in gold leaf I did not abandon my little idea, which seemed to gleam even more richly now, played with it, formulating it as Korneff explained the tripod pointing machine for sculptural work, rapped on plaster models of the crucified Christ, facing left or facing right, with his knuckle: "So you might take on an apprentice?" My little idea was off and running. "I gather you're looking for an apprentice, am I right?" Korneff rubbed the tape covering the boils on the back of his neck. "I mean, would you take on someone like me as an apprentice?" The question was badly put, and I corrected myself at once: "Please don't underestimate my strength, sir. My legs are a little weak, but that's all. I've got a strong grip!" Inspired by my own resolution and going for broke, I bared my left upper arm, offered my small but rawhide-tough muscle for him to feel, and when he didn't, grabbed a boasting chisel off the shell limestone, made the six-sided metal tool bounce up and down convincingly on my small, tennis-ball-sized mound, and interrupted my demonstration only when Korneff turned on the grinder, started running a blue-gray grinding disk over the travertine pedestal for the double slab, and finally, his eyes glued on the grinder, roared out over the noise: "Best sleep on it, boy. This here's no bed of roses. Then, if you still feel like it, I'll take you on as a trainee."

Taking the stonecutter's advice, I slept on my little idea for a week, while by day I weighed little Kurt's flintstones against the gravestones on Bittweg, listened to Maria's reproaches: "You're just living off us, Oskar. Get started in something: tea, cocoa, powdered milk maybe," but I started in nothing, basked in the approval of Guste, who held up the absent Köster as a model and praised me for keeping out of the black market, but was deeply hurt by my son Kurt, who, inventing columns of numbers and committing them to paper, ignored me in the same way I had seen fit to ignore Matzerath over the years.

We were having lunch. Guste had switched off the bell so the customers wouldn't catch us eating scrambled eggs and bacon. Maria said, "See, Oskar, we can only afford this because we don't sit around twiddling our thumbs." Little Kurt heaved a sigh. Flintstones had fallen to eighteen. Guste ate heartily in silence. I did the same, liked what I ate, but though I liked it, I was still unhappy, perhaps it was the powdered eggs, and biting down on something gristly in the bacon, I suddenly felt such an intense craving for joy that it radiated right to the rims of my ears, I longed for joy against all better judgment, beyond the power of cynicism to outweigh, I longed for boundless joy and rose while others, satisfied with powdered eggs, still ate, approached the cupboard as if it held that joy, rummaged through my drawer and found, not joy, but there beneath the photo album, beneath my tome, two packs of Herr Fajngold's disinfectant, pulled from one not joy, no, but my poor mama's thoroughly disinfected ruby necklace, which Jan Bronski, one winter night that smelled of snow, had taken from the window of a shop through which, not long before, Oskar, still happy then and slaying glass with song, had sung a circular hole. And with that necklace I left the flat, saw the necklace as the first step toward, made my way toward, rode off toward the railway station, thinking, If all goes well . . . then bartered long and hard, confident that . . . but the one-armed man and the Saxon everyone called the Assessor, who knew the price of things but not their value, had no idea what happiness they laid before me when, in return for my poor mama's necklace, they handed me a genuine leather briefcase and fifteen cartons of Yankee cigarettes, Lucky Strikes.

That afternoon I was back in Bilk with the family. I unloaded fifteen cartons of Lucky Strikes, a fortune, in packs of twenty, savored their astonishment, thrust the mountain of packaged blond tobacco at them, and said, That's for you, now leave me alone, they're worth that much I should hope, and I want a lunchbox from now on too, with my lunch in it, which I plan to take to work in this briefcase each day. I wish you joy with your honey and flintstones, I said without scorn or censure, I shall practice another art, henceforth my joy will be written, or, to put it more professionally, engraved, on gravestones.

Korneff took me on as his trainee for a hundred Reichsmarks a month. That was practically nothing, but it paid off in the end. After only a week it was clear my strength was not up to heavy stone work. I was supposed to rough-cut a slab of Belgian granite fresh from the quarry for a four-plot grave, but in less than an hour I could barely lift the point, and the hand in which I held the boasting mallet was totally numb. I had to leave the rough pointing to Korneff while I, showing real skill, took on fine pointing, notching, checking surfaces with dual marking levels, drawing lines for the four blows, and hatching the dolomite borders blow by blow. An upright squared block, above it, forming a T, the board on which I sat, guiding the point with my right hand, and in my left, over Korneff's objections, who wanted to make a right-hander of me, in my left, banging away, clanging away, with the wooden pears, the billets, with iron mallets, the bush hammer, with sixty-four bush-hammer teeth biting and softening the stone at the same time: here I found joy, though it was not my drum, found joy, though it was but a substitute, for joy too may be a substitute, may only come by way of substitution, joy always ersatz joy, laid down as sediment: marble joy, sandstone joy, sandstone from the Elbe, sandstone from the Main, sandstone always mine, sandstone beyond time, joy from Kirchheim, joy from Grenzheim. Hard joy: Blaubank. Cloudy, brittle joy: alabaster. Widia steel strikes joyfully on diorite. Dolomite: green joy. Gentle joy: tufa. Motley joy from the Lahn. Porous joy: basalt. Cooled joy from the Eifel. Joy erupted like a volcano and fell as a layer of dust, as grit between my teeth.

But my greatest talent and joy was engraving letters. I even surpassed Korneff, handled the ornamental features of the sculpture work: acanthus leaves, broken roses for children's stones, palm branches, Christian symbols like *PX* or *INRI*, fluting, astragals, eggs and darts, chamfers and double chamfers. Oskar blessed gravestones of all prices with all manner of ornament. And when, over an eight-hour period, repeatedly clouding the polished slab of diorite with my breath, I provided an inscription such as *Here rests in God my dear Husband* — new line — *Our dear Father, Brother, and Uncle* — new line — *Joseph Esser* — new line — *b. 3.4.1885 d. 22.6.1946* — new line — *Death is the Gateway to Life* — then, reading over this text, I felt a sort of ersatz joy, that is, was pleasantly happy, and repeatedly thanked Joseph Esser, dead at the age of sixty-one, and the small green clouds of diorite raised by my lettering point as I bestowed particular attention on the five *O*'s in Esser's epitaph; and so I did well with the letter *O*, for which Oskar felt a special affection, producing it with a fine regularity and endlessness, though it was always somewhat too large.

I started work as a stonecutter's trainee at the end of May. In early October Korneff developed two new boils and we had to set up a travertine slab for Hermann Webknecht and Else Webknecht née Freytag in South Cemetery. Up till then, the stonecutter, who still didn't trust my strength, refused to take me along to the cemetery. An almost deaf but hardworking man from the firm of Julius Wöbel usually helped him set up stones. In return Korneff stepped in for Wöbel, who employed eight men, whenever he was shorthanded. I kept offering to help out at the cemetery, but in vain; cemeteries still attracted me, even though no decisions were in the offing at the time. Fortunately by early October the busy season had set in for Wöbel and he couldn't spare any men before the first frost; Korneff was forced to turn to me.

The two of us tilted the travertine slab behind the three-wheeler, then placed it on hard wooden rollers, rolled it onto the truck bed, shoved the pedestal beside it, protected the corners with empty paper sacks, loaded on the tools, cement, sand, gravel, and rollers and crates for offloading, I fastened the tailgate, Korneff was already at the wheel starting the engine, then stuck his head and boil-infested neck out the side window and yelled, "Come on, boy, get moving. Grab your lunch box and hop in!"

A slow drive around and past City Hospital. Outside the main entrance white clouds of nurses. Among them a nurse I know, Sister Gertrud. I wave, she waves back. My luck's back, I think, or I've never lost it, ought to ask her out sometime, even if I can't see her anymore, since we've turned toward the Rhine, ask her out to something, heading for Kappes-Hamm, maybe see a movie or Gründgens at the theater, there it is now, that yellow brick building, ask her out, doesn't have to be a play, smoke rising from the crematorium above the half-bare trees, how would you feel about a little change of scenery, Sister Gertrud? Another cemetery, other gravestone firms: a lap of honor for Sister Gertrud before the main entrance: Beutz & Kranich, Pottgiesser's Natural Stone, Böhm's Mortuary Art, Gockeln's Cemetery Landscaping and Gardening; questions at the gate, it's not that easy to get into a graveyard, staff with cemetery caps: travertine for a double plot, Number Seventy-nine, Section Eight, Webknecht, Hermann, hand raised to cemetery cap, lunch pails left to warm at the crematorium; and standing outside the mortuary Crazy Leo.

I said to Korneff, "Isn't that Crazy Leo, the fellow with the white gloves?"

Korneff, reaching back and feeling his boils: "That's not Crazy Leo, it's Weird Willem, he lives here!"

How could I rest content with this information? After all, I'd been in Danzig before, and now I was in Düsseldorf, but I was still called Oskar: "There was a fellow back home who hung around cemeteries and looked just like him, and his name was Crazy Leo, and early on, when he was just plain Leo, he was a student at the seminary."

Korneff, his left hand on his boils and turning the three-wheeler toward the crematorium with his right: "You might be right about that. There's a bunch of them look like that used to be in the seminary living in graveyards now, using other names. That there's Weird Willem!"

We drove past Weird Willem. He waved a white glove at us and I felt at home in South Cemetery.

October, graveyard paths, the world losing its teeth and hair, that is, yellow leaves ceaselessly drifting down from above. Silence, sparrows, strolling visitors, the three-wheeler's engine heads for Section Eight, still a long way off. Old women here and there with watering cans and grandchildren, sun on black Swedish granite, obelisks, columns with symbolic cracks or actual war damage, a tarnished green angel behind a yew tree or something yewlike. A woman shading her eyes with a marble hand, dazzled by her own marble. Christ in stone sandals blessing the elms, another Christ in Section Four blessing a birch. Lovely daydreams on the path between Sections Four and Five: the sea, for instance. And this sea, among other things, casts a corpse on the shore. Violin music from the pier at Zoppot and the bashful beginnings of a fireworks display in support of those blinded in war. I bend down, a three-year-old Oskar, over the flotsam, hoping it may be Maria, or Sister Gertrud perhaps, whom I ought to ask out some time. But it is fair Luzie, pale Luzie, as the fireworks rushing toward their climax reveal and confirm. And as always when she's up to no good, she's wearing her knitted Berchtesgaden jacket. Wet is the wool I strip from her body. And wet the little jacket she wears beneath her knitted jacket. Yet another Berchtesgaden jacket blooms before me. And toward the very end, when the fireworks have died down at last and only the violins remain, I find beneath the wool upon the wool within the wool, wrapped in a League of German Girls singlet, her heart, Luzie's heart, a cold, tiny gravestone, on which stands written: *Here lies Oskar — Here lies Oskar — Here lies Oskar . . .*

"Don't fall asleep, boy!" Korneff interrupted my lovely reveries, laved by the sea, illuminated by fireworks. We turned left, and Section Eight, a new section with no trees and few gravestones, lay flat and hungry before us. Above the monotony of the other graves, all still too fresh to be tended, the most recent five rose clearly: moldering mounds of brown wreaths with faded, rain-soaked ribbons.

We quickly found Number Seventy-nine at the top of the fourth row, right by Section Seven, which boasted a few young, fast-growing trees, and was stocked with meter-high stones, mostly of Silesian marble, lined up with some regularity. We pulled up behind Seventy-nine, unloaded the tools, cement, gravel, sand, the pedestal and the travertine slab, with its slightly oily sheen. The three-wheeler sprang up as we rolled the load from the truck bed onto the crate with boards for tilting. Korneff pulled out the temporary wooden cross, with a crossbar bearing the names H. Webknecht and E. Webknecht, from the head of the grave, had me hand him the post-hole digger, and started digging two holes five feet three inches deep, one meter sixty by cemetery regulations, for the concrete posts, while I fetched water from Section Seven, then mixed the concrete, so it was ready by the time, having dug five feet, he said he was finished, and I could begin tamping in both holes while Korneff sat panting on the travertine slab and reached back to feel his boils. "Coming to a head. I can always feel when they're about to bust." I kept on tamping, my mind nearly blank. Coming from Section Seven, a Protestant funeral procession crawled across Section Eight to Section Nine. As they passed us, three rows away, Korneff slid off the travertine slab, and in compliance with cemetery regulations, we pulled off our caps for them, from the pastor through the next of kin. A solitary figure walked behind the coffin, a small, lopsided woman in black. Those who followed were all much taller and sturdier.

"God almighty, Katie bar the door!" Korneff groaned beside me. "I got a feeling they're going to bust before we get that slab up!"

Meanwhile the funeral procession arrived at Section Nine, rearranged itself, and gave birth to the rising and falling voice of the pastor. We could have placed the pedestal on the base, since the concrete was starting to set. But Korneff lay belly down across the travertine slab, shoved his cap between his forehead and the stone, and jerked back his jacket and collar, laying his neck bare, while details from the life of the dearly departed in Section Nine were announced to us in Section Eight. Not only did I have to clamber up on the travertine slab, I squatted on Korneff's lower back and took in the whole bag of tricks: there were two side by side. A straggler with an enormous wreath hurried toward Section Nine and the sermon that was slowly drawing to a close. After removing the tape with a single jerk, I wiped off the Ichthyol salve with a beech leaf and examined both indurations, tar-brown shading into yellow, and of approximately equal size. "Let us pray" drifted over from Section Nine. I took that as a sign, turned my head away, pressed and pulled at the beech leaves under my thumbs. "Our Father . . ." Korneff ground his teeth: "Pull, don't squeeze." I pulled. ". . . be Thy name." Korneff managed to join in the prayer: ". . . Thy kingdom come." Then I squeezed anyway, since pulling didn't work. "Will be done, on, as it is in." It was a miracle there was no explosion. And again: "Give us this day." Now Korneff had found his place in the text: "Trespasses and . . . not into temptation . . ." There was more than I expected. "Kingdom, the power, and the glory." Squeezed out the last colorful remnants. "Forever and ever, amen." While I pulled again, Korneff: "Amen," and squeezed again: "Amen," while over in Section Nine they turned to their condolences, Korneff groaned another: "Amen," lying flat on the travertine slab heaved a sigh of relief: "Amen," and "Got any concrete left for the base?" I had, and he: "Amen."

I dumped the final shovelfuls as a binder between the two posts. Then Korneff slid off the polished, lettered surface and had Oskar show him the autumnal beech leaves with the similarly colored contents of his boils. We straightened our caps, took hold of the stone, and set the monument for Hermann Webknecht and Else Webknecht née Freytag in place as the funeral in Section Nine dispersed into thin air.

Fortuna North

ONLY PEOPLE WHO LEFT something of value behind on earth could afford gravestones back then. It didn't have to be a diamond or a yard-long string of pearls. Five sacks of potatoes would get you a full-fledged meter-high slab of shell limestone from Grenzheim. We took in enough cloth for two three-piece suits in exchange for a double-plot Belgian granite monument on a triple pedestal. The tailor's widow, who had the cloth and an apprentice, offered to make the suits for us if we would throw in a dolomite border.

So one evening after work, Korneff and I boarded the Number Ten and headed toward Stockum, where we looked up the widow Lennert and had our measurements taken. Absurd as it sounds, Oskar was wearing an antitank gunner's uniform in those days, one Maria had altered for him, and even though the buttons on the jacket had been moved, given my unusual build, it proved impossible to button.

The apprentice, whom the widow Lennert called Anton, hand-tailored a suit for me from dark blue material with a pinstripe: single-breasted, lined in ash gray, the shoulders well padded but creating no false sense of size, my hump not concealed but handsomely empha-sized, cuffs for the trousers but not too wide; Master Bebra remained my well-dressed ideal. Thus no loops for a belt, but buttons for sus-penders instead, the vest shiny in back and matte in front, lined in an-tique rose. The whole thing took five fittings.

While the tailor's apprentice was still bent over Korneff's double-breasted suit and my single-breasted suit, a shoe salesman tried to get a meter-high stone for his wife, who had been killed in an air raid in forty-three. At first the man tried to palm off redeemable coupons on us, but we wanted to see real merchandise. For Silesian marble with a synthetic stone border plus installation Korneff obtained a pair of low, dark brown shoes and a pair of carpet slippers with leather soles. I received a pair of black shoes with laces, which, though old-fashioned, were wonderfully soft. European size thirty-five; they offered my weak ankles firm and elegant support.

I laid a bundle of Reichsmarks on the synthetic-honey scales for Maria, who handled the shirts: "Could you get me two white dress shirts, one with pinstripes, and a light gray tie and a chestnut-colored one? The rest is for little Kurt and for you, dear Maria, who never think of yourself but only of others."

In a burst of generosity, I also gave Guste an umbrella with a genuine bone handle and a deck of nearly new Altenburger skat cards, since she enjoyed laying them out but was reluctant to borrow a deck from the neighbors every time she wanted to find out when Köster was coming home.

Maria rushed off to carry out her commission, bought a raincoat for herself with the considerable remaining cash, and a school satchel of imitation leather for little Kurt, which, ugly as it was, would have to do for the time being. To my shirts and ties she added three pairs of gray socks, which I'd forgotten to ask for.

When Korneff and I picked up our suits, we stood in some embarrassment before the mirror in the tailor's workshop, yet quite impressed with each other. Korneff scarcely dared turn his neck, furrowed with the scars of his boils. He leaned forward, his arms dangling from his drooping shoulders, and tried to straighten his crooked legs. As for me, when I folded my arms across my chest, thereby enlarging the horizontal mass of my upper body, placed my weight on my feeble right leg and angled my left nonchalantly, my new clothes gave me a daemonic, intellectual look. Smiling at Korneff and enjoying his astonishment, I approached the mirror, stood so close to the surface dominated by my reversed image that I could have kissed it, but instead simply breathed on it and said, as if in passing, "Hey there, Oskar. You still need a tie pin."

When, on Sunday afternoon a week later, I entered City Hospital to visit my nurses and present my new, vain self in tiptop form, showing all my best sides, I was the proud owner of a silver tie pin, set with a pearl.

The dear girls were speechless when they saw me sitting in the nurses' ward. This was late in the summer of forty-seven. I folded the arms of my suit across my chest in my accustomed manner and played with my leather gloves. I had been a stonecutter's trainee and master of fluted grooves for over a year now. I placed one trouser leg over the other, being careful to maintain the crease. Our good Guste cared for my suit as though it had been tailor-made for Köster, who was going to make some changes when he returned. Sister Helmtrud asked to feel the cloth. In the spring of forty-seven I bought little Kurt a mouse-gray loden coat for his seventh birthday, which we celebrated with homemade eggnog and Madeira cake — recipe: add freely! I offered the nurses, Sister Gertrud now among them, some candy that, in addition to twenty pounds of brown sugar, we'd been given for a slab of diorite. It seemed to me little Kurt was enjoying school a bit too much. The young lady teacher, not yet worn down, and certainly no Spollenhauer, praised him, said he was bright but a trifle solemn. How gay nurses can be when you bring them sweets. When I was alone with Sister Gertrud for a moment in the nurses' ward, I inquired about her free Sundays.

"Well, today, for instance, I get off at five. But nothing's happening in town," Sister Gertrud said with resignation.

I told her it was worth a try. At first she declined, she'd rather get a good night's sleep. Then I was more direct, came out with my invitation, and since she still couldn't make up her mind, concluded mysteriously with the words: "Show a little spirit, Sister Gertrud. You're only young once. There'll certainly be no lack of cake stamps." I illustrated this by giving the breast pocket of my jacket a slightly stylized tap, offered her another sweet, and, strangely enough, felt a mild wave of terror when I heard this strapping young Westphalian, who was not at all my type, turn away toward a small medicine cabinet and say, "All right then, if you think so. At six, let's say, but not here, at Corneliusplatz."

I would hardly have expected Sister Gertrud to meet me in the lobby or at the entrance to the hospital. At six o'clock I was waiting for her under the city clock on Corneliusplatz, which was still suffering the effects of war and could not tell time. She was punctual, as I could see from the relatively inexpensive pocket watch I had purchased a few weeks before. I almost didn't recognize her, and if I had seen her step off the tram in time, some fifty paces away say, at the tram stop across the street, before she noticed me, I would have slipped away, sidled off in disappointment; for Sister Gertrud did not arrive as Sister Gertrud, did not appear in white with her Red Cross pin, but as just another woman in civilian clothes of the poorest cut, just another Fräulein Gertrud Wilms from Hamm or Dortmund or some other place between Hamm and Dortmund.

She didn't notice my dismay, but said she'd almost been late because the head nurse had given her something to do shortly before five, just to be mean.

"Now, Fräulein Gertrud, may I offer a few suggestions? Perhaps we could go to a pastry shop first and relax a while, and whatever you want after that: a movie perhaps, I'm afraid it's too late for theater tickets, but how about a little dancing?"

"Oh, yes, let's go dancing!" she cried with enthusiasm, then realized too late, with a distress she could scarcely conceal, that although I was well dressed, I would cut an impossible figure as her dancing partner.

With mild schadenfreude — why hadn't she appeared in the nurse's uniform I so admired? — I seconded the plan, one she herself had approved, and, lacking any true power of imagination, she soon recovered from her shock and joined me in some cake that seemed filled with cement, one slice for me and three for her, and after I'd paid with cake stamps and cash, we boarded the Gerresheim tram at Koch am Wehrhahn, since, according to Korneff, there was a dance hall below Grafenberg.

The tram only went as far as the incline, so we made our way slowly up the last stretch on foot. A picture-perfect September evening. Gertrud's wooden sandals, no redeemable coupons necessary, clattered like the mill on the floss. That made me feel gay. People coming downhill turned around and stared at us. Fräulein Gertrud was embarrassed. I was used to it and took no notice: after all, my cake stamps had helped her to three slices of cement cake at Kürten's Pastry Shop.

The dance hall was called Wedig's and was subtitled Löwenburg, or The Lions' Den. The giggling started at the ticket window, and when we entered, heads began to turn. Sister Gertrud was ill at ease in her civilian clothes and almost tripped over a folding chair before a waiter and

I caught her. The waiter led us to a table near the dance floor and I ordered two cold drinks, adding in an undertone, so only the waiter could hear, "And put a little something in them, please."

The Löwenburg consisted of one large room that might once have served as a riding academy. The upper regions of the room, including its heavily damaged ceiling, were festooned with paper streamers and garlands from last year's Carnival. Dim colored lights revolved overhead, casting reflections on the tightly slicked-back hair of young black marketers, some quite elegant, and on the taffeta blouses of the young women, who all seemed to know one another.

When the cold drinks with a little something in them were served, I bought ten Yankee cigarettes from the waiter, offered one to Sister Gertrud and another to the waiter, who stuck it behind his ear, and after giving my lady a light, pulled out Oskar's amber cigarette holder and smoked about half a Camel. The tables near us quieted down. Sister Gertrud dared look up. And when I crushed out the stately stub of the Camel in the ashtray and left it there, Sister Gertrud picked up the butt smoothly and tucked it away in a side pocket of her oilcloth handbag.

"For my fiancé in Dortmund," she said, "he smokes like crazy."

I was glad I wasn't her fiancé, and that the music had started up.

The five-man band played "Don't Fence Me In." Young men in crêpe soles dashed diagonally across the dance floor without colliding and angled for young ladies who entrusted their handbags to friends as they rose.

Some couples danced with a smoothness born of long practice. Quantities of chewing gum in motion, a few fellows stopped dancing for several beats, held their partners, who continued impatiently bobbing up and down in place, by the arm—scraps of English now leavened the stock of Rhenish words. Before the couples returned to their dance, small items had been passed on: true black marketers never have a night off.

We sat out that dance, and the next foxtrot as well. Now and then Oskar glanced at the men's feet and, as the band struck up "Rosamunde," asked Gertrud, who reacted with dismay, to dance.

Recalling Jan Bronski's choreographic skills, realizing I was nearly two heads shorter than Sister Gertrud, well aware that our alliance offered a note of the grotesque and even wishing to emphasize it, I tried a one-step: placing my hand on her bottom, I turned my palm outward, felt thirty percent wool, and with my cheek on her blouse as she gave in to my lead, shoved a strong Sister Gertrud back lock, stock, and barrel, followed hard on her heels, cleared the way to our left with arms stretched out, and crossed the dance floor from corner to corner. It went better than I had dared hope. I allowed myself a few fancy steps, clung to her blouse above and her hips below, to the hold that they offered, left and right, dancing about her, maintaining the classical one-step position, where the lady looks as if she were falling, and the gentleman pushing her over seems ready to fall right on top of her; yet because they're such good dancers, they never fall.

We soon had an audience. I heard cries like: "Didn't I tell you he could dance! Look at 'im go! A real Jimmy the Tiger. *Come on,* Jimmy! *Let's go,* crazylegs! Go, man, go!"

Unfortunately I couldn't see Sister Gertrud's face and could only hope that she was accepting this youthful ovation with proud composure, having resigned herself to their applause, just as she resigned herself as a nurse to the often awkward flattery of her patients.

They were still clapping when we sat down. The five-man band gave a flourish, their drummer leading the way, then another and yet a third. "Hey you, Jimmy!" they called out, and "Did you see those two?" Then Sister Gertrud rose, mumbled something about the ladies' room, picked up the handbag with the cigarette butt for her fiancé in Dortmund, and, blushing furiously, pushed her way out, knocking into chairs and tables on every side, heading toward the ladies' room near the ticket window.

She never came back. From the fact that she'd downed her drink in one gulp before leaving I gathered that draining a glass signaled farewell: Sister Gertrud had jilted me.

And Oskar? A Yankee cigarette in his amber holder, he ordered a straight schnapps from the waiter, who was discreetly removing the nurse's glass, drained to the dregs. Oskar forced a smile. Painfully, it's true, but he smiled, crossed his arms above, his legs below, wagged his delicate black shoe, size thirty-five European, and enjoyed the moral superiority of the abandoned.

The young people, regular guests at the Löwenburg, were kind, waved to me as they swung by on the dance floor. "Hey, there!" the fellows yelled, and the girls, *"Take it easy!"* I thanked these representatives of true humanity by waving my cigarette holder and grinned indulgently as the percussionist gave an elaborate drumroll, reminding me of my good old days in the grandstands, launched into a solo on snare, bass drum, cymbals, and triangle, and announced a ladies' choice.

The band played a hot number, "Jimmy the Tiger." This was meant for me, no doubt, though no one in the Löwenburg could possibly have known of my career as a drummer under grandstands. At any rate the young quicksilvery thing with a mop of henna-red curls who'd singled me out as the man of her choice whispered tobacco hoarse and chewing-gum wide into my ear, "Jimmy the Tiger." And while we danced a fast Jimmy, conjuring up the jungle and all its dangers, the tiger prowled on tiger paws for almost ten minutes. Again a flourish, applause, and another flourish, because I had a well-dressed hump, was nimble on my feet, and didn't cut a bad figure at all as Jimmy the Tiger. I invited the young lady so favorably disposed toward me to sit at my table, and Helma — that was her name — asked if her friend Hannelore could join us. Hannelore was silent, sedentary, and hard drinking. Helma in turn had a thing for Yankee cigarettes, and I had to order more from the waiter.

The evening went well. I danced "Hey Ba Ba Re Bop," "In the Mood," and "Shoeshine Boy," made small talk in between, and entertained two easily pleased young women who told me they both worked at the long-distance telephone exchange on Graf-Adolf-Platz, and said even more girls from the exchange came to Wedig's on Saturdays and Sundays. At any rate they came every weekend, unless they had to work, and I promised I would come often too, because Helma and Hannelore were so nice, and because girls who worked long distance — and here I made a little play on words they both caught at once — also knew how to work up close.

It was a long time before I dropped by the hospital again. And when I resumed my occasional visits, Sister Gertrud had been transferred to the women's ward. I no longer saw her, except once, briefly, waving in the distance. I became a regular and welcome guest at the Löwenburg. The girls exploited me a good deal, but not excessively. Through them I came to know several members of the British Army of Occupation, picked up dozens of English words and phrases, and even became close friends with a couple of the band members at the Löwenburg, but as for drumming I held back, never sat down at the drums, and instead rested content with the modest joy of tapping out letters in stone at Korneff's workshop.

During the hard winter of forty-seven to forty-eight I remained in contact with the girls from the telephone exchange, and was warmed from time to time, at no great cost, by the silent, sedentary Hannelore, though we always maintained a certain distance and restricted ourselves to noncommittal manual labor.

In winter the stonecutter rests and restores. Tools are resharpened, the surfaces of a few old slabs are pounded flat for inscriptions, missing corners are ground into chamfers and fluted. Korneff and I replenished the gravestone display, which had thinned out during the fall season, and cast a few synthetic slabs from a mixture of shell limestone, sand, and cement. I also tried my hand at some of the easier sculptural elements with the pointing machine — reliefs of the heads of angels, Christ's head with a crown of thorns, the dove of the Holy Spirit. When it snowed I shoveled snow, and when it didn't snow I thawed the water line to the grinder.

Toward the end of February forty-eight, shortly after Ash Wednesday — I'd lost weight during Carnival and may have been looking a bit wan and intellectual, for some of the girls at the Löwenburg took to calling me Doctor — the first farmers from the left bank of the Rhine arrived to inspect our stock of gravestones. Korneff was away. He was taking his annual rheumatism cure, working at a blast furnace in Duisburg, and when he returned fourteen days later, dried out and sans boils, I had already managed to sell three stones, one of them for a triple plot, at a good price. Korneff sold off another two slabs of Kirchheim shell limestone, and in mid-March we began installing them. One of Silesian marble went to Grevenbroich; the two Kirchheim meter-high stones are in a village graveyard near Neuss; the red Main sandstone with my angel heads may still be admired today at the cemetery in Stomml. At the end of March we loaded up the diorite slab for the triple plot with Christ's thorn-crowned head and drove off slowly, because the three-wheeler was overloaded, toward Kappes-Hamm and the bridge crossing the Rhine at Neuss. From Neuss by way of Grevenbroich to Rommerskirchen, then right on the road to Bergheim Erft, leaving Rheydt and Niederaußem behind us, we delivered the block and its base without breaking an axle to the cemetery in Oberaußem, which lay on a hill that sloped gently toward the village.

What a view! At our feet the soft-coal district of Erftland. The eight chimneys of the Fortuna Works, steaming heavenward. The new Fortuna North power plant, hissing as though about to explode. Midrange mountains of slag, topped by cable cars and tipping wagons. Every three minutes an electric train, full of coke or empty. Coming from the power plant or headed toward it, small and toylike; next, leaping over the left corner of the cemetery, a toy for giants: high-voltage wires in triple ranks, buzzing with high tension, racing off toward Cologne. Other lines in rank rushing toward the horizon, toward Belgium and Holland: hub of the world—we set up the diorite slab for the Flies family—electricity is generated when . . . The gravedigger and his helper, who substituted for Crazy Leo on this occasion, arrived with tools, we stood in a field of electric tension, the gravedigger began unearthing a grave three rows down from us to relocate its occupant—war reparations rushed on their way—the breeze brought us the typical smells of a premature exhumation—not too disgusting, it was still March. Slag heaps of coke on the March fields. The gravedigger wore a pair of glasses held together with string and argued in an undertone with his Crazy Leo till the siren at Fortuna expelled its breath for one long minute, we were out of breath too, not to mention the woman being moved, only the high-tension lines kept right on working as the siren tipped, toppled overboard, and drowned—while smoke curled up in noonday fashion from the slate-gray slate roofs of the village and church bells chimed in: Pray now, work now—industry and religion hand in hand. Change of shift at Fortuna, bacon sandwiches for us, but no rest for those moving the woman or for the high-voltage current rushing restlessly through to the victorious powers, lighting up Holland, while here the current was still constantly being cut off—and yet the dead woman was brought to the light.

While Korneff dug the five-foot holes for the base, she came up for fresh air, had not been down in the dark that long, just since last fall, yet still she'd made progress, kept pace with improvements under way on all sides; and just as progress had been made dismantling the industrial Rhineland and Ruhr, so too had this woman, in the course of the winter—which I'd frittered away at the Löwenburg—made serious progress, taking herself so gravely to task beneath the frozen crust of the soft-coal district that now, while we poured concrete and set the pedestal, she could be persuaded to move her remains only piecemeal. But that's what the zinc casket was for, so not even the tiniest piece would be lost — just as children ran along behind the overloaded trucks when coal was distributed in Fortuna, collecting the fallen chunks, because Cardinal Frings had decreed from the pulpit: Truly I say unto you, pilfering coal is no sin. But no fire was needed to warm her now. I don't think she was cold in the proverbially chill March air, she still had plenty of skin, though leaky and filled with runs, compensated for by patches of clothing and scraps of hair in a permanent wave — hence the name — and the coffin fittings were worth relocating too, even small splinters of wood wanted to go along to the next cemetery, where there would be no farmers or miners from Fortuna, no, the big city was where she wanted to go, where there was always something happening, and nineteen movie houses playing at once, for she was an evacuee, the gravedigger told us, and not from here: "The girl came from Cologne, and now she's headed for Müllheim, across the Rhine," he said, and would have said more, had not the siren sounded another minute's worth of siren, and taking advantage of the siren, I drew near the remains, making my way stealthily beneath the siren's cover, wanting to witness the transfer, taking something along that later, by the zinc coffin, proved to be my spade, which I now put into action, not meaning to help but simply because I had it with me, lifting something on the blade of the spade that had fallen off to the side: a spade that had once belonged to the Reich Labor Service. And what I picked up on the RLS spade was the middle finger and — I still believe today — the ring finger that had once belonged or still belonged to the evacuated woman, and had not dropped off, but had been hacked off instead by the motorized digger, which had no feeling. They seemed to me, however, to have once been lovely and agile, just as the woman's head, already in the zinc casket, had preserved a certain regularity throughout the postwar winter of forty-seven/ forty-eight, well-known for its severity, so that here too one could speak of loveliness, though lapsed. Moreover the woman's head and fingers struck me as much more intimate and human than the beauty of the Fortuna power plant. True, I may have enjoyed the pathos of the industrial landscape, just as I had once enjoyed Gustaf Gründgens in the theater, but I still remained skeptical of such staged beauty, artful though it was, while the evacuated woman was only too natural. Granted, the high-voltage wires, like Goethe, gave me a cosmic feeling, but the woman's fingers touched my heart, even if I imagined the evacuee as a man because that was more compatible with my penchant for making decisions, and fit the comparison that transformed me into Yorick, and the woman—half in the grave, half in the zinc casket—into Hamlet the man, if you wish to call Hamlet a man. And I, Yorick, Act Five, the fool, "I knew him, Horatio," Scene One, on all the stages of the world—"Alas, poor Yorick!"—loaning my skull to Hamlet, so some Gründgens or Sir Laurence Olivier can ponder over it as Hamlet: "Where be your gibes now? your gambols?"—I held Gründgens' Hamlet fingers on the blade of my Labor Service spade, stood on the firm soil of the Lower Rhenish soft-coal district, between the graves of miners, farmers, and their families, gazed down upon the slate roofs of the village of Oberaußem, and transformed that village cemetery into the center of the world, the Fortuna North power plant into my daunting, demigod antagonist, the fields into the fields of Denmark, the Erft my Belt, what rotted here was something rotten in the state of Denmark—and I was Yorick; strung taut, filled, crackling, and singing above me, not actual angels, yet high-voltage angels singing away in triple ranks toward the horizon, toward Cologne with its central train station by that fabulous Gothic monster, sending current to the Catholic welfare center, heavenly hosts hurrying over the turnip fields, and the earth brought forth coal and the corpse, not of Yorick but of Hamlet. But those who had no part in the play remained below—"Which have solicited. The rest is silence"—weighed down with gravestones, as we weighed down the Flies family in their triple plot beneath a ponderous diorite slab. But for me, Oskar Matzerath Bronski Yorick, a new age was dawning, and scarcely aware of that new age, I took another quick glance, before it had passed, at the ravaged fingers of Hamlet on my spade—"He is fat and scant of breath"—heard Gründgens ask, Act Three, Scene One, to be or not to be, rejected this foolish formulation, and paired things far more concretely: my son and my son's flintstones, my presumptive earthly and heavenly fathers, my grandmother's four skirts, my poor mama's immortal beauty in photos, the labyrinth of scars on Herbert Truczinski's back, the blood-blotting mail baskets of the Polish Post Office, America—ah, what is

America compared to the Number Nine streetcar to Brösen? — sent the still occasionally sharp scent of Maria's vanilla drifting into the triangular face of Luzie Rennwand offering madness, asked Herr Fajngold, still disinfecting death, to find the missing Party pin in Matzerath's windpipe, and said to Korneff, or perhaps to the high-tension pylons above, said — since I was slowly reaching a decision, yet still felt the need, before that decision, to ask a suitably theatrical question, one that would cast doubt on Hamlet and make of me, Yorick, a true citizen — said to Korneff when he called me over, since it was time to mount the diorite slab on the pedestal, said softly, wishing to be a solid citizen at last, said — with just a touch of Gründgens, though he could hardly have played Yorick — said over the blade of the spade: "To wed or not to wed, that is the question."

After this turning point in the cemetery facing Fortuna North, I gave up Wedig's Löwenburg dance hall and broke off all connections with the girls from the telephone exchange, whose primary merit had been the quick and satisfying connections they offered.

In May I took Maria to the movies. After the show we went to a restaurant, dined fairly well, and I talked with Maria, who was worried sick because little Kurt's flintstone source was drying up, because the synthetic-honey business was slowing down, and because I'd been supporting the whole family for months with — as she put it — my limited strengths. I comforted Maria, told her Oskar did so gladly, that he liked nothing better than having to bear a great responsibility, complimented her on her appearance, and finally proposed to her.

She asked for time to think it over. My Yorick question was ignored or avoided for weeks, till it was answered at last by the currency reform.

Maria offered all sorts of reasons, stroking my sleeve as she did so, called me "dear Oskar," told me I was too good for this world, hoped I would understand and that this wouldn't damage our friendship, wished me all the best for my future as a stonecutter and in general, but, when pressed again and even more urgently, declined to marry me.

And so Yorick did not become a solid citizen, but a Hamlet instead, a fool.

Madonna 49

THE CURRENCY REFORM arrived too soon, made a fool of me, compelled me to reform Oskar's currency in turn; from then on, even if I couldn't convert it into capital, I found myself forced to make a living from my hump.

I would have made a good citizen. The period following the currency reform, which — as we see today — included all the necessary preconditions for the current blossoming of bourgeois comfort, would have brought out the bourgeois in Oskar. As a married man, a solid citizen, I could have taken part in the reconstruction of Germany, would have had a good-sized stonecutting business by now, providing a livelihood for thirty journeymen, handymen, and apprentices, would have been the man adorning all those newly constructed office high-rises and insurance palaces with their ever popular shell-limestone and travertine façades: a businessman, a solid citizen, a family man — but Maria turned me down.

Then Oskar recalled his hump and fell prey to art. Korneff's existence as a stonecutter was also threatened by the currency reform, so before he could fire me, I fired myself, stood about on street corners, when I wasn't twiddling my thumbs in Guste Köster's kitchen–living room, gradually wore out my elegantly tailored suit, began to neglect my appearance, and while I didn't fight with Maria, I feared I might, and so would often leave the apartment in Bilk well before noon, drop by the swans on Graf-Adolf-Platz, then visit the ones in the Hofgarten, and sit small, pensive, but not embittered in the park, diagonally across from the Employment Agency and the Art Academy, which are next-door neighbors in Düsseldorf.

You sit and sit on a park bench like that till you turn wooden yourself and feel the need to talk. Old men brought out by good weather, elderly women who slowly revert to garrulous girlhood, the changing seasons, black swans, children who chase one another screaming, and pairs of lovers you'd like to watch until, as one could predict, they have to part. Now and then someone drops a piece of paper. It flutters a while, tosses and turns till it's stabbed with a sharp-tipped pole by a man in a cap who's paid by the city.

Oskar knew how to sit and flare his trouser legs evenly with his knees. Of course I had noticed the two lean young men and the fat girl in glasses well before the girl, who was wearing a leather jacket with an ex-Wehrmacht belt, spoke to me. The idea apparently originated with the young men, who were dressed in anarchistic black. No matter how dangerous they looked, they hesitated to speak point-blank and directly to a humpbacked man in whom they sensed a hidden greatness. They talked the fat, leather-clad girl into it. She came, stood straddle-legged on solid pillars, stuttering, till I invited her to sit down. She sat, her glasses clouded by the mist, nearly a fog, drifting in from the Rhine, talked and talked till I asked her to stop, wipe her glasses, and state her request in a manner I could understand. With that she called over the somber youths, who introduced themselves, without being prompted, as artists: painters, draftsmen, and sculptors seeking a model. They concluded by telling me, not without some passion, that they thought I would make a good model, and when I made a rapid rubbing motion with my thumb and forefinger, they quickly detailed the potential earnings of an academic model: the Art Academy paid one mark eighty an hour, and for posing in the nude—but there was probably no question of that, the stout girl said—two German marks.

Why did Oskar say yes? Was it the lure of art? Was it the lure of cash? Art and cash both lured me, made Oskar say yes. So I stood up, left the park bench and the possibilities of a park bench existence behind me forever, followed the resolutely marching girl in glasses and the two youths, who walked with a stoop as though carrying their genius on their backs, past the Employment Agency to Eiskellerbergstraße and into the partially demolished building of the Art Academy.

Professor Kuchen—black beard, coal-black eyes, bold black slouch hat, black rims beneath his fingernails—he reminded me of the black sideboard from my childhood — saw in me the same splendid model his students had seen in the man on the park bench.

For a time he walked around me, his coal-black eyes circling, snorted black dust from his nostrils, and then spoke, throttling an invisible enemy with his black nails: "Art is accusation, expression, passion. Art is black charcoal crushing white paper."

I posed as a model for this crushing art. Professor Kuchen led me to his students' studio, lifted me with his own hands onto a revolving pedestal, turned it about, not to dizzy me, but to display Oskar's proportions from all sides. Sixteen easels drew closer to Oskar's form. Yet another brief lecture from the charcoal-dust-snorting professor: he asked for expression, seemed in love with the word, demanded expression, pitch-black and desperate, saw in Oskar the shattered image of humanity, an accusation, a challenge, a timeless expression of the madness of our century, and ended by thundering across the easels: "Don't draw this cripple — slaughter him, crucify him, nail him to the paper with charcoal!"

That must have been the signal to start, for charcoal ground sixteen-fold behind easels, cried out as it softened, turned to dust as it sketched my expression — that is, my hump — and turned it black, blackened it thoroughly, got it all wrong; for every one of Professor Kuchen's students tried to capture my expression with a blackness so thick they couldn't help exaggerating it, kept overestimating the size of my hump, reached for larger and larger sketchpads and still couldn't get my hump down on paper.

Then Professor Kuchen gave the sixteen charcoal crushers the sage advice not to start with the outline of my all too expressive hump — which seemed to exceed all known formats — but to begin instead on the upper fifth of the pad, as far left as possible, by blackening in my head.

My beautiful hair gleams dark brown. They turned me into a scraggly-haired gypsy. Not one of the sixteen artists noticed Oskar's blue eyes. When, during one of the breaks — for every model gets to rest fifteen minutes after posing for forty-five — I inspected the upper left fifth of the sixteen pads, I was struck at each easel by the social indictment in my careworn face, but slightly taken aback to find the brilliance of my blue eyes missing: where there should have been a clear, winning sparkle, strokes of blackest charcoal rolled, narrowed, crumbled, and glared at me.

Keeping in mind artistic freedom, I said to myself: These young sons of the Muses and devoted daughters of Art have recognized the Rasputin in you, but will they ever discover and awaken the slumbering Goethe within, will they ever capture him on paper, not as expression but with the delicate, measured touch of a silver point? Neither the sixteen students, gifted though they might have been, nor Professor Kuchen, with his supposedly unique charcoal stroke, succeeded in passing on to posterity an acceptable portrait of Oskar. But I was well paid, treated with respect, posed for six hours a day on the turntable, with my face first toward the constantly clogged sink, then with my nose to the gray, sky-blue, slightly cloudy studio windows, then toward a folding screen, dispensing expression at one mark eighty pfennigs an hour.

After a few weeks the students managed to produce several nice little sketches. They'd toned down their dark expressionism and no longer exaggerated my hump so wildly, even got me on paper now and then from head to toe, and from the jacket buttons on my chest to the hindmost reaches of the cloth marking the back of my hump. On several pads there was even room for a background. In spite of the currency reform, these young people still felt the war's influence, constructed ruins behind me with accusing black holes where windows had been, portrayed me as a forlorn, undernourished refugee among blasted tree stumps, even interned me in a camp, wove a ferociously barbed barbed-wire fence behind me in painstaking black charcoal, erected watchtowers in that same looming background, forced me to hold an empty tin bowl while prison windows behind and above me lent their graphic appeal – Oskar was shown in prisoner's garb – all in the name of artistic expression.

But since it was as a black-haired gypsy-Oskar that I was made to witness all this misery, through coal-black eyes instead of my own blue ones, knowing full well that barbed wire couldn't be drawn, holding still even so as a model, I was nonetheless pleased when the sculptors, who as everyone knows must make do without backgrounds reflecting the times, asked me to pose for them, and in the nude.

This time it was not a student but the master in person who spoke to me. Professor Maruhn was a friend of Professor Kuchen, my charcoal master. One day, as I was posing motionless in Kuchen's private studio, a gloomy loft filled with framed strokes of charcoal, allowing the master, whose beard you could almost hear rustling in the wind, to record me on paper with his unique stroke, Professor Maruhn dropped by, a sturdy, thickset fifty-year-old in a white modeling smock, who, had not a dusty beret borne witness to his artistic calling, might have been taken for a surgeon.

Maruhn, an admirer of classical form, as I could see at a glance, regarded me with hostility, given my proportions. He jeered at his friend: weren't the gypsy models enough, the ones he'd been blackening in charcoal up to now, the ones who'd earned him the nickname Gypsycakes in artistic circles? Was he going to try his hand at freaks now, did he plan to follow up the commercial success of his gypsy period with an even more lucrative and successful gnomic period?

Professor Kuchen transformed his friend's mockery into raging, pitch-black strokes of charcoal: it was the blackest portrait he ever made of Oskar, totally black in fact, except for a few highlights on my cheekbones, nose, forehead, and hands, which Kuchen always spread wide with expressive power, overly large and swollen with gout, in the middle ground of his charcoal orgies. In this drawing, however, much admired at later exhibitions, my eyes are blue, by which I mean they are lighter in tone, not scowling darkly. Oskar attributes this to the influence of the sculptor Maruhn, who was not, after all, a fanatic of charcoal expression, but a classicist alert to the Goethean clarity of my gaze. It can only have been Oskar's eyes that led this lover of classical harmony to see in me a fit model for his own sculpture.

Maruhn's studio was bright with dust, nearly empty, and contained not a single finished work. Nevertheless, frameworks of projected sculptures stood everywhere, so perfectly conceived that even without modeling clay, the wire, iron, and curves of bare lead tubing proclaimed a future perfect harmony.

I posed nude for the sculptor five hours a day and received two marks an hour. He chalked a point on the turntable to show me where my right leg was to take root from then on as the engaged leg. A vertical line rising straight up from the instep of the engaged leg must meet the base of my neck precisely between my collarbones. My left leg was the free leg. But the term is misleading. Even though I was to keep it slightly bent and relaxed to one side, I was not to move it, and certainly not freely. The free leg too was rooted to a chalk outline on the turntable.

During the weeks I posed for the sculptor Maruhn he could find no set position for my arms comparable to the fixed position of my legs. He had me dangle my left arm and angle my right over my head, cross my arms over my chest, clasp them under my hump, stand with arms akimbo; there were a thousand possibilities, and the sculptor tried them all, on me and on the iron framework with the flexible lead-tubing limbs.

When, after a month's strenuous search for the right pose, he finally decided to begin modeling me in clay, either with my hands clasped behind my head, or as a torso with no arms at all, he was so worn out with constructing and reconstructing the framework, that though he reached for the clay in the clay box, and even made a start, he then dumped the dumb, formless mass back into the box, crouched before the frame, and stared at me and my frame, his fingers trembling in despair: the framework was too perfect.

Sighing in resignation, feigning a headache, but bearing no ill will toward Oskar, he gave up and placed the humpbacked framework with its engaged leg and its free leg, with its raised, tubular arms, with its wire fingers clasped at the back of its iron neck, in the corner with all the other prematurely finished skeletons; gently, not mockingly, but conscious instead of their own uselessness, the wooden strips — also known as butterflies — intended to bear the weight of the clay, swayed in the spacious framework of my hump.

After that we drank tea and chatted for an hour or so, which the sculptor counted as an hour of posing. He recalled the early days, when as an uninhibited young Michelangelo he slapped clay on frameworks by the ton and actually completed sculptures, most of which were destroyed in the war. I told him about Oskar's work as a stonecutter and engraver of inscriptions. We talked shop for a while; then he took me to his students so they could recognize the sculptor's model in Oskar and shape frameworks based upon me.

If long hair is any indication of gender, six of Professor Maruhn's ten students could be designated as female. Four were ugly and gifted. Two were pretty and talkative — real girls. Posing in the nude never bothered me. Yes, Oskar even enjoyed the astonishment of the two pretty, talkative sculptresses as they examined me for the first time on the turntable and ascertained, to their dismay, that Oskar, despite his hump, despite his parsimonious size, carried a male member with him which, should the need arise, could match that of any so-called normal man.

Maruhn's students differed from the master in their approach. After only two days they had constructed their skeletons, seemed totally inspired, slapped the clay on the hastily and inexpertly mounted lead tubes in a rush of inspiration, but must have added too few wooden butterflies to the frame of my hump: for no sooner had the weight of the damp modeling clay been applied to the skeleton, giving Oskar a wild, rugged look, than ten freshly modeled Oskars began to sag, my head fell between my feet, the clay slumped down from the tubing, my hump drooped to the hollows of my knees, and I came to appreciate Maruhn, the master, whose frames were so perfect that he had no need to conceal them beneath cheap clay.

The ugly but gifted sculptresses even shed tears when the clay Oskar parted from the frame Oskar. The pretty but talkative sculptresses laughed as the flesh slid rapidly, almost symbolically, from my bones. Yet when the novice sculptors finally managed, after several weeks, to finish a few passable sculptures, first in clay, then in shiny plaster for the end-of-term exhibition, I had a chance to make several new comparisons between the ugly, gifted girls and the pretty but talkative ones. The ugly but not entirely artless maidens reproduced my head, limbs, and hump with some care, yet were strangely shy about my sexual organs, either neglecting or stylizing them in some silly fashion, while the sweet, wide-eyed maidens with their lovely though hardly agile fingers wasted little time on the articulated proportions of my body, but instead devoted their entire energy to reproducing my imposing genitals to a hair. Lest we forget the four young men who were sculpting away, I can report that they abstracted me, clapped me into a quadrangle with flat grooved boards, and, with dry male rationality, let the very thing the ugly maidens neglected and the sweet young maidens allowed to bloom as fleshy nature, jut out into the room as an elongated, quadrangular log above a pair of matching cubes, like the sex-crazed organ of a building-block king.

Was it my blue eyes or the sun-bowl reflectors the sculptors set up around me, the nude Oskar: in any case, the young artists who visited the lovely sculptresses discovered a picturesque charm in either the blue of my eyes or my irradiated skin, glowing lobster-red, and carried me off from the sculpture and graphics studios on the ground floor to the upper stories, where they then mixed the paints on their palettes to match my colors.

At first the painters were so taken with my blue eyes that their brushes rendered me entirely blue. Oskar's healthy flesh, his wavy brown hair, his fresh, flushed lips shriveled, moldered in macabre shades of blue; at best, here and there, accelerating the decay, a moribund green, a nauseous yellow, crept in between patches of blue flesh.

Oskar did not take on other colors until, in the course of a weeklong celebration of Carnival in the cellars of the Academy, he discovered Ulla and brought her to the artists to serve as their Muse.

Was it Shrove Monday? Yes, it was on Shrove Monday that I decided to join the festivities, to put on a costume and mix in with the crowd as a costumed Oskar.

When Maria saw me standing at the mirror, she said, "Stay home, Oskar. They'll just trample you." But then she helped me with my outfit, cut scraps of cloth that her sister Guste sewed with garrulous needle into a jester's costume. I'd been thinking at first of something in the style of Velázquez. And I would have gladly appeared as General Narses, or possibly Prince Eugen. When I stood at last before the full-length mirror, which the war had endowed with a diagonal crack that slightly canted the surface, and saw the entire brightly colored, baggy, slashed outfit hung with bells, which moved my son Kurt to laughter and a fit of coughing, I said softly to myself, not entirely pleased: Now you're Yorick the fool, Oskar. But where is the king you'll play the fool to?

In the tram on the way to Ratinger Tor, near the Academy, I noticed that the other passengers, all those cowboys and Spanish señoritas trying to forget their offices and shop counters, weren't laughing at me but were frightened instead. Everyone edged away, and so I was accorded the pleasure of a seat in the otherwise jammed tram. Outside the Academy, policemen were swinging their hard rubber truncheons, which were by no means merely cosmetic. "The Tumble of the Muses" — as the young artists had christened their ball — was packed, but the crowd still tried to push their way into the building, resulting in a confrontation with the police that was somewhat bloody but in any case colorful.

Oskar jingled the little bell hanging on his left sleeve, the crowd parted, and a policeman, professionally attuned to recognize my true stature, saluted down at me, asked if he could be of help, and, swinging his truncheon, escorted me into the cellar festivities — where things were cooking but not yet done.

Now no one should imagine that an artists' ball is a ball where artists have a ball. Most of the students at the Academy stand behind cleverly decorated but somewhat wobbly counters with serious, strained expressions on their painted faces, trying to earn a little extra money by selling beer, champagne, Vienna sausages, and clumsily poured schnapps. Those having a ball are everyday citizens who throw their money around once a year and try to live it up like artists.

After I'd spent an hour or so on stairways, in nooks and crannies, and under tables, startling couples on the point of wringing a thrill from their discomfort, I made friends with two Chinese girls who must have had some Greek blood flowing in their veins, for they were practitioners of a love praised centuries ago in song on the island of Lesbos. Though they went at each other all fingers and thumbs, they left my vital zones in peace, put on a show I found amusing at times, drank warm champagne with me, and, with my permission and apparent success, tested the resistance of my hump, which thrust out solidly at its extremity — once again confirming my theory that a hump brings good luck to women.

Nevertheless, the longer I was with these women, the sadder I got. Thoughts plagued me, the political situation worried me, I traced the blockade of Berlin in champagne on the tabletop, sketched in the airlift, despaired of the reunification of Germany while contemplating those two Chinese girls, who could never unite, and did something very unlike me: Oskar, as Yorick, pondered the meaning of life.

When the ladies could think of nothing more worth watching — they subsided in tears, leaving telltale traces on their painted Chinese faces — I arose, slashed, baggy, jingling my bells, two-thirds of me wanting to head home and one-third still hoping for some further Carnival encounter, and saw — no, he spoke to me — Corporal Lankes.

Do you remember? We met him on the Atlantic Wall during the summer of forty-four. He was guarding concrete and smoking my master Bebra's cigarettes.

I was trying to squeeze my way up the stairs, thickly populated with necking couples, and was just lighting up, when someone tapped me on the shoulder and a corporal from the last war said, "Say, friend, got a cigarette?"

Small wonder that I recognized him at once, given this familiar request and his field-gray costume. Yet I would never have tried to renew our acquaintance had not the corporal and concrete artist held the Muse in person on his field-gray knee.

Let me speak with the corporal first and describe the Muse later. I not only gave him a cigarette but held out my lighter for him, and said, as the first puff of smoke rose, "Do you remember, Corporal Lankes? Bebra's Theater at the Front? Mystical, barbaric, bored?"

The painter stopped in shock at my words; he managed to hold on to his cigarette, but the Muse slipped from his knee. I caught the totally drunk, long-legged child and handed her back to him. As the two of us, Oskar and Lankes, swapped old memories, cursed Lieutenant Herzog, whom Lankes called a nut, recalled my master, Bebra, and the nuns who'd been looking for prawns in the Rommel asparagus, I gazed in amazement at the Muse. She'd come as an angel, in a hat of molded cardboard of the sort used for egg cartons, yet in spite of her advanced state of inebriation and the melancholy droop of her wings, she still radiated the slightly artsy-craftsy charm of a heavenly being.

"This here's Ulla," Lankes, the painter, explained. "She studied dressmaking, but now she wants to do something in art, and I can't see that, because she can make some money with dresses, but she'll make nothing in art."

Oskar, who made good money in art, offered to introduce Ulla the dressmaker to the painters of the Art Academy as a model and Muse. Lankes was so delighted by my proposal that he helped himself to three cigarettes from my pack, inviting me in return to come see his studio, if, he quickly added, I didn't mind paying for the taxi.

Off we rode, leaving Carnival behind, I paid for the taxi, and Lankes, whose studio was on Sittarder Straße, made us coffee over an alcohol stove, which revived the Muse. After throwing up with the help of my right forefinger, she seemed almost sober.

Only then did I note the light blue eyes from which she stared in constant amazement, and hear her voice, which was slightly squeaky and tinny but not without a certain touching charm. When Lankes explained my proposal to her, ordering more than suggesting that she pose at the Art Academy, she refused at first, saying she didn't want to be a muse or a model for the Art Academy, but only for Lankes. But, as gifted artists sometimes do, matter-of-factly and without saying a word, he slapped her a few times with his big hand, asked her again, and chuckled contentedly, good-natured once more, as, sobbing and weeping like an angel, she declared her willingness to become a well-paid model for the painters at the Art Academy, and possibly their Muse as well.

You have to visualize Ulla as roughly five foot ten, extremely slender, lovely and fragile, reminiscent of both Botticelli and Cranach. We posed together in the nude. Her long, smooth flesh is about the color of spring-lobster meat, covered with soft, childlike down. The hair on her head is somewhat fine, but long and straw-blond. Her pubic hair curls reddishly, covering only a small triangle. Ulla shaves her armpits weekly.

As might be expected, the run-of-the-mill art students didn't know what to do with us, made her arms too long, my head too big, falling prey to the beginner's standard error: they couldn't get us the right size and shape.

It was only when the Goat and Raskolnikov discovered us that paintings were produced worthy of Oskar and the Muse.

She's sleeping, I'm startling her awake: Faun and Nymph.

I'm crouching, she's leaning over me with small, always slightly shivering breasts, stroking my hair: Beauty and the Beast.

She's lying there, I'm playing between her long legs with the mask of a horned horse: the Lady and the Unicorn.

All this in the style of the Goat or Raskolnikov, sometimes in color, then in elegant grays, sometimes detailed with a fine brush, then again, in the Goat's manner, splattered on with the spatula of genius, sometimes hinting at the mystery surrounding Ulla and Oskar; and then it was Raskolnikov who found his way, with our help, to surrealism: Oskar's face became the honey-yellow dial of our grandfather clock; roses bloomed in mechanical profusion from my hump and were picked by Ulla; Ulla was smiling above and long-legged below as I sat in her cut-open body, crouching between her spleen and liver, leafing through a picture book. They liked to costume us too, transforming Ulla into a columbine and me into a mournful, white-faced mime. Finally it fell to Raskolnikov — they called him that because he was always talking about crime and punishment, guilt and atonement — to paint the truly great picture: I sat on Ulla's lightly downed left thigh—naked, a deformed child—she was the Madonna; Oskar held still for Jesus.

This painting, entitled *Madonna 49,* was later shown at several exhibitions, and also proved effective as a poster, thus reaching the respectable bourgeois eyes of my Maria and initiating a domestic quarrel, yet nevertheless was purchased for a tidy sum by a Rhenish industrialist—and no doubt still hangs today in the conference room of some high-rise office building influencing members of the board.

I was amused by all the gifted shenanigans occasioned by my hump and proportions. In addition, given the high demand for our services, Ulla and I were taking in two marks fifty an hour each for posing together in the nude. Ulla enjoyed being a model too. Lankes the painter, with his big, slaphappy hand, treated her better once she started bringing money home on a regular basis, and hit her only when his abstract paintings required the angry hand of genius. Even though, speaking purely in visual terms, he never used her as a model, she was his Muse too in a sense, for only the slaps he gave her could lend his painter's hand its true creative power.

In fact Ulla's lachrymose delicacy, which was in reality the indestructibility of an angel, made me feel like slapping her myself at times; but I was always able to control these urges, and whenever I felt inclined toward the whip, would invite her to a pastry shop, or, with a tinge of snobbery engendered by my intercourse with artists, take her for a stroll along a crowded and gaping Königsallee, a tall, rare plant set off against my own special proportions, or buy her lilac stockings and pink gloves.

It was a different story with Raskolnikov, who, without actually approaching her, knew her most intimately. He had her pose on the turntable with her legs spread wide, yet did not paint, but sat instead a few steps away on a stool and, staring at her private parts, whispered urgently of guilt and atonement till the Muse's sex grew moist, opened, and Raskolnikov too, merely by speaking and staring, achieved the release he sought, sprang from his stool to his easel, and set to work with grandiose sweeps of his brush on Madonna 49.

Raskolnikov sometimes stared at me as well, but for different reasons. He felt I was missing something. He spoke of a vacuum between my hands, had me hold a series of objects one after another, never at a loss for ideas, given his surrealistic imagination. He armed Oskar-Jesus with a pistol and had me aim at the Madonna. I had to hold out an hourglass toward her, then a convex mirror that distorted her terribly. I held scissors, fish bones, telephone receivers, death's-heads, model airplanes, tanks, steamships in both hands, and still — as Raskolnikov quickly saw — the vacuum was not filled.

Oskar dreaded the day when the painter would bring the object that alone of all objects was made to be held by me. When he finally brought the drum, I cried out, "No!"

Raskolnikov: "Take the drum, Oskar, I know who you are."

I, trembling: "Never again. All that has ended."

He, darkly: "Nothing ends, all returns, guilt, atonement, guilt again."

I, with my last strength: "Oskar has repented, spare him the drum, I'll hold anything, but not the drum."

I wept as the Muse Ulla leaned over me, and blinded by tears could not prevent her kiss, could not prevent the terrible kiss of the Muse — and all of you who have ever been kissed by the Muse will surely understand that, branded by that kiss, Oskar took up the drum at once, the drum he had rejected years before and buried in the sand of Saspe Cemetery.

But I didn't drum. I simply posed and was painted — which was bad enough — as a drumming Jesus on the bare left thigh of Madonna 49.

That's how Maria saw me on the poster announcing an art exhibition. Unbeknownst to me, she went to the exhibition and must have stood before the painting a long time, her anger building, for when she took me to task, she struck me with my son Kurt's school ruler. Having found a well-paid job in a large delicatessen some months earlier, first as a salesclerk and soon thereafter as cashier, given her talents, Maria was no longer an Eastern refugee trading on the black market, but now a well-established citizen of the West, and could thus call me, with some conviction, a pig, a pimp, and a total degenerate, and scream that she wanted nothing more to do with the filthy money I was earning with such smutty filth, or with me either.

Though Maria soon retracted this last statement, and two weeks later restored a not inconsiderable portion of the money I was earning modeling to the household budget, I still decided to stop living with her, her sister Guste, and my son Kurt, and to move far away, to Hamburg or perhaps to the seashore again, but Maria, who had quickly accepted my plans to leave, persuaded me, backed up by her sister Guste, to look for a room near them and little Kurt, or at least in Düsseldorf.

The Hedgehog

BUILT UP, CHOPPED DOWN, wiped out, hauled back, dismembered, remembered: Oskar first learned the art of drumming up the past as a lodger. It wasn't just the room, the Hedgehog, Herr Münzer, and the coffin warehouse in the courtyard that helped—Sister Dorothea offered a special stimulus.

Do you know *Parsifal?* I don't know it very well either. The only thing I recall is the story about the three drops of blood in the snow. That story seems true because it fits my case so well. It probably fits anyone who gets an idea. But Oskar is writing about himself, so it's almost suspiciously well tailored to him.

I was still serving Art, letting myself be painted in blue, green, yellow, and earth tones, letting them blacken me in charcoal and place me before backgrounds, fructifying the Art Academy in collaboration with the Muse Ulla for the entire winter semester—we gave our Muses' blessing to the summer semester that followed as well—but the snow had already fallen which received those three drops of blood that transfixed my gaze as they did that of the fool Parsifal, of whom the fool Oskar knows so little that he can effortlessly identify with him.

My clumsy image will be clear enough to you: the snow is the uniform of a hospital nurse, the red cross, which most nurses, including Sister Dorothea, display in the center of the pin that closes their collar, shone like the three drops of blood. There I sat and couldn't take my eyes off it.

But before I could sit in the former bathroom of Zeidler's flat, I had to look for that room. The winter semester had just ended, students were giving up their rooms, heading home for Easter, and were either coming back or gone for good. My colleague Ulla, the Muse, who helped me search, went along with me to Student Administration. There I was given several addresses and a written recommendation from the Art Academy.

Before looking at flats, I visited Korneff the stonecutter, whom I hadn't seen in some time, in his workshop on Bittweg. I made the trip in part because I liked him, but I was also looking for work during the semester holidays; the small number of hours I'd set up to pose privately for a few professors, with and without Ulla, would barely feed me for the next six weeks — and I had to come up with enough money to rent a furnished room too.

I found Korneff unchanged, with two nearly healed boils on his neck and one still ripening, bending over a slab of Belgian granite that he had smoothed and was now providing with hatching, blow by blow. We chatted a while and I played with a few lettering chisels by way of a hint, looking around for benched slabs, cut and polished, ready for their carved inscriptions. Two standard meter-high stones, one of shell limestone and another of Silesian marble for a double grave, looked as if they'd been sold by Korneff and were crying out for an expert letter carver. I was happy for the stonecutter, who'd had a rough time after the currency reform. Yet even back then we'd consoled ourselves with the wise observation that no matter how life-affirming the currency reform was, it couldn't keep people from dying and ordering gravestones.

That proved to be true. People were dying and buying again. And the currency reform brought in new business: butchers had their shops lined inside and out with colored Lahn marble, and many a bank or department store removed damaged squares of sandstone or tufa from its façade and had them replaced to make it look respectable again.

I praised Korneff's industry, asked him if he was able to handle all the work. He was evasive at first, then admitted he sometimes wished he had four hands, and finally proposed I work half days at his place doing lettering; he paid forty-five pfennigs a letter for inscriptions in limestone, fifty-five a letter for granite and diorite, and sixty and seventy-five pfennigs for lettering in relief.

I started right in on shell limestone and was soon back in the swing of things, attacked the letters, incised in cuneiform script: *Aloys Küfer —*

b. 3 Sept. 1887 — d. 10 June 1946 — finished all thirty-one letters and numbers inside of four hours and received as I left, per scale, thirteen marks and ninety-five pfennigs.

That was about a third of the monthly rent I thought I could afford. I didn't want to pay more than forty marks, nor could I, for Oskar felt duty bound to continue contributing, at least modestly, to the household finances in Bilk, for Maria, the boy, and Guste Köster.

Of the four addresses provided by the friendly staff of the Academy's Student Administration, my first choice was Zeidler, at Jülicher Straße 7, because I would be near the Art Academy.

Early in May, on a hot, hazy Lower Rhenish day, I set out, provided with sufficient cash. Maria had brushed my suit and I looked quite presentable. Zeidler's three-room flat was on the third floor of a building with a crumbling stucco façade hidden by a dusty chestnut tree. Since almost half of Jülicher Straße was in ruins, one could hardly speak of buildings to either side or across the way. A huge mound to the left, shot through with rusty T-beams and sprouting greenery and buttercups, suggested the prior existence of a four-story building. To the right a partially destroyed property had been restored as far as the second floor. But the funds had apparently run out. The façade of polished black Swedish granite was badly cracked and had gaps here and there which were still in need of repair. The inscription *Schornemann's Funeral Parlor* lacked several letters, I don't recall which ones. Fortunately the two deeply carved palm branches decorating the still mirror-smooth granite remained intact, and helped lend the damaged shop a halfway pious air.

The coffin warehouse of this seventy-five-year-old firm was in the courtyard, and was often worth viewing from my room, which looked out to the back. I watched the workers roll a few coffins out of the shed in good weather and place them on wooden sawhorses, then use various polishing agents to brighten up the caskets, which tapered toward the foot in such familiar fashion.

Zeidler himself opened the door when I rang. Short, squat, breathless, and hedgehoggy, he stood in the doorway wearing thick glasses, the lower half of his face hidden beneath fluffy shaving lather, holding the brush to his cheek with his right hand, looked like an alcoholic and sounded like a Westphalian.

"If you don't like the room, just say so. I'm shaving and I've still got to wash my feet."

Zeidler didn't stand on ceremony. I looked at the room. I could hardly like it, since it consisted of a nonfunctioning bathroom half-tiled in turquoise green, with the rest uneasily wallpapered. Nevertheless I didn't say I didn't like it. Disregarding Zeidler's drying lather and unwashed feet, I rapped on the bathtub and asked if we couldn't just as well dispense with it, since it had no drainpipe in the first place.

Smiling, Zeidler shook his gray hedgehog head and tried in vain to whip up more lather with his brush. That was his reply, whereupon I declared myself willing to take the room and tub for forty marks a month.

When we stood once more in the dimly lit, tubular corridor, lined with several doors painted various colors, some partly glassed, I asked who else lived in Zeidler's flat.

"Wife and lodgers."

I tapped on the frosted-glass door in the middle of the corridor, which could be reached with a single step from the entrance to the flat.

"The nurse lives there. But that's no concern of yours. You'll never see her anyway. She only sleeps here, and sometimes not even that."

I won't say Oskar gave a start at the word "nurse." He nodded, didn't dare ask about the other rooms, knew about his own room with tub; it was on the right, behind the door at the end of the hall.

Zeidler tapped me on the lapel: "You can cook in your room if you've got an alcohol stove. And use the kitchen now and then for all I care, if the stove's not too high for you."

That was his first allusion to Oskar's stature. He took a cursory glance at my letter of recommendation from the Art Academy, which did its job, since it was signed by the director, Professor Reuser. I responded to all his do's and don'ts with yes and amen, noted to myself that the kitchen was on the left next to my room, and promised to have my laundry done elsewhere, since he was worried the steam might damage the bathroom wallpaper, a promise I could make with some assurance, for Maria had agreed to do my washing.

I should have left then, fetched my luggage, filled out the change-of-residence forms. But Oskar didn't do so. He couldn't bear to leave the flat. For no reason at all, he asked his future landlord where the toilet was. The latter gestured with his thumb toward a plywood door reminiscent of the war years and their aftermath. As Oskar prepared to make immediate use of the toilet, Zeidler, starting to itch from the lather now crumbling on his face, switched on the light in the little room.

Once within I was irked, for Oskar felt no need at all to go. I waited stubbornly, however, till I could pass a little water, trying hard not to wet the seat or tile floor in the cramped space, which was difficult, given my insufficient bladder pressure, and because the wooden seat was so near. My handkerchief dabbed traces from the worn-down wood; the soles of Oskar's shoes had to efface a few unfortunate drops on the tiles.

In spite of the unpleasantly hardened soap on his face, Zeidler had not sought a shaving mirror and hot water in my absence. He was waiting in the corridor, seemed to have taken a fancy to the joker he sensed in me. "You're really something. Haven't even signed the lease and already using the john!"

He approached me with a cold, crusty shaving brush, probably planning some silly joke, but then, without pestering me, opened the door leading out of the flat. While Oskar backed past the Hedgehog into the stairway, keeping an eye on him as he did so, I noticed that the door to the toilet was located between the kitchen door and the one with frosted glass, behind which, from time to time, on an irregular basis, a hospital nurse bedded down for the night.

When Oskar rang again at Zeidler's flat late that afternoon with his luggage, including the new tin drum given to him by Raskolnikov, painter of madonnas, and brandished his change-of-residence papers, a freshly shaved Hedgehog, who by now had no doubt washed his feet as well, ushered me into his living room.

It smelled of cold cigar smoke. Of cigars lighted several times. To which was added the effluvia of several possibly quite valuable carpets piled on top of one another and rolled up in the corners of the room. It also smelled of old calendars. I saw no calendars, however; the smell came from the carpets. Strangely enough, the comfortable leather-upholstered chairs had no smell at all. That disappointed me, for Oskar, who had never sat in a leather chair, nonetheless had so vivid a notion of the redolent leather on which one sat that he suspected the leather on Zeidler's armchairs and side chairs of being artificial.

In one of these smooth, odorless, and, it later turned out, genuine leather armchairs sat Frau Zeidler. She wore a gray, sportily tailored outfit that didn't quite fit her. She'd let her skirt scoot up over her knees and showed three fingers' worth of slip. Since she didn't adjust her dress and—it seemed to Oskar—had been crying, I didn't risk introducing myself and greeting her. My bow remained silent and was already turning in its final stages toward Zeidler, who introduced me to his wife by jerking his thumb toward her and briefly clearing his throat.

The room was large and square. The dark shadow of the chestnut tree in front of the building enlarged and diminished the space by turns. I left my suitcase and drum by the door and carried my registration papers over to Zeidler, who was standing between the windows. Oskar could not hear his own footsteps, for he was walking on four—I counted them later—superimposed carpets, each smaller than the one beneath, their fringed or fringeless borders of differing hues forming a multicolored staircase, the lowest step of which began near the wall in reddish brown and disappeared under the next, more or less green step, covered for the most part with furniture such as the heavy sideboard, the display cabinet filled with liqueur glasses, dozens of them, and the spacious marriage bed. Even the border of the third carpet, in a blue pattern, lay in full view from corner to corner. To the fourth carpet, a wine-red velour, fell the task of supporting the round pull-out table protected by oilcloth, and four leather-covered chairs with evenly spaced metal studs.

Since several more carpets that weren't tapestries hung on the walls or slouched in corners rolled up, Oskar assumed the Hedgehog had traded in rugs prior to the currency reform and was stuck with them afterward.

The only picture was a framed and glazed portrait of Prince Bismarck hanging between two small rugs of an Oriental cast on the window wall. The Hedgehog sat in a leather armchair, beneath the Chancellor, with whom he shared a certain family resemblance. As he took the change-of-residence form from my hand and studied both sides of the preprinted document carefully, critically, and impatiently, his wife's whispered query if anything was wrong threw him into a rage that made him look even more like the Iron Chancellor. The armchair spewed him forth. He stood on four carpets, held the form to one side, filled himself and his waistcoat with air, reached the first and second carpet with a single bound, and showered his wife, who had bent over her sewing again, with a sentence that ran somewhat as follows: Youshutyourmouthwhenyourenotaskedandkeepitclosedilldothetalkinghereandnobodyelsesee! Notanotherword!

Since Frau Zeidler restrained herself nicely, didn't say another word and stuck to her sewing, the problem the Hedgehog faced as he stood impotently kicking the carpets was how to allow his rage to reverberate and fade in a credible manner. He took one stride to the display case, rattled it open, reached in cautiously with outspread fingers, grasped eight liqueur glasses, withdrew his overloaded hands from the case, leaving all within intact, tiptoed — like a host planning to divert himself and seven guests with an exercise in dexterity — toward the green-tiled slow-combustion stove, and flung the fragile freight — casting all caution now to the wind — against the cold cast-iron door of the stove.

Amazingly enough, throughout this scene, which required a certain accuracy, the Hedgehog managed to keep his bespectacled eye on his wife, who had arisen and was trying to thread a needle by the right-hand window. An instant after he had shattered the glasses, she brought this delicate task, which required a steady hand, to a successful conclusion. Frau Zeidler returned to her still warm chair and sat down in such a way that her dress scooted up again, clearly revealing three fingers' breadth of her pink slip. Bent forward, with a critical yet submissive eye, the Hedgehog had followed his wife's trip to the window, the needle threading, and her return. She was scarcely seated again when he reached behind the stove, pulled out a dustpan and whiskbroom, swept up the shards, and shook the sweepings onto a newspaper that was already half-covered with shattered liqueur glasses and would be hardpressed to hold a third outburst of glass-breaking wrath.

If the reader now asserts that Oskar recognized in this glass-smashing Hedgehog a version of the Oskar who sangshattered glass over the years, I can't say you're entirely wrong; I too once loved to transform my rage into shards of glass — but no one ever saw me reach for a dustpan and brush.

Once Zeidler had cleared away the traces of his wrath he returned to his armchair. Once more Oskar handed him the registration form, which the Hedgehog had dropped when he reached into the display cabinet with both hands.

Zeidler signed the form and gave me to understand that he ran an orderly house, where would we be otherwise, after all, he'd been a salesman for fifteen years, sold hair clippers in fact, did I know what hair clippers were?

Oskar knew what hair clippers were, and made a few explanatory motions in the air from which Zeidler could infer that I was au courant with regard to hair clippers. His neatly clipped crew cut showed he represented his product well. After explaining his work schedule to me—one week on the road, two days at home—he lost all interest in Oskar, just rocked hedgehoggishly in the creaking light brown leather, glared through his glasses, and kept repeating apropos of nothing: jajajajajaja—it was time for me to go.

Oskar took his leave of Frau Zeidler first. She had a cold, boneless, but dry hand. The Hedgehog gestured from his chair, waving me toward the door, where Oskar's luggage stood. My hands were already full when his voice sounded: "What have you got there hanging on your suitcase?"

"My tin drum."

"You plan on drumming here?"

"Not necessarily. I used to play it a lot."

"That's fine with me. I'm never home anyway."

"It is unlikely I shall ever drum again."

"And why are you still so small, huh?"

"An unfortunate fall stunted my growth."

"Just don't give me any trouble with fits and all."

"The state of my health has improved steadily over the past few years. Just look how nimble I am." Then Oskar performed a few flips and semi-acrobatic exercises he'd learned back when he was with the Theater at the Front, reducing Frau Zeidler to giggles and leaving the Hedgehog still slapping his thighs as I entered the hall and carted my luggage and drum past the nurse's frosted door, the toilet, the kitchen, and into my room.

That was early May. From that day forward, I was tempted, possessed, overwhelmed by the mystery of the hospital nurse: nurses made me ill, perhaps incurably so, for even today, when all that is behind me,

I still contradict my keeper Bruno, who flatly maintains that only men can be proper nurses, the patient's addiction to female nurses being simply one more symptom of the disease; while the male nurse conscientiously cares for the patient and sometimes cures him, the female nurse follows the feminine path: she seduces the patient toward recovery or toward death, which she imbues with a tinge of eroticism that renders it palatable.

Thus says my keeper Bruno, whose view I am reluctant to support. Whoever needs to have his life reconfirmed by hospital nurses every other year or so, as I do, maintains his gratitude, and is not so quick to allow a grumpy if likable keeper filled with professional envy to alienate him from his Sisters.

It began with my fall down the cellar steps on the occasion of my third birthday. I think she was called Sister Lotte and came from Praust. Sister Inge was with me for several years at Dr. Hollatz's. After the defense of the Polish Post Office I fell into the hands of several nurses at once. I recall only one of them by name: Sister Erni or Berni. Nameless nurses in Lüneberg, at the university clinic in Hanover. Then the sisters of City Hospital in Düsseldorf, first and foremost Sister Gertrud. But then she came along, and I didn't even have to visit a hospital. While in perfect health, Oskar succumbed to a nurse who, like him, lived as a lodger in Zeidler's flat. From that day on my world was filled with nurses. When I left for work early each morning to carve inscriptions for Korneff, my tram stop was at St. Mary's Hospital. Nurses came and went outside the brick gateway and in the flower-laden forecourt of the hospital. Sisters with their strenuous work before or behind them. Then the tram arrived. I often found myself sitting in the same rear car with several of the exhausted or at least weary nurses with worn faces, or standing on the car's platform with them. At first I inhaled their scent reluctantly, then soon sought it out, stationing myself near or even among their uniforms.

Then Bittweg. I worked outside in good weather, carving letters among the gravestones on display, saw them passing by, arm in arm, two by two or four by four, on their break, chatting, forcing Oskar to look up from his diorite, to neglect his work, for every upward look cost me twenty pfennigs.

Movie posters: there had always been plenty of films in Germany about nurses. Maria Schell lured me into the movie houses. She wore a nurse's uniform, laughed, cried, nursed selflessly, smiling and still in her nurse's cap, played somber music, then in a fit of despair nearly tore her nightgown, renounced her love after her attempted suicide—Borsche played the doctor—stayed true to her profession, retained her cap and Red Cross pin. While the upper and lower levels of Oskar's brain laughed and wove a steady stream of smutty remarks into the film, Oskar's eyes wept tears, I wandered half-blind through a desert of anonymous good Samaritans in white, seeking Sister Dorothea, of whom I knew only this: she had rented the room behind a frosted-glass door at Zeidler's.

Sometimes I heard her steps when she returned from the night shift. Heard her around nine in the evening too, when her day shift was over and she went to her room. Oskar didn't always remain seated in his chair when he heard the nurse in the hall. Often he would play with the door handle. For who could resist? Who doesn't look up when something passes by that might be passing by for him? Who can stay seated when every neighboring sound seems to serve the sole purpose of sending a calmly seated person springing to his feet?

Still worse is the silence. We know this from the ship's figurehead, who after all was wooden, silent, and passive. There lay the first museum guard in his blood. They said: Niobe killed him. The director looked for a new guard, since the museum could not be closed. When the second guard was dead, they cried: Niobe killed him. The museum director had difficulty finding a third guard—or was it the eleventh he sought by now?—it hardly matters. One day this long-sought guard lay dead as well. Niobe, they cried, Niobe of the green paint, Niobe gazing from amber eyes. Niobe, wooden, nude, who neither flinches, freezes, sweats, nor breathes, untouched even by woodworms since she'd been sprayed against them, her historical value retained. A witch was burned because of her, the man who carved her lost his gifted hand to the ax, ships sank, but she floated on. Niobe, wooden and fireproof, killed others yet did not lose her value. She silenced with her silence the head of his class, students, an elderly priest, a whole chorus of museum guards. My friend Herbert Truczinski mounted her and sprang a fatal leak; yet Niobe stayed dry and her silence deepened.

When, in the early morning around six, the nurse left her room, the hall, and the Hedgehog's flat, things grew very still, though she made no noise when she was there. Unable to stand the silence, Oskar had to make his bed creak a time or two, move a chair, or roll an apple against the bathtub. Around eight there was a rustling. This was the mailman, dropping letters and postcards through the slot onto the hall floor. Aside from Oskar, Frau Zeidler too listened for this sound. Her job as a secretary at Mannesmann didn't start until nine, so she let me go first, and it was Oskar who reacted to the rustling. I moved quietly, though I knew she could hear me, left my door open so I wouldn't have to turn on the light, scooped up all the mail, checked for the weekly letter Maria sent me reporting in detail on herself, the child, and her sister Guste, stuck it in my pajama pocket if it had come, then quickly looked through the rest of the mail. Everything addressed to the Zeidlers or a certain Herr Münzer, who lived at the other end of the hall, I let slide back onto the floor, since I was crouching rather than standing; as for the nurse's mail, Oskar turned it about, smelled it, felt it, and, last but not least, checked the return address.

Sister Dorothea seldom received any mail, though she got more than I did. Her full name was Dorothea Köngetter, but I just called her Sister Dorothea, and occasionally forgot her last name, which was superfluous anyway, since she was a nurse. She got mail from her mother in Hildesheim. Letters and postcards arrived from hospitals scattered throughout West Germany. These were from nurses she'd gone through training with. Now she was struggling, somewhat haltingly, to keep up with them by postcard, and was receiving these replies, which, as Oskar hastily noted, seemed rather silly and trite.

I did learn a few things about Sister Dorothea from these postcards, however, most of which showed pictures of hospitals covered with ivy: she had spent some time at St. Vincent's Hospital in Cologne, at a private clinic in Aachen, and had worked in Hildesheim too. That's where her mother was writing from. So she either came from Lower Saxony or was a refugee from the East like Oskar, and had settled there after the war. I also learned that Sister Dorothea was working nearby, at St. Mary's Hospital, and was evidently close friends with a certain Sister Beate, for several postcards referred to this friendship, and bore greetings for Beate.

She disconcerted me, this girlfriend. Her existence gave Oskar all sorts of ideas. I composed letters to Beate, requested her intercession in one, then suppressed all mention of Dorothea in the next, planning to approach Beate first and then switch to her friend later on. I drafted five or six letters, even stuck one or two in envelopes, was on my way to the mailbox, and yet sent none.

But perhaps, in my madness, I might still have sent such a missive to Sister Beate one day, had I not, on a certain Monday — Maria had just begun her affair with her boss, Stenzel, which, strangely enough, left me completely cold — found that letter in the hall which transformed my passion, lacking nothing in love, into jealousy.

The preprinted return address told me that a certain Dr. Erich Werner — St. Mary's Hospital — had written a letter to Sister Dorothea. On Tuesday a second letter arrived. Thursday brought a third. What was that Thursday like? Oskar returned to his room, fell onto one of the kitchen chairs that served as furniture, pulled Maria's weekly letter from his pajama pocket — in spite of her new lover Maria continued to write punctually, neatly, and clearly, omitting nothing — even opened the envelope, read without reading, heard Frau Zeidler in the hall, then her voice calling for Herr Münzer, who failed to answer, though he must have been home, for she opened his door, handed the mail to him, and kept right on talking.

Though she continued to talk, I no longer heard Frau Zeidler's voice. I surrendered myself to the wallpaper's madness, its vertical, horizontal, diagonal madness, its curving, thousandfold madness, saw myself as Matzerath, shared with him the suspiciously wholesome daily bread of the betrayed, costumed with ease my own Jan Bronski as a cheaply and poorly drawn seducer in satanic makeup, appearing first in the traditional overcoat with velvet collar, then in the hospital smock of Dr. Hollatz, quickly followed by that of the surgeon, Dr. Werner, all to seduce, to corrupt, to ravish, to desecrate, to whip, to torture — to do everything a seducer must do to retain his credibility.

Today I can smile when I recall the thought that then turned Oskar as yellow and mad as the wallpaper: I decided to study medicine and graduate as quickly as possible. I would become a doctor, at St. Mary's Hospital of course. I would drive Dr. Werner out, expose him, reveal his incompetence, even accuse him of manslaughter for botching a larynx operation. It would transpire that Herr Werner never went to medical school. He'd served in a field hospital during the war and picked up a thing or two: away with the charlatan! And Oskar becomes head surgeon, so young and yet such a responsible position. A new Sauerbruch strides through echoing corridors with Sister Dorothea, his surgical assistant, at his side, surrounded by a retinue clad in white, visiting patients, making a last-minute decision to operate. How fortunate that film was never made.

In the Wardrobe

NOW, NO ONE SHOULD believe that Oskar thought only about nurses. After all, I had my professional life. Summer semester had begun at the Art Academy and I had to give up the part-time work I'd had chiseling letters over the holidays, for now Oskar sat still for good wages, challenging old styles to prove themselves, while new styles tested themselves on me and Ulla the Muse; the latter destroyed our substance, denied us, negated us, covering canvas and sketchpads with lines, squares, and spirals, stuff learned by heart, fit at best for wallpaper, and endowed those commercial patterns, which contained everything but Oskar and Ulla and thus lacked all mystery and tension, with pretentious titles that reeked of the marketplace: *Woven Upward. Song above Time. Red in New Spaces.*

This latter style was favored mostly by new students who still couldn't draw very well. My old friends working with Professors Kuchen and Maruhn, top-flight students like the Goat and Raskolnikov, were too rich in charcoal and color to sing a song in praise of poverty with pale curlicues and anemic lines.

But Ulla the Muse, who, when she descended to earth, revealed a distinct taste for arts and crafts, warmed to the new wallpaper designs so thoroughly that she quickly forgot Lankes, the painter who had abandoned her, and turned to the decorative patterns in various sizes of a somewhat older artist named Meitel, which she found pretty, cheerful, funny, fantastic, awesome, and even chic. That she was soon engaged to the artist, who had a special fondness for forms suggesting sugary-sweet Easter eggs, meant little; she was constantly getting engaged, and at this very moment—as she told me the other day when she came by with sweets for Bruno and me — she's about to enter into what she always refers to as a serious relationship.

When the semester began, Ulla wished to limit the vision she offered as Muse solely to those heading in this new direction, which she failed to see was such a sadly blind alley. Meitel, her Easter-egg painter, had put that flea in her ear and as an engagement present had provided her with a vocabulary she tried out on me in our conversations about art. She spoke of relationships, of constellations, accents, perspectives, irrigative structures, processes of fusion, phenomena of erosion. She, whose daily fare consisted solely of bananas and tomato juice, now spoke of proto-cells, of color atoms, which not only reached their natural positions through dynamic flat trajectories within their force fields, but could even be said to . . . That's more or less what Ulla came out with during our breaks, or now and then over a cup of coffee on Ratinger Straße. Even when her engagement to the dynamic Easter-egg painter was a thing of the past and, after the briefest of episodes with a lesbian, she'd taken up with one of Kuchen's students and been drawn back into the world of solid objects, she still retained this vocabulary, which put such a strain on her little face that two sharp and somewhat fanatical creases formed on either side of her mouth.

Here I must admit that it was not solely Raskolnikov's idea to paint Ulla as a nurse beside Oskar. After *Madonna 49* he portrayed us as *The Rape of Europa* — I was the bull. And immediately following the somewhat controversial *Rape* came *The Fool Heals the Nurse.*

It was a little suggestion on my part that inflamed Raskolnikov's imagination. Brooding darkly and furtively in his redheaded way, cleaning his brushes, staring fixedly at Ulla, he began speaking of guilt and atonement, so I suggested he picture me as Guilt, Ulla as Atonement; my guilt was obvious and Atonement could be dressed as a nurse.

That this fine painting was subsequently given a different and quite misleading title was Raskolnikov's doing. I would have called it *Temptation,* because my painted right hand was holding a latch, pressing it down, and opening the door to a room in which the nurse was standing. Or it might simply have been called *The Latch,* for if I had to give a new name to temptation I'd recommend latch, since that handy protuberance cries out to be seized, and since the latch on the frosted-glass door to Sister Dorothea's room tempted me whenever I knew that Zeidler the

Hedgehog was away for the day on business, that the nurse was at the hospital and Frau Zeidler in the office at Mannesmann.

Oskar would leave his room with the drainless tub, step into the corridor of Zeidler's flat, station himself outside the nurse's room, and try the latch.

Until around the middle of June, and I tried it almost every day, the door had not yielded. I had almost concluded that the nurse had been so schooled in orderliness by the responsibilities of her profession that it would be advisable to abandon all hope of a door left open by accident. Thus the mindless mechanical reaction that caused me to close it again immediately on the day I found it unlocked.

For what was surely several minutes, Oskar stood there, almost bursting at the seams, assailed by so many thoughts of the most varied origins simultaneously that his heart was hard-pressed to suggest even the hint of a plan.

It was only after I'd managed to graft other relationships to myself and my thoughts—Maria and her lover, I thought, Maria has a lover, the lover gives Maria a coffeepot, Maria and her lover go to the Apollo on Saturday night, Maria cozies up to her lover after hours, at work she calls him sir, he owns the business—not till I considered Maria and her lover from various angles did I manage to bring my poor brain into some sort of order—and I opened the frosted-glass door.

I had already pictured the room as windowless, for the dimly translucent upper section of the door had never betrayed a strip of daylight. Reaching to the right, just as in my room, I found the light switch. The forty-watt bulb was perfectly adequate for a chamber of this size, which was much too narrow to be called a room. I was annoyed to find myself immediately confronted by my upper half in a mirror. However, Oskar did not turn aside from this reversed image, though it told him so little; for the objects on the equally wide washstand before the mirror attracted him strongly, raised Oskar on tiptoe.

The white enamel of the washbowl showed chipped spots of bluish black. The marble washstand top in which the bowl was sunk up to its overlapping rim revealed some damage as well. The missing left corner of the marble top lay before the mirror, showing the mirror its veins. Traces of flaking glue on its broken edge testified to an awkward attempt at repair. My stonecutter's fingers itched. I thought of Korneff's homemade marble cement, which transformed even the most fragile Lahn marble into those durable tiles affixed to the façades of large butcher shops.

Now, after these familiar thoughts of limestone allowed me to forget my badly distorted image in that nasty mirror, I succeeded in naming the smell that had struck Oskar immediately upon entering the room.

It was vinegar. Later, till just a few weeks ago in fact, I justified the acrid odor by assuming that the nurse must have washed her hair the day before and added vinegar to the water before rinsing. True, there were no vinegar bottles on the washstand. Nor could I detect any vinegar in containers with other labels; nor, I kept telling myself, would Sister Dorothea heat water in Zeidler's kitchen, which would require advance permission on his part, and go to all the bother of washing her hair in her own room, when she had the most modern facilities at St. Mary's Hospital. Of course a general prohibition may have been issued by the head nurse or the hospital administration forbidding the nurses to use certain sanitary arrangements in the hospital, so that Sister Dorothea had no choice but to wash her hair in the enamel washbowl before that distorted mirror. Even if there was no vinegar bottle on the washstand, there were plenty of little jars and tins on the clammy marble. A package of cotton wool and a half-empty box of sanitary napkins discouraged Oskar from further investigation of the little jars and their contents. But I still believe today they contained only cosmetics, or at most harmless salves.

The nurse had stuck her comb in her hairbrush. It cost me some effort to draw it forth from the bristles and take a look. It's a good thing I did, for in that moment Oskar made his most important discovery: the nurse had blond hair, perhaps ash blond; but one should be cautious in drawing conclusions from dead hair on a comb, so let's just leave it at that: Sister Dorothea had blond hair.

In addition the comb's suspiciously abundant content implied that the nurse suffered from hair loss. I immediately placed the blame for this embarrassing condition, certainly distressing to any woman, on her nurse's caps, but did not indict them; you can't do without caps in a well-run hospital.

As unpleasant as Oskar found the smell of vinegar, the fact that Sister Dorothea was losing hair aroused only anxious love in me, refined by sympathy. Indicative of my state and feelings, several products said to promote hair growth came to mind, ones I intended to give Sister Dorothea at some opportune moment. Already dreaming of this meeting — Oskar imagined it beneath a warm, windless summer sky, amid fields of waving grain — I stripped the leftover hair from the comb, bunched and tied it in a knot, blew off a little dust and dandruff from the bundle, and shoved it quickly into my wallet.

I'd placed the comb on the marble top to deal with my wallet, but once trophy and wallet were safe in my jacket, I picked up the comb again. I held it up to the naked light bulb so I could see through it, checked the two distinct rows of teeth, noted two teeth missing from the finer set, insisted on running the nail of my left index finger with a whir along the tips of the coarser ones, and delighted Oskar during the whole of this playful episode by bringing to light a few smaller hairs that I had deliberately neglected to remove so as not to arouse suspicion.

The comb sank back into the hairbrush once and for all. I turned away from the washstand, which was giving me far too one-sided a picture. On the way to the nurse's bed, I bumped against a kitchen chair to which a bra clung.

Oskar had nothing but his fists with which to fill the concavities of those cups, which were faded from repeated washing and discolored at the rims, but his fists failed to fill them, fidgeted about instead, alien and unhappy, too hard, too nervous in those bowls from which I would gladly have spooned a daily sustenance, even with the nausea it now and then would bring, for too much of any brew will make you retch at times, then turn sweet again, too sweet, so sweet it makes one relish retching, and puts true love to the test.

I thought of Dr. Werner and removed my fists from the bra. Dr. Werner faded at once and I was able to approach Sister Dorothea's bed. The nurse's bed. How often Oskar had pictured it, and now it was the same ugly bedstead, painted brown, that framed my own repose and intermittent insomnia. I would have wished for her a white-enameled metal bed with knobs of brass, the lightest, most delicate of railings, not this cumbersome, loveless fixture. Motionless, with heavy head, devoid of all passion, incapable even of jealousy, I stood for some time before an altar to sleep whose eiderdown might well have been of granite, then turned away, shunned that disconcerting sight. Never would Oskar have imagined Sister Dorothea and her slumbers in such an odious tomb.

As I was on my way back to the washstand, perhaps intending to open at last those jars that might hold salves, the wardrobe commanded me to note its dimensions, to call its paint black-brown, to trace the contours of its cornice, and, finally, to open it: for every wardrobe insists on being opened.

I turned the nail that held the doors closed to a vertical position: immediately and without any effort on my part the wooden panels swung open with a sigh and offered such a vista that I had to step back a few feet to regard it coolly above my crossed arms. Oskar had no desire to lose himself in detail as he had at the washstand, nor to pass a judgment burdened by prejudice, as he had with the bed; he wanted to approach the wardrobe with total freshness, as on the first day of Creation, for the wardrobe was welcoming him too with open arms.

Nevertheless, Oskar, the incorrigible aesthete, could not totally forgo criticism: some barbarian had hurriedly sawed off the feet of the wardrobe, leaving splinters behind, and set it flat and disfigured on the floor.

The internal arrangement of the wardrobe was flawless. To the right, three deep compartments held lingerie and blouses. White and pink alternated with a light blue that was surely colorfast. Two red-and-green-checkered oilcloth pouches tied together hung by the linen compartments on the inside of the right-hand door of the wardrobe, the upper pouch holding the mended stockings, the lower one those with runs in them. Compared with the stockings Maria received, and wore, from her boss and lover, those in the oilcloth pouches seemed just as fine, but of a tighter and more durable weave. In the spacious area of the wardrobe to the left, dully gleaming starched nurse's uniforms dangled on clothes hangers. On the hat shelf above them perched a row of simple, pretty nurse's caps, fragile, shunning the touch of an inexpert hand. I cast only a cursory glance at the civilian clothes placed to the left of the linen compartments. The cheap, haphazard selection confirmed my secret hope: Sister Dorothea devoted only limited attention to this portion of her clothing. And the three or four pot-shaped items of head gear on the shelf by the caps, carelessly and loosely stacked atop one another, crushing their comical imitation flowers, gave the overall impression of a fallen cake. The hat shelf also held a scant dozen books with colored spines leaning against a shoebox filled with scraps of wool yarn.

Oskar tilted his head, had to step closer to read the titles. Smiling indulgently, I returned my head to the vertical position: our good Sister Dorothea read crime novels. But enough about the civilian sector of the wardrobe. Lured closer by the books, I maintained my favorable position and even leaned forward into the interior, no longer resisting the increasingly strong desire to take my place within, to join the contents of that wardrobe to which Sister Dorothea entrusted no small part of her outward appearance.

I didn't even have to move the sensible, low-heeled shoes that stood on the plank floor of the wardrobe, carefully polished and ready to go. The arrangement of the wardrobe, which seemed almost intentionally inviting, was such that Oskar had room, crouching on his heels and drawing up his knees, to take shelter in the middle, without crushing a single garment. And so, filled with anticipation, I climbed in.

Nonetheless my mind was not immediately at rest. Oskar felt he was being watched by the furniture and the light bulb. To make my stay inside cozier, I tried to pull the doors to the wardrobe shut. This proved difficult, for the hinges on the doors were worn and left a gap at the top: light entered, but not enough to disturb me. The smell, on the other hand, intensified. It smelled old and clean, no longer like vinegar, but unobtrusively of mothballs; it smelled good.

What did Oskar do while he sat in the wardrobe? He leaned his forehead against Sister Dorothea's nearest uniform, a sleeved smock that fastened about the neck, and the door to every room of hospital life opened at once before him — then my right hand, perhaps seeking support to lean back on, reached behind me, through the civilian clothes, groped its way, found no hold, grasped something, something smooth and flexible, then found at last — still gripping the smoothness — a supporting slat, and felt along a crossbar that was nailed horizontally and offered support both to me and to the back of the wardrobe; Oskar's hand returned to his side, he could now rest content, and I looked at what I'd found behind me.

I saw a black patent-leather belt, but I saw more than a belt, since in the wardrobe it was so dark that a belt could easily be something else, something equally smooth and long, something I stared at as a stalwart three-year-old drummer on the harbor jetty at Neufahrwasser: my poor mama in her navy blue spring coat with the raspberry-colored lapels,

Matzerath in his overcoat, Jan Bronski with his velvet collar, Oskar's sailor's cap with its ribbon with *SMS Seydlitz* embroidered in gold, were all there, and overcoat and velvet collar jumped from stone to stone ahead of me and Mama, who because of her high heels couldn't jump, headed toward that sea marker with the man fishing at its foot with his clothesline, and a potato sack filled with salt and movement. Seeing the sack and the line, we asked the man sitting at the foot of the sea marker why he was fishing with a clothesline, but the fellow from Neufahrwasser or Brösen, wherever he was from, just laughed and spat a thick brown gob into the water, where it rocked back and forth by the jetty and didn't stir from the spot till a seagull carried it off; for a seagull will carry off anything, it's no squeamish dove, and certainly no nurse — tossing everything white into one basket, or into one wardrobe, is far too simple, and the same goes for black, for I did not yet fear the Black Cook back then, sat fearless in the wardrobe, then outside it too, stood fearless on the windless jetty at Neufahrwasser, held something else black and slippery, but not a belt, sat in the wardrobe, cast about for comparisons, for wardrobes force comparisons, tried the Black Cook by name, but she didn't make my skin crawl yet, white was what I thought about, could scarcely keep a gull and Sister Dorothea apart in my mind, but at last I shoved doves and all similar nonsense aside, for it was not Pentecost but Good Friday when we rode out to Brösen and walked to the jetty — and there were no doves circling the sea marker where the fellow from Neufahrwasser sat with his clothesline, sat and also spat. And when the fellow from Brösen hauled in the line, hauling until the line came to an end, and showed what made it so hard to pull from the brackish waters of the Mottlau, my poor mama laid her hand on Jan Bronski's shoulder and velvet collar, because her face had turned the color of cheese, because she wanted to leave and yet had to watch as the man slung the horse's head down on the stones, as the smaller, sea-green eels dropped from the matted mane, as he struggled to draw the larger, darker ones from the cadaver, as if they were screws he had to remove, and someone tore open a featherbed, which is to say that seagulls came and fell upon them, for three or more seagulls can easily handle a small eel, while the larger ones give them a harder time. But then the man pried open the horse's jaws, forced a stick between them, which made the horse laugh, and reached in with his hairy arm, groped for something, felt for something, just as I groped for something, felt for something in the wardrobe, so too did he, and pulled them forth, as I did the belt, but in his case two at once, and slung them in the air, slapped them on the stones, so that breakfast sprang from my poor mama's mouth, coffee and milk, egg white and yolk, a little jam and clumps of white bread, so copiously that the gulls angled down at once, descended one story, fell to with spread wings, I need hardly mention their screams, nor their well-known evil eyes, and could not be driven off, certainly not by Jan, who was afraid of the gulls and covered both his blue eyes, by now like saucers, nor did they listen to my drum but kept on gorging instead, while I, enraged and inspired, beat out a few new rhythms on tin, all of which meant nothing to Mama, totally occupied as she was with gagging and gagging, though no more came forth, she'd not eaten that much, wanted to stay slim, exercised twice a week at the Women's Association, though it did little good since she snacked in secret and always figured some way out, as did the fellow from Neufahrwasser who, casting all theory aside, when everyone was thinking, that's it, there's nothing more, finished by pulling an eel out through the nag's ear. Covered with white gruel it was, since it had been rummaging about in the horse's brain. He swung it about till the gruel flew off, till the eel showed its sheen and gleamed like a patent-leather belt, for what I'm trying to get at is this: Sister Dorothea wore a belt like that when she went out on her own, without the Red Cross pin.

But we headed home, though Matzerath wanted to stay longer because an eighteen-hundred-ton Finn was coming in and making waves. The man left the horse's head on the jetty. Soon after, the black horse was white and screaming. Not screaming as horses scream, but as a cloud screams that's white and loud and voracious, hiding a horse's head. Which was pleasant enough back then, for that meant we no longer saw the nag, even if we could imagine what lay behind the frenzy. The Finn diverted us too, now loaded with lumber and rusty as the graveyard gate at Saspe. My poor mama, however, did not turn to look at the Finn or the gulls. She had had enough. Although she once both played and sang "Fly, Little Seagull, Away toward Helgoland" on our piano, she no longer sang that little song, no longer sang anything, at first refused to eat fish as well, but one fine day she started in and ate so much fish, such oily fish, that in the end she could eat no more, wanted no more, had

had enough, was sick not just of eels but also of life, and of men in particular, of Oskar too perhaps, at any rate, she, who never denied herself anything, suddenly turned frugal and abstemious and had herself buried in Brentau. I've probably inherited that from her, since I deny myself nothing and hardly need anything; the only thing I can't live without, regardless of the price, is smoked eel. I felt the same way about Sister Dorothea, whom I had never seen, whose patent-leather belt I found only moderately appealing—and yet I couldn't tear myself away from that belt, it was endless, it even multiplied, so that I unbuttoned my trousers with my free hand in order to picture once more the nurse whose image had been blurred by all those shiny eels and the Finn putting into port.

Oskar, repeatedly banished to the harbor jetty, gradually managed, with the help of the seagulls, to find his way back to the world of Sister Dorothea, at least to that half of the wardrobe that sheltered her empty but still alluring uniforms. As I finally felt that I saw her clearly again and recognized details of her features, the bolts slipped from the worn-out grooves: the wardrobe doors fell apart with a discordant groan, bright, annoying light flooded in, and Oskar had to take care not to soil Sister Dorothea's sleeved smock hanging next to him.

If only to provide a necessary transition and offer a playful denouement to my stay in the wardrobe, which had been more strenuous than I'd expected, I drummed a few random measures—something I hadn't done for years—more or less skillfully against the dry rear wall, then left the wardrobe, and checked again to be sure it was neat and clean—I couldn't really fault myself—even the belt had retained its sheen; no, a few dull spots had to be breathed on and rubbed until the belt became once more an object reminiscent of those eels caught on the harbor jetty at Neufahrwasser when I was a little boy.

I, Oskar, left Sister Dorothea's chamber, cutting off the current to the forty-watt light bulb that had watched me throughout my visit.

Klepp

THERE I STOOD in the corridor, with a wad of pale blond hair in my wallet, trying for a second to feel the wad through the leather, through the lining of my jacket, vest, shirt, and undershirt. But I was too weary, and in that strangely morose way, too satisfied, to see anything more in the trophy I had stolen from her chamber than loose hair of the sort picked up by combs.

Only then did Oskar admit to himself that he'd sought quite different treasures. What I'd wanted to prove during my stay in Sister Dorothea's chamber was that this Dr. Werner must surely be in evidence there, if only through one of the envelopes I knew about. I found nothing. No envelope, let alone a page from a letter. Oskar admits that he pulled the crime novels down one by one from the hat compartment, opened them, looked for dedications and bookmarks, and also for a photo, for Oskar knew most of the doctors at St. Mary's Hospital by sight, though not by name—but there was no picture of Dr. Werner.

He seemed unfamiliar with Sister Dorothea's room, and if he'd ever seen it, he hadn't managed to leave any traces. So Oskar had every reason to be pleased. Wasn't I way ahead of Dr. Werner in that regard? And didn't the lack of any trace of the doctor prove that the relationship between doctor and nurse was confined to the hospital and thus purely professional, or if not professional, then at least unilateral in nature?

But Oskar's jealousy clamored for a motive. Though the slightest vestige of Dr. Werner would have been a blow to me, it would have provided an equally strong satisfaction with which the minor, short-lived outcome of my sojourn in the wardrobe could hardly compare.

I no longer recall how I made it back to my room, but I do remember hearing a forced cough meant to attract my attention coming from behind the door at the other end of the hall, where a certain Herr Münzer lived. What was this Herr Münzer to me? Didn't I have my hands full with the Hedgehog's female lodger? Why add Münzer to my burdens — who knew what the name might conceal? So Oskar ignored the cough's demand, or, more accurately: I didn't understand its import, didn't realize till I was in my room that this Herr Münzer, whom I neither knew nor cared about, had tried to lure me, Oskar, to his room by coughing.

Granted: for a long time I regretted not having reacted to the cough, for my room seemed so terribly cramped and yet so vast that a conversation with the coughing Herr Münzer, no matter how tedious and forced, would have come as a relief. But unable to summon up courage, belatedly, to establish contact with the gentleman at the other end of the hallway, perhaps by producing a cough of my own in the hall, I surrendered passively to the unyielding rectangle of the kitchen chair in my room, grew restless, as always when I sit on chairs, picked up a medical reference book from my bed, dropped the expensive tome, purchased with my hard-earned modeling money, leaving it crumpled and creased, picked up Raskolnikov's gift, my tin drum, from the table, held it, but could not ply the tin with my sticks, nor could Oskar find the tears that might have fallen on the round white lacquer and granted a relief without rhythm.

Here one might begin a tract on lost innocence, comparing the drumming, eternally three-year-old Oskar to the humpbacked, voiceless, tearless, and drumless Oskar. But that would not accord with the facts: Oskar lost his innocence on several occasions while still drumming, recovered it or let it grow back; for innocence flourishes like a weed — just think of all those innocent grandmothers who were all once wicked, spiteful infants — no, it wasn't the little game of innocence and innocence lost that made Oskar jump up from his kitchen chair; it was love for Sister Dorothea that commanded me to replace the drum undrummed, made me leave the room, corridor, and Zeidler's flat to head for the Art Academy, though Professor Kuchen was not expecting me till later that afternoon.

When Oskar impetuously fled his room, stepped into the hall, and opened the outer door to the flat noisily and with a good deal of fuss, I listened for a moment in the direction of Herr Münzer's room. He didn't cough, and so, ashamed, offended, content and craving, tired of life and hungering for it, smiling here and there, in other places nearly in tears, I left the flat and then the house on Jülicher Straße.

A few days later I carried out a long-cherished plan, the continued rejection of which had proved an excellent method for planning it in detail. That day I had the whole morning free. Oskar and Ulla weren't due to pose for the imaginative Raskolnikov till three that afternoon, when, as the returning Ulysses, I was to surprise Penelope with the gift of a hump. I'd sought in vain to dissuade the artist from this notion. In those days he was successfully exploiting Greek gods and demigods. Ulla felt at home in the world of mythology, and so I gave in, let myself be portrayed as Vulcan, as Pluto with Proserpina, and, in the end, that afternoon, as a hunchbacked Ulysses. But it's the morning I want to describe. So Oskar won't reveal what Ulla looked like as Penelope and simply say: silence reigned in Zeidler's flat. The Hedgehog had taken his hair clippers on a business trip, Sister Dorothea was on the day shift, having left the house at six, and Frau Zeidler was still in bed when, shortly after eight, the mail arrived.

I went through it at once, found nothing for me — Maria's letter had come just two days before — but discovered at first glance an envelope posted from the city that bore the unmistakable handwriting of Dr. Werner.

First I put the letter back with the others for Herr Münzer and the Zeidlers, went to my room, and waited until Frau Zeidler entered the hall, gave her lodger Herr Münzer his letter, returned to her kitchen, then her bedroom, and in less than ten minutes left the flat and the house, for her office job at Mannesmann started at nine.

Oskar waited just to be sure, donned his clothes with unhurried deliberation, cleaned his fingernails with apparent calm, and only then resolved to act. I went to the kitchen, set an aluminum kettle half-filled with water on the largest burner of the three-burner gas stove, set the flame on high to begin with, turned the dial to the lowest setting as soon as it started to steam, then, carefully collecting my thoughts and focusing them as closely as possible on the action at hand, reached Sister Dorothea's door in two strides, took the letter that Frau Zeidler had shoved halfway under the frosted-glass door, went back to the kitchen, and cautiously held the back of the envelope over the rising steam till it could be opened without damage. Naturally Oskar had turned off the gas before venturing to hold Dr. Werner's letter over the kettle.

I didn't read the doctor's tidings in the kitchen, but lying on my bed. At first I was disappointed, for neither the salutation nor the standard formula that closed the letter shed any light on the doctor/nurse relationship.

"Dear Fräulein Dorothea!" it said—and: "Sincerely yours, Erich Werner."

Nor did I find a single truly tender word in the letter. Werner was sorry he hadn't spoken to Sister Dorothea the day before, though he had seen her outside the door to the men's ward for the privately insured. For reasons that remained unclear to Dr. Werner, she had turned away when she had come upon the doctor conversing with Sister Beate — Sister Dorothea's friend. Dr. Werner simply sought some explanation, since his conversation with Sister Beate had been of a purely professional nature. As Sister Dorothea no doubt knew, he had always taken pains, both in the past and at present, to maintain a proper distance from the somewhat impetuous Beate. This was no easy matter, as she, Dorothea, knowing Beate, must surely realize, for Sister Beate often declared her feelings quite openly, feelings that he, Dr. Werner, had certainly never reciprocated. The last sentence of the letter ran: "Please believe that I would be happy to speak with you at any time about this matter." In spite of the formality, coldness, and even arrogance of these lines, I did not find it difficult, in the end, to see through Dr. Werner's epistolary style and recognize the missive for what it was: a passionate love letter.

Mechanically I restored the letter to its envelope, and with no thought at all for hygiene, moistened the flap, which Werner may well have wet with his tongue, with Oskar's tongue in turn, then burst out laughing, and slapped my head front and back, still laughing, till I finally managed, in mid-slap, to divert my right hand from my brow to the latch on the door to my room, to open the door, to step into the hall, and carefully push the letter from the good Dr. Werner halfway under the door that sealed off the well-known room of Sister Dorothea with gray paint and frosted glass.

I was still squatting on my heels, with one or possibly two fingers on the letter, when I heard Herr Münzer's voice from the other end of the corridor. He spoke slowly and clearly, as though giving dictation, and I understood every word: "My dear sir, would you be so kind as to bring me some water?"

I straightened up, said to myself, The man must be sick, but knew as I did so that the man behind the door wasn't sick, that Oskar was simply saying this to himself as an excuse to bring him water, since a simple, unmotivated call could never have lured me to the room of a total stranger.

At first I was going to bring him the lukewarm water in the aluminum kettle that had helped me open the doctor's letter. But then I poured that water into the sink, ran fresh water into the kettle, and carried kettle and water to the door behind which must dwell the voice of Herr Münzer that had cried out for me and for water, or perhaps for water alone.

Oskar knocked, entered, and ran point-blank into Klepp's characteristic odor. If I call his effluvium acrid, I omit its equally strong sweetness. The air surrounding Klepp had nothing in common with the vinegary air of the nurse's chamber, for example. To call it sweet and sour would be equally false. This Herr Münzer, or Klepp as I call him today, this corpulent, lazy yet not immobile, readily perspiring, superstitious, unwashed yet not derelict flautist and jazz clarinetist, had and still has, though something was always preventing him from dying, the smell of a corpse about him, a corpse that can't stop smoking, sucking on peppermints, and exuding a haze of garlic. So smelled he then, and so he smells and breathes today, descending upon me on Visitors Day, bearing both lust for life and transience in his scent, forcing Bruno to throw open the windows and doors to air things out the moment his elaborate farewells, filled with promises to return, have ended.

Today Oskar is bedridden. Back then, in Zeidler's flat, I found Klepp in the remnants of a bed. He was cheerfully rotting away, remaining within reach of an old-fashioned, extremely baroque-looking alcohol stove, a good dozen packages of spaghetti, cans of olive oil, tubes of tomato paste, moist clumps of salt on newspaper, and a case of bottled beer that turned out to be lukewarm. He would urinate into the empty beer bottles while lying down, and, as he told me in confidence an hour or so later, seal the greenish containers, which held just about as much as he did and were for the most part full, and set them aside, clearly separated from those that were still literally beer bottles, to prevent any chance that while tending his bed he would get thirsty and grab the wrong one. Although the room had running water—with a little initiative he could have urinated in the sink—he was too lazy, or, more accurately, too hindered from getting up because of the way he lived, to leave the bed he had shaped to his body with such effort and fetch fresh water in his spaghetti pot.

Since Klepp as Herr Münzer was always careful to cook his pasta in the same water, and guarded the multiply drained-off and increasingly viscous brew like the apple of his eye, he often managed, with the help of his store of empty beer bottles, to maintain the horizontal position suited to his bed for upward of four days at a time. The critical stage came when the spaghetti brew had boiled down to an oversalted, glutinous sludge. Of course at that point Klepp could have gone hungry; but in those days he lacked the necessary ideological presuppositions for such an act, and his asceticism seemed limited from the very start to periods of four to five days, for otherwise a larger spaghetti pot and a water container of sufficient size to match his store of pasta, or Frau Zeidler, who brought him his mail, might have made him still more independent of his surroundings.

On the day Oskar violated the privacy of the mail, Klepp had been lying independently in bed for five days: he could have pasted posters on pillars with his spaghetti sludge. Then he heard my irresolute steps in the corridor toward Sister Dorothea and her letters. Having learned that Oskar does not react to forced coughs meant to attract attention, on the day I read Dr. Werner's coolly passionate letter he tried his voice: "My dear sir, would you be so kind as to bring me some water?"

And I took the kettle, poured out the lukewarm water, turned on the faucet, let it run till the little kettle was half-full, added a little more, and brought him fresh water, was the dear sir he assumed I was, introduced myself as Matzerath, stonecutter and letterman.

He, equally polite, raised his upper body a few degrees, introduced himself as Egon Münzer, jazz musician, but asked me to call him Klepp, since Münzer had been his father's name. I understood his wish all too well; after all, I myself preferred Koljaiczek or simply Oskar, used Matzerath out of sheer humility, and only rarely called myself Oskar Bronski. So I found it easy enough to address this portly, recumbent young man — I guessed he was thirty, but he proved to be younger — as just plain Klepp. He called me Oskar, since Koljaiczek was too much work.

We struck up a conversation, but took pains to keep to small talk at first. We touched on the most trivial of topics: I asked if he thought the fate of man was unalterable. He thought it was. Was he of the opinion that all men must die, Oskar asked. The death of all men he thought certain too, but was by no means sure that all men must be born, spoke of his own birth as a mistake, and once again Oskar felt a kinship with him. We both believed in heaven — but when he said heaven he gave a nasty little laugh and scratched himself under the bedclothes: one could assume Herr Klepp was planning indecent acts in the here and now that he would carry out in heaven. When we came to politics, he waxed almost passionate, named over three hundred German noble houses he would immediately grant title, crown, and power; the Duchy of Hanover he ceded to the British Empire. When I asked about the fate of the former Free City of Danzig he was sorry to say he didn't know the place, but had no problem naming a count from the Bergisches Land, who, as he said, descended in a more or less direct line from Jan Wellem, as prince of the little city he was sorry to say he'd never heard of. Finally — we were engaged in defining the concept of Truth, and making good progress — I skillfully interpolated a few questions into the conversation from which I learned that Herr Klepp had been paying rent to Zeidler as a lodger for three years now. We expressed our regrets at not having met sooner. I blamed the Hedgehog for failing to provide me with sufficient information about this man who was tending his bed, just as it had not occurred to him to convey more about the nurse than the paltry comment: A nurse lives behind this frosted-glass door.

Oskar didn't want to start right in burdening Herr Münzer or Klepp with his troubles. So instead of seeking information about the nurse, I expressed my concern for him: "Apropos of health," I threw in, "aren't you well?"

Klepp again raised his upper body a few degrees, then, realizing he would never make it to a right angle, sank back again and informed me that in fact he was lying in bed in order to find out whether his health was good, middling, or poor. He hoped within a few weeks to discover that it was middling.

Then what I'd feared might happen did, something I'd hoped to avoid by an extended and wide-ranging conversation. "My dear sir, do join me in a plate of spaghetti." So we ate spaghetti cooked in the fresh water I'd brought. I wanted to ask him for the sticky pot, so that I could take it to the sink and give it a thorough washing, but didn't dare. Turning on his side, Klepp cooked our meal in silence with the sure motions of a somnambulist. He drained the water carefully into a large tin can, then, without noticeably altering the position of his upper body, reached under the bed and pulled out a greasy plate crusted with tomato paste, seemed to hesitate a moment, then fished around under the bed again and brought to light a wad of newspaper, wiped the plate with it, tossed the wad back under the bed, breathed on the smeared platter as if to remove a final speck of dust, then, with an almost noble gesture, handed me the most loathsome plate I'd ever seen, and invited Oskar to help himself.

After you, I said, hoping he would go first. Having provided me with a fork and spoon so greasy they stuck to my fingers, he heaped a huge portion of the spaghetti onto my plate with a soup spoon and fork, then, with elegant motions, squeezed a long worm of tomato paste in decorative patterns onto it, added a generous portion of oil from the can, did the same for himself, sprinkled pepper over both plates, stirred up his share, and with a glance urged me to do the same. "Ah, dear sir, forgive me for not having grated parmesan in the house. Even so, *bon appétit!*"

To this day Oskar doesn't know how he summoned up the courage to ply fork and spoon. Amazingly, it tasted good. In fact Klepp's spaghetti set a culinary standard against which, from that day on, I measured every menu set before me.

During the meal I had time to appraise the bedkeeper's room discreetly. The main attraction was a round hole for a stovepipe just below the ceiling, breathing darkly from the wall. It was windy outside. Apparently it was the gusts of wind that puffed occasional clouds of soot through the hole into Klepp's room. The clouds settled evenly on the furnishings, conducting a burial rite. Since those furnishings consisted only of the bed in the middle of the room and a few of Zeidler's rolled-up rugs covered with wrapping paper, it was safe to say that nothing in the room was blackened more thoroughly than the once-white bedsheet, the pillow beneath Klepp's head, and a hand towel the bedkeeper spread over his face whenever a gust of wind ushered a cloud of soot into the room.

The room's two windows, like those in Zeidler's bed–sitting room, looked out on Jülicher Straße, or, more precisely, out into the leafy gray-green garb of the chestnut tree outside the building. The only picture gracing the room hung between the two windows, fastened with thumbtacks, a color photo, probably taken from some magazine, of Elizabeth of England. Beneath the picture, hanging from a hook, was a set of bagpipes, its Scottish plaid barely discernible beneath a layer of soot. As I gazed at the color photo, thinking less of Elizabeth and her Philip than of Sister Dorothea, standing, perhaps in despair, between Oskar and Dr. Werner, Klepp explained to me that he was a loyal and enthusiastic supporter of the English royal family, and had even taken bagpipe lessons from the pipers of a Scottish regiment in the British Army of Occupation, since Elizabeth commanded the regiment; he, Klepp, had seen her in the weekly newsreel, in Scottish kilts, plaid from top to toe, reviewing the regiment.

Strangely enough, the Catholic in me rose up at this point. I said I doubted that Elizabeth understood the first thing about bagpipes, and added a few comments about the disgraceful end of the Catholic Mary Stuart; in short, Oskar let Klepp know that he considered Elizabeth tone-deaf.

Actually I had expected an angry outburst from the Royalist. Instead he gave a superior smile and asked me why he should give any weight to what such a little man — that's what the fat fellow called me — had to say about music.

Oskar stared steadily at Klepp for some time. He had spoken to me without knowing that he spoke to something deep within me. A shiver ran through my head to my hump. It was as if all my old, battered, worn-out tin drums were celebrating Judgment Day on their own. A thousand drums I had thrown on the scrap heap and the one drum that lay buried in the cemetery at Saspe rose up, rose renewed, were resurrected whole and intact, sounded forth, filled me with their resonance, boosted me from the edge of the bed, pulled me, as I begged Klepp to excuse me for a moment, from the room, drew me past Sister Dorothea's frosted-glass door — the half-covered rectangle of the letter still lay on the hall

floor—whipped me along toward my room and the drum Raskolnikov
had given me while painting *Madonna 49;* and I seized the drum, held it
and both drumsticks in my hands, turned or was turned, left the room,
sprang past that cursed chamber, entered Klepp's spaghetti kitchen like a
man who has survived long wanderings, and without further ado, seated
myself on the edge of the bed, adjusted my red and white lacquered tin,
dallied in the air with the drumsticks, still a little embarrassed no doubt
and looking past an astonished Klepp, then let one stick fall, as if at random, on the tin, and ah, the tin replied to Oskar, who quickly followed
with the second stick; and I began to drum, told it all in order, in the beginning was the beginning: the moth between the light bulbs drummed
out the hour of my birth; I drummed the cellar stairs with their sixteen
steps and my fall down those steps during the celebration of my legendary third birthday; I drummed the schedule at the Pestalozzi School
from top to bottom, climbed the Stockturm with the drum, sat with
it beneath political grandstands, drummed eels and gulls, and carpet
beating on Good Friday, sat drumming on my poor mama's coffin that
tapered toward its foot, then used the scar-studded back of Herbert
Truczinski as a score, and noticed, as I drummed up the defense of the
Polish Post Office on Heveliusplatz, as if from a great distance, a movement at the head of the bed on which I sat, saw with half an eye a Klepp
now sitting up, pull from beneath his pillow a ludicrous wooden flute,
place it to his lips, and bring forth tones so sweet, so unnatural, so attuned to my drumming, that I could lead him through Saspe Cemetery
to Crazy Leo, that I could, once Crazy Leo was done with his dance, let
the fizz powder of my first love foam up before him, for him, and with
him; I even led him into the jungles of Frau Lina Greff, let the seventy-
five-kilo counterweight drum machine of the greengrocer Greff whir
and run down to silence, had Klepp join Bebra's Theater at the Front,
let Jesus speak on my drum, drummed Störtebeker and all the dusters
off the diving board—while Luzie sat below—but I let ants and Russians
take over my drum, though I didn't lead Klepp back to Saspe Cemetery,
where I threw my drum into Matzerath's grave, but instead took up my
never-ending theme: Kashubian potato fields in October rains, there
sits my grandmother in her four skirts; and Oskar's heart almost turned
to stone when I heard October rain drizzling from Klepp's flute, as, be-

neath the rain and her four skirts, Klepp's flute found my grandfather, Joseph Koljaiczek, the arsonist, and both demonstrated and celebrated my poor mama's hour of conception.

We played for several hours. After multiple variations on the flight of my grandfather across the timber rafts, we brought the concert to a close, slightly exhausted but happy, with a hymnlike intimation of a possible miraculous rescue of the vanished arsonist.

With the final note still half in his flute, Klepp sprang forth from his form-furrowed bed. Cadaverous smells clung to him. He threw open the windows, stuffed newspaper in the chimney hole, tore the color photo of Elizabeth of England to shreds, declared an end to the Royalist Era, let water gush from the tap into the sink, and washed himself: he washed himself, Klepp did, he washed everything away boldly, this was no mere washing, it was a purification, he was washing himself clean; and as the purified man turned from the water and stood before me, fat, dripping, naked, nearly bursting, his unsightly member hanging at an angle, and lifted me, lifted me up in his outstretched arms — for Oskar was and still is a lightweight — as the laughter erupted from him, poured forth and dashed against the ceiling, I realized that Oskar's drum was not alone in being resurrected, that Klepp too had risen from the dead — and so we congratulated each other, kissed each other on the cheek.

That same day — we went out toward evening, drank beer, ate blood sausage with onions — Klepp suggested we form a jazz band. I asked for time to think it over, but Oskar had already made up his mind, not only to give up carving inscriptions for Korneff the stonecutter, but to stop modeling with Ulla the Muse and become the percussionist in a jazz band.

On the Coco Rug

So oskar supplied his friend with reasons for getting out of bed. Though Klepp sprang joyfully from the musty bedclothes, even let water touch him, and became the sort of man who says Let's go! and I'll take on the world!, I would claim today, when Oskar's the one keeping to his bed, that Klepp is taking his revenge, wants to spoil my bed for me at the mental institution the way I spoiled his for him in the spaghetti kitchen.

Once a week I have to put up with his visits and listen to his upbeat jazz tirades, his musico-Communist manifestos, for no sooner had I deprived him of his bed and his bagpiping Elizabeth than this bedkeeper who styled himself a true Royalist and devotee of the English monarchy became a dues-paying member of the German Communist Party, an illegal hobby he pursues to this day by drinking beer, devouring blood sausage, and holding forth about the benefits of collectives like a full-time jazz band or a Soviet kolkhoz to the harmless little men who stand at bars and study the labels on bottles.

These days there aren't many possibilities left for a dreamer who's been startled awake. Once alienated from his form-furrowed bed, Klepp could become a Communist comrade — illegally, which further increased its appeal. Jazz was the second religion open to him. Third, as a baptized Protestant, he could convert to Catholicism.

You have to hand it to Klepp: he kept all religious avenues open. Caution, his heavy, glistening flesh, and a humor that feeds on applause inspired in him a recipe that, with a peasant's practical wit, combined the teachings of Marx and the mythos of jazz. If one day he runs into a left-wing priest catering to the working class who also owns a collection of Dixieland records, a jazz-ruminating Marxist will start receiving the sacraments on Sundays from then on, mingling the body odor described above with the effluvia of a Neo-Gothic cathedral.

May my bed, from which this fellow tries to lure me by promises warm with life, protect me from that fate. He submits petition after petition to the court, works hand in hand with my lawyer, demands a retrial: he wants to see Oskar acquitted, to see Oskar free — get our Oskar out of that place — and all simply because Klepp begrudges me my bed.

Nonetheless I'm not sorry that while lodging with Zeidler I transformed a recumbent friend into a standing, stomping-about, and sometimes even walking friend. Apart from the strenuous hours I devoted to Sister Dorothea, deep in thought, I now had a carefree private life. "Hey, Klepp!" I would clap him on the shoulder. "Let's start a jazz band." And he would fondle my hump, which he loved almost as much as his own belly. "Oskar and I are starting a jazz band," Klepp announced to the world. "All we need is a decent guitarist who can handle the banjo too."

A second melodic instrument is indeed needed with a drum and flute. A plucked bass would not have been bad, even in purely visual terms, but bass players were always hard to come by, even in those days, so we undertook an eager search for the missing guitarist. We frequented the movie houses, had our photographs taken twice a week as you may remember, and played all sorts of silly tricks with our passport photos over beer, blood sausage, and onions. Klepp met Red Ilse back then, thoughtlessly gave her his photo, and for that reason alone had to marry her — but we couldn't find a guitarist.

Even though modeling at the Art Academy had familiarized me to some extent with Düsseldorf's Altstadt, with its bull's-eye windowpanes, its mustard and cheese, its beery atmosphere and Lower Rhenish coziness, I first came to know it well at Klepp's side. We looked for guitarists all around St. Lambert's Church, in all the taverns, and in particular on Ratinger Straße at The Unicorn, because Bobby, who led the dance band there, let us join in on flute and tin drum at times and praised my playing, though Bobby himself was an excellent percussionist, unfortunately missing a finger on his right hand.

Though we didn't find a guitarist at The Unicorn, I picked up a few routines, and with my own experience in the Theater at the Front, I would soon have passed for a fair percussionist had not Sister Dorothea made me miss my cue now and then.

Half my thoughts were always with her. I could have endured that if the other half had remained totally focused from one note to the next in the vicinity of my tin drum. Instead a thought would start out with my drum and wind up at Sister Dorothea's Red Cross pin. Klepp, who managed to bridge my lapses brilliantly on his flute, was worried each time he saw Oscar half-submerged in thought. "Are you hungry, shall I order some sausage?"

Klepp sensed a wolfish hunger lurking behind each of the world's sorrows, and thought that any sorrow could be cured by a helping of blood sausage. Oskar ate great quantities of fresh blood sausage with onion rings and washed them down with beer back then, just so his friend Klepp would think his sorrow was named hunger and not Sister Dorothea.

We generally left Zeidler's flat on Jülicher Straße early in the morning and had breakfast in the Altstadt. I only went to the Academy when we needed money for the cinema. Ulla the Muse was engaged to Lankes for the third or fourth time, and thus unavailable, since Lankes was receiving his first major industrial commissions. But Oskar didn't like to pose without the Muse—they were totally distorting him again, painting him in the blackest of colors, and so I devoted myself entirely to my friend Klepp; for I found no peace at the flat with Maria or with little Kurt. Her boss and married lover Stenzel was installed there every evening.

One day in the early fall of forty-nine, as Klepp and I stepped out of our rooms and met in the hall near the frosted-glass door to leave the flat with our instruments, Zeidler called out to us from the door of his bed-sitter, which he had opened a crack.

He shoved a narrow but bulky roll of carpet toward us and asked us to help him install it. It was a coco runner. The runner was eight meters twenty long, or about twenty-seven feet. Since the corridor in Zeidler's flat was only twenty-four feet six inches long, Klepp and I had to cut seventy-five centimeters, or about thirty inches, off the runner. We did this sitting down, for cutting through the coco fibers proved hard work. When we were finished, the runner was short by about an inch. Since the runner matched the width of the corridor, Zeidler, who supposedly had trouble bending over, asked us to nail it to the floorboards. It was Oskar's idea to stretch the runner as it was being nailed. In this way we managed to wrangle the missing inch from it, leaving only a small gap. We used broad, flat-headed nails, because small-headed ones would not have held the coarsely woven coco runner. Neither Oskar nor Klepp hit his thumb. Of course we did bend a few nails. But that was due to the quality of the nails, which came from Zeidler's stock and pre-dated the currency reform. After we had fastened the runner halfway down the hall, we crossed our hammers and looked up, not insistently but expectantly, at the Hedgehog, who was supervising our work. He disappeared into his bed-sitter, returned with three liqueur glasses from his liqueur-glass store and a bottle of Doppelkorn. We drank to the runner's durability, then pointed out, again not insistently but expectantly, that coco fibers made a man thirsty. Perhaps the Hedgehog's liqueur glasses were happy that they held several more rounds of Doppelkorn before a familiar temper tantrum from the Hedgehog reduced them to shards. When Klepp accidentally knocked over an empty liqueur glass on the coco runner, the little glass neither broke nor made a sound. We all praised the runner. When Frau Zeidler, who was watching our work from the door of the bed-sitter, joined us in praising the runner for protecting falling liqueur glasses from harm, the Hedgehog flew into a rage. He stamped on the still unfastened portion of the runner, seized the three empty liqueur glasses, disappeared thus burdened into the Zeidlers' bed-sitter, the glass doors of the display case rattled — he was grabbing more glasses, since three weren't enough for him — and soon thereafter Oskar heard a familiar tune: in his mind's eye he saw Zeidler's slow-combustion stove, eight shattered glasses lay at its foot, and Zeidler was bending over for the dustpan and brush, sweeping up the shards Zeidler had produced as the Hedgehog. Frau Zeidler, however, remained standing in the doorway while all the scraping and tinkletinkle went on behind her. She took a considerable interest in our work, for we had picked up our hammers again following the Hedgehog's angry outburst. He didn't return, but he'd left the bottle of Doppelkorn with us. At first we felt awkward as we took turns tipping the bottle to our mouths in Frau Zeidler's presence. But she gave us a friendly nod, though it couldn't induce us to pass her the bottle for a nip. Nevertheless we worked neatly, hammering nail after nail into the runner. As Oskar nailed down the runner outside the nurse's chamber, the frosted-glass panes rattled at each blow of the hammer. That caused him pangs of anguish, and for an anguished moment he let the hammer drop. As soon as he was past

Sister Dorothea's frosted-glass door, however, both he and his hammer felt better. As all good things must come to an end, so too the nailing down of the runner. The nails ran from one end to the other with their broad heads, stood up to their necks in the floorboards and held their heads just barely above the flowing, swirling, whirlpool-forming coco fibers. Pleased with ourselves, we strode up and down the corridor, enjoyed the full length of the carpet, praised our own work, pointed out that it was no mean task to lay down a coco runner and nail it fast on an empty stomach, and at last induced Frau Zeidler to venture out upon the brand-new, virgin coco runner, make her way along it to the kitchen, pour us coffee, and fry us eggs. We ate in my room, Frau Zeidler toddled off, since she was due at the Mannesmann office, we left the door open, and chewing and pleasantly weary, contemplated our work, the coco runner flowing toward us.

Why so many words about a cheap rug, which at most might have had some barter value prior to the currency reform? Oskar anticipates this legitimate question and answers it in advance: upon this coco runner, in the course of the following night, I first met Sister Dorothea.

I came home late, toward midnight, full of beer and blood sausage. I'd left Klepp behind in the Altstadt. He was looking for the guitarist. I found the keyhole of the Zeidler flat, found the coco runner in the hall, found my way past the dark frosted glass to my room, found my way to my bed, after first finding my way out of my clothes, but found I couldn't find my pajamas — they were in the laundry at Maria's — found the thirty-inch-long piece of coco runner we'd cut from the overly long carpet, placed it beside the bed as a bedside rug, found my way into bed, but found no sleep.

There's no point in telling you everything that went through Oskar's mind, consciously or unconsciously, because he couldn't fall asleep. Today I think I know why I couldn't sleep. Before climbing into bed I'd stood barefoot on my new bedside rug, the remnant from the runner. The coco fibers pressed against my bare feet, penetrated my skin, and entered my blood: long after I had gone to bed, I was still standing on coco fibers and thus could not drift off; for nothing is more stimulating, sleep-dispersing, and thought-provoking than standing barefoot on a coco fiber mat.

Long after midnight, till almost three in the morning, Oskar was still standing and lying sleepless on the mat and the bed, at one and the same time, when he heard a door and then another door in the corridor. That must be Klepp, I thought, coming home without a guitarist but stuffed with blood sausage, yet I knew it wasn't Klepp opening first one door and then the other. And I had a further thought: if you're lying in bed for no reason anyway, feeling those coco fibers pricking the soles of your feet, you might as well get up and actually stand on the mat by your bed instead of just imagining it. Oskar did just that. This had consequences. I had barely set foot on the mat when the thirty-inch-long remnant reminded me via my soles of its source, the twenty-four-foot-five-inch coco runner in the corridor. Whether it was because I felt sorry for the cut-off remnant, or because I'd heard the doors in the corridor and assumed, without believing it, that Klepp had returned, Oskar bent down, and, having failed to find his pajamas when he went to bed, took one corner of the bedside rug in each hand, spread his legs till he was no longer standing on the fibers but on the floorboards, pulled the mat high between his legs, held its thirty inches in front of his bare body, which measured four feet, thus covering his nakedness decently, but exposing himself to the sensation of the coco fibers from his collarbone to his knees. This sensation was further intensified as Oskar, shielded by his fibrous garment, passed from his dark room into the dark corridor and thus onto the coco runner.

Small wonder, given the fibrous encouragement of the runner, that I took quick little steps, tried to escape the sensation beneath me, to save myself, that I strove to reach the one place where no coco fiber covered the floor — the toilet.

The toilet was dark, like the corridor and Oskar's room, yet occupied. A small, feminine shriek told me so. My coco-fiber pelt also knocked against the knees of someone seated. Since I made no move to leave the toilet — for the coco runner threatened behind me — the person sitting before me tried to order me out of the toilet: "Who are you, what do you want, go away!" came the command, in a voice that could not possibly be that of Frau Zeidler. Somewhat plaintively: "Who are you?"

"Well, Sister Dorothea, take a guess," I said, venturing a joke intended to ease our slightly embarrassing encounter. But she wasn't in the mood for guessing, stood up, reached for me in the dark, tried to push me from the toilet onto the runner in the hall, but reached too high, into the void over my head, tried lower down, but grabbed not me but my fibrous apron instead, my coco-fiber pelt, shrieked again — why do women always have to shriek first thing? — and mistook me for someone else, for Sister Dorothea began to tremble and whispered, "Oh God, it's the devil!" which drew a small giggle from me, but one without malice. Nevertheless she assumed it was the devil's giggle, but that little word devil was not to my liking, and when she asked again, but now quite timorously, "Who are you?" Oskar replied, "I am Satan, come to call on Sister Dorothea." And she: "Oh God, but why?"

Slowly feeling my way into the role and using the Satan in me as a souffleur, I replied, "Because Satan loves Sister Dorothea." "No, no, no, I don't want that," she burst out, then tried to break away, but encountered the satanic fibers of my coco pelt again — her nightgown must have been quite thin — and her ten little fingers too encountered that seductive jungle, and she went weak, could hardly stand. A slight faint caused Sister Dorothea to sink forward. I caught the falling woman with my pelt, which I lifted away from my body, held her long enough to make a decision in keeping with my satanic role, released her gently so that she fell to her knees, but made sure that her knees did not touch the cold tiles of the toilet and came to rest instead on the coco runner in the hall, then let her glide onto her back lengthwise, with her head pointing west, toward Klepp's room, and since her body was in contact with at least five foot three of the coco runner, covered her with the same fibrous material, of which I had only thirty inches of course, pulled it up under her chin, then found that the other end came too far down over her thighs, pulled the mat up another three or four inches, over her mouth, but with Sister Dorothea's nose uncovered, so she could breathe; and she was panting hard as Oskar now lay down upon his erstwhile bedside mat, set a thousand fibers quivering, but sought no direct contact with Sister Dorothea, let the coco fibers do their work, struck up another conversation with Sister Dorothea, who was still feeling slightly faint and whispered, "Oh God, oh God," kept asking Oskar who he was and where he came from, shuddering between the coco runner and the mat when I said I was Satan, pronounced the word Satan with a satanic hiss, sketched Hell as my home with a bold stroke or two, and bounced all the while on my bedside mat, keeping it in motion, for I couldn't help hearing that the coconut fibers were giving Sister Dorothea a feeling much like the feeling fizz powder had given my beloved Maria all those years ago, except that the fizz powder allowed me to hold up my end fully and triumphantly, while here on the coco mat I was a total and humiliating flop. I just couldn't cast anchor. What had been stiff and purposeful in those fizz-powder days, and often enough thereafter, hung its head under the sign of the coco fibers, remained listless, puny, with no goal in mind, responding neither to my purely cerebral persuasive skills nor to the sighs of Sister Dorothea, who whispered, moaned, and whimpered, "Come, Satan, come!" as I tried to calm and comfort her: "Satan's coming, Satan's almost there," I murmured in my most satanic tone, all the while conversing with the Satan who had dwelt within me since baptism—and was still lodged there—growled at him: Don't be a killjoy, Satan! Pleaded: Please, spare me this disgrace. Cajoled: This is not at all like you, Satan, remember Maria, or better yet the widow Greff, or how we made merry with lovely Roswitha in gay Paree. But he replied morosely, without worrying about repeating himself: I'm not in the mood, Oskar. When Satan's not in the mood, virtue triumphs. Even Satan has the right not to be in the mood every now and then.

So, rattling off these and similar old saws, he refused to support me, while, slowly tiring, I tried to keep the coco-fiber mat in motion, chafing and tormenting the flesh of poor Sister Dorothea, and finally responded to her thirsting "Come, Satan, please come!" with a desperate, absurd, utterly unmotivated assault beneath the coco fibers: I aimed an unloaded gun at the bull's-eye. She tried to help her Satan, drew her arms from under the coco mat, tried to wrap them around me, managed to do so, found my hump, my warm, human, and by no means fibrous skin, failed to find the Satan she sought, ceased murmuring "Come, Satan, come," cleared her throat instead, and repeated her original question in a new tone of voice: "For heaven's sake, who are you, what do you want?" I was forced to draw in my horns, admit that according to my official papers I was Oskar Matzerath, that I was her neighbor, and that I loved her, Sister Dorothea, from the depths of my heart.

To those now enjoying my discomfort who think that Sister Dorothea flung me down on the coco runner with a curse and a clout, Oskar reports, sadly but with a certain satisfaction, that Sister Dorothea removed her hands and arms slowly, one might almost say reluctantly and thoughtfully, from my hump, in what seemed like an infinitely sad caress. And when soon thereafter the sound of her weeping and sobbing arose, it too lacked all violence. I hardly noticed it when she wriggled out from under me and the mat, let me slip to the floor, and slipped away herself, her steps absorbed by the rug on the floor. I heard a door open and close, a key turned, and all at once the six frosted-glass panes of Sister Dorothea's chamber glowed with inner light and reality.

Oskar lay there and covered himself with the mat, which still retained some warmth from that satanic game. My gaze was held by the glowing rectangles. Now and then a shadow crossed the frosted glass. Now she's going to the wardrobe, I told myself, now she's going to the washstand. Oskar tried a canine, cringing approach. Taking my mat with me, I crept along the runner to her door, scratched at the wood, pulled myself up partway, sent a seeking, imploring hand wandering across the two lower panes; but Sister Dorothea didn't open up, moved tirelessly between the wardrobe and the washstand with its mirror. I knew it and would not admit it: Sister Dorothea was packing her things, fleeing, fleeing from me. Even the feeble hope that she would show me her electrically illumined face as she left her chamber was to be buried. First, things went dark behind the frosted glass, then I heard the key, the door opening, shoes on the coco runner — I reached for her, struck a suitcase, a stockinged leg; then she kicked me in the chest with one of those sturdy hiking shoes I'd seen in her wardrobe, throwing me onto the runner, and as Oskar pulled himself back together and pleaded, "Sister Dorothea," the door to the flat slammed shut: a woman had left me.

Now you and all those who understand my grief will say: Go to bed, Oskar. What business do you have in the corridor after this shameful episode? It's four o'clock in the morning. You're lying naked on a coco runner, barely covered by a fiber mat. You've scraped your hands and knees raw. Your heart bleeds, your member aches, your disgrace cries out to high heaven. You've awakened Herr Zeidler. He's awakened his wife. They're going to get up, open the door of their bed-sitter, and see you. Go to bed, Oskar, it will soon strike five.

I gave myself that exact advice back then lying on the runner. But I just lay there and shivered. I tried to call back Sister Dorothea's body. I felt nothing but coconut fibers, even had a few caught in my teeth. Then a strip of light fell on Oskar: the door to Zeidler's bed-sitter fell open a crack. Zeidler's hedgehog head, above it a head full of metal curlers,

Frau Zeidler. They stared, he coughed, she giggled, he called out, I didn't reply, she giggled again, he shut her up, she asked me what was wrong, he said it wouldn't do, she said this was a decent house, he threatened to evict me, but still I lay silent, for my cup was not yet full. The Zeidlers opened their door, and he switched on the light in the hall. They came toward me, giving me little tiny nasty looks, and this time he wasn't going to vent his anger on liqueur glasses, he stood over me, and Oskar awaited the Hedgehog's rage—but Zeidler could not vent his rage, for just then a commotion came from the stairwell, a shaky key sought the door to the flat, found it at last, and Klepp entered, bringing with him someone equally drunk: Scholle, the long-sought guitarist.

The two of them calmed Zeidler and his wife down, bent over Oskar, asked no questions, picked me up, carried me and the satanic scrap of coco runner back to my room.

Klepp rubbed me warm. The guitarist brought me my clothes. Together they dressed me and dried my tears. Sobs. Morning arrived outside the window. Sparrows. Klepp hung my drum around me and brought out his little wooden flute. Sobs. The guitarist shouldered his guitar. Sparrows. Friends surrounded me, took me between them, led a sobbing but unresisting Oskar out of the flat, out of the house, onto Jülicher Straße and to the sparrows, led him forth from the influence of coconut fibers, led me down dawning streets, through the Hofgarten to the Planetarium and the banks of the river Rhine, wending its way grayly toward Holland, bearing barges on which washing fluttered.

From six till nine on that misty September morning the flautist Klepp, the guitarist Scholle, and the percussionist Oskar sat on the right bank of the river Rhine making music, getting in a groove, drinking from the same bottle, squinting off toward the poplars on the other bank, regaling barges on their way upriver, having taken on coal in Duisburg, with the hot and happy, sad and slow music of the Mississippi, and tried to think of a name for their newly formed jazz band.

When a bit of sun began to tint the morning mist, and the craving for a leisurely breakfast crept into our music, Oskar, having put his drum between himself and the preceding night, arose, took money from his coat pocket, which meant it was time to eat, and announced to his friends the name of their newborn band: "The Rhine River Three," we called ourselves, and headed off for breakfast.

The Onion Cellar

WE LOVED THE RHINE meadows, and the tavern owner Ferdinand Schmuh loved the same stretch of the Rhine's right bank between Düsseldorf and Kaiserswerth. We generally rehearsed our music just above Stockum. Schmuh took his rifle to hunt sparrows among the hedges and bushes of the sloping riverbank. That was his hobby, his way of relaxing. When business got on Schmuh's nerves, he put his wife behind the wheel of their Mercedes and they drove along the river, parked the car just above Stockum, then, slightly flat-footed, his rifle angled downward, he set off across the meadows, dragging along his wife, who would have preferred to stay in the car, deposited her on a comfortable rock on the riverbank, and disappeared among the hedges. We played our ragtime, he banged away in the bushes. While we made music, Schmuh shot sparrows.

At the first crack from the bushes, Scholle, who, like Klepp, knew every tavern owner in town, would announce:

"Schmuh's shooting sparrows."

Since Schmuh has passed away, I may just as well add my obituary here: Schmuh was a good shot, and perhaps a good man as well; for when Schmuh shot sparrows, though he kept shells in his left coat pocket, he kept his right coat pocket stuffed with birdseed, which, after hunting and not before — Schmuh never shot more than twelve sparrows in an afternoon — he scattered among the sparrows with generous sweeps of his hand.

On a cool November morning in the year forty-nine, when Schmuh was still among the living — we'd been rehearsing on the bank of the Rhine for several weeks by then — he addressed us in an overly loud and far from gentle voice: "How am I supposed to hunt here when you're playing music and scaring away the birds?"

"Oh," Klepp apologized, and held his flute as though presenting arms, "you're the gentleman with the fine musical ear who's been blasting away in the hedges in perfect time with our tunes, allow me to pay my respects, Herr Schmuh!"

Schmuh was flattered that Klepp knew his name, but asked him how that happened. Klepp, with a show of indignation: Why, everyone knows Schmuh's name. You heard it on the streets: there goes Schmuh, here comes Schmuh, did you see Schmuh just now, where's Schmuh today, Schmuh's shooting sparrows.

Transformed by Klepp into a figure of public note, Schmuh offered us cigarettes, asked our names, wanted to hear a little something from our repertoire, was offered "Tiger Rag," then waved his wife over, who'd been sitting on a rock in her fur coat, contemplating the waters of the Rhine. She arrived in fur and we had to play another tune, obliged her with "High Society," and after we'd finished she said in fur, "Why, Ferdy, that's just what you're looking for at The Cellar." He seemed to share her opinion, to think he'd found just what he'd been looking for, but he skimmed a few flat stones across the waters of the Rhine first, thinking things over, perhaps running through a few numbers before making his offer: play at The Onion Cellar evenings from nine till two in the morning, at ten marks apiece per night, or say twelve — Klepp said seventeen so Schmuh could say fifteen — Schmuh made it fourteen marks fifty, and we called it a deal.

Seen from the street, The Onion Cellar looked like many of the newer nightclubs that differed from older taverns by being more expensive. The higher prices were justified by the extravagant décor of the bars, usually called artists' clubs, and by their names: the subdued refinement of "The Ravioli Room," the shadowy existentialism of "Taboo," the heady spice of "Paprika," and of course "The Onion Cellar."

The words *The Onion Cellar* and a crude but striking likeness of an onion were painted with deliberate clumsiness on an enamel sign that hung in the old German manner from an ornate wrought-iron gallows in front. Bull's-eye panes of beer-bottle green glazed the only window. Outside the iron door, which was painted with red lead and had no doubt shielded an air-raid shelter during the years of adversity, stood a doorman in a rustic sheepskin. Not just anyone was allowed in The Onion Cellar. On Fridays in particular, when paychecks turned to beer, some of the locals, for whom The Onion Cellar would have been too expensive in the first place, had to be turned away. Behind the red lead door, those allowed in faced five concrete steps, descended them, came to a landing three feet square—a poster from a Picasso exhibition rendered even this small landing striking and original—then descended another set of steps, four this time, and found themselves opposite the cloakroom. *Please pay when you leave!* a little cardboard sign stated, and the young man behind the cloakroom counter—usually a bearded apostle from the Art Academy—never took money in advance, for The Onion Cellar was expensive, but it was also a serious and respectable establishment.

The host received each guest in person with the most mobile of eyebrows and gestures, as if initiating the newcomer into some sacred rite. The host, as we know, was Ferdinand Schmuh, who shot sparrows now and then and had a keen understanding of the society that had sprung up in Düsseldorf—and in other cities as well, if more slowly—after the currency reform.

The Onion Cellar itself—and here the serious and authentic nature of this successful nightclub was clearly in evidence—was an actual cellar, and even slightly damp. It could be compared to a long tube, chilly under foot and measuring about fourteen by sixty, heated by two round cast-iron stoves, also authentic. The Cellar was not, to be sure, a true cellar. The ceiling had been removed to open things up into the former ground-floor flat above. The single window of The Onion Cellar was thus not an actual cellar window, but the former window of the ground-floor flat, which undermined the authenticity of the successful nightclub to a certain extent. But since the window had been glazed with bull's-eye panes, rendering it opaque, and since a gallery had been constructed in the expanded upper area of the cellar, reached by a highly original set of steep steps like a hen-house ladder, The Onion Cellar might well be termed a serious nightclub, even if the cellar wasn't really a cellar—and why should it have been?

Oskar has forgotten to tell you that the hen-house ladder to the gallery wasn't a true hen-house ladder either, but more a sort of inclined gangway, since there were two highly original clotheslines to grasp to the left and right of the dangerously steep ladder; it swayed slightly, making you think of an ocean voyage, and added to the price of The Onion Cellar.

Carbide lamps of the kind miners carry lighted The Onion Cellar, spread a smell of carbide — which also raised the price — and transported The Onion Cellar's paying guests to the gallery of a mine, a potash mine, say, three thousand feet below the surface of the earth; cutters stripped to the waist hack away at the rock, strike a vein, the scraper hauls salt, the winches whine, fill the carts; far to the rear, where the tunnel turns toward Friedrichhall Two, a light sways, here comes the head foreman, calls out, "Hey, boys!" and swings a carbide lamp that looks just like those hanging on the unplastered, thinly whitewashed walls of The Onion Cellar, emitting light, smelling, raising prices, and creating a highly original atmosphere.

The uncomfortable seating consisted of ordinary crates covered with onion sacks, but the gleaming wooden tables, neatly polished, lured the guests from the mine to the sort of peaceful farmhouse parlors you sometimes see in films.

And there you have it. What about the bar? No bar. Waiter, a menu please? No menu, no waiter. No one but us, The Rhine River Three. Klepp, Scholle, and Oskar sat beneath the hen-house ladder, which was in fact a gangway, came at nine, unpacked our instruments, and started playing around ten. But since it's only a quarter past nine now, we can talk about us later. For the moment we need to keep our eye on Schmuh, who keeps an eye on sparrows.

As soon as The Onion Cellar was filled with guests — half-full counted as full — Schmuh, the host, would don his shawl. The shawl, a cobalt-blue silk, was printed with a special pattern, and is mentioned because donning the shawl had a particular meaning. The pattern could be called Golden-Yellow Onions. Only when Schmuh wrapped his shawl about him could one truly say that The Onion Cellar had opened.

The customers: businessmen, doctors, lawyers, artists, actors, journalists, film people, well-known athletes, high-ranking officials from provincial and municipal government, in short, all those who call themselves intellectuals nowadays, sat on burlap-covered crates and talked with their spouses, girlfriends, secretaries, arts-and-crafters, and male mistresses too, their conversations subdued, slightly hesitant, almost forced, as long as Schmuh had not yet donned his shawl of golden-yellow onions. They've tried to start up conversations but failed, tried their best but talked around their true problems, tried to air things, get things off their chests, talk freely and openly, spill their guts, speak straight from the heart, tried to stop thinking and just let go, face the bloody truth, stand there naked and human—but they can't. Here and there hints of a botched career, a broken marriage. That gentleman with the massive head, the intelligent face, and soft, almost delicate hands seems to be having problems with his son, who doesn't approve of his father's past. The two women in mink, shown off to advantage by the carbide lamps, claim they've lost their faith: in what, remains an open question. We still know nothing of the past of the gentleman with the massive head, nor what problems he faces with his son because of that past; it's like—forgive Oskar for this comparison—trying to lay an egg: you push and push . . .

Those in The Onion Cellar pushed in vain till Schmuh, the host, suddenly appeared with his special shawl, graciously accepted their joyful cry of "Ah," disappeared for a few minutes behind a curtain at the end of the cellar where the toilets and a storeroom were located, and then returned.

But why is the host greeted with an even more joyful, half-relieved "Ah" when he reappears before his guests? The owner of a successful nightclub vanishes behind a curtain, gets something from the storeroom, aims a few harsh words in a low voice at the washroom attendant, who's sitting there reading a magazine, steps back outside the curtain, and is greeted like the Savior, like a long-lost rich uncle.

Schmuh moved among his guests with a little basket on his arm. This little basket was covered with a blue-and-yellow-checkered cloth. On the cloth lay a number of small wooden boards, shaped like pigs or fish. Schmuh distributed these nicely polished boards among his guests. He handed them out with little bows and compliments that revealed a youth spent in Budapest and Vienna; Schmuh's smile looked like the smile on a copy of a copy of what was presumably the real *Mona Lisa*.

The guests, however, received these small wooden boards with a grave air. Some people traded with each other. One preferred the pig shape, while another—man or woman, as the case might be—preferred the more mysterious fish to the ordinary domestic pig. They sniffed at the little boards, passed them around, and Schmuh the host waited, having served the guests in the gallery as well, till every board had come to rest.

Then—and every heart was waiting—he pulled away the cloth as a magician might: to reveal a second cloth still covering the basket. But on this cloth, though difficult to recognize at first, lay kitchen knives.

As with the boards, Schmuh now handed out the knives. But at this point he made his rounds more quickly, increased the tension that increased his prices, paid no compliments, left no time for trading knives, made each move with measured haste, cried, "Ready, set, go!" and whipped the cloth from the basket, reached in and doled out, dispensed, distributed among the multitude, giver of alms, host to his guests, gave them all onions, like the slightly stylized, golden-yellow onions on his shawl, plain ordinary onions, onion bulbs, not tulip bulbs, onions such as housewives buy, onions women sell at market, onions farmers and their wives or hired farm girls plant and harvest, the onions one sees, more or less faithfully portrayed, in the still lifes of Dutch miniature masters, such were the onions Schmuh gave to his guests, till all had onions, and no sound was heard but the roar of round stoves and the song of the carbide lamps. Such was the silence that followed the grand distribution of the onions—when Ferdinand Schmuh cried, "Ladies and gentlemen, help yourselves!" and threw one end of his shawl across his left shoulder like a skier set to take off, which was their signal.

The guests peeled their onions. An onion has seven skins, they say. The ladies and gentlemen peeled their onions with the kitchen knives. They removed the first, third, blond, golden-yellow, rust-brown, or, better still, onion-colored skin, peeled till the onion turned glassy, green, whitish, moist, sticky-watery, till it smelled, smelled like an onion, then they sliced it the way onions are sliced, sliced awkwardly or deftly on little chopping boards the shape of pigs or fish, sliced this way and that, the juice spattering or spraying into the air above the onion—the older men who weren't used to handling kitchen knives had to take care not to cut their fingers, but a few did anyway and didn't notice—the women were more efficient, not all of them, but those who played housewife at home, and so knew how to slice onions for hash-brown potatoes, or liver with apple and onion rings; but Schmuh's Onion Cellar had neither, there was nothing whatever to eat, and those who wanted something to eat had to go somewhere like The Little Fish, for at The Onion Cellar you simply sliced onions. And why was that? Why, because the cellar was a hot spot and offered something special, because onions, sliced onions, if you looked at them carefully . . . but no, Schmuh's guests no longer saw anything, or some no longer saw anything, their eyes were overflowing, but not because their hearts were full; for the heart that's full to over-flowing does not always make the eye flow, some never manage it at all, particularly in the last ten years or past few decades, so that in times to come our century, though filled with so much pain and sorrow, will be called the tearless century — and it was precisely this lack of tears that led those people who could afford it to Schmuh's Onion Cellar, where the host handed them a small chopping board — pig or fish — a kitchen knife for eighty pfennigs, and an ordinary field-garden-and-kitchen-variety onion for twelve marks, which they sliced into smaller and smaller pieces till the juice brought forth — brought forth what? Brought forth what the world and the world's suffering could not: a round, hu-man tear. People wept. At long last, people wept again. Wept openly, wept without restraint, wept honestly. The tears flowed and washed everything away. The rains came. The dew fell. Oskar sees floodgates opening. Dams bursting in spring tide. What's the name of that river which floods each year and the government does nothing about it? And following this natural phenomenon for twelve marks eighty, human be-ings who had cried themselves out talked to one another. Hesitantly at first, astonished by the nakedness of their own words, the guests of The Onion Cellar, having sliced their onions, turned to their neighbors on the uncomfortable burlap-covered crates and answered every question, let themselves be turned inside out like a coat. Oskar, however, who along with Klepp and Scholle sat tearless beneath the quasi hen-house ladder, will be discreet; from among all the revelations, self-accusations, confessions, exposures, and admissions, he will relate only the story of Fräulein Pioch, who lost her Herr Vollmer many times over, and so ac-quired a heart of stone and a tearless eye, forcing her to pay repeated visits to Schmuh's expensive Onion Cellar.

We met, Fräulein Pioch said when she had finished crying, on the tram. I was coming home from work — she owns and operates an excellent bookstore — the car was full, and Willy — that's Herr Vollmer — stepped hard on my right foot. My knees went weak, it was love at first sight. Since I couldn't walk, he offered me his arm, practically carried me home, and from that day on cared lovingly for the toenail that had turned black and blue beneath his heel. Nor did he fail to love the rest of me, till the nail fell off my right big toe and no longer blocked the growth of a new one. The day the dead toenail fell off, his love began to cool. We both suffered from this loss. Then, since he was still attached to me, and because we had so much in common, Willy made a shocking suggestion: Let me step on your left big toe, he said, till the nail turns blue, then black and blue. I gave in and he did. Again I enjoyed the full benefits of his love, and continued to enjoy them till the left nail of my big toe fell like a withered leaf, and it was autumn again for our love. Now Willy wanted to step on my right big toe, where the nail had grown back, to love and care for me once more. But I wouldn't let him. If your love is true and deep, I said, it should outlast a toenail. He didn't understand, and left me. Several months later we met at a concert. After the intermission he sat down beside me without asking, since the seat was empty. When the chorus sounded in the Ninth Symphony, I stuck out my right foot, from which I had removed my shoe. He stepped down, and I managed not to disturb the concert. Seven weeks later, Willy left me again. Twice more we managed a few weeks together, since I held out first my left, then my right big toe. Today both toes are maimed. The nails won't grow back. Willy visits me now and then, sits at my feet on the carpet, shaken, filled with pity for the two of us, but without love or tears, and gazes at the two nailless victims of our love. At times I say to him: Come on, Willy, let's go to Schmuh's Onion Cellar and have a good cry. But so far he's never come. The poor man has no idea what comfort tears can offer.

Later—and Oskar discloses this merely to satisfy the curious among you—Herr Vollmer, who sold radios by the way, did visit The Cellar. They wept together and, as Klepp told me yesterday during visiting hours, are said to have recently married.

Although the true tragedy of human existence was spread fully before us after onions on Tuesday through Saturday—The Onion Cellar was closed on Sunday—Monday's guests, while not the most tragic of weepers, were certainly the most intense. Prices were lowered on Mondays. Schmuh handed out onions at half price to students. For the most part these were medical students, both male and female. And students from the Art Academy, particularly those who wanted to be drawing instructors, spent part of their stipends on onions. But I still wonder where all those schoolboys and schoolgirls got the money for onions.

Young people have a different way of crying. Young people have completely different problems. And they don't always involve exams or school. Of course there were father-son stories in The Onion Cellar, and mother-daughter tragedies as well. Though the young felt misunderstood, they hardly found it worth crying about. Oskar was pleased to see that the young still wept for love, and not just love of a sexual nature. Gerhard and Gudrun: at first they always sat down below, only later did they weep side by side in the gallery.

She was tall and strong, played handball, studied chemistry. She knotted her hair at the back. Gray-eyed and maternal, the type you used to see for years in Women's Association posters before the war ended, staring straight ahead with a clear, forthright gaze. Though the curve of her brow was creamy, smooth, and healthy, she bore her misfortune clearly on her face. From her Adam's apple past her round, strong chin, including both her cheeks, a manly growth of beard, which the poor girl kept trying to shave, left its distressing traces. Her tender skin suffered from the razor. Gudrun wept for this reddened, cracked, pimply disaster in which the beard kept growing back. It was only later that Gerhard started coming to The Onion Cellar. The two didn't meet on the tram, like Fräulein Pioch and Herr Vollmer, but on the train. He sat across from her, they were both coming back from semester break. He fell in love with her at once, in spite of her beard. Because of her beard, she didn't dare love him, but admired the very feature that caused him so much unhappiness — Gerhard's chin, smooth as a baby's bottom; the young man couldn't grow a beard, which made him bashful around young women. Nevertheless Gerhard spoke to Gudrun, and by the time they got off at the station in Düsseldorf, they were at least friends. From then on they saw each other daily. They spoke of this and that, shared most of their thoughts, but never alluded to the missing beard or the one that kept growing. Gerhard tried to spare Gudrun and, knowing how sensitive her skin was, never kissed her tormented face. Thus their love remained chaste, though neither set much store by chastity, for she was committed to chemistry and he to medicine. When a mutual friend suggested they try The Onion Cellar, they both smiled disdainfully, with that skepticism so often found in doctors and chemists. But they went in the end, just for purposes of research, as they assured themselves. Oskar has seldom seen young people cry like that. They came again and again, went without food to pay their six marks forty, wept over the missing beard, over the beard laying waste to the young girl's tender skin. Sometimes they tried to stay away from The Onion Cellar, even missed a Monday once, but were there again the following Monday, rubbing chopped onion between their fingers, admitting through tears that they'd tried to save the six marks forty by experimenting with a cheap onion in her room, but it wasn't the same as in The Onion Cellar. You needed an audience. It was easier to cry in company. A true community formed when, to your left and right, fellow students from all fields, even artists and schoolboys, were weeping with you.

The case of Gerhardt and Gudrun too resulted not only in tears, but little by little in a cure. The eyewash must have washed away their inhibitions. They drew closer, as they say. He kissed her flayed skin, she delighted in his smooth one, and one day they stopped coming to The Onion Cellar, no longer needed it. Oskar ran into them months later on Königsallee and hardly recognized them at first: he, Gerhardt the glossy, was sporting a full reddish blond beard that practically rustled in the wind; she, Gudrun the granular, showed only a faint brownish down on her upper lip that looked good on her. Gudrun's cheeks and chin gleamed, without a sign of vegetation. They looked like a pair of married students — Oskar hears them fifty years hence telling their grandchildren: Gudrun — "That was back before your grandpa had a beard." Gerhardt — "That was back when your grandma still suffered from facial hair and we went to The Onion Cellar every Monday."

But why, you ask, are three musicians still sitting under the ship's gangway or hen-house ladder? Given all the weeping, wailing, and gnashing of teeth, did the onion shop really need live music on a regular basis?

Once the guests had cried and talked themselves out, we took up our instruments and provided a musical transition to more mundane conversations, made it easier for them to leave The Onion Cellar so new customers could take their place. Klepp, Scholle, and Oskar didn't like onions. There was also a clause in our contract forbidding us from using onions the way customers did. But we had no need of onions. Scholle, the guitarist, had nothing to complain about, he always looked happy and content, even when two strings on his banjo snapped at the same time in the middle of a rag. My friend Klepp confuses the notions of crying and laughing to this very day. He finds tears funny; I've never seen him laugh as hard as he did at his aunt's funeral, the one who used to wash his shirts and socks before he got married. But what of Oskar? Oskar had good reason to cry. Didn't he need to wash away Sister Dorothea, and that long, futile night on an even longer coco runner? And my Maria, did she not offer grounds for sorrow? Was not her boss, Stenzel, passing freely in and out of the flat in Bilk? And little Kurt, my son, was he not calling the delicatessen owner and part-time Carnival worker first "Uncle Stenzel," then "Papa Stenzel"? And behind my Maria, lying beneath the loose, distant sand of Saspe Cemetery, the clay of Brentau Cemetery, my poor mama, the foolish Jan Bronski, Matzerath the cook, who could express his emotions only in soup—did they not all require my tears? But Oskar belonged to the fortunate few who could still cry without onions. My drum helped me. Just a few specific drumbeats and Oskar was in tears, no better or worse than the expensive tears of The Onion Cellar.

Nor did Schmuh abuse the onions. The sparrows he shot from the hedges and bushes in his free time were all he needed. Often enough after hunting, Schmuh would lay out the twelve sparrows he'd shot on a newspaper, sometimes shedding tears over the little feathered bundles, still lukewarm, and with tears in his eyes scatter birdseed over the Rhine meadows and riverbank stones. In the onion shop he'd found yet another way to vent his sorrow. He'd fallen into the habit of giving the washroom attendants a tongue lashing once a week, using strangely old-fashioned terms of abuse: hussy, harlot, wench, jade, stew. "Out!" Schmuh would shriek. "Depart from my sight, you harridan!" He would fire these women on the spot and hire new ones, but that proved difficult after a time, for he couldn't find any more, and so had to rehire those he had already thrown out once or twice. These washroom attendants returned to The Onion Cellar gladly, since they hadn't understood most of the names they'd been called, and earned good money. Tears drove more guests to the facilities than in other nightclubs, and a crying man tends to be more generous than one with dry eyes. Particularly the gentlemen who disappeared "in the back" with streaming faces swollen and inflamed reached deeply and gladly into their purses. The women who tended the washrooms also sold customers the famous onion-print handkerchiefs with *The Onion Cellar* printed diagonally across them. These looked quite cheerful, and could be used both to dry tears and as headscarves. Male guests at The Onion Cellar had the colored rectangles sewn into triangular pennants and hung them in the rear windows of their cars, carrying Schmuh's Onion Cellar with them on holiday to Paris, the Côte d'Azur, to Rome, Ravenna, Rimini, even to far-off Spain.

Our band and music served yet another function: occasionally some of the guests would slice two onions in succession; then there were eruptions that could all too easily have degenerated into orgies. Schmuh disliked this final loss of restraint, and the moment a few gentlemen started loosening their ties and a few ladies began fumbling at their blouses, he would order us to strike up the music to counteract these stirrings of lewdness, yet it was Schmuh himself who repeatedly paved the way toward an orgy by providing particularly susceptible customers with a second onion.

The most violent eruption I can recall at The Onion Cellar was, if not a turning point, at least a decisive moment in Oskar's life. Schmuh's wife, the vivacious Billy, seldom visited the Cellar, and when she did, she came with friends Schmuh had no desire to see. One evening she turned up with Woode, the music critic, and Wackerlei, a pipe-smoking architect. Both were regular customers at The Onion Cellar, burdened with thoroughly boring sorrows: Woode wept for religious reasons — he longed to convert, or had already converted, or was converting for the second time — and the pipe-smoking Wackerlei bewailed a professorship he'd turned down in the twenties for the sake of a flashy Danish woman who'd run off instead with some South American and bore him six children, all of which grieved Wackerlei so deeply that his pipe kept going out. It was the slightly malicious Woode who persuaded Schmuh's wife to cut up an onion. She did so, burst into tears, and started spilling the beans, laid poor Schmuh bare, told stories about him Oskar has the tact to spare you, at which point several strong men were required to keep Schmuh from flinging himself upon his wife; after all, kitchen knives were lying all around on the tables. The enraged man was forcibly restrained long enough for an indiscreet Billy to disappear with her friends Woode and Wackerlei.

Schmuh was both agitated and stunned. I could see it in his flighty hands, which kept rearranging his shawl. He disappeared behind the curtain several times to lash out at the washroom attendant, returned in the end with a full basket, and announced to the guests in a strained and overly cheerful voice that he, Schmuh, was in a generous mood, this round was on the house, and started handing out onions.

Even Klepp, who thought most human situations, no matter how painful and embarrassing, a good joke, appeared pensive, or at least tense, and held his flute at the ready. After all, we knew how dangerous it was to allow this sensitive and refined company a chance to release their inhibitions through tears twice in rapid succession.

Schmuh, who saw that we had taken up our instruments, forbade us to play. The knives on the tables set to work. The first oh-so-beautiful rosewood skins were cast carelessly aside. Glassy onion flesh with pale green stripes went under the knife. Strangely enough, the ladies weren't the first to weep. Gentlemen in the prime of life—the owner of a large mill, the proprietor of a hotel with his lightly rouged friend, a nobleman representing his firm, a whole table of clothes manufacturers in town for a board meeting, and a bald actor we nicknamed the Gnasher, because he gnashed his teeth when he cried—were all in tears before the ladies joined in. But these ladies and gentlemen did not dissolve in the tears of relief that the first onions called forth; instead they fell prey to convulsive fits of weeping: the Gnasher gnashed so fiercely he would have moved any audience to tearful gnashing, the mill owner kept pounding his carefully groomed gray head on the table, the hotel owner blended his crying jag with that of his graceful friend; Schmuh, standing by the stairs, let his shawl dangle, eyed the unleashed company with a pinched mouth, but not without pleasure. And then an older woman tore off her blouse before the eyes of her son-in-law. Suddenly the hotel owner's friend, whose slightly exotic appearance had already attracted attention, stood on a table, his naturally brown body bare from the waist up, moved on to the next, and launched into some sort of Oriental dance, signaling the advent of an orgy that was lively enough to begin with, but was so lacking in imagination, so downright silly, that it's not worth describing in detail.

Schmuh was not the only one disappointed; Oskar too lifted his eyebrows in bored disgust. A few silly striptease acts, gentlemen wearing ladies' underwear, amazons donning ties and suspenders, a couple or two who vanished beneath the tables; only the Gnasher distinguished himself by chewing up a bra and apparently swallowing part of it.

It was probably the terrible din, all the ouhhhs and uahhhs signifying little or nothing, that caused a disappointed Schmuh to give up his place beside the stairs, perhaps fearing the police. He bent down to us where we were sitting under the hen-house ladder, poked Klepp, then me, and hissed, "Music! Play something, for God's sake. Put an end to this."

But it turned out that Klepp, who was easily pleased, was having a good time. He was shaking so hard with laughter he couldn't lift his flute. Scholle, who looked on Klepp as his master, followed his lead in everything, including laughter. So that left only Oskar — but Schmuh could count on me. I pulled my tin drum out from under the bench, nonchalantly lit a cigarette, and began to drum.

With no plan in mind, I made myself understood on tin. I forgot all the standard nightclub routines. No jazz for Oskar either. I didn't like being taken for a maniacal drummer by the crowd anyway. Though I considered myself a decent percussionist, I was no purebred jazz musician. I love jazz, just as I love Viennese waltzes. I could have played either, but didn't feel I had to. When Schmuh asked me to step in with my drum, I didn't play what I could play, but what was in my heart. Oskar pressed his drumsticks into the hands of a three-year-old Oskar. I drummed up and down former paths, showed the world as a three-year-old sees it, and the first thing I did was harness that postwar crowd incapable of a true orgy to a cord, that is, I led them down Posadowskiweg into Auntie Kauer's kindergarten, had them standing with their mouths hanging open, holding one another by the hand, turning their toes inward, waiting for me, their Pied Piper. And so I left my post beneath the hen-house ladder, took the lead, began by drumming up a sample of "Pat-a-cake, pat-a-cake, baker's man," then, when childish glee from all corners indicated its success, sent them into a paroxysm of terror with "Better start running, the Black Cook's coming!" I feared her now and then as a child, but in recent days she scares me more and more, and now I sent her raging through The Onion Cellar, monstrous, coal-black, vast, and accomplished something Schmuh could only manage with onions: the gentlemen and ladies shed big, round, children's tears, were scared to death, begged me for mercy, so that to comfort them, and help them back into their clothes, their underwear, their silk and satin, I drummed "Green, green, green are all my clothes," and "Red, red, red are all my clothes," and "Blue, blue, blue . . ." and "Yellow . . ." too, through every shade and color till all stood decently clad once more, then lined the kindergarten up to leave, led them through The Onion Cellar as though it were Jäschkentaler Weg, climbed up the Erbsberg, past the creepy Gutenberg Memorial, and on to Johanniswiese, as though real daisies bloomed there, which they, those ladies and gentlemen, were free to pick in childish joy. And then I gave them all permission, all those present, including Schmuh, to leave a little souvenir of that playful kindergarten afternoon, to do their business, told them on my drum — we neared the deep, dark Devil's Gorge, gathered beechnuts on the way — go right ahead now, children: and they did their little children's business, all wet themselves, gentlemen and ladies, Schmuh the host, my friends Klepp and Scholle, even the washroom attendant in the back, went peepee peepee in their pants, crouched and listened to themselves as they did so. Once this music faded — Oskar merely tapped lightly along with that children's orchestra — I banged the drum loudly and ushered in a boundless joy. With a rollicking:

> Glass, glass, little glass,
> Sugar and no beer,
> Mother Holle runs upstairs
> And sheds a tiny tear . . .

I led the cheering, giggling, childishly babbling company first to the cloakroom, where a bewildered bearded student handed out coats to Schmuh's childish guests, then drummed the ladies and gentlemen up the concrete steps with the popular little song "If Washerwomen You Would See," past the doorman in sheepskin, and out. Beneath a night sky studded with fairy-tale stars, slightly cool, but seemingly made to order for the occasion, in the spring of nineteen-fifty, I dismissed the gentlemen and ladies, who carried on for some time with their childish nonsense in the Altstadt and did not return home till the police finally helped them recall their age, social position, and telephone numbers.

As for me, I returned to The Onion Cellar, a giggling Oskar caressing his drum, to find Schmuh still clapping his hands, standing knock-kneed in wet trousers by the hen-house ladder, and seemingly as happy in Auntie Kauer's kindergarten as he had been on the Rhine meadows, when a grown-up Schmuh went shooting sparrows.

On the Atlantic Wall or
Bunkers Can't Cast Off Concrete

I'D ONLY MEANT to help Schmuh, the host of The Onion Cellar. But he couldn't forgive me for the tin drum solo that transformed his high-rolling guests into babbling, blithely merry children who still wet their pants and therefore cried — cried without onions.

Oskar tries to understand. How could he help but fear my competition when customers kept pushing aside his traditional crying onions and calling for Oskar, for Oskar's drum, for me, who could conjure up on tin the childhood of any guest, no matter how advanced in years?

Schmuh, who up till then had restricted himself to firing washroom attendants on the spot, now fired our band and hired a strolling fiddler who, if you squinted a little, might have been taken for a gypsy.

When we were tossed out, however, several of Schmuh's best customers threatened to boycott The Onion Cellar, and within a few weeks he was forced to accept a compromise: Three times a week the strolling fiddler fiddled. Three times a week we performed, having demanded and received a raise: our salary was now twenty marks a night, and increasingly generous tips poured in too — Oskar opened a savings account and looked forward to the interest.

All too soon my little savings book became a friend indeed in time of need, for Death came and carried off Ferdinand Schmuh, along with our work and wages.

As I've said before, Schmuh shot sparrows. Sometimes he took us along in his Mercedes and let us watch. Despite occasional quarrels over my drum, which also drew in Klepp and Scholle, who always stuck by me, relationships between Schmuh and the band remained friendly until, as I say, Death came.

We piled in. Schmuh's wife sat at the wheel as always. Klepp beside her. Schmuh between Oskar and Scholle. The rifle Schmuh held on his knees, stroking it from time to time. We stopped just short of Kaiserswerth. A backdrop of trees on both sides of the Rhine. Schmuh's wife stayed in the car and unfolded a newspaper. Klepp had bought some raisins and was eating them at a more or less steady pace. Scholle, who'd studied something or other before taking up the guitar, managed to recite a few poems about the Rhine River from memory. The river was showing its poetical side as well, bearing not only the usual tow barges, but autumnal leaves rocking their way toward Duisburg, even if the calendar claimed it was still summer; and if Schmuh's rifle hadn't spoken up now and then, that afternoon below Kaiserswerth might well have been called peaceful.

By the time Klepp had finished his raisins and wiped his fingers on the grass, Schmuh was finished too. To the eleven cold balls of feather lying on the newspaper he added a twelfth, still kicking, as he put it. The sharpshooter was already packing up his plunder — for some inexplicable reason, Schmuh always took what he shot home — when a sparrow settled on a nearby tree root that had washed onto the bank, and did it so openly, this gray, fine specimen of a sparrow, that Schmuh couldn't resist; he who never shot more than twelve sparrows in an afternoon shot a thirteenth — which Schmuh should not have done.

After he'd laid the thirteenth beside the other twelve, we walked back and found Schmuh's wife sleeping in the black Mercedes. First Schmuh got in front. Then Scholle and Klepp climbed in the back. I was to get in next, but I didn't, said I felt like a little stroll, that I would take the tram, not to worry about me, and so they headed off toward Düsseldorf without Oskar, who had wisely declined to get in.

I followed them slowly. I didn't have far to go. There was a detour around some roadwork. The detour led past a gravel pit. And in the gravel pit, over twenty feet below, lay the black Mercedes with its wheels in the air.

Some workmen in the gravel pit had pulled the three injured occupants and Schmuh's body from the car. The ambulance was already on its way. I clambered down into the pit, my shoes soon full of gravel, and gave what little help I could to the injured; in spite of their pain they tried to ask questions, but I didn't tell them Schmuh was dead. Stiff and startled he stared at the sky, which was mostly cloudy. The newspaper with its afternoon's plunder had been thrown from the car. I counted twelve sparrows, couldn't find the thirteenth, and was still looking for it when the ambulance was funneled down into the gravel pit.

Schmuh's wife, Klepp, and Scholle had suffered minor injuries: bruises, a few broken ribs. Later, when I went to see Klepp in the hospital and asked what caused the accident, he told me an amazing story: as they were driving past the gravel pit, slowly because of the poor condition of the detour, scores or even hundreds of sparrows rose in clouds from the hedges, bushes, and fruit trees, cast a shadow across the Mercedes, banged against the windshield, frightened Schmuh's wife, and by sheer sparrow power caused the wreck and Schmuh's death.

Whatever you may think of Klepp's story, Oskar remains skeptical, since he counted no more sparrows when Schmuh was buried in South Cemetery than he had in previous years among the gravestones as a stonecutter and letterman. Be that as it may, as I followed along with the train of mourners behind the coffin in a borrowed top hat, I saw the stonecutter Korneff with an assistant I didn't know, setting up a diorite slab for a double plot in Section Nine. As the coffin with Schmuh was carried past the stonecutter on its way to the newly opened Section Ten, Korneff doffed his cap in accordance with cemetery rules, failed to recognize me, perhaps because of the top hat, but did rub the back of his neck, indicating ripening or overripe boils.

Funerals! I've been obliged to take you to so many cemeteries already, and as I've said elsewhere, funerals always make you think of other funerals — so I won't report on Schmuh's funeral and Oskar's retrospective musings at the time — Schmuh's descent into the earth went smoothly, and nothing special happened — but I will tell you that after the funeral — the mood was fairly informal, since the widow was still in the hospital — a gentleman came up to me and introduced himself as Dr. Dösch.

Dr. Dösch ran a concert agency. But he didn't own the agency. Dr. Dösch also identified himself as a former customer at The Onion Cellar. I'd never noticed him there. Nevertheless he'd been present when I turned Schmuh's guests into babbling, joyful children. Dösch himself, he told me in confidence, had reverted to a state of childhood bliss under the influence of my tin drum, and now wanted to feature me and what he called my "cool trick" in a major production. He was fully authorized to offer me a fantastic contract; all I had to do was sign. He pulled it out in front of the crematorium, where Crazy Leo, who was called Weird Willem in Düsseldorf, was waiting in white gloves for the mourners; in return for huge sums of money, I would have to appear alone onstage in theaters seating two to three thousand people and offer solo performances as "Oskar the Drummer." Dösch was inconsolable when I said I couldn't sign right then and there. I offered Schmuh's death as an excuse, I'd been so close to Schmuh, I just couldn't go to work for someone else before I'd even left the cemetery, I needed time to think things over, perhaps take a little trip, and after that I'd look him up, Herr Dr. Dösch, and perhaps then I'd sign the piece of paper he called a work contract.

Though I signed no contract at the cemetery, in the lot outside, where Dösch had parked his car, Oskar found himself compelled by his uncertain financial situation to accept and pocket an advance that Dr. Dösch handed me discreetly, tucked away in an envelope with his business card.

And I did take that trip, and even found a traveling companion. Actually I would have preferred to travel with Klepp. But Klepp was in the hospital and didn't dare laugh because he'd broken four ribs. And I would gladly have gone with Maria. The summer holidays had not yet ended, we could have taken little Kurt along. But she was still tied up with Stenzel, her boss, who had little Kurt calling him Papa Stenzel.

So I wound up traveling with Lankes, the painter. You've met Lankes before as Corporal Lankes, and as the sometime fiancé of Ulla the Muse. When, with my advance and my savings book in my pocket, I looked up Lankes at his studio on Sittarder Straße, I was hoping to find Ulla, my former colleague; I intended to ask her to join me on the trip.

I found her with the painter. We've been engaged for two weeks, she told me in the doorway. Things hadn't worked out with Hänschen Krages, she'd had to break off their engagement; did I know Hänschen Krages?

Oskar was sorry to say he didn't know Ulla's former fiancé, extended his generous offer, then had to watch as Lankes stepped up and, before Ulla could say yes, elected himself Oskar's traveling companion and boxed the Muse, the long-legged Muse, on the ear because she didn't want to stay home and had burst into tears.

Why didn't Oskar defend himself? Why, if he wanted to travel with the Muse, did he not take her side? As attractive as the thought of a trip with the extremely slender, downy blond Ulla was, I still feared becoming too intimate with a Muse. You have to keep the Muses at a distance, I told myself, otherwise the Muse's kiss will start to taste like everyday fare. Better to travel with Lankes, who slaps his Muse when she tries to kiss him.

No lengthy discussions were required about our destination. Normandy was the only choice. We wanted to visit the bunkers between Caen and Cabourg. Because that's where we'd met during the war. The only difficulty was getting visas. But Oskar doesn't waste words on visa stories.

Lankes is a stingy man. The lavishness with which he flings cheap or scrounged paint on poorly primed canvas is matched only by his tight-fistedness when it comes to paper money or hard cash. He never buys cigarettes, but he's always smoking. To show how systematic his stinginess is, consider the following: the moment someone gives him a cigarette, he takes a ten-pfennig piece from his left trouser pocket, lifts the coin briefly, and slips it into his right trouser pocket, where it joins a greater or lesser number of small coins, depending on the time of day. He smokes constantly and once told me, when he was in a good mood, "I make about two marks a day smoking!"

The bombed-out lot Lankes bought in Wersten about a year ago was paid for, or perhaps we should say puffed for, with the cigarettes of his friends and acquaintances.

This was the Lankes with whom Oskar traveled to Normandy. We took an express train. Lankes would rather have hitchhiked. But since he was my guest and I was paying, he had to give in. We went by bus from Caen to Cabourg. Past poplars behind which were meadows bordered by hedges. Brown-and-white cows gave the countryside the look of an ad for milk chocolate. Of course the shiny paper wouldn't dare show the obvious war damage that still marked and disfigured every village, including the little town of Bavent, where I'd lost my Roswitha.

From Cabourg we walked along the beach toward the mouth of the Orne. It was not raining. Just before Le Home, Lankes said, "We're home now, boy! Got a cigarette?" Even while switching the coin from pocket to pocket, he pointed with his wolf's head stretched toward one of the numerous undamaged pillboxes in the dunes. Long-armed, he held his knapsack, the sketching easel, and a dozen stretched canvases on the left, put his right arm around me, and pulled me toward the concrete. Oskar's luggage consisted of a small suitcase and his drum.

On the third day of our stay on the Atlantic coast — in the meantime we had cleared the interior of Dora Seven of drifted sand, removed the unsightly traces of lovers who'd sought shelter there, and furnished the space with a crate and our sleeping bags — Lankes returned from the beach with a good-sized cod. Some fishermen had given it to him. He'd tossed off a sketch of their boat, they'd palmed off part of their catch.

Since we were still calling the pillbox Dora Seven, it's no wonder Oskar's thoughts turned to Sister Dorothea while cleaning the fish. Liver and milt from the fish flowed over both his hands. I was facing the sun as I scaled the cod, and Lankes took the occasion to dash off a quick watercolor. We sat behind the pillbox, sheltered from the wind. The August sun did a headstand on the concrete dome. I began larding the fish with garlic. The cavity once filled with milt, liver, and guts I stuffed with onions, cheese, and thyme, but didn't throw liver and milt away, lodged both delicacies between the fish's jaws, which I wedged open with a lemon. Lankes nosed about in the area. Scavenging, he disappeared into Dora Four, Three, and bunkers farther on. He returned with boards and some large cartons he could use to paint on, and bequeathed the wood to the little fire.

We had no trouble keeping the fire going all day, since the beach was pierced every step or two by dry, feather-light driftwood casting changing shadows. Over the hot, glowing coals, which were now ready, I laid part of an iron balcony railing that Lankes had torn off a deserted beach villa. I rubbed the fish with olive oil and set it on the hot grate, also oiled. I squeezed lemon over the crackling cod, and slowly — for you mustn't rush a fish — readied it for the table.

The table consisted of several empty buckets covered by a large piece of tar-board folded in several places. We had our own forks and tin plates. To distract Lankes — who was circling around the slowly steeping fish like a hungry gull after carrion — I brought my drum out from the bunker. I bedded it down in the sand and played against the wind, constantly changing rhythm, breaking up the sounds of the surf and the rising tide: Bebra's Theater at the Front had come to inspect concrete.

From Kashubia to Normandy. Felix and Kitty, the two acrobats, knotted and unknotted themselves on top of the pillbox, recited against the wind — just as Oskar played against the wind — a poem whose refrain proclaimed in the midst of war a coming age of primal gemütlichkeit: ". . . and Sunday's roast with leaves of bay: The bourgeois life is on its way!" Kitty declaimed in her slight Saxon accent; and Bebra, my wise Bebra, captain of the Propaganda Corps, nodded; and Roswitha, my Mediterranean Raguna, picked up the picnic basket, set the table on concrete, on top of Dora Seven; and Corporal Lankes too ate our white bread, drank our chocolate, smoked Captain Bebra's cigarettes . . .

"Man, Oskar!" Lankes called me back from the past. "I wish I could paint the way you drum; got a cigarette?"

So I stopped drumming, handed my traveling companion a cigarette, checked the fish and saw that it was good: its eyes bulged tender, soft, and white. Slowly, not missing a spot, I squeezed some lemon over the partially browned, partially cracked skin of the cod.

"Me hungry!" said Lankes. He bared his long, pointed yellow teeth and pounded his chest apelike with both fists against his checkered shirt.

"Heads or tails?" I put to him and slid the fish onto a sheet of wax paper covering the tar-board as a tablecloth. "What would you advise?" Lankes asked, pinching out his cigarette and stowing away the butt.

"As a friend I'd say take the tail. As a cook I've got to recommend the head. But if my mama, who ate a lot of fish, were here now, she'd say take the tail, Herr Lankes, then you know what you've got. The doctor, on the other hand, always advised my father . . ."

"I stay away from doctors," Lankes said distrustfully.

"Dr. Hollatz always advised my father, when it came to cod, which we call dorsch, always to eat the head."

"Then I'll take the tail. I can see you're trying to pull a fast one on me!" Lankes was still suspicious.

"So much the better for Oskar. I like a good head."

"Then I'll take the head, if you want it so bad."

"You have a hard life, Lankes," I said, to put an end to the conversation. "The head is yours, I'll take the tail."

"Hey, I put one over on you, didn't I?"

Oskar admitted that Lankes had put one over on him. I knew his fish would only taste good if seasoned with the certainty that he'd put one over on me. I called him a sharp customer, a lucky dog, he must have been born on Sunday—and we pitched into the cod.

He took the head, I squeezed the rest of the lemon juice over the white, crumbling flesh of the tail, from which the butter-soft garlic cloves loosened and fell.

Lankes pried bones from between his teeth, peered over at me and the tail piece: "Let me try some of your tail." I nodded, he tried some, still wasn't sure, till Oskar took a bite of the head and reassured him: as usual he had snagged the better piece.

We drank Bordeaux with the fish. I was sorry about that, said I'd have preferred white wine in the coffee cups. Lankes waved off my concerns, they always drank red wine in Dora Seven when he was a corporal, he recalled, right up till the invasion: "Man, were we drunk when it all started up. Kowalski, Scherbach, and little Leuthold, all buried back there in the same graveyard on the other side of Cabourg, they didn't have a clue what was happening. The English at Arromanches, and loads of Canadians in our sector. They were on to us, saying 'How are you?' before we could get our suspenders up."

Then, stabbing the air with his fork and spitting out bones: "By the way, I saw that nut Herzog today in Cabourg, you met him on your tour of inspection. A lieutenant."

Of course Oskar remembered Lieutenant Herzog. Lankes went on to tell me over fish that Herzog came to Cabourg year in and year out with maps and surveying instruments, because the pillboxes kept him awake nights. He planned to come by Dora Seven too, and take measurements.

We were still on our fish—which was slowly revealing its large, bony structure—when Lieutenant Herzog arrived. Khaki shorts, muscular bulging calves above tennis shoes, gray-brown hair sprouting from his open linen shirt. Naturally we stayed seated. Lankes introduced me as his friend and comrade-in-arms Oskar, and still called Herzog "Lieutenant," although he was now retired.

The retired lieutenant immediately began inspecting Dora Seven, starting with the outside, which Lankes allowed him to do. He filled out charts, pestered the countryside and oncoming tide with his telescope. He caressed the gun slits of Dora Six, right next to us, so tenderly you would have thought he was pleasuring his wife. When he wanted to inspect the interior of Dora Seven, our vacation cottage, Lankes resisted: "Man, Herzog, what is it you want? Fiddling around here with concrete. That was news once, but it's all passé now."

Passé is a pet term with Lankes. He tends to divide the world into contemporary and passé. But for the retired lieutenant nothing was passé, things still didn't add up, they'd all have to answer to history many times over in the coming years, and he was going to inspect the interior of Dora Seven now: "I hope I've made myself clear, Lankes."

Herzog had already cast his shadow across our table and fish. He started to go past us and into the pillbox, above the entrance of which concrete ornaments still bore witness to the artistic hand of Corporal Lankes.

Herzog didn't make it past our table. Without dropping his fork, Lankes's fist shot up and laid out retired Lieutenant Herzog on the sand. Shaking his head, deploring the disruption of our fish fest, Lankes rose, bunched the lieutenant's linen shirt at his chest, dragged him off to one side, tracing a smooth, straight track in the sand, and tossed him down the dune, where we could no longer see him but still had to listen to him. Herzog gathered up his surveying instruments, which Lankes had flung after him, and withdrew cursing, conjuring up all the ghosts of history that Lankes had called passé.

"He's not all that far off, is Herzog, even if he is a nutter. If we hadn't been so drunk when it all started back then, who knows what might have happened to those Canadians."

I could only nod in agreement, for just the day before, at low tide, I'd found among the seashells and empty prawn husks a telltale button from a Canadian uniform. Oskar stowed the button away in his wallet, as pleased as if he'd found a rare Etruscan coin.

Lieutenant Herzog's visit, brief though it was, had stirred up memories: "Do you remember, Lankes, when our frontline troupe was inspecting your concrete and we had breakfast on top of the pillbox, there was a slight breeze, just like today; and all at once six or seven nuns appeared, searching for prawns among the Rommel asparagus, and you were ordered to clear the beach, Lankes, and did, with a deadly round of machine-gun fire."

Lankes remembered, sucked on fish bones, even knew their names,

Sister Scholastika, Sister Agneta, named them in turn, described the novice as a rosy face framed in black, portrayed her so clearly that the image of my secular hospital nurse, Sister Dorothea, which I carry with me always, was not so much submerged as partially obscured; and was even further obscured when, a few minutes after his description — but not so surprisingly as to constitute a miracle — a young nun, pink and framed in black, could hardly be missed billowing across the dunes from the direction of Cabourg.

She was warding off the sun with a black umbrella of the kind elderly gentlemen carry. Above her eyes arched an intensely green celluloid shade resembling the visors worn by busy Hollywood filmmakers. They were calling for her in the dunes. There seemed to be more nuns out there. "Sister Agneta!" they called. "Sister Agneta, where are you?"

And Sister Agneta, the young thing who could be seen above our clearly delineated codfish skeleton, replied, "Here, Sister Scholastika. There's no wind at all here."

Lankes grinned and nodded complacently with his wolf's head, as if he had ordered up this Catholic parade, as if nothing could surprise him.

The young nun spotted us and stood to the left of the pillbox. Her rosy face, with two circular nostrils, said between slightly protruding but otherwise perfect teeth, "Oh."

Lankes turned his head and neck without moving his upper body: "Well, Sister, taking a little stroll?"

How quickly the answer came: "We visit the seashore once a year. But for me it's the first time. The ocean's so big."

There was no denying it. To this very day, that description of the ocean seems to me the only one that truly hits the mark.

Lankes played host, poked about in my portion of fish and offered her some: "Try a little fish, Sister? It's still warm." His free and easy French astonished me, and Oskar tried the foreign language too: "You don't have to worry, Sister. It's Friday."

But even this allusion to the no doubt rigid rules of her order could not convince the young woman so cleverly hidden beneath her habit to partake of our repast.

"Do you live here?" curiosity impelled her to ask. She found our bunker charming, if slightly odd. At this point, unfortunately, the Mother

Superior and five other nuns with black umbrellas and green reporter's visors entered the picture over the crest of the dune. Agneta dashed off and, as far as I could gather from the flurry of words clipped short by the east wind, was given a good scolding and taken back into their circle.

Lankes was dreaming. He held his fork upside down in his mouth and stared at the billowing group on the dune: "Those aren't nuns, they're sailing ships."

"Sailing ships are white," I pointed out.

"Those are black sailing ships." It was hard to argue with Lankes. "The one out on the left is the flagship. *Agneta*'s a speedy corvette. Good sailing weather: column formation, jib to stern post, mizzenmast, mainmast and foremast, all sails set, heading toward the horizon, toward England. Just think: the Tommies wake up tomorrow morning, look out the window, and what do they see? — twenty-five thousand nuns, flags flying from the mast tops, and here comes the first broadside . . ."

"A new religious war," I helped him. The flagship should be named the *Mary Stuart* or the *De Valera,* or better still, the *Don Juan.* A new, more mobile armada avenges Trafalgar. "Death to all Puritans" is the watchword, and this time the English don't have a Nelson on hand. Let the invasion begin: England's no longer an island.

The conversation was getting a little too political for Lankes. "Now they're steaming away, the nuns," he reported.

"Sailing away," I corrected him.

Sailing or steaming, they billowed off toward Cabourg. They held umbrellas to shield themselves from the sun. But one lagged a little behind, bent down between steps, picking up and discarding. The rest of the fleet — to stick with the metaphor — made their way slowly on, tacking into the wind, toward the burned-out shell of the former beach hotel.

"She didn't get her anchor up, or her rudder's damaged." Lankes was sticking with sea lingo. "Isn't that the speedy corvette *Agneta*?"

Corvette or frigate, it was the novice Agneta coming toward us, gathering and discarding seashells.

"What's that you're gathering, Sister?" Lankes could see very well what it was.

"Seashells." She pronounced the word very clearly and bent down.

"Are you allowed to do that? Those are earthly goods, after all."

I supported the novice Agneta: "You're wrong, Lankes. There's nothing earthly about seashells."

"Then they're stranded goods, goods in any case, and nuns aren't allowed to have them. For them it's poverty, poverty, and more poverty. Right, Sister?"

Sister Agneta smiled with protruding teeth: "I just take a few. They're for the kindergarten. The little ones love to play with them, and they've never been to the seashore."

Agneta stood at the entrance to the pillbox and cast a nun's glance inside.

"How do you like our little home?" I said, cozying up to her. Lankes was more direct: "Take a tour of our villa. Costs nothing to look, Sister."

She scraped the tips of her shoes below the sturdy stuff of her habit, stirring up sand that the wind lifted and sprinkled over our fish. Somewhat more uncertain now, with eyes distinctly light brown, she examined us and the table between us. "Surely I shouldn't," she replied, asking to be contradicted.

"Oh come now, Sister!" the painter said, sweeping all objections aside, and rising. "It's got a great view, the bunker. You can see the whole beach through the gun slits."

She still hesitated, her shoes now surely full of sand. Lankes extended his hand into the pillbox entrance. His concrete ornaments cast strong, ornamental shadows. "It's clean inside." Perhaps it was the artist's gesture of invitation that brought the nun into the bunker. "Just for a moment, then," came the decisive word. She whished into the pillbox ahead of Lankes. He wiped his hands on his trousers — a typical painter's gesture — and warned me before disappearing: "Don't eat my fish!"

But Oskar had had his fill of fish. I withdrew from the table, remained at the mercy of the sandy wind and the blustering noise of the tide and the sea, that swaggering old strongman. With my foot I dragged my drum closer and began drumming, tried to drum my way out of this concrete landscape, this pillbox world, this vegetable called Rommel asparagus.

First, and with scant success, I tried love: Once upon a time I too had loved a Sister. Not a nun, to be sure, but a nurse. She lived in Zeidler's flat, behind a door of frosted glass. She was beautiful, and yet I never saw her. A coco runner came between us. It was too dark in Zeidler's hall. And so I felt the coco fibers much more clearly than Sister Dorothea's body.

When this theme ended all too quickly on the coco runner, I tried to convert my early love for Maria to rhythm and plant it like rapidly growing ivy in front of the pillbox. But once again Sister Dorothea stood in the way of my love for Maria: the smell of carbolic acid drifted in from the sea, gulls beckoned in nurses' uniforms, the sun seemed to glow like a Red Cross pin.

Oskar was actually glad when his drumming was interrupted. The Mother Superior, Sister Scholastika, had returned with her five nuns. They looked tired, held their umbrellas at a forlorn slant: "Have you seen a young nun, our young novice? The child is so young. It's the first time the child has seen the ocean. She must have lost her way. Where are you, Sister Agneta?"

There was nothing I could do but send the little billowing squad, this time with the wind at their backs, off toward the mouth of the Orne, Arromanches, and Port Winston, where the English once wrested their artificial harbor from the sea. There wouldn't have been room for all of them in the bunker anyway. I'd been tempted, just for a moment, to let them pay Lankes a surprise visit, but then friendship, disgust, and malice combined to make me lift my thumb toward the mouth of the Orne. The nuns obeyed my thumb, turned into six steadily shrinking, wavering black dots on the crest of the dune; and their plaintive "Sister Agneta, Sister Agneta!" turned increasingly windswept, till it was buried at last in the sand.

Lankes left the pillbox first. The typical painter's gesture: he wiped his hands on the legs of his trousers, lounged about in the sun, bummed a cigarette off me, stuck it in his shirt pocket, and fell upon the cold cod. "That whets your appetite," he said suggestively, and set to pillaging the tail piece that was mine.

"She must be unhappy now," I said accusingly to Lankes, savoring the word unhappy.

"How so? She's got nothing to be unhappy about."

It was inconceivable to Lankes that his notion of human relations might make anyone unhappy.

"What's she doing now?" I asked, though I really had another question in mind.

"She's sewing," Lankes explained with his fork. "Ripped her habit a bit and now she's mending it."

The seamstress left the bunker. She immediately opened her umbrella, babbling gaily, yet I thought I detected a note of strain: "The view from your bunker really is nice. You can see the whole beach and the ocean."

She paused before the ruins of our fish.

"May I?"

We both nodded.

"Sea air whets your appetite," I said by way of encouragement, upon which she nodded, dug into our fish with reddened, chapped hands recalling her hard work in the nunnery, raised the fish to her mouth, and ate gravely, with pensive concentration, as if she were rechewing something along with it, something she'd had before the fish.

I glanced under her coif. She'd left her green reporter's visor in the pillbox. Small, uniform beads of sweat lined her smooth forehead, Madonna-like within its stiff white border. Lankes asked for another cigarette, though he still hadn't smoked the first one. I tossed him the whole pack. While he stowed three away in his shirt pocket and stuck a fourth between his lips, Sister Agneta turned, threw away her umbrella, and ran — only now did I see that she was barefoot — up the dune and disappeared toward the surf.

"Let her run," Lankes said in an oracular tone. "Either she'll come back or she won't."

I couldn't sit still for long watching the painter's cigarette. I climbed up on the pillbox and scanned the beach, the waves of the incoming tide closer now.

"Well?" Lankes wanted to know.

"She's undressing." That was all he could get out of me. "Probably wants to go swimming, to cool off."

That struck me as dangerous, given the tide, and so soon after eating. She was already in up to her knees, went in deeper and deeper, her back rounded. The water, which couldn't be all that warm with August drawing to a close, didn't seem to bother her: she swam, swam well, practiced different strokes, and dived into the oncoming waves.

"Let her swim, and come on down off the bunker."

I looked behind me and saw Lankes stretched out, puffing away. The bare bones of the cod glistened white in the sun, dominating the table.

As I jumped down from the pillbox, Lankes opened his artist's eyes and said, "What a painting that would make: *Tidal Nuns*. Or *Nuns at High Tide*."

"You monster!" I shouted. "What if she drowns?"

Lankes closed his eyes: "Then we'll call it *Drowning Nuns*."

"And if she comes back and throws herself at your feet?"

With open eyes the painter delivered his verdict: "Then I'll call her and the painting *Fallen Nun*."

With him it was always either/or, heads or tails, drowned or fallen. He bummed my cigarettes, tossed the lieutenant off the dune, ate my fish, showed the inside of a bunker to a child who'd given herself to Christ, sketched scenes in the air with his big, knobby foot as she swam out to sea, chose formats and titles: Tidal Nuns. Nuns at High Tide. Drowning Nuns. Fallen Nuns. Twenty-five Thousand Nuns. Seascape format: Nuns off Trafalgar. Portrait format: Nuns Conquer Lord Nelson. Nuns in a Headwind. Nuns in Fair Wind. Nuns Tacking into the Wind. Black, lots of black, dead white, and cold-storage blue: The Invasion, or Mystical, Barbaric, Bored — that old concrete title from his war days. And when we returned to the Rhineland, Lankes painted every one of them, in seascape format, in portrait format, a whole series of nuns, found a dealer who was crazy about nuns, exhibited forty-three nun paintings, sold seventeen to collectors, industrialists, art museums, and an American, spawned critics who compared him, Lankes himself, to Picasso, and by all this success, persuaded me, Oskar, to dig out the business card from Dr. Dösch, the concert agent, for Lankes's art was not alone in crying out for bread, my art did too: the time had come, by means of my drum, to transmute the prewar and wartime experience of Oskar, the three-year-old drummer, into the pure, ringing gold of the postwar period.

The Ring Finger

"So," said zeidler, "you clearly don't plan to work anymore." It riled him that Klepp and Oskar sat in either Klepp's or Oskar's room doing next to nothing. I'd paid the October rent on both rooms with what was left of the advance Dr. Dösch gave me after Schmuh's funeral at South Cemetery, but the prospects for November, financial and otherwise, looked bleak.

And yet we had plenty of offers. We could have played in various dance halls and nightclubs. But Oskar didn't want to play jazz. Klepp and I were at odds with each other. He said my new drum style had nothing to do with jazz. I didn't dispute that. Then he called me a traitor to everything jazz stood for.

It wasn't till early November, when Klepp found a new percussionist—and a good one too, Bobby from The Unicorn—and got a gig in the Altstadt, that we could speak like friends again, even if Klepp was starting to sound like a Communist at the time, all talk and not much thought.

The only door left open to me was Dr. Dösch's concert agency. I couldn't go back to Maria, nor did I wish to, since her lover Stenzel was getting a divorce so he could turn my Maria into a Maria Stenzel. From time to time I lettered a gravestone at Korneff's on Bittweg, dropped in at the Academy to be blackened and abstracted by eager apostles of art, and, with no ulterior motive, paid several visits to Ulla the Muse, who had been obliged to break off her engagement with Lankes shortly after our trip to the Atlantic Wall because Lankes now painted nothing but high-priced pictures of nuns, and didn't even bother to beat her anymore.

Dr. Dösch's business card lay with silent insistence on the table by my bathtub. One day, having torn it up and thrown it away, since I wanted nothing to do with Dr. Dösch, I discovered to my horror that I could reel off the agent's phone number and address by heart like a poem. I spent three days doing this, kept awake by the number, and so on the fourth day I went to a phone booth, dialed the number, Dösch answered, acted as if he'd been expecting my call at any moment, and asked me to come to the agency that very afternoon so he could introduce me to his boss, who was expecting me.

The West Concert Agency was located on the eighth floor of a new high-rise office building. Before entering the lift, I wondered if the agency's name might not conceal some annoying political agenda. If there was a West Concert Agency then there was sure to be an East Concert Agency in some matching high-rise. The name was cleverly chosen, for I immediately preferred the West, and as I left the lift on the eighth floor I had the good feeling that I was on my way to the right agency. Wall-to-wall carpet, plenty of brass, indirect lighting, totally soundproof, door-to-door harmony, long-legged, crisply rustling secretaries carrying the aroma of their bosses' cigars past me; I almost turned and ran from the West Concert Agency.

Dr. Dösch welcomed me with open arms. Oskar was glad it didn't turn into a hug. A green sweater girl's typewriter fell silent as I entered, then caught up with what it had missed on account of my entrance. Dösch let his boss know I'd arrived. Oskar sat down on the left front sixth of an armchair upholstered in English red. Then a double door opened, the typewriter held its breath, I was sucked from my chair, the doors closed behind me, carpet flowed through a bright room, bearing me along with it, till a piece of steel furniture told me: Oskar is now standing in front of the boss's desk, wondering how much it weighs. I lifted my blue eyes, sought the boss beyond the infinite, bare oak surface, and in a wheelchair that could be cranked up like a dentist's chair and swiveled, paralyzed and living now only through his eyes and fingertips, found my friend and master Bebra.

He still had that voice, though. It spoke from Bebra: "So we meet again, Herr Matzerath. Did I not say years ago, when you still preferred to face the world as a three-year-old, that our kind can never lose one another? But I see to my regret that you've altered your proportions in a major and senseless way to your own disadvantage. Didn't you measure barely three foot one back then?"

I nodded, on the verge of tears. On the wall, behind the steady hum of the master's electric wheelchair, hung the only picture in the room, a life-size, half-length portrait of my Roswitha, the great Raguna, in a Baroque frame. Without following my gaze, but well aware of its goal, Bebra spoke, hardly moving his mouth: "Oh yes, our dear Roswitha. Would she have liked the new Oskar? I doubt it. She had a thing for a different Oskar, a three-year-old, chubby-cheeked Oskar, madly in love. She worshiped him, as she admitted to me in what was more an announcement than a confession. But one day he didn't want to bring her coffee, so she got it herself and paid for it with her life. That is not, to the best of my knowledge, the only murder committed by our chubby-cheeked Oskar. Didn't he drum his poor mama into the grave?"

I nodded, was able to weep, thank God, and kept my eyes trained on Roswitha. Meanwhile Bebra was readying his next blow: "And what about that postal clerk Jan Bronski, whom Oskar used to call his presumptive father? He turned him over to the hangmen. They shot him in the chest. Perhaps, Herr Oskar Matzerath, since you dare appear in this new form, you can tell me what happened to our three-year-old Oskar's second presumptive father, Matzerath the grocer?"

I confessed to that murder too, admitted I'd rid myself of Matzerath, described how I'd made him choke to death, no longer hid behind a Russian machine gun but said instead, "It was I, Master Bebra. I caused it, and I caused the other one too, I caused that death, even there I am not innocent — have mercy on me!"

Bebra laughed. I don't know what he laughed with. His wheelchair trembled, winds ruffled through his white gnome's hair and across the hundred thousand wrinkles that formed his face.

Once more I begged fervently for mercy, lent my voice a sweetness I knew was effective, covered my face with hands I knew were beautiful and equally effective: "Mercy, dear Master Bebra, have mercy!"

Then, having cast himself in the role of judge and playing it to the hilt, he pressed a little button on a small ivory switchboard he held between his hands and knees.

The carpet behind me brought the green sweater girl. She held a file, spread it out on the oaken surface that stood roughly level with my collarbone on a pluck of steel tubing, so that I couldn't see what the sweater girl was spreading out. She handed me an ink pen: I was to purchase Bebra's mercy with my signature.

Nevertheless I ventured a question toward the wheelchair. I found it difficult to place my signature blindly on the spot indicated by a lacquered fingernail.

"It's a work contract," Bebra said. "You have to sign it in full. Write 'Oskar Matzerath,' so we know who we're dealing with."

As soon as I'd signed, the humming of the motor increased fivefold, I tore my eyes from the ink pen just in time to see a quickly rolling wheelchair, growing smaller as it departed, lower itself, cross the parquet floor, and disappear through a side door.

Now, some may think that the contract in duplicate I signed twice purchased my soul, or required some terrible misdeed of Oskar. Nothing of the kind. As I studied the contract in the outer office with the help of Dr. Dösch, I understood quickly and effortlessly that Oskar's task consisted of performing solo on his tin drum before an audience, that I was to drum as I did when I was three and as I did again in Schmuh's Onion Cellar. The concert agency agreed to organize my tour, and to beat the drum of publicity prior to Oskar's appearance with his own drum.

While the advertising campaign was under way, I lived on a second generous advance from the West Concert Agency. Now and then I visited the office building, talked to journalists, let myself be photographed, lost my way at times in that box which looked, smelled, and felt the same everywhere, like some highly indecent object with an infinitely expandable condom stretched over it, sealing it off. Dr. Dösch and the sweater girl treated me with consideration, but I saw no more of Master Bebra.

Actually I could have afforded better lodgings even prior to my first tour. I stayed at Zeidler's, however, because of Klepp, trying to make up with my friend, who didn't like my relationship with the agency, but I refused to give in, no longer accompanied him to the Altstadt, drank no more beer, ate no more fresh blood sausage with onion, but dined instead in the finest railway-station restaurants to prepare myself for future railroad journeys.

Oskar doesn't have space here to describe his successes in detail. A week before the tour began, the first scandalously effective posters appeared, setting the stage for my success, proclaiming my forthcoming appearance like that of a magician, a faith healer, a messiah. My first visitations were to cities in the Ruhr area. The halls in which I appeared seated from fifteen hundred to two thousand people. I sat alone onstage before a black velvet backdrop. A spotlight targeted me. A dinner jacket clothed me. Though I drummed, there were no young jazz lovers among my fans. My listeners, my fans, were mature adults over the age of forty-five. To be precise, I would say approximately one-fourth of my audience consisted of forty-five- to fifty-five-year-olds. Those were my younger fans. Another quarter were fifty-five to sixty years old. The oldest men and women made up the larger and more appreciative half of my listeners. I spoke to those advanced in years and they responded, no longer sat silently as I let the three-year-old's drum speak, but rejoiced, not in the language of the aged, of course, but with the childish babbling and prattling of a three-year-old, with "Rashu, Rashu, Rashu!" the moment Oskar drummed up something from the amazing life of the amazing Rasputin. I had even more success with certain themes than I did with Rasputin, who was too demanding for most listeners, themes with no particular plot, which merely described situations, to which I gave titles like Baby's First Teeth—That Awful Whooping Cough—Those Itchy Wool Socks—Dream of Fire and You'll Wet the Bed.

These pleased the old people. They were right there with Oskar. They suffered as they cut their milk teeth. Two thousand old people hacked long and hard from an outbreak of whooping cough I instigated. How they scratched at the long wool socks I pulled onto them. Many an old lady, many an old gentleman, wet their pants and their padded seats when I set the children dreaming of roaring fires. I don't recall whether it was in Wuppertal or Bochum, no, it was in Recklinghausen: I was playing to old miners, the company had paid for the performance, and I thought these old comrades, having spent years handling black coal, could handle a little black fright. So Oskar drummed up "The Old Black Cook" and watched fifteen hundred comrades who had suffered through firedamp, collapsing tunnels, strikes, and unemployment send up a fearsome howl when she arrived, a howl—and that's why I mention the story—that shattered several thickly curtained windowpanes in the hall. And so by this detour I rediscovered my glass-slaying voice, but used it sparingly, not wanting to ruin our business.

For my tour was indeed good business. When I came back and settled accounts with Dr. Dösch, it turned out my tin drum was a gold mine.

Though I hadn't asked after Master Bebra—I had long since given up all hope of seeing him again—Dr. Dösch announced that Bebra was expecting me.

My second encounter with the Master went somewhat differently from the first. Oskar was not left standing before the steel desk, but found instead a motorized, swivel wheelchair made to his measurements placed opposite the Master's chair. We sat for a long time in silence, listening to press notices and reports on Oskar's percussive arts which Dr. Dösch had recorded and now played for us. Bebra seemed satisfied. I found all the talk in the newspapers a little embarrassing. A cult was being built up around me, attributing healing powers to me and my drum. They were said to cure memory loss; the term "Oskarism" made its first appearance, and soon became a catch phrase.

Afterward the sweater girl brought me tea. She laid two pills on the Master's tongue. We chatted. He was no longer my accuser. It was like the early years when we sat in the Café Vierjahreszeiten, except the Signora was missing, our Roswitha. When I couldn't help noticing that Master Bebra had fallen asleep during my somewhat long-winded tales of Oskar's past, I spent another quarter-hour playing with my electric wheelchair, sent it humming across the parquet floor, swiveled it left and right, made it grow and shrink, and found it difficult to part from this everyday item of furniture, which, with its infinite possibilities, offered an innocent vice.

My second tour took place at Advent. I adjusted my program accordingly and heard my praises sung in both Catholic and Protestant newspapers. And I did indeed manage to turn ancient, hard-boiled sinners into little children singing Advent hymns in touchingly quavery voices. "Jesus I live for thee, Jesus I die for thee," sang twenty-five hundred people one would not have believed capable of such eager, childlike faith at their advanced age.

My third tour, which took place during Carnival, was equally appropriate. No so-called Children's Carnival could have been more amusing and carefree than the atmosphere at my performances, which transformed every trembling grandma, every shaky grandpa, into naively comic gangland molls and rat-a-tat-tatting gangsters.

After Carnival I signed a contract with a record company. I recorded in soundproof studios, was put off at first by the overly sterile atmosphere, then had huge photos of old people like those in nursing homes and on park benches placed on the studio walls and drummed as effectively as I did at performances in the human warmth of concert halls.

The records sold like hotcakes, and Oskar grew rich. Did I give up my miserable former bathroom in Zeidler's flat as a result? I did not. Why not? Because of my friend Klepp, and the empty room behind the frosted-glass door in which Sister Dorothea had once lived and breathed. What did Oskar do with all that money? He made Maria, his Maria, a proposition.

I said to Maria: If you show Stenzel the door, if you not only refuse to marry him but throw him out once and for all, I'll buy you a new, modern delicatessen in a first-rate business location, because you, my dear Maria, were born for business, not for some good-for-nothing like Herr Stenzel.

I had not misread Maria. She gave up Stenzel, set up a first-class delicatessen on Friedrichstraße with my financial backing, and just last week—as Maria reported yesterday with joy, and not without gratitude—opened a branch in Oberkassel, only three years after starting the first one.

Was I on the way back from my seventh or my eighth tour? July was at its hottest. I hailed a taxi at the train station and went straight to the office building. As had happened at the station, a crowd of annoying autograph hunters stood outside the high-rise—retirees and grandmas who should have been taking care of their grandchildren. I immediately sent up word to the boss I was there, found the double door open and the carpet flowing toward the steel desk; but it wasn't the Master behind the desk, no wheelchair awaited me, but the smile of Dr. Dösch.

Bebra was dead. In fact the Master had been gone for several weeks. At Bebra's wish, I had not been informed that his condition was serious. Nothing, not even his death, was to interrupt my tour. At the reading of the will that soon followed, I inherited a small fortune and the portrait of Roswitha, yet also suffered a substantial financial loss, since I canceled without notice two tours to which I was firmly committed, one to southern Germany and one to Switzerland, and was sued for breach of contract.

Those few thousand marks aside, I was hit hard by Bebra's death and was slow to recover. I locked my tin drum away and refused to stir from my room. To make matters worse, my friend Klepp chose that moment to get married, made a redheaded cigarette girl his wife, just because he'd once given her his photo. Shortly before the wedding, to which I was not invited, he gave up his room, moved to Stockum, and Oskar remained Zeidler's sole lodger.

My relationship with the Hedgehog had altered somewhat. Now that almost every newspaper carried my name in banner headlines he treated me with respect, and in return for a small consideration, even gave me the key to Sister Dorothea's empty room; later I rented the room myself so no one else could have it.

A path was thus provided for my sorrow. I opened the doors to both rooms, wandered from the tub in my room across the coco runner in the hall to Dorothea's chamber, gazed into the empty wardrobe, faced the taunting washstand mirror, despaired beside the heavy bed stripped bare, escaped into the corridor, fled from the coco fibers to my room and couldn't even bear it there.

Expecting to find customers among the lonely perhaps, an enterprising businessman from East Prussia who'd lost an estate in Masuren opened a shop near Jülicher Straße with a simple, straightforward name: Dogs for Rent.

There I rented Lux, a black Rottweiler, powerful, gleaming, and slightly overweight. I went walking with him so I wouldn't have to pace back and forth between my bathtub and Sister Dorothea's empty wardrobe in Zeidler's flat.

Lux would often lead me to the Rhine. There he barked at the ships. Lux would often lead me to Rath, in Grafenberg Forest. There he barked at the lovers. Toward the end of July of fifty-one, Lux led me to Gerresheim, a suburb of Düsseldorf, which, with its few factories and a large glassworks, was doing its best to deny its rural origins. Just beyond Gerresheim were allotment gardens, and among them pastures had fenced themselves in, and fields of grain were billowing, rye I think it was.

Have I already said it was hot the day the dog Lux led me to Gerresheim, and beyond Gerresheim to the allotment gardens and fields of grain? Not till we'd left the last houses of the suburb behind did I let Lux off the line. Even so he stayed at my heel, a loyal dog, an extremely loyal dog, since as a dog-rental dog he had to be loyal to many masters.

In other words, Lux obeyed me, positively dogged my steps. I found this dogged obedience overdone, wished he would run ahead, kicked him so he would; but he strayed with a bad conscience, kept turning his smooth black neck, kept his doggedly devoted dog eyes on me.

"Beat it, Lux!" I ordered. "Scram!"

Lux obeyed several times, but so briefly that I was delighted when he stayed away for slightly longer, disappeared into the grain, which was rye here, swaying in the wind, wait, not swaying in the wind — the wind had dropped and it was sultry.

Lux must be chasing a rabbit, I thought. Or perhaps he simply wants to be alone, to be his doggy self, just as Oskar would like to be a man awhile, without a dog.

I paid no attention to my surroundings. Neither the allotment gardens nor Gerresheim nor the city lying flatly in the haze beyond attracted my eye. I sat down on an empty, rusted cable reel, which I will now call a cable drum, for Oskar had barely taken a rusty seat before he was drumming his knuckles on the cable drum. It was hot out. My suit weighed down on me, it was too heavy for summer. Lux was gone, and stayed gone. The cable drum didn't replace my tin drum, but even so: I slowly drifted back, and when things didn't seem to be going anywhere, when the images of the past few years with all those hospitals kept coming back, I picked up two dry sticks, and told myself: Hang on a moment, Oskar, let's see what you are and where you came from. And there they were, shining, those two sixty-watt bulbs of the hour of my birth. The moth chattered between them, a distant storm shoved heavy furniture about, I heard Matzerath speak, then Mama. He pledged me the store, Mama promised a toy, I'd have a tin drum when I turned three, and so Oskar tried to make those three years pass as rapidly as possible: I ate, drank, spit up, gained weight, let them weigh me, diaper me, bathe me, brush me, powder me, vaccinate me, admire me, call me by name, smiled when asked, chortled on command, went to sleep on time, woke up on time, and showed in sleep the special face that grownups call angelic. I had diarrhea several times, caught a number of colds, had whooping cough, clung to it awhile, and did not let go till I had grasped its difficult rhythm, kept it forever in my wrists; for, as you know, "Whooping Cough" was part of my repertoire, and when Oskar drummed the whooping cough before an audience of two thousand, two thousand little old ladies and men hacked and coughed.

Lux whined before me, rubbed against my knees. This dog from the dog rental my loneliness made me rent. There he stood four-legged, wagged his tail, was a dog, had a doggy look, and held something in his slavering muzzle: a stick, a stone, whatever a dog might find of value.

Those all-important early years slipped slowly from me. The pain in my gums heralding my first milk teeth receded, I leaned back wearily, a grown-up hunchback, neatly but somewhat too warmly dressed, with a wristwatch, an identification card, and a bundle of banknotes in my wallet. I placed a cigarette between my lips, held a match to it, and left it to the tobacco to dissolve the clear-cut taste of childhood left in my mouth.

And Lux? Lux rubbed against me. I pushed him away, blew cigarette smoke at him. He didn't like that, but held his ground and rubbed against me. His gaze licked at me. I searched the nearby wires between the telegraph poles for swallows, hoping to use them as a remedy for pushy dogs. But there were no swallows and Lux refused to be driven off. His muzzle found its way between my trouser legs, hit the spot so unerringly it seemed the East Prussian rental agent must have trained him to do it.

I struck him twice with the heel of my shoe. He retreated, stood there trembling, four-legged, yet still offered me his muzzle, holding its stick or stone so steadfastly he might have been holding not a stick or a stone but the wallet I felt in my jacket or the watch I felt ticking on my wrist.

What was he holding? What was so important, so worthy of display?

I reached between his warm jaws, soon held it in my hand, saw what I held, yet still acted as if I were searching for the word that might describe what Lux had found and brought from the field of rye.

There are parts of the human body which can be examined more easily and more accurately when they are detached, alienated from the whole. It was a finger. A woman's finger. A ring finger. A woman's ring finger. A tastefully ringed woman's finger. Between the metacarpal and the first finger joint, approximately three-quarters of an inch below the ring, the finger had allowed itself to be hacked off. A clean and clear cross-section preserved the sinews of the tendon.

It was a lovely, agile finger. I immediately identified the gemstone of the ring — correctly, as it later turned out — as an aquamarine, held by six golden claws. The ring itself proved so thin in one spot, worn to the point of fragility, that I judged it to be an heirloom. Though a line of dirt, or rather soil, showed beneath the fingernail, as if the finger had been forced to scratch or dig into the earth, from its shape the nail appeared well manicured. Beyond that the finger, once removed from the warm living muzzle of the dog, felt cold, and its yellowish pallor matched the cold.

For months Oskar had been carrying a triangular silk handkerchief peeking out of his left front breast pocket. He pulled forth this piece of silk, spread it out, bedded the ring finger down in it, noting that the inner surface of the finger showed lines extending to the third joint that bore witness to hard work, energy, and tenacity.

After wrapping the finger in the handkerchief, I rose from the cable drum, patted Lux on the neck, set out with handkerchief and finger in handkerchief in my right hand toward Gerresheim, headed home with various plans for my find, made it as far as a nearby garden fence — when Vittlar, who was lying in the fork of an apple tree and had been watching me and my retriever, addressed me.

The Last Tram or Adoration of a Canning Jar

THE VOICE ALONE: that arrogant, affected nasal whine. He lay in the fork of the apple tree and said, "That's quite a dog you've got there, sir!"

I, at a loss: "What are you doing in that apple tree?" He preened on the forked branches, stretched his long upper body languidly: "They're just cooking apples, you've nothing to fear."

Time to put him in his place: "Who cares if they're cooking apples? What do I have to fear?"

"Well," he hissed, darting his tongue, "you might think I'm the snake, straight from Paradise, there were cooking apples even then."

I, angrily: "Allegorical rubbish!"

He, slyly: "So you think only fancy fruit's worth sinning for?"

I was ready to leave. The last thing I wanted to do right then was discuss the fruits in paradise. Then he took a more direct approach, jumped down nimbly from the apple tree, stood tall, willowy, and wily at the fence: "What's that your dog found in the rye?"

I don't know why I said, "A stone."

"And you stuck the stone in your pocket?" This was degenerating into an interrogation.

"I like to keep stones in my pocket."

"What I saw the dog bring back looked more like a stick."

"I'm sticking with stone, stick or stone."

"So it was a stick?"

"Whatever: stick or stone, cooking apples or fancy fruit . . ."

"A flexible stick?"

"The dog wants to go home, I'm off."

"A flesh-colored stick?"

"You just tend to your apples. Come on, Lux."

"A flesh-colored, flexible stick with a ring on it?"

"What is it you want? I'm just a man out for a stroll with a borrowed dog."

"Well, you see, I'd like to borrow something too. Could I just put that pretty ring on my little finger for a moment or two, the one that gleamed on the stick and turned it into a ring finger? Vittlar's my name. Gottfried von Vittlar. I'm the last of our line."

That's how I met Vittlar, made friends with him that very day, still call him my friend, and said to him not long ago, when he came to visit, "I'm so glad, dear Gottfried, that it was you who turned me in to the police and not just any stranger."

If angels exist, they surely look like Vittlar: tall, willowy, vibrant, collapsible, more likely to hug the most barren of all lampposts than a gentle maiden who might ensnare him.

You don't notice Vittlar at first. Presenting a certain side, depending on his surroundings, he can turn himself into a length of string, a scarecrow, a coat rack, the recumbent fork of a tree. That's why I didn't notice him when I was sitting on the cable drum and he lay in the apple tree. Even the dog didn't bark; for dogs neither smell nor see nor bark at angels.

"Be a good fellow, my dear Gottfried," I said to him the other day, "and send me a copy of the statement you made to the court two years or so ago that led to my trial."

Here's the copy, in his own words, of his testimony in court:

On the day in question I, Gottfried von Vittlar, was lying in the fork of an apple tree in my mother's garden that bears enough cooking apples to fill our seven canning jars with applesauce each year. I was lying in the fork of the tree, lying on my side that is, with my left hip lodged in the lowest point of the fork, which was slightly mossy. My feet were pointing toward the glassworks at Gerresheim. I was looking—let's see now—I was looking straight ahead, waiting for something to happen within my field of vision.

The accused, who is today my friend, entered my field of vision. A dog accompanied him, circled about him, behaved like a dog, and, as the accused later told me, was named Lux, a Rottweiler rented from a dog-rental agency near St. Roch's Church.

The accused sat down on the empty cable drum that's been lying in front of my mother Alice von Vittlar's allotment garden since the end of the war. As the Court knows, the physique of the accused can only be described as small, and also hunchbacked. I was struck by that. But the behavior of that small, well-dressed gentleman seemed to me even stranger. He drummed on the rusty cable drum with two dry sticks. Bearing in mind that the accused is a drummer by profession, and, as has since been established, practices his trade whenever and wherever he can, and that a cable drum — which is not called a drum for nothing — could easily entice anyone, even a layperson, to drum, I can only state that on a sultry summer day, the accused Oskar Matzerath took a seat on the cable drum fronting Frau Alice von Vittlar's allotment garden and, with two dry willow sticks of unequal length, intoned rhythmically arranged sounds.

I further testify that the dog Lux disappeared for a considerable time into a field of rye ripe for harvest. If asked how long he was gone, I couldn't give an answer, since the moment I lie down in the fork of our apple tree I lose all sense of time, long or short. If I say notwithstanding that the dog disappeared for a considerable time, it means that I missed the dog, because I liked him, with his black coat and floppy ears.

The accused, however — I think it's safe to say — did not miss the dog.

When the dog Lux returned from the ripe rye, he was carrying something in his mouth. Not that I could tell what the dog held in his mouth. A stick, I thought, or a stone, or, less likely, a tin can or even a tin spoon. Only when the accused removed the corpus delicti from the dog's muzzle did I clearly recognize it for what it was. Yet, speaking conservatively, I would say that from the moment the dog first rubbed his muzzle, still holding the object, on what I believe was the left trouser leg of the accused, to that point in time, which I regret to say can no longer be precisely determined, at which the accused reached in and took possession of what he found there, several minutes passed.

No matter how hard the dog tried to get his temporary master's attention, the accused kept on drumming in that monotonously impressive yet inscrutably childlike fashion. Only when the dog resorted to rudeness, thrusting its damp muzzle between the legs of the accused, did he lower his willow sticks and kick the dog with, as I distinctly recall, his right foot. The dog made a half circle, returned a second time, trembling like a dog, and presented its full muzzle.

Without rising, seated that is, the accused — this time with his left hand — reached between the dog's teeth. Relieved of his find, the dog Lux backed away several meters. The accused remained seated, however, held the object in his hand, closed his hand, opened it again, closed it again, and when he opened his hand once more something glinted. When the accused had grown accustomed to the sight of the object, he held it up with his thumb and forefinger at approximately eye level.

Only then did I identify the object as a finger, extended the concept because of the glint, called it a ring finger, and without realizing it, had given a name to one of the most interesting trials of the postwar era: I, Gottfried von Vittlar, came to be known as the star witness in the Ring Finger Trial.

Since the accused remained calm, I too remained calm. In fact his composure communicated itself to me. And when the accused carefully wrapped the finger and ring in the handkerchief that had previously blossomed gallantly from his breast pocket, I felt a stirring of sympathy for the man on the cable drum: a neat and tidy gentleman, I thought, there's someone you ought to know.

So I called out to him as he started to leave with his rented dog in the direction of Gerresheim. He reacted with annoyance at first, seemed almost arrogant. I still can't understand why the accused saw me as the symbol of a snake, simply because I was lying in an apple tree. He was suspicious of my mother's cooking apples too, and said they must certainly be of the Paradise variety.

Now it may be true that the Evil One makes a habit of bedding down in the forks of trees. But in my case it was simply boredom, a state I attain with practiced ease, that moved me to seek a spot in the apple tree several times a week. Yet boredom may well be the very essence of Evil. And what had driven the accused beyond Düsseldorf's city walls? Loneliness, as he later confessed to me. And is not loneliness boredom's given name? I put these thoughts forward to explain the accused, not to incriminate him. After all, what made me take a liking to him, address him, and make friends with him was precisely his particular style of Evil, his drumming, which resolved Evil into its rhythmic components. Even this testimony before the bar of the High Court, which names me as a witness and him as the accused, is a game we invented, just one more small way of diverting and nourishing our boredom and loneliness.

In response to my request, the accused, after some hesitation, slipped the ring off the ring finger — it came off easily — and onto the little finger of my left hand. It fit well and pleased me. Of course I had descended from my customary fork before trying the ring on. We stood on either side of the fence, introduced ourselves, chatted, touching on various political topics, till we felt comfortable, and then he gave me the ring. He kept the finger, holding it carefully. We agreed that it was a woman's finger. While I wore the ring and let the light play on it, the accused began tapping out a lively little dance rhythm on the fence with his free left hand. The fence in front of my mother's garden is so naturally unstable that it responded in its wooden way to the drumming of the accused by rattling and vibrating. I don't know how long we stood like that, conversing with our eyes. We were engaged in this most innocent of games when an airplane's engines sounded at midrange above us. It was probably coming in for a landing at Lohausen. Though we were both curious to know if the incoming plane would land with two engines or four, we kept our eyes on each other and didn't look up at the plane; later on, when we had occasion to play the game now and again, we named it Crazy Leo's Asceticism, since the accused claims that he had a friend by that name some years ago with whom he played this little game, mostly in cemeteries.

When the plane had found its landing field — whether on two or four engines I really can't say — I gave back the ring. The accused placed it on the ring finger, used his handkerchief as packing material again, and asked me to come with him.

This was on the seventh of July, nineteen fifty-one. At the tram terminal in Gerresheim we took a taxi instead of a tram. The accused demonstrated his generosity toward me on many subsequent occasions as well. We drove into the city, asked the taxi to wait outside the dog-rental agency near St. Roch's Church while we turned in the dog Lux, reentered the taxi, which took us straight across the city, through Bilk and Oberbilk, to Wersten Cemetery, where Herr Matzerath had a fare of more than twelve marks to pay; only then did we visit the gravestone shop of the stonecutter Korneff.

The place was filthy and I was glad when the stonecutter had completed my friend's commission, which took about an hour. While my friend described the various tools and types of stone to me in loving detail, Herr Korneff, who said not a word about the finger, made a plaster cast of the finger, without its ring. I watched him work with only half an eye, but saw the finger had to be prepared; it was smeared with grease, sewing thread was run around it, then plaster was poured on and the mold split in two with the string before the plaster hardened. I'm a window dresser by trade, so making a plaster cast is nothing new to me, but the moment the stonecutter picked up the finger I felt it took on an unaesthetic quality, which it did not shed until the cast was made and the accused retrieved the finger, wiped the grease off and tucked it away in his handkerchief. My friend paid the stonecutter. At first he didn't want to take anything, since he considered Herr Matzerath a colleague. He also said Herr Oskar had popped his boils for him a while back and hadn't asked anything for that. When the plaster had hardened, the stonecutter opened the mold, placed the cast next to the original, promised to make more castings from the mold in the next few days, and accompanied us through his display of gravestones out onto Bittweg.

A second taxi ride brought us to the central train station. There the accused treated me to a lavish dinner at a fine restaurant. From his familiar tone with the waiters I gathered Herr Matzerath must be a regular guest there. We ate breast of ox with fresh horseradish, then Rhine salmon, followed by cheese, and finished with a small bottle of champagne. When the conversation drifted back to the finger and I advised the accused to regard it as lost property and turn it in, since he now had a plaster cast of it, the accused stated firmly and decisively that he considered himself its rightful owner, since he'd been promised just such a finger on the occasion of his birth, though in coded form, using the word drumstick; he also mentioned the finger-length scars on his friend Herbert Truczinski's back which had prophesied the ring finger; and then there was that empty shell at Saspe Cemetery, it too had the size and significance of a future ring finger.

Though I smiled at first at my newfound friend's reasoning, I have to admit that any open-minded person would easily grasp the sequence: drumstick, scar, shell, ring finger.

A third taxi took me home after dinner. We agreed to meet again, and when, three days later, I kept my appointment with the accused, he had a surprise in store for me.

First he showed me his flat, or rather his rooms, for Herr Matzerath lives as a lodger. He seems to have rented a shabby former bathroom to begin with, but later, when his percussive artistry brought him prestige and prosperity, he also paid rent on a windowless room he called Sister Dorothea's chamber, and did not balk at paying for a third room as well, which had been occupied by a certain Herr Münzer, a musician and colleague of the accused, laying out a huge sum, for Herr Zeidler, the landlord of the flat, had raised the rents shamelessly, knowing how prosperous Herr Matzerath had become.

It was in Sister Dorothea's so-called chamber that the accused had prepared his surprise. On the marble top of a mirrored washstand stood a jar the size my mother Alice von Vittlar uses for canning the applesauce she makes from our cooking apples. But this jar contained a ring finger floating in alcohol. The accused proudly showed me several thick medical books that had guided him in preserving the finger. I leafed quickly through the books, barely glancing at the illustrations, but admitted that the accused had done an excellent job of preserving the ring finger's appearance, and that the jar with its contents looked quite pretty and decorative in front of the mirror, which, as a professional window dresser, I was in a position to confirm.

When the accused saw I had accustomed myself to the sight of the jar, he confessed that he occasionally prayed to the jar. Curious, I inquired somewhat boldly if he could give me a sample of his prayers. He requested a favor in return, gave me pencil and paper, and asked me to write down his prayer and pose questions about the finger, which he would answer to the best of his ability as he prayed.

I herewith offer in testimony the words of the accused, my questions, his answers — the Adoration of a canning jar: I adore. Which I? Oskar or I? I piously, Oskar distractedly. Devotion, perpetual, without fearing repetition. I discerning, lacking all memory. Oskar discerning, filled with memories. I cold, hot, warm. Guilty if questioned. Innocent if not. Guilty because, came to grief because, guilty in spite of, absolved myself from, shifted all onto, fought my way through it, kept myself free of it, laughed over at in, cried about for without, blasphemed in speaking, blasphemed in silence, don't speak, don't stay silent, adore. I adore. What?

Jar. What jar? That jar. What does the jar hold? The jar holds the finger. What finger? Ring finger. Whose finger? Blond. What blond? Medium height. Medium height five foot four? Medium height five foot five. Distinguishing features? A mole. Mole where? Inner upper arm. Left right? Right. Ring finger where? Left. Engaged? Yes, but not married. Religion? Protestant. Virgin? Virgin. Born when? Don't know. When? Near Hanover. When? In December. Sagittarius or Capricorn? Sagittarius. Character? Timid. Good-natured? Hardworking, talkative. Sensible? Thrifty, levelheaded but cheerful. Shy? Likes sweets, sincere and bigoted. Pale, dreams of travel, irregular periods, lazy, likes to suffer and talk about it, lacks imagination, passive, takes things as they come, a good listener, nods in agreement, folds her arms, lowers eyelids when speaking, opens eyes wide when addressed, light gray with brown near the pupil, ring was a gift from her boss, a man who was married, refused it at first and then took it, shocking event, fibrous, Satan, lots of white, took trip, moved out, came back, couldn't stop, jealous for no reason, illness but not mine, death but not mine, yes, no, don't want to, picking cornflowers, came later, no, took her there first, can't go on . . . Amen? Amen.

I, Gottfried von Vittlar, append this copy of the prayer to my testimony before the Court only because, as confused as it may appear when read, the details regarding the owner of the ring finger coincide in large part with the official description of the murdered woman, the hospital nurse Sister Dorothea Köngetter. I am not trying to cast doubt on the accused's statement that he neither murdered the nurse nor saw her face to face.

The devotion with which my friend knelt before the canning jar, which he had placed on a chair, and plied his tin drum, which he held clamped between his knees, still strikes me today as a noteworthy fact that speaks well for him.

I had numerous opportunities over the following year or so to watch the accused pray and drum, for he hired me as a traveling companion at a generous salary and took me along on his tours, which he had interrupted for a considerable period but resumed shortly after finding the ring finger. We traveled all over West Germany, received offers from the East Zone as well, and even from abroad. But Herr Matzerath wanted to remain within the borders of the Federal Republic, wishing to avoid, as he put it, getting caught up in the usual concert-tour racket. He never drummed or prayed to the jar before a performance. But after an appearance and a leisurely meal we would repair to our hotel room: he drummed and prayed, I asked questions and wrote, and afterward we compared the prayer with those of previous days and weeks. Of course there are longer and shorter prayers. At times the words clash violently, then the next day they flow, almost tranquil and expansive. Nevertheless all the prayers I've gathered here and submit herewith to the High Court tell us nothing more than the first transcript I appended to my statement.

During this year of travel, between one tour and the next, I met in passing several friends and relatives of Herr Matzerath. He introduced me to his stepmother, Frau Maria Matzerath, whom the accused adores, though with a certain restraint. The half brother of the accused, Kurt Matzerath, also greeted me that day, a well-behaved eleven-year-old schoolboy. Frau Maria Matzerath's sister, Frau Auguste Köster, made an equally positive impression on me. As the accused confessed to me, relationships with his family had been more than a little strained during the early postwar period. It was only when Herr Matzerath set up a large delicatessen for his stepmother, one that even carried tropical fruit, and helped out financially whenever the store ran into difficulties, that a friendly relationship developed between stepmother and stepson.

Herr Matzerath also introduced me to a few of his former colleagues, mostly jazz musicians. Though Herr Münzer, whom the accused calls Klepp, struck me as cheerful and easygoing, to this day I've had neither the heart nor the will to develop these contacts further.

Even though, thanks to the generosity of the accused, I had no need to continue my career as a window dresser, I still decorated a few shop windows whenever we returned from a tour, out of sheer love for the profession. The accused was kind enough to take a personal interest in my craft, often standing on the street late into the night, and never tired of providing an audience for my modest talents. Now and then, when my work was finished, we would stroll through nighttime Düsseldorf, avoiding the Altstadt, since the accused didn't like the sight of bull's-eye windows and old-fashioned German tavern signs. One such post-midnight stroll through nighttime Unterrath—and here I come to the final portion of my statement—led us to the tram depot.

We stood side by side, at peace with the world, watching the last of the scheduled trams arrive. It was a pleasant show. The darkened city about us. In the distance, since it's Friday, a drunken construction worker roars. Otherwise all is silent, for the last trams, even if they jangle and make the curved rails squeal, are silent. Most of the trams continued directly into the depot. A few, however, sat there pointing in different directions, empty, but festively lit. Whose idea was it? We both had it, but I was the one who said, "Well, my friend, what do you think?" Herr Matzerath nodded and we boarded without haste, I took over the driver's stand, settled in at once, took off gently, quickly gaining speed, proved to be a skilled motorman, as Herr Matzerath — the brightly lit depot already behind us — acknowledged with these friendly words: "You must surely have been baptized a Catholic, Gottfried, or you couldn't drive a tram so well."

I did indeed enjoy this little part-time job. Apparently the depot had not noted our departure, for no one came after us, and they could easily have ended our journey by simply cutting off the power. I headed the tram toward Flingern, passed right through it, considered turning left at Haniel's for Rath and Ratingen, but Herr Matzerath suggested the stretch toward Grafenberg and Gerresheim. Though I feared the hill at the Löwenburg dance hall, I acceded to the accused's wishes, made it up the hill, and had left the dance hall behind when I had to hit the brakes; three men were standing on the line, not so much requesting as forcing us to stop.

Shortly after Haniel's, Herr Matzerath retired to the interior of the car to smoke a cigarette. So it was I, as motorman, who had to call out, "All aboard, please!" I noticed that the third, hatless man, whom the two others, both in green hats with black bands, held between them, kept missing the running board, either because he was clumsy or had poor eyesight. His companions, or guards, guided him almost brutally onto my driver's platform, and from there into the car.

I had started off again when I heard behind me, from the interior of the car, a pitiful whimpering and what sounded like someone being slapped, then, to my reassurance, the firm voice of Herr Matzerath, admonishing the newly arrived passengers, warning them not to strike an injured, half-blind man who had lost his glasses.

"You stay out of this," I heard one of the green hats roar. "He's going to get what's coming to him now. It's taken long enough."

As I continued on slowly toward Gerresheim, my friend Herr Matzerath asked what the poor man had done wrong. The conversation quickly took a strange turn: within two sentences they were back in the war, or more specifically at its outbreak, on the first of September in thirty-nine; it seems the half-blind man was an irregular who had illegally defended a Polish post office. Strangely enough, Herr Matzerath, who couldn't have been more than fifteen at the time, knew all about it, and even recognized the man as Viktor Weluhn, a poor, nearsighted fellow who had carried money orders for the post office, lost his glasses in the course of the fighting, fled without them, and escaped the bloodhounds, who had never given up, however, but pursued him instead till the end of the war, even into the postwar years, and now produced a document issued in thirty-nine ordering his death by firing squad. We've finally caught him, one of the green hats shouted, and the other one said he was damned glad to see this account settled. It seems he'd devoted all his free time, including holidays, to making sure a document issued in thirty-nine was finally enforced; he had his own job as a salesman, and his friend, an Eastern refugee, had his troubles too, since he'd lost a successful tailoring business back East and had to start life all over again, but now their work was done and they could relax; we'll carry out that order and put paid to the past tonight — good thing we caught this last tram.

So, against my will, I became the motorman on a tram carrying a condemned man and two executioners with an order for death by firing squad toward Gerresheim. When I reached the deserted, somewhat irregularly shaped marketplace in the suburb, I turned right, heading for the terminal near the glassworks, where I planned to drop off the green hats and the half-blind Viktor, then return home with my friend. Three stops before the terminal Herr Matzerath left the car and placed his briefcase, in which, as I knew, the jar stood upright, on the spot where professional motormen usually keep lunch boxes with their sandwiches.

"We've got to save him. It's Viktor, poor Viktor!" Herr Matzerath was clearly upset.

"He still hasn't found glasses that fit. He's very nearsighted. He'll be looking the wrong way when they shoot him." I thought the executioners had been unarmed. But Herr Matzerath had noticed bulges in the coats of both green hats.

"He delivered money orders for the Polish Post Office in Danzig. He's doing the same thing now in the Federal Republic. But they hound him after working hours because they still have an order to shoot him."

Though I couldn't follow everything Herr Matzerath said, I promised to be at his side at the execution and, if possible, help him prevent it.

Beyond the glassworks, just before the first of the allotment gardens — I could have seen my mother's garden with its apple tree in the moonlight — I stopped the tram and called into the interior: "All out, end of the line." They emerged at once with their green hats and black hatbands. The half-blind man had trouble with the running board again. Then Herr Matzerath got off, first pulling his drum from under his overcoat, and asked me as he descended to bring along his briefcase with the canning jar.

We left the tram glowing brightly far behind us and stuck to the heels of the executioners and their victim.

We passed along garden fences. I was getting tired. When the three men came to a stop ahead of us, I noticed they had chosen my mother's garden as the execution site. Herr Matzerath and I both protested. They paid no attention, knocked down the fence, which was rotten anyway, bound the half-blind man Herr Matzerath called poor Viktor to the apple tree beneath my fork, and, since we kept up our protest, showed us again by flashlight the tattered execution order signed by a military court officer named Zelewski. It was dated, as I recall, Zoppot, the fifth of October, thirty-nine, the stamps seemed right too, there was little we could do; nevertheless we talked about the United Nations, democracy, collective guilt, Adenauer, and so on; but one of the green hats swept all our objections aside with the remark that we had no right to get mixed up in this, there was still no peace treaty, he'd voted for Adenauer just like us, but the order was still valid, they'd taken the document to the highest authorities, consulted with them, they were doing their damned duty, and we should just leave.

We didn't leave. Instead Herr Matzerath lifted his drum as the green hats opened their coats and swung out their tommy guns — at that same moment a nearly full moon with only a slight dent broke through the clouds, causing the edges of the clouds to gleam metallically like the jagged edge of a tin can — and Herr Matzerath began desperately stirring his sticks on similar but undamaged tin. It sounded strange and yet familiar. Again and again the letter O rounded itself: lost, not yet lost, is not yet lost, Poland is not yet lost! But that was poor Viktor's voice, he knew the words to Herr Matzerath's drum: Poland is not yet lost, as long as we still live. And even the green hats seemed to know that rhythm, for they cowered behind their metal guns outlined in moonlight, as well they might, since the march Herr Matzerath and poor Viktor struck up in my mother's garden plot awakened the Polish cavalry. The moon may have helped as drum, moon, and the cracked voice of the nearsighted Viktor called forth all those stamping horsemen from the soil: hooves thundered, nostrils snorted, spurs jingled, stallions whinnied, hurrah, hooray! . . . but not in the least, nothing thundered, snorted, jingled, whinnied, nothing cried hurrah, hooray; silently they glided over the harvested fields outside Gerresheim, yet still it was a squadron of Polish uhlans, for red and white like Herr Matzerath's lacquered drum the pennants tugged at their lances, no, didn't tug, but floated instead, just as the whole squadron floated beneath the moon, perhaps came from the moon, wheeled to the left toward our garden, floated, seemed neither flesh nor blood, yet floated, like homemade toys for children, conjured up, akin perhaps to the knotworks Herr Matzerath's keeper makes from string: a knotted Polish cavalry, silent yet thundering, bloodless, fleshless, yet Polish and unbridled, heading right toward us, so that we threw ourselves to the ground, submitted to the moon and Poland's squadron as they swept over my mother's garden, over all the other carefully tended gardens, but laying waste to none, took only poor Viktor and his executioners, and were lost in the open fields beneath the moon — lost, not yet lost, riding off eastward, toward Poland, toward the far side of the moon.

We waited, breathing heavily, till the night was once again devoid of incident, till the heavens closed once more, shut off that light which had persuaded a long-dead cavalry to mount one final attack. I rose first and congratulated Herr Matzerath on his great triumph, though without underestimating the influence of the moon. But he waved me off, tired and downcast: "Triumph, my dear Gottfried? I've had far too many triumphs in life. I'd like to fail for once. But that's hard to do and takes a great deal of work."

I disliked this little speech, since I'm the hardworking type but have had no triumphs. Herr Matzerath seemed a bit ungrateful to me, and I told him so: "You're being arrogant, Oskar," I ventured, for we were on a first-name basis by then. "You're in all the newspapers. You've made a name for yourself. I'm not talking about money. But do you think it's easy for someone like me, who never even gets his name in the papers, to go around with someone famous like you? Just once I'd like to perform some deed, perform some great act, as you just have, all on my own, and be in the newspapers making headlines: Gottfried von Vittlar did that!"

Herr Matzerath's laughter hurt my feelings. He lay on his back, burrowed his hump in the soft earth, tore up the grass with both hands, threw tufts of grass into the air, and laughed like an inhuman god who can do anything: "My friend, nothing could be easier. Here's my briefcase. It has miraculously escaped the hooves of the Polish cavalry. I give it to you, its leather harbors the jar with the ring finger. Take the whole thing, run back to Gerresheim, where the brightly lit tram will still be standing, get in, take my gift to the police station on Fürstenwall, turn me in, and tomorrow you'll find your name printed in every newspaper."

At first I tried to refuse his offer, pointed out that he surely couldn't live without the finger in the jar. But he reassured me, said he was fed up with the whole finger business, and besides he had several plaster casts of it, and even one in pure gold, I might as well go ahead and take the briefcase, go back to the tram, take the tram to the police station, and turn him in.

So I walked away, and could still hear Herr Matzerath laughing behind me. For he stayed there, savoring the night, tearing up grass and laughing as I jangled my way toward the city. But when I turned him in — which I did the following morning — I did indeed, thanks to Herr Matzerath's kindness, make it into the newspapers several times.

Meanwhile I, Oskar, the kindly Herr Matzerath, lay laughing in the night-black grass outside Gerresheim, rolling with laughter beneath a few visible and deadly serious stars, burrowed my hump into the warm earth, thinking: Sleep Oskar, sleep, another hour or so, till the police awaken you. You'll never lie so free beneath the moon again.

And as I awoke, I noticed, before I could notice it was broad daylight, that something, someone, was licking my face: warmly, roughly, evenly, damply licking.

Surely that can't be the police, roused and sent here by Vittlar, licking you awake? Still, I was in no hurry to open my eyes, but let myself be licked awhile, warmly, roughly, evenly, damply, enjoying it, not caring who was licking: Either it's the police, Oskar figured, or a cow. Only then did I open my blue eyes.

She was spotted black and white, lay beside me, breathed and licked me till I opened my eyes. It was broad daylight, clear to partly cloudy, and I said to myself: Oskar, don't linger with this cow, no matter how divinely she gazes at you, no matter how earnestly she soothes and weakens your memory with her rough tongue. It's broad daylight, flies are buzzing, you have to flee. Vittlar is turning you in, hence you must flee. A serious accusation deserves a serious flight. Let the cow moo, and flee. They'll catch you, here or somewhere else, but that hardly matters to you.

And so, licked, washed, and combed by a cow, I made my getaway, burst out in a gale of bright morning laughter a few steps into my flight, and left my drum with the cow, who lay there mooing as I fled laughing.

Thirty

AH YES, MY FLIGHT. There's still that to tell you about. I fled to en-hance the value of Vittlar's accusation. No flight without a goal, I told myself. And whither, Oskar, do you wish to flee? Political factors, the so-called Iron Curtain, ruled out the East. So I was forced to eliminate as a goal my grandmother Anna Koljaiczek's four skirts, still billow-ing protectively on Kashubian potato fields, though flight toward my grandmother's skirts, if flight there must be, was the only destination I felt held any real promise.

Just in passing: today I celebrate my thirtieth birthday. At the age of thirty, one is obliged to speak about flight like a man and not like a boy. Maria, who brought me the cake with the thirty candles, said, "You're thirty now, Oskar, it's about time you started acting sensibly."

Klepp, my friend Klepp, gave me some jazz records as always, and used five matches to light the thirty candles on my birthday cake: "Life begins at thirty!" said Klepp; he's twenty-nine.

Vittlar, however, my friend Gottfried, who's dearest to my heart, gave me candy, leaned over my bedrails, and said in his nasal voice, "When Jesus was thirty years old, he went forth and gathered disciples."

Vittlar has always loved to confuse me. I'm supposed to abandon my bed and gather disciples just because I'm thirty. Then my lawyer came in brandishing a document, trumpeted his congratulations, hung his nylon hat on my bed, and proclaimed to all and sundry: "What a happy coincidence! My client is celebrating his thirtieth birthday, and on this very same thirtieth birthday I've received word that the Ring Finger Case is being reopened, they have a new lead, this Sister Beate, you know her of course . . ."

Thus, on my thirtieth birthday, the announcement arrives that I've feared for years, feared from the moment I fled: they've found the real murderer, they reopen the case, acquit me, discharge me from the mental institution, deprive me of my beloved bed, toss me out on the cold street, exposed to all the elements, and oblige a thirty-year-old Oskar and his drum to gather disciples.

So now they say Sister Beate murdered my Sister Dorothea, out of yolk-yellow jealousy.

Perhaps you still remember? A certain Dr. Werner, as happens all too often in films and in life, stood between two nurses. A terrible tale: Beate loved Dr. Werner. But Dr. Werner loved Dorothea. Dorothea meanwhile loved no one, except perhaps, in secret, little Oskar. Then Werner fell ill. Dorothea nursed him because his bed was in her ward. Beate could not stand this. So she talked Dorothea into taking a walk with her, and then, in a rye field near Gerresheim, killed her, or perhaps better, got rid of her. Now Beate was free to care for Dr. Werner undisturbed. But it seems he didn't recover under her care, far from it. Perhaps the love-crazed nurse said to herself: As long as he's ill, he's mine. Did she give him an overdose? Did she give him the wrong medicine? At any rate, Dr. Werner died, either from an overdose or the wrong medicine, though Beate confessed to neither, nor to the walk in the rye field that became Sister Dorothea's final stroll. Oskar, who likewise confessed to nothing but owned an incriminating finger in a canning jar, was found guilty of the rye-field deed, but since they were not sure he was all there, they placed me in a mental institution for observation. Of course Oskar fled before they found him guilty and committed him, for by my flight I hoped to enhance substantially the value of my friend Gottfried's accusation.

I was twenty-eight when I made my getaway. Just a few hours ago, thirty glowing candles dripped calmly onto my birthday cake. It was September back then too, when I fled. I was born in the sign of Virgo. But it's my flight we're talking of here, not my birth beneath light bulbs.

Since, as I've said, the escape route eastward toward my grandmother was closed, I was forced like everyone else these days to flee westward. If the world of high-level politics keeps you from your grandmother, Oskar, then flee toward your grandfather who lives in Buffalo, USA. Head for America: let's see how far you get.

Grandfather Koljaiczek in America had come to mind while my eyes were still closed and the cow was licking me in the meadow near Gerresheim. It must have been around seven in the morning and I said to myself: The shops open at eight. I ran off laughing, leaving my drum by the cow, telling myself: Gottfried's tired, he probably won't turn you in till eight or eight-thirty, take advantage of what little head start you've got. It took me ten minutes to raise a taxi by phone in the sleepy little suburb of Gerresheim. It carried me to Central Station. I counted my money on the way, miscounting several times because I kept bursting out in fresh gales of bright morning laughter. Then I leafed through my passport and found that, thanks to the good offices of the West Concert Agency, I had valid visas for both France and the United States; Dr. Dösch's fondest wish had always been to grant those countries a concert tour with Oskar the Drummer.

Voilà, I said to myself, let's flee to Paris, it looks good, sounds good, could happen in the movies, with Gabin smoking his pipe and chasing after me good-naturedly. But who would play me? Chaplin? Picasso? Laughing and stimulated by these thoughts of flight, I was still slapping the thighs of my slightly rumpled trousers when the taxi driver asked me for seven marks. I paid and had breakfast in the station restaurant. I placed a railway schedule next to my soft-boiled egg, found a good train, had enough time after breakfast to buy some foreign currency, purchased a small suitcase of fine leather, filled it with expensive but ill-fitting shirts, since I was afraid to return to Jülicher Straße, packed a pair of pale green pajamas, toothbrush, toothpaste, and so on, bought a first-class ticket, since there was no need to economize, and was soon comfortably ensconced in a cushioned window seat: I was fleeing without having to run. The cushions aided my reflections: the moment the train pulled out and the flight proper began, Oskar cast about for something worth fearing; for not without reason did I say to myself: No fright, no flight! But what, Oskar, frightens you enough to make you flee, since the police only make you burst out in bright morning laughter?

Today I am thirty, both flight and trial are behind me, but the fear I talked myself into when I fled remains.

Was it the jolting of the tracks, was it the song of the train? The words emerged monotonously, I noticed them just short of Aachen, they took firm hold of me as I sank back on the cushions in first class, still gripped me, increasingly distinct and terrifying, beyond Aachen — we crossed the border about ten-thirty — so that I was glad when the customs officers, showing more interest in my hump than in my name and passport, provided some distraction — and I said to myself: That Vittlar, the sluggard! It's almost eleven and he still hasn't reached the police station with the canning jar under his arm, while I've been fleeing since the break of dawn for his sake, scaring myself to motivate my flight; what a fright I had in Belgium when the train sang out: Better start running, the Black Cook's coming! Ha! Ha! Ha!

Today I am thirty, my trial will be reopened, the expected acquittal will force me back on my feet, riding trains, trams, exposed to those words: Better start running, the Black Cook's coming! Ha! Ha! Ha!

Yet, apart from my dread of the Black Cook, whose terrifying arrival I expected at every station, the trip was pleasant enough. I had the whole compartment to myself — perhaps she was sitting in the one next to me — made the acquaintance of first Belgian, then French customs officers, dozed off for five minutes or so now and then, awoke with a small cry, and to provide some sort of shield against the Black Cook, leafed through the weekly magazine *Der Spiegel*, which had been passed to me through the compartment window in Düsseldorf, amazed as always by the breadth of knowledge of the journalists, and even found a story on my manager, Dr. Dösch of the West Concert Agency, confirming what I already knew: Dösch's agency was supported by a single mainstay, Oskar the Drummer — not a bad photo of me. And so, all the way to Paris, Oskar the Mainstay contemplated the collapse of the West Concert Agency that would inevitably result from my arrest and the terrifying arrival of the Black Cook.

Never in my life had I feared the Black Cook. It was not till my flight, when I wished to be frightened, that she crawled under my skin, and has remained there in various forms, sleeping for the most part, to this very day, on which I celebrate my thirtieth birthday: it may be the name Goethe, for instance, that makes me cry out and flee beneath the bedcovers in fear. No matter how carefully I studied the poet-prince, even as a boy, his Olympian calm always struck me as slightly sinister. And when he now stands by the rails of my bed disguised in black as a cook, no longer luminous and classical, but darker than any Rasputin, and says on my thirtieth birthday, "Better start running, the Black Cook's coming!" I'm terrified.

Ha! Ha! Ha! sang the train that carried the fleeing Oskar toward Paris. I actually expected the Interpol agents at the Paris North station – Gare du Nord, as the Parisians say. But the only person who spoke to me was a porter who reeked so strongly of red wine that I couldn't for the life of me see him as the Black Cook, and so entrusted him with my suitcase as far as the gate. The Interpol agents and the Cook won't have wasted any money on a platform ticket, I told myself, they'll accost and arrest you outside the gate. You'd be wise to retrieve your suitcase before you pass through. So I wound up carrying my own suitcase as far as the metro, since not even the officials were there to take it from me.

I won't go on about that world-famous metro smell. I read recently that you can buy it as perfume and spray yourself. I noticed that the metro sang about the Black Cook too, but in a different rhythm from the train, and I saw that those around me must know and fear the Black Cook as I did, for they exuded anxiety and dread. My plan was to take the metro as far as Porte d'Italie, and then a cab from there to Orly Airport; if I couldn't be arrested at the Gare du Nord, I thought the famous airport of Orly – with the Black Cook as airline hostess – would be an amusing and original spot. I had to change trains once, glad that my suitcase was so light, and then headed south on the metro as I pondered: Where will you get off, Oskar – my God, the things that can happen in a single day: this morning you were still being licked by a cow outside Gerresheim, fearless and cheerful you were, and now you're in Paris – where will you alight, where will she come toward you, black and terrible? Place d'Italie or not till the Porte?

I got off one stop before the Porte, at Maison Blanche, thinking: They think, of course, that I think they'll be waiting for me at the Porte. But she knows what I think and what they think. Besides, I was fed up with the whole thing. My flight and the effort to keep up my fright had exhausted me. Oskar had lost all desire to go to the airport, now thought Maison Blanche would be more amusing than Orly Airport, and turned out to be right: for the metro station had an escalator that was to inspire several lofty notions in me, while adding its escalator clatter: "Better start running, the Black Cook's coming! Ha! Ha! Ha!"

Oskar is somewhat at a loss. His flight is drawing to a close, and with it this report: Will the rattling escalator at the Maison Blanche metro station be high, steep, and symbolic enough to serve as a final image for his recollections?

But now there is my thirtieth birthday. To all those who find the escalator too noisy, to those who don't find the Black Cook sufficiently frightening, I offer my thirtieth birthday as an ending. For of all birthdays, is not the thirtieth the most significant? It contains Three, and foreshadows Sixty, rendering it superfluous. As the thirty candles were burning on my birthday cake this morning, I could have wept for joy and rapture, but was ashamed to do so in front of Maria: at thirty a man may no longer weep.

The moment I mounted the first step of the escalator — if an escalator can be said to have a first step — and it carried me upward, I burst out laughing. I laughed despite my fear, or because of it. Slowly, steeply I rose — and there they were, waiting at the top. There was still time for half a cigarette. Two steps above me a nonchalant pair of lovers were carrying on. A step below me stood an old woman, whom I suspected at first, for no reason at all, of being the Black Cook. She wore a hat decorated with artificial fruit. While I smoked, I tried my best to conjure up a whole range of escalator-related comparisons: first Oskar played the poet Dante, who returns from the inferno and is greeted at the top, where the escalator ends, by manic *Spiegel* reporters who ask, "Well, Dante, what was it like down there?" I went through the same little scene as Goethe, prince of poets, and reporters for *Der Spiegel* asked how I liked it down below with the Mothers. Finally I grew tired of poets and said to myself: It's not reporters for *Der Spiegel* or men with tin badges in their coat pockets waiting up there, it's the Black Cook, the escalator rattled, the Black Cook's coming, and Oskar replied, "Better start running!"

There was a normal flight of stairs next to the escalator. It led people from the street down into the metro. It must have been raining outside. The people looked wet. That worried me, because I hadn't had time to buy a raincoat in Düsseldorf. Glancing upward, however, Oskar saw that the men with the conspicuously inconspicuous faces were carrying civilian umbrellas — none of which cast any doubt on the existence of the Black Cook.

What will I say to them? I wondered, slowly savoring my cigarette on a slowly rising escalator that lifted my emotions and enriched my knowledge: you grow younger on an escalator, you grow older and older on an escalator. The choice was up to me: I could step off the escalator at age three or age sixty, greet the Interpol agents as a child or an old man, fear the Black Cook at either age.

It must be getting late. My metal bed looks so tired. And my keeper Bruno showed his anxious brown eye twice at the peephole. There, beneath the watercolor of the anemones, stands my uncut cake with its thirty candles. Maria may already be asleep. Someone, I think it was Maria's sister Guste, wished me luck for the next thirty years. I wish I could sleep like Maria. But what was it my son Kurt, the schoolboy, the model pupil, always first in his class, wished me on my birthday? When Maria sleeps, the furniture around her sleeps too. Now I have it: for my thirtieth birthday Kurt wished me a speedy recovery. But what I would like is a slice of Maria's sleep, for I'm tired and running out of words. Klepp's young wife made up a silly but well-intentioned birthday poem addressed to my hump. Prince Eugen was hunchbacked too, and yet he captured the city and fortress of Belgrade. Maria should know by now that a hump brings luck. Prince Eugen also had two fathers. I'm thirty now, but my hump is younger. Louis the Fourteenth was Prince Eugen's presumptive father. Beautiful women used to touch my hump on the open street to bring them luck. Prince Eugen was hunchbacked, that's why he died a natural death. If Jesus had been a hunchback, they could hardly have nailed him to the cross. Just because I've turned thirty, must I really go out into the world and gather disciples?

But those were merely escalator notions. Higher and higher it bore me. Before and above me the nonchalant lovers. Behind and below the old woman with the hat. Outside it was raining, and above, at the very top, stood the agents from Interpol. Slats lined the escalator steps. When you're on an escalator, you should really reconsider everything: Where do you come from? Where are you going? Who are you? What's your name? What do you want? Smells assailed me: The vanilla of a young Maria. The sardine oil my poor mama warmed up and drank hot till she grew cold and lay beneath the earth. Jan Bronski, who sprinkled cologne so liberally, yet an early death still seeped through all his buttonholes. In Greff the greengrocer's storage cellar it smelled of winter potatoes. Once more the smell of dry sponges on the slates of first graders. And my Roswitha, redolent of cinnamon and nutmeg. I floated on a carbolic cloud as Herr Fajngold sprinkled his disinfectants over my fever. Ah, and the Catholicism of the Church of the Sacred Heart, all those unaired vestments, the cold dust, and I, at the left side-altar, loaning my drum, to whom?

Yet those were merely escalator notions. Today they want to nail me down, they say: You're thirty. That means you have to gather your disciples. Think back to what you said when they arrested you. Count the candles on your birthday cake, leave your bed and gather disciples. But there are so many possibilities open to a man of thirty. For example, if they actually toss me out of the institution, I might propose a second time to Maria. My chances would certainly be better today. Oskar set her up in the delicatessen, he's well-known, he's still earning good money with his records and he's older, more mature. At thirty a man should marry. Or I might stay single, choose one of my professions, buy a good shell-limestone quarry, hire stonecutters, sell direct from the quarry to the builders. At thirty a man should start a career. Or—if prefabricated slabs for façades bored me to death in the long run—I could look up Ulla the Muse, serve the Fine Arts at her side as an inspiring model. I might even marry her one day, my Muse so often and so briefly engaged. At thirty a man should marry. Or if I grew tired of Europe I could emigrate, head for America, for Buffalo, my old dream: search for my grandfather, the millionaire and former arsonist Joe Colchic, formerly Joseph Koljaiczek. At thirty a man should settle down. Or I could give in and let them nail me down, go out, simply because I'm thirty, and play the Messiah they take me for, make more of my drum than it is, turn my drum, against my better judgment, into a symbol, found a sect, a party, or perhaps merely a lodge.

In spite of the lovers above me and the woman with the hat below, these escalator notions arose in me. Did I say earlier that the lovers stood two steps above me, not one, and that I'd placed my suitcase between me and the lovers? Young people in France are very strange. As the escalator carried us upward, she unbuttoned first his leather jacket, then his shirt, and fondled his bare, eighteen-year-old skin. But she did this in such a businesslike manner and so unerotically that it aroused my suspicions: these young people were being paid by the government to act madly in love on the open streets so as to maintain the reputation of France's great city. When the couple kissed, however, my suspicions faded: he nearly choked on her tongue, and was still in the midst of a fit of coughing when I stubbed out my cigarette, preferring to greet the police agents as a nonsmoker. The old woman below me and her hat — her hat being level with my head, because my height made up the difference between the two steps — did nothing of note, except mumble a bit, grumbling to herself; but many old people do that in Paris. The rubber handrail of the escalator traveled upward with us. You could place your hand on it and let it ride along. I would have done so if I'd brought gloves on the trip. The tiles on the staircase walls each reflected a flicker of electric light. Pipes and bundles of thick cables kept cream-colored company with us as we rose. There was nothing infernal about the escalator's din. Instead it seemed gemütlich, despite its mechanical nature. In spite of the clattering lines about the terrifying Black Cook, the Maison Blanche metro station struck me as comfortable, almost cozy. I felt at home on the escalator, and would have counted myself happy, in spite of my dread and the bogeywoman, if instead of total strangers it had carried my friends and relatives, living and dead, upward with me: my poor mama between Matzerath and Jan Bronski; Mother Truczinski, the gray-haired mouse, with her children Herbert, Guste, Fritz, Maria; the greengrocer Greff and his slovenly Lina; Master Bebra of course and the graceful Roswitha — all those who framed my questionable existence, all those who had run aground on my existence — if I had only seen above, where the escalator ran out of breath, in place of agents of the law, the Black Cook's very opposite: my grandmother Anna Koljaiczek, resting like a mountain, receiving me and mine, upon our successful ascent, beneath her skirts, taking us into the mountain.

But two men stood there, wearing American-style raincoats instead of wide skirts. And toward the end of my ascent, with all ten toes smiling in my shoes, I had to admit to myself that the nonchalant lovers above me and the mumbling old lady below were simply police agents.

What more can I say: born beneath light bulbs, interrupted my growth at the age of three, was given a drum, sangshattered glass, smelled vanilla, coughed in churches, stuffed Luzie with food, watched ants as they crawled, decided to grow, buried the drum, moved to the West, lost what was East, learned to carve stone and posed as a model, went back to my drum and inspected concrete, made money and cared for the finger, gave the finger away and fled as I laughed, ascended, arrested, convicted, confined, now soon to be freed, and today is my birthday, I'm thirty years old, and still as afraid of the Black Cook as ever — Amen.

I stubbed out my cigarette and let it fall. It came to rest between the slats of the escalator step. After traveling heavenward for some time at a forty-five-degree angle, then horizontally three steps, following the nonchalant police lovers and preceding the police grandmother, Oskar let himself be carried from the slats of the escalator step onto a firmly fixed iron grid, and when the police agents identified themselves and addressed him as Matzerath, he said first in German, true to his escalator notions, "Ich bin Jesus!," repeated it in French, since he was facing Interpol agents, and finally in English: "I am Jesus!"

Nonetheless I was arrested as Oskar Matzerath. Offering no resistance, I placed myself under the protection of the authorities and, since it was raining outside on the Avenue d'Italie, their umbrellas, but still glanced about nervously in fear, and saw several times — she can do that — the terrifyingly calm countenance of the Black Cook in the crowd on the street, and among those pressing around the police van.

I've run out of words now, but still have to think over what Oskar's going to do after his inevitable discharge from the mental institution. Marry? Stay single? Emigrate? Model? Buy a stone quarry? Gather disciples? Found a sect?

These days all the possibilities offered to a man of thirty must be considered, and how else but with my drum? So I'll drum out the little song that's become more and more real to me, more and more terrifying, I'll conjure up the Black Cook, consult her, so that tomorrow morning I can tell my keeper Bruno what sort of life the thirty-year-old Oskar plans to lead from now on in the shadow of an increasingly black bogeywoman; for what frightened me years ago on the stairs, what shouted boo in the cellar when I went to fetch coal, startling me to laughter, remained there forever, talking with fingers, coughing through the keyholes, moaning in the stove, screeching with the door, billowing up the chimney, when ships blew their horns in the fog, when a fly took hours to die between panes, when eels craved Mama, and my poor mama craved eels, when the sun vanished behind the Turmberg yet lived on as amber. Who did Herbert think of as he assaulted the wooden figure? Behind the high altar too—what would Catholicism be without the Cook who blackens every confessional? She cast her shadow as the toys of Sigismund Markus shattered, and the brats in the courtyard at the apartment building, Axel Mischke and Nuchi Eyke, Susi Kater and Hänschen Kollin, they declared it, they sang it, while brewing the brick powder soup: "Better start running, the Black Cook's coming! You're to blame, and you're to blame, and you are most of all. Better start running . . ." She was always there, even in the woodruff fizz powder, foaming so greenly and so innocently; in every wardrobe I ever crouched in, she crouched too, and later on she borrowed Luzie Rennwand's triangular fox face, ate sausage sandwiches, skin and all, and led the Dusters up the diving tower—Oskar alone remained, watched the ants, and knew: that's her shadow, multiplied, now seeking sweetness, and all the words: blessed, sorrowful, full of grace, virgin of virgins . . . and all the stones: basalt, tufa, diorite, nests in the shell lime, alabaster so soft . . . and all the songshattered glass, transparent glass, glass blown paperthin . . . and all the groceries: flour and sugar in blue pound and half-pound bags. Later on, four tomcats, one of them named Bismarck, the wall that had to be freshly whitewashed, Poles exalted in death, special communiqués, who sank what when, potatoes rattling down from the scales, everything that tapered toward the foot, cemeteries in which I stood, flagstones on which I knelt, coconut fibers on which I lay . . . all things mixed in concrete, the juice of onions that called forth tears, the ring on the finger and the cow that once licked me . . . Don't ask Oskar who she is. He's run out of words. For what was once behind my back, then kissed my hump, is now and forever coming toward me:

Black was the Cook always somewhere behind me.
And now she comes toward me at last all in black.
Her words and her garments all twisted and black.
And the debts she pays are all paid in black.
And children who sang: Is the Black Cook coming?
No longer need ask, they'd better start running.
Better start running, the Black Cook's coming!
Ha! Ha! Ha!

Translator's Afterword

*Or you can start by declaring that novels can no longer
be written, and then, behind your own back as it were,
produce a mighty blockbuster that establishes you as the
last of the great novelists.*

WHEN RALPH MANHEIM was asked to translate *Die Blechtrommel*
in 1959, Günter Grass was a young man in his early thirties, largely unknown in the English-speaking world, who had written a novel so linguistically complex and innovative that even German readers found it
difficult. Yet Manheim's English version was so successful that *The Tin
Drum* became a runaway best-seller and catapulted its young German
author to the forefront of world literature. Grass was well aware how
much he owed to Ralph Manheim, both then and in the years to follow.
So impressive was the novel, and its English counterpart, that from our
present-day vantage point it remains the most important work of German literature since the Second World War.

Nevertheless, Grass voiced his concerns about certain aspects of the
English version soon after it appeared, and began, over thirty years ago,
to inquire gently of Helen Wolff if a retranslation might be possible. In
a letter to her of 20 December 1976, he raised the issue directly:

> I'd also like to bring Ralph around, given the distance of years now,
> and all the experience he's gained with my language, to rework
> and fill in his translation of *Die Blechtrommel;* after all, there are
> substantial omissions. I believe *The Tin Drum* has gained a firm
> place in English-language literature in the meantime, so that it
> could hold up happily and well under a revision.

A week later, Helen Wolff replied briefly, and in passing: "I'll think about
a new reworking of *The Tin Drum.*" Although no revised version was
ever undertaken, Grass never dropped the idea, and thirty years later,

having obtained the rights to the novel from Pantheon, Harcourt finally commissioned one, with an eye toward the celebration that would mark the fiftieth anniversary of the original German publication.

Ralph Manheim did not live to offer his own reworking of *The Tin Drum,* but I was privileged to know him in my early years as a translator, to spend time with him, both on my visits to Paris and on his first trip in many years to America, his homeland, and to learn from him. His tenacity in the face of difficult texts, the gifted nature of his solutions, and his enduring integrity were a constant inspiration to me, whether I experienced them face to face in conversation or saw them exemplified in the steady stream of major works he translated — not only from the German, but from French and other languages as well. This new translation is offered against that background, and in gratitude to him.

Oskar Gets a New Tin Drum

On a warm summer day in 2005, the citizens of Gdańsk, Poland, were treated to an unusual sight: one of their favorite sons, Günter Grass, had returned, and he appeared to be conducting a tour. As he pointed out the special features of historical buildings in the Altstadt, the dozen or so men and women gathered around him seemed to be paying unusually close attention. And well they might, for each of them was hard at work retranslating Grass's most famous novel, set in Danzig, into his or her respective language.

The puzzled onlookers had no way of knowing the true nature of this tour. For over a week, the Nobel Prize–winning author had been conferring for hours each day with his translators, going over *Die Blechtrommel* page by page, then emerging from the workshop atmosphere to show them the heart and soul of the novel's geography and history — the potato fields of the Kashubian countryside, the beach and jetty at Neufahrwasser, the city and suburbs of Danzig, Oskar's home, the grocery store, the old city hall: in short, the still living features of his past.

Grass first raised the idea of his now famous "Übersetzertreffen" (translators' meetings) in a letter to Helen Wolff in 1976:

Not long ago I was in Bergneustadt (near Bonn) at a gathering of translators. . . . During the symposium an idea came to me: to arrange such a meeting of my translators three or four months after the appearance of a new text, one which I would attend as author for three or four days, making myself available, discussing the major problems, and helping to get this important process under way. Luchterhand and the foreign publishers could bear the cost. . . . What do you think of the idea?

With his publishers' blessing, such gatherings, which soon achieved a certain fame of their own, were to become a regular feature of Grass's literary life, and have recurred with each new novel.

Few authors have the power to generate financial support of this magnitude from their publishers, but, more significantly, few seem to care deeply enough about translation even to ask for it. Grass's desire to meet and discuss a new work with his translators sprang directly from a belief that rendering the style, substance, and linguistic complexity of his writing required a closer bond. And on that summer day in Gdańsk, translators both old and new had gathered once again with a special goal in mind—new translations to celebrate the fiftieth anniversary of *Die Blechtrommel*.

Making It New

The most common question I faced while working on the new *Tin Drum* was, "What was wrong with the old one?" This question reveals a fundamental misunderstanding about the nature of literary translation. It is precisely the mark of a great work of art that it demands to be retranslated. What impels us toward new versions is not the weakness of existing translations, but the strength and richness of certain works of literature. The works that are never retranslated are those we only care to read once.

We translate great works because they deserve it — because the power and depth of the text can never be fully revealed by a single translation, however inspired. A translation is a reading, and every reading is necessarily personal, perhaps even idiosyncratic. Each new version offers, not a better reading, but a different one, one that foregrounds new aspects of the text, that sees it through new eyes, that makes it new.

We also retranslate for new generations of readers. Language constantly changes, and although most original texts, by some mystery yet to be explained, maintain their freshness, translations, for better or worse, do not. After a few decades they become dated. If we are to perpetuate the life of a masterpiece in another language, we need new versions as the years pass.

We retranslate from a new vantage point, with a wealth of detailed scholarship behind us, with a wide range of newly available reference works, including specialized dictionaries, illustrated guidebooks, and wordlists of dialects. And we can now turn — as we do so often — to the Internet for rapid answers to even the most arcane of questions. All these aids are crucial to producing a new and more accurate version of *The Tin Drum,* since its pages teem with the detailed vocabulary of brick making, stonecutting, petrography, mining, sculpture, musicology, and warfare, with the rules of skat, with ecclesiastical paraphernalia, and with the perverse coinages of the Nazi era.

And if we're lucky, we may retranslate with the help of the author.

In Gdańsk, each morning at nine, we took our places around a long table and set to work. We were free to ask any question we wished, and Grass always answered directly and clearly, with unfailing good humor. In more than twenty-five hundred instances, carefully noted page by page in a protocol each translator later received, he clarified the meaning of a word or phrase, noting a particular linguistic effect, urging us to capture a special nuance.

He called our attention to his own idiosyncratic style — his penchant, for example, for writing numbers and dates out in full, rather than using Arabic numerals. He requested that we indulge him in this, pointing out that this practice struck German publishers as strange too. He asked us to follow Oskar's odd predilection for the use of the superlative, a verbal tic seldom noted in previous versions. He asked that we differentiate the characters more carefully in spoken dialogue, particularly with regard to variations in dialect, grammatical usage, and vocabulary.

He was anything but dictatorial, however. In passages involving complicated wordplay, or strongly marked by rhythm, he told us just to do our best, trusting us to come up with similar effects in our own languages, and encouraging us to coin new words where he had invented new ones in German (thus *zersingen* becomes "singshatter" in the new version, *Betthüter* becomes "bedkeeper"). And on almost every page, he read one or more passages aloud, stressing the musicality of the language. Over the course of those days in Gdańsk, nothing made a more lasting impression on us than the sound of his voice, the melody of the text, the rhythm of Oskar's drum.

But it is not information alone that comes to our aid in retranslating a text, even when that information comes directly from the author. Our notion of the nature of translation itself changes over time. Should a translation transport the text into our own life and culture, or should a translation convey the reader into the world and culture of the original? Should the translation of a difficult and innovative work be rendered into a more readable and simplified form for readers, or should they be treated to an equally difficult and innovative text in their own language? Do we owe our allegiance to the author or to the reader? Can we be true to both?

Two brief examples may serve to sharpen the sense of these contrasting translation styles. During the trial of the gang called the Dusters in Book Two of *The Tin Drum,* Oskar looks down from the metaphorical heights of a diving tower and sees the world spread out below him. He watches as the threads of current events are woven into history. As Ralph Manheim's version continues:

> I also saw that activities such as thumb-twiddling, frowning, looking up and down, handshaking, making babies, counterfeiting, turning out the light, brushing teeth, shooting people, and changing diapers were being practiced all over the world, though not always with the same skill.

This is a smooth and readable sentence that conveys the sense of Grass's original text quite clearly. But what makes this sentence special is something Grass does with language:

> Auch fiel mir auf, das Tätigkeiten wie: Daumendrehen, Stirnrunzeln, Köpfchensenken, Händeschütteln, Kindermachen, Falschgeldprägen, Lichtausknipsen, Zähneputzen, Totschießen und Trockenlegen überall, wenn auch nicht gleichmäßig geschickt, geübt wurden.

Here a translator can achieve a similar rhythmic and semantic effect by stretching the language a little:

And I saw too that activities like thumb-twiddling, brow-wrinkling, head-nodding, hand-shaking, baby-making, coin-faking, light-dousing, tooth-brushing, man-killing, and diaper-changing were being engaged in all over the world, if not always with equal skill.

The sense of the sentence is still clear. One version draws nearer to the reader; the other clings closer to the author.

This may be seen at a syntactic level as well. To take only one example:

Auch war er der Chef der Formellabrüder und freute sich, wie wir uns freuten, uns kennengelernt, ihn kennengelernt zu haben.

He was also the Formella brothers' boss and was glad to make our acquaintance, just as we were glad to make his.

Here Manheim renders the German in a smoothly flowing sentence unlikely to attract special notice. Grass, however, catches his German reader's attention by allowing the introductions to cross each other, as they often do in real life, rearranging and interlocking the parts of the sentence. Retaining that effect in English is not difficult; it is simply a matter of taking the same linguistic liberty:

He was also the Formella brothers' boss, and was pleased, as we were pleased, to meet us, to meet him.

The difference between these two versions — one smooth and readable, the other deliberately playful and inventive — hints at a difference in philosophical approaches. A small matter in a single sentence, but over the whole of a novel the cumulative effect is considerable. Ralph Manheim could have translated *The Tin Drum* in either mode. A gifted writer of extraordinary linguistic skills, Manheim produced, often against the grain of standard literature, a timely and literate translation that played a major role in the international success of Günter Grass's novel and helped propel its author to a Nobel Prize. The new version I offer is meant for our present age, one that is increasingly open to the foreignness of the text, to the provocative innovation of linguistic play, to a syntactic complexity that stretches language.

A few general comments on this new translation may help the reader sense the broader implications of this approach.

Better Start Running, the Black Cook's Coming!

One of the most memorable figures in *Die Blechtrommel* is the Black Cook, whose frightening presence pervades the novel. Grass recalled her to life from an old German folksong, first recorded at the end of the nineteenth century:

> *Ist die schwarze Köchin da? Nein, nein, nein!*
> *Dreimal muß ich rum marschiren,*
> *Das vierte Mal den Hut verlieren. Eins für mich!*
>
> *Ist die schwarze Köchin da? Ja, ja, ja!*
> *Da steht sie ja, da steht sie ja,*
> *da steht die schwarze Köchin da! Zisch, zisch, zisch!*

This song was sung by little girls standing in a circle. The game consisted of reducing the circle one by one until only the "schwarze Köchin" remained, who then hid her face in shame as the other girls whirled around her, singing the final verse.

The Black Cook not only haunts Oskar's nights and days but adds an important thematic motif to *The Tin Drum*, from the disgusting brew forced on Oskar by the children of the courtyard, to the dish of eels that sickens his mother Agnes, to the sausage sandwich devoured by Luzie as she urges the boys to jump to their death. It is no wonder that Luzie and the Black Cook coalesce in the course of the novel, or that the taste of that courtyard soup stays with Oskar forever. When the novel was first translated, however, there was no way to know the important role that cooks would continue to play in Grass's later works. So the Black Cook was reduced to a generic "witch, black as pitch" in *The Tin Drum*, and one important motif vanished. There were no doubt reasons for this choice, which was obviously a conscious one, and it is interesting to speculate on what they might have been. Whatever they were, the Black Cook is called back in the new version, and woven once more into the fabric of the novel.

The Long and the Short of It

One of the most pervasive stylistic changes in the new version of *The Tin Drum* is made in direct response to a plea Grass voiced long ago. In a letter to Helen Wolff of 6 February 1978, Grass lamented "the tendency [of English translations] to break up the structure of my (necessarily) long periods into easily consumed, practical, sensible sentences, and thus to flatten the dramatic and temporal buildup of tension, and so destroy the effect; particularly since such longer periods are often followed by a series of short, staccato sentences which depend on the gradient of what has gone before. . . . Please don't tell me this doesn't work in English, that it runs counter to the rules— my prose doesn't follow German rules either, and is an offense to [standard grammars like] *Duden*."

This same issue was raised by Grass during our meeting in Gdańsk, and I have responded. Each sentence in the new *Tin Drum* now faithfully replicates the length of the sentence in Grass's original text, and no sentences are broken up or deliberately shortened. As a result, long sentences reign in this version, as they do in the German. Grass does not write long sentences just to be difficult. Time and again, the length and cadence of a sentence underlines a mood, reinforces the impact of the moment, or reflects a central theme.

In a passage in Book Two, Maria slips into bed for the first time with Oskar, the apparent three-year-old who is nearly her own age. The paragraph consists of two sentences, one short and one long. The second sentence, after an initial caesura marked by a colon, glides along smoothly, in a mixture of humor and sexual tension, toward Maria's final words:

> As soon as Maria put down the comb, the whistling stopped. She turned, shook her hair out, and arranged things on her chest of drawers with a few deft movements, which put her in high spirits: she threw a kiss to her mustached father, photographed and retouched in a black ebony frame, then leapt into bed with exaggerated energy, bounced up and down a few times, grabbed the eiderdown on her last bounce, and disappeared up to her chin under the mound, didn't touch me at all as I lay under my own quilt, reached out from under the eiderdown with a round arm from which the sleeve of her gown slid back, felt over her head for the cord to click off the light, found it, clicked it, and only when it was dark, said to me much too loudly, "Good night!"

The old version broke this passage into six short sentences, and while the humor was by no means lost, the steadily increasing syntactic tension Grass sought was missing.

Another example of a single sentence broken into five shorter ones in the earlier English version occurs near the close of Book One. In a mood of uncertainty and fear, Oskar meditates on the menacing present-day figures who may be hiding behind the beard of Santa Claus, those false messiahs of Hope, Faith, and Love who are ready to turn on the gas again, ready to butcher both people and language. For almost an entire page, the lament pours forth like a true purgation, of which any fragment has power: ". . . and we'll never know who had to fall silent, to say not a word, so guts could be filled and books could be heard, stuffed tight, jam-packed, thickly written . . ." All this erupts from Oskar's inner core in one long spasm of nausea — and in one long sentence.

Not a Button Missing

Throughout *The Tin Drum,* Grass renders Oskar's story with the loving detail of a historical painting tinged with surreal fantasy. As with Joyce in *Ulysses,* or Alfred Döblin in *Berlin Alexanderplatz,* every detail counts: street names, geography, dates, the time of day, but also whether it is the right or left hand that is raised, the cloth from which a suit is made, the particular odor of a damp cellar. These details are never merely photographic (although photography is also central to the novel) but are the touches that turn life into art, and bring that art to life.

If every button counts in Grass, one aspect of the translator's task is surely to be certain that none are missing. Yet in the history of translation this has been anything but a foregone conclusion. In an attempt to make the text more readable, to smooth the way, to iron out difficult passages, translators have long omitted or blurred such details in the name of a style domesticated for the home audience.

Of course no translator, even one emboldened to render every facet of the text fully, insists on a slavish word-for-word correspondence. But acting on the assumption that Grass's stylistic innovations, his attention to detail, and even his deliberate provocations are crucial to the work as a whole, I have chosen to err on the side of inclusion. As a result, in hundreds of instances, a word, a phrase, or a sentence has been restored.

Among many other items I have returned to the English text of *The Tin Drum* a pair of polished boots, a missing mustache, a lifted little finger, a disquisition on the ABCs, a head of tousled hair, some day-old pastries, a Norwegian barrel, the battered rim of a cook pot, the conservators of a bell tower, a Number Five streetcar, four seats at a Christmas play, an early Mass, the Mirror of Confession, Judas, several boxes of Persil, a daddy longlegs, a Prince Heinrich Memorial Cap, a guitar and apron, the churches of Rechtstadt, Altstadt, Pfefferstadt, and several streets along which Oskar walked or onto which the windows of various buildings and apartments opened.

Even small omissions may be telling. Throughout the first third of the novel, Oskar calls his mother "mama." Following her funeral, however, he invariably refers to her as his "poor" mama — a note of lament I have restored in the English version wherever it was missing. Here a consistent rendering restores one small indication of the depth of Oskar's emotional attachment to his mother.

The inclusion of such small details often serves a wider purpose. Like Grass himself, Oskar is left-handed, and the overtones, both artistic and at times literally sinister, of this left-handedness (or, on occasion, left-footedness) reverberate throughout the novel. In more than two dozen places I have restored Grass's specific references to left (as opposed to right) where it was missing. Thus Greff the greengrocer now pulls "a boy of perhaps thirteen with overly large eyes" toward him with his left hand; now it is Jan's gray-stockinged left foot that he allows to wander between Agnes's thighs beneath the table as Oskar watches; now, as Oskar looks on in supposed innocence, Maria steps from her rolled-up shorts and kicks them off into a corner with her left foot; now it is Maria's left leg that Oskar sees "hooked over the backrest, as if it weren't involved" on the couch with Matzerath; now it is Maria's left hand into which Oskar pours fizz powder before she kicks him, and her left hand she washes clean; now the fatal Nazi pin remains open in Oskar's left hand. In these and other similar instances, overtones of sexual transgression, crime, and art are reinforced almost subliminally by that little word "left."

But the missing buttons to be restored in the new version go beyond single words. On several occasions entire sentences have been reinserted into the text. Such gaps can occur, as every translator knows, for reasons that are innocent enough: simple oversight, an editorial decision to smooth out the text, moments when the translator is fatigued, rushed, and simply at a loss as to meaning. At times, however, editorial squeamishness may have been involved. Although it would be unfair to refer to the text as bowdlerized—for much of what remained in *The Tin Drum* was certainly shocking enough fifty years ago—there were instances where the publishers may have wished to spare the reader. Today, when condoms are ubiquitous in public life, we would scarcely think of omitting the italicized phrase from this sentence in Grass's novel:

> Now and then I visited the office building, talked to journalists, let myself be photographed, lost my way at times in that box that looked, smelled and felt the same everywhere, *like some highly indecent object with an infinitely expandable condom stretched over it, sealing it off.*

And in the passage where Matzerath and Maria are found coupling on a couch, the omission can hardly have been accidental:

> Then they would fall apart *and let the snot splat down somewhere, onto a towel they'd brought, or if they couldn't reach that, onto the sofa or even on the carpet.* But I couldn't bear to see that.

Apart from one other brief phrase, however, that seems to have been the extent of omissions intended to spare the reader.

It was in part the complexity of Grass's style in *The Tin Drum* that led to other gaps. For example, the opening words of the chapter entitled "The Hedgehog"—aufgebaut, abgeholzt, ausgemerzt, einbezogen, fortgeblasen, nachempfunden—must have seemed quite unintelligible and therefore were simply omitted in the first version. Ironically, when the translators met with Grass in Gdańsk, he referred to this opening paragraph as a key passage in the work. Those opening words, he told us, refer to memories themselves and how we deal with them, tapped out to the beat of a drum. In the new version, I've taken the sort of liberty Grass encouraged in order to convey this effect:

> Built up, chopped down, wiped out, hauled back, dismembered, remembered: Oskar first learned the art of drumming up the past as a lodger.

The English words have a different rhythm, and the German prepositional pairs—auf/ab, aus/ein, fort/nach—are only approximately matched in English by up/down, out/back, and dis/re, but drum and memory are now linked as Grass intended.

From the day of his birth beneath two sixty-watt light bulbs, the rhythm of Oskar's life is rapped out on his drum. The novel itself is generated to that sound, which resonates from one passage to the next, at times soft and gentle, at times strident and insistent. As Oskar wears out drum after drum, the chapters rise in turn. And by the closing page those drumbeats have been transformed to poetry.

In German the effect is often like jazz, with riffs on words instead of notes. In such freewheeling passages Grass urged us to find equivalents in our own language, but to sense and maintain a rhythmic flow. Encouraged by Grass, I have sometimes placed the sound and rhythm of a sentence above normal syntax and grammar.

Chapter and Verse: Concluding Words

The precision with which Grass weaves the verbal web of *The Tin Drum* is remarkable, and one of the major challenges of a new translation is to follow each thread in detail. Again and again Grass echoes earlier passages, building a cumulative effect by the end of the novel that is particularly powerful.

Tracing these motifs in translation is sometimes difficult, but it is far easier today than it was fifty years ago, because we now have a technology that makes it easier for us to identify repetitions. As a collateral benefit, it has been possible to correct several dates, facts, and figures in *The Tin Drum,* including one or two instances of authorial inconsistency. (Thus the number of stairs Oskar threw himself down when he took his plunge into the cellar has now been firmly established as sixteen.)

Even chapter titles in *The Tin Drum* are often precisely echoed in the text. In the new translation the episode formerly entitled "No Wonder" is now called "No Miracle," since in the chapter itself the phrase refers straightforwardly to the failure of the boy Jesus to perform a miracle for Oskar. The chapter title "He Lies in Saspe" remains unchanged, but when the phrase occurs in the text, it now, as in the German, repeats the title.

These small points are multiplied many times over throughout the novel, and although the reader may not note and react to every one of them, they are central to the aesthetics of Grass's text, as they are to music and art itself. In the new version, something of the beauty and complexity of Günter Grass's novel should be felt on every level, both in the macrostructure of the work and in its smallest details.

The challenge of *The Tin Drum* has been remarkable. But nothing can match the challenge it must have posed almost fifty years ago. I am only too aware of the shortcomings of my own translation, of the debt I owe to Ralph Manheim, and of the good fortune I have had to share some part of this long journey with him.

BREON MITCHELL
January 2009

Glossary

Atlantic Wall (Atlantikwall): an extensive system of coastal fortifications built by the Germans along the western coast of Europe during World War II to defend against an anticipated Allied invasion of the continent from Great Britain.

Baron Münchhausen (1720–1797): a German baron famous for his outrageous tall tales about his adventures. The tales were later collected and published by others.

Belisarius (ca. 500–565): one of the greatest generals of the Byzantine Empire.

Biedermeier: a term used to refer to Central European culture from ca. 1815 to 1848, marked by the rise of an urbanized middle class that was focused on domestic affairs, with a sentimental taste in art and literature.

Bollermann and Wullsutzki: popular characters in Danzig jokes and stories, symbolizing German and Polish elements.

Bonbon: used colloquially to refer to the Nazi Party pin, which was round in shape.

Burckhardt, Carl Jacob (1891–1974): a Swiss diplomat and historian who served as League of Nations High Commissioner of Danzig, 1937–1939.

Cold Storage Medal: the colloquial name given to the medal for service in the German Army on the Arctic Front.

Crossing the T: in naval battles, an attack against the flank of another ship.

Currency reform: the West German monetary policy established in 1948. The introduction of the German mark (Deutsche mark) to replace the inflated Reichsmark had a highly beneficial psychological effect on German businessmen and was considered the turning point in the postwar reconstruction and economic development of West Germany.

Der Cherubinische Wandersmann (The Cherubic Pilgrim) (1674): a collection of mystical poetry assembled by Angelus Silesius.

De Gaulle's cross; the cross of Lorraine: the Cross of Lorraine was adopted by Charles de Gaulle as the official symbol of the Free French Forces during World War II.

Draußen vor der Tür (Outside the Door; The Man Outside) (1947): a drama by Wolfgang Borchert (1921–1947) describing the hopeless situation of the returning prisoner of war after World War II.

Edelweiß Pirates of Cologne: the most notorious of the armed bands of youths that appeared in Germany toward the end of World War II.

Elective Affinities (Die Wahlverwandtschaften) (1809): a novel by Goethe, based on the metaphor of chemical attraction.

Flex, Walter (1887–1917): a popular German writer who died from battle injuries in World War I.

Forster, Albert (1902–1952): the Gauleiter, or Nazi district leader, of Danzig from 1930. On September 1, 1939, Forster declared the Free City Treaty provisions null and void, suspended the constitution, and proclaimed the annexation of Danzig to the German Reich with himself as sole administrator.

Frings, Josef Cardinal (1887–1978): an outspoken critic of Nazism who served as Archbishop of Cologne from 1942 to 1969 and was elevated to Cardinal in 1946 by Pope Pius XII.

Greiser, Arthur (1897–1946): the president of the Danzig Senate from 1934 who signed a treaty with the Nazis regulating Danzig's relations with Poland. After World War II he was condemned to death in Poland as a war criminal.

Gulden: the currency of Danzig from 1923 through 1939, when it was replaced by the German Reichsmark. It was divided into 100 pfennigs (pennies). Until 1923, Danzig issued paper money denominated in marks.

Hartmannsweilerkopf: a pyramidal rocky spur in the Vosges Mountains fiercely contested by the French and the Germans in World War I.

Heil dir im Siegerkranz (Hail to Thee in Victor's Crown): the unofficial national anthem of the German Empire from 1871 to 1918.

Hitler Youth Quex and SA Man Brand: leading characters in popular books and propaganda films who represent ideal members of the Hitler Youth (aged fourteen to eighteen) and the SA and who become martyrs for the Nazi cause. Quex, for example, is murdered by Communists. On his deathbed he converts his father, who is a Communist, to National Socialism.

Home to the Reich (Heim ins Reich): the standard slogan in Nazi Germany promoting annexation of territories.

Jan Wellem: the popular name for the elector palatine Johann Wilhelm (1679–1716), whose monument still stands today in Düsseldorf.

July 20th conspiracy: a group, led by high-ranking German generals, who made an attempt on Hitler's life in 1944.

Kashubes: a Germanized West Slavic people living in the northwestern part of the earlier province of West Prussia and in northeastern Pomerania. Until 1945, some 150,000 people spoke Kashubian as their mother tongue. The language forms a transitional dialect between Polish and West Pomeranian.

Käthe Kruse dolls: individually designed, handmade cloth dolls from the workshop of the onetime actress Käthe Kruse.

Kyffhäuser Bund: a right-wing, monarchist, ex-servicemen's association of a paramilitary nature founded in 1900. Its merger with other servicemen's groups after World War I resulted in a combined membership of over four million.

Matka Boska Częstochowska (Black Madonna of Częstochowa): an icon representing the Virgin Mother which hangs in a monastery church in Częstochowa and is traditionally believed to have been painted by Saint Luke. Its miraculous power is said to be responsible for the lifting of a Swedish siege in the seventeenth century. One of the most famous religious and national shrines in Poland, it is still visited annually by throngs of pilgrims.

Narses (478–573): along with Belisarius, one of the great generals in the service of the Eastern Roman Emperor Justinian I.

Niemöller, Pastor Martin (1882–1984): a Protestant clergyman and the leading figure in the anti-Nazi Confessional Church who spent seven years in a concentration camp.

Pan Kichot: Polish for Don Quixote.

Pay book: unlike American soldiers, who carried no identification but their dog tags, German soldiers carried a booklet containing full information as to their vital statistics, military history, and pay.

Peace of Oliva (1660): a treaty that cost Poland considerable territory. Seven years later the Ukraine was ceded to Russia.

Persil: a popular German brand of laundry detergent invented in 1907.

Poland is not yet lost, etc.: in reference to the Polish national anthem ("Jeszcze Polska Nie Zginęła").

Prince Eugen: François-Eugène, Prince of Savoy-Carignan (1663–1736), a famous military commander and patron of the arts who served three Hapsburg emperors with great distinction.

Prince Heinrich at the Helm (Prinz Heinrich steht am Steuerrad): a well-known German song—"ein Volk, das solche Fürsten hat, das leidet keine Not" (a Volk that has such princes lacks for nothing).

Rauschning, Hermann (1887–1982): the president of the Danzig Senate, 1933–1934. Rauschning ended his association with Hitler and the National Socialists in 1934 when he became opposed to the policies of the Danzig Gauleiter Forster. He fled from Germany in 1936 and subsequently wrote several books criticizing the Nazi regime.

Realm of the Mothers: a reference to Goethe's *Faust II* (1832).

Rentenmark: the temporary currency established in 1923 to stabilize money during the inflationary period in Germany following World War I.

Röhm putsch: an alleged SA plot against Hitler in 1934 led by Ernst Röhm (1887–1934), used as an excuse for purging the SA on the "Night of the Long Knives."

Rommel's asparagus (Rommelspargel): Early in 1944, under the direction of Field Marshal Erwin Rommel (1891–1944), the Germans built a series of reinforced concrete pillboxes housing machine guns and light artillery along the beaches of Normandy to strengthen the Atlantic Wall. The beaches themselves were mined and provided with antitank obstacles, including slanted poles with sharpened tops, which the troops called "Rommelspargel."

Rydz-Śmigły, Edward (1886–1941): a Polish political figure, the General Inspector of Poland's armed forces during the invasion of Poland in 1939.

SA (Sturmabteilung): a paramilitary organization of the Nazi Party. These "stormtroopers" played a key role in Adolf Hitler's rise to power in the 1920s and 1930s. They were often referred to as "brownshirts," from the color of their uniforms. The SA differed from the SS (Schutzstaffel), who were directly loyal to Hitler, by being seemingly more independent.

Sauerbruch, Professor Ferdinand (1875–1951): a famous German surgeon.

Schwedensprung: a site from which the Swedes launched a major attack against Poland in the seventeenth century.

Sea marker (Seezeichen): a tall mast with nautical insignia marking the entrance to a harbor—here, the entrance from the Baltic into the Mottlau River.

Siegfried Line: the defensive military line, called the West Wall by the Germans, built during the 1930s, opposite the French Maginot Line.

Speicherinsel: an island formed by the Mottlau River in the middle of Danzig, so called because of its famous half-timbered grain warehouses.

Spinach shirts of the PX (Chi Rho, the first two letters of Christ's name): members of this religious movement wore green shirts.

SS (Schutzstaffel): the SS ("Shield Squadron") grew from a small paramilitary unit to a powerful force of almost a million men directly loyal to Hitler and the Nazi Party, with almost as much political influence as the German Army. Built upon Nazi racial ideology, the SS, under Heinrich Himmler's command, was responsible for most of the worst crimes of the Nazi Party, and was the primary organization that enacted the Holocaust.

Störtebeker: the nickname of the leader of the Dusters. Klaus Störtebeker (ca. 1360–1401) led a group of privateers hired during a war between Denmark and Sweden to fight the Danish and supply the besieged Swedish capital, Stockholm, with provisions.

Strength through Joy (Kraft durch Freude): a Nazi organization that provided regimented leisure for members of the German working class. It provided theater, sports, travel, and vacation opportunities at reduced prices. No organized social or recreational group was allowed to function in Germany except under the control of this official, all-embracing organization.

Sütterlin script: the standard German script developed by Ludwig Sütterlin (1865–1917) and taught in schools from 1915 to 1945.

Swedish punch: a form of torture in which peasants were forced to drink warm urine.

Todt Organization: the organization directed by the engineer Fritz Todt (1891–1942) which conscripted forced labor—often children—for construction work, notably on the fortification of the West Wall (Siegfried Line) in 1938 and the Atlantic Wall in 1940.

Vyazma and Bryansk: two important engagements in the Battle of Moscow (1941–1942).

Wessel, Horst (1907–1930): a German Nazi activist who was made a posthumous hero of the Nazi movement following his violent death in 1930. He was the author of the song usually known as the "Horst-Wessel-Lied" (Horst Wessel Song), which became the Nazi Party anthem and Germany's official co-national anthem from 1933 to 1945.

Wiechert, Ernst (1887–1950): a German writer popular in the 1930s and 1940s.

Winter Aid (Winterhilfe): the major Nazi charity, set up under the slogan "War on Hunger and Cold," to which the German people made compulsory contributions.

Women's Association (NS-Frauenschaft): a Nazi organization for women. Gymnastics, including swinging Indian clubs, was a favorite form of exercise for such organizations.

Yellow cross: another name for mustard gas, first used in World War I.

Young Volk (Jungvolk): Nazi youth organization for ten- to fourteen-year-olds.

ŻOB (Żydowska Organizacja Bojowa): "Jewish Combat Organization," an underground movement formed in the ghetto in 1942–1943.

Confident Data Science

Confident Data Science

Discover the essential skills of data science

Adam Ross Nelson

KoganPage

First published in Great Britain and the United States in 2023 by Kogan Page Limited

2nd Floor, 45 Gee Street	8 W 38th Street, Suite 902	4737/23 Ansari Road
London	New York, NY 10018	Daryaganj
EC1V 3RS	USA	New Delhi 110002
United Kingdom		India

www.koganpage.com

Kogan Page books are printed on paper from sustainable forests.

ISBNs

Hardback   978 1 3986 1234 1
Paperback   978 1 3986 1232 7
Ebook   978 1 3986 1233 4

British Library Cataloguing-in-Publication Data
A CIP record for this book is available from the British Library.

Library of Congress Cataloging-in-Publication Data
2023942926

Typeset by Integra Software Services, Pondicherry
Print production managed by Jellyfish
Printed and bound by CPI Group (UK) Ltd, Croydon, CR0 4YY

Contents

List of figures and tables

About the author

Adam Ross Nelson JD PhD is a career coach and a data science consultant. As a career coach, he helps others enter and level up in data-related careers. As a data science consultant, he provides research, data science, machine learning and data governance advisory services. He holds a PhD from the University of Wisconsin-Madison. Adam is also formerly an attorney with a history in working in higher education, teaching all ages and working as an educational administrator.

Adam sees it as important for him to focus time, energy and attention on projects that may promote access, equity and integrity. In the field of data science this focus on access, equity and integrity means opening gates and removing barriers to those who have not traditionally been allowed access to the field. This commitment means he strives to find ways for his work to challenge systems of oppression, injustice and inequity. He is passionate about connecting with other data professionals in person and online. If you are looking to enter or level up in data science, one of the best places to start is to visit these sites:

coaching.adamrossnelson.com
www.linkedin.com/in/arnelson
www.linkedin.com/company/data-science-career-services
twitter.com/ adamrossnelson
adamrossnelson.medium.com
https://www.facebook.com/upleveldata

Preface

This book begins with a history of the field before providing a theoretical overview and then also multiple specific examples of data science. In the section on 'getting oriented' as a source of theory this book provides a discussion of the history of the field, data ethics, data culture and data processes. There are also detailed typologies of analyses and data types.

This book also feature projects that call for readers to apply newly acquired knowledge. Instead of providing opportunities to dabble in every conceivable method in data science, machine learning, artificial intelligence or advanced analytics, the 'getting going' section first delivers a look at data exploration, followed by preparing data and sentiment analysis.

The third major section of this book, called 'getting value', focuses on tools in data science and also on how practitioners can derive value for employers, clients, and other stakeholders.

If you are interested in filling your personal bank of knowledge with the essential skills in data science, this book is for you.

For example, if you are a university or bootcamp student pursuing a major or certification in data science or related fields, this book will help you master many of the field's core concepts and skills. This holds true for both undergraduate and graduate students. Moreover, the first section, 'getting going', provides you with a starting point for projects that allow you to apply this book's information in scenarios that mirror those you may encounter later in your professional practice.

By reading this book, you will learn how to apply data science in a way that can create value for your future career.

If you are leading an organization, then this book could become your secret weapon. It contains extensive references to on-the-job experiences where I describe my successes and also a

few mistakes. You can use this book to help you and those at your organization deal with common mistakes in data science. By using this book in the course of staff and professional development, you can help your team gain valuable skills that will serve them and their organizations well.

Overall, this is a valuable resource for business and organizational leaders who are looking to improve their data science skills or develop a culture of data within their organization.

Acknowledgements

To my teachers, mentors, colleagues, classmates, students, and family – thank you. Together, we have learned with and from each other, and I am grateful for the knowledge and experiences we have shared.

I also wish to acknowledge those who donated data from their social media activity to this book's effort, including Mike Jadoo, Becky Daniels and Sharon Boivin.

Links for the book

From time to time in the book I refer to supporting material which can be downloaded from:

github.com/adamrossnelson/confident

A full set of data sources for the book appears on page 372. You can download the same list with hyperlinks from koganpage. com/cds.

Introduction

Imagine you stand accused of a crime, that you are in a court-room, in front of a judge, across from a prosecutor, wearing smart glasses. The smart glasses, more than a fashion statement, can observe what you see and hear and they have an earpiece through which a computer-generated voice is helping you make your case. This is not a new courtroom drama. This is also not a virtual reality (VR) game. Also, you may be glad to realize, you are not in a high-tech law school classroom. Instead, thanks to data science, this may be how the future of law will unfold.

Or, at least, it could have been the future of law. A company tellingly named Do Not Pay, that claims to have built the first robot lawyer, was looking to test its AI-powered legal defence in a California court in early 2023. But then there were angry letters of protest and threats. A number of state bar organiza-tions even threatened to sue the company. A state bar official protested and implied that since practising law without a licence is a misdemeanour crime, the people at Do Not Pay, or the

company itself, could face criminal penalties such as jail time if they pursued their AI-powered legal experiment.

BUILDING A FANBASE Data science is a team sport

To help you and your organization grow in its ability to use data science in new and innovative ways, you, and data science itself, you will need a fan base. This fan base will help surface thoughts and ideas that seek to leverage data science move past inevitable resistance.

However, building a fan base for data science can be challenging, especially when many people may be defensive or fearful of change. In these situations, it can be helpful to approach data science as a team sport, rather than an individual pursuit. By emphasizing the collaborative nature of data science, you can help disarm others who may feel threatened or defensive. This collaborative mentality can create a sense of shared ownership and responsibility for data-driven initiatives.

One way to build a fan base for data science is to identify key stakeholders and champions within your organization who are supportive of data-driven decision-making. These individuals can help spread the word about the benefits of data science and encourage others to get on board.

Ultimately, building a fan base for data science requires a combination of persistence, creativity and strategic thinking. By emphasizing the collaborative and team-oriented nature of data science, you can help build support and excitement for data-driven decision-making within your organization. As a favourite saying of mine goes, data science is a team sport, and by working together.

The company cancelled its plans. Do Not Pay continues to assert that AI, powered by robust data science, could help individuals who might not otherwise be able to afford lawyers. As a formerly

practicing lawyer myself, I remain excited by the possible benefits of further introducing data science into the practice of law. AI could help level the playing field. These technologies may equalize access to legal information and assistance. Better and more equal access to legal information and legal assistance is a good outcome.

I also empathize with the worry from many critics of the Do Not Pay case, who said their concern was for the clients who may potentially receive bad advice based on incomplete or faulty inputs. As you will see throughout this book, an important limitation of data science is that the quality of its outputs are always limited by the quality of their inputs. The output in the Do Not Pay case would only be as good as the data on which it is built.

Across history, advances in technology have led to both job loss and to the creation of new jobs. Typically speaking, many of those job losses have been in blue collar fields and areas of work. For a long while so-called highly skilled professionals, such as attorneys, may have felt insulated from the threat that technology could change or even replace the profession. As the pace of development in data science quickens, attorneys and other highly skilled professionals have less reason to feel protected. For example, the rise of ChatGPT, which we will cover later in this book, may very well change the writing profession. One day it could be possible for ChatGPT, or similar tools, to write this book better than I can. We will take a look at ChatGPT's capabilities as a writer in Chapter 7.

If you stop reading my book now (please keep going – there is much more to learn!), at least you will know this much: whether it is the law or writing books about data science, one thing I know for certain is that we are still at the beginning of learning how data science will continue to change both our work and personal lives.

Though the world may not be ready yet for AI-powered legal proceedings, data science has already permanently changed our lives. You might use GPS in your car or on your phone to choose

a route that minimizes travel time. During lunch, you might quickly fill your online shopping cart from a list of personalized recommendations. In the afternoon, you might discuss a family member's magnetic resonance imaging (MRI) scan with a doctor to learn about their risk profile for Alzheimer's or other similar disease. On the way home, you might listen to music curated from an expansive catalogue, tailored to your own specific tastes based on what you listened to over the past several weeks. After dinner, you might even spend an hour playing your favourite *Battle Royale* game. All of these scenarios, including the video games, are powered by data science.

Data science in any number of forms could be responsible for you holding this book in your hands right now. You might be part of a demographic that received a targeted advertisement about this book, for example. One thing I know at a high level of certainty is that the algorithms which brought you this book did so at least in part because they had information that suggests you are interested in learning more about data science.

So let us get into that.

Broadly speaking, data science makes sense of large and complex bundles of information. The methods associated with data science bring you actionable insights and predictions. Take the GPS example. In concert with GPS technology, the software in your phone (the maps application) uses multiple algorithms that have been informed by historic data about traffic patterns (vehicle density, speed, road and weather condition information, live data from other drivers, historic traffic patterns and similar). With these data, the algorithms generate predictions about the traffic or road conditions you may face as you move around town.

Similarly, physicians also use software that detects Alzheimer's-associated patterns in images from brain MRI scans. Armed with data from previous scans, and their associated diagnoses, medical practitioners can make predictions by asking predictive algorithms to review new scans. In concert the physicians, the

computers, the imaging technicians and practitioners in data science have assembled a pile of technology that can assist in estimating Alzheimer risk.

So, yes, we feel the impact of data science in many, if not all, aspects of our lives. To fully understand these developments, it is important to also know how we arrived here; how and when data science became important; who the pioneers of the field were. This chapter will introduce you to some of the lesser-known history of the field. In that sense, this chapter is a tribute to the unsung heroes of data science.

Unsung founders of data science

Given the examples above, you might think data science is a relatively new field. Though many of the applications we have discussed have been implemented in the last fifteen to twenty years, the roots of the field go much deeper. Many people, including data scientists, would attribute the origins of data science to the efforts of scholars such as the brilliant chemist-turned-mathematician John Tukey and the visionary astronomer-datalogist Peter Naur, starting in the 1950s and 1960s.

However, the birth of data science can be traced back at least one century earlier. An important early systematic work in data science dates to the early 1800s. At least two of the earliest practitioners in this field were women, and in their day the field was not yet called data science – that name would emerge many decades later.

The technical visionary: Ada Lovelace

Ada Lovelace is often credited with having written the world's first computer program. This is ground-breaking in itself; what is less well known is that Lovelace's mathematical acumen led her to recognize the tremendous potential of the Analytical

Engine, Charles Babbage's computing machine, for which she wrote code.

Lovelace correctly foresaw that such a machine could perform diverse complex tasks, ranging from understanding language to analysing paintings to composing music. Her notes reveal that she prophesied how computing would give rise to signal detection, machine learning, and artificial intelligence.

> Supposing, for instance, that the fundamental relations of pitched sounds in the science of harmony and of musical composition were susceptible of such expression and adaptations, the engine might compose elaborate and scientific pieces of music of any degree of complexity or extent.[1]

The mathematical mastermind: Florence Nightingale

The widely known image of Florence Nightingale, or 'The Lady of the Lamp', is one of a compassionate nurse who worked tirelessly to save the lives of wounded soldiers during the Crimean War (1853–56). The other side to the story is that Florence Nightingale was an astute mathematician and statistician who used her numerical expertise to bring about radical changes to the British military's policies on the care of wounded men.

Nightingale meticulously collected data on soldiers' mortality rates from battle wounds and contrasted these with the much higher mortality arising from preventable illnesses contracted due to unsanitary hospital conditions. She then used a revolutionary data visualization to present her data to British bureaucrats and politicians. Given our modern sensibilities, we would look back at Nightingale's visualization and call it an infographic. These visualizations are only one example of how Nightingale pioneered many of the modern techniques now widely used in data science today.

Rewriting history

Besides Ada Lovelace and Florence Nightingale, of course, there are others whose invaluable, yet largely unrecognized contributions have advanced the field. These unsung heroes have shaped data science into the ubiquitous and potent tool that it is today. Some of these individuals and their works are now garnering more recognition. In addition to the role of women in data science, contemporary recitations of the field's history are now better recognizing the contributions of people of colour. One of the first women of colour to receive widespread recognition for her role in advanced math is the gifted mathematician Katharine Johnson, whose complex calculations helped launch humans to the moon. You may recognize the name as it now adorns the recently inaugurated Katherine Johnson Computational Research Facility at the United States National Aeronautics and Space Administration (NASA).

More recently, Dr Emery Brown, the distinguished neuroscientist and statistician, became the first African American to be elected to the National Academies of the Sciences, Engineering as well as Medicine for his work in neural signal processing algorithms. Likewise, young data scientist Yeshimabeit Milner is widely respected as the founder of the Data 4 Black Lives movement. Her work reduced abnormally high black infant mortality rates in Miami by spearheading policy reforms informed by conscientiously, responsibly and inclusively collected and analysed data.

Dr Meredith D. Cox is the founder of Black Data Matters, another organization that seeks to empower the African American community through data science and statistics. She has dedicated her life to creating more equitable opportunities for people of colour in data-related fields and ensuring that everyone has access to the resources they need to succeed.

Through her organization, Black Data Matters, Dr Cox works to increase data literacy and help people of colour navigate the data-driven world. She provides educational programmes, workshops, and webinars that focus on data science fundamentals like machine learning, programming languages (Python and R), and how to interpret advanced statistical analyses. With her efforts, she is making a lasting impact on data science representation and helping to bridge its gap.

At last, it seems, the history of data science is being rewritten to better and more fully reflect the rich and varied contributions of scientists from diverse disciplines and many formerly less well represented, less well honoured and less well acknowledged backgrounds.

Broadening the field, and the recorded history of data science does not diminish the legacy of more often recognized contributors like Tukey and Naur. Instead, telling a more complete story of the field's history sets everyone's star in a brighter galaxy. Everyone who takes the mantle of data science, from those listed, to those still unknown, and to you who are reading this book, is building upon those early discoveries.

The dangers of data science

Data science tools, like any tool, can be used in positive or negative ways. In the GPS example above, collecting data from drivers on the road can help understand the most up-to-date traffic patterns and help people get where they need to go sooner and more safely. Great. But we also know that data often perpetuate societal detriments including, for example, systemic racism, classism and other forms of prejudice and oppression.

In her book *Weapons of Math Destruction*, Cathy O'Neil makes this point well.[2] She shows how algorithms used in credit scoring perpetuate inequality by unfairly down-rating borrowers from certain neighbourhoods and of certain racial heritages.

These parameters, in a technical sense, are otherwise illegal to consider when making mortgage and lending decisions. However, when obfuscated as a part of data science the implication here is that the technology may nullify the law's prohibitions on referencing these factors in lending decisions. Computer assisted algorithms in credit rating make it difficult for otherwise qualified borrowers to access credit. When credit ratings can sometimes be reviewed by prospective employers, data science assisted lending decisions may also limit employment prospects.

O'Neil further discussed more than a handful of additional scenarios that involve scaling data science in ways that produce racially biased outcomes. For example, she discusses how predictive policing algorithms can result in racial profiling, as they are often trained on biased data that reflect historical patterns of discrimination. In these ways, these algorithms perpetuate stereotypes and disproportionately target already disadvantaged, marginalized and vulnerable populations.

Safiya Umoja Noble further exposes these prejudicial algorithms in her book, *Algorithms of Oppression*.[3] She focuses on the ways the algorithms we have been implemented in our lives reinforce oppressive social hierarchies, including racism, sexism and classism. For example, she extensively explores how search engines seem to provide racially biased results. On her observations, search results over-represent mugshots of Black men as 'criminals'. Algorithms used to screen job candidates filter out applicants from those with names that are 'ethnic'. A student who searches online for colleges to attend but whose geo location information indicates they are searching from a wealthy and an affluent community will see nationally representative results from highly rejective, expensive and widely regarded as elite school choices; while a student conducting the same search from a location that is less affluent will see results that point towards less costly, more local and less well-regarded as prestigious options.

The problem of course is not with the job applicant and not with the aspiring college applicant. The problem is with the bias,

unconscious or otherwise, of the persons who created, collected and prepared the data, and then also implemented the work that used the data to train how the tools to decide which results to return for which users and for which use cases. These same algorithms have no problem prioritizing male applicants, or over-representing white men in search results like 'CEO' or 'teacher'.

In a related example that also exposes bias, see here how a prompt given to a popular artificial intelligence (AI) image generation tool produces biased results. When asked to generate 'a CEO speaking at a company event' these are the results – no women and no people of colour.

FIGURE 1.1   Images generated by artificial intelligence in response to the prompt 'a CEO speaking at a company event' (18 February 2023)

Source: Generated by Jasper AI

Naming these biases and unreservedly characterizing them as harmful is a start. There are many engaged in reducing and fighting the harms we have and continue to introduce through the field. Another important way to combat these harms is to encourage folks from diverse backgrounds to join the field. When the people collecting data are not diverse, it is easier for unconscious and even conscious bias to find its way into the collection, preparation, processing, analysis and interpretation of data. There are thankfully many organizations that are working to help address this representation gap.

I, and others in the field, have proposed the creation of a Hippocratic Oath specific to data science. These oaths include important language like, 'I will apply, for the benefit of society, all measures which are required, avoiding misrepresentations of data and analysis results,' and 'I will remember that my data are not just numbers without meaning or context, but represent real people and situations, and that my work may lead to unintended societal consequences, such as inequality, poverty, and disparities due to algorithmic bias. My responsibility must consider potential consequences of my extraction of meaning from data and ensure my analyses help make better decisions'.[4]

My proposal simplifies and also takes the notion of assigning to practitioners in the field another kind of affirmative obligation. I say, we have an obligation to prevent others from using our work in ways that may harm others.

One last way we can ameliorate any potential harm is to create plans that can address unforeseen problems. The first step in creating that plan is to ask the question, 'What do we do if we produce a result that is unflattering or that indicates we may have harmed others?' The next step is to answer that question fully for your specific context, document the answer, and make sure you are ready to deploy the solutions you documented.

Asking this kind of question, and having this kind of conversation – about unflattering results – before the analysis also establishes a reference point for if or when you and your team do encounter unflattering results. So, instead of the conversation sounding like:

Oh no, what should we do now?

The conversation will be more along the lines of:

When we last discussed how we would manage this kind of finding, we said that we would want to know the results. We also said that we would want to share the results and that we would want to contextualize those results. Further, we agreed that we would use this as an opportunity to explain what we will do to remedy the fault.

Asking this kind of question early (and also often as the analysis proceeds) builds a sense of shared responsibility.

The two biggest families of data science techniques

Both major families of machine learning involve using data to generate a prediction. Consider, for example, the task of making predictions about a shopper who uses an online shopping platform. Based on information about that shopper, about other shoppers, about the market, and other factors, the store's online platform can make predictions about that shopper. The platform can then deliver to the shopper those predictions in the form of recommendations for the shopper. Sometimes the shopping platforms produce recommendations that seem a bit unsettling. For example, at times the platform might recommend items the shopper will want, or feel they need, but when they had not yet previously known existed.

Another example are algorithms that are exceedingly good at 'learning' to review an email and then predicting whether that

email is spam or not spam. The predictions are not always correct, which is why sometimes you need to comb through your spam folder for an important email the computer mistakenly identified as spam.

Supervised machine learning

In the first biggest family of data science techniques there is supervised machine learning. Supervised machine learning involves generating an algorithm that can make its predictions based on patterns the algorithm learned (figuratively speaking) from training data. The training data are often historic data. For example, when training spam detection algorithms, data scientists used emails from users who had previously marked those emails as either spam or not spam. The algorithms are capable of recognizing patterns characteristic of spammy emails, and conversely the patterns characteristic of not-spammy emails. Based on those patterns, the algorithms review new emails and then generate a prediction that indicates whether newly arrived emails might be spam.

In the case of the MRI scan example, the training data came from previous patient scans. The previous scans had already been reviewed by doctors in order to diagnose whether the patient may be at risk for Alzheimer's. Or, in some cases, doctors and data scientists may have collaborated to collect scans over time. By collecting survey scans from healthy patients and then later observing which patients developed Alzheimer's, the doctors and data scientists used that information as labelled training data.

In this way, the training data can teach (again, figuratively speaking) the algorithm how to make its predictions. The algorithm does not learn in the same way humans learn. Instead, the algorithm mimics the results of the human learning process.

Once fully developed and put into production, a supervised machine learning algorithm has a set of specific inputs and also

a specific output. In the case of email spam detection the specific inputs are data from the newly arriving email messages and the specific output is a prediction as to whether the newly arrived email is spam or not. In the case of the MRI scan that might assist in identifying Alzheimer's risk, the specific input will be the images from the MRI scan and the specific output will be a prediction as to whether that patient may develop Alzheimer's.

Unsupervised machine learning

The second biggest family of data science techniques is called unsupervised machine learning. Where supervised machine learning has a specific input and a specific output, unsupervised machine learning is much more open ended. Unsupervised machine learning is usually a set of tools data scientists turn to when they are looking to better understand large amounts of highly complex data.

Consider, for example, your own email inbox. If you are like many, you have more emails than you can truly read. It might be helpful for you to look at your emails and to devise a classification system. The classification system could help you organize your emails by topic. An unsupervised machine learning technique known as topic analysis could help in this scenario.

The topic analysis would take as its input all of your emails. Maybe you have thousands of emails. No human could review those thousands of emails on their own. But a computer can review those thousands of emails quickly. After reviewing (figuratively speaking) your emails, the unsupervised topic analysis techniques could provide for you a list of topics in which your emails may group.

Notice how the unsupervised topic analysis approach has no clear predetermined output. The topics could have been numbered in the dozens, or perhaps the number of topics could have been more succinct. Despite being more open ended, the topic analysis approach has a useful result. The useful result is

that you will have new insights on how you might group or categorize your emails.

A more general use case would be emails sent to a role-based email address. For example perhaps customer_service@acme. com receives hundreds or thousands of emails each day. Acme corporation would benefit from knowing what topics customers write about. Topic analysis would assist in discerning what topics customers mention in those emails.

Data science in concert

Data science techniques often work in concert. For example, Acme corporation might first screen emails sent to customer_ service@acme.com with a spam filter (supervised techniques) before feeding the email data to a topic modelling (unsupervised) machine learning algorithm. Of course only the not-spam emails need to go into the topic modelling algorithm.

In this way, data scientists use supervised and unsupervised machine learning techniques in concert with other forms of automation to both better understand and also make better use of large data sets. The result is often increased efficiency, improved accuracy and cost savings.

The more complex these systems grow over time, the more they begin to resemble human intelligence. But the machines involved are not actually thinking. Instead, there is usually a long workflow of algorithms strung together, operating in concert, to perform human-like results.

Overview of the book

Earlier I mentioned the stars in the galaxy of data science. As you read, use this book as your own kind of star chart through the field. A note to know about the field, as I have defined it for

this book, is that I use the term 'data science' in a manner that is broad and inclusive. I mean for my references to data science to also include work or topics in machine learning, artificial intelligence and advanced analytics.

Part One of this book, 'Getting oriented', seeks to do exactly that. You will learn about the genres and flavours of data analysis in Chapter 2, ethics and data culture in Chapter 3 and data science processes in Chapter 4.

Part Two of this book, 'Getting going', is more hands-on. Chapters 5, 6 and 7 are about putting data science into practice, including some hands on projects that you can do on your own. Chapter 8 provides you with a weekend crash course, using a sentiment analysis project.

Part Three of this book, 'Getting value', is about how you can use data science to generate valuable, meaningful output. Data science professionals call these valuable outputs 'predictions'. Chapter 9 is about data and how it is in and of itself also a tool. The chapter reviews multiple popular data sources for training, testing, education and demonstration purposes. Chapter 10 is about data visualizations and it works with data introduced in Chapter 9. Importantly the work accomplished in Chapter 10 sets the stage for the work that happens next in Chapter 11. Chapter 11 ties together how you can use the data to generate rigorous and reliable predictions.

Through this star chart you can choose your own adventure. Here are three of many potential paths. The first, not surprisingly, is to start at the beginning, and read until the end. That's a classic choice! Second, if you want to dive straight in to a deep exploration of the data and code, I recommend starting with Chapters 5, 6, 9, 10 and 11. The third option would be for those who are more interested in the background and overview of the field, the ways we use data science broadly, the philosophy of the field including data culture and ethics, for which I recommend starting with Chapters 2, 3, 4 and 7.

Whichever way you read the book, I am glad you're here. Enjoy!

Conclusion

Imagine being wrong. I mean so wrong that the feelings of embarrassment overwhelm you. My sincere wish for readers of this book is that the information that follows will inspire you to risk being that wrong. I do not wish you harm. But I do wish you the confidence that is necessary to risk making mistakes as you grow in your knowledge of, and trust and confidence towards, data science. Put another way, among the best ways to truly get it right in data science is to get it wrong – a lot. But do not be deterred! Mistakes are among the surest paths to progress.

This book is about data. About confident data science, in particular. You might expect it to double down on the importance of investing in data. Instead, this book is primarily about the importance of investing in yourself and in other people. This book is about building confidence in two things. First, it is about building confidence in data science. Second, it is about building your confidence in yourself as a professional who works with or in the field of data science.

In this book I will share some of my own experiences, struggles and successes as a data scientist. I will also offer practical advice on how to sharpen your skills in data science, build strong teams and navigate the ever-changing field of technology.

Ultimately, this book is about empowering you to be confident in your ability to understand and use data effectively in whatever role you hold. Whether you are just beginning your journey into the world of data or have been working with data for years, I hope that this book will serve as a valuable resource for building your confidence and expertise in the realm of data science.

PART ONE

Getting oriented

In the first major section of this book the learning objective is, as the title implies, to readers to the history of data science, and also to the functions of data science in terms of what I call the genres and flavours of analysis. This initial section minimizes its focus on technical aspects of the field as it instead focuses on culture, ethics and process. Chapter 4 on data science processes is, as you will see, an extension of the Chapter 3, which focuses on culture. The major learning objectives of Part One are:

OBJECTIVES

- To continue lessons from Chapter 1 that convey the history of data science with an emphasis on the rich and varied contributions of scientists from traditionally underrepresented backgrounds.

- To understand the functions of data science in systematic terms that relate to a taxonomy of analysis. I call these taxonomic levels the flavours or genres of analysis.

- To be able to give examples of projects that utilize specific analytical flavours and also to be able to articulate the strengths, weaknesses and limitations of each.

- To know that the primary driver of value in any given analysis is not the method or technique, but rather it is the research question under scrutiny or the business problem to be solved.

- To articulate what data culture is and to understand how to build data culture.

- To describe eight major phases of data analysis that can form the basis of any organizational approach to planning and documenting its analytical processes.

Genres and flavours of analysis

The parable of the elephant and the blind is a useful starting point when looking over the field of data science. In this well-known parable that first appeared hundreds of years ago in early human literature, religion and philosophy, there is an elephant. Aside from the elephant there are several humans who cannot see. Each person observes the elephant with senses other than sight including touch, smell and hearing. Through these senses the humans gather an impression of what the elephant is. However, each person's experience is limited. As a result of their limited experiences they all reach different conclusions about the elephant.

For example, one person has an opportunity to touch the elephant's leg, which feels solid, crinkly, tall and wide. Eventually this person concludes the elephant is like a tree. Another person has an opportunity to touch and feel the trunk. Relying primarily on the sense of touch the trunk leads this person to conclude

the elephant is a snake. As the parable continues various persons have the opportunity to touch the ears, tusks, tails and other portions of the elephant.

While everyone is talking about the same thing (the elephant), their different experiences lead them to talking about that elephant in different ways. They have disagreements over what the elephant is. In some version of this parable, the persons who have an opportunity to observe the elephant (via touch, smell, and hearing but not sight) often conclude that others who claim to know about the elephant have no idea what the others are talking about or that others are lying about the nature of the elephant.

Data science is an elephant. The field is broad enough that no practitioner or observer could fully experience the whole. As a result there are many who speak about data science in terms that differ broadly from the terms that many others may use.

Another useful analogy that I often use is that of flavours, or ingredients in a recipe. Imagine that you had an opportunity to taste only one ingredient of the many ingredients needed for a chocolate chip cookie. Most will choose the chocolate chips. Many might choose the brown sugar. Fewer will choose the flour, butter or baking soda bicarbonate.

Just as it is helpful to think of data science as the elephant, it is also helpful to think of data science in terms of this flavours analogy. Not only are there many in the field who have yet to taste the full range of flavours available, there are some who have unfortunately only tasted the unsavoury flour, butter or baking soda bicarbonate. This flavours analogy is one I write more about later in the chapter.

This chapter aims to present a partial solution to a problem: when many professionals from across broad and diverse fields contribute to data science, they bring their own different experiences and reference points with them. Many in the field only

know their own favourite specific flavours and combinations of flavours, which are often heavily influenced by their own paths into the field.

Ultimately, the solution presented is to seek out and embrace new flavours, by learning from diverse sources, seeking out diverse perspectives and actively attempting to understand the experiences of others. The first step in understanding the experiences of others is going to be to gather a full inventory of the flavours of analysis. Only after fully understanding all the flavours can we begin to piece together a more complete understanding of data science. In other words, by expanding our taste palates, we can expand our understanding of data science in its entirety.

DATA SCIENCE VS DATA ANALYTICS   Far more alike than different

One of my least favourite ongoing discussions in data science is 'What is the difference between data science and data analytics?' Or also, 'What is the difference between a data scientist and a data analyst?'

The reason I find these questions frustrating, counter-productive and even distasteful is that they usually seem to serve a gatekeeping purpose. Asking, thinking about and labouring over this question is a gatekeeping behaviour. That gatekeeping behaviour is problematic because we know that women and people of colour are under-represented in the field and especially under-represented in the roles that many perceive to carry more esteem and prestige, such as 'data scientist' and 'machine learning engineer'.

By reinforcing and buttressing the often superficial distinctions between 'data analyst' and 'data scientist' we are reinforcing and buttressing the gates that keep under-represented populations and identities in the perceived-to-be more junior and elementary 'analytics' roles and away from the perceived-to-be more senior 'scientific' roles.

Here is an analogy. Imagine a crowded airport and someone fainting in the crowded concourse. A handful of folks run over to help. Some of them are nurses. Does the person who fell turn the nurses away because they are not doctors? No. The nurses can help. Likewise, what if the patient knows the trouble may be heart-related? Then also suppose a doctor intervenes – but is an oncologist, a specialist in cancer, not heart disease. Does the patient turn that oncologist away? No.

Such is the case in data. A data analyst and a data scientist can perform many of the same functions. In some cases maybe a specific data analyst can do as much as or more than the next closely associated data scientist. Data science is a team sport and it requires both analysts and scientists on the team. It is important to focus less on how you name the roles and more on how to best position your players so as to move the ball down the field for the sake of the work at hand.

Analytical flavours

For this book I have defined five flavours of analysis. These flavours form a sort of analytical taxonomy. An analytical taxonomy, like any taxonomy, is a classification scheme in which we can systematically organization thoughts, ideas or things into groups or types. Some might call these genres of analysis. Others have also offered similar outlines that frame these flavours as levels of analysis or levels of analytical maturity.

Even though others have provided similar outlines, the version I present here is unique in multiple ways. First, most other versions of this model present one to two questions that fit within each flavour of analysis. My examples provide up to nine questions that may fit within each flavour of analysis.

This book also differs from other similar outlines which tend to ascribe a measure of value to each flavour. For example, the

first flavour is descriptive analysis. Other previous example outlines relegate descriptive analysis to the lowest value. For reasons on which I will elaborate shortly, it is not the flavour that drives value. When combining data science flavours they are often all of equal value. To suggest that one flavour is less valuable than the other would be, returning to the baking analogy, similar to suggesting that the bitter-tasting baking soda bicarbonate is the least valuable. Just as you should not discard soda bicarbonate (because it tastes bad) you should not discard or overlook the importance of descriptive analytics. To imagine any data science project without descriptive analytics would not be to imagine a meaningful result.

I also reject the notion that the difficulty differs from one flavour to another. To suggest that descriptive analysis is the easiest, as many versions of this taxonomy do, is short-sighted. While other similar outlines emphasize that these flavours may form a hierarchy, the model I present here rejects the notion of a hierarchy – each flavour is equally valuable and, depending on the nature of the project, equal in difficulty.

Other similar models also often list data science as a flavour of analysis. Or, to be consistent with other model terms and phrases, they identify data science (in and of itself) as a level or genre of analysis. Classifying data science as a flavour of analysis is wrong. Instead, I compare data science to the elephant or the baked good. While data science is the elephant or the baked good, then each flavour of analysis contributes to a final product that is data science (or the whole elephant or baked good).

Broadly speaking, the five analytical flavours are descriptive, interpretive, diagnostic, predictive and prescriptive. I summarize these flavours in Table 2.1. After elaborating on each of these flavours I then proceed to a discussion of each flavour.

TABLE 2.1   Flavours of analysis

Analytical Flavour	Associated Questions
Descriptive analysis	What happened? When did it happen? How often does it happen? How much of it happened? Are there outliers? What are the averages? Are there trends? Do any of the variables correlate? What data are missing?
Interpretive analysis	What does it mean? What are the implications? What (how much) does it cost us? What other questions should we consider? What other data sources should we examine? What was happening beforehand? What happened afterwards?
Diagnostic analysis	How did it happen? Why did it happen? Is it a problem? How big (or costly) is the problem? What are the symptoms? Have we previously missed important symptoms? What are the causes? What potential solutions might there be?
Predictive analysis	What will happen next? When will it happen? What are the odds of this happening again? Will the trend continue? Can we accurately forecast?
Prescriptive analysis	What should we do about it when (if) it happens again? How can we make it happen?

Descriptive analysis

Some of the primary tools employed in support of descriptive analysis include an area of statistics known as descriptive statistics. Descriptive statistics are the counts, tabulations, means, medians, modes, minimums, maximums, percentiles and distributions of the data. Other tools include visualizations, such as histograms, boxplots, correlation matrices, pair plots, frequency tables and cross-tabulations.

The typical range of example questions you can answer with descriptive analysis are:

1 What happened?
2 When did it happen?
3 How often does it happen?
4 How much of it happened?
5 Are there outliers?
6 What are the averages?
7 Are there trends?
8 Do any of the variables correlate?
9 What data are missing?

Interpretive analysis

This flavour of analysis is the process of making useful sense of the data. Making useful sense of the data includes understanding what the data represents, and what the data might not represent. This flavour of analysis is about generating information that can articulate, in plain language, what the data mean.

In other words, this flavour is also often the beginning of developing a story about the data. Interpretive analysis is important because it provides context for the data. Alternatively, interpretive analysis can also identify what context may be missing. Context is key for understanding the implications of data. Without interpretive analysis other flavours of analysis will be less meaningful.

In a book about data science (numbers) it is important to also note that some of the tools used in support of interpretation and analysis will include a measure of qualitative (non-numerical) methods. The extent and rigor of those qualitative methods could be as extensive as employing interviews and focus groups. However, in many cases it is common and sufficient to tap into the domain knowledge of subject matter experts who know well the processes that generated the data. Other tools that often provide meaningful insights for this flavour of analysis include natural language processing and text analytics.

The typical range of example questions you can answer with interpretive analysis are:

1 What does this mean?
2 What are the implications?
3 What other questions should we consider?
4 What other data sources should we consider?
5 What was going on before hand?
6 What happened afterwards?

QUALITATIVE METHODS MATTER TOO Data science should not be exclusive of qualitative methods

In the world of data science there is often a strong emphasis on quantitative methods – using statistical analyses and numerical data to draw insights and make decisions. While quantitative methods can be incredibly powerful, they are not the only tool in the data science toolkit. Qualitative methods – which focus on understanding the meaning and context behind data – can provide valuable insights that quantitative methods alone cannot capture.

Qualitative methods are a broad category of research approaches that are used to explore and understand human behaviour, experiences and perceptions. These methods are often

used to gather data through observation, interviews, focus groups and other techniques that involve direct engagement with research participants. The data gathered through qualitative methods are typically non-numerical and focus on the narrative and contextual details of the research subject.

In contrast, quantitative methods are focused on gathering numerical data through surveys, experiments and other techniques that are designed to produce numerical data that can be analysed statistically. While quantitative methods are often used to test hypotheses and make predictions, they may not provide a full understanding of the context and meaning behind the data.

There are many reasons why data science should be inclusive of qualitative methods. One of the key advantages of qualitative methods is that they can provide a more nuanced and in-depth understanding of complex phenomena. By focusing on the narrative and contextual details of data, qualitative methods can capture the richness and complexity of human experiences and behaviours in a way that quantitative methods often cannot.

Another advantage of qualitative methods is that they can help identify gaps and limitations in existing data. Additionally, including qualitative methods in data science can help to promote a more diverse and inclusive approach to research. Qualitative methods are often used to explore the perspectives and experiences of marginalized and underrepresented groups, and can help ensure that their voices are heard before, during and after decision-making processes.

Despite the benefits of qualitative methods, they are often seen as less rigorous and objective than quantitative methods. As such, qualitative methods may be overlooked or undervalued in data science. However, this perception is based on a misunderstanding of the nature and purpose of qualitative methods. Qualitative methods are not intended to replace quantitative methods, but rather to complement them and provide a more complete understanding of complex phenomena.

Diagnostic analysis

Some might appropriately perceive diagnostic analysis as a form of causal analysis. Diagnostic analysis is the process of identifying the causes and conditions that then lead to a specific result or outcome of interest. This flavour is diagnostic in ways that are similar to medical diagnoses. In diagnostic work it is also common to consider whether an outcome of interest is problematic. If problematic, then the next question is, how problematic? Or, how big is the problem? How costly is the problem? Scientists and analysts often characterize measuring the size of the problem as 'quantifying the problem'.

This type of analysis is important because it may eventually allow us to fix the problem plus understand how and why the problem occurred, or at least understand the problem (if there is one) better.

The typical range of example questions you might answer with diagnostic analysis are:

1 How did it happen?
2 Why did it happen?
3 Is it a problem?
4 How big (or costly) is the problem?
5 What are the symptoms?
6 Have we previously missed important symptoms?
7 What are the causes?
8 What potential solutions might there be?

Predictive analysis

Predictive analysis is not necessarily quite what it sounds like. Predictive analysis is the best term we have for a family of analytical methods and techniques that can use past data to make informed estimations (probabilities, odds and odds-ratios) about what will happen in the future. Predictive analysis is at the heart of supervised machine learning techniques.

To elaborate on how this flavour might benefit from a name change is to look at an example of predictive analysis that does not involve predicting the future in the lay sense. One of the best examples of predictive analytics is the spam filter on your email. These are less about predicting future behaviour or events and more about using previous emails that had been marked as spam to 'train' a tool that can look at newly arrived emails and 'predict' if that email is spam. The trained tool then screens new emails as they arrive in your inbox. When a spam filter that relies on predictive analysis sees an email that appears to be similar to other emails that the filter knows to be spam, the filter can then use that information to 'predict' whether the new email is also spam.

While predictive analytics can be accurate, valid, reliable and valuable, it is important to note that this flavour of analysis is not without limitations. An average online banking platform user likely understands the limitations of predictive analysis because it is common for banks to ask you to verify your identity before they allow you into their online banking platforms. To do this the banks will often email you a confirmation code. You will need the confirmation code to enter the banking platform. Sometimes, spam detection gets in the way of proper delivery of these confirmation codes. Perhaps a handful of times you may have experienced how the bank's identify verification email can easily land in your spam filter instead of your inbox because the spam filter inadvertently 'predicted' that email to be spam.

All analytical techniques have their limitations. For this flavour, the largest assumption is that past behaviour is a predictor of future behaviour. However, data about the past, depending on how well they were collected and encoded, can only provide a limited view into the future.

The typical range of example questions you can answer with predictive analysis are:

1 What will happen next?
2 When will it happen?

3 What are the odds of this happening again?
4 Will the trend continue?
5 Can we accurately forecast?

By extension, this predictive flavour of analysis has another important use. By closely evaluating the statistics generated through the process of training a predictive model we can often use these methods to report which factors are most or least predictive of our outcome of interest. This is beneficial because it can provide actionable insights which add value above and beyond a trained predictive model.

For example, if an employer sought to improve its employee retention it could build a model related to predicting employee longevity. By examining the statistics underlying that predictive model the employer could derive actionable insights that would inform the employer as to how it can improve retention. The predictive model could provide information about specific employee attributes that seem to be most predictive of longevity. Perhaps employees who fully used their vacation, instead of allowing unused vacation balances to lapse, stayed longer. With this information the employer could design efforts to encourage employees to fully use vacation balances.

Prescriptive analysis

When in the midst of academic or corporate training, I introduce this topic in one of two ways. Sometimes both. The first is to explain that prescriptive analysis is a flavour of analysis that takes its name from the same etymological roots as does medical prescription. When a doctor provides a prescription, the doctor gives you a recommendation for what you should do. Thus prescriptive analysis tells us what we should do.

The second way I often introduce this flavour of analysis is to point to my wrist where I frequently have a smart watch. I ask the audience if they have smart watches that monitors body temperature, heat rate, time spent sitting, time spent standing,

time spent walking. Many will reply, yes. Then I ask, has the watch suggested you stand or go for a walk today? If yes, then you have benefitted from the output of prescriptive analysis. That watch is telling you what you should do.

Likewise, if you have ever made or adjusted plans as the result of a weather forecast you have both benefitted from and also conducted your own prescriptive analysis. If the forecast says rain and you respond by deciding to take an umbrella with you, that decision of yours is prescriptive result. You have made a decision based on what you should do given the forecasted weather condition.

The typical range of example questions you can answer with prescriptive analysis are:

1 What should we do about it?
2 How can we make it happen?

The relative value of each flavour

Many taxonomies, whether of data analysis or of other areas, emphasize a hierarchical relationship when outlining, classifying, sorting and organizing each individual level. I reject the notion that descriptive, interpretive, diagnostic, predictive and prescriptive analysis may be sorted from most valuable to least valuable or from most difficult to least difficult.

To sort descriptive, interpretive, diagnostic, predictive and prescriptive by some measure of perceived value or difficulty is to imply that the method drives value. The analytical flavour, technique and method do not drive value. Related, the analytical flavour, technique and method do not drive difficulty – at least not to the extent often thought. It is more true and realistic to state that each flavour is of equal importance, value and difficulty.

What will drive value and difficulty is the research question, the analytical question or the business problem you are looking

to answer or solve. Consider again the baking analogy. If you are planning a birthday celebration the typical business need for that occasion is a birthday cake. To make a birthday cake you will need many of the same flavours of ingredients that you would also need to make chocolate chip cookies. However, if you perceived cookies as easier to make (which is likely a false assumption), and produce cookies for that occasion the solution does not fit the need. And thus, given the specific scenario (a birthday celebration) the cake is going to be the most valuable output.

As data science practitioners you must be well versed in a range of analytical capabilities that will address the specific research question, the specific analytical question or the specific business problem at hand. Remember, it is not the flavour that matters, but rather what you can bake with them in combination to address the question or problem at hand that drives value.

R + PYTHON Choosing the best tool

It was not long ago that 'R or Python' was a serious question. Many continue to ask, 'Should I learn R?' 'Should I learn Python?' 'Should I learn both?' Today the best answer from many seems to be, 'Go for Python.'

The reason for Python's growth seems clear. Over the years Python has been a general purpose language suitable for multiple fields of work outside data science. Some of the more popular uses for Python have been game development and also web design and development.

Another reason for Python's success in the data science field is its ease of use and readability. Python's syntax is designed to be intuitive and easy to understand, making it accessible to developers and data scientists of many skill levels. All of this has led to a world in which Python has a large and active community of developers who have created a wide range of libraries and tools specifically for data science (or science in general) such as NumPy, Pandas, and SciKit Learn.

In contrast, R was designed specifically for statistical computing and graphics, and although it is still widely used in the data science community, it generally has a more limited scope than Python. While R and Python are now commensurate with each other in terms of statistical modelling and visualization, many regard R as more difficult to learn with a steeper learning curve than Python.

Given that Python has long been in use by a wide, broad and diverse community it seems that the pervasiveness of Python has given it the upper hand in its race with R.

General analytical advice

Avoid thinking of data science as new

As discussed in Chapter 1, the history of data science traces back at least to the early 1800s. It is a disservice to the field to mistakenly view data science as 'new'. Data science has been around for a long time and its development has been rooted in the work of many both well known and lesser known.

While Naur and Tukey are often credited with having coined the term data science in the middle of the 20th century, it is important to recognize that their works were based on the principles others established much earlier in our history. For example, Ada Lovelace lived and worked more than 100 years before Naur and Tukey. It was her ability to recognize that computers could be used beyond simple calculations that set forth a vision for entirely new fields of study.

In the course of my career I've developed a series of core beliefs on the topic of data science. Among those core beliefs is that data science is not a new field of study or practice. You will not find me in an academic, corporate or written context speaking about the wonders of data science as a new field.

Another important reason I maintain that data science is not new is that it is an extension of our human nature. Data science is about building models, mathematical and statistical, that help us understand how the world works. Sometimes these models help us understand or predict human behaviour. Often, depending on the flavour of analysis, these models can make recommendations to us about what we should do now, next or later.

There is nothing magic or mysterious about this. Humans naturally create models. So-called models are natural and universal. We use them, often subconsciously and informally, to understand our world, make decisions and solve problems. For example, if we see that it is raining outside, we have a mental model that tells us to dress in a raincoat or take an umbrella to avoid getting wet from the rain.

Another example of a mental model many may be familiar with is that body weight is a function of diet, exercise, genetic disposition and height. More formally we could say:

$$BodyWeight = f\ (\beta_1 Diet + \beta_2 Activity + \beta_3 GeneticDisposition + \beta_4 Height)$$

This equation is a scientific, mathematical and statistical notation or representation of the model that a person's body weight is going to be some combination of what you eat, the amount and type of activity you perform, your genetic disposition and your height.

The newness, or the perception of newness, of data science is due to our digital age's technological advancements. In the modern digital age we have access to more data and computational power than ever before. With access to that data, and access to powerful computers, we can create computer models that mimic the mental processes of humans. For anyone involved in data science, it is best to stop viewing it as something mysterious or shiny and new, but rather as a natural extension of who we are as humans.

An important reason to embrace this reality is that just as human models are biased,[1] so too are our scientific, mathematical, and statistical models.[2] Which also means, as I discuss next, that all models are wrong.

Data science is not unbiased

The field of data science is highly dependent on machine learning algorithms, which are developed by humans. As we humans possess bias but simultaneously lack a strong capacity to recognize bias (especially not our own biases)[3] we undoubtedly build algorithms that include our biases. It is important for data scientists to understand the potential sources of bias in their models and take steps to mitigate these biases.

One source of bias within algorithms comes from the data used when developing the model. A clear example of this that has been well-reported is how judges, attorneys and consultants in criminal law built and rely on algorithms designed to predict a criminal's propensity for recidivism. These algorithms create risk assessment profiles, scores and other 'predictions' that can inform sentencing decisions. The creators of these algorithms acknowledge that the models train on previously collected data that include inherently biased patterns we know to pervade worldwide criminal justice systems. While relying on these algorithms, judges, attorneys and consultants in criminal law perpetuate past injustices that are the result of human and systematic racial prejudices and biases.

REDUCING BIAS   Two pragmatic approaches

Finding, reducing and mitigating bias in data science is an important topic to understand at both the conceptual and also the practical level. Here are three techniques that can assist in reducing bias.

Sanity checks

This is a preliminary attempt that is meant to expose results that are obviously wrong or of low quality. For example, as discussed in later chapters when we look at regression analysis, a key evaluation metric from regression analysis is known as R squared (R^2). In short, this R^2 metric quantifies the proportion of the data's

---

variation explained by the model. If the R^2 is high, close to 98 or 99%, that is a red flag. A high R^2, absent other information that explains the reasons for that high value, fails a sanity check. The reason an R^2 that approaches 100% fails a sanity check, generally speaking, is because no model can fully explain all variation in the data. After a sanity check it then makes sense to continue checking for bias with falsification and disconfirmation attempts.

Falsification analysis

Falsification is an attempt to disprove the assumptions on which you relied when selecting your model of choice. For example, in general a primary assumption shared by nearly all techniques in data science is that past behaviour is a predictor of future behaviour, or that past results are a predictor of future results. This assumption is not always sound.

Another assumption associated with regression analysis is that the relationship between predictor feature variables and predicted target variables is linear. A close inspection of a Seaborn pair plot (discussed in Chapters 5 and 10) shows how they may be useful in evaluating this assumption of linearity.

Disconfirmation

When you seek evidence that contradicts your primary results you are engaging in a disconfirmation attempt. One of the best ways to pursue disconfirmation as a strategy that can help identify bias, or other analytical flaws, is to conduct the analysis with multiple methods, multiple data sources and multiple data preparation strategies. If the results from multiple methods, multiple data sources and also multiple data preparation strategies match and agree then you have confirmed your results. If the results disagree then you have disconfirmed your results, which means you may have introduced a source of bias into one or more of your attempts or that there may be other analytical flaws that need redress.

All models are wrong

Even a casual observer should note obvious errors in the body weight model I specified above. Activity, for example, is likely operating as a proxy for calories burned. As is usual, many models reference proxies instead of the actual casual factor. As a result of this nuance, I can say the body weight model above is wrong. As all models are wrong.

George Box was an American statistician who made important contributions to the field of statistics. For example, he is often credited with first proposing the boxplot. He is also well known for the quotation often attributed as his original spin: 'All models are wrong but some are useful'.[4] This quotation appeared in an article of the proceedings of a workshop on robustness in statistics held on 11–12 April 1978 at the Army Research Office in Research Triangle Park, North Carolina. The proceedings are entitled *Robustness in Statistics*. Accompanying this quotation, Box also wrote: 'Now it would be very remarkable if any system existing in the real world could be exactly represented by any simple model. However, cunningly chosen parsimonious models often do provide remarkably useful approximations.'[5]

Some rephrase or elaborate this idea by explaining that the usefulness of a model is inversely proportional to its complexity. In other words, the simpler a model is, the more likely it is to be useful. To simplify is one of the many reasons we reference proxies, such as activity instead of calories burned.

Returning to the body weight example above. If we endeavoured to collect information about a person's diet, their activity, their genetic disposition and height, we would be able to estimate that person's body weight using this model. However, because the model is wrong, we would be unable to accurately predict every person's precise body weight. For many people, we would be close. But for most there would be a margin of error. That margin of error is why this and all other models are wrong.

Some of the reasons this specific model is wrong is that we have not included environmental influences. We also have not modelled for changes over time. Another significant contribution to this model's wrongness, and any model's wrongness, is going to be error. There are many forms of error. In this example, I will point to one error type, measurement error. Our ability to accurately measure height might be good. The tools, units, and conventions associated with measuring a person's height are well known and highly standardized. However, with fewer standards and less consensus on the best tools, our ability to accurately measure diet, activity, genetic disposition and environmental factors is more limited.

Despite measurement and other error types, and despite being wrong by missing important factors, our body weight model can be useful. We can use this model to estimate a person's body weight if we know their diet, their activity, their genetic disposition and height. We can thus use this model to provide recommendations related to a person's health and wellness goals.

When we remember that all models are wrong, we are reminded of the importance of scepticism. We must question the assumptions of any model and determine whether they hold up to scrutiny. We must also be willing to change our models when new information arises that disproves them. Box's famous quotations also remind us of the role of humility. No practitioner in data science is perfect. Thus the models we build will reflect, and if we are not careful amplify and scale, our weaknesses, flaws and limitations.

Finally, when we remember that all models are wrong, we are reminded of the importance of patience. Models take time to build and test. The need to plan for more time than you think you will need is a topic I revisit in the section that outlines the data science and analytical process.

Less is often more

My advice that less is often more flows from two quotations and a poem called 'The Zen of Python'. The first quotation is that 'everything should be made as simple as possible, but no simpler'. The second quotation is, 'If you can't explain something simply, you don't understand it well enough.' 'The Zen of Python' says, 'Simple is better than complex. Complex is better than complicated.'

Simplicity is key. As a data science practitioner, it is important to remember that complexity is often counter-productive. Often the simplest solutions are the best solutions.

Fully embracing and putting the 'less is often more' advice into practice means looking back to the flavours of analysis. Each of the flavours involve different kinds of complexity. You can use the flavours of analysis as a guide when you seek to establish whether you have unnecessarily introduced a measure of complexity that will limit your project's ability to succeed. The flavours of analysis discussed above can help you ascertain whether you are asking just the right question in just the right way – nothing more complex than is required to answer your research question or solve your specified business problem.

The downstream benefits of this 'less is often more' advice are also clear. When working with stakeholders, it is imperative to be able to explain what you are doing and why in a simple way. Once you begin producing and disseminating results your work it will be easier to communicate if you control and limit the amount of complexity at the front end. When you reduce complexity, and consequently communicate better, not only does this increase buy-in from stakeholders, but it helps ensure you and your colleagues truly understand the problem and solution yourself.

It can often be tempting to add additional variables or layers of analysis in order to improve model performance. However, in doing so we run the risk of over-fitting our models, leading to

them performing well on the data we have given them for training purposes, but then not to generalize well to new data. Thus, the 'less is often more' advice can also serve as a guard against over-fitting.

Experiment and get feedback

Data science is a team sport. As with any team sport, having the right players who know and understand each other is essential. It is important for the team to share an understanding that the work occurs over multiple rounds of effort. Each round of effort can be thought of as a mini-experiment.

Here is how the multiple rounds of effort will look in practice. When a practitioner is making a visualization, for example, they should prepare multiple versions. Maybe both a vertical bar chart and also a horizontal bar chart. Of course, both charts will have a title, a legend (if necessary), readable fonts and well-conceived labels.

The practitioner can then turn to the team to review both versions of the chart. The team will be a group that knows and understands that this share-out is a kind of mini-experiment. The author of the charts will know and trust the team to give honest feedback. The team can provide input as to which visual is more successful. Then finally the practitioner who authored the chart can take that feedback and use it to prepare the final version of the visual.

The above example that involves comparing and contrasting two versions of the same chart is one of many ways teams can conduct experiments and also use them to get feedback. It is important to involve the team in these experiments and mini-experiments so that the final product is better than what was originally envisioned.

Chapter 4 discusses data science processes and how the principle of getting feedback can also extend to gathering feedback from external experts who might not be on the core team. The

process of getting feedback from external experts means gaining the value of insight from a pair of fresh eyes.

Be ethical

A casual survey of the books involving data science in my shelf shows that only around 10% of them discuss ethics. The implication of this finding is that we need more discussion of data ethics. Anyone interested in seeking discussion on the topic of data ethics, at least until others follow this book's example, will need to seek specialized resources.

I point to at least three important angles on the topic of ethics in data science. I often introduce the first through a story about a well-known scientist, Daryl Bem, who is on record saying:

> I'm all for rigor, but I prefer other people do it. I see its importance – it's fun for some people – but I don't have the patience for it. If you looked at all my past experiments, they were always rhetorical devices. I gathered data to show how my point would be made. I used data as a point of persuasion, and I never really worried about, 'Will this replicate or will this not?'[6]

If it is not testable, verifiable and replicable, it is not science. Even though he was primarily a psychologist, Bem's flippant and cavalier comments represent some of the most unsettling kinds of thought you can find in any scientific area of work and study.

Beyond being transparent about your motives and biases, it is important to minimize those biases. In addition to working to minimize the harmful or detrimental effects of your motives and biases, there are at least two other important angles I tend to teach on the topic of data ethics, including building a shared sense of ethical responsibility and also respect for privacy.

Build shared ethical responsibilities

Beyond transparency and efforts to reduce bias, under the banner of ethics I also teach that data scientists have an

affirmative obligation to avoid allowing others to use our work in ways that may harm others. One of the best ways to meet this affirmative obligation is to build a shared sense of responsibility for ethics.

One of the most egregious examples that may show how our work can be used, against our wishes and in ways that may cause harm to others, comes from information made public during the Facebook (now Meta) whistleblower incidents in the Fall of 2021.[7] The whistleblower, Frances Haugen, provided revelations that she said evidences potential harms to children, and that encourages division which may undermine democracy, in the pursuit of money.

At Facebook, Haugen studied the company's algorithms. According to Haugen, the algorithms that controlled the display and distribution of social media activity amplified misinformation. Haugen also claims foes of the United States exploited the algorithm to its detriment. Before she left the social network, she copied thousands of pages of confidential documents and shared them with regulators, lawmakers and *The Wall Street Journal*. In a less controversial scenario Haugen may have been empowered, and may have been able to better prevent the potential harms she had revealed.

When advising clients I work to avoid ethical dilemmas with an important question. I ask clients 'What will we do…' 'How will we respond…' 'What additional steps will be necessary…' '…if our work provides insights that are unflattering or that show we may be causing harm to anyone or any group?' In other words, 'What happens if we produce a result that makes us look bad?'

No single strategy can completely avoid ethical dilemma. Posing these tough questions works to reduce the risk of dilemma because it establishes a baseline response on how the analyst should proceed if or when the project finds unflattering results.

Having this dialogue before the analysis is conducted helps set a benchmark for when unfavourable results may occur.

Asking this question prepares everyone involved in advance and establishes clear expectations. Consequently, instead of the conversation sounding like:

Oh no, what should we do now?

The conversation will instead be more along the lines of:

When we last discussed how we would manage this kind of finding, we said that we would want to know the results. We also said that we would want to share the results and that we would want to contextualize those results. Further, we agreed that we would use this as an opportunity to explain what we will do to remedy the fault.

Establishing a sense of shared accountability from the beginning by asking ethical questions builds trust and reinforces moral responsibility. It clearly signals that both the analyst and their team are aware of this obligation, setting expectations for future contributions throughout the analysis process.

Respect privacy

Closely related to data ethics is privacy. As a former attorney I often point to sources of law in support of this topic. Many governments from local (city, state, provincial), to national and international have legislated on the topic of data privacy. The legislation on this topic is extensive enough that those in the field of data science have little excuse to ignore this important topic.

Many prominent sources of law, guidance and best practices summarize the topic of data privacy as follows.

1 **Lawfulness:** When you collect, maintain, store, move, analyse, distribute or publish any data be sure you do so in a manner that complies with applicable law.
2 **Fairness:** Legal folk will euphemize fairness as a matter of good faith. Acting in good faith means acting with honesty

and sincerity of intention. One reasonable test for fairness would be, would those who provided these data be comfortable, happy with, or care about how you plan to maintain, store, move, analyse, distribute or publish any of the data. A high standard of fairness will also involve a system of notification that also includes the opportunity to opt in, opt out or otherwise update preferences.

3 **Transparency:** A key component of achieving transparency is to have clearly written policies regarding the collection, maintenance, storage, movement, analysis, distribution and publication of any data. Of course, publishing those policies is also crucial. The highest standard would be to ensure that anyone with a concern for your data to be fully and affirmatively notified that you are collecting data plus how you will maintain, store, move, analyse, distribute or publish them. It is also important to clearly and transparently communicate the purposes for which you will collect, maintain, store, move, analyse, distribute or publish data.

4 **Minimization:** Minimize the data you collect, maintain, store, move, analyse, distribute or publish. It is important to only collect the data you transparently communicated you would collect. It is also important to only collect, maintain, store, move, analyse, distribute or publish the data you need for your specific purposes.

5 **Accuracy:** Data accuracy, as it sounds, ensures that the data are useful for the purpose you collect, maintain, store, move, analyse, distribute or publish them. The accuracy principle includes making reasonable steps to check for inaccuracy and to have policies, processes and procedures in place to repair those inaccuracies.

6 **Limitations over time:** The limitations over time principle limits for how long you should maintain and store the data. If you no longer need the data for the purposes that you communicated then you should execute any data destruction policies you, of course, also transparently communicated.

7 **Confidentiality:** Confidentiality protects privacy overall. Achieving confidentiality means processing collecting, maintaining, storing moving, analysing, distributing or publishing data in a secure manner. The goal is to avoid unauthorized, inadvertent and unlawful access to the data. The highest ideal here involves limiting individual human access only to those who must have that access. Additionally, it is important that those with access are correctly and thoroughly trained on data privacy and ethics.

8 **Audit:** The last principle I list here involves building systems that will permit objective verification of all of the above. For example, an auditor should be able to, and perhaps should frequently, check with individuals who have any role in collecting, maintaining, storing moving, analysing, distributing or publishing data. The auditor should be able to know exactly what that person's role is and why they have access to the data. And there should be tools and mechanisms in place that will allow each individual who accesses the data to also demonstrate that their own operational practices day-to-day, week-to-week, month-to-month, and year-to-year comply with all of the other data privacy principles.

In reviewing these privacy principles you see how they interact and interrelate. For example a practice that aims to observe the minimization principle likely also contributes to other principles. Or, without clear policies in place an auditor could not verify that individuals involved in collecting, maintaining, storing moving, analysing, distributing or publishing data (or that the organization as a whole) are adhering to the data privacy principles. In this way having a transparent and well-documented set of policies also contributes to the ability to conduct an audit.

Anticipate problems

Especially remember to anticipate ethical problems and dilemma. Anticipating problems is an important aspect of doing well in

life and business, anyway. I use anticipating problems as general advice regarding data science as an opportunity to double and triple mention the importance of ethics.

Here I remind that it is a best practice to always ask at the beginning of any project, 'What happens if our results are unflattering, shameful, or otherwise somehow open us to criticism or embarrassment?'

In reading the above question, now for a second time, I hope you will see that I place this obligation, to avoid allowing others to use our work in ways that may harm others, on par with similar obligations among educators, medical, legal, architectural, engineering, accounting and other licensed professionals. As of yet, there is no formal obligation in law or in a professional code of responsibility (other than general prohibitions against fraud, tort law and criminal law) for those who work in data science. If we do not anticipate these and other ethical dilemma, we risk undermining the credibility of our work. Worse, if we do not observe these ethical obligations we risk causing real harm to others.

No single practice will fully prevent an ethical dilemma. A collection of safeguards will be necessary to protect our work against ethical perils. The practice I propose here, asking and documenting what would happen if the results are unflattering or shameful, is just one of many opportunities to anticipate and mitigate risks.

The emphasis on ethics in this and other sections of this book might at first glance seem overdone. They are not, I assure you. Finding an unflattering or undesirable result is not an uncommon analytical outcome. Such results appear in nearly any area of practice from pharma research to political investigations to other scientific disciplines.

Conclusion

In the first few days of starting a new data science role, I was once speaking with the organization's director of development

operations (DevOps). I was asking DevOps to help me get set up with access to production data (read only, of course). The organization had not previously employed a data scientist – I was the first. The DevOps team pointed me to a set of tools they had in place that would produce a series of rudimentary descriptive statistics.

I explained that I needed the original underlying data because I needed to see the shape of the data. The DevOps team scratched their head. They asked, 'What do you mean? The number or rows and number of fields?' I said, 'Sure, that would be useful too.' But, also pointed out that you can get the number of rows and the number of fields from the, mostly SQL, tools they already pointed me towards. I continued to explain, 'I need to see the standard deviation, and the standard errors, plus it would also be useful to generate and inspect boxplots, histograms and other similar graphics.'

Because the organization I was at was eager to expand its capacity for data science the conversation continued and remained productive. We eventually arrived at common understandings that surrounded the needs of data scientists and how the DevOps team could engineer solutions that would meet those needs. We did not solve these problems on week one. It took multiple conversations spanning many months to build the common understanding that would be necessary to implement a data science operation within the organization.

This story was around a point in my career where I introduced data science to an organization that had not yet worked with data science. Introducing a data-rich organization to data science is an experience that I hope others may experience in their careers. The lessons about data science and developing a data culture from such an experience are profound. Much of that wisdom is landing here in your hands via this book. This story also illustrates the most important takeaway from this chapter: that data science can mean many things to many

different practitioners or observers. This diversity of perspective is both a strength and a weakness.

The diversity of perspective is a weakness when it leads to arguments, disagreements, or miscommunication. The hard truth is that often those who teach, speak, write, practise and interact with data science often use broadly different terminology.

As a field, data science can find strength in this diversity of perspective by working towards a more common set of terms and phrases to describe our work. This chapter does not call for readers to take the burden of unifying the entire field. However, I do encourage readers, data scientists along with those who are adjacent to the field, to strive for a more common set of terms and phrases to describe the work of your teams and of those within your own organizations.

The process of building your own organization's common understanding of data is the process of building your organization's data culture. Data culture is a topic to which I will return in the next chapter.

This chapter also provided a dose of general analytical advice. Some of that advice revisited the notion that data science is not a new field. And by looking under the hood of data science, and understanding it as a process that involves building models of the world, the chapter also demystified the field.

## CHAPTER THREE

Ethics and data culture

In the midst of the Covid-19 pandemic, in the fall of 2021, the whistleblower who famously exposed multiple controversial practices at Facebook (now known as Meta) was a data scientist. Some have speculated that the controversy surrounding the former Facebook data scientist's revelations to world media and the United States Congress hastened Facebook's decision to rebrand and reorganize as Meta. The rebranding and reorganization, it was thought, was meant to take attention away from the controversy.

Ethics in data science is a meaningful centrepiece for the topic of 'data culture' because ethical norms serve to illustrate what data culture is. Culture is a set of shared thoughts, understandings, values, traditions, practices, institutions, language and other customs that are passed from one generation to the next.

Data culture is more than ethics, of course. I have a specific reason to display the topic of data culture through the lens of ethics. Not long ago I attempted an experiment. You can do this experiment yourself if you have a pile of data-related books

nearby. I looked around and found 10 books on various data-related topics. I intentionally chose a broad range of book 'types'. Some of the books were more technical, and others were less technical. Some of the books were broadly applicable to the practice of data science in any industry. Other books were specific to just one individual industry.

After collecting these books I looked in the index for each. All 10 books had extensive indices. Some had glossaries. Across all of the book indices and glossaries, only two mentioned ethics in the index or glossary. And that same number discussed data ethics in any meaningful depth.

As a result of this experiment, I aim to correct for the field's oversight and only minimal reference to ethics.

First this chapter will define what culture is and then it will also explore what data culture is. And second, this chapter also offers guidance on how data science professionals can build data culture.

Culture and data culture

Culture is a shared set of thoughts, understandings, values, traditions, practices, institutions, language and other customs that groups of people pass from one generation to the next. All organizations have culture, some are more intentional than others.

My best evidence for the notion that all organizations have a culture is the reactions students in my corporate seminars have for me when I ask them questions like 'What is that "flip-flop" that you just mentioned?' Or sometimes I need to say something like 'Thank you for sharing that story. Can you fill me in on what the "hidden spaces" are that you were talking about?' The 'flip-flop' and 'hidden spaces' in these examples are generic terms I invented to stand in for what I call 'ACME-isms'.

A specific example of an ACME-ism is the Zoom slinky. The Zoom slinky is a reference employees at Zoom know well. It is a graphic that showcases the features and capabilities of the Zoom platform. It also makes for a fun artefact that folks at Zoom know about. Knowledge of the slinky pervades the organization and, as employees come and go, the artefact remains.

ACME-isms are specific terms and phrases that often, but not always, have an intuitive meaning but that are really only used by folks who work at ACME Corporation. To use a specific company name, the publisher of this book Kogan Page, there might be a specific term or phrase at Kogan Page that I could call a 'KP-ism' because it would be meaningful to folks who work at Kogan Page but it might not be as meaningful for anyone else.

An ACME-ism is an example of a shared thought, understanding, tradition, practice and language that the group of people at ACME pass from one generation to the next. Another example of a shared thought, understanding, value, tradition, practice, or institution is a concern to behave and operate ethically.

Building data culture

Therefore, data culture comprises data-related thoughts, data-related understandings, data-related values, data-related traditions, data-related practices, data-related institutions, data-related language and other data-related customs that a group passes from one generation to the next.

Because data culture is a specific, observable and measurable phenomenon, it is possible to build it. Those working in data science either as individual contributors or as leaders can build data culture through multiple strategies. Most of these strategies map back to a specific exercise.

The specific exercise is to speak as a group about a specific data-related question and then arrive at a shared understanding

or conclusion. The remainder of this section reviews questions that organizations can answer for themselves and that in doing so will foster discussions that build data culture.

What are data?

This is one of the many questions I most enjoy. There is no correct answer. In full view of the definition of data culture, given above, the correct answer for any given organization is the one that members of that organization find most meaningful for and useful for themselves.

If you seek to build data culture at your organization, consider setting aside time at a gathering or a series of gatherings. Often weekly or monthly staff meetings will work well for this. Provide for everyone in the meeting a plain, clean sheet of paper. And then ask everyone to quietly write on the paper what they believe is 'the definition of data'. After sufficient time passes, ask everyone to give their paper to someone else. Ask everyone to read what the previous colleague wrote and then to write out a response. Continue the process of passing the papers around so that everyone can read and respond to what others say.

Later you can collect the papers, compile the thoughts, and then use the compilation as reading material that your organization can use for more discussion. The goal is to determine, for your own purposes and your own use, what the definition of data is.

A common finding from exercises like this one is that data are raw material. But that we use data to make information. Eventually, after sufficient effort the data transform into new knowledge, which is information about how the world works but that did not exist before. Your results will vary.

What is an analysis?

This is a question that many organizations would do well for themselves to answer. Again, there is no right or wrong answer.

The goal is not to arrive at a textbook answer. The goal is to find a common and shared understanding that members of the organization find useful. Also that members of the organization can pass from one generation to the next.

A failed, stalled or disappointing analytical project often roots back to an insufficient shared understanding of what it means to conduct an analysis. Related questions under this heading that organizations should consider are:

- What are the expected inputs for an analysis?
- What are the expected outputs of an analysis?
- Who will prioritize what analyses we perform? How will we know which analyses to perform ourselves? How can we know which to delegate? And, on what basis will we know that it is safe to postpone an analysis for later work?
- How do we know what success is when we conduct an analysis?

Common findings from the discussions under the 'what is an analysis' heading include a documented process that organizations can follow through the course of an analysis. For organizations that wish to further reinforce and infuse the data culture within other traditions, an option is to place the results of this discussion in an operational manual or handbook. To help those that are interested in this topic of discussion, Chapter 4 outlines an overview of the data science process. I suggest readers use this book's outline from Chapter 4 as a point of departure when developing their organization's own documentation.

What is our analytical process?

Knowing and having documented your analytical process is an important aspect of building and maintaining a strong data culture. There are many ways to know about and document your process. Often it can begin with simple discussions in which members of the organization share their own thoughts. Later the

documentation work can proceed by writing summaries of the discussions. Building diagrams related to those discussions is also an effective way of documenting the process.

As it turns out, discussing, formulating, writing out and diagramming your process will build team cohesion and also build culture. As a team, through these discussions and planning activities you will build shared values and understandings that can be passed down from one generation to the next. As mentioned, Chapter 4 provides a starting point for planning and documenting your process. It is not necessary to follow Chapter 4's plan exactly. Instead it is useful to go through the experience of building and documenting your own process. You need to arrive at a process that works for you and that represents your own behaviours, habits and practices.

To effectively answer the question 'What is our analytical process?' and also to effectively document that answer, you will need to consider the steps or stages of your analytical process. Determine what inputs are required for each step and what outputs are generated. Additionally, it is important to consider how you will assign authority and responsibility for initiating an analysis. By documenting your process, you can create a shared understanding of how data analysis is conducted in your organization, which is critical for a strong data culture.

What is data literacy?

Data literacy is often a notion that evokes mixed feelings. For example, how many professionals have you encountered who stated with pride, in gist, 'I am not the numbers person here.' Or, 'I hate math!' For unknown reasons, it is often socially acceptable and even sometimes a badge of honour to brag about innumeracy, when we would not consider it acceptable to brag about illiteracy. For the savvy data-driven organization with a strong data culture the notions of numeracy or data literacy need not be evocative of mixed or negative feelings.

Devoting staff development time to discussing data literacy, which simultaneously builds data literacy, will cultivate a culture that leads to more people who are adept at coping with data. The organizations that have thought about what it means to be data literate will be more well equipped to measure the data literacy of their members. When there is shared thought, understanding, value, tradition, practice, institution, language and other customs on the topic of data literacy, the organization's attempts to measure (in essence, assess) that data literacy will be more welcome and less intimidating.

What is data our infrastructure?

Tackling this infrastructure question as an organization presents a massive opportunity to build and strengthen data culture. For this topic I point to a plumbing analogy. Your organization's building has plumbing that supports the delivery and removal of water. It is well designed to deliver water, at the desired temperature, to the right places at the right time and in the right way. Everyone who needs access to the water has access to the water.

Data infrastructure is similar in that it is the foundation that supports the collection, management and dissemination of data within an organization. A well-designed data infrastructure can enable data-driven decision-making, facilitate collaboration and promote transparency and accountability. In contrast, a poorly designed data infrastructure can lead to data silos, poor data quality and limited data access, all of which can undermine data culture.

To build an adequate data infrastructure requires a shared understanding of what infrastructure is and what it does for the organization. This is why answering the question 'What is our data infrastructure?' as an organization can be a powerful and productive way to build data culture.

PRIVACY PRINCIPLES   A quick reference

There is a rough consensus that there are eight privacy principles. Here is a quick reference.

1 **Lawfulness:** When you collect, maintain, store, move, analyse, distribute or publish any data, be sure you do so in a manner that complies with applicable law.

2 **Fairness:** Legal folk will euphemize fairness as a matter of good faith. Acting in good faith means acting with honesty and sincerity of intention.

3 **Transparency:** A key component of achieving transparency is to have clearly written policies regarding the collection, maintenance, storage, movement, analysis, distribution and publication of any data. Of course, publishing those policies is also crucial.

4 **Minimization:** Minimize the data you collect, maintain, store, move, analyse, distribute or publish. Only collect the data you transparently communicated you would, and ensure that those who provided the data fairly opt in, opt out or otherwise updated their preferences.

5 **Accuracy:** Ensure that data are useful for the purpose for which you collect, maintain, store, move, analyse, distribute or publish them.

6 **Limitations over time:** Just as the minimization principle aims to limit the data you collect, maintain, store, move, analyse, distribute or publish only to the data that are necessary for the original purposes, the limitations over time principle limits for how long you should maintain and store the data.

7 **Confidentiality:** Achieving confidentiality means processing, collecting, maintaining, storing, moving, analysing, distributing or publishing data in a secure manner – only those who require access have access.

8 **Audit:** The last principle involves building systems that will permit objective verification of all of the above.

Can we reduce the risks of ethical dilemmas?

With respect to my former colleagues in the legal profession, we as current or former attorneys often have ideas about reducing the risks of ethical dilemmas (or ethical lapses) that feel like a full and complete solution. We say, write policy. Also, document standard operating procedure. Or, establish consequences for not following those procedures. And then audit for compliance.

The legalistic approach can be helpful and valid. A more complete approach is to build a culture that encourages frequent discussion or debate on what it means to behave ethically when collecting, analysing, storing, transferring, updating, producing and disseminating data-related products. These discussions will build data culture.

Try this experiment that can help measure your organization's culture on the topic of ethics. Find 10 people in your organization and ask: 'How do we reduce the risk of ethical dilemma in our data-related work?' If you receive clear answers that match each other then those clear and consistent answers are a good sign. If you receive unclear answers, or no answers, or answers that are in no way consistent then you know your organization has room to grow in this area.

Organizations should create a safe and open environment where employees can discuss ethical concerns or dilemmas related to data usage. This environment should be free of judgement or repercussions, and employees should feel comfortable sharing their experiences or concerns without fear of retribution. These discussions can lead to a better understanding of ethical dilemmas and promote a culture of shared responsibility for ethical data practices.

The discussions themselves become an aspect of the data culture. Earlier in Chapter 2 I discussed the Fall 2021 Facebook (now Meta) whistleblower news stories. In connection with that story I also suggest that organizations ask at the beginning of

any data-related project: 'What will we do if the results are unflattering?' Also, in Chapter 1 I introduced the notion of a data scientist's Hippocratic Oath. Consider prompting informal discussions at your organization on this topic by asking casually, 'What do you think about a Hippocratic Oath for data scientists?'

Why these discussions work

These discussions work to build data culture for at least three reasons. First, merely providing the opportunity for discussion will help the organization form, develop and enhance its shared understanding of data.

Second, this works because from the information generated by your organization's discussion, you have an empirical basis on which you can base and document your organization's shared understanding of data.

Third, the discussions begin for many organizations, or continue for others, other important conversations throughout your organization. Let those conversations flourish.

Organizations who are committed to building data culture can encourage the conversations by asking managers to include an agenda item on their team meetings to discuss the topics. It is not necessary to ask managers to 'report back' how those conversations go or what anyone says. As usual, managers should share with other managers and organizational leaders any information they feel is important to share. Otherwise, the value in those conversations is the conversations on their own. The conversations build data culture. The conversations also become a part of the data culture. When done well, the conversations persist and then become a tradition that will pass from one generation to the next.

Measuring data culture

When looking to measure data culture at your organization consider a worksheet like the one in Figure 3.1.

Working on data culture at many organizations can be a difficult sell for at least two reasons. The first is that measuring data culture is a challenging task since it encompasses a wide range of less-tangible organizational aspects and factors, such as values, beliefs, customs and practices. The second is because building data culture almost never contributes to the profit and loss statement or the balance sheet, at least not directly so. There is no line on the assets section of the balance sheet for 'data culture'.

The mere act of making an effort to measure data culture can also promote data culture. The practice of measuring and tracking data culture over time can become its own data-related custom that the organization builds and values collaboratively and also passes from one generation to the next.

One of the most common methods of measuring data culture is through employee surveys. These surveys can provide valuable insights into how employees perceive data ethics, data policies and procedures, data literacy and other aspects of data culture. In addition to the survey shown in Figure 3.1, another popular survey option is the *Harvard Business Review*'s measure. This is a tool designed to help organizations assess their data and analytics capabilities. The tool measures an organization's data culture along multiple dimensions including culture, leadership commitment, operations and structure, skills and competencies, analytics–strategy alignment, proactive market orientation and employee empowerment. One of the strengths of this tool is that it is well-recognized from its distribution through the *Harvard Business Review*. The tool specifically helps organizations identify themselves as data laggards, data strivers or data leaders.[1]

FIGURE 3.1   Nelson's Brief Measure of Data Culture

		Yes	Some-times	No	Not sure
1	When you have questions about your organization's data do you believe you know who can provide knowledgeable responses?	O	O	O	O
2	When others have questions about your organization's data do most others know who can provide knowledgeable responses?	O	O	O	O
3	Generally, do you believe you can access the data you need for your work?	O	O	O	O
4	Do you believe you can access the data you need for your work when you need it?	O	O	O	O
5	Do you believe you can access the data you need for your work, without asking for assistance from others?	O	O	O	O
6	Generally, do you believe most others can access the data they need for their work?	O	O	O	O
7	Do you believe most others can access the data they need for their work when they need it?	O	O	O	O
8	Do you believe most others can access the data they need for their work, without asking for assistance from others?	O	O	O	O
9	Do you believe your organization provides the professional development you need to effectively use data in your work?	O	O	O	O
10	Do you believe your organization gives most others the professional development they need to use data effectively?	O	O	O	O
11	Do you have a high level of confidence that the data you get at work is accurate?	O	O	O	O
12	Do you believe others have a high level of confidence that the data they get at work is accurate?	O	O	O	O
13	Do you believe you understand what data is available from your organization?	O	O	O	O
14	Do you believe most members of your organization understand what data is available from your organization?	O	O	O	O

Score 1 for each Yes or Sometimes. 0 for No or Not sure.

Total the score (maximum of 14 points, minimum zero). Calculate average score across units, teams, divisions etc. Keep track of your results over time.

Total

Conclusion

Some of the most painful experiences in my data science career relate to one thing. Failure of communication. The truism that the greatest barrier to communication is the illusion that it happened applies here.

As a data scientist I received invitations to meetings that I sometimes knew little about. The invitation usually indicated the group wanted the so-called 'data perspective' over whatever agenda items they had in store. Of course, I would happily oblige and offer to attend. I always said, 'Please send me the data ahead of time so I can look them over.' The folks asking me to attend their meeting usually sent a few data visualizations or a pivot table. The problem here is that a data visualization or a pivot table is not data. Instead, the data visualization and the pivot table are the results of an analysis. When someone asks for the data, but instead receives the results of an analysis, there has been a miscommunication.

This chapter, and the topic of building data culture, is largely aimed at preventing the miscommunication I describe here. The problem is that the meaning of *data*, and the meaning of an *analysis*, were not yet fully shared by all. When organizations have stronger data cultures, usually built through conversations surrounding questions like those discussed in this chapter, the data-related work grows to be more valuable, efficient, productive and meaningful.

Another important focus of this chapter, along with subsections of previous chapters, has been the topic of data ethics. This chapter used multiple examples related to letting a strong data culture also strengthen a culture of ethics.

Lastly, this chapter also offered perspectives on how organizations can measure data culture. Culture is a specific, observable, and measurable phenomena. There are at least two important takeaways on the topic of measuring data culture. First, there is

no one-size-fits-all approach to measuring data culture. Second, making an effort to measure and track data culture over time pays a return on investment for organizations who seek to build an enhance their data culture. The return on investment comes not only from the ability to track and measure progress on an empirical basis, but also because the practice of measuring and tracking data culture can become a part of the organization's culture.

Data science processes

In data science, I do not recommend that you hope for the best and expect the worse. There is a better way to practise in the field. The business of predicting outcomes is a scientific endeavour. To qualify as science, the work must be reproducible. For you and others to reproduce your work, it is important to document your process. This chapter offers a model process.

The core issue of this chapter is not what your process should be. Instead, the deeper goal is to help you define and establish a process that will be effective for the work you and your teams perform.

Ask a dozen data scientists what the 'data science process' is and you will have at least a dozen different responses. Some of those responses may be similar. But all will be unique in some manner. There are multiple reasons for the likelihood that a survey of multiple scientists will produce a list of different responses. At least one reason for the diversity of thought on this

topic is that the field has rapidly evolved over time. The field will likely continue evolving rapidly into the distant future. Another important reason for this diversity is that the field is born of many disciplines. Each discipline brings its own specialties, priorities and quirks.

To improve your opportunities for high-quality scientific results it is important for data scientists, data science teams and data-driven organizations to have a process in mind. At the risk of disappointing anyone looking for a definitive overview of how the data science process should look, I say it may be unhelpful to look for a definitive overview. I do not offer a definitive proposal here. I also caution against relying too extensively on any resources that characterizes its own brand of wisdom as definitive or ultimate.

Instead of looking for a process that others have defined and then working to adopt that process, data science leaders and organizations should review multiple processes from multiple sources and multiple disciplines.

As discussed in Chapter 3, the discussions, conversations and collaborations that mean to define those processes are at least as important as the process itself. It is also important to have documented that process. How that process looks can differ from one organization to the next. Sometimes that process can differ from one team to another even within the same organization.

As suggested in Chapter 3, the data science process any organization derives for itself, follows for its work, and documents for its files will become a part of that organization's data culture. An organization's data science process will constitute a tradition or institution (data-related) that the organization will share and pass from one generation to the next.

THE BIGGER PICTURE, ABOVE PROCESS   Creating new knowledge

When thinking about data science, machine learning, artificial intelligence and advanced analytics processes, it is also important not to lose sight of the bigger picture. An aspect of the bigger picture is to think through and also build consensus on why you have a process, why you focus on data, and what data can do for you.

One short and sure answer to these questions is that data science can generate new knowledge that the world did not previously possess. The pursuit of new knowledge, and the competitive advantage that comes with possessing knowledge others do not, can be a significant aspect of the bigger picture when it comes to thinking about data science processes. Consider the definition of these terms:

New (njuː) ADJECTIVE Not existing before; made, introduced, or discovered recently or now for the first time.

Knowledge ('nɒlɪdʒ) NOUN Understanding of the world derived from empirical testing or observation. Often derived from scientific processes.

The goal of generating new knowledge is at the heart of all scientific disciplines, including data science. It is about finding patterns and relationships in the data that can help us make better decisions or solve complex problems.

New knowledge is not limited to prominent scientific discoveries or breakthroughs. It can be simpler. Knowledge of simple, but unexpected, correlation can often be helpful.

Specifying an organization's data science process as a matter of culture highlights two important considerations. First, the focus shifts away from establishing the so-called best process *in general*

and towards the importance of meaningful discussions that establish the best process *in specific* for the organization. Second when there are challenges or when the organization faces upset, as any organization will, its data science process will be firmly grounded in the organization's culture. Consequently, the organization's data culture will better withstand challenges and upset.

Iterative and cyclical processes

To assist readers with finding a starting point, this chapter presents an eight-stage processes that may fairly represent many generalizable data science processes.

As you read through Figure 4.1 keep the following three thoughts in mind. One, this process and its elements will work best as a place for you and your organization to start as you look to specify your own data science processes. Two, for your purposes you may modify any given step. Likewise, you may add, delete, reorder, merge or further subdivide the steps. And three, this process assumes that the data science team is working iteratively and cyclically, which means the team works through this process over multiple or repeated cycles.

An eight-stage starting point

Figure 4.1 shows eight-stages in a process that could reasonably represent the workflow of many data science teams as they move through many projects.[1] To read this figure start at the upper left with 'Question or problem' and then move clockwise around the diagram.

FIGURE 4.1   An eight-stage model of the data science process (1 March 2023)

Question or Problem
Ask a question or specify a business problem to solve.

Look + Check Around
See if question has been asked and/or problem solved. If yes, with which data + methods?

Disseminate
Communicate results. Plan next steps + new questions.

Justify
If previously studied, justify replication. Define success.

Interpret
Answer or solve the original question or problem.

Wrangle
Find, collect, extract, wrangle, summarize, validate, formulate + organize data.

Check + Recheck
Check + recheck results. Validate + test models. Assess for + work to reduce bias.

Select + Apply
Select + apply analytical techniques designed to answer the question; Solve the problem.

Source: Adam Ross Nelson in *How to Become a Data Scientist: A guide for established professionals*, Up Level Data, LLC

To simplify visualization and communication of this process I have abbreviated the name of each step. Please do not let these shorthand abbreviations obscure the depth and complexity associated with each step. For example, the first step is to specify a research question to answer or a business problem to solve but it appears in Figure 4.1 as 'Question or problem'. It is possible to write entire books on the topic of specifying quality research questions.[2]

Question or problem

In this step data scientists seek to specify analytical questions or business problems that require data-driven decisions or insight. As conventional wisdom often advises that a problem well defined is a problem half-solved, specifying the question or business problem is important.

Data scientists and teams that work in data science sometimes neglect spending sufficient time, energy and effort on the processes associated with specifying the research question to study or the business problem to solve. This stage is an important opportunity to avoid moving deeper into an analysis before everyone fully understands the question to answer or problem to solve. Moving directly into working with data equipped only with an off-hand notion or vaguely defined analytical question or a business problem is a mistake.

Fully understanding the question or business problem requires more time, energy and effort than many often appreciate. Albert Einstein is often credited with the sentiment that if he had an hour to solve a problem, he would spend 59 minutes defining and understanding the problem. Then, he would spend the last minute executing the solution.

The step requires inputs from an operational professional, team or manager. The input indicates that there is an operational problem or opportunity. For example, loss prevention at a larger grocer might report that there is a rise in the number of store visitors who end up leaving without making a purchase. Simultaneously, there is no rise in inventory shrinkage that could correspond to a rise in theft. The initial conclusion is that potential customers are visiting the store, not finding what they were looking for, and then leaving the store.

The general manager of the store will recognize this as a potential problem or opportunity. After additional review, the manager also notices that the rise in visitors who make no purchase before leaving seems to occur mostly on Fridays

between the hours of 11 am and 4 pm. A manager with access to a data science team may present this observation as one to take through the grocer's data science processes.

Often the output of this first step can be simultaneously expressed both as a research question and also as a business problem to solve. To continue with the example from the grocer, an analytical question will be something like 'How can we model the products demanded from customers who visit the store on Fridays between 11 am and 4 pm?' The specific dependent variable will be customer product demands while the specific independent variables will be the time a customer visits the store. To express this as a business problem is more straight forward: 'How can we better serve customers who are visiting the store on Friday's between 11 am and 4 pm but who are leaving without making a purchase?'

Look and check around

When looking and checking around, the goal is to gather knowledge and inspiration from existing data and information sources. One of the primary purposes of the look and check around step is to avoid duplication of effort. In this stage the first component task is to look closely at the analytical question or business problem from the previous stage. It is necessary to ascertain whether the question has been asked and answered or if anyone else has already solved the business problem.

If yes, the subsequent question to ask and answer is: on what data did the previous efforts rely? Also, which methods did the previous efforts employ? And, what were the strengths, weaknesses and limitations of previous efforts? If the question has not been studied or if no one has already solved the problem, then consider why not. Are there factors, challenges, difficulties or other resource constraints that prevented others from previously working to answer the question or solve the business problem?

While looking and checking around it is also important to note what data sources may be available. During this phase is when the team may begin the work of extracting or collecting data for review and analysis.

This step also resembles the academic exercise known as literature reviews. As such, this step should involve a review of relevant literature, broadly defined. Teams should review canonical sources of research in addition to other sources of corporate intelligence such as internal or external white papers, position papers, case studies, marketing materials and other related sources of information that may provide insights.

Data scientists have significant contributions to offer teams and organizations during this look and check around stage. A daily expectation for data scientists is to be familiar with common data sources and common methods. With this contextual knowledge of sources and common methods, the data scientist can expedite the team's process as it looks and checks around.

Justify

During the justification step is when teams and organizations need to know whether the question has been studied or the problem has been solved. If the answer to these is yes, then the justification step involves specifying why the replication work is now worthwhile. Perhaps there are new sources of data now available that were not previously available. Likewise, there may be additional methods or techniques available that were previously not yet available, or well understood.

Related, if the question has not been studied or the problem has not been solved, perhaps previous teams have already considered the questions or problems but then rejected them due to costs or other resource constraints. If previous efforts rejected the research question or business problem, the justification step involves articulating why circumstances have changed that now

increase the value of answering the question or solving the problem.

This phase also often involves quantifying the benefits of answering the research question, or solving the business problem. Returning to the grocery store example above, quantifying the problem would involve identifying exactly how many customers entered the store without making a purchase. Then, also identifying how much they might have spent. The information generated through this quantification effort will help understand what level of resources the grocer can reasonably assign to solving this problem. Ascertaining the value of answering the question or solving the problem also better enables a meaningful return on investment analysis.

It is not uncommon for the research question or the business problem to fail justification. If the question or the business problem fails justification the data science process will need to circle back to earlier stages, discussed above. While revisiting the earlier stages, the team will need to either select an entirely new question or business problem or it will need to revise and restate the existing question or business problem. Assuming the research will progress after the justify stage, the team will then proceed to the fourth stage, wrangle.

Wrangle

Following justification comes the wrangle step. This data wrangling step involves obtaining the data that will be necessary for future steps ahead. Wrangling also often involves inventorying, further analysing, cleaning and preparing any data previously collected.

This stage may also involve finding additional data. Finding additional data involves determining whether the data already exist and what would be involved in extracting them. Often, additional data will exist within databases used for operational or transactional purposes. Likewise, many times data can be

purchased from data brokers. Finding data for analysis might also involve collecting new data. After finding data, further wrangling means cleaning and preparing the data.

An example of cleaning or preparing data could involve checking to make sure the data 'make sense'. Chapter 5 more fully explores the considerations and steps that are necessary when cleaning and preparing data for analysis. Specific topics discussed further in Chapter 5 include error checking, working with missing data, converting qualitative data to a numerical format and discarding data that provide little analytical value.

Related to the grocery hypothetical continued from above, consider a data set that includes observations from loss prevention who note the time a customer enters the grocery store and then also the time they depart the grocery store. A rudimentary step in checking for data quality will be to ensure that the time of entry is earlier than the time of departure. If the time of departure appears earlier than the time of entry in any of the observations this would be a sign of error. Before proceeding with analysis, this kind of error will need further redress during the data wrangling process. The data wrangling, cleaning, preparing and validation procedures would involve deciding what to do with the apparently erroneous records.

The wrangling stage's specific inputs will be the research question or business problem, plus any information discovered in the look and check around stage. As an output, teams will produce one or more sets of data. In general, these data will be suitable for answering the analytical question or solving the business problem. In specific, these data sets will include dependent and independent variables as detailed earlier in the process.

Select and apply

The earlier stage, look and check around, will often heavily inform the select and apply stage. Ideally during the look and check around stage, the team will have reviewed previous efforts

to answer similar questions or solve similar problems. The review of those previous efforts will have highlighted what tools, methods and techniques worked well (or not so well) in the past.

This select and apply stage is where a data scientist will review a range of tools and techniques to find those that are most appropriate for the research question or business problem specified earlier in the process. A data scientist may review multiple statistical techniques or algorithms during daily practice or in any given project. Often this stage may involve revisiting literature or other materials the team gathered during the look and check around stage.

Also important at this stage may be documentation review. Documentation review often means a review of documentation that supports prospective tools or techniques. In cases where previous efforts identified tools, methods or techniques that did not perform as well as expected, a data scientist may search through the documentation for those tools, methods and techniques to better understand their strengths and weaknesses.

At times, making a final selection as to which tools and techniques to apply can be difficult. This is especially true if the team has identified multiple options that are suitable for the research question or business problem. In such cases a data scientist may apply multiple techniques to compare the results.

Another theme that can surface during this stage is that the entire data science process is not necessarily linear. A complication that might occur during this select and apply stage is that the data scientist might form an opinion that the analysis would be better if additional variables could also be available but that were not collected earlier (or that were perhaps discarded) earlier in the wrangle stage. When a data scientist decides that more, or different, data may be desirable it could be necessary for the team to return to earlier phases for additional wrangling.

Another reason the process might require a departure from the linear outline presented here is that a data scientist might ascertain one or more of the variables available for analysis is not

sufficient to answer the question as originally specified. In this case, the team may need to revisit the process's first stage in order to consider what alternate questions may be appropriate given the new information that has been acquired through the process.

While this stage will take wrangled data, previous research results, and a specific research question or business problem as inputs, the output will be specific statistics and figures associated with one or more predictive model. From the grocery store example, a reasonable output associated with this stage would be a model that can predict what products shoppers might seek based on the day of the week and time of day they enter the store.

Check and recheck

This stage is an opportunity to make sure all of the preceding stages have been completed as expected. This means that the original question or business problem was well specified; that all available useful and helpful information turned up in the look and check around stage; and that the work has been properly justified. In some cases, during the check and recheck stage teams may discover that the value of the project had previously been understated (happy outcome) or overstated. The work during check and recheck also means assessing that data wrangling is complete and accurate and then that all tools and techniques were applied as intended.

A significant focus of the check and recheck stage is that it also involves testing the original data and the results. Data scientists can work to verify the results. During this portion of the data science process, a data scientist will perform multiple checks to ensure that the data were sufficient, prepared appropriately and that the analysis was executed as expected. In the case of developing predictive models, the data scientist will ensure the models generalize well to previously unseen data. It is common to challenge the results in order to measure and assess how robust they will be to changing, shifting or unforeseeable future

circumstances. Checking the results also involves reviewing any assumptions that had been made throughout the earlier stages.

This stage is a chance to make sure that the results are ready for interpretation and then later dissemination or deployment. A thorough range of activities during this check and recheck stage helps to ensure the results, once interpreted, can be trusted.

Though ethics and concerns for fairness need to be infused throughout the practice of data science, the check and recheck stage is also a stage in which practitioners can guard against letting their work cause harm to others. In this stage, in addition to double checking the review of previous work, double checking how the data were wrangled, double checking the selection and application of tools or techniques, it is important to check for bias that may cause harm. When teams encounter forms of bias it is also important to make efforts in this stage to reduce that bias. The data scientist must work with others to evaluate, identify and then reduce bias (or otherwise reduce the harmful effects of that bias).

Finally, this stage can also involve a review of the process and its results by data scientists and data professionals other than those who executed the earlier stages. By introducing an external or peer review, this stage can give an opportunity for a fresh pair of eyes to identify anything that may have been overlooked or to suggest any other improvements that may lead to a better result. External reviewers may also be helpful and useful in identifying important points to highlight in the subsequent interpretation and dissemination steps.

Interpret

Interpretation means explaining what the results mean. What the implications are. What the next steps might be. And how the results can be actionable and otherwise valuable. Interpretation also involves detailing any strengths and weaknesses that surfaced during check and recheck (or elsewhere in the process).

Interpretation can also involve explaining and documenting the tools, techniques, logic and methods used throughout the process. Another important aspect of interpretation work can involve comparing newer results with earlier results. When newer results disagree with previous results it is important to address those disagreements.

The specific inputs for this stage are all of the decisions, determinations and lessons from each of the process's earlier stages. The specific outputs will include a collection of visualizations, charts, tables, models and reports that explain why the analysis turned out as it did. Often at least some of the visualizations, charts, tables, models and reports can serve double as information that supports the next stage, dissemination.

For example, a data scientist may create a dashboard that not only allows the business to easily and quickly review results, but also serves as a way to disseminate those same results. During this interpretation stage a data scientist, and the team as a whole, may work to augment the dashboard with supplemental information, or annotations, that will anticipate viewer's questions and provide answers to those questions.

WHAT DATA CAN DO FOR YOU   More on why a process is important

For an angle on why it is important to have a process, on why you focus on data anyway and on what data can do for you, consider these three specific thoughts. Use these ideas as a guide while you communicate with others the value of data science. First, finding proverbial needles in a hay stack. Second, prioritizing and optimizing work and resources. Third, expediting and simplifying decision making.

Finding needles in a hay stack

A clear data process can help businesses find needles in a haystack. This refers to the ability to identify valuable insights

---

hidden within large sets of data. The best processes comb through vast amounts of data to identify patterns, trends and outliers that might otherwise go unnoticed. For example, in the family of techniques known as cluster analysis, an online retailer can use their data to understand customer feedback and preferences, which can reveal which products, among hundreds, thousands, or more, sell best, which do not, and why.

Prioritizing and optimizing work and resources

Consider, for example, the opportunity to precisely identify which operational areas at your organization are performing well and which may need improvement. One of the many ways this knowledge will help is by supporting decisions related to prioritizing and allocating resources. For example, an auditor at a bank might benefit from a classification algorithm that can assist in identifying which transactions might be fraudulent. With the computer's assistance, fraud detection specialists can focus more of their time and energies on reviewing potentially fraudulent transactions and less of their time searching for potentially fraudulent transactions.

Expediting and simplifying decision making

Another important reason to have a clear process at your organization, and to pursue data-related initiatives in general, is that doing so can expedite and simplify decision making. For example, a warehouse manager who is responsible for the tasks associated with deciding what to stock could benefit from a recommendation engine that suggests which products or supplies to order and when. Of course, a warehouse manager would not need to rely entirely on the computer's recommendation. Instead the data can support the manager's decision by providing a recommendation that will serve as a reliable starting point that will expedite and simplify the decision making process.

Disseminate

Dissemination is the process of reporting results, which can occur in many ways, including internal memos, reports, journal publications, articles, white papers, presentations, briefings and discussions. Because data science is often about solving a problem, rather than the more academic exercise of answering a research question, this disseminate step may often be better thought of as implementation. Often, data science professionals will call implementing a solution built with and rooted in data science as putting a model into production. Thus dissemination may also involve preparing models and other technical specifications for engineers to implement in production. In short, dissemination or implementation means either sharing the answer to the original research question or implementing a solution for the original business problem.

In the grocery example, putting a model into production could involve using the predictive model to display or deliver reminders to clerks at the store who are responsible for ordering product. The deployed implementation could deliver just-in-time recommendations to have on hand products thought to be sought after by those customers who were visiting at higher rates but then leaving the store without making a purchase.

Related, instead of putting into production a recommendation and reminder algorithm the, grocer's internal communications and training teams could also play a part in dissemination. The communications and training team may use this new information to better train store personnel as to what customers may demand at specific times on specific days. Knowing which items customers may demand at specific times on specific days is actionable in at least two ways. First, make sure the items are in the store and on the shelves. Second, make sure the items are in prominent and easily visible places throughout the store.

A word of caution regarding dissemination. It can be a mistake to reserve dissemination to occur on a specific schedule.

As data science continues to be a growing field, that is not new, but that has yet to be well understood. It is important to showcase the work so that others will learn about it and also appreciate its full value. It is important to ensure you communicate your work along the way.

While the answer to the original question or a solution to the business problem may seemingly be the most obvious output of this dissemination stage, there is at least one other output that is as important and also at least as valuable: new questions and new problems. Through the data science process the team will uncover new questions and discover new business problems. The discovery of new questions and business problems again illustrates how this process is not linear, because the new questions and business problems then operate as inputs for the first question or problem stage discussed above. To assist in emphasizing how the outputs of this dissemination stage often operate as additional inputs for a new round or work, I illustrated this process in a circular fashion, as shown in Figure 4.1.

Conclusion

This chapter builds on previous chapters by providing an overview of an eight-stage process you can use when planning data science projects.

Earlier chapters pointed out that data culture is a shared set of data thoughts, data understandings, data values, data traditions, data practices, data institutions, data language and other data customs that groups of people pass from one generation to the next. When well conceived and managed, an organization's data science process becomes a data tradition, data practice, data institution (a cultural artefact).

It is not necessary that an organization adopt this book's eight-stage process. Related, it is important to be cautious of sources that claim to recite in a definitive way what the data

science process should be. A definitive process, in my view, would not be helpful. Every organization and team is too unique. Instead, organizations should use this book's eight-stage process as a point of departure when reviewing its current practices and also when planning for future practices.

The process of discussing, devising and documenting a data science process can also contribute in positive ways to an organization's data culture. The goal for this chapter is to help you work through the experience of defining and establishing a process that will work well for the work you and your teams perform.

Getting going

Now that Part One of this book has introduced you to the untold story of data science, the genres and flavours of analysis, the notions of data culture, a thorough discussion of data ethics, and the importance of a data science process, Part Two will help you obtain or expand your hands-on experience with data science. As you move into Part Two of this book be sure to keep in mind Part One's general analytical advice, the philosophy regarding data ethics and culture, and the overview of data science processes. Part Two aims to help readers accomplish the following specific learning objectives:

OBJECTIVES

- An enhanced ability to recognize data types and structures as data scientists use the terms.
- An enhanced ability to conduct exploratory data analysis, and also to prepare data for data science, machine learning, artificial intelligence and advanced analytics.

- A renewed or expanded ability to write code in Python that can accomplish many common data exploration and preparation tasks.
- An expanded familiarity with multiple tools commonly used for data exploration and manipulation.
- A close understanding of multiple platforms currently in production, that employ data science, machine learning, artificial intelligence and advanced analytics.
- The ability to examine and review a new platform and then to recognize how data science may be enabling that platform.
- The ability to identify new opportunities that can apply data science to improve your work, or the work of your organization.
- A renewed or expanded ability to write code in Python that will execute sentiment analysis and then compare the results across multiple platforms.

This section, and indeed the entire book, does not aim to provide an exhaustive review of data science. Instead, in keeping with the book's aim to introduce the essential skills of data science, there is a curated and selected range of topics designed to build a reader's confidence in working with data science. Part Two assumes some of the following:

- Those who wish to follow along with the coding examples and exercises have access to a coding environment or an integrated development environment (IDE) such as Jupyter Notebooks or Google Colaboratory. For a guided overview of these topics see Appendices A and B.
- You have a general understanding of how to install new packages with pip or conda. For a guided overview of this topic see Appendix C.
- Related, those who wish to follow along with the coding examples will already be familiar with introductory topics in Python – or computer programming in general.

## CHAPTER FIVE

Data exploration

Some will say exploratory data analysis comes before data preparation. Others will say it is the other way around. Ask 10 data professionals which comes first and you might get 10 different answers.

On the one hand, without at least some preparation, an exploratory analysis might reveal less than fully useful insights. Simultaneously, without at least some exploration it is not fully possible to know what preparation tasks will be necessary before a full analysis.

In practice these two portions of a project happen iteratively and hand-in-hand. For example, the first task is often to open data and then display a small sample of observations. Strictly speaking, opening and displaying a small portion of the data is exploratory analysis.

The very next step might be to check how many columns have missing data and also what proportion of the columns contain missing entries, if any. Again, this rudimentary task is

exploratory analysis. While many exploratory techniques lay ahead, it natural to begin making initial determinations related to data preparation. For example, an analyst might choose to fill missing continuous variables with a mean. Another approach would be to fill missing values with an outlier that categorically designates the value as having formerly been missing. For categorical data a common practice involves filling missing entries with a new 'unknown' category that can be better represented and interpreted for visualization or analytical purposes. Of course, later, after knowing the data, it will be necessary to revisit those initial preparation steps. Later in the process analysts can make more informed decisions as to which methods will be the most sensible for the given data.

To simplify the discussion and to set aside the debate over which step goes first and second, this chapter will first discuss and demonstrate exploratory data analysis with relatively well-known data that have few missing values. Then Chapter 6 will discuss and demonstrate data preparation with other data that are more problematic.

For those that have yet to work in a coding environment that allows you to write Python code, look at see the appendices provided at the end of this book, which offer advice and instruction on how to access a Python environment and get started in writing computer code. The appendices also provide additional information on how you can access and make use of this book's companion Jupyter Notebooks, which are at:

github.com/adamrossnelson/confient

While this chapter intends to provide a high-level and largely theoretical discussion on the topics of exploratory data analysis and data preparation, I will also use this and the next chapter to survey the existence and capabilities of multiple popular tools. Many of these tools are low or no code.

Exploratory data analysis

One of the best ways to explore data is through data visualization. Also important to execute are correlation analyses and cross-tabulations (often known as contingency tables or pivot tables). Instead of providing a specific section on each strategy (visualization, correlation, or cross-tabulations) this chapter on exploratory data analysis is organized around four major tools.

The first of the tools are low-code (Google Sheets and Microsoft Excel) while the third tool (Python) requires a moderate amount of coding. This chapter will also show how you can easily produce an interactive exploratory data analysis report using a tool widely known as Pandas Profiling that in 2023 was renamed YData Profiling.[1]

The interactive report produced with YData Profiling is easy to share with others. Before moving into tool-specific discussions, this chapter also provides an introduction of the data. Chapter 5 is also the first chapter to include a companion Jupyter Notebook, available at github.com/adamrossnelson/confident.

CORRELATION ANALYSIS A closer look at interpretation and understanding

Throughout, this book references correlation analysis. Correlation analysis is useful in data science for many purposes.

Among those purposes is to analyse for a potentially causal relationship. For example, imagine hypothetical data that consist of crop yields and rainfall amounts. In the data each observation is a specific farmer's field. There is a column that reports crop yield in tons per acre, and another column that reports rainfall on the fields. A correlation matrix for these data might look as follows.

TABLE 5.1   Rain and crop yield correlation matrix results

	Yield	Rain
Yield	1.0000	0.6235
Rain	0.6235	1.0000

To read a correlation table such as this you can start with the first column of results, which in this case is the middle column, and in all cases will be the second column from the left. Moving downward on the first column of results which is headed 'Yield' we see that the correlation coefficient for 'Yield' with itself is 1.0000 meaning that 'Yield' is perfectly correlated with itself (all variables are always perfectly correlated with themselves).

Then moving downward again we see a correlation coefficient of 0.6235 meaning that the correlation coefficient for 'Yield' and 'Rain' is 0.6235. Many will interpret this coefficient as a strong positive relationship. And because we also have a theoretical basis to believe that the amount of precipitation may be related in a causal way to crop yield we would also take this correlation result as causal evidence of that relationship.

In a correlation table such as this one, the upper right portion of the table will mirror the lower left portion. And you will always see a diagonal from the upper left to the lower right that shows a series of 1.0000 perfect correlations.

Correlation can be but is not always evidence of causation. Alone, without other evidence or a strong theoretical reason to believe there is a causal relationship, or without both we cannot take correlation results alone as evidence of a causal relationship. However, when combined with other evidence correlation can be strongly indicative of a causal relationship.

Correlation may help identify predictor variables. In a data science, machine learning, artificial intelligence, or advanced analytics project we would take this high correlation coefficient of 0.6235 as an indication that we could use rainfall to predict yield.

A means to identify potential predictors is a key use for correlation as an analytical technique.

Correlation may also help simplify your work. When in the process of choosing which predictors to use we can also use correlation analysis to ascertain which predictors are also highly correlated with each other. When we have a high level of correlation among multiple predictors it is often best to choose one of those predictors, not all of them, because doing so will simplify your model by allowing you to use fewer predictors.

The data

The data I select for demonstrating exploratory data analysis in this chapter come from a popular data visualization library known as Seaborn. The Seaborn library provides quick access to multiple data sets that are useful for training, testing, demonstration or educational purposes.

The creators of Seaborn provide convenient access to its data sets via GitHub at github.com/mwaskom/seaborn-data. You can preview the data via any web browser. We will use the mpg.csv data for these demonstrations. After browsing to the web address listed above you can click on the mpg.csv filename which will then, on most browsers, display the data. Browsing the data from your web browser will help you understand them. An excerpt of the data is shown here:

As you can see, the web-based GitHub platform displays CSV data files with a small measure of helpful summary information such as the number of lines in the file. Here we see 399 lines. Each line is one record or observation. In this case one record, or one observation, for each automobile. Since the first line is a set of column names (or, as data scientists would say, variable names) there are 398 records or observations.

FIGURE 5.1   The first four observations – automobile data from Seaborn

```
399 lines (399 sloc)    20.7 KB          Raw    Blame    🖉  ▾  ⧉  🗑
```

🔍 Search this file...

	mpg	cylinders	displacement	horsepower	weight	acceleration	model_year	origin	name
2	18.0	8	307.0	130.0	3504	12.0	70	usa	chevrolet chevelle malibu
3	15.0	8	350.0	165.0	3693	11.5	70	usa	buick skylark 320
4	18.0	8	318.0	150.0	3436	11.0	70	usa	plymouth satellite
5	16.0	8	304.0	150.0	3433	12.0	70	usa	amc rebel sst

Source: github.com/mwaskom/seaborn-data/blob/master/mpg.csv

Each record (often called observations by many in data science) is one vehicle. For each record we know the vehicle's efficiency (mpg), number of cylinders (cylinders), horsepower (horsepower), weight (weight) and other factors. A visual scan of the data (which at this stage means a scroll through the display provided by GitHub in any web browser) reveals there are some missing data in the horsepower column.

If you want to load these data into a local or Cloud-based tool you might be tempted to first download the data. However, there are more efficient methods for bringing these data into your preferred tool, as we will explore below.

Before moving to a specific discussion of the tools, we will need to find and then save for later reference the URL that returns the raw comma separated (delimited) values (CSV). To get this URL return to your browser in GitHub and click on the button labelled 'Raw' located in the upper right just next to the 'Blame', pencil, copy, or trash icons. The 'Raw' button will navigate your browser to a version of the data that represents the data in their base CSV format. The last step will be to save the URL, which I also place here to make sure you find the same result I do: raw.githubusercontent.com/mwaskom/seaborn-data/master/mpg.csv

Loading data in Google Sheets

The quickest way to bring these data into Google Sheets is not to download the file and then import or upload the file to your Google drive. Rather, the quickest way to import these data will be to use a formula available in Google Sheets known as =IMPORTDATA (url, delimiter, locale). To use this formula replace url with the URL we saved from above and place double quotation marks around the URL as shown here in Figure 5.2.

FIGURE 5.2   Importing into Google Sheets

| A1 | ▾ | ƒx | =IMPORTDATA("https://raw.githubusercontent.com/mwaskom/seaborn-data/master/mpg.csv" |

	A	B	C	D	E	F	G	H
1	=IMPORTDATA("https://raw.githubusercontent.com/mwaskom/seaborn-data/master/mpg.csv"							
2								
3	IMPORTDATA(url, delimiter, locale) ⌄							
4				⋮				
5								

Immediately after executing the formula shown in Figure 5.2 you can begin exploring the data. Google Sheets offers you the opportunity to sort, filter, slice, validate and perform a range of other data exploration or manipulation tasks.

For this demonstration we will focus on the 'Column stats' option found in the data menu. Place your cursor on any of the columns by selecting any cell within that column. In this case I have selected the mpg column. Once you have selected a column of interest you can then choose the 'Column stats' data menu option.

Here Figure 5.3 shows selected results from the mpg column where the column stats menu option produces a histogram. In this histogram we see that the majority of vehicles appear to have an efficiency above 10 miles per gallon and below 37 miles per gallon.

Moving on to another column type, the origin column, we see different plots and results. Because the origin column includes nominal or categorical data, it is not possible to produce a histogram. Instead the most useful output is a frequency table, as shown here in Figure 5.4.

FIGURE 5.3   A histogram of the mpg column from mpg.csv

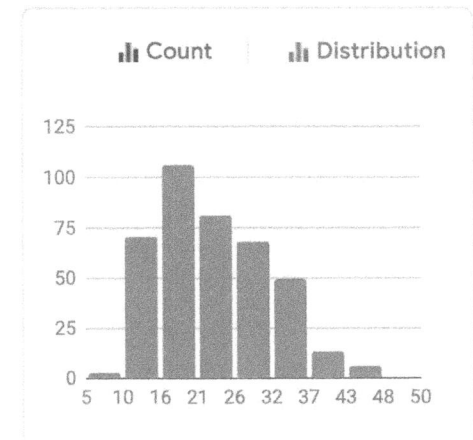

FIGURE 5.4   A contingency table, or value count tabulation, of the origin column from mpg.csv

	⤴ Most	⤵ Least
VALUE		FREQUENCY
usa		249
japan		79
europe		70
origin		1

This table shows the counts of each category shown in the origin column. The results show that there are 249 vehicles manufactured in the 'USA', 79 in 'Japan' and 70 in 'Europe'. Note that this table incorrectly shows one vehicle from someplace named 'Origin'. The reasons for this incorrect tabulation show a limitation in the tool. Google Sheets has incorrectly interpreted the first row of the mpg.csv file, the row that lists column names, as an observation.

Noting this incorrect tabulation is an advisory to check, double check and recheck analytical results as often and as frequently as possible. Often, an appropriate strategy is to conduct an analysis using multiple tools. Some tools will often make incorrect assumptions about the data. In this case Google Sheets incorrectly assumed the first row is an observation. Other tools might make different assumptions that may influence the results. When the results disagree across multiple tools, that disagreement can assist in identifying those assumptions and then also in adjusting for them.

Loading and exploring data in Excel

For Excel we can produce a similar demonstration with the same data. We will also use a different process for importing the data.

Instead of a formula we will use the 'Import' option found in the File menu. When you choose the import option Excel will then first ask what kind of file you seek to import. For this demonstration, choose the 'CSV' option.

We do not need to first download the CSV data before we import them. Instead, in the Data tab there is an option called 'New query'. Under the 'New query' menu option is another option that reads 'From other data sources'. The next option will let you choose 'From the web' where you can provide the URL we saved from above.

One of the best-kept secrets in the world of exploratory data analysis is Excel's 'Analyze data' feature, which in some older versions is called the 'Ideas' feature. The 'Analyze data' icon can be found on the far right of the ribbon under the 'Home' tab.

One click on the 'Analyze data' feature produces multiple automated exploratory data analyses. At the time I tested the feature for this chapter, Excel returned for me more than thirty data visualizations and tables. In some cases the automated output will be suitable for copy-and-past to a final report with minimal, or no, revision.

To manage expectations, it is also useful to note that some of the automated output is not useful at all. Figures 5.5a, 5.5b, and 5.5c show three of the more useful (and nearly ready to present) outputs.

Figure 5.5a shows that vehicles made in the United States seem to have a higher average displacement. The tool thought to analyse how weight might be related to efficiency and shows the results of that analysis in Figure 5.5b. Excel shows that as a vehicle's weight seems to increase the efficiency seems to decrease – a useful insight. If you are familiar with scatter plots as shown here in Figure 5.5b, you will know that each dot represents a single vehicle from the data.

This second visual, a scatter plot strategy, places each dot on the visual where the vehicle's weight and mpg value intersect. Thus, the dots representing vehicles with higher weights (and

FIGURE 5.5A   A bar chart produced by Excel's automated exploratory data analysis features

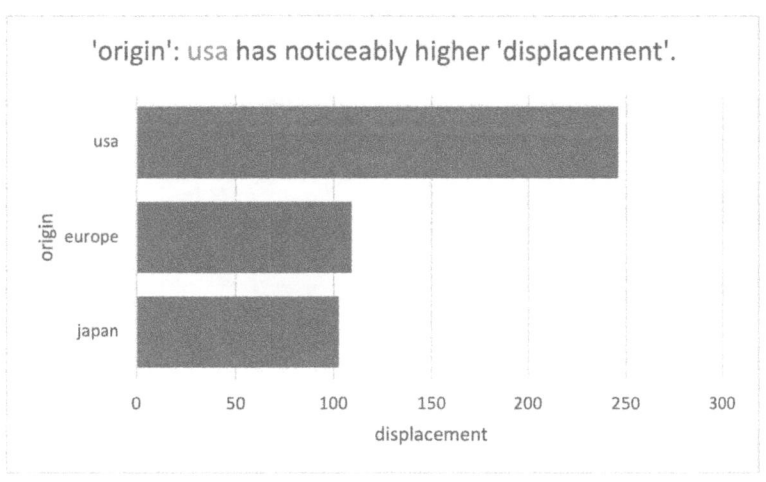

FIGURE 5.5B   A scatter plot produced by Excel's automated exploratory data analysis features

FIGURE 5.5C   A bar chart produced by Excel's automated exploratory data analysis features

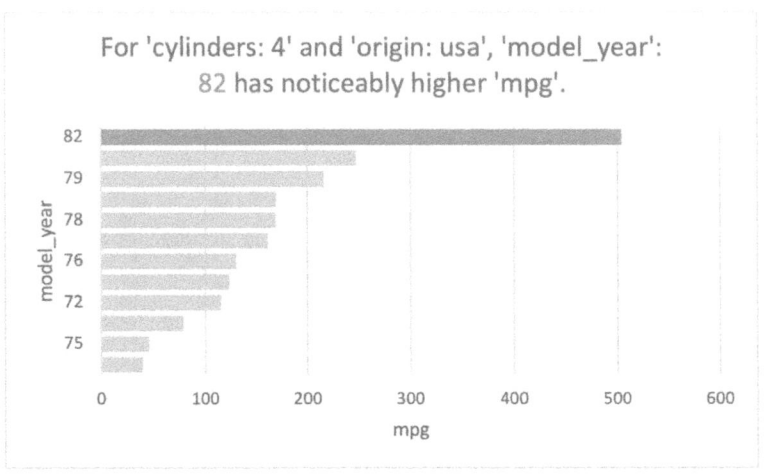

correspondingly lower efficiency) appear in the upper left portion of this visual, while the dots with lower weights (and correspondingly higher efficiency) appear on the lower right portion of this visual.

In Figure 5.5c Excel again found a pattern, worth deeper exploration, that even a highly experienced and gifted analyst may have missed without the assistance of automated exploratory data analysis. It seems that for vehicles with four cylinders and that were manufactured in the United States, 1982 was a year with a bump in efficiency. For anyone interested in the history of fuel efficiency standards among US-manufactured vehicles, a logical next question would be to investigate whether there were new regulations in effect beginning in 1982 that we should consider as we further analyse these data.

As Microsoft has further developed this tool it has added new and impressive features. I am convinced that even the most seasoned data professional will be pleasantly surprised after

FIGURE 5.6   A scatter plot chart produced by Excel's automated exploratory data analysis features

exploring the ability to ask questions of the data in plain English. Microsoft implemented the ability to ask Excel these questions in plain language even before ChatGPT.

Here I asked, 'What is the relationship between acceleration and mpg?' And, you can see the results in Figure 5.6.

Though the results are uninteresting from an analytical perspective, Excel did provide the precise data visualization I would have worked to produce if I were working without the assistance of this automated tool. In this case, you see here a scatter plot that shows each car's mpg and acceleration as a dot. Since the dots seem to clump together in no apparent pattern, line, trend, direction, or grouping, it seems that the relationship between these two variables is minimal.

At one time I previously made an added attempt at giving Excel a harder test. I asked 'Does mpg decrease with model_year?' The earlier attempt produced a helpful data visual in the form of a bar chart as shown in Figure 5.7.

FIGURE 5.7 A bar chart produced by Excel's automated exploratory data analysis features

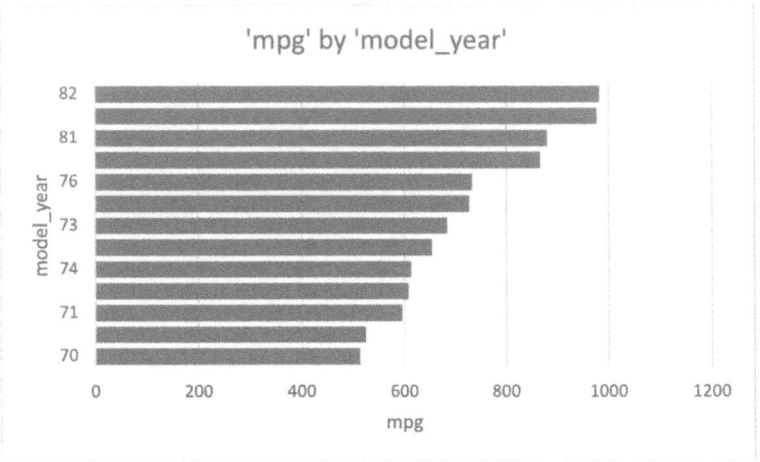

'mpg' by 'model_year'

I would have chosen a line plot (not a bar plot). A subsequent test, on another computer, on another day, produced a table instead of a chart for the same question.

Finding different results on different computers and on different days, but when starting with the exact same data, raises a concern about reproducibility. One of the significant disadvantages of low- or no-code tools is that their results may often be more difficult to reproduce. When it is difficult to reproduce the same results from the same data we tend to lose trust and confidence in the process and the results.

Here is an opportunity to look ahead towards the coding tools discussed later in this chapter (Python and YData Profiling). Despite the higher learning curve associated with tools that require users to write computer code, the added advantages associated with better reproducibility outweighs the cost of learning to use these tools by a significant measure.

There are some additional limitations associated with this automated data exploration tool in Excel – and with automated

data exploration tools in general. As I have observed the development of this tool, I have also noticed that newer versions seem to handle missing data differently than older versions. These changes over time are another threat to reproducibility.

Also, a clear miss was that the automated output did not include a simple table of summary statistics showing the minimum, maximum, median, mean, standard deviation and other similar statistics for each of the numerical columns. Another feature I would suggest for Microsoft to add here would be to generate word Clouds from text columns.

Regarding the relatively minor, and also to be expected, limitations I discuss here it is also important to note that a skilled analyst can easily overcome those limitations with manual processes, tools and techniques available from other portions of Excel (or other tools altogether).

If you aim to be a confident data science professional you should keep an eye on Microsoft's automated exploratory data analysis tools. Microsoft's documentation claims that its Office software continues to grow 'smarter' over time. To make Excel smart enough to do data analysis (or at least exploratory data analysis – to automate the process of finding patters in data) Microsoft is enhancing its Office products with Cloud infrastructure. As an observer of this tool I anticipate Microsoft to find ways to integrate ChatGPT or other similar tools with Excel.

Before moving to explore data in Python, we will review one additional data exploration task in Excel. We will visually inspect the data for missing values. To inspect for these missing values we will use one of the most straight forward approaches possible – we will browse the data on screen.

However, to assist us in spotting missing values we will also use conditional formatting. The conditional formatting will highlight missing information for us. To use conditional

formatting we will first highlight the automobile data in the Excel spreadsheet by placing our cursor in any column and any row of the automobile data and then press Control + A on the keyboard. The key stroke combination Control + A will highlight the table for us.

Then in the ribbon under the Home tab there is a button called 'Conditional formatting' as shown in Figure 5.8a.

By selecting 'Less than' in the pick list to the right of the 'Cell value' pick list and then entering 1 in the text input box we will ask Excel to colour cells with missing data bright red (or pink). An important note to make here is that this method will only work for data sets in which we do not expect negative numbers. The following shown in Figure 5.8b will be your result.

In Figure 5.8b we see a missing value in observation number 33 (Excel shows this observation as row 34 because Excel's row number one contains variable names, thus this missing value is in the data's 33rd observation). We will see this same missing value again when we conduct a similar exploratory exercise in Python.

FIGURE 5.8A   The 'new formatting rule' dialogue box from Excel

FIGURE 5.8B   Observations 30 through 45 of mpg.csv from Excel

	A	B	C	D	E	F	G	H	I
1	mpg	cylinders	displacement	horsepower	weight	acceleration	model_year	origin	name
30	9	8	304	193	4732	18.5	70	usa	hi 1200d
31	27	4	97	88	2130	14.5	71	japan	datsun pl510
32	28	4	140	90	2264	15.5	71	usa	chevrolet vega 2300
33	25	4	113	95	2228	14	71	japan	toyota corona
34	25	4	98		2046	19	71	usa	ford pinto
35	19	6	232	100	2634	13	71	usa	amc gremlin
36	16	6	225	105	3439	15.5	71	usa	plymouth satellite custom
37	17	6	250	100	3329	15.5	71	usa	chevrolet chevelle malibu
38	19	6	250	88	3302	15.5	71	usa	ford torino 500
39	18	6	232	100	3288	15.5	71	usa	amc matador
40	14	8	350	165	4209	12	71	usa	chevrolet impala
41	14	8	400	175	4464	11.5	71	usa	pontiac catalina brougham
42	14	8	351	153	4154	13.5	71	usa	ford galaxie 500
43	14	8	318	150	4096	13	71	usa	plymouth fury iii
44	12	8	383	180	4955	11.5	71	usa	dodge monaco (sw)
45	13	8	400	170	4746	12	71	usa	ford country squire (sw)

Loading and exploring data with Python

The last tool to discuss here, and one that is useful for exploratory data analysis, is Python. If you are not new to Python you might be familiar with its other uses. It is a versatile and powerful programming language that can be used for a variety of purposes. Some of its more popular uses are web development or game development. Python also, as it turns out, happens to be a powerful data analysis tool that also is well known for its capabilities as a tool that supports data science.

As with any tool, there are usually multiple paths to accomplishing any single task or objective. In this subsection we turn to Python to explore data and to focus the discussion we will reproduce some of the visuals that Google Sheets and Excel provided. Then we will also look at investigating missing values in our data for a demonstration on identifying missing data. And lastly, before moving onward in Chapter 6 to a discussion on manipulating data to prepare them for further analysis, we will also explore the correlation matrix and the pair plots.

A hallmark of working in data science is to find methods and techniques that will automate our work and make it more reproducible. One of the ways we will make our work more reproducible is that we will not use a web browser to first download the data before we open them in the tool. We will use the tool to download and open the data via the internet. In Python here is how that will look:

```
# Standard Pandas + Seaborn import
import pandas as pd
import seaborn as sns

# Load data using Pandas from online (option A)
df = pd.read_csv('https://raw.githubusercontent.com/' + \
                 'mwaskom/seaborn-data/master/mpg.csv')
# Load data using Seabotn (option B)
df = sns.load_dataset('mpg')
```

First, this code imports the pandas library, which is a widely used data analysis library in Python. Notice how in option A the URL for the mpg.csv file appears in this code. This code uses a function from the Pandas library known as `pd.read_csv()`.

The `pd.read_csv()` function is a Pandas function that reads a CSV file and returns a DataFrame object. In this code, it is used to read a CSV file from a GitHub repository, which contains data about the fuel efficiency of various cars.

By passing the URL web address location of the CSV file into the `pd.read_csv()` function the code finds the CSV file via the computer's internet connection and then stores those data as a Pandas DataFrame in the object we have named `df`.

The resulting DataFrame object `df` will contain the data from the CSV file, with rows and columns corresponding to the rows and columns in the file. By default, the first row in the CSV file is assumed to contain column names.

With this `df` object we can quickly reproduce many of the visuals we saw earlier in Google Sheets and Excel. In Google Sheets, using the 'Column stats' menu option we saw a histogram of the mpg column. To reproduce that histogram here in Python is a relatively simple accomplishment only requiring one line of code, `df['mpg'].plot.hist()`, which will produce a histogram but one that is not well-labelled. The following code produces a better result, as shown in Figure 5.9.

```
# Generate a histogram with Pandas .plot.hist
df['mpg'].plot.hist(bins=9,
                    title='Histogram of Vehicle
                    Efficiency')
```

Google Sheets also produced a frequency table of the values found in the origin column. In Python we can reproduce the frequency table with `df['origin'].value_counts()`. This

FIGURE 5.9   A histogram of vehicle efficiency from mpg.csv. Produced with the code shown here

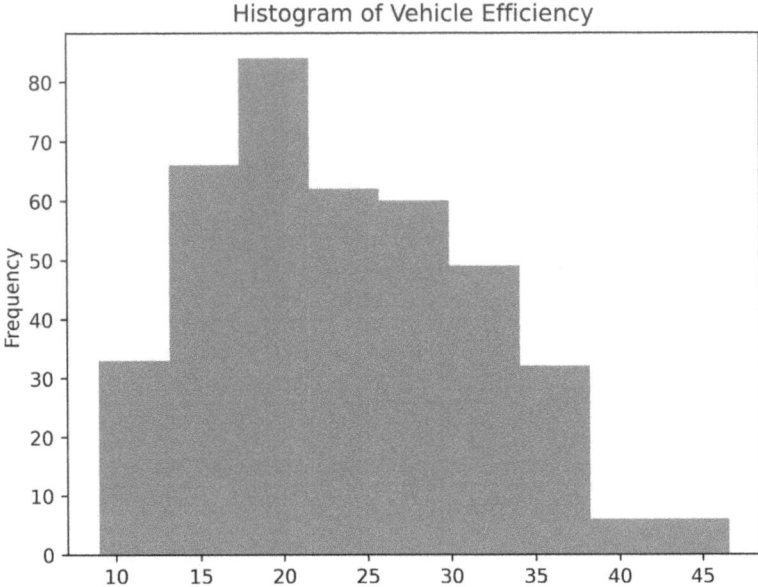

code produces output that lists 249 vehicles from the 'USA', 79 from 'Japan' and 70 from 'Europe'. Note how, unlike the result from Google Sheets, there are three categories instead of four. The reason for this different result is that Python has correctly identified and interpreted the data's first row as variable names instead of as an observation.

One of the key visuals we looked at in Excel was the scatter plot that evaluated the relationship between a vehicle's weight and a vehicle's efficiency. To reproduce that visual in Python we will use the following code:

```
# Generate a scatter plot with Pandas .plot.scatter()
df.plot.scatter(y='mpg', x='weight',
                title='Efficiency & Weight: Scatter Plot')
```

For the result:

FIGURE 5.10   A scatter plot that shows how vehicle efficiency seems to decrease as vehicle weight increases. Produced with the code shown here

As before, we can see the relationship between these two variables. As weight increases, it seems that the efficiency decreases. Here again we see that each dot represents a single vehicle from the data. The scatter plot strategy places each dot on the visual at the place where the vehicle's weight and mpg value intersect. Thus, the dots representing vehicles with higher weights (and correspondingly lower efficiencies) appear in the lower right portion of this visual, while the dots with lower weights (and correspondingly higher efficiencies) appear on the upper left portion of this visual.

Notice also how this visual is a transposed version of the visual Excel automatically produced above. The reason this visual is transposed is because I placed mpg on the vertical y-axis while Excel placed mpg on the horizontal x-axis. Typically, when

designing scatter plot visuals such as this one we would place the resulting (the dependent) variable on the vertical. The resulting or dependent variable in many contexts is difficult to discern and there is no exact rule. However, in this case it is a matter of logic. A vehicle's efficiency does not influence the weight of the vehicle. Instead, it is the weight that influences the efficiency.

Thus efficiency results from the weight, or we say efficiency is *dependent* upon the vehicle weight. As a general rule, remember to design visuals that place the dependent variable on the vertical instead of the horizontal.

INSPECTING FOR MISSING VALUES

Inspecting for missing values is likely one of the earliest steps in any project. When inspecting for missing data in Google Sheets or Excel it is usually a simple matter of scrolling through your data to inspect visually for missing data. To assist you in finding missing data within Google Sheets or Excel there are some additional techniques such as conditional formatting that can help you spot the signs of a missing cell.

When working in Python, it is more difficult to browse your data. One option that mimics the conditional formatting (combined with a visual browse) of your data in Excel or Google is to export your data to an html table, then open that table in a web browser. Converting the data to a conditionally formatted HTML table, for display in a web browser is an operation that requires three lines of code in Python.

```
# Create df, zeros=non-missing, ones=missing
to_browse = (df.isnull() * 1)

# Create a 'base' record that will be all missing
to_browse.loc['base'] = 1
```

```
# Style and save the result as html
to_browse.style.highlight_max(
    color='red').to_html('to_browse.html')
```

In the first line of code here we create a new object called to_ browse which we will eventually save to disk as an html file. In this first line of code we set to_browse to be equal to df. isnull() * 1 which creates a version of the original DataFrame where each missing value is coded as 1 and each non-missing value as 0. To ensure that the coding scheme works correctly, the DataFrame needs at least one 1 value in each column. The second line of code adds a row of 1s onto the bottom of the DataFrame. Lastly, the third line of code chains multiple methods to conditionally format and save the to_browse object to disk. The .style.highlight.max(color='red') and the .to_ html() method conditionally format and then write a new file called to_browse.html that you can view in any web browser.

After executing this code you will have a new file called to_ browse.html in your working directory. Open that file in any

FIGURE 5.11   An excerpt of the to_browse.html. Produced with the code shown here

	mpg	cylinders	displacement	horsepower	weight	acceleration	model_year	origin	name
30	0	0	0	0	0	0	0	0	0
31	0	0	0	0	0	0	0	0	0
32	0	0	0	1	0	0	0	0	0
33	0	0	0	0	0	0	0	0	0
34	0	0	0	0	0	0	0	0	0
35	0	0	0	0	0	0	0	0	0
36	0	0	0	0	0	0	0	0	0
37	0	0	0	0	0	0	0	0	0
38	0	0	0	0	0	0	0	0	0
39	0	0	0	0	0	0	0	0	0
40	0	0	0	0	0	0	0	0	0
41	0	0	0	0	0	0	0	0	0
42	0	0	0	0	0	0	0	0	0
43	0	0	0	0	0	0	0	0	0

web browser and you be able to browse, as shown in Figure 5.11, and quickly spot the bright red cells that contained missing data.

In this visual we see that the horsepower value is missing from observation number 33. Another simple line of code allows us to more closely inspect the missing observation, and the others near it, `df.loc[30:35]`.

By inspecting your data for missing observations, records and cells, you can begin to make decisions about how to manipulate that missing data to include it in your analysis, or to exclude it. Chapter 6 discusses how to accomplish those manipulations and how to make those decisions.

Before moving to the data manipulation and preparation in Chapter 6, we conclude Chapter 5 with three additional aggregate approaches that will let you more quickly see missing data, and other important characteristics of the entire data set as a whole.

A clever way to report the overall number of missing records, column-by-column, is to string two methods together on the DataFrame object. In practice it looks like this: `df.isnull().sum()`.

The reason this `.sum()` method reports the number of missing values is because the `.isnull()` method first converts the entire DataFrame to an array of True and False values – True for missing, False for not missing. The `.sum()` method interprets the True values as 1 and the False values as 0. The essence of taking the sum, is to count the number of missing values.

In the resulting output we see that there are six missing observations from the horsepower column. Instead of the `.sum()` method we can also use the `.mean()` method which will report the proportion of missing observations from each column.

The reason `df.isnull().mean()` reports the proportion of missing observations is because, as before, the `.isnull()` method first changes the entire DataFrame to an array of True and False values, discussed above. The `.mean()` method then again interprets True as 1 and False as 0. When you find the mean of any group of 1s and 0s you will have a result that is

equivalent to the proportion of 1 values (or the proportion of True values). To improve the output and to make it more readable the following code also uses the .apply() method along with an anonymous lambda function.

```
# Further explore with isnull().mean()
df.isnull().mean().apply(
    lambda x: '{:f} % Missing'.format(x * 100))
```

FIGURE 5.12   The proportion of missing values in each column of mpg.csv. Produced with the code shown here

```
mpg            0.000000 % Missing
cylinders      0.000000 % Missing
displacement   0.000000 % Missing
horsepower     1.507538 % Missing
weight         0.000000 % Missing
acceleration   0.000000 % Missing
model_year     0.000000 % Missing
origin         0.000000 % Missing
name           0.000000 % Missing
dtype: object
```

From the output shown in Figure 5.12 it appears that those six missing observations in the horsepower column equate to about 1.5 % of the column as missing.

INSPECTING FOR MISSING VALUES (GRAPHICALLY)

Another opportunity to evaluate an entire DataFrame quickly is to visualize missing values with a heat map. In this section on Python we have relied entirely on one package, Pandas. To expand the available functionality we will now also turn to Seaborn. To import Seaborn we used the code import seaborn as sns as shown above, following import pandas as pd. After importing Seaborn the following code quickly produces a heat map that highlights which data in our DataFrame are missing.

```
# Further explore missing values with Seaborn heatmap
sns.heatmap(df.isnull().transpose(), cmap='Blues_r')
```

The above code contains `sns.heatmap()` which accepts any matrix with numbers and then returns a colour-encoded matrix. The `df.isnull()` code evaluates to a matrix of True (where the data are missing) and False (where the data are not missing) values. The heat map will evaluate and then colour accordingly, True values as 1 and False values as 0.

A more readable version of this code would use line continuation to differentiate between key functions and portions with the code.

```
# A more readable Seaborn heatmap syntax
sns.heatmap(
    df.isnull().transpose(),
    cmap='Blues_r')
```

As before, this code contains the `sns.heatmap()` code with two arguments. The two arguments are indented on subsequent lines which make the code more readable. The first indented line contains two methods chained together on a DataFrame (`df`) object. The `.isnull()` method converts the DataFrame to a matrix that only contains True or False values. The values will be True where the data are missing and False where the data are not missing. Together these two methods provide the number matrix `sns.heatmap()` needs to produce its visual. The `sns.heatmap()` function will interpret True values as 1 and False values as 0.

The heat map this code produces is similar to the conditionally formatted spreadsheets and conditionally formatting HTML files we discussed above. However, the heat map approach visualizes the missing data more efficiently in a 'smaller' space.

By default the heat map will encode the missing values as a bright pink and the non-missing as a dark black. By adding the `cmap='Blues_r'` option in line 4 the missing values display as nearly white and the non-missing graph as dark blue.

The `transpose()` method then rotates the matrix 90 degrees. This rotation places the columns as rows and the rows as columns and allows readers to view the output from left to right. I use the `transpose()` method often when working with data in Pandas because I find when I do the output is frequently more readable. As shown here in Figure 5.13 the transposition means you can inspect for missing values in each column by scanning the image from left to right. Reading from left to right, for many, may be more natural than reading from top to bottom (which would have been the default).

Figure 5.13's data visualization shows the six missing observations in the horsepower column as bring white slivers.

THE CORRELATION MATRIX AND PAIR PLOT

Python provides dozens of tools for additional data exploration. This section reviews two more before moving onto the topic of data manipulation and preparation.

The first is to review a correlation matrix. Correlation analysis is a statistical technique used to measure the strength of a relationship between two or more variables. It can be used to determine the degree of association between variables, as well as to identify potential causal relationships between variables.

For example, we already began looking at correlation above when we looked at scatter plots that showed the relationship between two variables (mpg and weight). We saw that as the weight of a vehicle increased, the efficiency of that vehicle decreased. Another example above looked at how the amount of rain that falls on a famer's field might also correlate with the tonnage of crop harvested from that field. In the automobile example we saw negative correlation values and in the crop harvest example we saw positive correlation values.

FIGURE 5.13 A heat map that shows missing values in mpg.csv. Produced with the code shown here

To produce a correlation matrix for an entire DataFrame with Pandas the code is df.corr(). With these automobile data we will see the result shown here in Figure 5.14.

Returning to the vehicle efficiency and vehicle weight example, we can find the correlation coefficient for weight and mpg in the first column under the heading 'mpg' and the fifth row labelled 'weight.' We see the result of –0.8317. The negative and relatively low correlation coefficient (where correlation coefficients are bound between –1 and 1) is consistent with the scatter plots, which also suggested a strong negative correlation.

While the correlation matrix is useful, relying only on the correlation matrix risks missing important patterns in the data that would only be visible with other forms of analyses. In Python, the Seaborn library that we first used to investigate missing data provides another important plot, known as the pair plot. The pair plot visualizes an entire DataFrame as a matrix of scatter plots. The code for a pair plot is sns.pairplot(df). To add nuance to this pair plot visualization we will add the hue option so that we can include the non-numeric (nominal) variable origin.

```
# Generate pair plot, visually explore data
sns.pairplot(df, hue='origin')
```

In Figure 5.15 we can again return to the vehicle efficiency and vehicle weight example. Finding the column labelled mpg (the column labels are across the bottom of the visual) and then the row labelled weight, we again see a scatter plot that suggests there is a negative relationship between these two variables. Specifically as one variable increases the other decreases.

Using a matrix of scatter plots such as this one, again called a pair plot, is also one of the first ways to look for opportunities to verify or falsify relevant assumptions that you will need to be

FIGURE 5.14 A correlation matrix from the values in mpg.csv. Produced with the code shown here

	mpg	cylinders	displacement	horsepower	weight	acceleration	model_year
mpg	1.000000	-0.775396	-0.804203	-0.778427	-0.831741	0.420289	0.579267
cylinders	-0.775396	1.000000	0.950721	0.842983	0.896017	-0.505419	-0.348746
displacement	-0.804203	0.950721	1.000000	0.897257	0.932824	-0.543684	-0.370164
horsepower	-0.778427	0.842983	0.897257	1.000000	0.864538	-0.689196	-0.416361
weight	-0.831741	0.896017	0.932824	0.864538	1.000000	-0.417457	-0.306564
acceleration	0.420289	-0.505419	-0.543684	-0.689196	-0.417457	1.000000	0.288137
model_year	0.579267	-0.348746	-0.370164	-0.416361	-0.306564	0.288137	1.000000

FIGURE 5.15   A pair plot matrix for selected variables from mpg.csv.
Produced with the code shown here

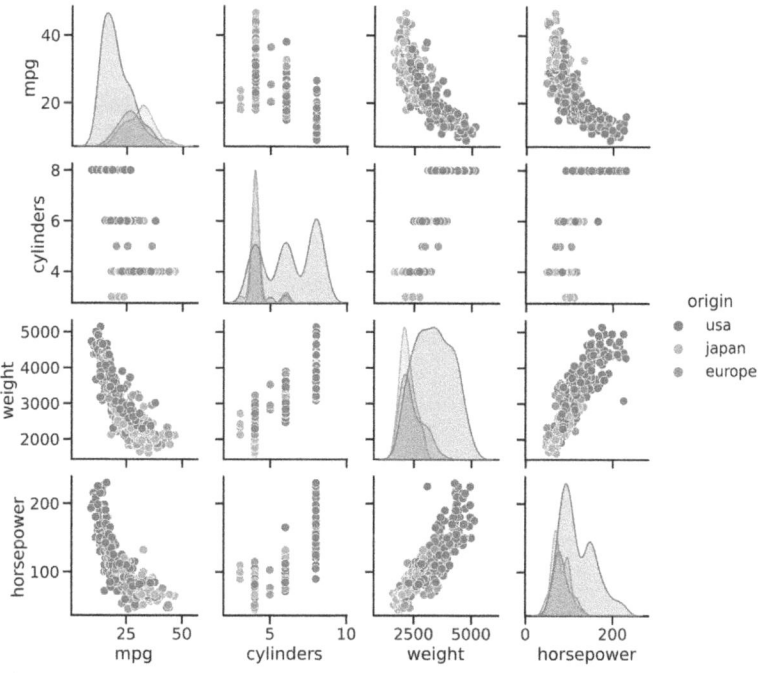

true as you select which models to apply in your predictive work. For example, as discussed later, a key assumption of k-means cluster analysis and k-nearest neighbors analysis is that similar items will both group closely together and also distinctly apart from other groups. A key assumption of regression analysis is that there are linear relationships in the data. In the case of this scatter plot we see that it confirms the assumption that there is a linear relationship between vehicle efficiency and vehicle weight. Not only does efficiency seem to decrease as weight seems to increase, but we also see that the vehicles plot in roughly a linear fashion across the scatter plot region.

Pandas (YData) Profiling

Before concluding this chapter there is one more subsection that introduces readers to a tool that will largely automate many of the exploratory tasks we reviewed in this chapter. Until recently, this tool has been known as Pandas Profiling. Following its latest release of 4.00 it is now known as YData Profiling.

In addition to automating many of the exploratory tasks discussed in this chapter, the YData Profiling package also makes it easy to explore the data interactively and to share HTML files with others so they may quickly explore the data – but without the need for those with whom you share to know or understand computer code.

Before getting started with YData Profiling you may need to execute the following pip installation command.

```
pip install -U ydata-profiling
```

For this demonstration we will return to the automobile efficiency data from Seaborn. The following code will set the stage for this demonstration.

```
# Import standard libraries
import pandas as pd
import numpy as np

# Import additional necessary library
from ydata_profiling import ProfileReport

# Load data using Seaborn
df = sns.load_dataset('mpg')
```

```
# Generate report using ydata_profiling
pr = ProfileReport(df,
        title="MPG Seaborn Confident Data Science Report")
```

This code again uses common standard imports import pandas as pd and import numpy as np. In Python, a standard import is a commonly used import statement that is considered a best practice and is used by convention. Standard imports are

FIGURE 5.16 The headers from YData Profile's report on mpg.csv. Produced with the code shown here

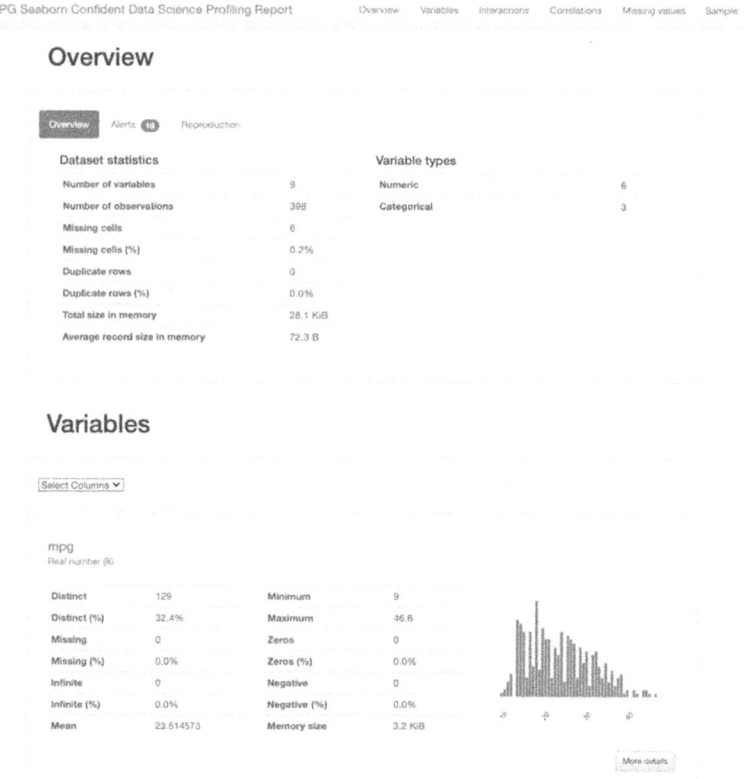

widely used in the Python community and are generally under-stood by most Python programmers. This code also imports `ProfileReport` from `ydata_profiling`.

After loading a data file, in this case mpg.csv and then instan-tiating a `ProfileReport` from YData Profiling, the report may be rendered in a Jupyter Notebook by evaluating `pr` in a cell. The top of that report will appear as shown in Figure 5.16.

The title given to the report will appear at the upper left of the report. Along the upper portion of the report is a menu system that will let you navigate between six sections. There is a section for Overview, Variables, Interactions, Correlations, Missing Values and also a Sample of the data.

In this example within the Overview section we also see tabs for Alerts (there are 10 of them) and Reproduction. Clicking on the Alerts tab will reveal list various patterns in the data you should consider closely, including high correlations, missing values and unexpected distributions.

The Reproduction tab provides information that may be useful to know if you seek to reproduce the work including the time you generated the report and also information about the settings that were in place when you generated the report.

Because the YData Profiling package is well documented, this section does not seek to provide readers with a complete over-view. Instead there are two more important features I have selected for discussion.

The first is the interactions feature. To navigate to the interac-tions section click on the Interactions menu choice near the top middle portion of the report. After navigating to the Interactions section Pandas Profiling gives you a set of tabs, one for each variable. You may use those tabs to browse the data's scatter plots. In this case we can again look at the relationship between vehicle weight and vehicle efficiency, as in Figure 5.17.

FIGURE 5.17 The interactions section of the YData Profile's report on mpg csv. Produced with the code shown here

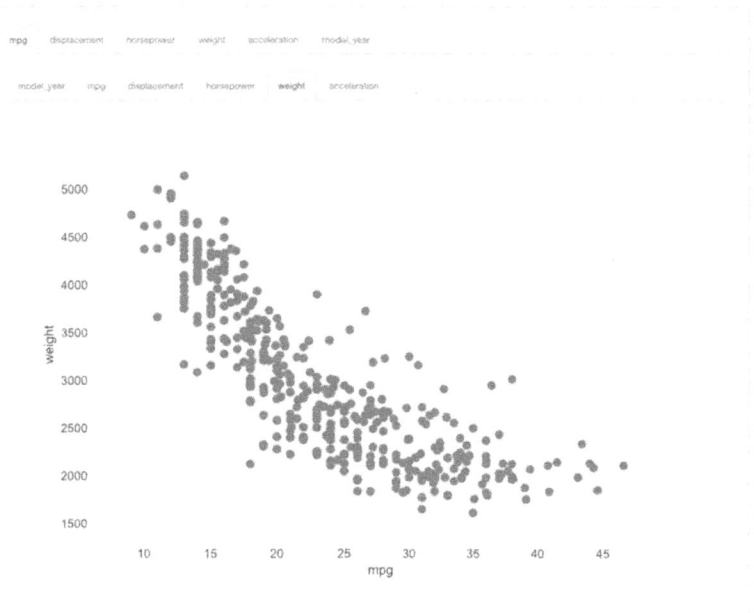

The final feature of YData Profiling to explore is the ability to export the `pr` object as a self-contained HTML file.

```
# Save the profile report as an html file
pr.to_file('Automated Automobile Data Report.html')
```

Once exported, you can share that self-contained HTML file with others who can use the file, and its interactive features, to explore the data. Once you execute the code for this you will find the file under the name you specified in your working directory.

Conclusion

This chapter surveyed and explored multiple tools and techniques involved in exploratory data analysis. The next chapter will explore tools and techniques suitable for data preparation and wrangling. Many of the tools presented here offer convenient and highly automated output. I do not mean to suggest that these low-code tools, in all of their impressive automation, replace skilled data professionals. These tools are good at analysing data in a rudimentary way only. They cannot replace data science professionals on your team or in your organization.

Despite the availability of these automated tools, the field continues to need more confident data scientists. Comprehensive analysis and a deep understanding of any given data set cannot be fully automated. Likewise, even when in the hands of human practitioners no two exploratory analyses will be the same. Data science professionals who can bring a critical eye to the data and the tools we use to explore the data can serve the field by knowing, understanding and exposing known limitations.

Given their weaknesses, automated exploratory data analysis tools are most appropriate for preliminary analysis and as a supplement to the work of skilled professionals. We need to choose our exploratory data analysis tools with care and a healthy measure of scepticism. It is also a prudent practice to avoid relying solely on one tool. By comparing results across and among multiple tools we can more easily reveal added insights that one tool may have missed.

Nevertheless, the future is bright for these tools. Microsoft is not alone in building or enhancing its existing product lines with Cloud-based infrastructure which will make the tools act, feel and at least appear smarter over time. Microsoft and other software produces have begun enhancing the existing tool sets with interactive artificial intelligences similar to ChatGPT.

For those who have followed along with the coding examples, a helpful next step that will continue your learning journey will be to select and work with another data set other than the mpg. csv data from Seaborn. Use the code in this chapter as a cookbook or template as you practise with new data.

This chapter also reviewed many rudimentary analytical techniques, including correlation analysis, scatter plots, crosstabulations (often otherwise known as contingency or pivot tables), pair plots (which combine multiple other techniques and visuals into one) and more. Without exploring and analysing data it is not possible to understand what may be necessary to fix that data. Chapter 5 leaves off where Chapter 6 picks up, with data manipulation and preparation.

Data manipulation and preparation

After having thoroughly explored the automobile data set above we now turn to the next logical topic, which is to manipulate and prepare data for further exploration. We also turn to a new data set discussed below. The reason I chose a new data set for the data manipulation and preparation discussion is because there are specific topics I wish to discuss and these contrived data help us touch on those topics in a context that is sensible for the data. This custom data set also easily displays on a single page, which makes it easier to review and also discuss each individual data point in context with the entire data set.

The data

To demonstrate processes associated with data preparation, this chapter uses a custom data set that you can download at github.com/adamrossnelson/confident.

As a Python dictionary, the data for this chapter are as follows.

```python
# Import Pandas + Numpy libraries
import pandas as pd
import numpy as np

data = {'PackageID':list(range(1001,1011))+[1010],
        'Length':[12.5,12.5,12.5,12.5,12.5,np.nan,12.5,12.5,
                  np.nan,12.5,12.5],
        'Width':[7]*3 + [8]*3 + [9]*4 + [9],
        'Height':[4,5,6,5,6,4,np.nan,5,7,6]+[6],
        'Liquid':[1,0,0,1,0,0,0,0,0,0]+[0],
        'Perishable':[1] + [0]*9 + [0],
        'Origin':['FL','FL','GA','SC','SC','GA','SC','SC',
                  'GA','GA'] + ['GA'],
        'Destination':['FL','NC','NC','SC','FL','NC','GA','SC',
                       'NC','GA'] + ['GA'],
        'Insurance':[100,100,200,150,10009,150,100,100,
                     150,200] + [200],
        'ShipCost':[19.99,19.99,24.99,21.99,19.99,
                    21.99,19.99,19.99,21.99,24.99] + [24.99],
        'ShipDate':pd.to_datetime(['1/6/2028','1/8/2028',
                                   '1/7/2028','1/8/2028',
                                   '1/9/2028','1/10/2028',
                                   '1/11/2028','1/14/2028',
                                   '1/12/2028', '1/12/2028',
                                   '1/12/2028']),
        'ArriveDate':pd.to_datetime(['1/7/2028','1/6/2028',
                                     '1/9/2028', '1/9/2028',
                                     '1/11/2028', '1/15/2028',
                                     '1/14/2028', '1/11/2028',
                                     '1/15/2028', '1/13/2028',
                                     '1/13/2028'])
       }
```

As you examine this dictionary, and this example data, you may note multiple peculiarities, errors or other problems that we will further explore in this chapter. After converting these data to a Pandas DataFrame it is easy to display these data in tabular format as follows.

```
# Create a Pandas df from the Python dictionary
df = pd.DataFrame(data)

# Evaluate the df to display data in tabular format
df
```

Alternatively, if you seek to load these data directly into a new notebook or coding environment of your own you can also use this code.

```
# Specify the data location, path, and file name
location = 'https://raw.githubusercontent.com/'
path = 'adamrossnelson/confident/main/data/'
fname = 'confident_ch6.csv'

# Load the csv from online into a Pandas df
df = pd.read_csv(location + path + fname)

# Evaluate the df to display the in tabular format
df
```

Both code blocks will result in a display that resembles the output in Figure 6.1.

FIGURE 6.1   The 11 observations from the shipping and mailing data we will examine in this chapter. Produced with the code shown here

	PackageID	Length	Width	Height	Liquid	Perishable	Origin	Destination	Insurance	ShipCost	ShipDate	ArriveDate
0	1001	12.5	7	4.0	1	1	FL	FL	100	19.99	2028-01-06	2028-01-07
1	1002	12.5	7	5.0	0	0	FL	NC	100	19.99	2028-01-08	2028-01-06
2	1003	12.5	7	6.0	0	0	GA	NC	200	24.99	2028-01-07	2028-01-09
3	1004	12.5	8	5.0	1	0	SC	SC	150	21.99	2028-01-08	2028-01-09
4	1005	12.5	8	6.0	0	0	SC	FL	10009	19.99	2028-01-09	2028-01-11
5	1006	NaN	8	4.0	0	0	GA	NC	150	21.99	2028-01-10	2028-01-15
6	1007	12.5	9	NaN	0	0	SC	GA	100	19.99	2028-01-11	2028-01-14
7	1008	12.5	9	5.0	0	0	SC	SC	100	19.99	2028-01-14	2028-01-11
8	1009	NaN	9	7.0	0	0	GA	NC	150	21.99	2028-01-12	2028-01-15
9	1010	12.5	9	6.0	0	0	GA	GA	200	24.99	2028-01-12	2028-01-13
10	1010	12.5	9	6.0	0	0	GA	GA	200	24.99	2028-01-12	2028-01-13

These data mimic data that might pertain to a set of packages distributed by a shipping business. The following is a data dictionary of these data:

- PackageID: An individual identification number for each package.
- Length: The length of each package (in inches).
- Width: The width of each package (in inches).
- Height: The height of each package (in inches).
- Liquid: Whether the package contains liquid material. 1 if yes. 0 if no.
- Perishable: Whether the package contains perishable material. 1 if yes. 0 if no.
- Origin: The two-letter abbreviation of the US state from which the business shipped the package.
- Destination: The two-letter abbreviation of the US state to which the business shipped the package.
- Insurance: The cost of shipping insurance purchased for the package.
- ShipCost: The total cost spent on shipping the package.
- ShipDate: The package's ship date.
- ArriveDate: The package's arrival date.

As you further review the data above, again notice that there are multiple issues and concerns. Before reading the pages that follow, review these data and name as many issues or concerns you can spot. If you are following along with these data on your own, consider applying the exploratory steps we discussed in Chapter 5.

As you review these data there are at least five issues or concerns to address in data cleaning:

1 There are missing data in the Length column (observations 5 and 8) and Height column (observation 6).
2 The Length column seems to have only one value (which for analytical purposes diminishes that column's value).

3 There is a potentially erroneous entry in observation number 4 of the Insurance column.

4 Also there are two observations (numbers 1 and 7) that show the ArriveDate as before the ShipDate. These date entries must be erroneous.

5 It also seems that entry number 10 may be a duplicate of entry number 9.

Replacing missing continuous data

One of the first strategies many turn to when facing missing data is to replace missing values with the mean (for discrete and continuous data) and to replace missing nominal with the most common occurrence. Frequently, there are better options. Let's review this example data for specifics.

First consider the Length column with missing entries in observation 5 and 8. Notice how all other entries in that column are 12.5 inches. This is a clue that the missing values should probably be 12.5. There are at least two ways to correct those missing values. The first would be to set the entire column equal to 12.5 with `df['Length'] = 12.5`. In a twist of fate and logic, replacing the missing value with the column mean is going to produce the same result. Since the entire column is 12.5 the mean of that column will be 12.5 so we could also execute `df['Length'] = df['Length'].mean()`.

In another scenario, we might have operational or business knowledge that tells us the values of those missing should actually be 22.5. Perhaps the input validation systems that supported user input incorrectly disallowed an accurate entry. In this hypothetical scenario, suppose we have an email from operations professionals telling us that a glitch in the computer user interface prevented shipping clerks from entering the correct value of 22.5. One of the quickest ways to fill those missing with 22.5 would be to execute `df['Length'].fillna(22.5)`.

Finding a suitable replacement strategy for the missing value in the Height column is a different challenge. There are multiple values. The `df['Height'].value_counts()` method reveals that we have four distinct values 4.0, 5.0, 6.0 and 7.0. The computer will recognize these data as continuous floating point data. As such we could replace the missing value with the column mean of 5.4.

However, as a confident data scientist we discern that replacing with 5.4 when all other values are specifically 4.0, 5.0, 6.0, and 7.0 may not be the best approach. Instead we could replace with the median. But the median of 5.5 does not seem to fit well either.

A categorical review of these data would be to use a cross-tabulation (often known as a contingency table) to compare the Height values with the Width values via the following code.

```
# Create a cross-tabulation table from two columns of data
# Fill missing values in 'Height' with 99
pd.crosstab(df['Width'],
            df['Height'].fillna(99))
```

Which will show a version of Figure 6.2.

FIGURE 6.2   A cross-tabulation of height and width. Produced with the code shown here

Height	4.0	5.0	6.0	7.0	99.0
Width					
7	1	1	1	0	0
8	1	1	1	0	0
9	0	1	2	1	1

By adding the `.fillna(99)` method to the `df['Height']` column we have the opportunity to inspect the missing values. Without the `.fillna(99)` method, the `pd.crosstab()` function would have omitted the row with missing data from the analysis.

From this result it appears that most of the observations with a width of 9.0 inches have a corresponding height of 6.0 inches. This output also quickly reveals that both the mean and median value of Height for packages with a Width of 9.0 is 6.0. From this output it is reasonable to infer that the missing value should have been 6.0. After seeing this finding we will proceed by filling the missing value in the Height column with 6.0.

Before moving on to adjusting outliers it is also important to note that there is rarely ever a fully correct and likewise rarely ever an outright wrong way of replacing missing data. Every choice will have strengths and weaknesses. Instead of looking for the correct or best method (which is non-existent), be sure to choose the method you feel you can best defend as appropriate. For example, we could also have dropped the observations with missing data.

In practice, you must keep track of your choices, which you will at least in some measure automatically track in the code you write and save for later reference. You must then later be prepared to document your choices along with their attendant strengths and weaknesses as you report your results.

Given these data, and the context discussed above, an efficient method of replacing the missing value in the Height column would be to use `df.fillna(6.0)`. The following demonstrates this code.

```
# Fill missing values in 'Height'
# with a default value of 6.0.
df['Height'] = df['Height'].fillna(6.0)
```

By passing the value 6.0 into the .fillna() method we use this code to replace any missing values in the Height column of a pandas DataFrame with a default value of 6.0.

To confirm the code performed as expected we can again use the pd.crosstab() function.

```
# Check manipulation performed as expected
pd.crosstab(df['Height'], df['Width'])
```

Replacing missing nominal or ordinal data

Above I explained that one of the most common approaches to adjusting missing nominal data is to replace the missing values with the most common nominal occurrence. While replacing with the otherwise most frequent occurrence may be appropriate in some cases, there are frequently better approaches.

For example, we know that 'in the presence of missing data, careful use of missing indicators, combined with appropriate imputation, can improve both causal estimation and prediction accuracy'.[1]

At first glance, it may appear there are no missing (or problematic) nominal or ordinal data. As shown in the next section on adjusting outliers, there are data that would seem reasonable to treat as ordinal. In specific, the Insurance variable appears continuous, but with only three distinct values (aside from the outlier in observation number 4). These insurance data are arguably better treated as ordinal. Upon discovering the ordinal nature of these data, the next section further explains how it might be appropriate replace missing (or problematic) nominal and ordinal data.

Adjusting outliers

In reviewing these data it appeared as though there was an erroneous entry in the Insurance column. This erroneous entry will also reveal itself as an outlier. Using df.describe().transpose() we can quickly inspect the summary statistics which will resemble the table in Figure 6.3.

FIGURE 6.3   Summary statistics from the shipping and mailing data. Produced with the code shown here

	count	mean	std	min	25%	50%	75%	max
PackageID	11.0	1005.909091	3.176619	1001.00	1003.50	1006.00	1008.50	1010.00
Length	9.0	12.500000	0.000000	12.50	12.50	12.50	12.50	12.50
Width	11.0	8.181818	0.873863	7.00	7.50	8.00	9.00	9.00
Height	11.0	5.454545	0.934199	4.00	5.00	6.00	6.00	7.00
Liquid	11.0	0.181818	0.404520	0.00	0.00	0.00	0.00	1.00
Perishable	11.0	0.090909	0.301511	0.00	0.00	0.00	0.00	1.00
Insurance	11.0	1041.727273	2974.397892	100.00	100.00	150.00	200.00	10009.00
ShipCost	11.0	21.899091	2.165851	19.99	19.99	21.99	23.49	24.99

The value of this potentially erroneous, but also outlying, entry of 10009 is far above the 75th percentile value of 200.00.

A common initial instinct in eliminating outliers is to drop observations that contain outliers from the data. However, as with many default choices, dropping the outliers may not always be the best choice. Often the outliers contain useful information. Another important step in reviewing outliers is to consider whether the data have been erroneously recorded. If the data were erroneously recorded, we may be able to infer a meaningful replacement entry.

For this analysis we will again turn to pd.crosstab() which will let us see how the data in the Insurance column interact with the data in the ShipCost column.

```
# Evaluate the outlier + extreme insurance value
pd.crosstab(df['Insurance'],
            df['ShipCost'])
```

Which will show a table that matches the information shown in Figure 6.4.

FIGURE 6.4   A cross-tabulation of Insurance and ShipCost. Produced with the code shown here

ShipCost	19.99	21.99	24.99
Insurance			
100	4	0	0
150	0	3	0
200	0	0	3
10009	1	0	0

The results in Figure 6.4 reveal an important pattern. Moving from the upper left of this table to the lower right of its first three rows we see that there is a perfect correlation between Insurance and ShipCost (except for the one outlying entry). It seems plausible to infer that the outlying entry, with its ShipCost of 19.99, should have had an entry of 100 in the Insurance column.

There are multiple techniques that can accomplish this replacement. Here are a few of them.

```
# Update data with list comprehension
[x if x < 2000 else 100 for x in df['Insurance']]

# Udpate data with np.where()
np.where(df['Insurance'] < 2000, df['Insurance'], 100)
```

```
# Update data with .apply() method and a lambda
df['Insurance'].apply(lambda x: x if x < 2000 else 100)
```

Again all three examples of code, update the data in the Insurance column. The first example uses list comprehension with a conditional statement. The second example uses NumPy's np.where(). The third example uses the .apply() method with an anonymous lambda function.

In each of these examples I used an arbitrary threshold (2,000) that I knew would distinguish between the correct (all less than 2,000) and the erroneous (well above 2,000) entry. Another approach would have been to use a different conditional that would then address the specific entry as follows.

```
# Updates specific entry with list comprehension
[x if x != 10009 else 100 for x in df['Insurance']]

# Update specific entry with .apply() method
df['Insurance'].apply(lambda x: x if x != 10009 else 100)
```

Removing duplicates

Duplicates can be difficult to spot. However, Pandas provides a simple method that will explore for and assist in inspecting the duplicates, called df.duplicated(). This code quickly produces easy-to-read output that identifies which observations are duplicative of other observations.

In our shipping and mailing data this code correctly identifies the 10th observation as a duplicate. Somehow this last package has

been recorded twice. The quickest way to drop the duplicate observations is with the code `drop_duplicates(inplace=True)`.

Addressing incorrect date entries

Whenever I see date data in a set similar to this mailing and shipping information, I check that the dates proceed in the correct order. In this case, ArriveDate should always be after ShipDate.

A quick way to check for this among these data would be to add a new column that tests for the proper conditions. With the following code, I choose to name the new column Sequence because it tests whether the sequence of the dates appear logical.

```
# Generate a new column to inspect data order
df['Sequence'] = df['ArriveDate'] > df['ShipDate']

# Display data with new column
df
```

Which will produce output that matches what we see in Figure 6.5.

In this new column, shown on the far right, apparently erroneous dates flag as False because the ShipDate was less than the ArriveDate. Given a large data source it would be more difficult to review dozens, hundreds, thousands or more observations. A quicker way to check these data would be to make a summation of the Sequence column. Python will treat True values as 1 and False values as 0.

Thus, if the sum of the sequence column is equal to the length of the DataFrame we can then conclude that all ShipDate values are less than ArriveDate values. We can test whether the sum of the sequence column is equal to the length of the DataFrame with the following code.

	PackageID	Length	Width	Height	Liquid	Perishable	Origin	Destination	Insurance	ShipCost	ShipDate	ArriveDate	Sequence
0	1001	12.5	7	4.0	1	1	FL	FL	100	19.99	2028-01-06	2028-01-07	True
1	1002	12.5	7	5.0	0	0	FL	NC	100	19.99	2028-01-08	2028-01-06	False
2	1003	12.5	7	6.0	0	0	GA	NC	200	24.99	2028-01-07	2028-01-09	True
3	1004	12.5	8	5.0	1	0	SC	SC	150	21.99	2028-01-08	2028-01-09	True
4	1005	12.5	8	6.0	0	0	SC	FL	10009	19.99	2028-01-09	2028-01-11	True
5	1006	NaN	8	4.0	0	0	GA	NC	150	21.99	2028-01-10	2028-01-15	True
6	1007	12.5	9	6.0	0	0	SC	GA	100	19.99	2028-01-11	2028-01-14	True
7	1008	12.5	9	5.0	0	0	SC	SC	100	19.99	2028-01-14	2028-01-11	False
8	1009	NaN	9	7.0	0	0	GA	NC	150	21.99	2028-01-12	2028-01-15	True
9	1010	12.5	9	6.0	0	0	GA	GA	200	24.99	2028-01-12	2028-01-13	True

```
# Perform a logic check to see if any values are False
(df['ArriveDate'] > df['ShipDate']).sum() == len(df)
```

In the case of these data, with two erroneous entries, the code will return a False value. This False value means it will be necessary to address the erroneous dates.

The next question will be, how many erroneous entries are there? Again, with a large data set consisting of hundreds, thousands or more observations it will not be as convenient to just count. To simplify the counting we can turn to the .value_counts() method as shown in the following code.

```
# Count the number of True and False values
df['Sequence'].value_counts()
```

This code will tabulate and display the total number of True values (9) and the total number of False values (2). This result indicates that there are two observations that do not meet the condition we specified above (df['ArriveDate'] > df['ShipDate']).

The next step will be to correct these apparently incorrect dates. There is no clearly perfect solution. And as is always the case, there is no such thing as a correct solution. This means we will need to proceed with a solution we believe we can best defend as most appropriate given the information available to us.

To address these apparently incorrect dates, a preliminary step would be to calculate the average number of days in transit among the correct observations.

```
# Make array of number of days in transit.
days = (df['ArriveDate'] - df['shipDate']).dt.days

# Keep only those observations above zero.
days = np.array([x for x in days if x > 0])

# Find the mean
days_mean = days.mean()

# Display the result
days_mean
```

These data produce a result of 2.1111. A subsequent step could be to take the ShipDate as accurate and then calculate a new ArriveDate based on the ShipDate.

Following the code above we can use days_mean in that code as follows.

```
# Create a column with an imputed correct arrival date.
df['Corrected'] = np.where(df['Sequence'],
                           df['ArriveDate'],
                           df['ShipDate'] +
                           pd.Timedelta(
                               days=round(
                               int(days_mean))))
# Display the data with the new corrected column
df
```

This code uses the np.where() function with three arguments. The first argument df['Sequence'] governs which values the code will update. Where the values are True there will be no update and where the values are False there will be

updates. The next argument `df['ArriveDate']` is the original data that need adjustments. The final argument `df['ShipDate'] + pd.Timedelta(days=round(days_ mean)` provides a corrected date.

Final results and checking the work

In one block of code, choosing no particular method over any other, the final results of our data manipulation and preparation will be as follows.

```
# Replace missing values in the Length column.
df['Length'] = df['Length'].fillna(12.5)

# Replace missing value in the Height column.
df['Height'] = df['Height'].fillna(6.0)

# Replace the erroneous value in the Insurance column.
df['Insurance'] = [x if x < 2000 else
                   100 for x in df['Insurance']]

# Remove duplicates from the DataFrame.
df.drop_duplicates(inplace=True)

# Correct the erroneous date entries.
df['Corrected'] = np.where(df['sequence'],
                           df['ArriveDate'],
                           df['shipDate'] +
                           pd.Timedelta(
                           days=round(
                           int(days_mean)))))
# Display the results of these manipulations
df
```

FIGURE 6.6 The 10 updated, corrected and manipulated observations from the shipping and mailing data. Produced with the code shown here

	PackageID	Length	Width	Height	Liquid	Perishable	Origin	Destination	Insurance	ShipCost	ShipDate	ArriveDate	Corrected
0	1001	12.5	7	4.0	1	1	FL	FL	100	19.99	2028-01-06	2028-01-07	2028-01-07
1	1002	12.5	7	5.0	0	0	FL	NC	100	19.99	2028-01-08	2028-01-06	2028-01-10
2	1003	12.5	7	6.0	0	0	GA	NC	200	24.99	2028-01-07	2028-01-09	2028-01-09
3	1004	12.5	8	5.0	1	0	SC	SC	150	21.99	2028-01-08	2028-01-09	2028-01-09
4	1005	12.5	8	6.0	0	0	SC	FL	100	19.99	2028-01-09	2028-01-11	2028-01-11
5	1006	12.5	8	4.0	0	0	GA	NC	150	21.99	2028-01-10	2028-01-15	2028-01-15
6	1007	12.5	9	6.0	0	0	SC	GA	100	19.99	2028-01-11	2028-01-14	2028-01-14
7	1008	12.5	9	5.0	0	0	SC	SC	100	19.99	2028-01-14	2028-01-11	2028-01-16
8	1009	12.5	9	7.0	0	0	GA	NC	150	21.99	2028-01-12	2028-01-15	2028-01-15
9	1010	12.5	9	6.0	0	0	GA	GA	200	24.99	2028-01-12	2028-01-13	2028-01-13

After executing these manipulations in preparation for further analysis it is important to check the results. With a small data set, such as this one, we can inspect the entire data set in a single page or a single computer screen by evaluating the df in Python which will produce the output you see in Figure 6.6.

However, it is often not easy to view an entire data set in one screen. Sometimes a data set could consist of hundreds, thousands, millions or even more rows. When working with larger data sets it is necessary to check results with more aggregated approaches.

There are many sensible approaches to performing these checks, some of which I introduced above. Here I provide reminders. It is important to check (and recheck) every data manipulation in at least one way, or more when possible. The following reviews each of the manipulations we executed.

To check that the missing values in the Length column correctly updated to 12.5, indeed that the entire column is equal to 12.5, simple comparison operators will work best. In our case the code (df['Length'] == 12.5).sum() == len(df['Length']) should return True. The reason we should see true here is because the (df['Length'] == 12.5) expression will return a Pandas Series of True and False. Each item in the series will be True where the expression was True and then False where otherwise. The .sum() method then counts the True values by treating each as a 1 and then finding the total sum. Logically, if all values were 12.5 the sum should equal the length of the series. The .value_counts() method can also be useful in this context.

```
# Check that length updated correctly
(df['Length'] == 12.5).value_counts()
```

Using this code the output will include a tabulation that counts the number of True values. In this context, with these data, that value will be a count of 10, which is the number we expect because we know there are 10 observations.

To check that we correctly fixed the missing value in the Height column we can return to the same cross-tabulation that helped us infer the best replacement entry. In this case, after executing the correction we add the `margins=True` option which will give a column for the row totals and a row for the column totals. The totals columns are called 'All'.

```
# Check Height manipulation performed as expected
pd.crosstab(df['Height'].fillna(99),
            df['Width'].fillna(99),
            margins=True)
```

In the output following this code we will see the bottom-right cell, with its value of 10, will indicate that all 10 observations are accounted for. We also see that there are no missing values (which would display as 99).

Regarding the outlier in the Insurance column, we decided to replace that with a new value that we inferred to be correct by comparing the entries in that column to entries in the ShipCost column. To check the work of this manipulation and replacement, the original cross-tabulation will show that all went according to plan (or otherwise if not). Again we will use the `.fillna(99)` methods to check for missing data and the margins=True option for the benefit of the total column and row.

```
# Check the Insurance column updated correctly
pd.crosstab(df['Insurance'].fillna
           df['shipCost'].fillna(99),
           margins=True)
```

From this output we will again see in the lower right a value of 10 that confirms all observations are accounted for. The rows and columns show that there are no further outlier, or apparently erroneous, entries to worry over.

To double-check that we corrected ArriveDate as desired, the following code should return True, as discussed above.

```
# Check that ArrivalDate updated correctly
(df['Corrected'] > df['shipDate']).sum() == len(df)
```

Simplifying and preparing for analysis

Another preparatory step that many analytical projects may require is to simplify the data. In this section we will simplify the data in five ways. We will:

- remove columns that can add little value to our analysis
- review and potentially discard highly correlated columns
- combine columns into a single column that we know (or suspect) to be closely related
- convert nominal categorical variables as arrays of zeros and ones (also known as dummy arrays)
- reduce the ShipDate and ArriveDate columns to a single column

For the first step we will again review the correlation matrix (using df.corr()) shown here in Figure 6.7, which now shows different results than earlier because we have changed more than a few of the data points.

FIGURE 6.7   A correlation matrix of the revised shipping and mailing data. Produced with the code shown here

	PackageID	Length	Width	Height	Liquid	Perishable	Insurance	ShipCost
PackageID	1.000000	NaN	0.943042	0.531816	-0.522233	-0.522233	0.289749	0.273724
Length	NaN	NaN	NaN	NaN	NaN	NaN	NaN	NaN
Width	0.943042	NaN	1.000000	0.472866	-0.361158	-0.441415	0.046241	0.025240
Height	0.531816	NaN	0.472866	1.000000	-0.490990	-0.509175	0.307339	0.320256
Liquid	-0.522233	NaN	-0.361158	-0.490990	1.000000	0.666667	-0.128037	-0.157243
Perishable	-0.522233	NaN	-0.441415	-0.509175	0.666667	1.000000	-0.298753	-0.279543
Insurance	0.289749	NaN	0.046241	0.307339	-0.128037	-0.298753	1.000000	0.993221
ShipCost	0.273724	NaN	0.025240	0.320256	-0.157243	-0.279543	0.993221	1.000000

One of the most unusual components or aspects of this correlation matrix is that we see NaN values for the Length row and column. The reason for this is, as discussed above, there is no variation in Length. All observations contain the same value. Since all variables contain the same data (in essence there is no variation) and since correlation measures how variables covary it is not possible to produce a correlation coefficient between Length and any other variable. Related, since Length does not covary with any other variable we can consider excluding this variable from further analysis. It is a common step to remove any variables that do not vary (or that vary very little) from most analyses.

In this correlation matrix we also see that Insurance and ShipCost are highly correlated with a correlation coefficient of 0.993221. Because these two variables are highly correlated we will consider removing one of these two columns from further analysis.

From reviewing our data, when ShipCost is 19.99 Insurance is always 100, when ShipCost is 21.99 Insurance is always 150, and when ShipCost is 24.99 Insurance is always 200. Since Insurance seems to be a direct function of ShipCost it will make sense for us to exclude Insurance.

Additionally, since our goal is to reduce the number of columns, in order to simplify our analysis we should consider combining closely related columns. In this example Length, Width, and Height are closely related. Indeed, we can combine them by finding the product of these three columns for a new, interpretable column we would call Volume.

Again, there are many ways to accomplish each of these tasks. The following code shows one of the many options.

```python
# Remove Insurance (highly correlated with ShipCost)
df = df.drop(columns=['Insurance'])

# Create a Volume colum
df['Volume'] = df['Length'] *
                df['Width'] *
                df['Height']

# Remove Length, Width, and Height columns
df = df.drop(columns=['Length','Width','Height'])

# Replace ArriveData with the Corrected column
df['ArriveDate'] = df['Corrected']

# Review the revised and updated data
df
```

This code uses multiple coding strategies. The first is the `.drop()` method and the second is to create or replace a column with the `df['ColumnName']` = expression. After performing the above actions, the new DataFrame will be as shown in Figure 6.8.

FIGURE 6.8 The 10 simplified observations from the shipping and mailing data. Produced with the code shown here

	PackageID	Liquid	Perishable	Origin	Destination	ShipCost	ShipDate	ArriveDate	Corrected	Volume
0	1001	1	1	FL	FL	19.99	2028-01-06	2028-01-07	2028-01-07	350.0
1	1002	0	0	FL	NC	19.99	2028-01-08	2028-01-10	2028-01-10	437.5
2	1003	0	0	GA	NC	24.99	2028-01-07	2028-01-09	2028-01-09	525.0
3	1004	1	0	SC	SC	21.99	2028-01-08	2028-01-09	2028-01-09	500.0
4	1005	0	0	SC	FL	19.99	2028-01-09	2028-01-11	2028-01-11	600.0
5	1006	0	0	GA	NC	21.99	2028-01-10	2028-01-15	2028-01-15	400.0
6	1007	0	0	SC	GA	19.99	2028-01-11	2028-01-14	2028-01-14	675.0
7	1008	0	0	SC	SC	19.99	2028-01-14	2028-01-16	2028-01-16	562.5
8	1009	0	0	GA	NC	21.99	2028-01-12	2028-01-15	2028-01-15	787.5
9	1010	0	0	GA	GA	24.99	2028-01-12	2028-01-13	2028-01-13	675.0

Categorical and nominal variables are variables that contain information that has no natural numeric or ordered representation. In these data we have the State of origin and also the State of destination. We can arbitrarily assign numbers to each State but doing so will produce results that will have no meaning. The solution is to represent these categorical values as an array of dummy values. Here is how that looks with these data.

For the Origin column there will be three new columns. One column will be a set of 1s and 0s that represent True or False and that indicate whether the package was from Florida (FL). Similarly there will be two more equivalent columns for Georgia (GA) and South Carolina (SC).

The following code shows how this dummy array creation works.

```
# Display dummy array (one-hot-encoding)
pd.concat([
    df[['Origin','Destination']],
    pd.get_dummies(df[['Origin','Destination']])],
    axis=1)
```

Which produces a result consistent with that shown in Figure 6.9.

To further learn how this encoding works, let's review observation 5, which, because the numbering starts at 0, is numbered 4. Working across that row we see that the Origin was SC and the destination was FL. Correspondingly, the Origin_SC column contains a 1 while the Destination_FL column also contains a 1. These 1 values correspond to the value in the original Origin

FIGURE 6.9   The origin and destination information from the shipping and mailing data following the dummy encoding procedure. Produced with the code shown here

	Origin	Destination	Origin_FL	Origin_GA	Origin_SC	Destination_FL	Destination_GA	Destination_NC	Destination_SC
0	FL	FL	1	0	0	1	0	0	0
1	FL	NC	1	0	0	0	0	1	0
2	GA	NC	0	1	0	0	0	1	0
3	SC	SC	0	0	1	0	0	0	1
4	SC	FL	0	0	1	1	0	0	0
5	GA	NC	0	1	0	0	0	1	0
6	SC	GA	0	0	1	0	1	0	0
7	SC	SC	0	0	1	0	0	0	1
8	GA	NC	0	1	0	0	0	1	0
9	GA	GA	0	1	0	0	1	0	0

and Destination columns. Notice also that all other columns of observation 5 contain 0.

Notice also that for the Origin array there are three columns. The reason for this is that there were three possible categories in the original data. For the Destination array there are four columns because there were four possible categories in the original data.

The last step in the process of creating dummy variables will be to choose one of the columns from each array to drop. The dropped column in each array will operate as a reference category. The reason it is necessary to drop a column from each dummy array is because the remaining columns will always predict the value of the dropped column.

Since the remaining columns predict the value of the dropped column, the essence of this operation is to simplify the data but without any loss of information. While the above code executes the dummy array creation and places the arrays alongside the original data for demonstration purposes, the following code creates the arrays, drops the original variables, and then also drops Florida as the reference category for both the Origin and Destination arrays.

```
# Generate dummy arrays and join with original
df = pd.concat([
    df.drop(columns=['Origin','Destination']),
    pd.get_dummies(df[['Origin','Destination']])],
    axis=1).drop(columns=['Origin_FL',
                          'Destination_FL'])

# Evaluate the results
df
```

FIGURE 6.10   The 10 simplified observations, now ready for analysis, from the shipping and mailing data. Produced with the code shown here

	PackageID	Liquid	Perishable	ShipCost	Volume	Origin_GA	Origin_SC	Destination_GA	Destination_NC	Destination_SC	TransitTime
0	1001	1	1	19.99	350.0	0	0	0	0	0	1 days
1	1002	0	0	19.99	437.5	0	0	0	1	0	2 days
2	1003	0	0	24.99	525.0	1	0	0	1	0	2 days
3	1004	1	0	21.99	500.0	0	1	0	0	1	1 days
4	1005	0	0	19.99	600.0	0	1	0	0	0	2 days
5	1006	0	0	21.99	400.0	1	0	0	1	0	5 days
6	1007	0	0	19.99	675.0	0	1	1	0	0	3 days
7	1008	0	0	19.99	562.5	0	1	0	0	1	2 days
8	1009	0	0	21.99	787.5	1	0	0	1	0	3 days
9	1010	0	0	24.99	675.0	1	0	1	0	0	1 days

One additional step that may be useful in simplifying the data for analysis would be to calculate transit time from ShipDate and ArriveDate and then to discard ShipDate, ArriveDate and Corrected. This operation will convert the information about travel to an easy-to-interpret continuous variable and also further reduces the total number of columns.

```
# Add column that represents transit time
df['TransitTime'] = df['Corrected'] - df['shipDate']

# Drop ShipDate, ArrivalDate, and Corrected columns
df = df.drop(['ShipDate','ArriveDate',
              'Corrected'], axis=1)

# Evaluate the results
df
```

All of which produces a final set of data, as shown in Figure 6.10, that is ready (or at least more ready than before) for analysis than the original data were.

As a result of the work shown in this chapter, we now have a DataFrame that we believe contains no missing data, no erroneous data, no outliers, and that is fully numeric. Of course, we are not sure that the data are error-free because we made choices as we deliberated on how to address missing or apparently erroneous data. We made the best choices we could, with the information we had, and as such, the data are now more ready for use in data science.

THE WILD LIVES OF DATA   Data in captivity – data in the wild

The pristine data presented in classes and books are not always reflective of real-world data, which are often complex and messy. Learning to inspect and clean data is vital for navigating the whole

---

life and world of data. Missing values, inconsistencies and errors must be identified and corrected using a range of tools and techniques, including data profiling, visualization and statistical analysis.

The ability to deal with missing values is especially important. Data scientists, machine learning, artificial intelligence and advanced analytics professionals who best develop a deep understanding of data structures and patterns can learn and grow to be more confident in the field.

Conclusion

Data preparation is a critical part of any analytical project. After deciding on a research question or business problem to solve, and also after looking at previous similar efforts, in many data science projects the first steps will be exploratory data analysis and also data preparation. Using a custom data set, consisting of 11 observations, and 12 variables, this chapter surveyed five major problems with the data. I then proceeded to show a collection of methods, among many, that work to fix those problems. Finally, I demonstrated multiple procedures related to preparing the data for analysis.

In order to ensure accuracy and validity in the results, it is important to understand and use best practices for data preparation. To begin, replacing missing values with the mean or most common occurrence can be effective. However, other strategies are often better. This chapter's examples explained how to replace with the mean, should you choose to do so. Importantly, it also demonstrated how to see when other approaches will be better. Additionally, it is important to consider the information outliers may offer your analysis rather than automatically dropping them.

Furthermore, it is smart and wise to simplify data before analysis. For example, this chapter showed how the Length, Width, and Height columns may be combined into a single Volume column. Likewise, I also showed how to convert shipping and arrival dates to simpler data that consisted of the number of days each package spent in transit.

Another important task for preparation, when there is nominal or ordinal data, such as package origin and destination, is to convert these data to a numeric representation. This chapter demonstrated how to use Pandas to convert nominal and ordinal data into an array of binary dummy variables.

Overall, data preparation requires careful consideration of how best to handle missing values, outliers and duplicates so that you can best obtain meaningful results. It is difficult to imagine a chapter that could fully explore every possible task or operation involved in preparing data for analysis along with every possible nuance. In lieu of a complete, definitive or exhaustive resource, this chapter, in conjunction with Chapter 5, provided an overview of many common tasks. This overview aims toward helping readers discover essential skills in data science.

Data science examples

Ok, that was a lot of technical information. If you did not quite follow it all, do not be discouraged. It was a lot of code and you can look back and review. Practised repetition is one of the best ways to learn the more technical information that is fundamental to data science.

I opened Chapter 1 of this book with examples of how data science enables computers to help navigate roads and highways (GPS), obtain personalized recommendations for online shopping carts, receive better health care in the form of computer assisted medical diagnostics (MRI scans), and facilitate online gaming. In this chapter I move away from the technical content and back into broader examples of data science in production.

CHATBOTS Yesterday's news

Chances are you have interacted with one or more chatbots. They live on websites, often in the lower right hand portion of the site's main page. They help you find information about the website's products or services. Often they can connect you with a real person, but they are designed to help you with little or no actual human intervention.

Often, despite a few awkward replies, chatbots have been successful at reducing the need for human intervention in matters related to customer service. As we move forward, those awkward chatbots are likely to grow more fluent and more helpful. A computer's ability to converse with humans has advanced far beyond what is required for yesterday's notion of a chatbot.

With the advent of multiple generative artificial intelligent tools, computers can now converse with you while understanding complex relationships between pending topics throughout the conversation.

Computers can also question, challenge and enquire further about any errors in your logic and reasoning. If the premise of what you suggest is not reliable, computers can spot that and tell you so.

In one simple example, imagine you are conversing with a chatbot at your favourite airline. Imagine that the chatbot is assisting you with a reservation change. If, in the course of your conversation, you told the chatbot that you needed to extend your stay, and then later inadvertently asked for a flight that would reduce the length of your stay, the artificial intelligence would likely spot the error or ambiguity. That artificial intelligence will stop and let you know that you have provided conflicting information and ask for clarification.

While not all chatbots have been enabled with this new level of reasoning and logic, this level of human-like reasoning from computers is now well-developed and growingly more widely implemented.

This chapter shows examples of how data science transforms the way we work, live, and interact. Each tool discussed here has been enabled by data science, machine learning, artificial intelligence or advanced analytics.

For each tool in this chapter I will provide a description of how its features and capabilities are examples of data science as well as examples of how you might use it in your work, business or personal life. An important note is that, for proprietary reasons, many of these tools and platforms do not reveal their precise inner workings. As a result, when we review these tools we make educated guesses as to the data science techniques that may be involved in their production.

I divide the chapter into three topical sections. The first section will focus primarily on tools that use natural language processing (NLP). The second section focuses on tools that provide image processing solutions. And the third section captures a range of additional examples that examine the lighter side of how data science has influenced our work and life.

Examples that provide NLP solutions

Natural language processing is a topic I will cover further in Chapter 8 with an example of how one of its analytical techniques can calculate a metric that aims to quantify reading difficulty. Chapter 8 also focuses on how NLP can analyse text and produce a score that will indicate the sentiment of the text.

Generally speaking, the sub-field of NLP borrows from multiple other fields. Importantly, this sub-field draws extensively from non-computational fields including linguistics and communications in addition to the computational fields of computer science, statistics, and ultimately also artificial intelligence. Natural language processing also requires a dose of acoustical and sound engineering. The goal of NLP is to enable computers to communicate and interact with humans in a natural and intuitive way.

NLP tasks include language translation (converting text from one language to another such as from French to German), text classification (grouping text into meaningful groups such as identifying a list of topics discussed in a massive collection of emails), sentiment analysis (identifying whether text expresses a positive or negative sentiment), and text generation (such as for use in chatbots).

If you have ever muttered out loud in a room where you are the only person there 'Hey Google' or 'Hey Siri' or 'Hey Alexa' you know the power of voice assistants. A popular portrayal of voice assistants you may consider reviewing for an alternative perspective is the 2013 movie *Her* where a writer named Theodore (portrayed by Joaquin Phoenix) is lonely and forms a close personal relationship with a voice-driven artificial intelligence (voiced by Scarlett Johansson). While the movie exaggerates the relationship between Theodore and the voice assistant, there is an active area of research in data science that involves looking for how voice assistants can help with mental health and anxiety.

In 2023 a corporation known as Embodied, Inc., released for purchase a robot powered by artificial intelligence known as Moxie. Its lifetime subscription was $1,499. The marketing material for this robot suggests that by interacting with child companions it can encourage social, emotional and cognitive development. While a host of data science techniques enable this robot's full range of features, a key element, the ability to interact with humans via spoken language, is enabled by natural language processing.

There are many tools that rely on NLP to help in personal, business and work contexts. In the examples that follow I first discuss those that assist in writing and second those that use a computer's ability to recognize human speech.

AI-assisted writing

AI writing assistants use artificial intelligence and machine learning techniques to assist in the writing process. There are a

number of tools and platforms that use these techniques to help writers generate ideas, structure their writing and improve the overall quality of their work.

Two of the most popular AI-assisted writing tools are Jasper and Copy AI. Both Jasper and Copy AI provide access to their tools via monthly or annual subscription plans. A third emerging tool is ChatGPT, which in 2023 also delivered a monthly subscription plan.

Jasper uses natural language processing and machine learning techniques to help writers generate ideas, structure their writing and improve the overall quality of their work. It includes features that can analyse the user's writing style, tone and content, while also providing suggestions and feedback to help the user improve their writing. Copy AI can help writers generate ideas and structure their writing. A frequent criticism of Jasper, Copy AI and other similar tools is that they often provide redundant or repetitive output.

ChatGPT, developed by OpenAI, which became widely available towards the end of 2022, provides writing support similar to Jasper and Copy AI. The primary innovation that ChatGPT brought to the range of platforms that assist in writing is a chat-like interface. Earlier tools relied primarily on a system of templates. The earlier templates called for users to provide starting text in response to specific prompts. The templates would then have a highly structured point of departure while generating new text. ChatGPT's chat-like interface is more open-ended and it permits users to speak with the artificial intelligence and ask for specific outputs in plain human language. Shortly after the release of ChatGPT, other AI-enabled writing assistants also introduced chat-like interfaces.

OpenAI's advances in NLP as available through ChatGPT extend the potential of these tools beyond serving as mere writing assistants. By having been trained on massive corpora, they can often provide a form of 'research' that rivals the results many might produce on their own via Google's web-search

platform (or via other more sophisticated research services such as LexisNexis, JStore, Westlaw and similar). I demonstrate these research capabilities (you might say pseudo-research capabilities) by asking these platforms to write about e-commerce below.

ChatGPT's evolving capabilities also move the state of the art above and beyond mere writing assistance in two additional ways. First, open AI designed ChatGPT for a broad range of purposes, including chatbots and other conversational interfaces. ChatGPT is capable of generating human-like text responses to user-submitted prompts. Second, ChatGPT is capable of understanding and questioning the validity of incorrect premises or assumptions. For example, ChatGPT could review two separate passages and then compare the two passages. If you asked ChatGPT to compare and contrast two passages but then you provided it with two identical passages, ChatGPT would recognize the problematic prompt and alert you to the apparent issue plus ask for clarification.

AI-ASSISTED WRITING IN ACTION

To compare the performance of Jasper, Copy AI and ChatGPT, I gave each tool the same input. I prompted each tool with 'Paragraph about benefits of e-commerce'.[1]

If you attempt to replicate this experiment you will likely see different results. Each of these tools respond with some measure of randomness.

Below are the results that we can compare and contrast.

Jasper's result (330 words):   E-commerce has become an increasingly important part of the modern business landscape, offering many benefits to both businesses and consumers. Some of the key advantages of e-commerce include greater convenience, increased functionality, and enhanced security for customers.

One of the main benefits of e-commerce is its convenience. With e-commerce platforms like Amazon or eBay, consumers can easily shop from anywhere in the world at any time of day. This makes

it much easier for people with busy schedules to buy what they need without having to plan ahead or go out of their way to find a physical store. Additionally, with online shopping there are no lines to wait in or crowds to navigate, making the entire experience more pleasant and less stressful.

In addition to convenience, e-commerce also offers enhanced functionality for consumers. With online shopping, people can easily search for products by criteria such as price or brand and quickly find exactly what they're looking for. They can also compare different products more easily with features like user reviews and detailed product information. And since many businesses offer free shipping on orders over a certain amount, shoppers don't have to pay extra fees or wait long periods of time for their items to arrive.

Another key benefit of e-commerce is the increased security that it offers consumers. Many businesses use secure payment systems like PayPal or credit card processing to protect customer data from being accessed or stolen by third parties. Additionally, many platforms provide built-in fraud detection tools that automatically flag suspicious transactions and alert customers about possible risks. With these security measures in place, people can shop online with greater confidence that their information will remain private and safe from hackers and other malicious actors.

Overall, e-commerce is an important part of the modern economy, offering a wide range of benefits to both businesses and consumers alike. Whether you're looking for convenience, enhanced functionality, or increased security while shopping online, e-commerce has something to offer everyone.

Copy AI's result (195 words): E-commerce is a big part of the world we live in. It's convenient, it's easy to use, and it can help us do things that would otherwise be difficult or impractical.

For example, imagine you're trying to find a job in your field – maybe you're looking for something short-term or part-time, or maybe you want something full-time. You might think about

searching through Craigslist or Monster.com, but what if you don't have access to those platforms? What if you don't have your own computer? Or what if you don't feel comfortable using the Internet on a regular basis? E-commerce can be a solution to all of these problems!

ebay is another great example: eBay allows people to buy goods online without having to pay for shipping costs or time spent waiting at the post office. Etsy is another great example: Etsy allows artists around the world to sell their goods directly from their own websites. Upwork allows freelancers around the world to find jobs with employers who pay them when they complete work for them. These are just some examples of how e-commerce helps us solve problems we might not otherwise be able to solve.

ChatGPT's result (217 words):   E-commerce, or electronic commerce, refers to the buying and selling of goods and services through the internet. There are several benefits to conducting business through e-commerce platforms:

- Convenience: E-commerce allows consumers to shop from the comfort of their own homes, without the need to physically visit a store. This is especially useful for people who live in rural areas or those who have limited mobility.
- Increased reach: E-commerce allows businesses to reach a wider audience, as they are not limited to a physical location. Customers can access the business's website from anywhere in the world, as long as they have an internet connection.
- Cost-effectiveness: Setting up and running an online store is generally cheaper than maintaining a physical storefront. This is because there are fewer overhead costs, such as rent and utilities.
- Increased efficiency: E-commerce can streamline the sales process, as it allows businesses to automate many tasks, such as inventory management and order processing.
- Personalization: E-commerce platforms can collect data on customer preferences and behaviour, which can be used to personalize the shopping experience and offer targeted recommendations.

Overall, e-commerce has revolutionized the way we shop and do business, and it continues to grow in popularity as more and more consumers and businesses turn to the internet for their shopping needs.

AI-ASSISTED WRITING STRENGTHS AND WEAKNESSES

There are several potential strengths of AI-assisted writing. First among these potential benefits are speed and accuracy. For example, AI-assisted writing tools can process and analyse large amounts of data quickly, which can help writers generate content more efficiently. For example, imagine you have prepared a 4,000 or 5,000 word report. Next imagine that a colleague has asked for a 1,000 word summary or a 500 word synopsis. AI writing assistants can make quicker work of that summarization task. A growing sentiment among AI enthusiasts is that if AI can

TABLE 7.1 Key metrics from example passages written with the assistance of AI

	Jasper	Copy-AI	Chat GPT
Words	330	195	212
Characters	1,828	932	1,196
Paragraphs	5	3	7
Sentences	16	11	10
Sentences per paragraph	3.2	3.6	1.4
Words per sentence	20.6	17.7	20.2
Characters per word	5.4	4.6	5.4
Flesch Reading Ease	34.1	64.7	31.3
Flesh-Kincade Grade Level	13.6	8.6	13.9
Passive sentences	6.2%	0%	20%

perform a task as well as humans, perhaps it should. Accuracy also connects with speed. For example, AI-assisted writing tools can help avoid mistakes in spelling or grammar.

When appropriately trained and correctly prompted to do so, AI-enabled writing assistants can also help draft text that is more engaging and relevant for specifically intended audiences. For example, a popular template from Jasper, as discussed above, is 'explain it to a child'. The previous sentence, adjusted by AI specifically for a reader in grade 8 reads: 'AI-enabled writing assistants can help people write better. They can make sure the text is interesting and that it's right for the audience. But only if they have been taught properly and given good instructions.'

There are also several potential weaknesses of AI-assisted writing. For many, the first concerns about potential weaknesses might be related to the danger of growing overly reliant on AI-assisted writing. By relying too heavily on AI-assisted writing, authors, editors and publishes may eventually produce a feedback loop that involves re-training and revising the generative models with new text that may have also been previously generated with the assistance of artificial intelligence. The demand for new text that can serve as training data may outstrip the supply.

At the top of my list of concerns for the future of AI-assisted writing are the issues related to ethics and law. The ethical concerns pertain to at least two main worries. The first is that AI-assisted writing relies on training data that are biased. As such, AI-assisted writing will produce biased outputs. As shown in Chapter 1, and in other related publications, it is not difficult to expose these biases.[2]

The second ethical consideration pertains to how the developers of generative AI models source training data. The debate here is conceptual, social, political, economic, cultural and psychological. The debate is whether these tools create new text or images based on the training data or merely copy the work of others. In other words, are the tools using training data as

inspiration, in a manner that is conceptually, socially, politically, economically, culturally and psychologically similar to the way humans draw inspiration from previous exposure to literature and art? Or, are the AI-enabled tools merely parroting the training data in a manner that, due to their scale, can be passed off as something that is new?

The final drawback I point to here is the legally ambiguous status of AI generated text (or images). With multiple class actions, or other legal actions, it is not clear that the generative AI of the 2020s will survive legal challenges that argue they are more like a parrot that imitates others rather than a human-like creator that draws creative inspiration.[3]

At present, there is a general understanding that while AI-assisted writing tools can be useful for certain tasks, they are not a replacement for human writers and editors, and should be used as part of a larger writing process rather than as a standalone solution.

Speech recognition

To work well, tools that employ speech recognition require a broad range of expertise, technologies and techniques from multiple fields. The ultimate goal of these tools is to enable computers to understand and interpret human spoken language. Speech recognition is an opportunity to revisit a key topic from the first chapter of this book – that data science is a concerted production involving a pile of many technologies that existed before and continue to exist independently of data science. The full combination and range of technologies involved in speech recognition is extensive.

Speech recognition lets computers encode and understand casual or naturally spoken human language. In addition to relying on the non-computational fields of linguistics and communications which involve making sense of syntax and semantics, plus

the computational fields of computer science and statistics, speech recognition also involves acoustical sciences, sound recording and sound reproduction. For example, acoustical sciences play a crucial role in analysing sound waves, which are essential in capturing and processing speech. Before a computer can recognize speech, it must first be recorded in a manner that encodes the invisible vibrations in the air, transforming them into a format that can be understood and analysed by a computer.

Here is how this looks in practice. When training a speech recognition model, the process begins with recording spoken audio, which captures the sound vibrations and converts them into digital data. The data then require further processing and manipulation. This processing and manipulation may involve tasks such as removing or eliminating data that carry no meaning, such as background noise. Other manipulations may specifically help the speech recognition cope with accents or dialects. Only with the involvement of the work rooted both in data science and in other sciences can voice assistants including Google Assistant, Siri, Alexa or others mimic how humans understand your speech and then also mimic how a human assistant might respond.

In short, to put these tools into production, the platforms must also leverage a combination of many algorithms that work in concert. The end result, for tools that employ speech recognition, is platforms that can help individual users with translation, home automation, setting reminders, communicating with others and other forms of assistance around the home or office.

Beyond the personal voice assistants, there are other tools built more specifically for business, work and commercial uses. Here is a brief overview that focuses on three examples of commercial tools that provide features that have been enabled at least in part by speech recognition, including Descript (video editing platform), Rev.com (audio transcription), and Zoom's automatic captions feature.

Descript is primarily a video and audio editing tool that makes extensive use of speech recognition and NLP. Nearly all of Descript's key features rely on NLP. For example, Descript

will transcribe video and audio. Once transcribed, Descript supports edits to the audio by allowing users to make edits to the text. However users edit the text, Descript will make corresponding edits to the audio and video. Descript's transcription also enables captions and subtitles.

Rev.com is a transcription and translation service that uses NLP tools and technologies that are similar to the range of those used by Descript to transcribe audio and video files.

Zoom is a video conferencing platform that enables users to communicate with each other using audio, video, chat and other media. While Zoom and most other tools using NLP do not publicly disclose the finest and most specific ways in which they use data science, it is likely that they employ a collection of technologies, in a broad number of ways, to improve the transcription results and related voice-to-text transcriptions.

These tools also evolve over time. When monitored and maintained properly, the specific models trained and deployed by the platforms can continue to learn from the new data they process and the feedback they receive from users.

A broad range of businesses and organizations use these tools that work with human speech through NLP. Among the clearer use cases, for example, are those required by transcription and translation services (rote conversion of audio to text), media and entertainment companies (as a method to quickly and efficiently make video and audio more accessible) and corporate training and development departments (as a way to quickly create written training documentation that may accompany audio and video materials).

Image processing

Consider the images in Figures 7.1 and 7.2. It is not always easy to see the difference between photographs and artificially generated images.

FIGURE 7.1   Side-by-side images of fruit in a bowl. The image on the left is from photographer NordWood Themes via Unsplash and on the right is from Jasper's AI assisted art generator

Source: medium.com/illumination/real-photo-or-artificial-intelligence-bcb52240e2d1

FIGURE 7.2   Side-by-side images of toy trucks. The image on the left is from Jasper's AI assisted art generator and on the right is from photographer Alessandro Bianchi via Unsplash

Source: medium.com/illumination/real-photo-or-artificial-intelligence-bcb52240e2d1

Image processing is a branch of artificial intelligence that uses computer algorithms to analyse, manipulate and generate images. Beyond making games that challenge you to spot the fake, this family of analytical techniques has many applications, including facial recognition (for identify verification), medical imaging analysis (for diagnostic purposes), industrial inspection (for quickly counting inventory), and more. For example, the computer assisted MRI analysis discussed near the top of Chapter 1 uses image processing enabled by data science.

Image processing, even more so than other techniques, is computationally intense. Recent advances in computation engineering have led to a surge in the development of tools that use image processing capabilities over recent years. These tools are also now capable of producing video.

In this section, we will review a small sample of tools that use image generation to assist with tasks such as art creation and image enhancement.

Jasper Art is an AI-powered art tool that uses image generation to help create new images. It uses machine learning algorithms to analyse text input and generate new images inspired by the text. Other platforms provide similar capabilities including Canva for example. I demonstrated this tool (and its biases) in Chapter 1 where I showed the results produced from the prompt 'a CEO speaking at a company event'. I also showed the results of these tools at the top of this section where I asked whether you were able to spot the artificially generated image next to a traditional photograph.

Lensa is a tool that uses image generation to enhance and modify images and videos. It allows users to apply a range of effects to images, including colour adjustments and more sophisticated filters and adjustments. Lensa uses machine learning algorithms to analyse the input image or video and then generate a modified version that is based on the original but is modified according to user specifications.

Here again, the image and video creation or modifications enabled by data science require entire teams to accomplish. There are teams involved in the development and still more teams involved in the deployment. The platforms enabled by image generation techniques and the techniques themselves are evolving and improving. Just as is the case for text transcription and NLP tools, these image generation tools have the ability to learn from the data they process and the feedback they receive from users. While in production is when data scientists monitor and maintain the work.

To look a bit deeper into the ways image generation works with data science is also to have an opportunity to appreciate one of the less well understood but especially clever techniques in the entire field. Think for a moment and in your imagination picture how a computer can produce images that will trick human observers into believing those images are real. In the context such as the one above involving fruit bowls and toy trucks, computers can produce hundreds of candidate images using a technique commonly called convolutional neural networks (CNNs). Of all the possible candidate images, it then becomes important to discern which images will indeed trick human observers.

To create an image that will appear real to most human observers, data scientists have devised techniques that take the science beyond learning to mimic patterns found in the training data. In a manner of speaking, the field has produced a family of techniques designed to challenge or test itself. Another technique often called generative adversarial networks (GANs) involves a second neural network. The first neural network generates candidate images while the subsequent neural network has been separately trained to ascertain whether an image will appear to humans as real. By configuring these networks to work together it is possible to build a system that generates images that humans consider high quality and perceive as real. In a manner of speaking, the generative model is not trained to create an image that looks like its training data, but rather to

create an image inspired by its training data that will trick the separately trained model into believing the image is real.

The people and businesses that use these tools include artists, photographers and anyone or any organization that is interested in creating or modifying images and videos.

Artists, in particular, can use these tools to create new works of art, either by generating images from scratch or by tweaking existing images. Photographers can enhance and modify their photos by adjusting colour, brightness and contrast, or by applying filters and effects. Graphic designers can create new graphics or modify existing ones by changing colour schemes or adding special effects.

Business organizations can benefit too. Just as I wrote about how many organizations might use NLP tools, there are similar use cases for image generation. Among these use cases, are products created by media and entertainment companies (as a method to make new video and audio for entertainment purposes) and by corporate training and development departments (as a way to quickly create new video and audio for training and professional development).

Consider also how marketing professionals can use image and video generation tools which are well suited to create eye-catching promotional materials such as banners, posters, or social media graphics.

Many observers are enthused by the rise of these image and video generation tools while others are more cautious. Many of the same advantages and limitations associated with tools that assist in writing also apply to the case of image generation tools. When appropriately trained and correctly prompted to do so, AI-enabled image and video generators create art, or images, that are engaging and relevant for specifically intended audiences or specific business purposes. However, it is not clear to what extent the ethical and legal drawbacks will undermine the value of image and video generation.

However, there is a lighter side to these topics, too.

The lighter side of machine learning

One of the simplest implementations of data science in the realm of image manipulation is that of filters. These filters make what appear to be simple modifications to images or videos. Photo filters on Instagram, Snapchat, Facebook, and other social platforms use machine learning algorithms to analyse and modify the images.

As explained in earlier chapters, no single technique or algorithm is responsible for accomplishing the work of these filters. Common approaches include image segmentation, which divides the image into regions and modifies each region separately; style transfer, which uses deep learning to mimic the style of one image and apply it to another; and object recognition, which can identify specific objects in an image and modify them. These three, and other techniques, work in concert to produce a final result.

These filters can be fun to use with friends and family. Of course, context is everything. You would not want to get stuck with a cat filter during an important business meeting. If you have not yet seen this unwanted cat filter, look online for my esteemed colleague the 'Cat Lawyer' for a good example of how not to use these filters. This example also shows how important it is to be sure you know how to disable the filters when you need to.

Filters are not all fun and games, however. There are more than a few potential downsides and reasons for caution. Photo filters can contribute to unrealistic and unattainable expectations of beauty and personal appearance. It is dangerous to push towards these unrealistic standards, especially for more vulnerable younger users of the technology.

Conclusion

Any data science tool is only as good as the data used to build and train the underlying models. In light of the potential harms

we discussed in this chapter, I believe now is another opportunity to revisit the affirmative obligation the field has to avoid causing harm for others. There is perhaps a discussion to have here that extends the Hippocratic Oath rules I proposed earlier. We should regard no tool as more important than the wellbeing of its users. It is up to those who develop the tools and teach about them to convey an ethical framework that ensures these tools support positive (not harmful) or entertaining (not harmful) purposes.

It should be clear that data science tools pervade all industries, and most industries have welcomed their arrival. As discussed, one of the very few exceptions are lawyers. Lawyers are not quite ready to take advice from AI in open court, and apparently not quite ready to permit anyone to do so, nor are they ready to let others in on the practice.

You can use AI-assisted writing, for example, to help create summaries. The debate is ongoing as to whether these assistants should replace portions of your writing responsibilities or whether their role should only be limited to one that provides a way to help guide your writing.

To get started on your own, visit one of the AI-assisted writing platforms I have discussed here. Prompt the assistant to tell you about a topic that you have had an interest in learning about. See where it takes you.

Whether you seek opportunities to interact with AI or not, you will undoubtedly interact with AI in future, and you probably already have. For example, many people are gathering more and more via online video. In order to make those gatherings more accessible, you will benefit from NLP that provides transcripts of those videos and also that makes those videos easier to find, as the transcriptions make those videos more discoverable via text-based online searches. As we grow more comfortable about talking to our technology, and as NLP continues to evolve, it is exciting to think about the yet-to-be developed and more sophisticated ways in which our technologies will be able to respond.

A weekend crash course

To fully master data science, it is important to understand both the theoretical and pragmatic sides of the field. This final chapter in Part Two gives you the opportunity to dig further into the pragmatic side of data science.

On the one hand, data science is a highly technical field that requires specialized knowledge which requires a deep understanding of the field's history, origins, culture and ethics. On the other hand, data science also involves understanding how data work to address specific, tangible and concrete problems. To provide value, data scientists need also to leverage data to provide actionable insights.

A helpful way to grow in your knowledge and confidence of data science is to work through a specific problem that calls for a solution that leverages one or more techniques from the data scientist's tool set. With the exception of Chapters 5 and 6, the earlier portions of this book discussed data science from a theoretical perspective. This chapter marks a transition from the theoretical to the pragmatic.

This chapter proposes that readers implement a sentiment analysis project. Readers should seriously consider writing, re-writing, working with, exploring, executing and examining the code in this chapter. One particularly useful way to learn more about data science is through the hands-on use of a key tool in the trade. This chapter will walk readers through the hands-on use of sentiment analysis tools. It will clarify what sentiment analysis is, how to execute two sentiment analyses, and then ultimately how to compare the results from each analysis.

To get the most out of this chapter, you will need access to a coding environment that allows you to write and execute Python code. You will also need an active connection to the internet. If you have not yet worked in a coding environment that allows you to write Python code, see the three appendices provided at the end of this book, which offer advice and instruction on how to access a Python environment and get started in writing computer code.

The examples shown here will use a popular coding environment that most readers can access for no cost, known as Google Colaboratory. Google Colaboratory is available to anyone with a Gmail account. Google also provides multiple examples and tutorials that can help you get started at: colab.research.google. com. To access this book's companion notebooks, which provide versions of the code from this book, visit github.com/ adamrossnelson/confident.

What is sentiment analysis?

Sentiment analysis allows you to quickly process large amounts of written or spoken data and extract meaningful insights related to the sentiment expressed in those texts. With this powerful tool, you can gain a better understanding of any large collection of text. The ability to analyse text from any target audience can help

you make data-driven decisions about product development, marketing campaigns, customer service strategies and more.

Relating this topic to previous chapters, it is helpful to mention that sentiment analysis is a supervised machine learning task. Sentiment analysis uses historic training data that have trained a model to recognize positive and negative sentiments. With the training, the model can evaluate new text that it has not yet evaluated and predict how a human might perceive the sentiment of that text. The target variable, in the case of sentiment analysis, is the sentiment score, while the predictor variables are the text passages.

Sentiment analysis is a family of techniques that falls within a larger family of techniques known as natural language processing (NLP). Natural language processing involves systematically dissecting language, from speech or writing, usually for analytical purposes.

A simple example of NLP would be to calculate a reading level or difficulty. Consider the first three sentences of Chapter 2, for example.

In this passage there are 54 words and three sentences, giving an average sentence length of 18 words. Nine words have three or more syllables, which have been underlined in Figure 8.1. Using the well-known Gunning Fog Index we can calculate a grade reading level for this passage. The Gunning Fog Index defines difficult words as those with three or more syllables. Then it adds the average sentence length to the proportion of difficult words. In this passage the proportion of difficult words is 16.66. Lastly, the Gunning Fog Index multiplies everything by .4. As shown in this figure, the level for the passage is about 13th (or almost 14th) grade. Calculating reading difficulty is one of many possible examples of natural language processing.

Sentiment analysis builds on natural language processing with more complex algorithms that can also detect and measure textual expressions of human emotion. Simply put, 'sentiment

FIGURE 8.1   A demonstration of the Gunning Fog Index readability calculations

The parable of the elephant and the blind is a useful starting point when looking over the field of data science. In this well-known parable that first appeared hundreds of years ago in early human literature, religion and philosophy, there is an elephant. Aside from the elephant there are several humans who cannot see.

Total words	54
Average sentence length	18
Total hard words	9
% hard words	16.66
Total sentences	3

$$\textbf{Fog Index} = 0.4 \left(\left(\frac{\text{words}}{\text{sentences}} \right) + 100 \left(\frac{\text{hard words}}{\text{words}} \right) \right)$$

$$= (0.4 \times (54/3)) + (100 \times (9/54))$$
$$= 0.4 \times (18 + 16.66)$$
$$= 13.864, \text{ i.e. 13th or 14th grade}$$

Source: Author's illustration

analysis' is a general term for a series of techniques and tools that leverage data science, and other sciences, to detect and measure textual expressions of human emotion.

The simplest detection algorithms only detect either positive or negative sentiment. Sentiment analysis can sometimes also make finer distinctions, including measuring the strength of the emotion.

The two most prominent methods of performing sentiment analysis are lexicon-based approaches and machine learning-based approaches. Both approaches have their advantages and limitations.

Lexicon-based approaches

Lexicon-based approaches take advantage of established diction-aries called 'lexicons' that include basic words and their associated sentiment. For example, a lexicon might contain the word 'love' and indicate that it is strongly positive. Later in this chapter, we will explore the results of a lexicon-based approach using Natural Language Toolkit's VADER sentiment analysis tools. The term VADER stands for Valence Aware Dictionary and Sentiment Reasoner.

The following code will show you specific examples.

```python
# Import the Pandas and the NLTK libraries
import pandas as pd
import nltk

# For the first run only (download the dictionary)
nltk.download('vadr_lexicon')

# Import SentimentIntensityAnalyzer
from nltk.sentiment.vader import SentimentIntensityAnalyzer

# Load VADER lexicon
vader_lexicon = SentimentIntensityAnalyzer().lexicon

# Specify a list of adjectives
adjectives = [
        'Adoringly', 'Brave', 'Creative', 'Daring',
        'Doomed', 'Energetic', 'Friendly',
        'Generous', 'Grin', 'Honest', 'Intelligent',
        'Joyful', 'Kind', 'Lost', 'Loyal',
        'Magnificent', 'Noble', 'Optimistic',
        'Playful', 'Questionable', 'Rebellious',
        'strong', 'Trick', 'Trustworthy', 'Unkind',
```

```
      'Verdict', 'Wreck', 'Worry',
      'Youthful', 'Zealot']

# Declare empty lists to be populated in the for loop
word_col = []
sent_col = []

# Use for loop to populate list
for word in adjectives:
    word_col.append(word)
    sent_col.append(vader_lexicon[word.lower()])

# Convert lists to Pandas DataFrame for display
pd.DataFrame({'Word 1':word_col[:10],
              'sentiment 1':sent_col[:10],
              'Word 2':word_col[10:20],
              'sentiment 2':sent_col[10:20],
              'Word 3':word_col[20:],
              'sentiment 3':sent_col[20:]})
```

This will produce the output shown in Figure 8.2, a variety of words along with their associated reference sentiment values. The NLTK VADER sentiment analysis tool uses these reference values to calculate the sentiment for passages of text.

This code example starts by importing the necessary libraries, including Pandas and NLTK. It then downloads the VADER lexicon using the `nltk.download()` function, and loads the VADER sentiment analyser using the `SentimentIntensityAnalyzer()` function.

The code then specifies a list of adjectives (`adjectives`) to be analysed, and declares two empty lists to store the words

FIGURE 8.2   Thirty words and their and sentiment pairings from NLTK's VADER sentiment analysis lexicon. Produced with the code shown here

	Word 1	Sentiment 1	Word 2	Sentiment 2	Word 3	Sentiment 3
0	Adoringly	2.4	Intelligent	2.0	Rebellious	-1.2
1	Brave	2.4	Joyful	2.9	Strong	2.3
2	Creative	1.9	Kind	2.4	Trick	-0.2
3	Daring	1.5	Lost	-1.3	Trustworthy	2.6
4	Doomed	-3.2	Loyal	2.1	Unkind	-1.6
5	Energetic	1.9	Magnificent	2.9	Verdict	0.6
6	Friendly	2.2	Noble	2.0	Wreck	-1.9
7	Generous	2.3	Optimistic	1.3	Worry	-1.9
8	Grin	2.1	Playful	1.9	Youthful	1.3
9	Honest	2.3	Questionable	-1.2	Zealot	-1.9

Source: Author's illustration

(word_col) and their associated sentiment scores (sent_col). It uses a for loop to loop through each adjective in the list, and for each adjective, the code obtains the word's associated sentiment score from the VADER lexicon using the vader_lexicon[word.lower()] syntax, where word is the current adjective in the loop. The sentiment score is then appended to the sent_col list, and the word is appended to the word_col list.

Finally, the code creates a Pandas DataFrame to display the words and their associated sentiment scores in a table format. The DataFrame has three major columns which shows each word and the associated sentiment. Each column contains 10 adjectives and their associated sentiment scores.

Machine learning-based approaches

Machine learning-based approaches often rely on neural networks, and other classification algorithms in order to analyse text and

identify which words or collection of words convey positive sentiments, negative sentiments or neutral sentiments. The machine learning-based approaches have at least two main advantages over lexicon-based approaches: machine learning allows data scientists to detect more complex patterns within textual expressions of emotions; and machine learning methods also more closely mimic human learning based on pre-labelled training data. Because, due in part to how machine learning can figuratively learn how to mimic human interpretations, it can often better cope with difficult to decipher emotional expressions such as irony or sarcasm.

An added advantage of machine learning-based sentiment analysis tools is that they can often detect emotion in text when pre-defined lexicons do not exist for the data at hand. Later in this chapter we will explore the results of a machine learning-based approach through the assistance of Google Cloud's NLP application program interface (API).

Sentiment analysis in action

Before looking at advanced tools that involve writing and executing computer code, we can explore the results of sentiment analysis with the online web interface located at cloud.google. com/natural-language. At this website you will find a section called 'Natural language API demo' with the words 'Try the API' located just above a text box, as shown here in Figure 8.3. In that text box, you can paste your own example text.

For this example, I will use text from the first ten lines of 'The Zen of Python'.[1]

Beautiful is better than ugly.
Explicit is better than implicit.
Simple is better than complex.
Complex is better than complicated.

Flat is better than nested.

Sparse is better than dense.

Readability counts.

Special cases aren't special enough to break the rules.

Although practicality beats purity.

Errors should never pass silently.

After pasting your chosen example text online you can then click the 'Analyze' button. If you used the same text I used, once you click on the 'Sentiment' tab you will see results similar to those shown here in Figure 8.3.

From this output we see that Google's sentiment analysis tool detected a nearly neutral sentiment coded yellow and scored at 0.1 for the entire document. Moving downward through the list

FIGURE 8.3   The output from Google's sentiment analysis tool when given the first 10 lines from 'The Zen of Python'

Entities	Sentiment	Syntax	Categories

Document and Sentence Level Sentiment

	Score	Magnitude
Entire Document	0.1	4
Beautiful is better than ugly.	0.6	0.6
Explicit is better than implicit.	-0.2	0.2
Simple is better than complex.	0.7	0.7
Complex is better than complicated.	0.1	0.1
Flat is better than nested.	0.4	0.4
Sparse is better than dense.	0	0
Readability counts.	0.4	0.4
Special cases aren't special enough to break the rules.	-0.6	0.6
Although practicality beats purity.	0.1	0.1
Errors should never pass silently.	-0.6	0.6

Source: Google's Natural Language AI

of sentences, the tool also returns a sentiment score for each sentence. The first, third, fifth and seventh sentences express positive sentiments while the second, fourth, sixth and ninth sentences express neutral sentiments. The eighth and tenth sentences express negative sentiments.

Google's tool returns a sentiment score between −1.0 and 1.0, which corresponds to the overall emotion (negative numbers indicate negative emotions, positive numbers indicate positive emotions). As inferred by the lower and upper bounds, this tool normalizes the sentiment score. The accompanying magnitude score will be a number between 0.0 and infinity. The magnitude score, which Google's tool does not normalize, indicates how strong the sentiment is. The length of the document can also influence the magnitude score, because the tool does not normalize the magnitude score.

Google's documentation provides a more technical guide for interpreting these scores. 'The score of a document's sentiment indicates the overall emotion of a document. The magnitude of a document's sentiment indicates how much emotional content is present within the document, and this value is often proportional to the length of the document'.[2]

A final note regarding sentiment analysis, before moving on to implement it using Google's API for Python and then later NLTK's model. The tools generally are good at identifying the general direction of a text's sentiment (positive or negative) but not the specific sentiment. For example, texts that express anger, sadness, depression or general disappointment would all likely classify as negative. But, many sentiment analysis tools are not capable of distinguishing the difference between anger, sadness, depression or disappointment.

Standard imports

The following examples assume you have executed the following standard imports in a Jupyter Notebook or Google Colaboratory

environment. In earlier chapters we saw examples of these standard imports. Here I provide some additional context.

In Python, a standard import is a statement commonly used throughout the community as best practice. The standard syntax is used and agreed upon by many as a matter of convention. The Python community widely uses standard imports. Many of the most common standard imports are generally understood by most Python programmers.

For example, in this code snippet the `import pandas as pd` statement is a standard import for the Pandas library. It imports the Pandas library and renames it to `pd`. The use of `pd` is somewhat arbitrary; we could have named it anything, except to rename Pandas as `pd` is the most widely used and recognized convention. Similarly, the `import numpy as np` statement is a standard import for the NumPy library. The longstanding convention is to import and rename NumPy as `np`.

```
# Import the Pandas NumPy and Seaborn libraries
import pandas as pd
import numpy as np
import seaborn as sns
```

In addition to importing Pandas as `pd` and NumPy as `np`, this code also follows the standard convention for importing Seaborn, which is to rename it as `sns`. Subsequent code can now reference these tools by their renamed shorthand.

Using Google Cloud's NLP API

In addition to the standard imports, you will also need to import Google Cloud's Natural Language API modules, which will allow us to make calls to Google's proprietary Machine Learning NLP model and make sense of its return values.

```
# Additionally import Google cloud libraries
from google.cloud import language_v1
from google.protobuf.json_format import MessageToDict
```

The `language_v1` module is the Google Cloud Language client, and we will use it to instantiate a connection with Google Cloud's NLP Machine Learning API. This client lets us send requests to Google for analysis.

And while we are at it, we also import the `MessageToDict` function from the `google.protobuf.json_format` module.

As you will see shortly, Google Cloud returns most of its API responses as a response object. So if we want to make the returned values more readable and useful, this `MessageToDict` function will be very helpful.

Following these required imports, let me show you how to analyse sentiment scores in a simple three-step process.

First, we instantiate the API client as an object we will call `client` by assigning `LanguageServiceClient.from_service_account_json()` from the `language_v1` module.

Have in mind that this method takes as argument the file path pointing to your Google cloud's `.json` credentials.[3]

Second, after instantiating the client, we also need to instantiate another object we will call `document`. The `Document()` method on the `language_v1` module which instantiates the `document`.

For the sake of this example, we will have Google Cloud's API analyse the sentiment score of only one sentence. That sentence will be 'I am happy to announce a promotion at work!' We will revisit this sentence with future tools. Starting with a single sentence will help in understanding a simple example of how the API works.

The `Document()` method takes two arguments, including the text we wish to analyse and a `type_` argument. In this chapter's examples, `type_` will always be `language_v1.Document.Type.PLAIN_TEXT`.

Third, we send the document to Google's API and then convert the response to a dictionary for review and evaluation.

A ONE-SENTENCE EXAMPLE

To send the document to Google Cloud's NLP API we use the analyze_sentiment() method on the client object. By assigning the result of the client's analyse sentiment method we can then review the results. In the code below we assigned the API's response to an object called a_sentiment.

```
# Specify a services.json location (also referenced in
subsequent code blocks)
sl = '../services/services.json'

# Instantiate a google Cloud client
client = language_v1.LanguageServiceClient.from_service_account_json(sl)

# Save text to a variable
my_text = 'I am happy to announce a promotion at work!'

# Create a Google Cloud document from the text
document = language_v1.Document(
    content=my_text,
    type_=language_v1.Document.Type.PLAIN_TEXT)

# Send the document to Google's API
a_sentiment = client.analyze_sentiment(
    document=document)
```

Overall, this is only four lines of code. As discussed above, the response object a_sentiment consists of a response class. The document object is a Google Cloud document. We can inspect the object type names with assist from type().

```
# Further inspect results with the type() function
print(f'The type of document is {type(document)}')

print(
    f'The type of the a_sentiment is {type(
        a_sentiment)}'))
```

To see the information from Google Cloud's analysis we use the MessageToDict() function discussed above.

```
# Save and then display the results of the API call
result_dict = MessageToDict(
    a_sentiment.__class__.pb(a_sentiment))

# Evaluate the results for display
result_dict
```

For the result:

```
{'documentSentiment': {'magnitude': 0.9, 'score': 0.9},
 'language': 'en',
 'sentences': [{'text': {'content': 'I am happy to
announce a promotion at work!',
    'beginOffset': -1},
    'sentiment': {'magnitude': 0.9, 'score': 0.9}}]}
```

From the above output we see that the overall sentiment score of this text is 0.9 (very high or positive) while the magnitude score is 0.9. To see this a bit more clearly we can use the following code.

```
# print document's sentiment score.
print(
    'Doc Sentiment : {}'.format(
        result dict['documentSentiment'] ['score']))
# print document's sentiment magnitude score.
print(
    'Doc Magnitude : {}'.format(
        result_dict['documentSentiment'] ['magnitude']))
```

For the result:

```
Doc Sentiment : 0.9
Doc Magnitude : 0.9
```

If you have followed along you have successfully made calls to the Google Cloud API, analysed the sentiment score of the sentence we provided, and transformed the output to a Python dictionary with easy-to-read key-value pairs.

According to Google Cloud's documentation, the sentiment score represents the underlying emotion of the text, which can be negative, positive or neutral. Sentiment score values can range from −1 to 1. The closer it is to −1, the more negative most readers would perceive the sentence to be. On the other hand, the closer the sentiment score is to 1, the more positive most readers would view the sentiment to be. Of course, language is subjective, and reasonable readers may disagree. These results are how the Google Cloud NLP API predicts most readers will perceive the text. When sentiment scores land around zero, this means the text is neutral.

As you can see in the example above, Google Cloud's NLP API seems to be delivering a prediction many would regard as

accurate. There is an overall score of 0.9, meaning that the text is extremely positive (which is exactly what we would expect of someone announcing a work promotion).

SENTENCE-LEVEL EXAMPLES

To extend the power of this code and this tool we can use it to compare scores from multiple sentences and paragraphs. We are only a few loops and a simple function away from accomplishing this more sophisticated cross-comparison objective.

The code below builds upon the single-sentence example code above. This extended code declares a function that sends multiple sentences to Google Cloud API, compiles, and then returns their sentiment scores.

This function will take as argument a Pandas Series with text strings in each of its items. The function will then return a DataFrame with sentiment and magnitude scores from each sentence. Subsequent code below will look at how to aggregate the sentiment and magnitude scores to one per Pandas Series item.

```
def googleapi_sentence_scores(series: pd.Series) -> pd.DataFrame:
    """Returns sentiment scores of all sentences of
    a given Pandas Series that contains text using
    the Google Cloud API.

    Takes the text data contained within a provided
    Pandas Series and returns a DataFrame reporting
    sentiment scores for each sentence in the
    original Series. The DataFrame will have an
    index that matches the Series index.

    Parameters
    ----------
    series : pd.Series
```

```
    Pandas Series containing text data to be
    analyzed by the Google Cloud API.

Returns
----------
scores_df : pd.DataFrame
    DataFrame reporting each sentence's
    resulting sentiment scores.
"""

# Instantiate Google Cloud API's client
client = language_v1.LanguageServiceClient.from_service_account_json(s1)

# Define lists to contain sentence sentiments.
index = []
sentences = []
sentiments = []
magnitudes = []

# Loop through each Series item; have Google
# Cloud API analyze sentiment scores
for i in series.index:

    # Take the next item in the Pandas Series
    my_text = series.loc[i]
    # Create a Google Cloud document from text
    document = language_v1.Document(
        content=my_text,
        type_=language_v1.Document.Type.PLAIN_TEXT)
    # Send document to Google's API
    a_sentiment = client.analyze_sentiment(
        document=document)
    # Save API results as a Python dictionary
```

```
a_sentiment_dict = MessageToDict(
    a_sentiment.__class__.pb(a_sentiment))

# Extract each sentence score; append lists
try:
    # Iterate through each sentence
    for s in a_sentiment_dict['sentences']:

        # Append the sentiments list
        sentiments.append(
            s['sentiment']['score'])
        # Append the magnitude list
        magnitudes.append(
            s['sentiment']['magnitude'])
        # Append the original sentence
        sentences.append(
            s['text']['content'])
        # Append index list
        index.append(i)

    # When there is an error, skip that entry.
    except:
        pass
# Compile results of entire analysis in df
scores_df = pd.DataFrame(
    {'index':index,
     'sentence':sentences,
     'sentiment':sentiments,
     'Magnitude':magnitudes}
).set_index('index')

# Return the resulting DataFrame
return scores_df
```

And now that we have defined the function that can return sentiment scores for multiple sentences, let's try it out:

```
# Store sentiment analysis results in new df
txt=['I was not a fan of The Hobbit. This is not a fav.',
    'What were you thinking? That is a bad idea.']

# Put results of sentiment analysis in new df
df = google_api_sentence_scores(pd.Series(txt))

# Display the result
df
```

For the result:

```
                        Sentence  Sentiment  Magnitude
index
0 I was not a fan of The Hobbit.      -0.8        0.8
0               This is not a fav.    -0.8        0.8
1           What were you thinking?   -0.4        0.4
1              That is a bad idea.    -0.9        0.9
```

As you can see from the results above, both documents scored low sentiment scores. In three of the four sentences the sentiment score was –.08 or lower. Google Cloud's NLP API predicts that these sentences express negative emotions.

DOCUMENT LEVEL EXAMPLES

If you want to aggregate the scores for each one of the entries, you can easily group them by their index:

```
# Aggregate and group the scores by index for doc level results
df.groupby(by='index').mean()
```

For the result:

```
        Sentiment  Magnitude
index
0         -0.80      0.80
1         -0.65      0.65
```

A potential problem with this particular approach is that we lose the context provided by the text. There is a trade-off here. By aggregating the scores there is less granularity but it is easier to review and compare each document as a whole. A better approach may be to collect sentiment scores for the entire document, which we can do with a simplified version of the function from above.

The Google NLP API can analyse and return scores for an entire document. The following code follows this document-level approach. Instead of returning sentiment scores sentence by sentence this new function returns sentiment scores for entire documents where each document is a single entry in the Pandas Series.

```
def google_api_document_scores(series: pd.Series) -> pd.DataFrame:
    """Returns sentiment scores of a given text using
    Google Cloud API.

    Takes the text data contained within the provided
    Pandas Series and returns a DataFrame reporting
    sentiment scores for each item in the original
    Series. The DataFrame will have an index that
    matches the Series index.

    Parameters
    ----------
    series : pd.Series
        Pandas Series containing text data to be
        analyzed by the Google Cloud API.

    Returns
    ----------
    doc_scores_df : pd.DataFrame
        DataFrame reporting each document's resulting
        sentiment scores.
    """

    # Instantiate Google Cloud API's client
    client = language_v1.LanguageServiceClient.from_service_account_json(sl)

    # Define lists to contain sentence sentiments.
    index = []
    documents = []
    doc_sentiment_scores = []
    doc_magnitude_scores = []

    # Loop through each Series item; have Google
    # Cloud API analyze sentiment scores
    for i in series.index:
```

```
# Take the next item in the Pandas Series
my_text = series.loc[i]
# Create a Google Cloud document from text
document = language_v1.Document(
    content=my_text,
    type_=language_v1.Document.Type.PLAIN_TEXT)
# Send the document to Google's API
a_doc_sentiment = client.analyze_sentiment(
    document=document).document_sentiment

# Extract sentiment & magnitude for each doc
doc_magnitude = a_doc_sentiment.magnitude
doc_score = a_doc_sentiment.score

# Append original text, scores to each list
documents.append(my_text)
# Append the sentiment scores
doc_sentiment_scores.append(doc_score)
# Append the magnitude scores
doc_magnitude_scores.append(doc_magnitude)
# Append the index list
index.append(i)

# Compile results of entire analysis in df
doc_scores_df = pd.DataFrame(
    {'index':index,
     'Documents':documents,
     'Sentiment':doc_sentiment_scores,
     'Magnitude':doc_magnitude_scores}
).set_index('index')

# Return the resulting DataFrame
return doc_scores_df
```

And now that we have defined the function, let's have the API analyse the same documents and compare the results of both approaches.

```
# Store sentiment analysis results in new df

txt=['I was not a fan of The Hobbit. This is not a fav.',
    'What were you thinking? That is a bad idea.']

# Put results of sentiment analysis in new df
df = google_api_sentence_scores(pd.Series(txt))

# Display the result
df
```

For the result:

	Documents	Sentiment	Magnitude
index			
0	I was not a fan of The Hobbit. This is not a fav.	-0.8	1.7
1	What were you thinking? That is a bad idea.	-0.7	1.4

This second approach returned similar sentiment scores but much higher magnitude scores.

BUILDING YOUR OWN LIBRARIES   Exploring a best practice

The presentation of multiple lengthy functions in this chapter presents an opportunity to discuss, as an aside, the topic of user-defined libraries. Python is a versatile and powerful

programming language that has become a popular choice for data science and machine learning applications. One of the key reasons for this popularity of Python is its flexibility and extensibility, which allows users to define their own libraries and modules to suit their specific needs. Many programming languages permit the creation of user-defined libraries.

A user-defined Python library is a collection of reusable code written by a user to perform a specific set of tasks or functions across multiple projects. Once created as a library of its own, the code in these libraries can be imported and used by multiple Python programs. The import for a user-defined library works in much the same way as any other standard package import works. When users create their own libraries it saves time and effort by re-using code rather than having to write everything from scratch – or having to copy and paste code from one project to another, which is prone to error and over time is a practice that becomes exceedingly difficult to maintain.

Another advantage of user-defined Python libraries is their ease of use and accessibility. Python is an open source language, which means that users can access a wide range of libraries and modules created by other users and developers. This makes it easy to find and use existing code for common tasks such as data cleaning, analysis and visualization. As such, you can share your libraries with others who may be interested in using your good work.

Users should consider adding user-defined Python libraries to their programming and data science practice for several reasons. First, user-defined libraries can help to save time and effort by re-using code across multiple projects. This can be especially useful for large or complex projects that require a lot of code.

Second, user-defined Python libraries can improve the efficiency and quality of Python programs by allowing users to define new data structures. Preparing and using specialized data structures can help improve performance and reduce errors, while

also providing greater flexibility and control over program behaviour.

Finally, user-defined Python libraries promote collaboration and knowledge sharing. By creating and sharing your own libraries and modules, you can contribute to the development of the wider Python ecosystem, while also benefitting from the contributions of others.

Using Natural Language Toolkit

As discussed above, VADER stands for Valence Aware Dictionary and Sentiment Reasoner and, unlike the machine learning-based approach employed by Google's Cloud-based API, VADER is a lexicon-based approach. Lexicon-based sentiment analysis relies on a set of pre-defined terms and scores to measure the sentiment of a given phrase. VADER consists of lexicons that include sentiment weighted words, emojis, ascii-text art, along with basic rules for handling negations, punctuation, capitalization and other elements of text analysis. Above in Figure 8.2 I showed a collection of 30 words and their associated sentiments.

VADER has been especially useful for social media analysis due to its accuracy in detecting sentiment in short phrases or messages. Additionally, it can detect sentiment towards specific topics as well as 'mixed' sentiments, which occur when two or more sentiments are expressed within the same utterance. After demonstrating the code associated with implementing a VADER analysis using Natural Language Toolkit (NLTK) below, I elaborate on these capabilities.

In addition to the standard imports discussed above, the NLTK examples shown here also require the following additional imports.

```
# Import SentimentIntensityAnalyzer
from nltk.sentiment.vader import
SentimentIntensityAnalyzer

# Import NLTK's sentence tokenizer
from nltk.tokenize import sent_tokenize
```

If you have not yet worked with the nltk.sentiment.vader and its SentimentIntensityAnalyzer you will also need to add to your computing environment the vader_lexicon with the following one-time code executions.

```
# Import the Natrual Language Toolkit Library
import nltk

# for first run only (download dictionary)
nltk.download('vader_lexicon')
```

SHORT EXAMPLES

An advantage of using NLTK's out-of-the-box Sentiment-IntensityAnalyzer from nltk.sentiment.vader is that it, like Google's tool above, does not require data cleaning. This tool requires only a few lines of code, for example:

```
# Instantiate the sentiment analyzer
sid = SentimentIntensityAnalyzer()

# Execute sentiment analysis with sentiment analyzer

sid.polarity_scores(
    'I am happy to announce a promotion at work!')
```

Which will produce the following output.

```
{'neg': 0.0, 'neu': 0.619, 'pos': 0.381, 'compound':
0.6114}
```

We can interpret this output as follows. The neg score indicates 0.0, meaning there is no negative sentiment. The neutral score shows 0.619 and the positive score indicates 0.381. From this output, read as a whole, we understand the input 'I am happy to announce a promotion at work!' as expressing a positive sentiment.

When looking for a summary of the output, we can turn to the compound score. The compound score, which will range from –1 to 1, interprets as a summary, of sorts, for the other output. The compound score will be negative when the overall sentiment is negative and positive when the overall sentiment is positive.

Seeing both a negative and a positive score further shows why the VADER approach to sentiment analysis is capable of identifying passages that express both positive and negative sentiments. In such cases we would view both high negative and positive scores. The following example shows mixed sentiment.

```
# Sentiment analysis with sentiment analyzer
sid.polarity_scores(
    '''I am happy to announce a promotion at work!
    This makes be very happy because I hated my
    former tasks. The past few years were tough
    and I was sad or depressed all the time I do
    not like to complain much because I am happy
```

```
to have any job. I know what it is like to be
unemployed and it is also not fun. Next
year I anticipate growing and loving my new
work!''')
```

Which produces the following result:

```
{'neg': 0.214, 'neu': 0.583, 'pos': 0.203, 'compound':
0.2751}
```

Another strength of VADER is that it can ascertain sentiment scores for emojis and it is sensitive to punctuation. Consider the following code, which is the same as an earlier example above but omits the exclamation point and consequently produces lower positive scores.

```
# Sentiment analysis with sentiment analyzer
sid.polarity_scores(
    'I am happy to announce a promotion at work.')
```

For the results:

```
{'neg': 0.0, 'neu': 0.619, 'pos': 0.381, 'compound':
0.5719}
```

SENTENCE-LEVEL EXAMPLES

Just as we saw sentence-level examples from Google's API above we can conduct an equivalent analysis using NLTK. To do this we will define a function that submits each sentence to NLTK's sentiment intensity analyser then stores and ultimately returns the combined results as a Pandas DataFrame.

```python
# Name the function sentence_scores
def sentence_scores(series: pd.Series) -> pd.DataFrame:
    '''Returns sentiment scores of a given text using
    NLTK's VADER sentiment analysis tools.

    Takes a Pandas Series that contains text data.
    Returns a Pandas DataFrame that reports sentiment
    scores for each sentence in the original Series. The
    DataFrame will have an index that matches the Series
    index.

    Parameters
    ----------
    Series : pd.Series
        Pandas Series containing text data to be
        analyzed using NLTK's VADER sentiment analysis
        tools.

    Returns
    ----------
    doc_scores_df : pd.DataFrame
        DataFrame reporting each document's resulting
        sentiment scores.
    '''
```

```
# Define empty lists to contain results.
index = []
sentences = []
neg_scores = []
neu_scores = []
pos_scores = []
compounds = []

# Instantiate the VADER analyzer.
sid = SentimentIntensityAnalyzer()

# Loop through each item in the Series.
for i in series.index:

    # Loop through each sentence in the Series item.
    for s in sent_tokenize(series.loc[i]):

        # Extract sentence scores; append lists
        try:

            # Get sentiment scores from NLTK
            scores = sid.polarity_scores(s)
            # Append the index list
            index.append(i)
            # Append the original text
            sentences.append(s)
            # Append the negative scores list
            neg_scores.append(scores['neg'])
            # Append the neutral scores list
            neu_scores.append(scores['neu'])
            # Append the positive scores list
```

```
        pos_scores.append(scores['pos'])
        # Append the positive scores list
        compounds.append(scores['compound'])

    # When there is an error, skip that entry.
    except:
        pass

# Compile & return Pandas DataFrame
return(pd.DataFrame({'index':index,
                     'Sentence':sentences,
                     'Negative':neg_scores,
                     'Neutral':neu_scores,
                     'Positive':pos_scores,
                     'Compound':compounds}
                    ).set_index('index'))
```

After defining this function, you can test it with the following
code.

```
# Store sentiment analysis results in new df
txt=['I was not a fan of The Hobbit. This is not a fav.',
     'What were you thinking? That is a bad idea.']

# Put results of sentiment analysis in new df
df = google_api_sentence_scores(pd.Series(txt))

# Display the result
df
```

Which will return the following:

index	Sentence	Negative	Neutral	Positive	Compound
0	I was not a fan of The Hobbit.	0.282	0.718	0.0	-0.2411
0	This is not a fav.	0.453	0.547	0.0	-0.3570
1	What were you thinking?	0.000	1.000	0.0	0.0000
1	That is a bad idea.	0.538	0.462	0.0	-0.5423

The output here roughly matches the output for the same sentences when we had previously used Google's API. All these four sentences have 0.0 positive sentiment and all but one has greater than 0.282 negative sentiment. Likewise, all but one of these sentences have compound score below zero.

DOCUMENT-LEVEL EXAMPLES

To aggregate the scores, one for each entry in the Pandas Series, use the `pd.groupby()` method.

```
# Aggregate and group the scores by the index for
document level results
df.groupby(by='index').mean()
```

For the results:

```
         Negative  Neutral  Positive  Compound
index
0          0.3675   0.6325       0.0   -0.29905
1          0.2690   0.7310       0.0   -0.27115
```

As you may have anticipated, both entries appear mostly negative in sentiment. The Negative score aggregates as 0.3675 and 0.2690 for both passages while the overall Compound score aggregates as –0.29905 and –0.27115.

As before, another approach is to compile scores for each sentence, instead of for each sentence within each sentence. The following function uses one less nested loop which returns a set of scores for each item in the Pandas Series instead of a set of scores for each sentence within each item in the Pandas Series.

```
# Name the function post_scores
def post_scores(series: pd.Series) -> pd.DataFrame:
    '''Returns sentiment scores of a given text using
    NLTK's VADER sentiment analysis tools.

    Takes a Pandas Series that contains text data.
    Returns a Pandas DataFrame that reports sentiment
    scores for item within the Pandas Seires. The
    DataFrame will have an index that matches the
    Series index.
```

```
Parameters
----------

Series : pd.Series
    Pandas Series containing text data to be
    analyzed using NLTK's VADER sentiment analysis
    tools.

Returns
----------

doc_scores_df : pd.DataFrame
    DataFrame reporting each document's resulting
    sentiment scores.
'''

# Define empty lists to contain each result.
index = []
posts = []
neg_scores = []
neu_scores = []
pos_scores = []
compounds = []

# Instantiate the analyzer.
sid = SentimentIntensityAnalyzer()

# Loop through each item in the Series.
for i in series.index:

    # Extract sentence scores; append lists.
    try:
        # Get sentiment scores from NLTK
        scores = sid.polarity_scores(
            series.loc[i])
        # Append the index list
```

```
            index.append(i)
            # Append the original text
            posts.append(
                series.loc[i])
            # Append the negative scores list
            neg_scores.append(
                scores['neg'])
            # Append the neutral scores list
            neu_scores.append(
                scores['neu'])
            # Append the positive scores list
            pos_scores.append(
                scores['pos'])
            # Append the positive scores list
            compounds.append(
                scores['compound'])

        # When there is an error, skip that entry.
        except:
            pass

    # Compile & return Pandas DataFrame
    return(pd.DataFrame({
        'index':index,
        'sentence':posts,
        'Negative':neg_scores,
        'Neutral':neu_scores,
        'Positive':pos_scores,
        'Compound':compounds}
    ).set_index('index'))
```

To test this function, we can use the same passages from above.

```
# Store sentiment analysis results in new df
txt=['I was not a fan of The Hobbit. This is not a fav.',
    'What were you thinking? That is a bad idea.']
# Put results of sentiment analysis in new df
df = google_api_sentence_scores(pd.Series(txt))

# Display the result
df
```

Instead of returning a DataFrame with one record per sentence, there is one record for each item in the original Pandas Series. Here I show the results with an abbreviated sentence column.

index	Sentence	Negative	Neutral	Positive	Compound
0	I was not a fan of T...	0.357	0.643	0.0	-0.5334
1	What were you thinki...	0.333	0.667	0.0	-0.5423

Again, as we saw before, the entries appear mostly negative in sentiment. The Negative scores are 0.357 and 0.333 for both passages while the overall Compound scores are –0.5334 and –0.5423.

Comparing the results

The purpose of comparing results from Google Cloud's NLP API and NLTK is to see if they agree. There are a variety of contexts in which it would be valuable to compare the results across multiple models. In this context we can take Google's results and NLTK's results with a high level of confidence because both tools are well know, well document and well used. Given the strong show of support among multiple users of these tools, we are not concerned that they may be deficient.

However, it is possible that they may have slight differences in how they interpret text. Related, you may be working with model results that are less well known where it would be valuable to cross-compare in order to better test the results from the other less well-known models. You can use this example to study how you can use Pandas to compare the results across multiple models. For example, a data science practitioner (along with their team) may be in the process of creating a new predictive model. The general workflow demonstrated here in this subsection will be similar to the general workflow you would also use to compare the new predictive model's results with other previously known-to-be-successful model results.

We will first prepare a side-by-side look at the results from each tool and then we will also perform a correlation analysis to more precisely measure to what extent they agree.

The first task will be to find or create a set of data to use as a reference point. To support this subsection's demonstration I first took versions of sentences we used above. Then I asked a chat-based writing assistant known as Jasper to 'write short sentences expressing negative sentiment' and also to 'write short sentences expressing a positive sentiment'. The following code places this reference data in a Pandas Series.

```
# Data to cross-compare between Google and NLTK
text_data = pd.Series(
 ['I am happy to announce a promotion at work!',
  'I am happy to announce a promotion at work.',
  'I was not a fan of The Hobbit. This is not a fav.',
  'What were you thinking? That is a bad idea.',
  'My gift for you: @>-->---',
  'The Confident Series is a must read you will love it.',
  'Video games can sometimes destroy productivity.',
  'VADER sentiment analysis is extremely effect.ve',
  'Google also has a sentiment analysis API.',
  'Nothing ever works out for me.',
  'I never get a break.',
  'We always mess things up.',
  'Nothing good ever comes my way.',
  'You are so unlucky.',
  'No one understands me.',
  'Everything is going wrong today.',
  'It just is not fair!',
  'I can accomplish anything!',
  'Data Science is your destiny',
  'Nothing can stop me if I put my mind to it.',
  'I am grateful for everything that comes my way.',
  'I am killing it in the Data Science classes right now.'
 ])
```

The next task will be to use the functions we defined and discussed earlier in this chapter to retrieve sentiment analysis results. After retrieving the results we append _nltk and _ggl to the columns in results DataFrames.

```
# Retrieve sentiment score results from NLTK
results_nltk = post_scores(text_data)

# Retrieve sentiment score results from Google API
results_google = google_api_document_scores(text_data)

# Append '_nltk' to the columns in the NLTK results
results_nltk = results_nltk.add_suffix('_nltk')

# Append '_ggl' to the columns in the Google results
results_google = results_google.add_suffix('_ggl')
```

The code below then also concatenates the results in a new Pandas DataFrame we call combined. To the combined Data-Frame we add a column that tells us whether the NLTK results agreed with the Google results. And lastly we display the results.

```
# Concatenate results from both NLTK and Google
combined = pd.concat([
    results_nltk,
    results_google[['sentiment_ggl',
                    'Magnitude_ggl']]],
    axis=1)

# Create a column that flags if NLTK and Google agreed
combined['Agree'] = (combined['Compound_nltk'] >= 0) == \
                    (combined['sentiment_ggl'] >= 0)

# Display the results
# Focus on NLTK's compund, & Google's Sentiment
combined[['Sentence_nltk', 'Compound_nltk',
          'Sentiment_ggl','Agree']]
```

Which produces the following output (where I have again abbreviated the original sentence for better display on the page):

index	Sent	Compound_ nltk	Sentiment_ ggl	Agree
0	I am happy to a...	0.6114	0.9	True
1	I am happy to a...	0.5719	0.9	True
2	I was not a fan...	-0.5334	-0.8	True
3	What were you t...	-0.5423	-0.7	True
4	My gift for you...	0.7184	0.3	True
5	The Confident S...	0.8126	0.9	True
6	Video games can...	-0.5423	-0.7	True
7	VADER sentiment...	0.0000	0.0	True
8	Google also has...	0.0000	0.2	True
9	Nothing ever wo...	0.0000	-0.6	False
10	I never get a b...	0.0000	0.6	True
11	We always mess...	-0.3612	-0.4	True
12	Nothing good ev...	-0.3412	-0.6	True
13	You are so unlu...	0.0000	-0.9	False
14	No one understa...	-0.2960	-0.7	True
15	Everything is g...	-0.4767	-0.9	True
16	It just is not...	-0.3080	-0.8	True
17	I can accomplis...	0.4753	0.9	True
18	Data Science is...	0.0000	0.0	True
19	Nothing can sto...	0.2235	0.8	True
20	I am grateful f...	0.4588	0.9	True
21	I am killing it...	-0.6597	-0.2	True

From this output we can see that NLTK and Google disagree on the general sentiment for two of these 22 observations. For observation number 9, which reads 'Nothing works out for me' NLTK assigned a compound score of 0.0 (effectively neutral) while Google assigned a sentiment score of -0.6 (effectively negative). For observation number 13 which reads 'You are so unlucky', NLTK assigned a compound score of 0.0 (effectively neutral) while Google assigned a sentiment score of –0.9 (effectively negative).

There are at least two more ways to compare these results. The first is to produce a correlation matrix with the following code. This .corr() method quickly creates a correlation matrix that displays the correlation coefficients shared by each combination of all numerical columns in the DataFrame.

```
# A correlation matrix to compare NLTK & Google
combined.corr()
```

Which produces the output shown here in Figure 8.4.

According to the correlation matrix the compound sentiment score from NLTK and the sentiment score from Google are positively correlated, and strongly so. We see a correlation coefficient of 0.8295. You can find this statistic by reading the row called Compound_nltk (the middle row on the table) and then following over to the column headed Sentiment_ggl where you will find 0.8295. From this result we can conclude that there is a high level of agreement between the two tools.

A final way to inspect this correlation is with a scatter plot. Using Seaborn, as shown, below we can also see visually that there seems to be agreement between the two tools.

FIGURE 8.4   A correlation matrix of the sentiment scores from NLTK and Google's NLP API. Produced with the code shown here

	Negative_nltk	Neutral_nltk	Positive_nltk	Compound_nltk	Sentiment_ggl	Magnitude_ggl	Agree
Negative_nltk	1.000000	-0.360246	-0.513841	-0.816384	-0.734155	0.254446	0.260561
Neutral_nltk	-0.360246	1.000000	-0.615176	-0.176244	-0.115210	-0.344910	-0.453893
Positive_nltk	-0.513841	-0.615176	1.000000	0.852034	0.726410	0.102150	0.197205
Compound_nltk	-0.816384	-0.176244	0.852034	1.000000	0.829533	-0.062950	-0.006123
Sentiment_ggl	-0.734155	-0.115210	0.726410	0.829533	1.000000	-0.114057	0.325615
Magnitude_ggl	0.254446	-0.344910	0.102150	-0.062950	-0.114057	1.000000	-0.042942
Agree	0.260561	-0.453893	0.197205	-0.006123	0.325615	-0.042942	1.000000

```
# Set the Seaborn context to talk formatting
sns.set_context('talk')

# Use Seaborn to produce a scatterplot
sns.scatterplot(data=combined,
                y='Compound_nltk',
                x='Sentiment_ggl')
```

Which produces the image shown in Figure 8.5.

The scatter plot strategy places a single dot on the visual for each of the sentences we submitted to the sentiment analysers. The dots appear at the place where the Compound_nltk and the Sentiment_ggl scores intersect. A scatter plot confirms there is a relationship between two variables, or in this case an agreement between the scores from NLTK scores and the scores from Google, when the dots seem to show a general trend.

FIGURE 8.5   A scatter plot that compares the compound NLTK sentiment sore with Google's sentiment score. Produced with the code shown here

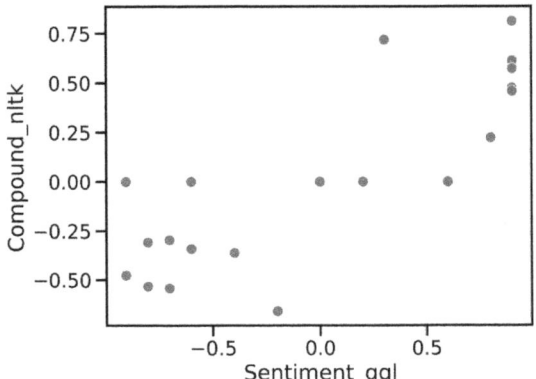

Conclusion

An important learning objective associated with this chapter was to provide for readers a renewed or expanded ability to write code in Python that will execute sentiment analysis and then compare the results across multiple platforms.

If you followed along with this chapter's proposed course of action and wrote, re-wrote, worked with, explored, executed and examined the code then you will have had a first-hand opportunity to learn more about data science through sentiment analysis. The chapter walked readers through what sentiment analysis is, how to execute sentiment analyses in two different tools, and then ultimately how to compare the results from each analysis. From the analysis we conducted in this chapter the primary conclusion seems to be that these two tools agree on sentiment most of the time, but not always. This type of comparison can also be used when developing new predictive models or assessing existing models. Reviewing the results of new models and also monitoring the performance of existing models is an important part of the field. The ability to perform these comparisons allows practitioners to make data-driven decisions about the accuracy and reliability of their work.

Before moving deeper into the finer points of sentiment analysis, this chapter also demystified sentiment analysis and the analytical family to which it belongs, known as natural language processing. In short, NLP is are methods that seek to systematically examine unstructured human communications.

Sentiment analysis is a powerful tool for gaining insights into large collections of text. With its ability to quickly process vast amounts of text, it has become an asset for those looking to gain valuable insights from text data such as customer feedback, market research and other similar sources. The next time you are faced with quickly examining large amounts of text, consider the power that sentiment analysis delivers.

In your business or organization you might, for example, find sentiment analysis helpful in managing a large caseload of customer services requests. Sentiment analysis could help you predict which requests for support may require a response ahead of others, meaning those with a strongly negative sentiment might need review sooner than those with a more moderate sentiment. If you or your organization provide a product or a service to a large group of customers or clients, and you regularly collect feedback, sentiment analysis might also help you identify which portions of that feedback need review for opportunities to improve the product or service. Conversely, by looking for feedback with positive sentiments you will potentially be well positioned to more quickly identify customer success stories.

Getting value

Part Three focuses on exploring how data science can deliver value to those who employ its techniques and strategies. This section also revisits the data science process outlined in Chapter 4. This aim is to demonstrate how the process of specifying and then solving an analytical question or business problem returns value.

Thus far, this book has referenced multiple analytical tools, including Google Sheets, Excel, Python and others. We also reviewed Google Cloud's NLP API, which assisted us in executing sentiment analysis. Within Excel we had a close look at its automated exploratory data analysis tool known as 'Analyze Data' that was formerly know as 'Ideas'.

Within the Python ecosystem, this book has also referenced Pandas (for data manipulations), Seaborn (for data visualization), NLTK (for natural language processing), YData Profiling (recently renamed from Pandas Profiling) (for automated exploratory data analysis) and others. Also, as is common for books in

this genre, the earlier chapters introduced readers to a series of companion Jupyter Notebooks. Chapters, 9, 10 and 11 continue with that practice and there are companion notebooks available at github.com/adamrossnelson/confident.

Within Part Three the book also provides a further, deeper overview of the tools previously referenced in earlier chapters. For example, a common problem experienced by those looking to grow or expand their knowledge of data science, machine learning, artificial intelligence or advanced analytics is the ability to find example data (real, fictional or otherwise) for training, education, testing or demonstration purposes. By framing data as a tool in and of itself, Chapter 9 at least partially addresses that problem by providing a review of data sources that are widely and freely available.

Additionally, this section introduces a newly created data set specifically compiled for this book. You may build on the examples herein by accessing the data for yourself. Part Three's learning objectives are:

OBJECTIVES

- To learn more, mostly through hands-on experience, about the range of tools and techniques data scientists use in our work.
- To explore multiple data sets.
- To understand how data visualization is itself an analytical too.
- To learn how two predictive algorithms known as k-nearest neighbors and ordinary least squares regression, work as tools to predict specific outcomes.
- To identify which data visualization can reveal which manner of insights, given the available data.
- To proceed through the eight-stage data science process outlined in Chapter 4.
- To implement both classification and regression analysis in Python.
- To evaluate the results of a classification or regression analysis.

Data

Of the many tools in data science, data are by the nature of the field one of the most valuable. It is not common to think about data as a tool. This chapter presents data as a tool and also presents a systematic discussion of that tool. Even if your initial reaction might be 'I already know what data are', this chapter also provides a story from my own experiences that I hope will convince you that it is important to better understand this tool we call data.

Finding the balance between jargon (which is often imprecise but catchy) and specific technical terms (which are dense, snoozy, but precise) is difficult. And there can be tough consequences for making the wrong decision for the wrong context.

For example, many years ago a colleague asked me when our company would start using data science. I was taken aback because we had already been employing data science. This question came within days of a presentation on logistic regression (a predictive algorithm commonly used in the field of data science) and some of our results on the organization's most important

projects. As I processed the experience I grew sullen. My colleague did not understand that we were using data science. Something was wrong. I had devoted my career to this work. I started it years earlier during my Ph.D. programme and continued the work at subsequent employers. And it felt like a significant failure that the work was so deeply misunderstood.

My colleagues were not aware that we were actively already using data science. As the organization's only data scientist on staff at the time, I realized that most of this was my fault. I had avoided using buzzwords (machine learning, artificial intelligence and predictive modelling) and instead used specific language (logistic regression) to describe our work. I thought the specific words would help others better understand and better appreciate the work we were doing and how we were doing it.

There are two solutions to the dilemma. First, meet your audience where they are. You can do this by using words they expect, which sometimes means using jargon. Second, educate your audiences. You can do this by learning with and from them. A thoughtful and compassionate application of both strategies will be best for most.

This chapter looks closely at specific types of data. As such, it leans in favour of the second solution: educating audiences by learning with and from them. By pursuing this joint learning goal, you will enhance your organization's data culture by building awareness around these specific technical terms and phrases.

In this chapter I will introduce the concept of a data typology and explain why it is important for data analysis. Having a shared understanding of this typology can improve your ability to communicate about data and data science. For example, many of the methods and techniques we employ in data science only work with specific types of data. Because some methods require a specific data type, this chapter will also cover how to convert between different data types.

In addition to an overview of data types, this chapter will also provide an overview of widely available online data sets that can

be used for practice, demonstration, education and training purposes. We will also introduce a social media data set created specifically for this book, which will serve as a useful resource throughout the remainder of the text.

Finally, I will revisit important thoughts from earlier in this book that there is no definitive source of truth about data, the data science process or related notions. No single definition of data could be correct for all scenarios or organizations. However, for organizations looking to build their data culture, this chapter can serve as a useful starting point for understanding what data are and how they can be analysed.

STRUCTURED VS UNSTRUCTURED DATA   Decoding the jargon

The terms structured and unstructured are common buzzwords and jargon. Let's explore them as an aside.

Unstructured data refers to any data without a predefined organized format, making them difficult to analyse or process. Examples of unstructured data include text documents, social media posts, images and videos.

Structured data refers to data that are organized and formatted in a conventional way. The organization means the data can be easily processed, stored and analysed. Examples of structured data include spreadsheets, databases and financial records.

While unstructured data are often touted as a valuable source of insights and information, they present unique challenges for data analysis and processing. Due to the lack of structure, unstructured data require specialized tools and techniques, such as NLP and machine learning, to extract meaningful insights. The first and often difficult task associated with analysing unstructured data is to model them in a structured way.

Structured data, on the other hand, are easier to process and analyse due to their organized format. However, structured data may not capture the full complexity of a particular phenomenon or system, and may require additional contextual information to provide a complete understanding.

Data typology

There are three broad types of data: quantitative, date and time and qualitative, as shown in Table 9.1. Qualitative data further consist nominal, ordinal, nominal binary and ordinal binary. Quantitative data also further consist of scale, discrete, continuous and ratio data.

TABLE 9.1   A typology of data including three main types, nine sub-types and their descriptions

Type	Sub-types	Descriptions
Quantitative	Scale Discrete Continuous Ratio	Quantitative data are often regarded as the most flexible. Meaning the kinds of analyses available for quantitative data are greatest. One of the reasons for this is that it is almost always possible to 'convert' quantitative data into qualitative data, but frequently not the other way around.
Time and date	Time and date	Not always described as a 'type' or 'family' on its own, but behave differently from both qualitative and quantitative data. For example, one of the quirks associated with time and date data is that they almost always go on the x-axis in a data visualization. Related, date and time in any given analysis as either a dependent or independent variable is often ambiguous.

(continued)

TABLE 9.1   (Continued)

Type	Sub-types	Descriptions
Qualitative	Nominal Ordinal Nominal binary Ordinal binary	Qualitative data are often the most difficult to analyse because computers do not naturally work well with non-numeric representations. A practical implication of this is that computers often 'cheat' by 'representing' these qualitative data in matrix or array forms. An important aspect of data science is understanding how computers use numbers to represent these non-numerical data. Another example of how and why qualitative data are difficult to analyse is that many analytical options are not possible. For example, we cannot create the average of a nominal variable – and technically it is dubious to create averages of ordinals.

For this discussion I treat date and time data as their own data type, which is a unconventional approach compared to many resources. The primary reason I regard date/time as a third data type in addition to qualitative and quantitative is because date/time data sometimes behave qualitatively, and sometimes more quantitatively. Related, date/time data are peculiar in the data visualization context. For example, as shown further in the next chapter, date/time data are almost always displayed on the horizontal axis of any chart or graph (when the same is not always true for qualitative and quantitative data).

Quantitative data

Quantitative data are a type of numerical data that are used to measure and describe. Unlike qualitative data, which describe quality or characteristics, quantitative data can be expressed numerically.

Quantitative data can be further classified into three types: continuous, discrete and scale data. Examples of continuous data include height, weight and temperature. Discrete data, on the other hand, can only take on certain distinct, separate values, such as counts of whole units. Examples of discrete data include the number of people in a room, the number of cars in a parking lot, or the number of goals scored in a soccer game.

Quantitative data can be easily summarized and analysed using statistical methods, such as means, medians and standard deviations. Additionally, the use of quantitative data permits objective, data-driven decisions based on empirical evidence.

However, the use of quantitative data also presents some limitations. For example, quantitative data can oversimplify complex phenomena by reducing complex systems to mere numeric values. Over-reliance on quantitative data can lead to the loss of important contextual information. Additionally, the validity and reliability of quantitative data can be affected by measurement error or bias.

CONTINUOUS

Continuous data are a type of quantitative data that can take any numerical value. In theory a truly continuous data variable has no limits, meaning any observation can consist of any number. However, in practice, continuous data are often bound within a certain range or interval. For example, drawing from the body weight example we introduced in Chapter 2, an adult person's body weight could be as low as 70 or 80 pounds (30 to 35 kilograms) – but not very much lower. If we saw a value closer to 10 pounds (4.5 kilograms) in data that purported to

represent adult human body weight we might assume the entry to be in error.

Quantitative continuous data are typically 'measured'. The measurement comes from a scale, a ruler or some other scientific instrument. Mathematically, these data can be infinitely subdivided, meaning that there are no intrinsically distinct values.

Examples of continuous data include height, weight and temperature. Examples of continuous data discussed within this book include the dimensions of a shipping package from Chapter 6 and human body weight from Chapter 2.

When analysing continuous data, we often turn to means, medians, minimums, maximums, modes, standard deviations and ranges. For more on these measures of central tendency and spread see the Glossary. We also often use Pearson correlation coefficient analysis and simple linear regression. To visualize continuous data we can use histograms, boxplots and scatter plots. For more on these data visualization strategies see Chapter 10.

DISCRETE

Discrete data are a type of quantitative data that can only take distinct, separate values. These data are often represented by whole numbers (but not always). For example, shoe size is arguably discrete but often contains decimals. Another common example of discrete data are counts of things where the 'thing' cannot be sub-divided (for example when counting the number of people in a room there cannot be a half of a person). Other examples of discrete data include the number of students in a class, the number of goals scored in a soccer game or the number of cars in a parking lot. Overall, unlike continuous data, which can be infinitely divided, discrete data are characterized by a distinct set of values that are countable and have clear boundaries.

When analysing discrete data we sometimes mistreat the data. For example, suppose there is a corporation with 3,025 employees and 101 business locations. We might be interested

in calculating the average number of employees per location (3025 / 100 = 30.25). Technically it is not possible to have a portion (¼th) of a person. But given the simplicity, and widely understood nature, of calculating averages, we often mistreat the discrete data by treating them as continuous.

If we had an interest in being less cavalier with these data we could choose to report the median number of employees at each location instead. The median count would be (in many contexts) a whole number, which holds truer to the discrete nature of the original data.

To visualize discrete data we can use many of the same visuals associated with continuous data, such as histograms, boxplots and scatter plots. Likewise when analysing discrete data, especially when we have relatively high numbers in our data, we often turn to measures of central tendency, measures of spread, Pearson correlation coefficient analysis and simple linear regression.

SCALE

Scale data summarize two or more variables (usually qualitative ordinal variables which I discuss below). Scale data usually summarize variables that are closely related. For example, it might be tempting to view customer satisfaction data as a scale. In such a case the customer may have responded to a set five of questions that each ask for similar information. One example of those questions could be as follows in Figure 9.1.

Scale data usually involve adding the individual responses to each question for a total score. In the above example, a hotel guest who answered between 3 and 5 to each of the questions would have a total score of 21 (5 + 4 + 5 + 4 + 3 = 21). Each response to each of the questions consists of a variable. The individual responses are ordinal (discussed below). Because the scale data are composed of (a mathematical summation) multiple other ordinal variables, these scale data are also sometimes called composite data or composite scores.

FIGURE 9.1   A set of survey questions intended to measure customer happiness

	1 (Very Un-Happy)	2 (Un-Happy)	3 (Neutral)	4 (Happy)	5 (Very Happy)
How happy are you with your overall experience at the hotel today?	O	O	O	O	⊙
How happy were you with the process of making your reservation for our hotel?	O	O	O	⊙	O
How happy are you with the reception staff?	O	O	O	O	⊙
How happy were you with the housekeeping services?	O	O	O	⊙	O
How happy are you with our catering services?	O	O	⊙	O	O

Source: Google Surveys

Due to how they are calculated, it is not possible to generate composite results with decimals. Because there are no decimals, scale data often resemble discrete data and usually fall within a specific upper and lower bound. In the above example that involved calculating a scale composite of a hotel guest's responses, the lowest possible composite score value will be 5 and the highest possible will be 25. Because scale data often behave like discrete or continuous we often turn to the same sets of analytical methods and visualization techniques, including

measures of central tendency, Pearson correlation, simple linear regression, box plots, histograms and scatter plots.

Ratio

Common examples of ratio data are percentages (also known as proportions) and rates such as the miles per gallon variable found in the automobile data referenced across other chapters in this book. A ratio is a number that represents the value of a numerator over a denominator.

Returning to the miles per gallon example, the mpg rating of any given vehicle represents the number of miles that a car will travel for each gallon of gasoline consumed. This rating thus provides a meaningful measure of efficiency, allowing comparisons between different vehicles. For instance, if one car achieves 30 miles per gallon and another achieves 20 miles per gallon, we can conclude that the first car is more fuel-efficient.

Percentages, another common ratio, represent a part of a whole. For instance, you are reading Chapter 9 of this book, and given that there are 11 chapters we can say that you are about 9/11ths or 81.81% of the way through reading it.

Qualitative data

Qualitative data are a type of non-numeric data that describe qualities and characteristics. Unlike quantitative data, which can be measured and expressed numerically, qualitative data are subjective and context-dependent. Qualitative data often may come from observations, interviews, open-ended survey responses, emails, texts, or other communications.

Qualitative data further divide into four sub-types of nominal, ordinal, nominal binary and ordinal binary. Qualitative data are less structured than quantitative. As such, a key challenge associated with analysing qualitative data is re-structuring the data to represent them numerically. The numeric representation is necessary so they can be mathematically analysed. This

book has previously discussed the process of converting qualitative nominal data to an array of dummies (zeros and ones) in Chapter 6.

Qualitative data are often used in social science research, including sociology, psychology and anthropology, to understand complex social phenomena and explore the meaning and experiences of individuals or groups. Qualitative data are also extensively useful in data science.

One of the key advantages of qualitative data is the depth of insight they can provide for the practice of data science when complex social phenomena are also involved.

ORDINAL AND ORDINAL BINARY

Ordinal data can be ranked or ordered and numbered based on an intrinsic order. But, unlike quantitative data, the differences between the ordered numbered values are not necessarily equal. For example, a Likert scale, which is often used in survey research, is an example of ordinal data. The values on a Likert scale can be ranked, but especially when you consider the subjective viewpoints of multiple different respondents the distance between each point on the scale is not necessarily the same, nor is it necessarily knowable. This means that even though we often assign numbers to Likert-like responses we cannot, while

FIGURE 9.2   An example survey question designed to measure customer happiness

	1 (Very Un-Happy)	2 (Un-Happy)	3 (Neutral)	4 (Happy)	5 (Very Happy)
How happy are you with your overall experience at the hotel today?	O	O	O	O	O

Source: Google Surveys

properly respecting the nature of the data, calculate an 'average' response. To understand this more fully, consider the question shown here in Figure 9.2.

If you collected three responses and one person responded 3 while the other two responded 4 the mathematical average would based on a be a total of 11 (3 + 4 + 4) divided by 3 for a result of 3.66 repeating. Since 3.66 repeating is not on the actual scale, the average result is not interpretable.

Ordinal binary data are a type of qualitative data that only have two possible values, and can be ranked, numbered or ordered based on an intrinsic order criterion. Examples of ordinal binary data include 'short or tall', 'slow or fast', 'cold or hot' and 'affordable or expensive'.

NOMINAL AND NOMINAL BINARY

Nominal data are a type of categorical data that do not have a natural order or ranking and are often used to classify or categorize data. Examples of nominal data include eye colour, movie genre and physical location (such as US zip or mailing codes).

Nominal binary data are a type of nominal data that only has two possible values. Examples of nominal binary data include 'on or off', 'hungry or not hungry' and 'working or not working'. Returning to the automobile place of manufacture example previously introduced in Chapter 5, nominal and binary data values might otherwise consist of 'foreign or domestic'. In the case of a survey where respondents respond to a question that calls for their opinion, typical example values might consist of 'agree or disagree' and 'no or yes'.

Nominal binary data can be useful for analysing and comparing differences between groups, and can be used to create simple models for prediction or classification.

While qualitative data do not have the same kind of precision and accuracy as quantitative data, they are often used in data science to provide rich and detailed descriptions of complex

phenomena. The interpretation of qualitative data is often highly context-dependent, which can make it difficult to generalize findings to other settings or populations.

Date and time

Date and time data are difficult to place as either qualitative or quantitative. Date and time data can behave as continuous quantitative data in some contexts, and as qualitative in others.

For example, consider age in years. When we record a person's age in years, we may be tempted to classify the variable as quantitative and discrete or continuous. In casual discussion we usually tell others how old we are in terms of whole years instead of giving decimals (unless we are under the age of five – no four-and-a-half-year-old ever misses the opportunity to proudly remind you of that half a year in age). However, consider this example: two people were born in the same year but on different days – just two days apart. One person's birthday was yesterday and the other person's birthday is tomorrow. If their birthdate and time data are collected on the intervening day ('today'), the person whose birthday was yesterday will count as a full year older than the person whose birthday is tomorrow, even though they are only two days apart in age.

When we calculate that one person is a year older than another we cannot be sure if they might actually be very nearly the same age. Thus age in years, is often better understood as an ordinal, because as we often collect and demark age, the level of precision is often low.

In practice, my advice is to carefully consider the purposes of your analysis before deciding how you will collect and then encode date and time data. In the above example, if it were important to know more precisely the difference in age between two people it would be better to collect birth date. With birth date you can calculate age in years, months, days, weeks. Without that truly continuous representation it is not possible to calculate differences in age.

Relative utility and type conversions

It is important to understand with which type of data you are working, because the type of data that is available influences the type of analysis you may conduct. For example, nominal data work well for chi square analysis but not for correlation analysis. Related, because it is almost always possible to convert continuous data to ordinal, nominal or binary (but not usually the other way around), the range of available analyses is greatest when you have collected continuous data at the outset.

This section provides a non-exhaustive list of techniques that can convert data from one data type to another. First, we explore how continuous or discrete data may be converted to ordinal. Second, I will show how to create a scale variable from a set of related ordinal variables. And third, I will also explore how ordinal data may be converted to continuous.

In this first example we will return to the automobile data frequently referenced in this book from Seaborn. We will evaluate the weight column, which is continuous data. Then we will convert that continuous data to ordinal data. To get started we will use the following code that loads the automobile data and then displays summary statistics for the continuous variable price.

```
# Import the Pandas and Seaborn libraries
import pandas as pd
import seaborn as sns
import numpy as np
import matplotlib.pyplot as plt

sns.set_context('talk')

# Open data from online.
df = sns.load_dataset('mpg')
```

```
# Show continuous nature of data with summaries.
df[['weight']].describe().transpose()
```

Which will produce the following output:

```
        count   mean      std     min     25%      50%     75%     max
weight  398.0   2970.42   846.84  1613.0  2223.75  2803.5  3608.0  5140.0
```

In the above output we see that the weight variable ranges from 1613 pounds on the lower end and 5140 pounds on the upper end. We can also use the .groupby() method to more carefully examine how these data differ by category. In this example we will use the categorical origin.

```
# Examine weight summaries by place of manufacture
df.groupby('origin').describe()['weight']
```

Which produces the following output:

```
        count   mean      std      min     25%      50%     75%      max
origin
europe  70.0    2423.30   490.04   1825.0  2067.25  2240.0  2769.75  3820.0
japan   79.0    2221.23   320.50   1613.0  1985.00  2155.0  2412.50  2930.0
usa     249.0   3361.93   794.79   1800.0  2720.00  3365.0  4054.00  5140.0
```

In the above output the qualitative categorical variable 'place of manufacture' origin appears along the rows while the statistics for vehicle weight within each category show along the columns. We see how many vehicles fall in each category in the count column, the mean weight in the mean column, etc.

The violin plot allows us to see how the continuous distribution of weight is different based on the place of manufacture. Violin plots are similar to boxplots. Both violin plots and boxplots visualize the information we displayed in tabular format with the .groupby().describe() method chain above. For a more extensive discussion of violin and boxplots see Chapter 10.

```
# Show continuous nature of data with violin plots.
sns.violinplot(data=df,
               x='weight',
               y='origin')
```

In the example violin plots shown in Figure 9.3, the qualitative categorical nominal variable place of manufacture origin appears on the vertical y-axis and quantitative continuous variable vehicle weight appears on the horizontal x-axis. We see that vehicles manufactured in the USA tend to weigh more than vehicles manufactured in Japan and Europe. We also see that the range of vehicle weight for vehicles manufactured in Japan and Europe is smaller.

CONTINUOUS TO ORDINAL

Consider a scenario where your audience does not understand well how to interpret a violin plot. But, you need to communicate how vehicle weight seems to be related to place of manufacture. One option would be to convert weight to an ordinal and then

FIGURE 9.3   A violin plot that compares vehicle weight across places of manufacture. Produced with the code shown here

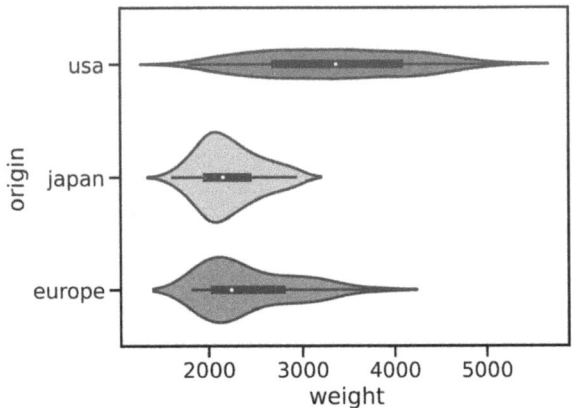

display the information about weight by place of manufacture as a cross-tabulation (also frequently known as a pivot table or contingency table). Here is the code that would accomplish the task and the resulting output.

```
# Establish bins with pd.cut, name the bins
df['weight_cat'] = pd.cut(df['weight'], 5,
                          labels=['Very Light','Light',
                                  'Moderate','Heavy',
                                  'Very Heavy'])

# Produce a crosstabulation show weight by origin
pd.crosstab(df['origin'], df['weight_cat'])
```

Which will produce the following output:

```
weight_cat Very Light  Light Moderate Heavy Very Heavy
origin
europe            39     21        9     1          0
japan             53     26        0     0          0
usa               29     66       68    62         24
```

Just as the violin plots communicated, this cross-tabulation shows that the moderate, heavy and very heavy vehicles originated nearly exclusively in the USA.

A trouble with converting data from continuous to ordinal is that the data cannot convert back to the original. This is why instead of replacing the weight column with categorical data the above code establishes a new column, called `weight_cat`.

ORDINAL TO SCALE

Even though ordinal data cannot naturally convert to continuous data, there is at least one technique that can create continuous-like data by combining multiple ordinal variables. When done, the resulting variable summarizes multiple closely related ordinal variables. Often this summarization is called a scale, a composite, or a composite score.

Imagine, for example, that you asked event attendees to provide feedback on the event and that you used the template shown here in Figure 9.4 (available from Google Forms).

The responses to each question on this survey is a classic ordinal response that produces classic ordinal data. To represent those data in a table you would see data that appears as follows here in Table 9.2.

FIGURE 9.4   A set of survey questions intended to measure customer satisfaction

How satisfied were you with the logistics? *
1 = Very dissatisfied   5 = Very satisfied

	1	2	3	4	5	N/A
Accommodation	◯	◯	◯	◯	◯	◯
Welcome kit	◯	◯	◯	◯	◯	◯
Communication emails	◯	◯	◯	◯	◯	◯
Transportation	◯	◯	◯	◯	◯	◯
Welcome activity	◯	◯	◯	◯	◯	◯
Venue	◯	◯	◯	◯	◯	◯
Activities	◯	◯	◯	◯	◯	◯
Closing ceremony	◯	◯	◯	◯	◯	◯

Source: Google Surveys

To simplify the analysis, it would make sense to add the number associated with each respondent's response for each aspect of the event. By adding these ordinal responses together, we create a new value that we would generally regard as a composite scale or as composite scale-data. Once calculated, we may treat these data as continuous variable. For a specific demonstration we look to the first response (Resp ID 1001) where this respondent's overall score would be 26 (2 + 3 + 5 + 5 + 5 + 2 + 5 + 4 = 26).

TABLE 9.2   A representation of data that could have been collected from survey questions shown in Figure 9.4

Response ID	Accommodation	Welcome Kit	Communication Emails	Transportation	Welcome Activity	Venue	Activities	Closing Ceremony
1001	2	3	5	5	5	2	5	4
1002	3	5	5	4	2	5	4	5
1003	3	3	5	5	5	4	3	5
1004	2	5	4	5	5	5	4	5
1005	2	5	4	3	5	5	5	5

NOMINAL TO BINARY

In a technical interview I was once given a data set that consisted of one categorical predictor, a few other continuous predictors and one continuous target variable. The task was to create a predictive model that used the categorical to estimate the continuous.

It seemed the employer was looking for a demonstration that involved converting the categorical to an array of dummy variables. As shown in chapter 6, converting nominal data to an array of dummy variables is not challenging. In the context of this technical interview, the categorical predictor variable described modes of transportation. In gist, The values were 'air', 'car', 'bus' and 'boat'. I realized I could simplify the data by converting this qualitative nominal categorical to a qualitative nominal binary, which would be more efficient. This conversion involved recoding 'car' and 'bus' as 'land transportation' but 'boat' and 'air' as 'not-land transportation'.

The risk of this kind of conversion that may involve losing information. The upside of this kind of conversion is that it simplifies the analysis and also potentially makes any prediction less computationally expensive.

For this interview, I submitted two solutions along with a comparison of the results from each solution. That employer explained they appreciate the creative approach and had not yet observed a candidate who took that extra step.

Below is example code that uses the Seaborn automobile data to convert the qualitative categorical nominal origin column consisting of 'europe', 'japan' and 'usa' as values to qualitative categorical nominal binary consisting of 'us' and 'abroad'.

```
# Frequently used data science imports.
import pandas as pd
import seaborn as sns

# Open data from online.
```

```
df = sns.load_dataset('mpg'))
# Create nominal binary from multi-categorical
df['origin2'] = df['origin'].map(
    {'usa':'us',
     'japan':'abroad',
     'europe':'abroad'})

# Show the results
df
```

The above code uses a Pandas method known as .map(). The .map() method accepts as its argument a Python dictionary that, in a manner of speaking, provides a map for the recoding process.

By setting the results of the map method equal to df['origin2'] the code simultaneously creates a new variable while preserving the original variable. Other methods may have been appropriate here. For example np.where() and also list comprehension could work as shown below.

```
# Use list comprehension to create nominal binary
df['origin3'] = ['us' if x == 'usa' else
                 'abroad' for x in df['origin']]

# Use np.where() to create nominal binary
df['origin4'] = np.where(
    df['origin'] == 'usa','us','abroad')
```

I introduced the `np.where()` and list comprehension techniques earlier in Chapters 5 and 6. I also provide additional explanation of list comprehension in Appendix B. For additional explanation of these techniques see Chapter 5, 6 and Appendix B.

Popular data sources

Choosing data for demonstration, practice, teaching, testing and related purposes is both a chore and an adventure. For readers who seek to be confident data scientists or machine learning, artificial intelligence and advanced analytics professionals, one of the toughest tasks, especially when starting out, is finding data to work with.

The good news is that finding data gets easier over time as you grow more familiar with the scope of data repositories across the world. You will also likely, whether by plan or by habit, develop a library of data that you reference often within your own organization. You will develop an interest in specific data sets for yourself over time. And you will have habits that help you save and find them more quickly. As I said, it gets easier but it is not ever a breeze.

This section outlines a collection of resources on which I have come to rely over the years. I hope you will find them equally useful.

FiveThirtyEight

One of the most under-appreciated data sources among newer data scientists is the news and media organization known as FiveThirtyEight. FiveThirtyEight, founded by former *New York Times* blogger Nate Silver in 2008, is a data-driven news and analysis website. It covers topics ranging from politics to sports, science to culture and beyond. Some of the earliest work FiveThirtyEight was most known for was analysis of election results and also election predictions.

FiveThirtyEight had become widely known for its accurate predictions during US elections since 2012. The organization's close association with politics led to its choice of name – there are 538 electors in the United States Electoral College. The site reports, 'We're sharing the data and code behind some of our articles and graphics. We hope you'll use it to check our work and to create stories and visualizations of your own.'[1]

It is not difficult to begin exploring data from the website with Python. The following code demonstrates loading multiple data sets from FiveThirtyEight in a single line of code.

```python
# U.S. House of Representative election predictions
house = pd.read_csv('https://projects.fivethirtyeight.com/' +
                    'polls/data/house_polls_historical.csv')
# Display an excerpt of the data
house.sample(5)

# U.S. Senate election predictions
senate = pd.read_csv('https://projects.fivethirtyeight.com/' +
                     'polls/data/senate_polls_historical.csv')

# Display an excerpt of the data
senate.sample(5).transpose()
```

The above data sets include 43 columns or variables each. Combined, they provide information from 10,247 polls. The columns range in data type from qualitative to continuous. Information about each poll includes its methodology (live telephone, online, text, mail, among others), its sample size, start date, end date, sponsoring organization and political affiliation of the sponsoring organization.

I recommend these polling data sets for anyone interested in learning to explore and inspect a data set. A wide variety of interests and skill levels may connect well with these data. For example, an intermediate-to-difficult level question would be to consider evaluating what the optimal sample size seems to be that will result in the most accurate results. A beginner-to-intermediate question might be to evaluate whether the political affiliation of the poll sponsor seems to drive the poll results. While a simpler question to start out with would be to consider whether the methodology might influence poll results.

From FiveThirtyEight you can also find a wide range of sports-related data. The following data include predictions related to World Cup soccer results.

```
# World Cup tournament predictions
cup = pd.read_csv('https://projects.fivethirtyeight.com/' + \
                  'soccer-api/international/2022/wc_matches.csv')

# Display an excerpt of the data
cup.sample(5)
```

For many reasons, a data set consisting of World Cup predictions may serve as a meaningful resource for a data science learner who wants to gain more knowledge and experience. This data set can help learners visualize data, compare multiple variables and draw conclusions about entertaining and well-understood real-world events.

In these data FiveThirtyEight created and estimated a Soccer Power Index (SPI) which is an 'estimate of team strength'.[2] To use these data for training, demonstration, or education, consider building a tournament bracket based on these ranking data.

UC Irvine Machine Learning Repository

The UC Irvine Machine Learning Repository is an online library of data sets that have been collected, studied and made available to the public for research. The repository was created in 1987 by Professor David Aha at the University of California, Irvine, and has grown to include over 600 data sets 'as a service to the machine learning community'.[3]

The data sets cover a range of topics, from chemical reactions and music to facial images and credit cards. Each data set includes a detailed description of its contents and usage guidelines as well as an associated data science task such as classification or clustering. It also provides links to relevant research papers that may facilitate further study.

The Machine Learning Repository's website also provides several other resources that are useful for machine learning practitioners. These resources help make the repository a valuable resource for students, educators, researchers and industry professionals alike.

The following code demonstrates how to load data from UC Irvine Machine Learning Repository using Python.

```
# Chemical analysis of wine samples
wine = pd.read_csv('https://archive.ics.uci.edu/ml/' + \
                   'machine-learning-databases/wine/wine.data',
                   names=['Alcohol','MalicAcid','Ash','Alcalinity',
                          'Magnesium','TotPhenols','Flavanoids',
                          'NonFlavanoidPhen','Proanthocyanins','
                          Color', 'Hue','OD280_OD315','Proline'])
# Display an excerpt of the data
wine.sample(5)
```

These wine quality data, and other similar beverage data, are frequently referenced resources for demonstrating data science processes in both educational and commercial settings. It can be used to explore the characteristics of wine, identify potential discrepancies between ratings and taste, or to analyse the impact of production techniques on quality.

Data science professionals can also use this and similar data sets to experiment with both supervised and unsupervised machine learning techniques. A common practice with this wine data is to take it as example data in the process of demonstrating clustering analysis. Clustering analysis is a process that can identify patterns in the data that are not otherwise readily discernable and that, before the analysis, were not known. In essence, clustering analysis will identify groups or kinds of wine that all have similar characteristics.

For use in supervised machine learning demonstrations, these data work well when using variables about chemical composition to predict taste and ratings. These data also work well when demonstrating predictive models that aim to classify wines by type, origin or colour. With their varied applications, wine quality data provide an excellent opportunity for those interested in learning about data science and exploring machine learning tools.

Additional libraries

There are dozens of data libraries worldwide. Here I provide a brief overview of a few other places to look for demonstration, testing and training data.

THE SEABORN LIBRARY

Seaborn is a popular data visualization library that that is built on top of the popular Matplotlib library. The library provides access to several example data sets. Earlier chapters in this book referenced the automobile efficiency mpg.csv data from Seaborn.

The primary intent of the library is to provide data with which you can demonstrate and test Seaborn data visualization code. However, these data also work well when looking to test, demonstrate or learn about tools in the field other than Seaborn or data visualization. After `import seaborn as sns` you can use the code `sns.get_dataset_names()` to see a list of available data. From there, loading a data set involves passing the data set name as a string into the `sns.load_dataset()` function.

```
# Load and display the mpg data from sns.load_dataset()
sns.load_dataset('mpg').sample(5)
```

Two other data sets that come with Seaborn, that we will briefly have a closer look at in the next chapter, include the tips data and the penguins data.

Tips data set   This data set contains information about tips in a restaurant, including the total bill, tip amount, and other attributes like whether the customer was a smoker or not. These data are a good place to look when studying supervised machine learning that might predict the total restaurant bill based on a variety of predictor variables including the day of the week, the number of diners, the gender of the server, among other factors. Typical methods for this task would include regression analysis. Regression analysis is a statistical method used to model the relationship between a dependent variable (in this case, the total bill) and one or more independent variables (the predictor variables, such as the day of the week, the number of diners, the gender of the server, etc.). Once the model has been trained and tested, it can be used to make predictions about the total bill based on new input data. For example, if we wanted to predict the total bill for a group of four diners on a Friday night with a

female server, we could input those variables into the model and it would output a predicted total bill.

Penguins data set   This is a recently added data set in Seaborn. It contains measurements for three penguin species, including their body mass, flipper length and bill length. These data are good for studying either supervised or unsupervised machine learning. For supervised machine learning these data are suitable for training classification models that will predict the penguin species based on the predictor variables including body mass, flipper length and bill length. For unsupervised machine learning these data are suitable for cluster analysis. Cluster analysis is a technique used to group similar observations or data points together based on their characteristics, without any pre-existing labels or categories. In the case of the Penguin data set, the predictor variables (body mass, flipper length and bill length) would be used to group the penguin observations into clusters. Once the clustering algorithm has been applied to the data, the resulting clusters can be compared to the otherwise previously known species column to ascertain how well the clustering algorithm identified (or mis-identified) the species groups.

TABLEAU

Tableau is a data analysis and visualization tool. Tableau allows users to quickly explore and analyse their data with interactive dashboards, visualizations and maps. It supports several types of charts such as heat maps, funnel charts, histograms and boxplots. Additionally, Tableau makes it easy to share insights with others through the platform's dynamic publishing capabilities.

For those looking for training, testing and demonstration data, the data set library from Tableau provides data categorized by business, entertainment, sports, education, government, science, lifestyle, technology and health. At the library website you can also find a list of other valuable libraries.[4]

One of the most popular data sets from the Tableau library is the Superstore data set. The Superstore data set is widely used in data visualization and business intelligence applications because it provides a rich source of sales data across a variety of different product categories and regions. The data set includes information such as order date, ship date, customer name, product category, sales and profit.

Much like many of the data previously mentioned above, the primary purpose for these data is to permit Tableau users to have it as a resource when learning Tableau. However, it can also be useful for those looking to learn, test or demonstrate data science. These data would be suitable for testing supervised machine learning that would involve regression analysis. A predictive regression model would have sales or profit as its target variable while other variables would serve as predictor variables in the feature matrix, such as product category, region or time. The related business use cases are to help retail organizations drive sales or profit, and to make predictions about future performance.

PEOPLE ANALYTICS DATA

The data that have been distributed with the *Handbook of Regression Modeling in People Analytics* have grown to be a popular and accessible data source for training, testing, education, and demonstration purposes.[5] There are 11 data sets that provide multiple opportunities to work with a range of data types.

To access these data with Python, first execute `pip install peopleanalyticsdata` in your terminal. Then in your notebook execute the following.

```
# import peopleanalyticsdata package
import peopleanalyticsdata as pad
import pandas as pd
```

```
print(f'There are {len(pad.list_sets())} sets.',
    end='\n\n')

# see a list of data sets
print(pad.list_sets())
```

Which will produce the following output.

```
There are 16 data sets.

['charity_donation', 'employee_survey', 'health_
insurance', 'job_retention', 'managers', 'politics_
survey', 'salespeople', 'soccer', 'sociological_data',
'speed_dating', 'ugtests', 'employee_performance',
'learning', 'graduates', 'promotion', 'recruiting']
```

At this point you can begin exploring the data listed above.

```
# load data into a dataframe
df = pad.managers()

df.sample(6)
```

Social media data

In addition to the data sources listed above, this book comes with two data sets. The first, discussed in Chapter 6, is fictional data that imagine the ship date, arrival date, shipping cost, insurance cost and package dimensions of approximately 10 packages.

This subsection provides another data source prepared specifically for this book. You can find these data along with the book's accompanying Jupyter Notebooks in a file called Confident_Ch9Social.csv at github.com/adamrossnelson/confident.

To load and begin inspecting these data use the following code.

```
# Specify file location, path, and name
location = 'https://raw.githubusercontent.com/'
path = 'adamrossnelson/confident/main/data/'
name = 'Confident_Ch9Social.csv'

# Load the csv file into a Pandas df
df = pd.read_csv(location + path + name + '.csv')
```

To prepare these data I asked multiple users of LinkedIn to share with me a portion of their LinkedIn data exports. Among LinkedIn data exports is a file called shares.csv. Each item in the shares.csv file is a post from that user on LinkedIn. From these share files I randomly selected approximately 40 posts from each user. Then I excluded posts that contained no text or that were re-shares. I also excluded a small number of posts that were exceedingly specific about dates, times, locations or events that may easily lead to identification of persons or entities associated with those dates, times, locations or events. Related, I removed or modified mentions of individual first and last names and I also removed URL web links. Similarly, I removed mentions of many specific companies (but not all). I left reference to specific companies that employed thousands or hundreds of thousands of people and that are well known internationally, such as Disney, for example. I also left references to governmental organizations.

To supplement the data, I created fictional with fictional posts. Adding fictional users accomplished two goals. First, the fictional users added a modicum of difficulty for anyone seeking to re-identify these posts (which will be impossible, but which I discourage). Second, the fictional posts add more data for our analytical work. To further de-identify these data I added noise to the date, reactions and the comments columns.

In these data each observation (or row) is a specific post from a specific user, actual or fictional, on LinkedIn. There is a column that identifies which user published the post. There is a column that contains the text of the post. The text of the post is what we will analyse using Google Clouds NLP API and NLTK's pre-trained models. The last two columns show the number of reactions and comments associated with that post. There is also a column that records the number of reactions that post received, and another for the number of comments on that post.

The final task in this chapter will be to retrieve sentiment data from NLTK and Google so that we can use the sentiment data in further demonstration and analysis in subsequent chapters. If you are following along, you can use the code here to also collect the sentiment information. If you prefer to move on to the subsequent chapters you can do so with the data file, included with this book's Jupyter Notebooks, called Confident_Ch9SocialSents.csv.

To collect the sentiment scores for these social data we must first re-define the functions we wrote in Chapter 8. We defined four functions. The first function (`google_api_sentence_scores()`) calculated sentiment analysis for each sentence using Google; the second function (`google_api_document_scores()`) calculated sentiment analysis for each document also using Google; the third function (`sentence_scores()`) calculated sentiment analysis for each sentence using NLTK; and the fourth function (`post_scores()`) calculated sentiment analysis for each document using NLTK.

Moving forward, we will use the document (or post) level functions. After performing the necessary imports, as described in Chapter 8, and also re-defining the functions, we can pass the ShareCommentary column of LinkedIn posts to the functions as follows.

```
# Collect sentiment data using Google API
results_google = google_api_document_scores(df['shareCommentary'])

# Collect sentiment data using NLTK
results_nltk = post_scores(df['shareCommentary'])

# Add identifier suffix to the columns
results_google = results_google.add_suffix('_ggl')
results_nltk = results_nltk.add_suffix('_nltk')

# Concatenate the results
concatenated = pd.concat([df,
                          results_google[['sentiment_ggl',
                                          'Magnitude_ggl']],
                          results_nltk[['Negative_nltk',
                                        'Neutral_nltk',
                                        'Positive_nltk',
                                        'Compound_nltk']]],
                          axis=1)

# Save the results to disk
concatenated.to_csv('Confident_Ch9SocialSents.csv')

# Show the results
concatenated.sample(8)
```

Once again, this code performs sentiment analysis on a column of data consisting of LinkedIn posts. The sentiment analysis is done using two different tools including Google's API and NLTK.

The first two lines of code use the `google_api_document_scores()` function to collect sentiment data for the `ShareCommentary` column in the DataFrame using the Google API. Subsequently, the code uses the `post_scores()` function to collect sentiment data for the same column using NLTK. The code then stores the resulting sentiment data in two separate DataFrames, `results_google` and `results_nltk`.

The next lines of code add a suffix to the column names in the `results_google` and `results_nltk` DataFrames. The suffix helps identify from which tool the data came.

The next line of code merges to the original DataFrame columns (`results_google` and `results_nltk`) that contain sentiment data. This merge is accomplished with the `pd.concat()` function. The resulting DataFrame is assigned to the variable concatenated.

The next line of code saves the concatenated DataFrame to a CSV file named `Confident_Ch9SocialSents.csv` using the `.to_csv()` method. This CSV file is the one you'll find with this book's GitHub repository.

The last line of code shows a sample of eight rows from the concatenated DataFrame using the `.sample()` method. Overall, this code performs sentiment analysis on textual data in a DataFrame using two different tools, concatenates the results along the columns axis and saves the resulting DataFrame to a CSV file.

One last note about social media data is that you can access your own data for analytical purposes. Doing so can be an informative and rewarding experience. You too can access your data from LinkedIn by clicking your 'Me' icon at the upper right of your LinkedIn main page, then 'Settings & privacy', then 'Get a copy of your data'.

It takes LinkedIn almost a full day to prepare your extract. Worth the wait. Once you get a copy of your data you may have as many as 40 CSV files to explore. Different users will have different results because not all users will have data from all of LinkedIn's feature sets.[6]

Implications for data culture

As explained earlier in this book, one of the most important and too often overlooked components of practising in data science is data culture. Building a strong data culture is often overlooked, but can greatly enhance the success of data-related projects. This book also specifically proposes in Chapter 3 that one of the best ways for an organization to build data culture is to talk about data. This means engaging in conversations about data and developing a common language and understanding of what data are and how they can be used.

In data-related conversations one of the first questions you will need to answer for yourself and your organization is, what are data? This chapter proposes several answers to that question by offering a typology that consists of qualitative, quantitative and date/time data. Each of these three categories further subdivide in ways that can help us in the field better understand our data and better understand each other as we talk about our data.

In other words, I propose you use this chapter's typology as a starting point when looking to facilitate these conversations. By understanding the different types of data and their properties, we can more effectively analyse and interpret our data, as well as communicate our findings to others. A stronger data culture also helps us communicate regarding our analytical plans before and during data collection.

Conclusion

I began this chapter with a note about an unfortunate data-related miscommunication. And I return to that story now. My story discussed the challenge of finding the balance between using catchy jargon and precise technical terms, and the consequences of making the wrong decision. In the midst of my true story I faced a situation where colleagues were unaware that we were already using machine learning and artificial intelligence. I realized this miscommunication was due to my own use of specific non-jargony language rather than the jargony buzzwords my audience had expected me to use. I suggested two solutions to this dilemma: using words that the audience expects (even if it means using jargon); or educating the audience about technical terms. This chapter focused on the second solution more that the first.

The main focus of this chapter is to help readers understand, in a deeper way, what are data, then to know where to go when looking for data to use in training, testing, demonstration and development purposes. This chapter also introduces a new data source consisting of posts from LinkedIn and associated sentiment scores. In doing so, this chapter also frames data as a tool among other tools. Subsequent chapters will reference this LinkedIn data for further demonstration purposes. In a manner of speaking, subsequent chapters will combine the LinkedIn data with additional tools including data visualization and predictive modelling.

In specific, this chapter delves into different types of data, including qualitative, quantitative and date/time data. Qualitative data describe the quality or characteristics of a phenomenon and are often subjective and context-dependent, while quantitative data can be measured and expressed numerically, and are often analysed using statistical methods. Date/time data can

behave as both continuous and qualitative, and present unique challenges for analysis.

The section on data sources provides helpful resources for finding data for practice, teaching and testing purposes. The chapter also includes a discussion of social media data, which can be a valuable resource for data scientists, machine learning, artificial intelligence and advanced analytics professionals.

Finally, the chapter highlights the importance of building a strong data culture within organizations. I propose that talking about data is one of the best ways to build data culture and enhance data literacy. By educating yourself and your audience, and fostering a culture of curiosity and learning, you can improve communication and analysis of data, and ultimately make more informed decisions.

## CHAPTER TEN

Data visualization

The next tool we need to look at closely in our confident data science journey is data visualization. In the previous chapter we explored what data are and how they can be categorized into different types. We also created a new data set consisting of posts from LinkedIn and the results of sentiment analysis. With this new data and also now with a better understanding of what data are, this chapter will be about how we can apply data visualization as an analytical technique.

This chapter on data visualization comes with a note of caution. While learning how to produce effective data visualizations can be a valuable skill, it can also be a mixed blessing. Once you have learned even a little bit about data visualization, your knowledge will likely exceed that of the average person. This can be both empowering and also it can be a source of frustration. Possessing this advanced specialized knowledge often means you will be capable of producing visuals that are rich and dense with information. You will be amazed by the insights you may reveal even when few others can understand the work.

It is important to remember that the most successful visuals are often those that convey one simple message. While it can be tempting to include as much information as possible in a visualization, doing so can result in a cluttered and confusing image that fails to communicate effectively. As such, while it is useful and powerful to learn about data visualizations in an advanced way, as this chapter will proceed to teach, it is important to keep in mind that with great power comes great responsibility.

The cautionary note aside, by learning how to create effective and impactful visualizations, you will be better equipped to communicate your findings to others and make informed decisions based on your data. However, it is important to approach data visualization with a clear understanding of its limitations and the responsibility that comes with the power to communicate complex information visually. This added responsibility means as your skills improve, you have an increased responsibility to create visuals that are not only informative but also accessible and easy to understand for a wide range of audiences. Striking the right balance between complexity and simplicity is an essential aspect of effective data visualization. You must strive to produce visuals that allow others to grasp key messages without feeling overwhelmed by overly intricate details.

Social media engagement

In this chapter we will begin exploring, through data visualization, how we might predict social media engagement in the form of comments and reactions. The primary predictor we will consider is a post's sentiment score. Having the ability to perform this kind of prediction can help us better plan posts that may achieve higher engagement rates and consequently wider distribution.

The ability to make these predictions relies on our ability to uncover complex relationships in the data. In order to inform

our statistical and mathematical work, this chapter starts with data visualization. After a preliminary section that demystifies data visualization, we will further explore multiple types of data visualizations and demonstrate how they can be used to explore the LinkedIn data set that we created in the previous chapter.

Specifically, we will demonstrate how scatter plots, scatter plots with a regression line, histograms, joint plots that combine scatter plots and histograms, violin plots, boxplots and heat maps can be used to explore and communicate patterns in our data. By the end of this chapter, you will have a better understanding of the power and potential of data visualization as a tool for exploring and communicating complex data.

VISUALIZATION FOR THE SAKE OF IT

Data visualization for the sake of data visualization is a mistake. I once worked with a group of clients who were reeling from a recent change in executive leadership. The new leadership introduced a range of new and exciting ideas for growth and innovation.

One of the newest and more executive C-suite members universally insisted that all reports and memos include one data visualization per page. The goal seemed obvious – to promote the use of data visualization throughout the organization.

However, the result was something else. Instead of promoting helpful, informative and efficient uses of data visualization, the demand for at least one visualization per page slowed the creation of crucial reports. Personnel were left to wonder what to visualize and what not to visualize. More often than not, the result was data visualization for the sake of data visualization and not for the sake of advancing the story or for better communication.

Tables as data visualizing

Tables count as a form of data visualization. When I teach the topic of data visualization I often include a special learning segment or

---

unit on producing a helpful and useful table that will add context to your message and enhance your ability to deliver the information you need to deliver. Tables inform, supplement and in some cases even underlie the accompanying data visualizations.

Whenever you find yourself thinking perhaps that a data visualization might improve your presentation, be sure to consider the option of producing a helpful table instead of or in addition to your graph or chart.

Demystifying data visualization

Data visualization is a form of data analysis that involves the creation of visual representations of data to help people better understand and interpret complex information. Many resources treat data visualization as its own separate topic, with extensive discussions on types of visualizations, how they work and when to use them. There are entire books (good books) on the topic. While this hyper-focused approach can be helpful in some ways, it can also be somewhat misleading. By treating data visualization as a separate topic, we may lose sight of the fact that it is really just one family of analytical techniques among many families.

By reframing data visualization as a family of analytical techniques, we can better understand how it fits into the broader context of data analysis. Instead of memorizing each type of visualization and its specific use cases, we can focus on the underlying principles of data visualization and how they can be applied in different contexts. This approach empowers us to more effectively think about what it is we want to know, and then devise a visual that can help us achieve our desired learning outcome.

Thinking about data visualization as a family of analytical techniques can also help us better understand the strengths and

limitations of different types of visualizations. Rather than simply selecting a visualization because it looks impressive or is popular, we can think more critically about what we are trying to communicate and which type of visualization will best serve that purpose. This approach requires a deeper understanding of the underlying principles of data typology and also of data visualization, but it also allows us to more effectively communicate our findings to others and make informed decisions based on our data.

Thus far this book has introduced a variety of data visualizations including:

- bar charts (Chapters 5)
- scatter plots (Chapters 5, 8)
- histograms (Chapter 5)
- heat maps (Chapter 5)
- pair plots (consisting of scatter plots and histograms) (Chapter 5)
- cross-tabulations (Chapter 6)
- violin plots (Chapter 8)

As this book references multiple types of data visuals throughout, it was also necessary to keep the discussion of each chapter's main topic flowing. As a result, some of the sections provided limited discussion of the finer points associated with interpreting each data visual. In the remainder of this chapter we will revisit many of these data visualization types and also explore additional visualization types. With each demonstration in this chapter, we will either be looking to generally explore the data, or more specifically understand how we can use sentiment to predict engagement (which we believe may also drive distribution).

Graphic components and conventions

Before moving into a specific discussion of charts and chart types, it is useful to lay a foundation that supplies a clear understanding

of common graphic components and conventions. This subsection provides a brief tour of axis, titles, legends, annotations, data labels and related topics.

Axes

An important convention to note is that almost all charts will involve at least two axes. On one axis will be a y variable and on the other will be the x variable. The y variable is usually a variable that is dependent on, or one that is a function of, the x variable. This is a topic we touched on in Chapter 5 when we explored the relationship between a vehicle's weight and its efficiency. Since efficiency is dependent on weight, the most conventional visualization strategy would be to place efficiency on the vertical y-axis.

Another common convention to keep in mind, at least as a starting proposition, is that the y variable typically appears along the vertical axis while the x variable will typically be along the horizontal axis.

One exception to this rule about y on the vertical and x on the horizontal is when there are date and time data. When there are date and time data, they almost always appear on the horizontal.

Titles

Titles are an important component of most data visualizations. When you prepare your title, consider stating the visual's main point or conclusion. Using the mpg data from previous chapters, here is an example of how that might look.

```
# Create a figure and axis object
fig, ax = plt.subplots(figsize=(10, 6))

# Scatter plot with title that states a conclusion
```

```
sns.scatterplot(data=sns.load_dataset('mpg'),
                y='mpg', x='weight', ax=ax).set_title(
    'Vehicle Efficiency Seems to be a Function of
    Vehicle Weight')

ax.text(3400, 40,
        'As weight increases we', size='small')
ax.text(3400, 38,
        'see efficiency decrease.', size='small')

plt.ylabel('Vehicle Efficiency (MPG)')
plt.xlabel('Vehicle Weight')
```

For the first major example of code in this chapter, the code uses the mpg data (efficiency in miles per gallon) from Seaborn to create a scatter plot of the mpg against a weight. This code adds a title to the plot that suggests a conclusion about the relationship between vehicle efficiency and weight. Additionally, using `ax.txt()` this code adds an annotation that further communicates the main message. The annotation locates this supplemental communication strategy at or near the portion of the chart that also reinforces the conclusion. Then with `plt.ylabel()` and `plt.xlabel()` the y-axis is labelled 'Vehicle Efficiency (MPG)' and the x-axis is labelled 'Vehicle Weight'. Which produces Figure 10.1.

Using the title or subtitle to state the main message of the visual in clear and unambiguous terms can be an effective data visualization and communication strategy.

Legends and annotations

Legends and annotations are another closely related topic. In Figure 10.1, I have added an annotation that reads 'As weight

FIGURE 10.1   A scatter plot of vehicle efficiency and vehicle weight. This rendition of this plot demonstrates how stating a conclusion in a chart title can reinforce the chart's key message

increases we see efficiency decrease.' This is one example of an effective annotation.

Chart legends help your audience understand your chart. However, a legend is often counterproductive. Consider the following two examples. Figure 10.2 uses a legend and Figure 10.3 removes the legend and adds informative annotations.

For the first code example that produces Figure 10.2, this code produces a simple scatter plot that shows data from Seaborn's penguins data set. For more on this penguins data see Chapter 9. This chart shows penguins by their bill and flipper length. Using hue='species' this code also identifies which observations belong to which species. The style='species' option changes the scatter plot symbols for each species, which will make the chart easier to read in black and white, and for those who experience colour-blindness.

While Figure 10.2 is sufficient, it may be difficult for some readers to track their eyes back and forth between the three

FIGURE 10.2   A scatter plot from the penguins data that includes a standard legend which helps readers understand the relative
physical attributes of each penguin species

large groupings (across the chart area) and the legend (appearing in the lower right corner). Instead, as produced by the next
code block and as shown in Figure 10.3, it may make sense to do
away with the legend and add annotations that directly label key
features of the chart.

```
# Create a figure and axis object
fig, ax = plt.subplots(figsize=(10, 6))

# Generate a scatter plot
sns.scatterplot(data=sns.load_dataset('penguins'),
                y='bill_length_mm',
                x='flipper_length_mm',
                hue='species',
                style='species',
```

```
                    legend=False,
                    s=200,
                    ax=ax).set_title(
          'Pengin Bill Length by Flipper Length')

ax.text(205, 36,
              'Adelie Blue ●',
              size='large',
              color='blue')

ax.text(171, 54.75,
              'Chinstrap Orange X',
              size='large',
              color='darkorange')

ax.text(204, 57.75,
              'Gentoo Green ■',
              size='large',
              color='green')

plt.ylabel('Penguin Length of Bill')
plt.xlabel('Penguin Length of Flipper')
```

Using the `legend=False` option in the `sns.scatterplot()` function and then later using `ax.txt()` this code redraws Figure 10.2 as Figure 10.3 with annotations in lieu of a legend.

Among these examples it may be easier for many to read and quickly understand how the bill length and flipper length differ by species of penguin.

Data labels

Data labels are almost always a good idea. In the case of a bar chart, data labels are often called height labels. Consider how the data labels (numbers at or near the top of each bar) improve the readability and interpretability of Figure 10.4.

FIGURE 10.3   A scatter plot from the penguins data that includes annotations in lieu of a legend

FIGURE 10.4   A bar chart, which includes data labels, showing the average tip amount on Thursday, Friday, Saturday and Sunday

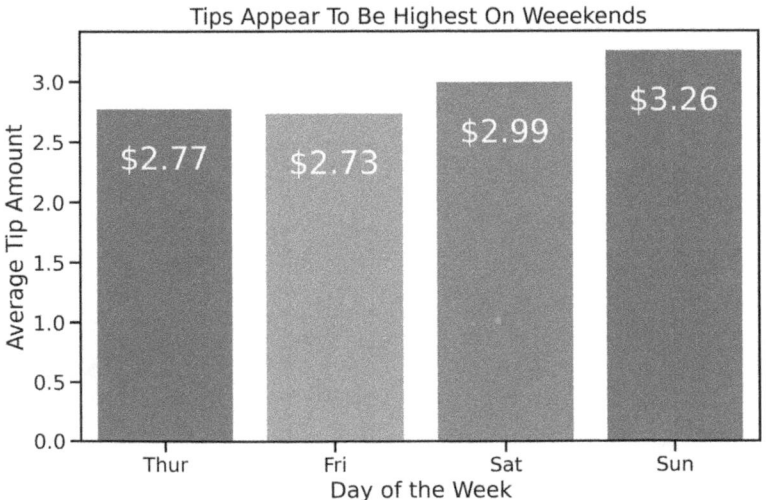

Source: Google Surveys

Instead of spending time drawing invisible lines from the tops of each bar over to the vertical y-axis, readers can simply look at the text that has been super-imposed on top of each bar. The text displayed on these bars clearly indicate the height of that bar.

The data science process

In this section we revisit many of the stages of the data science process I wrote about in Chapter 4, where I laid out an eight-stage model for conducting a data science project. There are two reasons why I only write about some of the eight stages here.

First, the analytical goal in this chapter is contrived for the purpose of presenting a coherent chapter. As such, some of the work associated with looking and checking around or with justification, for example, are beside the main point for this chapter. Second, it is also helpful to simplify for the purposes of this chapter. For example, the next chapter pertains more directly to the later stages in the eight-stage process, such as select and apply through to disseminate.

The question or business problem

First we must specify an analytical question to answer, or a business problem to solve. In this case we have both.

Our analytical question is: do we find a relationship between a LinkedIn post's engagement in the form of comments and reactions and that post's sentiment?

The business problem we can solve is: we can help LinkedIn users predict which posts may earn more engagement in the form of comments and reactions, and consequently then also further exposure and distribution.

In these analyses, our target variables are reactions and comments. All other data we have available to us may be useful as predictor variables; however, we will primarily focus on sentiment scores.

Wrangle

First using `pd.read_csv()` we must load the data that we prepared in Chapter 9. A version of that file is available with this book's notebooks. Here is the code to load and cursorily inspect these data.

```
# Load ConfidentDataCh9Social.csv
df = pd.read_csv(' Confident_Ch9SocialSents.csv ',
                 parse_dates=['Date'])
# Display the shape of the data
print(df.shape)

# Show the results
df.sample(3)
```

With these data there are at least two data wrangling steps that will be appropriate. The first will be to inspect for, and remove, outliers. The second will be to engineer additional feature variables. In this chapter we engineer three additional predictive feature variables. With information we gain here in Chapter 10 we also further demonstrate the creation of and engineering of additional feature variables later in Chapter 11.

FINDING AND MANAGING OUTLIERS

To inspect for outliers, we can first sort the data by our variables of interest in descending order and then display the results. Often this technique will make any outliers.

```
# View reaction counts that may be outliers
# Observe Index 0 (idx 0) = outlier
df.sort_values('Reactions', ascending=False).head()
```

Which produces a version of the following output that sorts the data from highest reaction count to lowest. As a result, any outliers show at the top of the list. Here we see that observation number 0 is an outlier with 221 reactions (more than four times as many reactions as the next most popular post at 55 reactions).

	Date	ShareCommentary	Reactions
0	2021-07-28	This is totally my youngest daughter...	221.0
1	2021-04-10	Ok, I'm just going to say it: I am not a guy. ...	55.0
2	2020-12-10	U.S. Department of Education has released its ...	53.0
138	2021-01-08	As someone who has experienced both high schoo...	46.0
3	2022-08-19	This week I lost a contract. A big one."\r\n""...	45.0

The next task is to review for observations with outlier comment counts.

```
# View comment counts that may be outliers
# Observe Index 86 (idx 86) = outlier
df.sort_values('Comments', ascending=False).head()
```

Which produces a version of the following output that sorts the data from highest comment count to lowest. Here we see that observation number 86 is an outlier with 314 comments (more than five times as many comments as the next most popular post at 58 comments).

To remove these observations the code is simple.

```
# Drop outliers
df.drop([0, 86], inplace=True)
```

ENGINEERING ADDITIONAL PREDICTIVE FEATURES

Feature engineering is the process of selecting and transforming raw data into a format that is more suitable for machine learning algorithms. In a more simple and pragmatic sense, feature engineering usually means creating new variables from other variables.

In this case we will calculate the length of the post in terms of the number of characters. We will also create a new grouping variable to complement the user identification numbers already in the data. A final new feature we will create will be to count the number of hashtags in each post.

Of course, we cannot yet know if these additional predictive features will be useful. The only way to learn is to engineer them and then analyse them.

```
# Engineer a new feature to show length of the post
df['len'] = df['ShareCommentary'].str.len()

# Engineer a new feature that will regroup users
df['group'] = df['User'].map({1010:'Biz Owner',
                              1011:'Biz Owner',
                              1020:'Biz Owner',
                              1021:'Biz Owner',
                              1030:'Economist',
                              1031:'Economist',
                              1040:'C-Suite',
                              1041:'C-Suite',
                              1050:'Marketing',
                              1051:'Marketing'})
```

```
# Count the number of hashtags in each post
df['hashtags'] = df['ShareCommentary'].str.count('#')

# Show the results
df.sample(6)
```

In gist, this code adds three new columns to the data including len, group and hashtags. For each observation in the data the code stores the post length in len. Based on hypothetical domain and also subject matter expertise, the code records career type based on user identification numbers in the group variable using the provided dictionary mapping and the .map() method. Lastly, this code also counts and records the number of hashtags in each post within the hashtag column.

First the code adds a new column len that contains the length of the text in the ShareCommentary.

A new column called group re-groups users based on the User column. For the purpose of this demonstration we can nod to a hypothetical source of domain knowledge that supplied us with information that indicates which type of career each user has pursued. Specifically this code used the .map() which recoded the data in the User column consistent with the Python dictionary passed into the method.

Lastly the code also creates a new column called hashtags which contains the number of hashtags (#) in the text of each row's ShareCommentary column.

Charts and graphs

Scatter plots

The first opportunity to review the relationships between our target variables and the feature predictor variables will be the

scatter plot. Recall that one of the best uses for a scatter plot is to show the relationship between two continuous variables. When making a scatter plot it is conventional to place the target variable on the vertical y-axis and the feature or predictor variable on the horizontal x-axis.

For each pair of continuous variables we could produce a scatter plot. With these data, that would be 100 plots (10 continuous variables by 10 continuous variables). Instead of writing code to produce 100 plots, we can use the pair plot from Seaborn.

A pair plot with 100 plots is difficult to read well. It is best practice to choose visuals that seem to indicate pairs of variables that may strongly relate to each other.

```
# Pairplot for the data's 10 continuous variables
sns.pairplot(df[['Reactions','Comments','Sentiment_ggl',
                 'Magnitude_ggl','Negative_ nltk',
                 'Neutral_nltk', 'Positive_nltk',
                 'Compound_nltk','len', 'hashtags']])
```

Because the visual is difficult to read, I have left it for you to inspect the pair plot on your own if you are following along. Instead, I also provide the correlation matrix for review in Table 10.1 which, in this context, is easier to read.

```
# Correlation matrix that matches pairplot
df[['Reactions','Comments','Sentiment_ggl',
    'Magnitude_ggl','Negative_nltk','Neutral_nltk',
    'Positive_nltk','Compound_nltk','len',
    'hashtags']].corr()
```

Which produces a table that matches Table 10.1.

In this early stage, choosing to arbitrarily look at correlations above 0.1 or below −0.1, it seems that reactions and comments may be related to five of our potential feature predictor variables. These potential predictors include Google's sentiment score `Sentiment_ggl`, Google's magnitude score `Magnitude_ggl`, NLTK's negative sentiment score `Negative_nltk`, the post length `len` and the number of `hashtags`.

To get a closer look at these specific relationships we can create 10 scatter plots with the following for loop.

```python
# Create a grid of subplots
fig, axes = plt.subplots(figsize=(12, 25),
                         ncols=2, nrows=5,
                         squeeze=False)
# Adjust the spacing between the subplots
plt.subplots_adjust(hspace=0.5, wspace=0.3)

# Tuple list containing var names + titles
variables = [
    ('Sentiment_ggl', 'Google Sentiment'),
    ('Magnitude_ggl', 'Google Magnitude'),
    ('Negative_nltk', 'NLTK Negative Score'),
    ('len', 'Length No of Chars'),
    ('hashtags', 'Hashtags Count')]

# Iterate through list of variables and titles
for i, (var, title) in enumerate(variables):
    # Iterate through outcomes
    # ('Reactions' + 'Comments')
    for j, outcome in enumerate(
            ['Reactions', 'Comments']):
```

```
# Create seaborn regplot for each
# variable combination and outcome
sns.regplot(
    data=df, ax=axes[i, j],
    x=var, y=outcome,
    scatter_kws={'s': 10}
).set_title(title)  # Set subplot title
```

Which gives the output shown in Figure 10.5.

From this output, reading across the top pair of scatter plots it appears that the number of reactions and the number of comments seem to decline as the Google sentiment score increases. The direction of the line shown in these top two scatter plots is consistent with the negative correlation coefficient we saw for these variables. The relationship is subtle. Without the trendline it would not be visually clear there is in fact a relationship.

Across the second row it appears that both reactions and comments increase when Google measures a higher sentiment magnitude, which is again consistent with the correlation coefficient we saw in Table 10.1 above.

Moving to the third row we see mixed results. The third row presents an opportunity to discuss the line and also the shaded regions shown in these scatter charts. The line is an estimate of the functional relationship between the y and the x variable in each chart. It is common to place this line on a scatter plot to better illustrate the potential relationship between continuous variables. The method used to estimate this line is simple linear regression, which calculates the intercept and the slope of the line where the line is a simple $y = mx + b$ and where m is the slope and b is the intercept. See Chapter 11 for more on the topic of linear regression. The shaded region around the lines in this image shows confidence intervals. The wider the confidence

TABLE 10.1   A table of correlations for use in evaluating which variables may be strongly related

	Reactions	Comments	Sentiment_ ggl	Magnitude_ ggl	Negative_ nltk	Neutral_ nltk	Positive_ nltk	Compound_ nltk	len	hashtags
Reactions	1.000000	0.636917	−0.157704	0.426088	0.119236	0.013979	−0.097863	−0.004379	0.230997	−0.173567
Comments	0.636917	1.000000	-0.145567	0.480816	0.119877	0.005344	−0.088964	0.048143	0.340855	−0.226637
Sentiment_ ggl	−0.157704	−0.145567	1.000000	−0.089720	−0.537168	−0.165442	0.552046	0.475427	−0.240813	−0.247328
Magnitude_ ggl	0.426088	0.480816	−0.089720	1.000000	0.209116	−0.195800	0.063747	0.207482	0.797749	−0.163028
Negative_ nltk	0.119236	0.119877	−0.537168	0.209116	1.000000	−0.424499	−0.242949	−0.592831	0.187724	0.025836
Neutral_nltk	0.013979	0.005344	−0.165442	−0.195800	−0.424499	1.000000	−0.775162	−0.108477	−0.024560	0.258551
Positive_nltk	−0.097863	−0.088964	0.552046	0.063747	−0.242949	−0.775162	1.000000	0.529394	−0.104885	−0.295371
Compound_ nltk	−0.004379	0.048143	0.475427	0.207482	−0.592831	−0.108477	0.529394	1.000000	0.084567	−0.347392
len	0.230997	0.340855	−0.240813	0.797749	0.187724	−0.024560	−0.104885	0.084567	1.000000	0.233969
hashtags	−0.173567	−0.226637	−0.247328	−0.163028	0.025836	0.258551	−0.295371	−0.347392	0.233969	1.000000

FIGURE 10.5   Ten scatter plots with lines of fit that show the relationship between the number of reactions, the number of comments, and five other factors including Google sentiment scores, Google magnitude scores, NLTK negative sentiment scores, the number of characters and the number of hashtags

interval, the less certain we are about the line. In the third row of graphs we see that the confidence interval is quite large. We see how the confidence interval is narrow towards the lower ends of the charts on the left, and then it widens towards the right ends of the charts. Thus, even though we see a potential relationship between NLTK's negative sentiment score and the number of reactions or comments, we need to be sceptical that NLTK's negative sentiment score will be helpful as a predictor.

For the number of hashtags and post lengths, charted in the last two rows, we see two more important patterns. Again, the length of the post seems to be positively related to the number of reactions and comments. However, the relationship between hashtags and the number of reactions and posts appears more difficult to summarize. We see a negative relationship, which means that the number of reactions and comments seem to decline with the number of posts. We also see that the number of reactions and comments dramatically declines for posts with something around more than four hashtags.

An important reason for reviewing scatter plots is that they can assist in verifying which predictive method may work best with your data. Earlier in Chapter 3 I mentioned that data science is not unbiased and that falsification analysis is one method of exposing bias in your work so that you can work to reduce it. For example, in Figures 10.2 and 10.3 showing penguins by flipper and bill length, we see that the three species of penguins seem to cluster naturally on the plot. In such a case where scatter plots show clusters, you will then know that the data are suitable for clustering or classification algorithms such as k-means clustering or k-nearest neighbors where a key assumption is that similar items are 'close' to each other.

Conversely, when you see linear, or seemingly nearly linear, relationships such as those shown in Figure 10.5 that compare reactions and comments to sentiment scores and hashtag counts, it is an indication that your data may be suitable for use in

regression algorithms where a key assumption is that there are linear relationships in your data.

In this way, a look at scatter plots is one method of falsification analysis, which is an effort to look for evidence that may invalidate one or more assumptions on which you rely when conducting your analysis.

Bar charts

A bar chart presents an opportunity to more fully explore some of the patterns we noticed above. For example, we might like to better understand how hashtags relate to engagement. To do this we will first recode hashtags into an ordinal and then create a bar chart that shows the average number of posts for each ordinal category of hashtags.

```
# Generate bar charts to explore hashtags
fig, axes = plt.subplots(figsize=(12, 15),
                         nrows=2, ncols=1)
plt.subplots_adjust(hspace=0.3, wspace=0.3)

# Define custom categories for the ordinal variable
categories = ['0-2', '3-4', '5-6',
              '7-8', '9-10', '11-12',
              '13-14', '15+']

# Convert the discrete variable to an ordinal
df['hash_cat'] = pd.cut(df['hashtags'],
                        bins=[0, 3, 5, 7, 9, 11,
                              13, 15, 1000],
                        labels=categories).astype(

    'category')
```

```python
# Calculate reactions + comments by hash_cat
reaction_by_hash = df.groupby(
    'hash_cat')['Reactions'].mean()
comments_by_hash = df.groupby(
    'hash_cat')['Comments'].mean()

# Create a bar chart for reactions by hash_cat
sns.barplot(x=reaction_by_hash.index,
            y=reaction_by_hash.values,
            ax=axes[0])

# Add labels to the bars
for i, v in enumerate(reaction_by_hash):
    axes[0].text(i, v-1.5, "{:.2f}".format(v),
            color='white',
            size='large',
            ha="center")

# Set the title and axis labels
axes[0].set_title(
    'Reactions Decrease After 4 Hashtags')
axes[0].set_xlabel(
    'Number of Hashtags')
axes[0].set_ylabel(
    'Average Number of Reactions')

# Create a bar chart for comments by hash_cat
sns.barplot(x=comments_by_hash.index,
            y=comments_by_hash.values,
            ax=axes[1])

# Add labels to the bars
for i, v in enumerate(comments_by_hash):
    # Place height label when value is >= 1
```

```
if v >= 1:
    axes[1].text(i, v-.5, "{:.2f}".format(v),
            color='white',
            size='large',
            ha="center")
# Place height lable when value is < 1
elif (v < 1) & (v != 0):
    axes[1].text(i, v+.15, "{:.2f}".format(v),
            color='black',
            size='large',
            ha="center")
# Set the title and axis labels
axes[1].set_title(
    'Reactions Decrease After 4 Hashtags')
axes[1].set_xlabel(
    'Number of Hashtags')
axes[1].set_ylabel(
    'Average Number of Comments')

# Display the charts
plt.show()
```

This code generates two bar charts that explore the relationship between the number of hashtags in social media posts and the average number of reactions and comments. This code and the resulting visualizations accomplish this analysis by first defining custom categories for a new ordinal variable hash_cat. To create hash_cat, the code converts the discrete variable hashtags to an ordinal using pd.cut(). It then calculates the mean number of reactions and comments for each level of hash_cat category using the Pandas .groupby() method. The code then displays the two bar charts using Seaborn's sns.barplot(). There is one

chart for average reactions by hash_cat and the other for average comments. The code also adds height data labels to the bars. All of which produces the results shown in Figure 10.6.

FIGURE 10.6   Two bar charts that explore the relationship between the number of hashtags in a LinkedIn post and the amount of engagement that post received

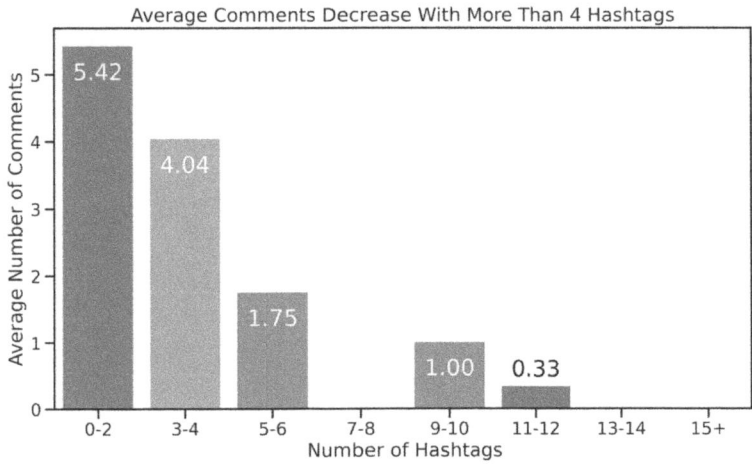

The practical implication of what we see in Figure 10.6 is that instead of relying on the number of hashtags as a discrete variable that may predict engagement, it may be smarter to convert hashtag counts to a binary variable with two levels of values. There will be one level of value for 0–4 hashtags and another level of value for 5 or more hashtags.

Violin plots and boxplots

To continue with how we explore these data, we can now turn to two closely related chat types – violin plots and boxplots. Violin plots and boxplots help visualize the measures of central tendency. They are also an excellent choice when looking to compare the measures of central tendency across categories. Here we can use both violin and boxplots to better explore how the number of hashtags might relate to engagement.

First, let's just look at the measures of central tendency in our measures of engagement by hashtag counts. Let's also take the lesson and conclusion found by looking at the bar charts. To take the lesson from those bar charts we will first covert the hashtag variable into a binary. The following code again uses the pd.cut() function to create this new hash_bins variable.

```
# Define the custom categories for the binary variable
hashbins = ['0-4', '5+']

# Convert the discrete variable to a binary
df['hash_bins'] = pd.cut(df['hashtags'],
                         bins=[0, 5, 1000],
                         labels=hashbins).
                         astype('category')

# Calculate reactions + comments by hash_bins
reaction_by_hashbins = df.groupby(
    'hash_bins')['Reactions']
```

```
comments_by_hashbins = df.groupby(
    'hash_bins')['Comments']

# Summary stats for reaction_by_hashbins
reaction_by_hashbins.describe()
```

Which produces the following output, which will be the summary statistics for reactions divvied out by our new binary hash_bins variable.

	count	mean	std	min	25%	50%	75%	max
hash_bins								
0-4	108.0	12.972222	11.353667	0.0	5.00	10.0	15.25	55.0
5+	32.0	6.937500	4.996370	1.0	3.75	6.0	8.00	21.0

Using similar code we can also see summary statistics for comments.

```
comments_by_hashbins.describe()
```

Which shows:

	Count	mean	std	min	25%	50%	75%	max
hash_bins								
0-4	108.0	5.101852	8.059289	0.0	0.0	3.0	6.0	58.0
5+	32.0	0.531250	1.106706	0.0	0.0	0.0	1.0	4.0

From this output, in tabular format we again see the pattern that both reactions and comments are higher among posts with 0–4 hashtags and much less for posts with 5 or more hashtags. However, it can be helpful to visualize with violin and boxplots.

```
# Create a 4x4 grid of subplots
fig, axes = plt.subplots(nrows=2, ncols=2, figsize=(10, 8))
plt.subplots_adjust(hspace=0.5, wspace=0.1)

# Upper left: box plot of Reactions by hash_bins
sns.boxplot(x='Reactions', y='hash_bins', data=df,
            ax=axes[0][0], palette='pastel')
axes[0][0].set_title('Box: Reactions by Hashtags')
axes[0][0].set_ylabel('No of Hashtags')

# Upper right: violin plot of Reactions by hash_bins
sns.violinplot(x='Reactions', y='hash_bins', data=df,
               ax=axes[0][1], palette='pastel')
axes[0][1].set_title('Violin: Reactions by Hashtags')
axes[0][1].set_ylabel('')
axes[0][1].set_yticklabels('')

# Lower left: box plot of Comments by hash_bins
sns.boxplot(x='Comments', y='hash_bins', data=df,
            ax=axes[1][0], palette='pastel')
axes[1][0].set_title('Box: Comments by Hashtags')
axes[1][0].set_ylabel('No of Hashtags')

# Lower right: violin plot of Comments by hash_bins
sns.violinplot(x='Comments', y='hash_bins',data=df,
               ax=axes[1][1], palette='pastel')
```

```
axes[1][1].set_title('Violin: Comments by Hashtags')
axes[1][1].set_ylabel('')
axes[1][1].set_yticklabels('')
```

This code creates a 4x4 grid of subplots using Matplotlib and Seaborn. The upper-left plot is a boxplot of Reactions by hash_bins, the upper-right plot is a violin plot of Reactions by hash_bins, the lower-left plot is a boxplot of Comments by hash_bins, and the lower-right plot is a violin plot of Comments by hash_bins. The code also sets the titles and y-axis labels for each plot using .set_title() and .set_ylabel(). Because the left- and right-hand plots share a y-axis, this code also removes the y-axis tick labels for the upper-right and lower-right plots. Which produces the output as shown in Figure 10.7.

As you can see here, a boxplot is a graphical representation of a data distribution using multiple key statistical measures including the first quartile (Q1), median, third quartile (Q3) and maximum. The box itself represents the interquartile range (IQR), which is the range of values between the first and third quartiles. The line inside the box represents the median. The whiskers extending from the box show the minimum and maximum values within 1.5 times the IQR. Any data points outside this range can be considered outliers and are plotted individually as circles, dots, diamonds or some other point.

To read a boxplot, first identify the median by looking for the line inside the box. Then, examine the large box which shows the middle range in which 50% of the observations lie. The whiskers will help to determine whether there are many outliers in the data. Outliers are data points that are significantly

FIGURE 10.7   Boxplots and violin plots that show how posts with more than four hashtags receive fewer reactions and fewer comments

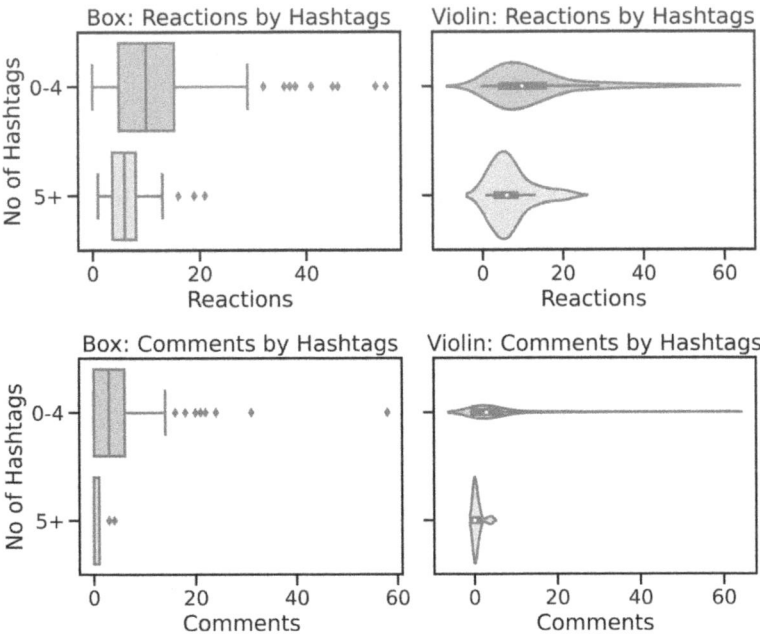

different from the rest of the data. In the context of boxplots outliers are often plotted as individual points. If there are outliers, they appear as individual points shown beyond the whiskers.

A violin plot is a type of data visualization that conceptually combines the notion of a boxplot with a kernel density plot. A kernel density plot shows the probability density function of a continuous variable. Thus, the violin plot shows the distribution of a continuous variable. Often, the profile of a violin plot can appear similar to the musical instrument. In this case we use the violin plot to see how the distribution is different between and among two categories' posts with 0–4 hashtags and posts with 5 or more hashtags.

The shape of the violin represents the density of observations along the x-axis. The wider parts of the violin represent regions where there are more observations, while the narrower parts represent regions with fewer observations. The white dot inside the violin represents the median of the data. The thick black bar inside the violin represents the interquartile range, which is the range between the 25th and 75th percentiles of the data.

In this chapter's current working context there is at least one other helpful use for box and violin plots. Here I will demonstrate with violin plots how we can examine engagement across our user group career type.

```
# Examine engagement across career type
fig, axes = plt.subplots(nrows=2, ncols=1, figsize=(10, 12))
plt.subplots_adjust(hspace=0.3, wspace=0.1)

# Upper: violin plot of Reactions by user career type
sns.violinplot(x='Reactions', y='group', data=df,
               ax=axes[0], palette='pastel')
axes[0].set_title('Reactions by Career Type')
axes[0].set_xlabel('Number of Reactions')
axes[0].set_ylabel('')
axes[0].set_xticklabels('')

# Lower: violin plot of Comments by user career type
sns.violinplot(x='Comments', y='group',data=df,
               ax=axes[1], palette='pastel')
axes[1].set_title('Comments by Career Type')
axes[1].set_xlabel('Number of Comments')
axes[1].set_ylabel('')
```

Which produces the output shown in Figure 10.8.

FIGURE 10.8   Two sets of violin plots that compare LinkedIn post engagement by users' career type

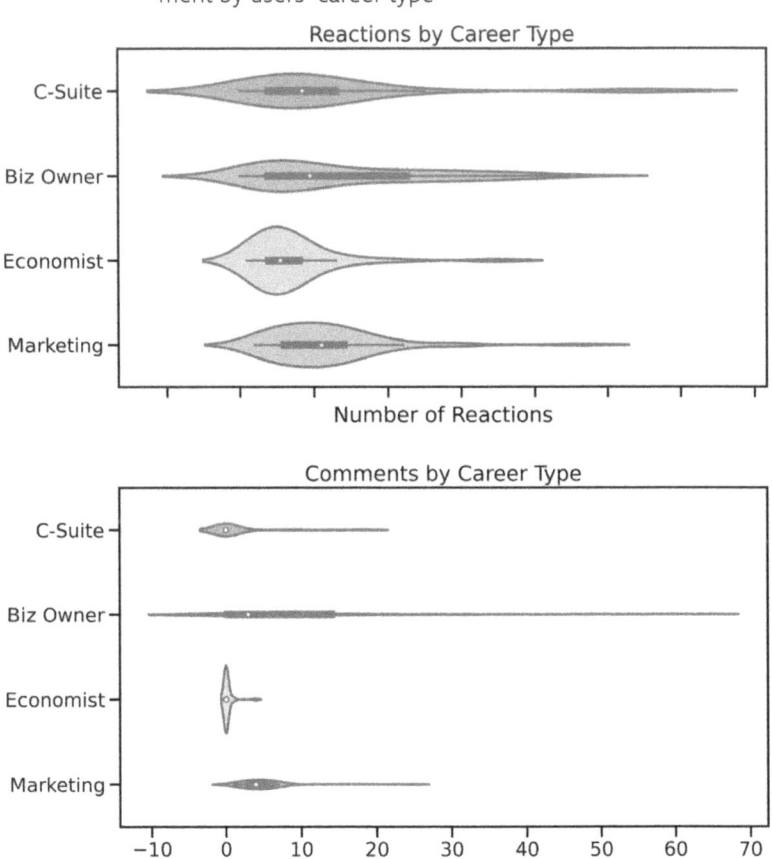

From these visuals we can see that the economist folks seem to have the lowest median engagement rates. With what appears to be the highest median number of comments and the highest median number of reactions, the marketing professionals seem

to have consistently the most engagement. However, the C-suite and business owner folks occasionally see spikes in their engagement as shown by the long tail we see to the right end of their violins.

In these examples we also observe one of the sometimes-perceived weaknesses of the violin plot. Sometimes the plot extends below zero, as shown here – even when there are not values below zero. Here we have counted the number of comments and reactions and there cannot be negative numbers on these counts. A violin plot sometimes extends below zero even when there are no values below zero because the plot is displaying the estimated probability density, which can take non-zero values outside the observed range of the data. This can happen if the distribution of the data is skewed or if there are outliers that extend the range of the data.

The box and violin plots can not only provide valuable information about the spread of the data, their central tendency and the presence of outliers, but also assist in comparing the measures of central tendency across multiple categories.

Heat maps

When well-prepared, heat maps can be quick to read and understand. Heat maps are a type of data visualization that can share information about and display up to three dimensions of data. For example, in Figure 10.9 there are three dimensions or variables to consider. The first is the career type of the person who posted, the second is the day of week they posted, and the third is the median number of reactions on posts from that day.

Figure 10.9 comes from the following code that proceeds in two major steps. The first major step is to prepare a pivot table that finds the median number of reactions from each type of LinkedIn user and from each day of the week.

FIGURE 10.9   A heat map showing the median number of post reactions by LinkedIn user type and day of week

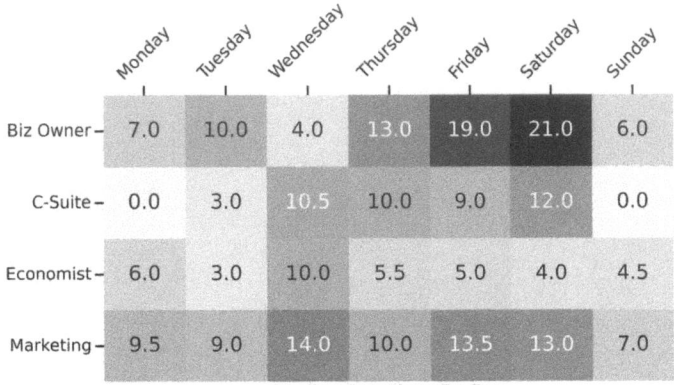

Median Reactions By Day

```
# Get the name of each day
df['day_name'] = df['Date'].dt.day_name()

# Pivot table; mean number of reactions by day
# Also review mean ractions by career type
reactions_x_day_x_group = pd.pivot_table(
    data=df, values='Reactions', index='group',
    columns='day_name', aggfunc='median').fillna(0.0)

reactions_x_day_x_group = \
  reactions_x_day_x_group.reindex(
  columns=['Monday', 'Tuesday', 'Wednesday',
            'Thursday', 'Friday', 'Saturday',
            'Sunday'])

reactions_x_day_x_group
```

Which produces the following output.

day_name	Monday	Tuesday	Wednesday	Thursday	Friday	Saturday	Sunday
group							
Biz Owner	7.0	10.0	4.0	13.0	19.0	21.0	6.0
C-Suite	0.0	3.0	10.5	10.0	9.0	12.0	0.0
Economist	6.0	3.0	10.0	5.5	5.0	4.0	4.5
Marketing	9.5	9.0	14.0	10.0	13.5	13.0	7.0

From this pivot table, the values that govern the shades of colour in Figure 10.9's heat map are again the third dimension. The second portion of the code that generates Figure 10.9 is as follows.

```
fig, ax = plt.subplots(figsize=(10, 5))

sns.heatmap(reactions_x_day_x_group,
            annot=True, fmt=".1f",
            cbar=False, cmap='Blues',
            annot_kws={"size": 20})

ax.set_xticklabels(ax.get_xticklabels(),
            rotation=45,
            ha='center')
ax.xaxis.tick_top()
ax.set_xlabel('Median Reactions By Day')
ax.set_ylabel('')
```

Heat maps are often used to show correlations or relationships between variables, and they can be useful for identifying patterns or trends in large data sets. The colour scale should be chosen carefully to ensure that the data are accurately represented and easily interpreted. In this case we see that engagement seems to increase for many users in the middle or later portion of the week. The higher engagement seems to be especially true for business owners.

Returning to our analytical question and business problem, to understand how we might predict engagement, it appears that day of week might be helpful in calculating that prediction. The number of reactions does seem to vary by day of the week. We will use this information later in Chapter 11 when we turn to using day of week in our predictive models.

Bubble chart

Similar to a heat map that shows the relationship between three variables, such as the type of career someone has, the day of the week and the median number of posts, we can also use bubble charts to look at three dimensions. The main difference is that for bubble charts we usually have a task that involves comparing three continuous variables.

For example, we have already observed that engagement seems to be related to both Google's sentiment and Google's magnitude score. We can include all three of these continuous variables in a single visualization using the notion of a bubble chart, as shown below in Figure 10.10 and produced with the code here.

```
plt.figure(figsize=(10, 8))
# Create a bubble chart
sns.scatterplot(data=df,
                x='Sentiment_ggl',
                y='Reactions',
                size='Magnitude_ggl',
                hue='Magnitude_ggl',
                sizes=(20, 800),
                alpha=0.5,
                edgecolor='k',
                palette='OrRd',
                legend='brief')
```

```
# Declare title in parts
t1 = 'Google Sentiment Score vs.'
t2 = ' Reactions with Magnitude Score'

# Set the title and axis labels
plt.title(t1 + t2)
plt.xlabel('Google Sentiment Score')
plt.ylabel('Number of Reactions')

# Move the legend outside the graph area
plt.legend(bbox_to_anchor=(1.05, 1),
           loc=2, borderaxespad=0.,
           title='Magnitude Score')

# Add an annotation that marks an observation of
interest
plt.annotate(text='Observation Of Interest',
             xy=(.5, 36), xytext=(.35,42),
             fontsize=15,
             arrowprops={
                 'arrowstyle':'->',
                 'connectionstyle':'arc3, rad=-.5'})
```

In this chart we see several large and small bubbles more towards the upper end of the range of reaction counts. When you look at this chart, recall that each bubble represents a specific post on LinkedIn. A common next step when visualizing data with a bubble chart is to individually inspect a specific data point. To

FIGURE 10.10   A bubble chart that shows the relationship between number of reactions, the Google sentiment score and the Google magnitude score

demonstrate the process of using a bubble chart in this way let's take a closer look at the large bubble located in the upper right portion of this chart, marked as an 'observation of interest'. The following code will show the data from that observation of interest.

```
# Using estimated filters search for a specific
observation
df[(df['Reactions'] > 30) &
   (df['Sentiment_ggl'] > .4) &
   (df['Magnitude_ggl'] > 10)].transpose()
```

Which produces the following output.

```
Date                           2021-11-11 00:00:00
ShareCommentary A week out from Thanksgiving,
and I have found...
Reactions                                      36.0
Comments                                       21.0
User                                           1021
Sentiment_ggl                                   0.5
Magnitude_ggl                                  14.5
Negative_nltk                                 0.014
Neutral_nltk                          0.776
Positive_nltk                         0.21
Compound_nltk                         0.9968
len                                   1875
group                                 Biz Owner
hashtags                              1
hash_cat                              0-2
hash_bins                             0-4
day_name                              Thursday
```

To see the unabbreviated version of that ShareCommentary text use the following code which passes the column name in square brackets and then 5 as an index also in square brackets that corresponds to the index displayed above.

```
# Read the actual post from that observation
df[(df['Reactions'] > 30) &
    (df['Sentiment_ggl'] > .4) &
    (df['Magnitude_ggl'] > 10)]['ShareCommentary'][5]
```

Which will display a version of the excerpted output.

```
'A week out from Thanksgiving, and I have found myself so
reflective of what I am thankful for this year. So, I think
I will share some of those things over the next week
(in no particular order)....."\r\n""\r\n"Today I am
thankful for flannel pajamas, king size down comforters,
and the ability to use them both while working."\r\n""\
r\n"That\'s right. I got up this morning, worked out,
got everyone to school,
showered, then PUT MY PJ\'s BACK ON!!!"\r\n""\r\n"Then I
draped myself with a king sized down comf...'
```

Histogram

A histogram is a special instance of a bar chart. The histogram uses the bar chart strategy, but instead of using the bar chart to understand how a qualitative variable relates to a continuous variable, the histogram provides a close look at a single continuous variable.

The histogram visualization strategy involves converting a continuous variable to an ordinal. Each level of the new ordinal is called a bucket, or a bin. The histogram places those buckets across the horizontal x-axis. Then along the vertical y-axis is usually the count of observations that fall in each of those buckets. Finally, the histogram includes a series of bars that corresponds to a height that shows the count of observations in that bin on the vertical y-axis.

Two example histograms shown in Figure 10.11 display the distributions of Reactions and Comments counts. The following code produces Figure 10.11.

```
# Examine the distributions of Reactions and Comments
fig, axes = plt.subplots(nrows=2, ncols=1, figsize=(8, 10))

# Adjust the space between the subplots
plt.subplots_adjust(hspace=0.4, wspace=0.1)

# Plot a histogram for 'Reactions'
sns.histplot(data=df, x='Reactions', bins=15, kde=True, ax=axes[0])
axes[0].set_title('Histogram of Reactions')    # 1st subplot title

axes[0].set_xlabel('Reactions')                # Set x-axis label
axes[0].set_ylabel('Frequency')                # Set y-axis label

# Plot a histogram for 'Comments'
sns.histplot(data=df, x='Comments', bins=15, kde=True, ax=axes[1])
axes[1].set_title('Histogram of Comments')     # 2nd subplot title
axes[1].set_xlabel('Comments')                 # Set x-axis label
axes[1].set_ylabel('Frequency')                # Set y-axis label
```

By reviewing these histograms, we can see that the majority of posts seemed to receive under 20 reactions and under 20 comments. However, the charts in Figure 10.11 also show that some posts received more than 50 reactions or comments. Using the bins=15 option, this code specifies that there will be 15 bins and also thus 15 bars in each histogram.

An added feature of histograms, as rendered in Figure 10.11, is a dark line that also traces the height of the bars. This line is a kernel density plot which is a method of estimating the probability density of the variable's distribution. When used well, the kernel density plot can provide a more visually appealing representation of the distribution than a histogram can provide alone. Importantly, to note in the context of this chapter on data visualization is that kernel density plots are also related to violin plots. The outlines of violin plots, such as those shown in Figures 9.3, 10.7 and 10.8, are estimated using the kernel density strategy.

With careful review, and by producing multiple versions with various bin counts, histograms provide valuable insights into the

FIGURE 10.11   Histograms of post reaction counts (above) and post comment counts (below)

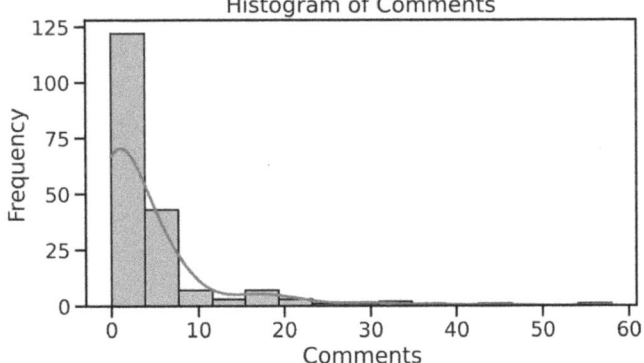

underlying structure and data patterns. By dividing the data into intervals or bins and plotting the frequency of observations within each bin, histograms allow for easy identification of trends, outliers and also potential issues regarding data quality that may need your attention.

Conclusion

In this chapter we discussed the role of data visualization in pursuing the answer to an analytical question or in working

towards the solution to an important business problem. Specifically we worked with data from LinkedIn users. And the analytical question was to understand if sentiment might help predict engagement with those posts in the form of reactions or comments.

We also built onto the data wrangling knowledge discussed earlier in Chapters 5 and 6 with three new data wrangling tasks. Here in Chapter 10 we inspected for and removed outlier data. We also created a new feature that measured the length of the posts on LinkedIn. And we applied hypothetical knowledge from others to inform how we coded the career type for each LinkedIn user.

Overall, this chapter highlighted the significance of data visualization in the data science journey, specifically in exploring data and extracting insights from them. I emphasized that the ability to create effective data visualizations is a valuable skill that can empower individuals to gain deeper insights, but I also urged a sense of caution. The cautionary note is that just because you can create information-dense data visualizations, in new formats, this does not mean you should. By learning more about data visualization, your knowledge of data visuals will quickly grow to exceed the knowledge of those with whom you work. Keep this in mind as you introduce new data visualizations to them.

I also specifically cautioned against creating cluttered and confusing visuals. I suggest that it is smart to let each visual convey one simple message (not many messages). I say again, while it can be tempting to include as much information as possible in a visualization, doing so can lead to ineffective communication. I also warned against the danger of producing data visualizations for the sake of data visualizations.

The chapter then explored multiple components and conventions of data visualization. I discussed axes, titles, legends, annotations, data labels and related topics in order to provide a

foundation as we looked at specific data visualizations through the remainder of the chapter.

Furthermore, the chapter also discussed the importance of reframing data visualization as a family of analytical techniques. By understanding the underlying principles of data visualization, and by understanding it as merely another analytical technique, individuals can better understand how it fits into the broader context of data analysis. This approach empowers individuals to think about what they want to know and then devise a visual that can achieve the communication goal. In this way, improving our knowledge about data visualization is more about learning to think about data and less about learning to memorize a gallery of data visualization types.

Finally, the chapter also showed how to produce and discussed how to interpret many of the most popular charts used in data visualization, including scatter plots, bar charts, boxplots, violin plots, heat maps, bubble charts and histograms.

Overall, the chapter provides a focused, rather than comprehensive, overview of data visualization, highlighting its importance in data analysis, and emphasizing the need for individuals to understand its underlying principles. The chapter sets the foundation for the next chapter, which focuses on generating business value with data, data visualization and data science.

Business values and clients

Through this book we have confidently journeyed through the history of data science. We have also discussed the topics of data culture and data ethics, and had a close look at what the process of data science looks like through an eight-stage model. Instead of comprehensive, our journey has been focused. We aimed for depth instead of breadth.

You may be bouncing around this book as you study the topic of data science. This chapter is one not to miss. Returning to the eight-stage process introduced in Chapter 4, this chapter focuses in new ways on the third (justify), fourth (wrangle), fifth (select and apply), sixth (check and recheck) and seventh (interpret) stages.

In specific, this chapter will continue with the data we introduced in Chapter 9 from users of LinkedIn. In Chapter 10 we used those LinkedIn data for data visualization work. We will carry the lessons learned in Chapter 10 forward here into

Chapter 11 where we will apply two data science models in a manner that may help us predict how extensively others may interact with a new proposed post on LinkedIn.

Justify the problem

Whether sentiment might, or might not, relate to engagement on social media is an important question. In 2021, at least one prominent former Facebook employee blew the whistle on what was likely the company's biggest scandal since its inception. Some may consider this scandal one of the most prominent in all of social media's history. Some viewed the contemporaneous company name change as a strategically timed attempt to deflect unfavourable attention.

For instance, the whistleblower, who worked for Facebook as a data scientist, accused Facebook of purposefully promoting and spreading controversial, divisive and hateful content in order to increase overall engagement on the Facebook platform.[1]

Before and since this scandal, accusations that companies like Facebook and other social media platforms deliberately promoted provocative content drew criticism. Haugen, the whistleblower, in her 5 October 2021 Congressional testimony, summarized: 'Facebook has realized that if they change the algorithm to be safer, people will spend less time on the site, they'll click on less ads, and [Facebook] will make less money'.[2]

As you can see, this topic is nuanced, and as such it is hard to find definite answers. Thankfully, now that you are armed with your newly acquired knowledge of NLP sentiment analysis, you can further explore this problem. For instance, in the previous chapter, we found there seems to be a relationship between the sentiment of a post on LinkedIn and the number of reactions and comments it receives.

Wrangle the data

For this work we again need to load and wrangle the data. Here again is the code that will load and cursorily inspect the data.

```
# Import the Pandas and Numpy libraries
import pandas as pd
import numpy as np

# Load ConfidentDataCh9Social.csv
location = 'https://raw.githubusercontent.com/'
path = 'adamrossnelson/confident/main/data/'
fname = 'confident_ch9socialsents.csv'
df = pd.read_cst(location + path + fname,
                 parse_dates=['Date'])

# Display the shape of the data
print(df.shape)
```

This block of code imports the Pandas and NumPy libraries. Then, it loads our LinkedIn data from a CSV file called confident_ch9socialsents.csv into a Pandas DataFrame. The code also parses the Date column because we specified it as a date with the parse_dates option in the .read_csv() function.

We already discussed some of the available data wrangling options presented by these data in Chapter 10 where we generated a variable to measure the length of the post (len), a variable to show information about the LinkedIn user's career (group) and a variable to count the number of hashtags (hashtags) in the post. In this chapter we repeat those steps and perform three additional data wrangling tasks.

Three added steps

Below, again, is the data wrangling code from Chapter 10 but with three additional data wrangling steps. The first additional step recodes the count of hashtags to a binary. We learned in the previous chapter that posts with more than approximately three or four hashtags seemed to have lower engagement. This means that we can simplify the analysis by converting the hashtag variable to a binary with two categories. In this hashtag binary there will be a 1 for those that included a hashtag count below the mean, and a 0 otherwise.

The second new step is to leverage information we also learned from Chapter 10 that Wednesday, Thursday, Friday and Saturday seem to be days with higher engagements. With this information we create a new binary predictor that informs us whether the post occurred on a Wednesday, Thursday, Friday or Saturday.

The third additional step creates a new set of binary target variables that we did not need for data visualization above, but which we will need for our classification predictive model here in Chapter 11.

```
# Engineer new feature that shows length of post
df['len'] = df['ShareCommentary'].str.len()

# Engineer new feature that regroups users
df['group'] = df['User'].map(
    {1010:'Biz Owner',1011:'Biz Owner',
     1020:'Biz Owner',1021:'Biz Owner',
     1030:'Economist',1031:'Economist',
     1040:'C-Suite',1041:'C-Suite',
     1050:'Marketing',1051:'Marketing'})

# Count the number of hashtags in each post
```

```
df['hashtags'] = df['ShareCommentary'].str.count('#')

# Convert hashtags to a binary predictor
# List comprehension to set posts with hashtag
# counts at or below 4 = 1 and otherwise = 0
df['hashtags'] = [1 if x <=4
                  else 0 for x in df['hashtags']]

# Create a binary predictor variable = 1 if post
# occurred on a Wed, Thu, Fri, or Sat
df['wed_t_sat'] = [1 if x in ['Wednesday','Thursday',
                              'Friday','Saturday']
                   else 0 for x in df['Date'].dt.day_
                   name()]
# New binary target (Reac short for Reactions. . .
# bin short for binary) - Preserve cut point record
mid_reac_cut = df['Reactions'].describe()['50%']
print(f"Median reactions: {mid_reac_cut}")

# List comprehension to set posts with reaction
# counts at or above median = 1, otherwise = 0
df['Reac_bin'] = [1 if x >= mid_reac_cut
                  else 0 for x in df['Reactions']]

# New binary target (Comm short for Comments . . .
# bin short for binary) - Preserve cut record
mid_comm_cut = df['Comments'].describe()['50%']
print(f"Median comments are: {mid_comm_cut}")

# List comprehension to set posts with reaction
# counts at or above the median = 1,otherwise = 0
df['Comm_bin'] = [1 if x >= mid_comm_cut
                  else 0 for x in df['Comments']]
```

```
# Show the results
df[['ShareCommentary','Reactions','Comments',
    'len','group','hashtags','wed_t_sat',
    'Reac_bin','Comm_bin']].sample(6)
```

This code first creates a hashtags column that counts the number of hashtags in each post. Next, the code converts the hashtags column to a binary predictor based on a threshold of 4. To assist in using information about the day of the post this code also created a wed_t_sat variable that is 1 when the post occurred on days known to produce higher engagement rates (Wednesday through Saturday) and 0 otherwise. In this code we also create two new binary target variables for Reactions and Comments based on whether the value is above or below the median. For later reference, the code also displays the median reactions and comments count. Finally, df.sample(6) displays six random observations from the modified DataFrame. For the following excerpted output.

	Reactions	Comments	len	group	hashtags	wed_t_ sat	Reac_ bin	Comm_ bin
189	3.0	1.0	661	Marketing	1	1	0	1
82	3.0	0.0	181	Biz Owner	1	1	0	0
92	5.0	0.0	1189	Economist	0	1	0	0
148	14.0	5.0	403	Marketing	1	1	1	1
52	9.0	0.0	744	Economist	1	1	1	0
181	7.0	2.0	585	Marketing	1	0	0	1

Inspecting for accurate wrangling

At this stage of the work, we have so many columns we cannot see all of them in one view without scrolling side-by-side. To inspect a subset of columns we can use the following code, which will better assist in inspecting new variables. Also notice how the following code lists the column names, not in the order the appear in the DataFrame but rather in an order that most easily allows us to inspect the data.

```
df[['Date','Reactions','Comments',
    'Reac_bin','Comm_bin','len',
    'hashtags','wed_t_sat']].sample(6)
```

For the following output.

	Reactions	Comments	Reac_bin	Comm_bin	len	hashtags	wed_t_sat
75	8.0	0.0	1	0	117	1	1
6	38.0	22.0	1	1	1575	1	1
87	6.0	1.0	0	1	691	0	0
172	6.0	2.0	0	1	659	1	1
39	15.0	9.0	1	1	124	1	1
80	7.0	3.0	0	1	1368	1	0

As explained in earlier chapters, it is important to further double-check the work. Here we can double-check this work in many ways. To start out, we can use cross-tabulations.

```
# Check the hastag work
pd.crosstab(
    df['ShareCommentary'].str.count('#'),
    df['hashtags']).transpose()
```

Which shows the following excerpted output that indeed confirms our code achieved the desired result. We see that the posts with 0, 1, 2, 3 or 4 hashtags are now recoded as 1, while all other posts with more hashtags are now recorded as 0.

	0	1	2	3	4	5	6	7	9	10	12	13	14	17	19	20	22
hashtags																	
0		0	0	0	0	0	7	5	3	1	2	1	2	2	2	1	12	1
1		52	16	27	40	18	0	0	0	0	0	0	0	0	0	0	0	0

We can also check the weekday coding results in a cross-tabulation.

```
# Check the wed_t_sat variable results
pd.crosstab(
    df['Date'].dt.day_name(),
    df['wed_t_sat']).transpose()
```

Which gives the somewhat disordered output (the days are out of order) that confirms the desired result. Wednesday, Thursday, Friday and Saturday are coded as 1, and all other days are coded as 0.

Date	Friday	Monday	Saturday	Sunday	Thursday	Tuesday	Wednesday
wed_t_sat							
0	0	30	0	7	0	22	0
1	33	0	19	0	57	0	24

Next, we can check that the binary `Reac_bin` coded correctly.

```
# Check for proper coding of the Reac_bin variable
pd.crosstab(
    df['Reactions'], df['Reac_bin']).transpose()
```

Which shows a version of the following excerpted output.

```
Reactions  0.0  1.0  2.0  3.0  4.0  5.0  6.0  7.0  8.0  9.0
Reac_bin
0               2    8    8   17   18    9   12   15    0    0
1               0    0    0    0    0    0    0    0   12    7
```

Because we see that posts with reaction counts 0 through 7 coded as 0 and that all others coded as 1 we know the recode procedure for `Reac_bin` performed as expected.

Next we can check the `Comm_bin` variable.

```
# Check for proper coding of the Comm_bin variable
pd.crosstab(
    df['Comments'], df['Comm_bin']).transpose()
```

Here in this excerpted output, because the column marked 0.0 for the count of `Comments` shows 81 posts coded as 0 and the remainder values coded as 1, we see that the coding process proceeded as planned.

Comments	0.0	1.0	2.0	3.0	4.0	5.0	6.0	7.0	8.0	9.0
Comm_bin										
0	81	0	0	0	0	0	0	0	0	0
1	0	20	9	12	15	10	9	9	1	3

It may seem excessive to check, and recheck the work. I promise you that when the stakes are high, and when your results are challenged later during dissemination, or even when there are troubles during implementation, taking the time to check and recheck your work will spare you hours awake at night wondering whether you correctly specified your code.

These rechecks guard against special kinds of mistake, known as 'silent' mistakes. They are silent because Python gives no error message. Recall that Python is ignorant of how you intended to manipulate the code. This means that just because Python gives no error, you cannot take it for granted that the code performed as expected.

A silent coding error is an error in code that does not generate error or warning messages. Nevertheless, the error produces incorrect or unexpected results. When these errors go unnoticed they can lead to serious problems later on. Checking and rechecking your work can help catch silent errors, preventing you from wasting time and effort debugging your code later.

Select and apply

So far, we have specified an analytical question, a business problem, we have looked around, we have justified the work, and we have wrangled the data. The next step in this book's eight-stage

process is to select and apply analytical techniques designed to answer the question or solve the problem. Broadly speaking, given these data and our current case, there are two main options for the select and apply stage. The first option will be to apply a classification technique and the second will be to apply a regression technique.

Both classification and regression are supervised machine learning. I introduced the topics of supervised and unsupervised machine learning in Chapter 1; we noted that supervised machine learning requires historic or past observations that we can use to train a model that will be able to make predictions when it sees new data.

In the case of classification, we will use a technique known as k-nearest neighbors to ascertain whether a post is highly engaging or not.

We will define 'highly engaging' as posts with `Comm_bin` == 1 or `Reac_bin` == 1. In other words, posts with more than two or more comments or eight or more reactions will be classed as highly engaging.

In the case of regression, we will use a technique known as simple linear regression, or ordinary least squares regression, to estimate the exact number of reactions or comments a post might be expected to receive.

K-nearest neighbors

HOW IT WORKS

Review Figure 11.1 as you consider the concepts that underlie how k-nearest neighbors works. The essence of this technique is that it will map the observations, in this case LinkedIn posts, in a scatter plot. Because the technique is supervised, the model will use the known classification of existing posts to predict to which class new posts will belong.

FIGURE 11.1   A scatter plot that shows hypothetical LinkedIn data in a manner that demonstrates k-nearest neighbors algorithms

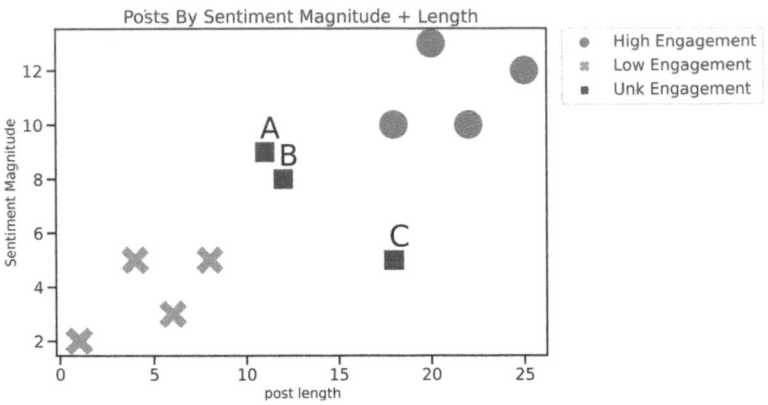

Here we see four green x symbols that represent posts with low sentiment magnitude and also that are short in length that, in this hypothetical, also experienced low engagement. We also see four red circles that represent posts with high sentiment magnitude and also that are of longer length that, again hypothetically, experienced high engagement.

I have labelled the three blue squares as A, B and C. The clever part about k-nearest neighbors is that the technique can help to ascertain, or predict, to which class points A, B and C belong by finding the k number of nearest neighbors and then classifying points A, B and C consistent with the majority of its neighbours on the scatter plot.

This technique also works in three-dimensional spaces, which is relatively easy to visualize by adding an imaginary z-axis to the x- and y- axis. Somewhat astoundingly to many observers who begin studying this method for the first time, these distances can also be measured and leveraged in the k-nearest neighbors algorithm in four dimensions, five dimensions or any number of dimensions. These multi-dimensional spaces where the number of dimensions exceeds three or four are often called hyper-dimensional or n-dimensional spaces.

In short, this algorithm makes predictions by plotting the unknown amongst a collection of known observations, then by calculating distances to the other known points in the hyper or feature space.

One of the key decisions in the process of implementing this algorithm is deciding how many neighbours you will direct the algorithm to use in making predictions. The processes ahead will show how to make that key choice.

SHOULD WE JUST 'EYEBALL' THIS?

We might be tempted to bust out a ruler, a pencil and a calculator to see for ourselves to which group or classification the unknown dots A, B and C belong. The visual is right there, no? Easy, right?

Not so. The computer is able to 'see' or discern distances much more quickly and efficiently than we can on our own. Relying on a human's calculations, even if well practised and well informed, would be a mistake. The human driven process would be subject to measurement error, perception error and more.

The computer is especially more capable than humans in the case of high n-dimensional spaces. The computer's k-nearest neighbors algorithm can literally memorize the locations of hundreds, thousands or even millions and billions of known observation locations in high n-dimensional space that most humans would struggle to merely comprehend.

After memorizing the locations of, and known classifications of, training data the algorithm can quickly produce new classifications for previously unobserved observations in a computational context that could demand hours of work from a single human.

MAKING IT WORK

To do this work we will also turn to a new collection of libraries from SciKit Learn, often abbreviated in writing and in spoken conversation as sklearn (pronounced s – k – learn). Here are those imports.

```
# Importing sklearn libraries
from sklearn.model_selection import train_test_split
from sklearn.preprocessing import StandardScaler
from sklearn.neighbors import KNeighborsClassifier
from sklearn.metrics import accuracy_score
from sklearn.metrics import classification_report
```

The `traint_test_split` function will help us divvy our data into separate training and testing data sets. The `StandardScaler` function will scale the data for us. Scaling the data is helpful because doing so will transform all variables to have a mean of 0 and a standard deviation of 1. This scaling procedure puts all variables on the same scale, which prevents any one variable from dominating the algorithm or skewing the results.

The `KNeighrborsClassifier` is the function that, as the name suggests, implements the algorithm we need for this technique. We will use `accuracy_score`, `classification_report` to evaluate the quality of the model and also to help us select the optimal number of k to specify in the model.

To begin this work we can use the data as prepared and wrangled above. To better identify exactly which variables are our predictor variables and exactly which is our target we will use the common convention to assign the predictors to capital X and the target to lower case y here in the following code, which will also split our data into `X_train`, `X_test`, `y_train` and `y_test`.

```
# Splitting the data into training and testing sets
X = df[['Sentiment_ggl', 'Magnitude_ggl',
        'len', 'wed_t_sat', 'hashtags']]
y = df['Reac_bin']
```

```
# Split the data for training and testing purposes
X_train, X_test, y_train, y_test = train_test_split(
    X, y, test_size=0.3, random_state=42)
```

The train_test_split function, as specified above by virtue of the test_size parameter, places 30% of the data in the test subset and reserves 70% for training.

After splitting the data we can then scale them using the StandardScaler function.

```
# Scaling the data
scaler = StandardScaler()
X_train_scaled = scaler.fit_transform(X_train)
X_test_scaled = scaler.transform(X_test)
```

At this point we are ready to begin training the model. We will iteratively use the KNeighrborsClassifier with multiple k which will allow us to test which specification is most accurate. Since one of the key decisions to make is how many k to specify, the iterative approach to training the model many times will help identify the optimal k. Remember that, discussed above in relation to Figure 11.1, the k parameter is the number of neighbours the model will look to when making predictions about new data.

To assist in finding the best k we also specify an empty list that will track the error rates associated with each k value.

```
# Find optimal k by starting empty list of errors
error_rates = []
```

The following code is the loop that will test the model with odd values of k, 1 through 41. The reason we choose odd values is to avoid the potential for ties in the number of nearest neighbours.

```
# Begin loop for all odd numbers from 1 to 41
for k in range(1, 41, 2):
    # Creating k-NN classification model
    knn = KNeighborsClassifier(n_neighbors=k)
    knn.fit(X_train_scaled, y_train)

    # Generate predictions on the testing data
    y_pred_kn = knn.predict(X_test_scaled)

    # Calculate predictions, record error rate
    error_rates.append(np.mean(y_pred_kn != y_test))
```

Through the course of the loop above, the code fits the KNeighborsClassifier, then it uses the results of that fit to make predictions using the testing data X_test_scaled, and finally compares y_pred and y_test to see what proportion of the predictions accurately matched the known results. The code stores the results of that comparison as a metric that is the proportion of incorrect matches in a Python list called error_rates.

With the error_rates list we can now visualize accuracy by the number of k.

```
# Plot the error rates
plt.figure(figsize=(12, 6))
plt.plot(range(1, 41, 2), error_rates, color='blue',
         linestyle=':', marker='x', markersize=5)
```

```
plt.title('Error Rates vs. K Values')
plt.xlabel('K Value')
plt.ylabel('Error Rate')

# Give annotation that documents optimal k
plt.annotate(text='Best Error-Rate With Fewest K',
             xy=(15, .29), xytext=(18, .32),
             fontsize=15,
             arrowprops={
                 'arrowstyle':'->',
                 'connectionstyle':'arc3, rad=-.3'})
```

Which produces output shown in Figure 11.2. When visualization the accuracy by the number of k we are looking for the most accurate result at the lowest number of k.

FIGURE 11.2   A line chart that shows error rates that correspond with each value of k

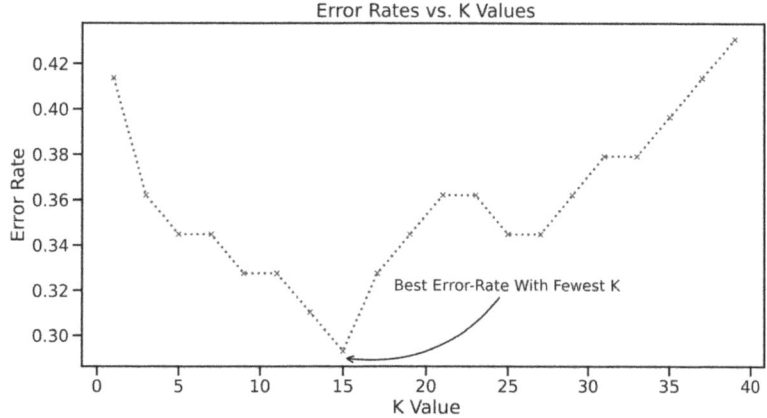

Choosing the most accurate result at the lowest number of k avoids overfitting the model. Overfitting is when the model is too complex and fits the training data too well. An overfit model

will make good predictions on known training data but likely not perform well on new data. Also notice how the graph makes what you might simply describe as an 'elbow' at the coordinates (k=15 and error rate=.29). The use of this visualization method to choose the optimal k is often known as the elbow method. As you continue your learning journey in data science you will see this elbow method in additional contexts.

Another important consideration here is whether accurately predicting the level of engagement 71% of the time, here in terms of a reaction count, at or above the median versus a reaction count below the median is an acceptable level of performance. Sure, 71% is much better than a coin flip, but it is far from perfect. Here is a good place to remember some of the general analytical advice from Chapter 3: all models are wrong and some are useful.

One last step before moving on to simple linear regression will be to generate again the k-nearest neighbors results with the optimal k = 15 and save additional performance metrics for later reference. The following code accomplishes these tasks.

```python
# Retrain the model with k = 15 (the optimal)
knn = KNeighborsClassifier(n_neighbors=15)
knn.fit(X_train_scaled, y_train)

# Generate predictions for later reference
y_pred_kn = knn.predict(X_test_scaled)

# Save performance results for later review
accuracy_kn = accuracy_score(y_test, y_pred_kn)
class_report_kn = classification_report(y_test, y_pred_kn)

# Display the accuracy score + classification report
print(accuracy_kn)
print(class_report_kn)
```

This code re-trains the k-nearest neighbors classification model with k=15, which was identified as optimal k. The KNeighborsClassifier() function instantiates the model, and the .fit() method trains the model on the scaled training data that had been prepared above. The .predict() then generates predictions on the testing data, and saves those predictions in y_pred_kn. The accuracy_score() function calculates the accuracy of the predictions, which the code saves to accuracy_kn. The classification_report() function generates a report of various classification metrics that the code then saves in class_report_kn. Finally the print() statement shows the classification results, shown here and discussed below under 'Check and recheck'.

	precision	recall	f1-score	support
0	0.62	0.65	0.64	23
1	0.76	0.74	0.75	35
accuracy			0.71	58
macro avg	0.69	0.70	0.70	58
weighted avg	0.71	0.71	0.71	58

Simple linear regression

HOW IT WORKS

Let us move on to simple linear regression to see if we can find results that may also be useful. Unlike k-nearest neighbors, which is often most closely associated with predicting a classification, we can use regression techniques to predict a continuous number as a target variable.

The process of understanding regression techniques begins in a way that is similar to the scatter plot in Figure 11.1 we used to understand k-nearest neighbors. Here we see Figure 11.3 where

in this case our target variable now appears on the vertical y-axis while the predictor variable appears on the x-axis.

In the example shown here in Figure 11.3, simple linear regression involves charting each post on the scatter plot according to the number of reactions it received and the post's sentiment magnitude score. Figure 11.3 includes fictional data to illustrate the method. The next step involves fitting a line through the scatter plot. Then we can use that line to estimate how many reactions a post might expect, given its sentiment magnitude score. As annotated, posts with a sentiment magnitude score of about 11 might expect approximately 14 reactions.

Just as I showed the k-nearest neighbors example in two dimensions, I also show this simple linear regression example in two dimensions. However, also like k-nearest neighbors, we can add multiple predictors to the technique, which means we will

FIGURE 11.3   A scatter plot with a regression line and a confidence interval that shows hypothetical LinkedIn data in a manner intended to demonstrate regression algorithms

be relying on the technique to find this line in a hyper-dimensional space. In two dimensions that line follows the functional form of $y = mX + b$. In hyper-dimensional spaces that line will follow a more complex form we can note as $y = m_1X_1 + m_2X_2 + m_3X_3 + \ldots + m_nX_n + b$. In the multi-dimensional space each X_n variable is an additional predictor variable.

MAKING IT WORK

Here again we turn to the SciKit Learn libraries. However, we also add another import `sm` from `statsmodels.api`. We will import the following.

```
# Importing sklearn libraries
from sklearn.model_selection import train_test_split
from sklearn.preprocessing import StandardScaler
import statsmodels.api as sm
from sklearn.metrics import mean_squared_error
```

If you have followed along the k-nearest neighbors example above, you will have already imported `train_test_split` and `StandardScalar` which help us divvy our training and testing data and also help us scale the data. Again, according to the procedure chosen for this book's illustrations, scaling the data centres the mean value of each variable at 0 and then adjusts the other values so that the distribution will have a standard deviation of 1. The scaling procedure prevents any one variable from, dominating the algorithm or skewing the results. Also the process of splitting data into training and testing sets is important so that we can more carefully evaluate the quality and performance of the model. The data held out for training can provide a clear look at how the model performs on unseen data.

The sm library from `statsmodels.api` will train and fit our linear regression model while the `mean_squared_error` function will help us to evaluate the results.

To proceed, we can continue working with the data as prepared and wrangled above. Just as we did before, to identify better exactly which variables are our predictor variables and exactly which is our target, we will use the common convention to assign the predictors to capital X and the target to lower case y here in the following code, which will also split our data into `X_train, X_test, y_train` and `y_test`. We also need to scale the data again with `StandardScaler()`.

```
# Splitting the data into training and testing sets
X = df[['Sentiment_ggl', 'Magnitude_ggl',
        'len', 'wed_t_sat', 'hashtags']]
y = df['Reactions']
X_train, X_test, y_train, y_test = train_test_split(
    X, y, test_size=0.25, random_state=42)

# Scaling the data
scaler = StandardScaler()
X_train_scaled = scaler.fit_transform(X_train)
X_test_scaled = scaler.transform(X_test)
```

For this technique we also need to add a constant, which will aid in interpreting our results. The constant will provide an intercept for us, which is the b value in the y=mX + b linear equation.

```
# Adding an intercept to the model
X_train_scaled = sm.add_constant(X_train_scaled)
X_test_scaled = sm.add_constant(X_test_scaled)
```

After adding the constant we can then turn to the y_train and the X_train_scaled data to fit the linear regression model.

```
# Training the OLS regression model
ols = sm.OLS(y_train, X_train_scaled)
ols_results = ols.fit()
```

In the next few lines of code we produce output that will let us interpret the results.

```
# Renaming columns in OLS regression results summary
column_names = ['Intercept'] + list(X.columns)
ols_results_summary = ols_results.summary(
    xname=column_names)
# Show the results of the regression estimations
print(ols_results_summary)
```

Which will give the following output.

```
                         OLS Regression Results
==============================================================================
Dep. Variable:               Reactions   R-squared:                       0.297
Model:                             OLS   Adj. R-squared:                  0.271
Method:                  Least Squares   F-statistic:                     11.66
Date:                 Mon, 10 Apr 2023   Prob (F-statistic):           2.09e-09
Time:                         19:22:35   Log-Likelihood:                -516.71
No. Observations:                  144   AIC:                             1045.
Df Residuals:                      138   BIC:                             1063.
Df Model:                            5
Covariance                   nonrobust
Type:
==============================================================================
```

	coef	std err	t	P>|t|	[0.025	0.975]
Intercept	11.4306	0.745	15.342	0.000	9.957	12.904
Sentiment_ggl	-2.1228	0.820	-2.589	0.011	-3.744	-0.502
Magnitude_ggl	8.0829	1.486	5.441	0.000	5.146	11.020
len	-4.8891	1.471	-3.324	0.001	-7.797	-1.981
wed_t_sat	1.9720	0.767	2.571	0.011	0.455	3.489
hashtags	0.1435	0.929	0.154	0.878	-1.694	1.981

Omnibus:	57.718	Durbin-Watson:	1.976
Prob(Omnibus):	0.000	Jarque-Bera (JB):	173.941
Skew:	1.562	Prob(JB):	1.70e-38
Kurtosis:	7.386	Cond. No.	3.83

Regression models are often favoured in the practice of data science because they are highly interpretable. Starting in the upper right of this output, we see an R-squared (R^2) value of 0.297. This value is a proportion calculated from the amount of variance explained by the model over the total amount of variance in the data. We can interpret this R-squared value as a proportion and it will always be between 0 and 1. Thus, this model, consisting of Google's sentiment score, Google's sentiment magnitude score, the length of the post, whether the post was from Wednesday to Saturday, and the number of hashtags, seems to explain 30% of the variation in the data.

The R-squared value also serves as a useful sanity check. If the R-squared value approaches 1.000 there may be flaws in the data preparation work. For example, if the R-squared approaches 1.000 it often means that some version of the predicted target variable may have inadvertently been included as a predictor feature variable. A high R-squared value that approaches 1.000 is not impossible, but when you observe a high R-squared value it often means you should carefully consider how, or whether, your model could possibly explain an exceedingly high level of variance in your working and analytical context.

From the Prob (F-statistic), which is a very small number 2.09e-09, we conclude that overall the model is statistically significance. Generally, we conclude a statistical result is statistically significant when the p-value is less than 0.0500.

Moving to the middle portion of the output, we see a column of coef values next to the words Intercept and also the names of each of our predictor variables. These coefficients represent the slopes associated with each of those predictor variables in the n-dimensional space. Since the space is n-dimensional and since we also standardized the predictors it is difficult to give precise meaning to each number in the coef column. Instead we can next turn to the P>|t| column which tells us whether the slope on that coefficient is statistically significant. In this case, most of the p-values shown here in the P>|t| column are small, less than 0.0500, and thus we conclude the slope coefficients, except for the one on hashtags, are statistically significant.

Then returning to the coefficients themselves we see that the coefficient on the `Sentiment_gg1` predictor is negative. This negative value means that as sentiment increases the number of reactions decreases. For `Magnitude_gg1` we see a positive coefficient, which means that as the sentiment magnitude score increases the number of reactions also increases. Likewise, for the `len` predictor we see that as length increases the number of reactions decreases. And ultimately for the hashtag predictor, recall that we coded that variable as 1 for posts with four or fewer hashtags, and 0 otherwise. Though the p-value is high, the positive coefficient on the hashtag predictor indicates that four or fewer hashtags indeed will generally mean higher reaction numbers.

There is another metric that can assist us in evaluating this model, called the root mean squared error. To display this metric we can use the following code.

```
# Evaluating the model
y_pred_lm = ols_results.predict(X_test_scaled)
mse = mean_squared_error(y_test, y_pred_lm)
rmse = np.sqrt(mse)
print('Root mean squared error: {:.2f}'.format(rmse))
```

Which will produce the following output, Root mean squared error: 8.91. Root mean squared error (RMSE) will be in the target variable's original units. Thus, we can say that this model is accurately predicting the number of reactions plus or minus about nine reactions.

Given that the standard deviation of reactions overall is 11.47, which you can find on your own with the code df['Reactions'].mean(), we can say that the error rate is under a full standard deviation at about .80 standard deviations.

Check and recheck

In this chapter we have thus far proceeded through an abbreviated example of the steps many might follow while selecting and applying an analytical technique designed to answer an analytical question or solve a business problem. The most significant abbreviation you may have noticed is that we proceeded to evaluate how well our models predict engagement in terms of reaction counts. This chapter has left out examples related to how you might evaluate models that predict engagement in terms of comment counts. With moderate modifications to the code, you can explore engagement in terms of comments on your own.

There are at least two more ways to check and recheck the results we have observed in this chapter. First regarding the k-nearest neighbors results we can take a more careful look at how well the model performed with the optimal k we found above using the elbow method (k = 15).

Because we saved accuracy_kn (the accuracy score at k=15) and class_report_kn (an overview of accuracy metrics at k-15) above, we can use those now to show the evaluation results.

```
# Display knn (k=15) classification metrics
print("Accuracy: {:.2f}".format(accuracy_kn))
print("Classification Report:")
print(class_report_kn)
```

Which produces the following output.

```
Accuracy: 0.71
Classification Report:
              precision    recall  f1-score   support
           0       0.62      0.65      0.64        23
           1       0.76      0.74      0.75        35
    accuracy                           0.71        58
   macro avg       0.69      0.70      0.70        58
weighted avg       0.71      0.71      0.71        58
```

From this output we again see that the accuracy of the knn with k=15 model is 0.71, which means that 71% of the predicted classifications were correct. The classification report shows precision, recall and f1-score for two classes (0 – reaction count below the median and 1 – reaction count at or above the median), as well as support (the number of samples in each class) for each class.

The precision score of class 0 is 0.62, which means that out of all the posts that were predicted to be in class 0 (low engagement), 62% actually belong to class 0. The recall score for class 0 is 0.65, which means that of all the posts that actually received lower engagement, the model predicted this outcome correctly 65% of the time. The f1-score is the harmonic mean of precision and recall, with a value of 0.64 for class 0 (in this case the math is 2 × (.62 × .65) / (.62 + .65) = .64).

The same measures are calculated for class 1, with precision of 0.76, recall of 0.74, and f1-score of 0.75. The macro-average f1-score is 0.70, which is the average of the f1-scores of both classes. Finally, the weighted average f1-score is also 0.71, which is the weighted average of the f1-scores, with weight proportional to the number of samples in each class.

A second major opportunity to further check and recheck the results from this chapter is to view a scatter plot that compares how well the simple linear regression predicted the number of reactions on the y-axis with the actual number of reactions on the x-axis. The following code will accomplish this task.

```
# Compare regression test with regression predictions
sns.lmplot(data=pd.DataFrame({'y_test':y_test,
                              'y_pred_lm':y_pred_lm}),
           x='y_test', y='y_pred_lm',
           height=6, aspect=1.5)
plt.title('Compare Predictions With Test Data')
plt.xlabel('Test Data (Actual Reactions)')
plt.ylabel('Predicted Data (Predicted Reactions)')

plt.annotate(text='', xy=(27, 17), xytext=(27,2),
             arrowprops={'arrowstyle':'<->'})
```

```
plt.annotate(text='', xy=(26.5, 17.75),
             xytext=(0,17.75),
             arrowprops={'arrowstyle':'<->'})

plt.annotate(text='Predicted 18 Reactions',
             xy=(25, 18), xytext=(18,25), fontsize=15,
             arrowprops={'arrowstyle':'->',
                         'connectionstyle':'arc3, rad=.3'})

plt.annotate(text='Received 27 Reactions',
             xy=(27.75, 16), xytext=(28,23),
             fontsize=15, arrowprops={
             'arrowstyle':'->',
             'connectionstyle':'arc3, rad=-.5'})
```

Which produces the output shown here in Figure 11.4. As with any scatter plot, each dot represents a single observation. I have annotated a specific observation near the middle of the plot. For this annotated post, the model predicted approximately 18 reactions but since that post received 27 reactions, the model underestimated the correct number of reactions.

However, overall it seems that there is a clear relationship between the number of predicted reactions and the actual number of reactions evident in Figure 11.4.

Some of the additional items that practitioners in data science might choose to pursue would be to consider applying other techniques beyond k-nearest neighbors and simple linear regression. When looking to predict Reac_bin we could have also turned to logistic regression, for example.

Related, there are also a handful of other pre-processing steps that we could have applied to the data. For example, instead of using the median number of reactions as the cut point between low and high engagement, we could have used the mean. Or, we

FIGURE 11.4   A scatter plot with a regression line and a confidence interval that demonstrates how to use a scatter plot in evaluating the results of a predictive regression algorithm

could have spent more time engineering additional specific and more precise predictor variables. For example, we could have also considered the topic of the post as a predictor, or the time of day as a predictor. Another step would have been to evaluate these models with other combinations of predictor variables other than the five we demonstrated here.

The check and recheck stage involves looking at research logs, notebooks and results to evaluate how extensively and how fully the data science team implemented all of these additional options through the select and apply stage. Related, this stage is an opportunity to make sure all of the preceding stages completed as expected.

Interpret

As I wrote about the results we saw above, I discussed the topic of interpretation. In the abbreviated context within this book we have already completed much of the interpretation stage. However, interpretation also involves explaining what the results mean.

In this case, is it a concern that negative sentiment seems to drive engagement on LinkedIn? Not really, no. Recall that a portion of the data used for this demonstration was synthetic. The results may or may not be exaggerated as a result of including that synthetic data. However, in another context where a similar project may have proceeded with entirely non-fictional data it would be worth a discussion for the team to think through how we could use this information to better drive social engagement without relying on expressing a negative sentiment.

Also, recall that interpretation involves explaining and documenting the tools, techniques, logic and methods used throughout the process. Overall, the interpretation work can be thought of as preparation for the work of dissemination.

Dissemination and production

Dissemination involves sharing the results and their implications with others. Dissemination can also mean putting the model into production. For this example, putting the predictive model into production could mean building software for a marketing and social media management team that would review its draft LinkedIn posts and then report the expected engagement rates.

With this tool, the marketing and social media management team could propose for the software multiple versions of their posts and have the opportunity to predict how their posts might perform in terms of engagement. With these models and the correct implementation in production, the marketing and social

media management teams could optimize for either reactions or comments, or both. Related, the right implementation could also lead to a tool that automatically suggests and recommends revisions that might drive engagement.

Starting over

I call this subsection starting over because, in the best case scenarios, after interpretation and dissemination you will have new questions. Often, by that stage in the process you will have more questions than you started with. Nice problem to have.

In most cases you can take those questions and feed them as input back into the first step of the process that requires an analytical question to answer or a business problem to solve. This tie-back and connection to the first step is one additional illustration of how the entire process is iterative and cyclical, not linear.

In case you skimmed past the advice from Chapter 4 where I discussed this eight-stage data science process, or perhaps in the case where you have yet to read that section of this book, let me reiterate the advice that I give to students, colleagues and clients alike.

The advice is to start building and tracking a backlog of analytical questions you want to answer and business problems you want to solve. You can keep track of these in a whiteboard, a wiki, or an online document that you and your team share. When you prioritize the items on this list, that will grow over time, and when you groom it, it can be a powerful tool for the data science enterprise, team or even individual professional.

Having ready access to a shared list of pre-prioritized analytical questions you want to answer and business problems you want to solve will help you and your team be more confident that you have a comprehensive understanding of the range of potential projects and that the projects on which you are now focused are indeed the highest priority.

Conclusion

In this chapter we again relied on the eight stages of the data science process from Chapter 4 as our main guideposts. The chapter moved through to select and apply a model, check and recheck the results, and then interpret those results. We also revisited how, when done well, this process permits itself to start afresh by taking any new questions that arise and using those as inputs to start the process anew.

Importantly, we continued working with the data we introduced in Chapter 9 from users of LinkedIn. To that LinkedIn data we applied two machine learning models that, if they were to be put into production, would help predict how others may interact with a new proposed post on LinkedIn.

To help us tackle this problem, we carried forward the lessons we learned in Chapter 10, where we used LinkedIn data to demonstrate data visualization work, and where we used those data visualizations to learn what factors may predict engagement. In the data visualizations we found a relationship between the sentiment of a post on LinkedIn and the number of reactions and comments it receives. We also found relationships between the day of the post, the length of the post and the number of hashtags. Thus, we used that information to select and apply k-nearest neighbors and simple linear regression that are well suited to answer our analytical question or solve our business problem.

We also looked at factors that may justify this research question. This chapter also revisited and built on previous examples of data wrangling. Both k-nearest neighbors and simple linear regression demonstrated promising results. The k-nearest neighbors model correctly classified the post as highly engaging or not highly engaging 71% of the time, while the simple linear regression model delivered a prediction that appeared accurate with a root mean square error of about 9 reactions.

This chapter also discussed how the process would proceed through a check and recheck of the results, what is involved in interpretation and then also dissemination. For this example, dissemination could mean putting the predictive models into production. Once in production, these models could support software for use by a marketing and social media management team that would review draft LinkedIn posts and then report the expected engagement rates. The right implementation could also lead to a tool that automatically suggests and recommends revisions that might drive engagement.

Glossary

Anaconda Navigator and Anaconda Prompt Anaconda Navigator is a desktop graphical user interface (GUI) that allows users to manage conda packages and environments. On the other hand, the Anaconda Prompt is a command-line interface that provides a convenient and consistent method to access many of the components of your Anaconda installation distribution. In a MS Windows environment, Anaconda recommends the Anaconda Prompt as the preferred command line interface when operating components of your Anaconda installation distribution.

application program interface (API) A set of programming instructions and standards for accessing an application or service. Allows developers to build software applications that interact with other systems' software components in a secure and predictable manner. For example, Google Cloud's natural language processing API.

average See mean.

bias Systematic errors or deviations in data analysis or decision-making processes that can lead to inaccuracies or unfairness. We can introduce bias through a variety of factors, such as flawed study design, imperfect data collection, or unconscious biases by individuals involved in the analysis or decision-making process. In data science and machine learning, bias can cause models that are inaccurate, unfair or perpetuate stereotypes. It is important to recognize and mitigate bias in order to ensure that data-driven decisions are objective and fair.

big data A term that has grown to include a range of meanings. A typical framework for understanding what may constitute big data is data sources that have a high volume (such as a high number of rows or observations), data with a high level of variety (such as data from multiple sources or that exist in multiple types and formats), and data that are generated with high velocity (such as a high number of new records or observations each second).

boxplot A visualization strategy that shows many of the measures of central tendency. A graphical representation of a data distribution using key statistical measures: first quartile (Q1), median and third quartile (Q3). The box itself represents the interquartile range (IQR),

which is the range of values between the first and third quartiles. The line inside the box represents the median. The whiskers extending from the box show the minimum and maximum values within 1.5 times the IQR. Any data points outside this range are considered outliers and are plotted individually as circles. See also violin plot.

chi square analysis A statistical method that examines the relationship between categorical variables by comparing observed and expected frequencies within a contingency table. If the differences between observed and expected frequencies exceed a predetermined significance level, it suggests that the categorical variables in the table may be related.

command line interface See command prompt.

command prompt A command prompt is a computer interface that relies on the user to specify and provide the computer with written text-based commands. A command prompt permits users to move, copy or manage files. Command prompts also permit users to review file contents, file directories and file attributes. A command prompt is also often referred to as a command line interface (CLI). A significant advantage of a command prompt is that the text input and output provide a prices record the commands issued along with the output that documents their results.

confidence interval The confidence interval is calculated by taking a data point such as a mean and creating an interval around the estimate. The width of the interval relates to a pre-specified level of certainty, often set at 95%. The level of certainty can be adjusted to provide narrower or wider intervals. Confidence intervals are used to assess the precision of predictions and estimates.

control flow A concept in computer programming that permits data scientists, and other programmers, to control under what conditions, for how many iterations or for how long specific code will execute. Control flow statements are programming language features that enable efficient implementation of complex logic, performance of repetitive tasks, handling of errors and creation of interactive programs. For example, in Python examples of control flow statements include if–else statements, for and while loops, pass and break statements, try–except blocks, among others. Other examples of control flow features in Python and other languages include functions and classes.

correlation matrix A correlation matrix is a table showing Pearson correlation coefficients between sets of variables. Each entry in the table shows the correlation between two variables. By analysing a correlation matrix, you can see which variables are most closely related to each other. The higher the correlation coefficient, the stronger the relationship between the variables.

correlation An analytical technique that seeks to understand whether two or more variables may relate to each other. There are many methods that can show or measure correlation including cross-tabulations, scatter plots, Pearson correlation coefficient calculation and regression analysis.

data steward An individual who is responsible for managing the collection, storage, quality, security and use of an organization's data assets. These professionals have or know where to find the data if they already exist, or how to collect them. Data stewards are also often knowledgeable about how the data were collected, or should be collected.

data types A concept in computer programming that governs how the computer will store data and what operations the computer may perform on the data. For example, in Python there are integers, floats, Booleans and strings. There are also lists, sets, dictionaries and tuples. Also a concept in data analysis that involves grouping data into a typology of data families that broadly include qualitative, quantitative and date/time.

Dependent variable See target variable.

Development operations (DevOps) A term used to describe the collaboration between data scientists, database administration, software developers, IT operations and related professionals. It encompasses practices such as continuous integration, automation, monitoring and configuration management that enable faster time-to-market for applications and services.

DevOps engineer A professional who oversees the operational aspects of a data science, database, software product or related system. The role involves configuring multiple computer systems, maintaining those systems with updates and monitoring system performance. This role also involves provisioning access to the systems. DevOps professionals also maintain processes for deployment, automation and troubleshooting production issues.

domain knowledge A set of skills and expertise related to a particular subject area or industry. Domain knowledge provides the basis for understanding customers, trends, competitors and technology to make informed decisions about product design and development. It enables teams to identify problems and create solutions that are tailored specifically to their industry. This knowledge is most often acquired through advanced academic study, extensive first-hand experience in the field, or both.

effect size A statistic calculated by subtracting the mean value of one group from the mean value of another group and then dividing the result by the pooled standard deviation of both groups. It is a standardized measure of the magnitude of the difference between two groups. The units on an effect size statistic are standard deviations.

ethics The study and consideration of the moral, legal, social and cultural equality and fairness in the collection, storage, use, sharing and dissemination of data. It involves analysing the ethical issues related to data privacy, security, transparency and bias, and the potential harm that may fall upon individuals or groups, especially those who are vulnerable as a result of data-related work. Data ethics aims to establish guidelines and principles to ensure that data are collected, used and managed in a responsible, ethical and socially conscious manner.

extreme values See outliers.

feature matrix A collection of feature variables (or predictor variable) that will be used to estimate or predict the value of a target variable. In a key example given in this book, which showed how body weight can be modelled as a function of other individual personal characteristics and habits, it is the personal characteristics and habits that compose the feature matrix.

feature variable See feature matrix and also predictor variable.

focus group A qualitative research method consisting of structured conversations between an interviewer and multiple group participants. Focus groups aim to obtain insights and opinions on a particular product, service or topic. Within the fields of data science, machine learning, artificial intelligence and advanced analytics, focus groups can be helpful in better understanding the domain associated with the research question or business problem.

function (computer programming) A function is a section of computer code that performs a specific task, and as such a function is also a core component of most computer programming languages. A function includes a specific sequence of operations that may operate on one or more inputs, or arguments.

function (statistical and mathematical modelling) For statistical modelling purposes a function defines the relationship between a set of input and one or more outputs. For example, body weight is a function of diet, activity, genetic disposition and height. Likewise, an automobile's efficiency (miles per gallon rating) is a function of its weight (among other factors).

Functional programming An approach to computer programming that focuses on writing programs that leverage well-defined functions, each of which perform discrete tasks. By writing code that leverages well-designed functions, data scientists and other programmers can produce code that is more concise, easier to read and easier to maintain. A functional programming approach also supports modularity, which means that the code may be easily repurposed for multiple projects. Functional code, which is more easily repurposed therefore also improves the efficiency of analytical work by reducing the need to rewrite redundant code that performs similar functions.

good faith A concept in law and ethics that implies actors proceed in an honest, cooperative and fair manner towards one another. In the context of data science this means operating in a manner that honours our obligation not to take unfair advantage of the data we collect or use from others.

Google Colaboratory An online and Cloud-based integrated development environment that provides a notebook interface. A notebook interface allows data scientists, artificial intelligence, machine learning and advanced analytics professionals to combine code and rich markdown text with charts, images, HTML, LaTeX and more in a cohesive presentation. More at: colab.research.google.com

histogram A specific kind of bar chart that assists in evaluating the scale (minimum and maximum), variance (the spread) and variable's central tendency (such as the mode). This visualization typically involves converting a continuous variable to an ordinal and then charting the frequency of observations within each ordinal bucket.

hyper-dimensional space See n-dimensional space.

independent variable See predictor variable.

input variable See predictor variable.

instantiate A concept in computer programming that refers to the process of creating a specific instance of an object. In concept this involves taking a template and creating an individualized version based on that template. Examples in this book included instantiating the sid from NLTK's sentiment analyser. Another common example from this book at other contexts is to instantiate an empty list in Python that subsequent code will then populate.

integrated development environment (IDE) Software that provides tools for software and computer code drafting, such as debugging, syntax highlighting and version control. Common IDEs in data science, machine learning, artificial intelligence and advanced analytics include notebooks such as Jupyter Notebooks and Google Colaboratory.

interview A qualitative research method often consisting of structured conversations between two or more people. Interviews are commonly used in fields such as psychology or marketing research. Within the fields of data science, machine learning, artificial intelligence and advanced analytics, interviews can be helpful in better understanding the domain associated with the research question or business problem.

iterable An object in Python or other programming languages that includes multiple data elements that may be looped through in a systematic or sequential manner. In Python, example iterables are lists, NumPy arrays and Pandas Series.

Jupyter Notebooks A web-based application that serves as an integrated development environment for drafting and debugging computer code. Often used by scientists, researchers, data scientists, engineers and software developers to create efficient and effective reproducible research. Jupyter Notebooks permit data science, machine learning, artificial intelligence and advanced analytics practitioners to combine code and rich markdown text with charts, images, HTML, LaTeX and more in a cohesive presentation.

K-nearest neighbors (KNN) A supervised machine learning algorithm suitable for both classification and regression problems. In KNN, the K refers to the number of nearest neighbours the algorithm will reference as it makes predictions. To make a prediction, KNN looks at the K

closest data points in the training set and based on the majority class (in the case of classification) or the average of the nearest neighbours (in the case of regression), it assigns a prediction to the new data point.

Kernel density estimation (KDE) plot A visualization strategy that shows the probability density function of a continuous variable. Often, KDE plotlines may be combined with histograms. Violin plots also utilize KDE plots. The probability density function describes the relative likelihood of observing a continuous random variable within a certain range of values.

logistic regression A statistical technique used to predict the probability of a binary event. It is used to measure the relationship between predictor variables and a binary outcome variable, such as yes/no, pass/fail or true/false. In data science, machine learning, artificial intelligence and advanced analytics, logistic regression is a supervised machine learning technique that requires training data from historic observations. Logistic regression permits practitioners to model the likelihood of future events under similar circumstances.

loop A loop is a control flow feature embedded in many programming languages that permits the performance of repetitive tasks. For example, the Python programing language features for and while loops.

maximum A statistic that identifies the highest value of a continuous variable.

mean A statistic (a measure of central tendency) that is calculated by adding all the values in a data set and dividing by the total number of values. The mean provides an overall measure of the centre of the data. It is also known as arithmetic mean, statistical mean or simply average. This statistic is highly sensitive to outliers or extreme values.

measures of central tendency A group of statistics that help understand the middle of a distribution. Common measures of central tendency include the mean, median and mode. These measures summarize the data and can be useful for a variety of techniques including comparison of a continuous variable across multiple categories, such as the mean or median incomes between college graduates and high school graduates.

measures of spread (dispersion) A group of statistics that describe the variation in a data set. These measures assess how far the values in a data set are spread out from each other and from the measure of

central tendency (e.g. mean, mode, median). Common measures of spread include range, interquartile range, variance and standard deviation.

median A statistic (a measure of central tendency) that is the middle value in a data set. It is calculated by ordering all the data points from least to greatest, and then choosing the midpoint. This is used to provide a measure of the centre of the data set. This statistic is often not strongly affected by outliers or extreme values.

minimum A statistic that identifies the lowest value of a continuous variable.

mode A statistic (a measure of central tendency) that identifies the most common value (or values) in a continuous variable.

N-dimensional space A mathematical concept that describes a theoretical space with multiple, often many, dimensions or axes. This is a fundamental concept in machine learning algorithms that involve multivariate analysis, such as clustering and classification.

natural language processing A specialty within data science, machine learning, artificial intelligence and advanced analytics that enables meaningful and linguistically driven interactions between computers and humans. It focuses on enabling computers to process and understand natural language input from humans in a way that is similar to how humans understand language. It also works to enable computers to respond in language that mimics how a human may respond. It uses a combination of computer science, linguistics and machine learning techniques to perform tasks such as language translation, sentiment analysis, speech recognition and text summarization.

ordinary least squares regression A statistical technique used to estimate the relationships between variables. As a supervised machine learning technique, this method permits data science, machine learning, artificial intelligence and advanced analytics practitioners to model an outcome variable, or target variable, as a function of one or more other predictor, or feature, variables. As a supervised method, it requires historic data that can train a predictive model to anticipate what the expected outcome may be when given new data from similar contexts in the future.

outliers Values in a variable that are distant from the measures of central tendency. Outliers can often have an influential effect on statistical

analysis. Because outliers can influence many data science, machine learning, artificial intelligence and advance analytical tasks, it is important to review data for outliers and carefully asses whether they should be modified, removed or left in place. This book discussed how sometimes an observation may appear as an outlier, at first, but how careful evaluation may reveal that dropping the observation is not the best approach for managing that outlier because instead of being an outlier there was other evidence that it was an erroneous value. Summarily removing outliers or extreme values can be a mistake as they may contain valuable information that could be useful for making better decisions.

output variable See target variable.

pair plot A plotting strategy that shows results similar to a correlation matrix. Instead of showing a matrix of correlation coefficients for each pair of variables in the matrix, the pair plot shows a scatter plot of each pair in the matrix.

pearson correlation coefficient A statistical measure that shows how two continuous variables are related. It ranges from –1 (perfectly negatively correlated) to +1 (perfectly positively correlated). A correlation of 0 means that there is no relationship between the two variables. Correlation measures linear relationships only. This method cannot measure non-linear relationships.

predicted variable See target variable.

predictor variable A variable that data science, machine learning, artificial intelligence and advanced analytics practitioners can use to estimate a target variable. Often also referred to as a feature variable, independent variable, input variable and similar terms. An example given in this book is a person's activity and also caloric intake which can be used to predict that person's body weight. Data science, machine learning, artificial intelligence and advanced analytics practitioners can use models consisting of one or more predictor variables to predict specific target variables such as body weight.

production data Data generated in the course of doing business. Often collected from various sources such as sensors, machines, software and other systems that are part of the production process. Also collected when humans interact and supply data in the course of conducting business electronically. Production data serve purposes related to

record keeping, system maintenance, delivery of services and related business functions.

qualitative data Non-numerical data that describe and provide insight into the quality or characteristics of an observation.

quantifying the problem This is a practice that involves understanding the impact of answering a research question or solving a business problem. By quantifying a business problem in terms of specific monetary figures (or in terms of specific value), data science, machine learning, artificial intelligence and advanced analytics practitioners can justify their work.

quantitative data Numerical data that are used to measure and describe a particular phenomenon or variable.

range A statistic (a measure of spread) calculated by subtracting the minimum value from the maximum value.

regression analysis In the context of data science, machine learning, artificial intelligence and advanced analytics, regression analysis refers to a type of predictive modelling task where the goal is to predict a continuous numerical value as the output. The objective of regression analysis is to find a mathematical function that relates one or more independent variables (also known as predictor variables) to a dependent variable (also known as the target variable). See also ordinary least squares regression.

response object Not to be confused with response variable, a response object is the result of a request to an API. The response object will provide information about the request that may include the original data sent for analysis, whether the analysis succeeded, and any important results from the API's analysis.

response variable See target variable.

sentiment analysis Uses multiple natural language processing techniques to quickly process written or spoken data and extract meaningful insights related to the sentiment expressed in those texts. The simplest detection algorithms detect only either positive or negative sentiment. In other words, sentiment analysis allows data scientists to detect whether text contains positive or negative sentiments.

shape of the data Can refer to a variety of data attributes and characteristics. For example, a violin plot and a histogram show data shape by plotting overall range, interquartile range, modes and other similar measures.

silent error This kind of error is due to an incorrect or imprecise specification in computer code that does not result in a warning or error message but that does produce incorrect, undesired or unexpected results. When these errors go unnoticed they may lead to serious problems later.

simple linear regression See ordinary least squares regression.

standard deviation A statistic (a measure of spread) calculated as the square root of the variance and expressed in the same units as the data points being measured. Standard deviation is often used to indicate how much variation there is between individual values in a data set. This statistic can be used in the calculation of other valuable statistics including t-test statistics, effect sizes and confidence intervals, or in the identification of outliers or extreme values.

subject matter expert (SME) An individual who has a high degree of knowledge and expertise in a particular area or discipline. These individuals possess extensive domain knowledge. SMEs acquire their domain knowledge through advanced academic study, extensive first-hand experience in the field, or both. Data scientists, machine learning, artificial intelligence and advanced analytic professionals seek the input of SMEs who can provide valuable insights that help to inform decision making processes, develop new products or services and understand the implications of changes in the industry or marketplace.

supervised machine learning Any technique that involves an algorithm that learns from historic labelled training data. These techniques involve using input predictor data that correspond to known output target values. By evaluating for how the predictor data relate to the target values, a supervised algorithm can, in a manner of speaking, learn how to predict target values when later also given new previously unseen data. Examples include regression, k-nearest neighbors, decision trees, support vector machines, logistic regression and neural networks. See also unsupervised machine learning.

target variable A predicted or estimated response value in a statistical model. It is also referred to as a dependent variable, output variable, predicted variable and other similar terms. An example given in this book is body weight, where a person's body weight can be modelled as a function of other personal characteristics, habits and behaviours.

Data science, machine learning, artificial intelligence and advanced analytics practitioners can use models consisting of one or more predictor variables to predict specific target variables such as body weight.

unsupervised machine learning Any technique that involves training an algorithm without supplying a pre-labelled target variable. Such algorithms identify patterns and relationships in the data on their own, with minimal prior knowledge or guidance. Common tasks accomplished with unsurprised techniques are clustering (identifying otherwise difficult to discern groupings), dimensionality reduction and anomaly detection. See also supervised machine learning.

violin plot A type of data visualization that conceptually combines the notion of a boxplot with a kernel density plot. Thus, the violin plot shows the distribution of a continuous variable.

Appendix A
Quick start with Jupyter Notebooks

Learning the essential skills of data science should be a fun, enjoyable and rewarding experience. However, the learning curve can be steep, which sometimes undermines a learner's ability to find the fun and joy in the journey. As described in the preface and throughout this book, most of the examples assume that readers have a moderate level of previous experience in Python plus handy access to an integrated development environment (IDE) such as Jupyter Notebooks or Google Colab.

In other words, while this book does not start in the deepest end of the data science pool, it also does not start in the shallowest end. These appendices are to help you wade into your journey along the way of discovering the essential skills of data science.

I developed the examples in this book using Anaconda's distribution of Python and Jupyter Notebooks. In a manner of speaking Jupyter Notebooks is a platform that supports data science work by serving an environment in which developers can write and execute computer code. While Jupyter Notebooks support many languages, the examples in this book are in Python.

This combined selection of tools, Anaconda's distribution of Python and Jupyter Notebooks, allows you to create and share your work in multiple easy to read formats. For example, this book's companion notebooks appear as shown in Figure A.1.

In this appendix, I will provide a quick-start guide to Anaconda's Jupyter Notebooks distribution, including what Anaconda is, more on what notebooks are, how to install the Anaconda distribution, and some additional key pointers to help users get started.

FIGURE A.1   A screen capture of how Chapter 11's companion Jupyter
Notebook appears when rendered in a notebook environment

CONFIDENT DATA SCIENCE
Discover the essential skills of data science
Companion Jupyter Notebooks + Coding Examples

Chapter 11 _Business Value + Clients_

To give citation to these coding examples give reference to an appropriate chapter and page of:

Confident Data Science: Discover the essential skills of data science
(Confident Series, 15) 1st Edition by Adam Ross Nelson (Author)
Publisher : Kogan Page (September 26, 2023).

Wrangle The Data

```
In [1]: # Import the Pandas, Numpy, & Seaborn libraries
        import pandas as pd
        import numpy as np
        import seaborn as sns
```

Source: github.com/adamrossnelson/confident

As with other chapters of this book, these appendices offer a companion Jupyter Notebook with coding examples at github.com/adamrossnelson/confident.

What is Anaconda?

Anaconda is a distribution of the Python programming language that includes a wide range of data science and machine learning libraries and tools. It is designed to simplify the process of setting up and managing a Python environment for data science and machine learning applications.

One of the key advantages of Anaconda is its package manager, which allows users to easily install and manage a wide range of Python packages and libraries. This package manager makes it easy to set up a customized Python environment with all of the tools and libraries that are needed for a specific project or application.

What are Jupyter Notebooks?

Jupyter Notebooks are a web browser-based interactive computing environment that allows users to create and share documents that combine live code, visualizations and narrative text. If you are familiar with the terminology integrated development environment (IDE), Jupyter Notebooks are a form of IDE. They are an ideal tool for data science and machine learning applications, as they allow users to explore and visualize data in a flexible and interactive way.

Jupyter Notebooks are organized into cells, which can contain code, text, or visualizations. Users can run individual cells or entire notebooks, and can save their work as a single file that can be easily shared with others.

Finding the Anaconda distribution

The Anaconda distribution can be found on the Anaconda.com website, which offers a free download of the latest version. Users can choose from among versions that are intended for a variety of operating systems. Download the option that best matches your computer.

Installing the Anaconda distribution

If you have not previously installed Anaconda, the process is relatively simple. It is similar to installing many other programs or software. The installation process is straightforward and should only take a few minutes to complete. Download the installer from the Anaconda website and follow the instructions provided.

After installation, there are at least three ways to initiate a new session in Jupyter Notebooks.

1. Using the Anaconda Navigator: The Anaconda Navigator is a graphical user interface that allows you to launch Jupyter Notebooks, as well as other tools and applications that are included with the Anaconda distribution. To initiate (start up) the Jupyter environment using the Anaconda Navigator, open the Navigator. Following most installations you will find the Navigator icon in your applications folder, your desktop or the start menu. Once within the Navigator, select the 'Jupyter Notebook' option, and click 'Launch'.
2. Using a command prompt or a terminal session: Open a command prompt or terminal window, navigate to the directory where you want to work, and type the command 'Jupyter Notebook'.
3. Using the Anaconda Prompt: If you prefer to use the Anaconda Prompt, you can start a Jupyter Notebook environment by opening the Anaconda Prompt and typing the command 'Jupyter Notebook'. Similar to the Anaconda Navigator, after installation of Anaconda you will find the Anaconda Prompt in the applications folder, your desktop or the start menu.

Using Jupyter Notebooks: Key pointers

Notebooks operate within a web browser. You can use any web browser including Chrome, Safari and Firefox. As shown in Figure A.1 the notebook allows you to write richly formatted text along with computer code. You will have a familiar looking menu system with a 'File' and 'Edit' menus among others, as shown here in Figure A.2. When you write and execute code in the Jupyter Notebook environment the output and results from your code will also display within the notebook.

FIGURE A.2   The upper portion of a Jupyter Notebook environment with its menu system and a single line of code that also shows the code's related output

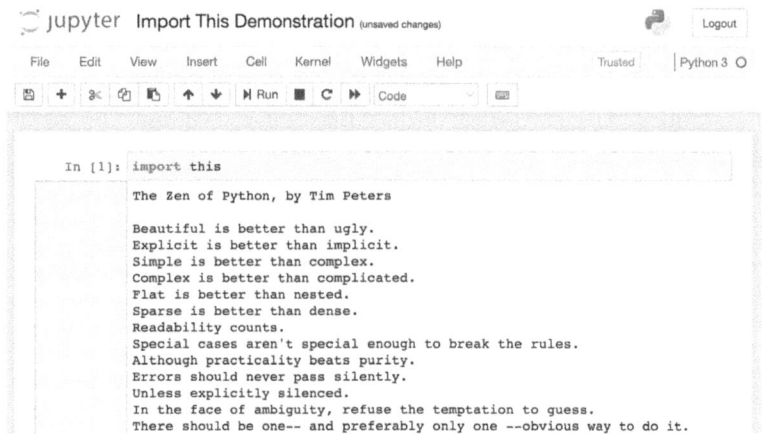

Source: Jupyter Notebooks

Here are some additional key pointers that can help users get started with Anaconda Jupyter Notebooks. Familiarize yourself with the Jupyter Notebook interface, including how to create and run cells, and how to save and share notebooks. For example, 'running' a cell means executing the code in that cell. In Figure A.2 the notebook has 'run' the code import this. If replicated, the code shown in Figure A.2 should also produce 'The Zen of Python' output. If you see the output as shown in Figure A.2, you also successfully ran the code import this. To run a cell you can press 'shift + return/enter' or you can also press the 'run' button shown at the top of the notebook.

Appendix B
Quick start with Python

If you are completely new to Python, or recently transitioning to Python from other languages, this quick start guide will help you. As you may know, Python is a popular programming language used in many fields, including data science. In this guide we will cover some basic concepts and examples to get you started with Python.

Look! I can swim

As you learn to swim in the data science pool and get better at operating in the deeper end of that pool you will want to share the news. To do that try the following code.

```python
print("Look Mom! I can swim!")
```

This code will print the string 'Look Mom! I can swim!' to the console (or to your notebook environment).

Data types

The types of data discussed here are a typology that is different from the types of data discussed in Chapter 9. The typology discussed in Chapter 9 organizes types of data for analytical purposes. The types of data discussed here organize data for efficient storage and reference within the Python computer programming language.

Python has several built-in data types, including:

- Integer: Whole numbers such as 1, 2, or –3. A specific example would be that there are three parts and eleven chapters in this book.

- Float: Numbers with decimal points, such as 3.14, –2.5, 1.0, or 2.1. A specific example from Chapter 8, in addition to other spots, would be sentiment scores which almost always include digits to the right of the decimal point.
- Boolean: True or false. For a specific example of these, we looked extensively at true and false values in Chapter 5 where we used them to visualize missing data, or in Chapter 11 where we created an array of Booleans to evaluate the results of predictive algorithms.
- String: A sequence of characters such as 'hello' or '123'. For more about strings, see the information under f-strings and the string `.format()` method discussed below.

Here are code-based examples of using these data types.

```
# Integer
depth = 12
print(x)

# Float
ss = 20.91
print(ss)

# Boolean
is_true = True
print(is_true)

# String
person = "César Augusto Cielo Filho"
print(person)
```

The following code puts these together in a more meaningful way.

```
# Write about the pool and swimming world record.

print('Most pools, at their deepest are about ' +
    str(depth) + ' feet deep.')
print('The fastest world record for the 50m ' +
    'freestyle belongs to' + person)
print('who finished in ' + str(ss) + ' str(ss) + ' seconds.')
```

Note how this code uses a function called str() to convert the numeric values of depth and ss into string so that the print() statement can properly handle the data. Later examples will show alternate coding options that will better manage those type conversions.

Common uses of data types

Integers and floats work for standard maths including addition, subtraction, multiplication and division. Booleans are used for logical operations such as checking whether a condition is true or false. Strings are for storing text such as names and messages.

```
# Arithmetic Operations
depth = 2    # Standard depth of olympic pool (meters)
width = 50   # Standard width of an olympic pool (meters)
length = 25  # Standard length of an olympic pool (meters)

print(depth + depth)          # Addition
print(depth - depth)          # Subtraction
```

```
print(depth * width * length)    # Multiplication
print(width / length)            # Division

# Arithmatic examples + With string manipulations
print('An olympic pool holds an estimated')
print(str(depth * width * length) +
    ' cubic meters of water, which is')
print('approximately ' + str(depth * width * length *
    str(depth*width*length*264.2) + 'gallons.')

# Logical Operations
is_raining = True
is_sunny = False
print(is_raining and is_sunny)    # And operator
print(is_raining or is_sunny)     # Or operator

# String Manipulation
message = "Congratulations to:"
first = "César"
middle = "Augusto"
family = "Cielo Filho"

# String concatenation
print(message + ' ' + first +
    ' ' + middle + ' ' + family)
```

F-strings

For string manipulation, concatenation and evaluation, programmers will use f-strings. This special syntax offers a more concise and readable way to format strings in Python.

This book includes many examples. With f-strings, you can embed expressions inside string literals, making it easy to insert

variables, function calls and even arithmetic operations directly into your strings.

```
# Working with f-strings
message = "Congratulations to:"
first = "César"
middle = "Augusto"
family = "Cielo Filho"

# An example of f-strings
print(f'{message} {first} {middle} {family}!')
```

This code will print the string 'Congratulations to: César Augusto Cielo Filho!' Note that the f before the opening quote indicates that this is an f-string. Any expression inside curly braces {} will be evaluated at runtime and its value will be inserted into the string. This can include variables, function calls and even arithmetic expressions. For example:

```
print(f"The volume of the pool is " +
      f"{depth * width * length} sq meters.")
```

This code will print the string 'The volume of the pool is 2500 sq meters.'

The string .format() method

Within this book you will also find multiple examples of the string .format() method. The .format() method is a built-in

function in Python that allows you to insert values into a string. As with f-strings you can use { } as placeholders in the string, which will be replaced by arguments passed to the .format() method. Here's an example:

```
print('{} {} {} {}!'.format(message, first, middle, family))

print('swam 50m freestyle in {} seconds!'.format(ss))
```

In this example, the values of the message, first, middle and family variables are inserted at the { } placeholders. The resulting strings are 'Congratulations to: César Augusto Cielo Filho!' 'Swam the 50m freestyle in 20.91 seconds!'

You can also use numbered placeholders and named placeholders to specify the order in which the values insert. When done well, using these place holder labels make the code more readable. Here's an example:

```
# Replicate above with named placeholders
print('{3} {2} {1} {0}!'.format(
    family, middle, first, message))
```

In this example, the numbered placeholders {3} {2} {1} and {0} specify the order in which the variables render to the string. The resulting string is: 'Congratulations to: César Augusto Cielo Filho!'

On most views, the .format() method creates a more dynamic, readable and flexible output.

Structured data types

Lists are a collection of ordered and changeable elements. Lists can also store elements that consist of mismatched data types. Lists are created using square brackets [ ]. Individual elements in the list are separated by commas. Importantly, the elements occupy memory in an ordered mutable way. This means that code can reference individual elements and also modify those elements. For example:

```
# Create two lists with data from above
pool_dimensions = [length, width, depth]
record_holder = [first, middle, family]

# Make a list of lists
my_list = [pool_dimensions, record_holder]

# Display the results
print(my_list[0])      # Call the first item in my_list
print(my_list[1])      # Call the second item in my_list
print(my_list)         # Print all items in my_list
```

Sets are an unordered collection of unique elements. No two elements in any set may be the same. Sets also store elements of different data types. Sets are created using curly braces { } or the set( ) function, and elements are separated by commas. Because they are unordered, it is not possible to reference specific elements in a set. They are an unordered, mutable collections of unique elements. For example:

```
# Declare a set
my_set = {1, 2, 'three', 4.0}
```

Dictionaries are a collection of key-value pairs, where each key must be unique. Dictionaries are created using curly braces { } and a colon : to separate key-value pairs. Key-value pairs are separated by commas. Also, keys and values can be of different data types. They are unordered, mutable collections of key-value pairs. But because of the key-value structure this dictionary data type is useful for creating readable code. For example:

```
# Using data from above create a dictionary
data = {'message':'Congratulations!',
         'swimmer':record_holder,
         'event':'50m freestyle',
         'time':ss}
# Report results from the data
print('{} {}!'.format(
     data['message'], ' '.join(
         data['swimmer']))))
print('You swam {} in {} seconds.'.format(
     data['event'],
     data['time']))
```

Notice how, in square brackets, the dictionary data provide 'keys' which identify more precisely what the data are within the 'values'. In a list or a set, the only meta clue as to what the data are within the object are the names of the object. The above code produces the following output: 'Congratulations! César Augusto Cielo Filho!' 'You swam 50m freestyle in 20.91 seconds.'

Tuples are a collection of elements just like lists. However, tuples are immutable, which means their contents cannot be changed

after creation. They are declared using parentheses instead of square brackets. They are ordered, immutable sequences of elements. For example:

```
# Declare a tuple with data from above
my_tuple = (message, first, middle, family)
```

List comprehension

List comprehension allows you to create a new list from an existing list using very little code. Many other programming languages would accomplish this task with the a verbose multi-line for loop. List comprehension often does this in a single line of code.

This book offers multiple examples of list comprehension. For an elementary example, suppose you have a list of numbers and you want to create a new list with only the even numbers. Here is an example of how to use list comprehension to achieve this.

```
numbers = [1, 2, 3, 4, 5, 6, 7, 8, 9, 10]
even_numbers = [x for x in numbers if x % 2 == 0]
print(even_numbers)
```

In this example, the new list even_numbers is the result of list comprehension with a conditional. The expression [x for x in numbers] generates a new list with all the numbers in the original list numbers, and the condition if x % 2 == 0 filters the list to include only the even numbers. The resulting list is [2, 4, 6, 8, 10]. List comprehension can be used with an iterable, including strings, tuples and dictionaries.

In another example, suppose you had a list of world records for the 50 meter freestyle. And you wanted to help set goals for new records. The new goals would be 98% of the previous record. The following code uses list comprehension to accomplish this result.

```
# A list of word records
former_records = [22.8, 23.5, 24.1, 24.9, 25.5]
record_goals = [x * .98 for x in former_records]

print(record_goals)
```

Declaring simple functions

As extensively shown in this book, for example in Chapter 8, within Python you can define your own functions to perform specific tasks or operations. Here is an example of a simple function that multiplies three numbers together and returns the result.

```
# Define a function to calculate volume
def calc_volume(l, w, h):
    """Multiply three numbers. Return result."""
    result = l * w * h
    return result
```

This function calculates volume. We can use this function with the length, width and depth variables from above.

In this function, we define three parameters l, w and h which represent the three numbers we want to multiply together. We

then define a local variable `result` which is assigned the product of `l`, `w` and `h`. Finally, we use the `return` statement to return the value of `result` as the output of the function.

To use this function, we can call it with the three variables length, width and depth that we had defined above as the function's arguments.

```
# Call the function with arguments 5 and 7
vol = calc_volume(length, width, depth)

# Print the result
print(vol)
```

Declaring anonymous functions

In Python, anonymous functions are created using the lambda keyword. Lambda functions are small, one-line functions that do not have a name.

Here is an example of an anonymous function that takes one argument and returns its square.

```
# Take one argument x and returns its square
square = lambda x: x**2
print(square(5))
```

In this example, we assigned a lambda function to the object `square`. The lambda function takes one argument `x` and returns its square. We then called the `square` function with the argument 5 and printed the result, which is 25.

Another example could be to take a string and return the first ten characters.

```
# Take a string and return the first ten characters
first_ten = lambda x: x[:10] + '...'
print(first_ten('The pool will be open all summer.'))
```

In this example, we assigned a lambda function to the object first_ten. The lambda function takes one argument x (which should be a string) and returns its first 10 characters plus an ellipse '...'.

Appendix C
Importing and installing packages

An important feature of Python and other programming languages is that programmers can easily extend the functionality of the language. In Python these extensions come from external code sources and are known as modules, packages or libraries. The `import` statement is responsible for importing this additional code and the attendant functionality.

Following a properly executed import statement, subsequent code may then reference the imported code. Most standard distributions of Python come along with multiple modules. Additionally, it is a relatively trivial matter to install new modules that do not routinely distribute with Python by default.

This appendix will demonstrate multiple modules plus some of the added functionality they bring. It will also demonstrate how to install new modules. For demonstration purposes we will look at the YData Profiling module, discussed earlier in Chapter 5.

One of the many modules that distributes with Python is the `random` module. The following line of code will provide a random number between 1 and 10.

```
>>> # Provide a random number between 1 and 10
>>> import random
>>> random.randint(1, 10)
6
```

You can also assign a module to an alias name as follows.

```
>>> # Import and assign to an alias
>>> import random as rn
>>> rn.randint(1, 10)
3
```

Another commonly referenced module is the math module. This provides access to common mathematical functions such as square roots or constants such as pi.

```
>>> Demonstrate pi and square roots with math module
>>> import math
>>> print(math.pi)
3.141592653589793
>>> print(math.sqrt(81))
9.0
```

The following demonstrates the syntax that imports specific objects from within a module.

```
>>> # Import specific portions of a module
>>> from math import sqrt
>>> from math import pi
>>> pi
3.141592653589793
>>> math.sqrt(81)
9
```

It is also an option to import multiple objects from the same module in an import statement.

```
>>> # Import multiple portions in one line
>>> from math import sqrt, pi
>>> pi
3.141592653589793
>>> math.sqrt(81)
9
```

Throughout, this book has used the following code that imports the Pandas, NumPy, and Seaborn modules.

```
>>> # Import pandas and give it the name pd.
>>> import pandas as pd
>>> # Import NumPy and give it the name np.
>>> import numpy as np
>>> # Import Seaborn and give it the name sns.
>>> import seaborn as sns
```

Installing new packages

Take note, installing and importing a package are not equivalent. It is possible to import the above-discussed packages, random, math, Pandas, NumPy and Seaborn, because they come with many popular distributions of Python. If you installed the Anaconda distribution of Python as suggested by this book you will have all of the above packages already installed.

Occasionally, this book and other sources will reference additional packages that you will need to install before you can import and them. One such package is YData Profiling.[1]

To install this package you will need access to your command prompt where you will type `pip install -U ydata-profil-ing`. After a successful installation you will then be able to import the `ProfileReport` components of this library with the code `from ydata_profiling import ProfileReport`.

For more on how to use `ydata profiling` see Chapter 5.

Another common error many may experience is that import statements often contain case-sensitive code. For example, even following proper installation the following lines of code will both return errors.

```
from Pandas_Profiling import ProfileReport
from pandas_profiling import profilereport
```

Only the following correctly capitalized import statements will work correctly.

```
from pandas_profiling import ProfileReport
```

Avoiding incorrect name assignments

Occasionally it is easy to incorrectly assign a module to an abbreviation that makes no sense or that breaks commonly accepted conventional practice. The following code will be problematic because it first imports Pandas and assigns it to the pd shorthand but then also imports NumPy and also assigns NumPy to the pd shorthand.

```
>>> import pandas as pd
>>> import numpy as pd
```

By convention, the above code is wrong. Technically, the code is runnable. This code will not return an error or a warning, and as such we call this kind of error a silent error.

As a programmer you will only know there has been an error when you write code that you meant to reference a method usually associated with Pandas but that is not associated with NumPy. Such as:

```
>>> df = pd.read_csv('name_of_csv_file.csv'
Traceback (most recent call last):
  File "<stdin>", line 1, in <module>
  File "/Users/book_code/anaconda3/lib/python3.9/site-
packages/numpy/__init__.py", line 313, in __getattr__
    raise AttributeError("module {!r} has no attribute "
AttributeError: module 'numpy' has no attribute
'read_csv'
```

The tell-tale signal to diagnosing the cause of this error message is that it tells you module 'numpy' has no attribute 'read_csv' – when you meant to reference the Pandas module. The reason for this error is that the earlier code imported NumPy as pd (import numpy as pd) instead of as np (import numpy as np).

List of data sources

Data sets are listed in the order presented throughout. You can download this list as a PDF with hyperlinks at koganpage.com/cds.

Chapter 6

mpg.csv – A set of data from the Seaborn data visualization library that includes information about vehicles, their price, their weight, efficiency, place of manufacture and additional factors. Available from: raw.githubusercontent.com/mwaskom/seaborn-data/master/mpg.csv

confident_ch6.csv – A fictional set of data that imagines information associated with series of packages shipped and mailed. Also available in HTML and Stata file formats. Available from: raw.githubusercontent.com/adamrossnelson/confident/main/data/confident_ch6.csv

Chapter 9

house_polls_historical.csv – Data from the news organization FiveThirtyEight.com that include information about polls in advance of US Congressional elections. Available from: projects.fivethirtyeight.com/polls/data/house_polls_historical.csv

senate_polls_historical.csv – Data from the news organization FiveThirtyEight.com that include information about polls in advance of US Senate elections. Available from: projects.fivethirtyeight.com/polls/data/senate_polls_historical.csv

confident_ch9social.csv – Data that include information on a collection of posts on LinkedIn. Chapters 9 produces these data then Chapters 10 and 11 make further use of them. Available from: raw.githubusercontent.com/adamrossnelson/confident/main/data/confident_ch9socialsents.csv

wc_matches.csv – Data from the news organization FiveThirtyEight regarding soccer's World Cup tournament predictions. Available from: projects.fivethirtyeight.com/soccer-api/international/2022/wc_matches.csv

wine.data – Data that report alcohol content, chemical characteristics, colour and other features associated with wine. Available from: archive.ics.uci.edu/ml/machine-learning-databases/wine/wine.data

tips.csv – Data from the Seaborn data visualization library that include information about restaurant dining bills, the amount of the bill, the amount of the tip, the number of diners and other information associated with each bill. Available from: raw.githubusercontent.com/mwaskom/seaborn-data/master/tips.csv

penguins.csv – Data from the Seaborn data visualization library that include information about three species of penguin. They also includes multiple observations from each species and information about each bird's physical attributes. Available from: raw.githubusercontent.com/mwaskom/seaborn-data/master/penguins.csv

sample_-_superstore.xls – Data provided by and often associated with Tableau data visualization software that include information from a variety of product categories and regions. Available from: public.tableau.com/app/sample-data/sample_-_superstore.xls

managers.csv – Fictional data about a group of employees, their performance scores and additional human resources information. Available from: raw.githubusercontent.com/keithmcnulty/peopleanalytics-regression-book/master/data/managers.csv

confident_ch9socialsents.csv – Data that include the data from confident_ch9social.csv but also six additional columns related to the sentiment scores of the LinkedIn posts. Chapter 9 produces these data then Chapters 10 and 11 make further use of them. Available from: raw.githubusercontent.com/adamrossnelson/confident/main/data/confident_ch9socialsents.csv

Notes

CHAPTER 1

1   R Hooper. Ada Lovelace: My brain is more than merely mortal, *New Scientist*, 15 October 2012. www.newscientist.com/article/dn22385-ada-lovelace-my-brain-is-more-than-merely-mortal (archived at https://perma.cc/J5HQ-36K2)

2   C O'Neil (2016) *Weapons of Math Destruction: How big data increases inequality and threatens democracy*, Crown Publishing Group, New York

3   S U Noble (2018) *Algorithms of Oppression*, New York University Press, New York

4   National Academies of Science, Engineering, and Medicine (2018) *Data Science For Undergraduates: Opportunities and options*, The National Academies Press, Washington DC

CHAPTER 2

1   A Oeberst and R Imhoff. Toward parsimony in bias research: A proposed common framework of belief-consistent information processing for a set of biases, *Perspectives on Psychological Science*, 2023. journals.sagepub.com/doi/full/10.1177/17456916221148147 (archived at https://perma.cc/3YXV-SYZC)

2   S U Noble (2018) *Algorithms of Oppression*, New York University Press, New York; C O'Neil (2016) *Weapons of Math Destruction: How big data increases inequality and threatens democracy*, Crown Publishing Group, New York

3   A Oeberst and R Imhoff. Toward parsimony in bias research: A proposed common framework of belief-consistent information processing for a set of biases, *Perspectives on Psychological Science*, 2023. journals.sagepub.com/doi/full/10.1177/17456916221148147 (archived at https://perma.cc/GR7P-SS3L)

4   G Box (1979) Robustness in the strategy of scientific model building, *Robustness in Statistics*, Academic Press, London, 202

5   G Box (1979) Robustness in the strategy of scientific model building, *Robustness in Statistics*, Academic Press, London, 202–03

6   D Engber. Daryl Bem proved ESP is real: Which means science is broken, Slate, 7 June 2017. slate.com/health-and-science/2017/06/daryl-bem-proved-esp-is-real-showed-science-is-broken.html (archived at https://perma.cc/56E5-TY3E)

7   A Nelson. Six months later: What data science (hopefully) learned from Facebook's whistleblower, Towards AI, 27 April 2022. pub.towardsai.net/six-months-later-what-data-science-hopefully-learned-from-facebooks-whistleblower-fe8049e5cac3 (archived at https://perma.cc/HKM8-AABX)

CHAPTER 3

1   P Sainam, S Auh, R Ettenson and Y S Jung. How well does your company use analytics? *Harvard Business Review*, 27 July 2022. hbr.org/2022/07/how-well-does-your-company-use-analytics (archived at https://perma.cc/X7CN-GF5C)

CHAPTER 4

1   A Nelson (2023) *How to Become a Data Scientist: A guide for established professionals*, Up Level Data, LLC
2   F Gemperle (2019) *Handbook of People Research: Deriving value by asking questions*, Lulu Publishing, Morrisville, NC; S Knowles (2023) *Asking Smarter Questions: How to be an agent of insight*, Routledge, Abingdon; J Keyton (2019) *Communication Research: Asking questions, finding answers*, McGraw-Hill Education, New York; T J Fadem (2009) *The Art of Asking: Ask better questions, get better answers*, FT Press, Upper Saddle River, NJ

CHAPTER 5

1   Changelog, nd. ydata-profiling.ydata.ai/docs/master/pages/reference/changelog.html#changelog (archived at https://perma.cc/PC4A-NCW2)

CHAPTER 6

1   M Sperrin and G P Martin. Multiple imputation with missing indicators as proxies for unmeasured variables: Simulation study, *BMC Medical Research Methodology*, 2020, 20 (185), 7. europepmc.org/backend/ptpmcrender.fcgi?accid=PMC7346454&blobtype=pdf (archived at https://perma.cc/6CC9-9RM9)

CHAPTER 7

1   I used artificial intelligence to generate these passages in early 2023. During the editing process in the summer of 2023 I also reprompted a selection of tools which, as expected, returned similar but different results. Another observation is that when prompted for 'paragraphs' the generative models sometimes produce only one paragraph and sometimes multiple. Conversely, when prompted for 'a paragraph' the generative models sometimes produce one paragraph and sometimes multiple.

2   A Nelson. Bias at work: An example of artificial intelligence bias at work, Towards Data Science, 29 August 2022. towardsdatascience.com/bias-at-work-adbd05b0c4a3 (archived at https://perma.cc/G6S7-SM9E); A Nelson. Exposing bias in AI: It isn't so difficult to show bias in AI, data science, machine learning and artificial intelligence, Illumination, 18 February 2023. medium.com/illumination/exposing-bias-in-ai-b6925227416 (archived at https://perma.cc/SLE7-3MDU)

3   P Kafka. The AI book is here, and so are the lawsuits: What can Napster tell us about the future? Vox, 2 February 2023. www.vox.com/recode/23580554/generative-ai-chatgpt-openai-stable-diffusion-legal-battles-napster-copyright-peter-kafka-column (archived at https://perma.cc/8BHA-8HFU)

CHAPTER 8

1   To access the Zen of Python you can search online for it. Or you can write the code `import this` in any Python environment, which will return the famous Zen of Python poem.

2   Google. Sentiment analysis response fields, Google, nd. cloud.google.com/natural-language/docs/basics (archived at https://perma.cc/M58Z-475J)

3   For more information on how to obtain .json credentials see: developers.google.com/workspace/guides/create-credentials (archived at https://perma.cc/UXE9-XQBQ)

CHAPTER 9

1   FiveThirtyEight. Our data, FiveThirtyEight, nd. data.fivethirtyeight.com (archived at https://perma.cc/P2BC-7JEF)

2   J Boice. How our 2018 World Cup predictions work, FiveThirtyEight, 2018. fivethirtyeight.com/features/how-our-2018-world-cup-predictions-work (archived at https://perma.cc/TLS9-3WC9)

3   UCI Machine Learning Repository. Welcome to the UC Irvine Machine Learning Repository! UCI Machine Learning Repository, nd. archive.ics.uci.edu/ml/index.php (archived at https://perma.cc/D84S-J58B)

4   Tableau. Resources: Sample data, Tableau, nd. public.tableau.com/app/resources/sample-data (archived at https://perma.cc/W85L-VCD5)

5   K McNulty (2021) *Handbook of Regression Modeling in Pople Analytics*, CRC Press, Boca Raton

6   A Nelson. LinkedIn: The best example data source you never knew, Towards Data Science. towardsdatascience.com/linkedin-the-best-example-data-source-you-never-knew-737d624f24b7 (archived at https://perma.cc/829S-7T22)

CHAPTER 11

1   S Ghaffary. Facebook's whistleblower tells Congress how to regulate tech, Vox, 5 October 2021. www.vox.com/recode/22711551/facebook-whistleblower-congress-hearing-regulation-mark-zuckerberg-frances-haugen-senator-blumenthal (archived at https://perma.cc/TK53-KT6Z); S Morrison and S Ghaffary. Meta hasn't 'really learned the right lesson', whistleblower Frances Haugen says, Vox, 6 September 2022. www.vox.com/recode/2022/9/6/23333517/frances-haugen-code-meta-facebook-whistleblower (archived at https://perma.cc/69SL-SLPV)

2   K Paul and D Anguiano. Facebook crisis grows as new whistleblower and leaked documents emerge, *Guardian*, 22 October 2021. www.theguardian.com/technology/2021/oct/22/facebook-whistleblower-hate-speech-illegal-report (archived at https://perma.cc/TE7D-4B8E)

APPENDIX C

1   You can find full reference information for YData Profiling here: ydata-profiling.ydata.ai/docs/master/index.html (archived at https://perma.cc/V3RC-SZAD)

Index

accuracy 46, 58
accuracy_score function 318, 320, 329
ACME 15, 52–53
acoustical sciences 165
additional data gathering 73–74
Aha, Professor David 246
AI (artificial intelligence) 1–3, 6,
10–11, 158
writing assistants 157–64, 172
see also chatbots; ChatGPT; Copy
AI; facial recognition; image
processing; machine learning;
robots; smart glasses; smart
watches; speech recognition
alerts tab 119
Alexa 157, 165
algorithms 4, 8–10, 37
Alzheimer's research 4–5, 13, 14
Anaconda 350–52
Navigator 338, 352
Prompt 338, 352
analysis 24–34, 54–55
chi-squared 234, 339
cluster 79, 247, 249
correlation 87–89, 112, 340
data exploration 85–122
falsification 38, 279
interpretive 77–78
k-means cluster 116
k-nearest neighbours 116, 314–21,
342–43
predictive 12, 76–77, 80
topic 14–15
see also regression analysis;
sentiment analysis
Analytical Engine 5–6
analytical processes 55–56
analytical questions logs 332–33
analytical taxonomies 24–34
Analyze Data 95
annotations 265–68
anonymous functions 364–65
application program interface
(API) 338

Google Cloud 180–82, 183–96,
209–15, 253–55, 278–80
art sector 170
artificial intelligence (AI) 1–3, 6,
10–11, 158
writing assistants 157–64, 172
see also chatbots; ChatGPT;
CopyAI; facial recognition;
image processing; machine
learning; robots; smart
glasses; smart watches; speech
recognition
audits 47, 58, 59, 79
automated exploratory analysis
tool 95–100, 121
axes 264
see also x-axis; y-axis
ax.txt code 265

Babbage, Charles 6
bar charts 42, 96, 97, 99, 268–70,
281–85
see also histograms
Bem, Daryl 43
bias 8–11, 37–38, 43, 77, 163, 338
big data 338
binary data
nominal 232, 234, 241–43
ordinal 232
Black Data Matters 7–8
body weight equation 36, 39–40
Boolean variables 356, 357
Box, George 39
boxplots 39, 236, 285, 288–89, 292,
338–39
Brown, Dr Emery 7
bubble charts 295–299
buckets (bins) 299, 300–01

Canva 168
categorical variables 86, 147
causation 88
central tendency 228, 285, 292, 344
see also mean; median

Printed in the USA
CPSIA information can be obtained
at www.ICGtesting.com
JSHW072105010923
47738JS00009B/12

9 781398 612327